COLOSSUS

Colossus

Stephen Marlowe

NEW ENGLISH LIBRARY
TIMES MIRROR

For Ann
who has the magic

First published in Great Britain by W. H. Allen & Co. Ltd., 1973
© Stephen Marlowe, 1972

❂

FIRST NEL PAPERBACK EDITION MARCH 1974

❂

NEL Books are published by
New English Library Limited from Barnard's Inn, Holborn, London, E.C.1.
Made and printed in Great Britain by Hunt Barnard Printing Ltd., Aylesbury, Bucks.

45001773 7

BOOK ONE

BOOK ONE

A GRIM OLD MAN, stocky and grizzled, walks with the aid of a Malacca cane through the crowd in the Salon des Beaux Arts. The exhibition has just opened. It is early autumn, 1824.

The high-crowned bolívar hat balanced deftly on his forearm, the plum-colored frock coat, the narrow tan trousers, all are in the height of fashion. The small case he carries is of good leather, old leather as seamed as his face. He smiles around the big dead Havana cigar protruding from his full lips, and the smile takes twenty years off his age like the single dexterous stroke of a portrait painter. The smile shows a set of good teeth, Spanish teeth, Aragonese teeth.

And what would they think, these dilettantes, these hangers-on, the old man wonders, the smile lingering in his dark, hooded eyes, if they knew what rested on red velvet inside the leather case?

Not that dueling is unknown in France. But at his age?

The old man detests his almost eighty years.

All his long life he has had a Spanish fondness for death, taunting it with the icy blues of his palette, challenging it with the slashing blacks. But someone else's death. He has too much to do. There is never enough time.

He stands squarely before a Delacroix canvas which has been awarded first prize. *Massacre of Chios,* it is called. He thinks of the Second of May and the Third of May, so long ago, and the grizzled old head shakes and the dead ash falls from the cigar and, distracted, he brushes it off his white silk cravat. No, this Delacroix does not know the disasters of war. Not Chios or Madrid or anywhere.

A tap on his shoulder. He turns, sees a pair of faces. One of them is speaking. He must concentrate on the lips. He is stone-deaf, and his French is not superb.

'Monsieur, you are in the way.'

The speaking face is effete. The French, after Napoleon. They used it all up then, all of it.

7

'Sorry, monsieur,' the old man grumbles in his execrable French, 'but I am deaf.'

He waits a few moments longer, with that Aragonese stubbornness, and then plods off, the Malacca cane thumping around the salon, through the gaily-dressed mob, through the eager, shallow chatter its bearer, thankfully, cannot hear.

And the dark eyes become more hooded, the full lips turn down in disapproval. Will they never learn?

Still the fake classical junk they expected him to paint sixty years ago. And here and there some of this new romantic foolishness. Ingres, Géricault, Constable. The names mean little. The paintings mean less.

And a voice, fifty years dead, tells him: 'You have the magic, Paco.' When he was ready to quit Madrid and return home and take up his father's trade, as his brother Tomás did.

You have the magic.

An unsteady hand now, and eyes so dim he cannot work without thick spectacles. But he had the magic. Truly, he had it.

Broad shoulders well back, the stocky figure moves through the salon and the foyer and outside. The air is cool and bracing. The gas lamps are lit, now, against the gathering Paris dusk. He can see the lamplighter, far off along the street, children dancing behind him. Gas lamps are a new thing, even in Paris.

A carriage comes jouncing by, drawn by high-stepping mules. The old man cannot hear the clatter of hooves and wheels on paving stones, but he can see the sparks fly.

The sparks, and briefly a face in the carriage as it hurtles past. He whirls, his heart pounding. The masses of black hair and that ivory skin. A certain aristocratic look to her, a certain arrogant elegance.

Foolish old man. She's dead these twenty years. But every time he sees that elegance. . . .

He fondles the well-worn leather case.

Tonight, he tells himself.

And, half an hour later, is seated at a café on the Rue de la Paix. He sips a coffee, lights another cigar and watches the fashionable traffic pass by.

Rue de la Paix. Street of the Peace. How fitting, he thinks, to be waiting here for a man once called the Prince of the Peace.

Called that, of course, by a fatuous cuckolded king, but still.

And the same fatuous cuckolded king, a weak-chinned, weak-willed royal idiot, sees the royal family portrait unveiled, twenty years and more ago, and says, with absolutely no expression on the fat, vapid, royal face: 'Yes, of course. Of course, I see, Don Paco.'

What he sees is a family of fishmongers dressed up as king and queen and princes and princesses of the realm.

And Don Paco will never have to paint for King Carlos again.

Three kings, the old man muses, painter to three kings. Santa Maria, how long I have lived!

The first Carlos, a small gnome of a man with that unfortunate Bourbon nose, the mahogany face under a black tricorn hat and a wistful half-smile on the homely features. 'Yes, Don Paco,' he says too, viewing his portrait with a kind of sad resignation. 'I really must have a new coat fitted, don't you think?' And the royal hand clasps the painter's shoulder to show that the king is pleased.

The third king, King Fernando, still sitting on the throne in the palace on its hill overlooking the river in Madrid, a big block of a jaw like his mother's in place of the weak Bourbon chin, said, not so very long ago, 'Goya, if we did not admire you so much we would have you garotted.'

So Paco Goya, age seventy-eight, having chosen exile before the king could blink his beady little eyes and change his mind, sits at a café on the Street of the Peace, in Paris, waiting for the former Prince of the Peace, an exile like himself, younger but not young, poor now, coming every night to this café to escape the mean fourth-floor room where he lives, writing his memoirs and perhaps remembering some of the things Paco remembers.

Perhaps? Does a man forget cold-blooded murder?

A cab pulls up before the café, under the gaslight-dappled leaves of the chestnut trees. The horse shakes its head, the driver receives his coins and the Prince of the Peace steps down. Probably overtips the cabman too, a gesture he can ill afford, as he can ill afford the cab and the finery he is wearing.

He passes the old man's table, walking with a swagger. The cab, the tip, the tall beaver hat, the gleaming shoes – how very Spanish, when likely the former Prince of the Peace wonders where his next meal will come from.

'Paco!'

The old man starts. But no, the voice is inside his head. He tells himself it is normal for a man his age, and one who is alone in a foreign place, and one who cannot hear, to invent such voices, to remember them.

9

'Paco!' the young voice of Martín Zapater insists, calling to him with a plaintive eagerness.

And he sees the New Tower in Zaragoza, thrusting its spire at the limitless Aragon sky. He stands, dusty and parched, among the vegetable stalls in the Plaza de San Felipe. Sixty years are flipped back like the pages of a book. Friend Martín, the old man thinks, good Martín, how I did abuse you.

Dead now. So many of them dead.

The old man's grip tightens on the leather case. In it, ironically a gift from the Prince of the Peace, is a pair of perfectly matched dueling pistols.

Tonight a duel. Tonight one of them will die.

CHAPTER ONE

Wanderers' Bell

'PACO! PACO!'

Martín ran toward him past the rows of vegetable stalls in the Plaza de San Felipe, up the lane between artichokes and eggplants and bright red tomatoes, dodging around a laden donkey.

'How did it go, Paco?' The voice was still high for seventeen, still scratchily uncertain. Martín was taller than Paco but less robust, with a long face, a big nose and brown eyes, usually solemn, which gleamed with excitement now.

Paco wanted to appear blasé, but he blurted: 'It's done – the whole reliquary cabinet. The Madonna and Child, the Virgin appearing to Santiago, even a canopy with cherubs. You never saw such real cherubs,' he added, not modestly.

'We missed you last night. We needed you,' Martín said.

'It took two days. The cherubs were extra. The cabinet needed cherubs.'

'You're a real painter now,' Martín cried, and the boys embraced and danced around, almost upending a cart heaped with carrots and lettuce.

Paco should have been exhausted. Few wagons passed along the hard, white road from the village of Fuendetodos to Zaragoza, and he had walked the twenty-five miles all day across the high, parched plain. It was a desolate landscape and a desolate journey – no trees, no farms, no sign that human footsteps had ever passed that way except for the dusty road: a single goatskin of water from the village well, a crust of bread, a stout walking stick, a clasp knife tucked into the sash between his sweaty white shirt and homespun knee breeches, rope-soled boots, almost worn through now, and the broad-brimmed black hat, covered with dust – as he himself was covered from head to toe.

But Paco felt exhilarated. It was as if he had been born suddenly those two days in Fuendetodos – the smell of oil and turpentine, the feel of the brush in his hand, and fat little Padre Gerónimo, who had baptized him, nodding and clucking

11

toothlessly while Paco brought the doors of the reliquary cabinet to life.

In a small drawstring pouch he had the proof of his birth, fifty reales. He had listened to their delightful clinking all the long journey back to Zaragoza.

Martín trailed after him as he went to the fountain in the middle of the plaza and doused his thick black hair with water. His broad face with its hooded eyes, flat nose, and stubborn jaw made him look older than he was.

'See,' he said, turning suddenly, spraying water. On his palm he clinked the bag of coins. 'Fifty reales.' His smile showed dazzling white teeth. Enough olive oil and garlic, the *baturros* of Aragon always said, and you'd have teeth like that until you were eighty. 'And that's only a start. Why, Padre Gerónimo said – '

'Listen, Paco,' Martín interrupted. 'There was trouble last night. A gang from the barrio of San Luis, they – '

'The float?' Paco said, his voice hard.

Next week was the festival of the Virgen del Pilar. All the city's barrios had built floats to honor their very own Maria del Pilar, elaborate structures carried by dozens of men hidden underneath, so that the floats seemed to move magically across the rough streets of the city to the basilica.

'No, no, our float's all right,' Martín said uneasily. 'There was a brawl. One more fight, the corregidor's police said, and they'll throw us all in jail.'

Paco shrugged. 'They always say that.'

'You don't understand,' Martín said, scuffing his rope-soled shoes in the dust. 'We burned their float down.'

The hooded eyes widened. 'The San Luis float?'

The barrio of San Luis had won the competition honoring the Virgin two years running. Pilar, Martín's and Paco's own barrio, had placed second each time.

'You, Martín?' Paco said, grinning broadly. 'You did that? I didn't know you had it in you, chico.'

'Then you're not angry?' Martín asked.

The grin faded from Paco's face. 'Martín,' he said slowly, 'who wants to be second best?'

He slapped the dusty hat against his breeches and covered his wet hair with it. 'They know who's responsible?'

Martín gulped. 'They said they'd get me.'

'We won't let them,' Paco told him with a confidence he hardly felt. The feud between the barrios, now, could develop into a bloody one. The San Luis toughs, led by a lumbering

12

oversized monster named Diego, were no laughing matter.

But Paco's assurance satisfied Martín. Paco was home and now everything would be all right. Hadn't Paco said so?

Martín punched his friend's shoulder. 'They're here, Paco. The bullfighters. A new troupe from Navarra.'

'Why didn't you say so, chico?'

And Paco Goya began to run. Donkeys, fruit vendors, water carriers, shoppers, all got out of his way.

From halfway across the Roman bridge Paco gazed back at the city.

The fairgrounds on the far side of the Ebro beckoned with a magic that made him forget the magic of what his right hand could do with a brush and some paints. But there was the city behind him too, and he loved the excitement of it, and the way the New Tower and the twin spires of the basilica rose against the late afternoon sky, higher with each step he took. Paco Goya, seventeen that Year of Our Lord 1763, already suffered from an artist's temperament. On his way to the fairgrounds, half his mind was back in the city. He lived in the past and in the future, and rushed impatiently through the present.

Soon would come the procession of the rosary, an army of carriages and floats (no prize for you this year, San Luis) with giant pasteboard figures walking on stilts, with flowers from all over Spain offered to the Pilar, their flaming colors contrasting with the sober garb of the priests. But first – ah, first! – would be the dancing of the jota, the girls with their dark Aragonese eyes flashing and under wide skirts their legs flashing too, soft dancing shoes red-laced high on shapely calves, so lovely you wanted to kiss them all.

And jugglers and acrobats and gypsies to tell your fortune or curse your enemy, and fireworks and bullfights. . . .

And, Paco reminded himself as they reached the first savory booths on the far side of the bridge, the finest food in the world. He bought some puff pastry for himself and Martín and two cups of vino-vino of Cariñena, surely the best wine in the world, and the strongest.

Perhaps tonight his mother would serve chilindrón chicken, red-pepper sweet, to celebrate his triumph. If he hadn't returned by wanderers' bell last night, then he would be home tonight, he had told his parents. He still had some time, though now the sun was low over the basilica across the river. He could run all the way home. He had to see the bullfighters first.

To be a torero, to face death and give death –

13

No. Didn't he want to be a painter?

'Paco,' Martín called.

'I'm coming.'

The great vans that had transported the bulls stood just outside the makeshift ring, and when you came close you could hear their pawing and snorting, and you could smell them and, pushing your way past the younger boys, you might catch a glimpse of a heavy dark something, or the white of a horn, or a baleful eye looking back at you, the little brain behind the eye wondering, probably, how it could propel the heavy-muscled body through that thickness of wood to impale you on that horn.

'There he is!'

One moment Paco stood near the larger of the two bull vans, and the next he saw Martín on the ground, blood spurting from his nose. Something struck him hard, between shoulder and ear, and he was down too and then up, still holding his walking stick and swinging it with both hands over his head to give Martín time to gain his feet.

He saw Diego of San Luis, as big as a bull, and a dozen other boys from the San Luis barrio. He swung the stick again. Diego backed off and one of the other boys fell down, and the smaller boys who had come to see the bulls quickly formed a ring, like their own miniature plaza de toros, and he stood in the middle of it.

'Run, Martín! Break through!'

He again swung the heavy stick with both hands. This time it was Martín they wanted, not him. Martín gave him one despairing look and broke through the circle of smaller boys with two of Diego's ruffians right behind him. Leaving Paco to face the rest of them.

They were everywhere, some with sticks like his own, some barehanded. They closed in.

'No, wait. He's mine,' Diego said contemptuously, and spat on the ground at Paco's feet.

The two of them circled warily, sticks clattering. The knuckles of Paco's right hand were struck, his painting hand. He almost dropped his stick but turned it suddenly like a sword and probed for Diego's belly, driving the stick home so that Diego's head came forward and down and he could smell the garlic on Diego's outrushing breath.

And then someone tripped him.

They swarmed all over him while he tried to protect his face

14

and his painting hand at the same time. He heard shouts, a scream. Someone stomped on his hand, his right hand. The scream was his own. He thought he heard a lazy voice say, 'That's not fair, now is it, brothers?'

He had unknown allies then, dressed all in white with red sashes. There were five of them, he saw as he got to his feet, four lithe and slender and whirling with dreamlike agility, and the fifth as big as Diego of San Luis. The big one lifted Paco's assailants off their feet like sacks of grain, and hurled them. The other four caught them as they landed, using elbows and fists and knees and feet deftly, like rapiers.

Diego of San Luis came at him with an open clasp knife.

They rolled over and over on the ground, the knife between them, each with a hand on it.

Diego rolled on top. His bulk turned the knife, and Paco suddenly and unbelievingly felt it sliding into the weight above him, a weight that now writhed and fell away.

'Police!' someone shouted, and someone took his arm and he was running. His right hand throbbed.

With the coming of darkness, a bone-chilling cold settled on the high plateau of Aragon. In October, they said, a man could bake to death by day and freeze to death by night.

'I feel like a block of ice,' Gaspar Apiñani said.

'It's colder than Navarra,' his brother Pascual said.

'It's colder than hell,' his brother Emeterio said. 'We should have gone to Sevilla. It's warm in Sevilla.'

The fourth brother, Juanito, was busily gathering brushwood. Unlike the others, he did not talk much. He struck a spark over tinder, hunkered down and blew on it. Soon he had a small, lonely fire burning to dispel the gloom and the cold. It did not help much. Paco joined the five brothers as they sat around it shivering.

Tuertillo, the leader of the brothers, squinted his single eye at Paco. He wore a patch over his left eye socket.

'You shouldn't have used that knife,' he said.

'It was his knife. All I –'

Tuertillo shrugged his massive shoulders. The leader of the Apiñani clan was bigger than any two of his brothers together. 'If he dies, what will you do?'

Paco sat there shivering. They had come two miles, Paco and Tuertillo running hard, the four other Apiñanis gliding like wraiths ahead of them.

'It always happens,' Gaspar Apiñani said.

15

'If there's trouble, we find it,' Pascual said.

'Like ants find honey,' Emeterio said.

Paco could not tell the three thin and talkative Apiñanis apart. He could identify Juanito because Juanito said little and did most of the work. Now he was gathering more brush-wood.

'There goes Zaragoza,' Gaspar said.

'It was a good opportunity for us,' Pascal said.

'We never fought the bulls outside Navarra before,' Emeterio said.

His two look-alike brothers nodded.

'If it had just been a brawl,' Gaspar said. 'Bullfighters fight. Like gypsies. It's expected of us.'

'But a knifing,' Pascual said.

'A knifing changes things,' Emerterio said.

'Still, we can't go back to Pamplona,' Gaspar said.

'We had a small difficulty in Pamplona,' Pascual said.

'Not that it was our fault, you understand,' Emeterio said.

And Paco, watching the three slender brothers, who could have been one brother and two mirrors, suddenly wished he had a crayon and some paper. He wanted to sketch them with the firelight on their gaunt faces like that.

Tuertillo stared at the flames with his single eye. 'Pamplona,' he said in his lazy voice. 'Zaragoza. Provincial cities. Who cares? We'll go to Madrid. A man can make his fortune in Madrid.'

Gaspar made a face. 'What about our horses?' he asked.

'What about our capes and banderillas?' Pascal asked.

'What about our swords?' Emeterio asked. 'The finest Toledo steel.'

Juanito put more wood on the fire. He was humming.

'Emeterio's right,' the one-eyed brother said. 'A knifing change things. We'll have to leave our things or face the corregidor's police.' He clapped a huge hand on Paco's knee. 'What do you do in life?'

Paco thought proudly of the reliquary cabinet in Fuende-todos. 'I'm a painter,' he said.

'Then why waste your time in Zaragoza? Madrid's the place for you. Throw in with us, man. What's a little trouble for, except to turn it to your own advantage? Take this eye.' He tapped a big forefinger against the cheekbone under the eye-patch.

'It happened in Pamplona,' Gaspar said. 'A big Navarra bull, red, with white patches under the forequarters.'

'Plucked that eye out with a single thrust of his horn, the way you pit an olive,' Pascual said. 'Left it dangling on my brother's cheek.'

'So Tuertillo hurls it on the sand and keeps on fighting,' Emeterio said. 'Ever since, he's been a madman with a cape.'

'Well, what do you say?' Tuertillo asked Paco. 'You can't go back. What if he dies? He may be dead already.'

Paco shuddered. He and Diego of San Luis had always hated each other. But dead?

'Have you money?' Tuertillo asked.

At first Paco was going to say no. What money he had was payment for his first commission as a painter. An artist. But he said: 'Not much. Almost fifty reales.'

'Fifty reales,' Gaspar said, awed.

'You'd be surprised what we can do with fifty reales,' Pascual said.

Emeterio whistled. 'We could stretch fifty reales from Barcelona to Cádiz.'

Why not? Paco thought. Go to Madrid with them. You can't learn anything more at José Luzán's studio. Your palette's as clear as his, even if he was a painter to the king. Maybe you're not the equal yet of Francisco Bayeu, Zaragoza's best painter, but in time that will come. He massaged the throbbing fingers of his right hand. With this hand, he told himself, you can do anything.

'Well?' Tuertillo asked.

Far off along the river, the wanderers' bell began to toll.

Every night of the year the bell rang out from the tower of the Church of San Miguel, to lead the lost traveler home to the safe familiar streets of the city, to a hot meal and a hearth, to a straw bed near the fireplace, to paints and plaster casts and to Martín, who had probably gone straight to Paco's house to tell his parents what had happened.

He could picture his mother – Doña Engracia everybody called her – waiting frantically, and his patient father trying to calm her, and his brothers Camillo and Tomás wondering what Paco was up to now and whether he would ever give the family any peace.

No, he couldn't go to Madrid, not yet. Maybe Diego wouldn't die. Maybe, somehow, things would work out.

'What's that bell?' Tuertillo asked him, and Paco explained. 'I'm going back,' he said. 'I've got to.'

'A wanderers' bell,' Gaspar said. 'Imagine that.'

'Like a lighthouse,' Pascual said.

'What will they think of next?' Emeterio said.

Paco stood up and impulsively held out the drawstring bag of money. 'It was my fault,' he told Tuertillo. 'Here, take it.'

'You don't have to do that,' Gaspar said.

'Santiago, a philanthropist,' Pascual said.

'We'll take it,' Emeterio said, and his one-eyed brother's hand closed on the drawstring bag.

'I think you're making a mistake,' Tuertillo told Paco. 'We'll wait here for you, until that bell of yours stops tolling. Then we're off.'

Paco nodded, turned away from the fire and faced the darkness.

'Adiós,' Gaspar said.

'Go with God,' Pascual said.

'You'll need all the help He can give you,' Emeterio said.

The family of José Goya and Engracia Lucientes lived in an apartment in an old brick building near the basilica – two large rooms, sparsely furnished: a bedroom for José and Doña Engracia and a big kitchen where the four children slept.

The city apartment represented something of a comedown for them, and Doña Engracia, who came from an old but poor hidalgo family, particularly resented it. Their holdings near the village of Fuendetodos, mean and grudging land that yielded a sparse crop of wheat, had been tended for several lean years by José Goya before he returned with his family to the city and, secretly pleased, resumed his trade as a gilder.

He just managed to keep the family's collective head above water. Farming in Fuendetodos, he had gone increasingly into debt. There was also the tax on meat, the tax on wine, the tax on candles, the tax on soap, all of them more begrudged by José than by his wife. The money found its way into the coffers of the Church and the nobility, and clearly, Doña Engracia maintained, they were entitled to it. José Goya was less sure, but he suffered in silence.

Paco's brother Tomás, hook-nosed and phlegmatic like his father, served as José Goya's assistant, which pleased Doña Engracia because the wages remained in the family. Paco's brother Camillo was studying for the priesthood, which pleased Doña Engracia even more. If you couldn't be of the landed gentry, she always said, at least you could be a priest. Paco's sister Rita, a pale girl of fourteen with delicate lungs and the face of a young El Greco martyr, fitfully helped her mother around the house. Doña Engracia liked that too; the

18

family could afford no serving girl. But Rita did not help with the cooking. No one touched Doña Engracia's iron cooking pots except Doña Engracia herself.

Doña Engracia's frustrations found a ready outlet at her charcoal stove. Her masterpiece was chilindrón chicken, the chicken cut into small pieces, bones and all, and cooked slowly and lovingly with red peppers, tomatoes, onions, and the ubiquitous garlic. It was this dish she had prepared for Paco's return from Fuendetodos, not last night but tonight, because if Paco said he might come early or might come late, then obviously he would come late.

The red-pepper aroma of the chilindrón now pervaded the apartment, but even Doña Engracia had lost interest in it. She sat, gathered with the family around the warmth of the stove, listening to the mournful tolling of the wanderer's bell.

'Paco's been in scrapes before,' said Tomás, who secretly envied his younger brother's escapades.

'He's a good boy,' said José Goya.

'Scrapes?' cried Doña Engracia. 'You call a stabbing a scrape? A good boy? Only last month you had to pay twenty reales to the corregidor because that good boy of yours – what was it last month? I can't keep track.'

'He only drew a picture,' said José Goya.

'A picture of the bishop, on the wall of the Seo itself, making the bishop look like a fat fish out of water.'

José Goya suppressed a smile. The bishop did, in fact, look like a fat fish out of water, with his bulging eyes and the way he puffed and blew.

'And the month before,' Doña Engracia went on. 'When he brought home that lamb, insisting he found it dead in the country?'

'He merely neglected to say he'd killed it,' José Goya said with a straight face.

'A lamb poached from the Count of Fuentes' own flock,' Doña Engracia said in a whisper that managed to be both furious and reverential. 'And the count a Pignatelli, the head of the family that pays for his schooling so he can draw a picture of the bishop that costs you twenty reales.' Abruptly, Doña Engracia was crying. The one thing she would never admit, least of all now, was that she loved her strange wild son Paco as much for the strangeness and the wildness as for any other reason.

The corregidor's police had come and gone. The boy Diego might live and then again he might not. Would the boy Paco

19

Goya be good enough to surrender himself to the police on his return home?

The fact that the police had not remained was significant, José Goya pointed out. It usually meant that if enough money exchanged hands, the fugitive was free to remain a fugitive. Not free in Zaragoza, of course, and not even in Aragon. But free, if he turned his back on the city and kept going.

'Paco? Alone in the world?' Doña Engracia cried. 'He wouldn't last a week, he can't take care of himself, he's like something wild and – and – '

She almost said wonderful.

On the stove the chicken simmered, and outside the wanderers' bell tolled; then there were quick footsteps on the stair and Paco stood in the doorway.

Camillo quickly crossed himself.

'Look at you,' Doña Engracia wailed. 'What are we going to do with you?'

Paco was dusty and dirty. His black hair stood in wild disarray. His shirt was torn. A big purple bruise discolored his swollen left cheek.

He was panting. He had run all the way. He looked at his two brothers, Camillo with chin on chest, sunk in thought or prayer, Tomás, the oldest, trying to appear stern; he looked at his sister Rita, who offered him that innocent martyr's smile; at his father, glowering like a stormcloud for Doña Engracia's benefit; and at Doña Engracia herself, whose full lips and dark, hooded eyes he had inherited, and he said:

'Chilindrón chicken?' He went to the stove.

'Get away from my pots,' Doña Engracia warned him, and kept herself so busy serving the meal that she had no time to scold her son. And no time to cry.

Like all the Pignatelli clan, Padre Nicolás Pignatelli was a collector of art and, within the limits of his modest wealth, a patron. His brother the Count of Fuentes had amassed a collection of paintings and statues that rivaled those of the Dukes of Osuna and Alba in Madrid. His brother Canon Ramón, remembering his antecedents, specialized in Italian art. The good padre himself, headmaster of the Jesuit school where Paco had studied, had festooned the walls of his quarters with native Aragonese art. There was, indeed, more canvas than wall, which suited Padre Pignatelli, who lived alone and had the paintings of Luzán and Bayeu for company. Both could thank Padre Pignatelli for their start. Still, it surprised them when he predicted: 'Someday these walls will be covered by the paintings of Paco Goya.'

'Goya?' they would say, and Luzán would shrug. He had accepted his limitations and become a teacher. Paco was no threat to him. But Francisço Bayeu, young, proud, seething with ambition, would say, 'Aren't you being somewhat premature, Padre?'

Now, seated by the blazing hearth in his sitting room Padre Pignatelli was inclined to agree.

The first requisite of art was to survive, and the way he was going, Paco Goya might not even reach his eighteenth birthday. The garotte could put a permanent end to a promising career.

Padre Pignatelli eased his bulk in the chair. His stout body covered a stubborn Aragonese heart and his round face hid a sharp, Jesuit-trained mind. He almost wished that Paco had the temperament of his brother Tomás, who would take his place among the artisans of Zaragoza, or of his brother Camillo, who would become a dull if well-intentioned priest. But no, great art did not grow out of mediocrity; it was tempered by discontent and pain; it needed a soul as unpredictable as a gypsy's.

Padre Nicolás Pignatelli sighed. He had eaten too much roast kid and drunk too much Cariñena, as usual, and he wanted nothing more than to crawl into bed.

Instead he waited up for a visit from the Goyas.

He had made some discreet inquiries. Well, yes, the corregidor's police had agreed, it might have been self-defense. The witnesses were all children – except for a troupe of Navarrese bullfighters who had taken part in the row and disappeared – so the corregidor would likely never get to the bottom of things.

Then if Paco Goya left Zaragoza?

The corregidor would not be displeased. The corregidor's calendar, as ever, was full. If an anonymous gift of, say, one hundred reales appeared on the corregidor's desk. . . . But naturally it was the duty of the good padre to turn the fugitive in if he could.

Yes, naturally, Padre Pignatelli had agreed – and said his Hail Marys in advance. Since Paco had undoubtedly acted in self-defense, it was only a mild sin, and in the name of art.

Perhaps, the padre told himself, just one more cup of vino-vino while he waited.

'And this second letter,' he told José Goya an hour later, pressing his family seal into the hot wax, 'for Don Pablo de Olavide. If it comes to that, he'll see to it the boy won't starve.'

The boy had paid no attention to the transactions of the past hour. He was studying the paintings on the walls, scowling before this one, exclaiming over that one.

José Goya took the two letters. 'You know Paco. He won't use them unless he *is* starving.'

'He'll use them,' Padre Pignatelli said, which could have meant anything.

Doña Engracia said: 'But Madrid. He's only seventeen. He doesn't know the first thing about taking care of himself.'

The Jesuit placed a plump hand over hers. 'Doña Engracia, he's no longer a child.'

'He's not a man.'

'No. Somewhere in between. An artist. He'll be like that all his life. Do you understand?'

'I understand,' Doña Engracia said, 'that you're avoiding the issue, Padre. Sometimes when he's working with those paints of his he forgets to change his clothing. He forgets to eat. He forgets to sleep. He – '

'Exactly. The true artist's temperament,' the Jesuit beamed.

'Will the true artist's temperament help him when he's alone in Madrid and starving? Or sick?'

'Look at him,' Padre Pignatelli urged in a soft voice.

Paco stood before the paintings on the opposite wall; he was in another world.

'Why should he rusticate here in Zaragoza?' Padre Pignatelli asked. 'He already paints better than his master Luzán. No, Doña Engracia. I almost wish I were seventeen and going to Madrid. The Puerta del Sol,' the Jesuit said raptly, 'the Plaza Mayor, the teeming life on the streets, the bold and beautiful majas – '

'Padre,' Doña Engracia said reproachfully, 'sometimes you don't sound like a priest at all.'

Times like that, Padre Pignatelli felt uncomfortable in his cassock. Doña Engracia was right, of course. He *had* let himself be carried away, envisioning a maja in a black lace dress, with a pair of castanets and a saucy look in her eyes as she danced for – whom? For Paco? For himself? He sighed. He'd be up half the night saying Hail Marys.

He cleared his throat with a deep rumble. 'Shall we tell the boy now?'

Reluctantly, Doña Engracia nodded.

'Paco,' Padre Pignatelli began, 'we've been discussing – '

'When do I leave for Madrid, Padre?'

Again the throat-clearing rumble. 'You will, of course, need money, my son. I'm willing to match the amount you earned in Fuendetodos.'

Paco looked down at the floor. 'I have no money, Padre.'

'What? Didn't they pay you?'

'Well, you see,' said Paco uncomfortably, 'I gave it to a bullfighter.'

'Santa Maria,' exclaimed José Goya.

'He won't survive his first night in Madrid,' wailed Doña Engracia.

Outside, the wanderers' bell tolled mournfully.

CHAPTER TWO

The Maja

MADRID, AS ANY SPANIARD who had been abroad conceded, was not the last word in capital cities.

The streets were crooked and narrow, and so dark at night that only cutpurses and cutthroats ventured forth after sunset, to chase the inadequate police patrols indoors and prey on one another. The municipal water supply was a trickle that could not cope with a population of almost two hundred thousand Madrileños. The municipal sanitation system was worse than non-existent. There was nowhere to walk, and no one to talk to whose ideas were worth hearing.

But all that was changing when the Apiñani brothers and their new friend Paco Goya reached Madrid.

Not that the government changed it consciously.

What they did was build a new royal palace.

It was a marvel of a palace with twelve hundred rooms. It had taken thirty years to build, and it did wonders for the city.

King Carlos, the story went, looked at his almost-completed palace, so impressive on its hill above the Manzanares River, and decided that while formerly there was no palace worthy of

23

a Bourbon king, now there was no city worthy of a Bourbon palace.

So broad avenues were thrust through the old quarters of the city and beyond, and five thousand oil lamps soon glowed on those avenues from dusk to midnight six months of the year. Water was piped in from the Guadarrama Mountains to the north, and sewage was collected as efficiently as in Paris or Rome.

Thus the new palace cost the royal treasury more than any built before, anywhere, because it changed an entire city.

As for talk, it was now everywhere.

It was political talk, which for a time did not interest Paco Goya, fresh from the provinces, and never really interested the Apiñani brothers at all. It was talk of the vast changes to the north, of men called Voltaire and Rousseau and Diderot, familiar names now in every chocolatería and café, and of how their Enlightenment would soon change the life of the people everywhere, in Spain as well as France. Or it was talk of the old soul of Spain, *castizo,* which was good enough for our grandfathers and therefore good enough for us, and the devil take those so-called Lights from France.

It was passionate talk in a passionate city, and it would lead inevitably to bloodshed. But not yet. Not for a little while yet.

There was talk, too, of the outlawing of bullfights.

This shocked the Apiñanis who, far from stretching Paco's fifty reales from Barcelona to Cádiz, had spent it all on their ten-day journey to Madrid. Their last half reale went for a ride, in style, in two open cabs on a fine afternoon in late October, to the office of Madrid's bullfight impresario.

The office was now occupied by the new Ministry of Sewage.

Paco and the Apiñanis went on foot to the bullfighters' café on the Puerta del Sol, where the brothers found a torero they had known in Pamplona. He was down-at-heel, he needed a shave, and he wore a waiter's black coat.

'King Carlos doesn't like bullfights,' he told them.

He scurried off to pour coffee and hot milk from two long-spouted pots for a fat man in a green velvet frock coat that surely must have been part of the French Enlightenment, because none of the Apiñanis had ever seen a garment like it before.

'Of course it won't last,' one-eyed Tuertillo assured Paco. 'They've tried to outlaw bullfights before. You'll see. A month or two, no more.'

'But the king himself?' said Gaspar.

'I'm not sure I'm going to like Madrid,' said Pascual.

'I'm hungry,' said Emeterio. 'A month or two is a long time to go without eating.'

Juanito's stomach rumbled. That was almost the most noise Paco had ever heard him make. He smiled apologetically.

Tuertillo waved a lazy hand at their waiter friend. 'A jar of red,' he said. 'The wine of the house, but not watered. A plate of country-cured ham, and before the ham, some shrimp. A great gleaming pink mound of shrimp.'

'Custard for dessert,' Gaspar suggested.

'And fresh peaches,' Pascual elaborated.

'And a big golden melon,' Emeterio concluded.

Paco's mouth began to water.

'The money,' the waiter said with a contemptuous glance.

'We'll have the money for you,' Tuertillo promised.

Soon they were all shelling shrimps and guzzling wine thirstily. Another jar came with the slices of dark red ham. All the brothers were eating as fast as they could convey the food to their faces.

Tuertillo kicked Paco under the table. 'Faster,' he said.

Uncomprehending, Paco stared at him. Why rush? Fast or slow, they didn't have a reale among them.

'The green velvet coat,' Tuertillo muttered.

The green velvet coat was the only other customer in the café. He sat lingering over his coffee and reading a newspaper.

Soon the custard, peaches, and melon came.

When the green velvet coat ordered a second cup of coffee, Tuertillo began to relax. 'Brandy,' he told the waiter expansively. 'With the sun of Andalucía in it.'

The waiter brought the brandy. 'That will be eight reales, friend,' he told Tuertillo.

'Disappear a few minutes, friend,' Tuertillo said, and winked his one eye.

Gaspar, Pascual, and Emeterio got up. They wandered around the café admiring the casks of wine and bottles of brandy and anís. They gazed at the mounted head of a fighting bull which had been killed in the Plaza Mayor in Madrid three years ago by the great matador Juan Romero. They turned slowly, one brother and two mirrors, and Juanito left the table and joined them. They seemed to see the green velvet coat for the first time. Awed, they drifted in the fat man's direction.

'Good afternoon, señor,' Gaspar said.

'A lovely day,' Pascual said.

25

'A splendid day to be alive,' Emeterio said.

Juanito scuffed his feet on the shell-littered floor and smiled a sweet, shy smile.

The fat man glanced up at all of them, mouthed a surly good afternoon and resumed reading the Madrid *Gazette*.

'We couldn't help noticing your coat,' Gaspar said.

'A magnificent garment,' Pascual said.

'In the height of fashion,' Emeterio said. 'You are to be commended for your taste, señor.'

They surrounded the fat man's table, three of the brothers looking awed and Juanito with that shy smile.

'Observe the softness of the collar,' Gaspar said. He touched the collar, just a light touch, really.

'And the broadness of the cuffs,' marveled Pascual, who touched the right cuff with the lightest possible touch.

'And the well-tailored sleeves. You don't mind, señor?' Emeterio asked politely. He touched the green velvet left sleeve, the politest of admiring touches.

Juanito just stood there smiling.

The fat man glowered at them. He looked around irritably for the waiter, but the waiter wasn't there.

Bowing low, the four brothers returned to their table. The fat man, relieved to be rid of that quartet of admiring rustics, was reading his *Gazette* again.

Tuertillo called the waiter. As he approached, Paco could see Juanito fumbling with something under the table and passing it to his brother. It was a green velvet purse, from which Tuertillo carefully counted out eight reales.

They left the café quickly. As they turned up a busy side street, they heard the fat man shouting.

That was Paco Goya's entrance into Madrid.

A month later he fell in love.

Madrileños insist their city has the worst climate in the world. Nine months of winter and three of hell is the way they put it. Madrileños are prone to extravagant statements, but in any event winter began that year early in November, right on schedule.

An icy wind blew down off the Guadarrama Mountains, and on a rare clear day you could see snow on the peaks and ridges. But mostly it rained, a cold, steady, drenching rain that sent the sodden Madrileños scurrying indoors. It rained for days on end, implacably. It rained diabolically, and after a while, in the poor quarters of the city, indoors was no dryer than out. Roofs leaked, ceilings dripped, cracked plaster walls became slimy with moisture.

As if all that water wasn't enough, Paco found work as a dishwasher in a restaurant on the Street of the Knifemakers, a narrow cobbled lane down a flight of stairs from the Plaza Mayor. Rain water rushed down those stairs and stood ankle-afternoon and four at night, washing dishes and silver. He plunged his hands into cold, greasy water four hours in the afternoon and four at night, washing dishes and silver. He spent another three hours each day scrubbing huge iron pots until his back ached and his hands were raw. At that, he considered himself lucky to be working. A full third of the able-bodied men living in the warren of streets south of the Plaza Mayor were unemployed.

Paco received no pay. But with the other dishwasher and the waiters he could eat leftovers, and he slept on a pile of straw in a corner of a storeroom behind the kitchen. The straw was almost dry, the storeroom was almost warm, and Paco was so tired by the early hours of the morning that he hardly noticed the glittering eyes of the foraging rats or their nocturnal squealings.

He did notice the majos and majas who frequented the restaurant, the men swaggering in their black jackets, broad crimson sashes and black breeches, the women saucy and bold in black mantillas, black bodices and black skirts. The majos entered the restaurant arrogantly, removing their drenched capes with a wet swirl to toss them negligently at a waiter. Their women cast bold glances around the red-brick cellar room, hoping to find majos more arrogant than their own. Paco would stand watching from the kitchen doorway until the proprietor sent him back to his slimy cold water with a well-placed kick.

But not a hard kick. The proprietor was a little frightened of Paco, which was how Paco got his job in the first place.

A few days after the incident of the green velvet frock coat, the Apiñani brothers had decked themselves out in majo costumes. These and the room they rented were the proceeds of other incidents like the green velvet coat, and the Apiñanis – all but shy Juanito – soon developed a swagger that outdid most other majos. It was as if they had been born to a way of life they hadn't known existed.

'What's bothering you?' Tuertillo had asked Paco one night. Paco was looking glum.

'I know you have to live somehow,' he said uncomfortably, 'until there are bulls to fight again. But I — '

'He's got scruples,' Gaspar said around a fat black cigar.

'He doesn't like stealing,' Pascal said in disbelief, also around a fat black cigar.

Emeterio blew smoke at Paco. 'Why, man, everybody preys on everybody else. You make knives, you sell them for a profit. You paint pretty pictures, somebody pays for them — more than they're worth, if you're lucky. We're more direct, that's all.'

'I'd feel better if I had a job,' Paco said.

'You won't find one,' Tuertillo told him. 'Everybody's out of work in Madrid these days.'

It was, of course, an overstatement. But not by much. Paco prowled the wet streets of the old quarter of Madrid for three days looking for work.

On the afternoon of the fourth day, Tuertillo said: 'If you really want a job, we'll get you one.'

The restaurant near the stairs that climbed to the Plaza Mayor was the first place of business they were blown to by the icy wind when they stepped outside. They swaggered donwstairs.

'Where's the proprietor?' Tuertillo asked in his lazy voice.

'Busy,' the waiter said curtly. He was used to majos. Majos and their majas filled the downstairs dining room right now.

Shy Juanito suddenly drew a clasp knife from his crimson sash. He flashed it in air an inch from the waiter's face.

That bit of activity disturbed none of the diners. Majos were always flashing knives. Even majas carried poniards tucked in their garters, and knew how to use them.

The proprietor came. He was as fat as the man in the green velvet frock coat.

'Our friend here wants work,' Tuertillo informed him.

'There is no work.'

'Any kind of job,' Gaspar said. 'Just one little job.'

'Or we'll wreck your restaurant,' Pascual said.

'We'll take it apart brick by brick,' Emeterio elaborated.

The proprietor looked at them. Majos were crazy. Majos were capable of anything. Besides, the restaurant really did need a second dishwasher.

'A dishwasher,' the proprietor said quickly, sizing Paco up. 'A place to sleep, all the leftovers he can eat, and no pay.'

Tuertillo was about to refuse the offer, or at least demand some small salary. But Paco said: 'I'll take it.'

Tuertillo's shoulders moved in a so-be-it shrug. Paco had a

lot to learn. Getting the worst of a bargain now would probably help him in the long run.

'By the way,' Gaspar said. 'We live in the neighborhood.'

'Just down the street,' Pascual said.

'So naturally we'll drop in from time to time,' Emeterio got to the nub of the matter. 'To see how our friend likes his work.'

Not all majos were petty thieves like the Apiñani brothers. Unless their majas supported them, they worked as tanners or butchers or smiths. The majas peddled oranges and nuts on the streets – when it wasn't raining. Their sexual liaisons were stormy and impermanent, they lived like pícaros, and if the spirit moved them they would spit in anyone's eye, including a policeman's. The spirit usually moved them.

They were the pride of Madrid's poor quarters. And human nature being what it is, they became the envy of Madrid's gentry.

Men of property, masquerading as majos, would often slip away from their big houses off the Alcalá or the Gran Vía, to descend into the maze of streets behind the Plaza Mayor and find themselves a maja.

Nor were wealthy women above slipping into costume and disappearing for a night in search of a majo.

It was, Paco soon learned, confusing. You often couldn't tell the real majos and majas from the fake ones.

Which, in a way, was how Paco fell in love.

Voices raised in anger drew Paco and the other dishwasher to the kitchen door. It was well past midnight, a clear night for once. It seemed that the rains of November might give way to a crisp, cold December.

'Going to be a fight,' the other dishwasher, a stooped old man, told Paco with relish.

A big, brutal-looking majo with the stub of a cigar clamped between his teeth had left his place and hovered menacingly over the only other occupied table.

At the table sat a majo and a dream.

The majo was a slender man, not much more than thirty, with a too-pretty face. He had fair, beardless skin, arched eyebrows and long-lashed eyes and a pouting, red-lipped mouth. He wore his dark, curling hair down to his shoulders where it hung unfashionably free.

The dream had dark red hair under her black mantilla and the largest, clearest blue eyes in the world. She had creamy

29

skin and high cheekbones which the red hair framed beautifully, and the most delectable mouth, small but full-lipped, that Paco had ever seen. She was young, not much older than Paco. His heart, as the poets say, skipped a beat. When it resumed beating, he was in love.

Just like that.

'The fellow's drunk,' the elderly dishwasher said. 'This is going to be good.'

Hovering over the table, the big majo pointed a forefinger the size of a garlic sausage at the too-pretty man. 'You heard me,' he said.

The pretty-faced man looked up at him through long eyelashes. 'Repeat it, my good man,' he suggested languidly.

The beautiful girl's hand touched his. 'Please take me home, Rafael. He's just looking for trouble.'

In, of course, the most beautiful voice Paco had ever heard.

The big majo bowed low and mockingly. 'A pleasure, señor. Two majas. That's what I thought when I saw you. I still do. Correct me if I'm wrong, ladies.'

'Rafael,' the girl said in warning, but she was too late.

Indolently, Rafael hurled the contents of a wing glass at the majo's face.

The proprietor looked at the ceiling in only mild despair; he lumbered away and returned hefting a barrel stave.

'Out,' he said. 'The lot of you.'

Only the girl seemed to think that was a good idea.

The big majo pawed elaborately at the red wine on his face. Then he reached for the clasp knife in his sash and at the same moment the proprietor sighed and swung the barrel stave. The big majo swiped at it casually with a ham of a hand, wrenched it from the fat man's grasp and hurled it against the brick wall with such force that it split in two.

Big majo and pretty majo faced each other across the table.

'Your knife,' the big majo said, but Rafael did not draw his knife.

'It's not that I enjoy fighting a woman,' the big majo taunted, and even that failed. Rafael would not be provoked again.

But the girl made a mistake. 'It's just part of his costume,' she tried to explain. 'He's no knife fighter.'

And Rafael shut his eyes and opened them, and stared at the knife in his own hand as if surprised that it was there.

It was there only a moment.

A huge hand grabbed him, slid him across the table. Crockery and glassware flew. His legs rose as he flipped over and landed on his back on the floor. The big majo set one booted foot on his wrist and kicked the knife away.

Rafael pushed himself off the floor slowly. His eyes took in the whole room as he rose – the fat proprietor, seated resignedly now with his double chin on his hand, Paco frozen at the kitchen door, the girl with her lips parted and her eyes wide, the majo and his knife. It was one of those moments that teach a man something about himself that with luck he would never have to learn.

Rafael turned and bolted up the stairs without looking back.

Returning the knife to his sash, the big majo bowed low before the girl and began: 'Now that you're alone, señorita – '

So swiftly that Paco could have missed it in the blink of an eye, the girl raised her black skirt to reveal a shapely silken leg, then turned with a poniard in her hand.

'Magnificent,' the elderly dishwasher said.

It was immediately clear to everyone including the big majo that the girl knew how to use her poniard. She came around the table, holding it low, moving it in small deadly arcs, her blue eyes flashing fire.

The majo backed off, then pivoted suddenly and swung an arm at the girl's hand. She darted in and out again quickly, the blade flashing like her eyes, and the majo withdrew his arm, clutching it with fingers that turned bright red.

'Spitfire, are you?' he said, almost with pleasure, and pulled the knife from his sash.

One moment Paco stood there, his jaw hanging like a *baturro's* at a fiesta, the next he was running hard across the room. By then the majo had feinted once with his knife, and as the girl's eyes followed the blurring gleam of the blade his free hand closed on her wrist. A wrenching motion, a cry, and the poniard clattered on the floor.

Paco jerked the majo's heavy cape from a peg on the wall. He whirled once, a movement the Apiñani brothers would have been proud of, to swirl the cape open, and dropped its billowing folds over the majo's head. Then the fat proprietor calmly stood, picked up his chair and swung it sideways at the majo, whose bellow was muffled by the cape as he fell.

'Better get out of here while you can, señorita,' the proprietor said.

'I'm going with her,' Paco heard himself saying.

'You've got work to do.'

'She can't go alone.'

31

'Go with her, and you won't have a job when you get back.'

The girl was pale and shaking. Even her lips had drained white. Her eyes met Paco's.

He took off his apron and dropped it on the floor.

Juanito Apiñani put the razor down and gave Paco a towel to mop soap from his face.

'Smooth,' Gaspar said.

'Pink,' Pascual said.

'Like a baby's bottom,' Emeterio said.

Tuertillo, though, was scowling. "That still doesn't settle the matter of clothing,' he pointed out. 'Will you go as a majo?'

Paco shook his head. 'Not to that house.'

'Then what? One of those Frenchified fellows with a powdered wig, a silk vest. and buckled shoes?'

Paco nodded. 'If I could.' He was very subdued.

'Well, brothers?' Tuertillo demanded. Gaspar, Pascual, Emeterio and shy Juanito left the Apiñanis' room jauntily.

An hour later they returned – three of them dancing in emptyhanded, Juanito so loaded down with clothing that even his face was hidden.

It took the brothers some time to dress Paco in the unfamiliar finery, four of them making suggestions and Juanito acting as valet. The costume dazzled them all – low, gold-buckled shoes, white silk stockings, off-white breeches, white shirt and neckcloth, gold silk vest, tan frock coat brocaded with gold, white doeskin gloves and tan tricorn hat with gold lace. Everything fit him perfectly. The brothers beamed their approval.

'Almost forgot,' Gaspar said.

'After all the trouble we had getting it,' Pascual said.

'The crowning glory,' Emeterio explained, and Juanito produced a white-powdered wig, neatly tied in back with a black ribbon. Off came the tricorn hat and on went the wig. Juanito set the hat back on Paco's head at a rakish angle. Tuertillo held the shaving mirror a short distance from Paco's nose and slowly retreated, the look of wonder on his face leaping the gap between them and appearing on Paco's face too.

Tuertillo supplied the finishing touch, a small leather purse clinking with coins. It was flat enough to fit into Paco's sleeve pocket with hardly a bulge.

The brothers surveyed him again, proudly.

'Handsome,' said Gaspar.

'Debonair,' said Pascual.

'To the manner born,' said Emeterio.

They prodded him toward the door.

At the Puerta del Sol, Paco hailed a cab and soon was seated against the soft cushions under the leather hood, watching the swaying withers of the mule and feeling the jounce of wheels on cobblestones.

They proceeded up the Alcalá, the newest and most fashionable of King Carlos' new avenues. It was late afternoon of a crisp sunny day, and Madrid had taken to the streets for its paseo.

The cab drew abreast of the Royal Academy of San Fernando. Paco stared at the gloomy façade of the building; its huge double doors opened on a dark courtyard. A slender man carrying a portfolio under his arm went in. The way he moved and his shoulder-length hair looked familiar; then he was gone.

He too, Paco told himself, would stride in there one day with a portfolio under his arm. Admission to the Academy of Fine Arts was every painter's dream.

A beggar darted beside the cab, an importunate hand extended, and called out in a croaking voice: 'Alms, alms for the love of the Virgin, good señor, noble señor!'

The good and noble señor negligently tossed the beggar a copper coin; the beggar vanished; the cab rumbled on.

The closer Paco came to his destination, the more he felt a fraud.

It had seemed so natural last night, after the fight in the restaurant. He had walked with the girl in the dark, silent streets, feeling mature and brave and saying very little. The girl clung to his arm and tried to match his strides.

'I really would rather not run, señor,' she said finally, and Paco blushed and slowed his pace.

They walked and walked, far enough, Paco thought, to go from one end of Zaragoza to the other. He had no cape; he was cold. The girl had a delicious scent of – of what? Of jasmine, or of moonlit nights in Andalucía. He could almost hear the guitars playing, and the sad voice of a spurned lover singing *cante hondo*.

He wanted desperately to talk, but could think of nothing to say. He began to hate the lonely sound of their footsteps.

Finally he blurted: 'Where do you live? France?'

And the girl laughed, a beautiful sound, and after that it was all right. He told her he was called Paco, he came from Zaragoza and would be a painter one day. She told him she was called Mariana and she lived in a big townhouse off the

Alcalá and they were almost there.

'Don't let the place frighten you,' she said. 'It's almost a palace.'

And they laughed together, the dishwasher from the Street of the Knifemakers and the girl who worked in a palace off the Alcalá. Paco wondered what she did there.

'Could you come tomorrow afternoon?' Mariana asked as they stopped before a pair of lamplit gateposts. Paco could see a driveway beyond and the dim shapes of great trees.

'Me?' he said, his heart leaping.

'Tomorrow at, shall we say, six? I want to thank you properly – Paco Goya y Lucientes.' And she ran between the gateposts and was gone.

He stood there dumbfounded. He hadn't told her his name. Just Paco. How could she know? It was impossible. It made him think of sorcery and witches.

All the way back to the street of Knifemakers he smelled the scent of jasmine.

Now his cab pulled in between the stone gateposts and he saw a huge house in the distance, its multitude of windows reflecting the twilight, its tile roof cluttered with enough chimney pots for an entire town.

The cab rolled over crushed stone and approached a carriage park. Horses and mules stood patiently while grooms curried them. Carriages were everywhere – gold-decorated berlins, cabs like Paco's own, a pair of black landaus, one great traveling coach and a single English milord. Footmen scurried about, polishing brightwork, polishing sidelamps.

Paco seemed to sink inside himself as his cab drew inexorably up to the porte-cochère. He had made a mistake; he should have asked for the servants' entrance. What, anyway, was Mariana doing in this monster of a house?

And how in the name of all the saints in Paradise had she known his name?

The cab creaked and swayed as its driver got down from his box. A footman approached and let down the step.

Driver waited, footman waited.

Far off in the interior of the huge house Paco heard a burst of laughter.

He climbed down. 'Wait,' he told the driver in an odd voice. About five minutes, he told himself, until they throw me out.

His stiff black shoes crunched over crushed stone. He went up three steps and through a wide doorway, and found himself in a white-walled hallway decorated with gold. A

34

young man in a tan tricorn and tan frock coat stared at him. The young man looked as frightened as Paco did.

It was himself, in a gold-bordered mirror.

A porter came into the mirror and stood at his image's shoulder. With a just-managed flourish, Paco stripped off his gloves, removed his hat, tossed gloves in hat. The porter took the hat, bowed and went away.

Paco advanced past the mirror and up three more steps into another white and gold hallway, bigger than the first. Beyond was a doorway and the sound of voices. Then a burst of laughter again, and he almost bolted.

Before he could, the most elaborately dressed man he had ever seen made his appearance. He was all in purple and gold with gold buttons up the length of his long frock coat, and a powdered wig. Paco was about to bow low. The elaborately dressed man bowed first.

'Whom shall I announce, señor?' he inquired.

The deferential tone coming from that awesome figure did something to Paco. He squared his shoulders and said: 'Francisco de Goya y Lucientes.' The 'de' was no lie; Doña Engracia, after all, had been born of an hidalgo family, if a poor one.

The major-domo bowed and preceded Paco toward the doorway. 'Don Francisco de Goya y Lucientes,' he bellowed.

Paco stood alone in the doorway, staring at a sea of curious faces. He could not move.

Then the sea parted miraculously, and Mariana came gracefully toward him with one hand outstretched.

'Hello, Paco. Hello,' she said with a dazzling smile. She wore a simple white gown with a pink sash that cinched her narrow waist. Her hand alighted with a feather touch on Paco's arm, and they entered the great salon together.

Nothing in Paco's life prepared him for that room.

Once more the walls were white, their panels gilded elaborately. Arched mirrors twice a man's height matched arched French doors opening on an interior garden. The bare floor was wood, not tile, and its squares gleamed brilliantly under a chandelier of a hundred candles and a hundred glittering crystals. Chairs and sofas of plump brocaded rose and gilded wood formed intimate conversational groupings. A huge gilt and marble table, a gilded fireplace, the gold scrollwork at juncture of walls and ceiling – all would have taken the gilder José Goya a year or more to produce.

Almost lost in one corner of that vast room stood a rose-wood harpsichord. A man made his way through the crowd, flipped back the tails of his frock coat, sat before the harpsichord and filled the room with a Scarlatti sonata.

'Scarlatti,' Paco whispered, pleased that he could identify the music.

Mariana nodded. 'Uncle Pablo was desolate when he died. They were great friends.'

Paco stood there, shifting his weight from one foot to the other. The gold-buckled shoes had begun to pinch. What the beautiful Mariana did in this house was live here.

The last notes of the harpsichord summoned polite applause. 'He's very talented,' Paco said. 'He works for your uncle?'

'The harpsichordist?' Mariana hid a quick smile behind her ivory fan. 'That's Fernando de Silva, the Duke of Alba.'

The Duke of Alba – most famous of all the grandees of Spain – playing the harpsichord here. Paco felt sweat trickling under the folds of his silk neckcloth. How, he wondered, could this beautiful white-gowned creature and the equally beautiful maja of last night, all in black, the one looking as if she had been born to this way of life, the other lustily wielding a poniard, be the same person? To be struck by love of the maja was one thing. He had even harbored a fantasy or two about her. She was young, hardly older than he; she was bold, she seemed to like him – anything could happen. But this aristocrat in white, hiding her amusement behind an ivory fan – he could as easily grow a pair of wings and fly to the moon.

'There you are, my dear.'

A handsome man, in his early forties and standing hidalgo-straight in a sky blue frock coat, approached them.

'Uncle.' Mariana curtseyed prettily.

'And this is our Aragonese artist?'

'Francisco Goya,' Mariana introduced them, 'my uncle, Don Pablo de Olavide.'

Paco bowed. Mariana's uncle bowed as low, without mockery.

'My niece,' he said, 'has a genius for ferreting things out, young man. I've been searching all over Madrid for you.'

'You have?' Paco asked.

Olavide surveyed his well-tailored clothing. 'But I can see your friends and family in Zaragoza had little reason to worry. You have a good job, no doubt?'

'Yes, señor,' Paco said, and Mariana again hid that quick smile behind her fan, a gesture not lost on her uncle.

'And I assume you aren't illiterate?' Olavide asked dryly.
'No, señor.' Paco bristled.

'Then might I take the liberty to suggest that you write to your parents, or to the good Padre Pignatelli?'

Paco clapped a hand to his head. 'Olavide,' he blurted. 'Of course, Padre Pignatelli gave me a letter for you, señor, but I – '

'Never got around to delivering it,' Olavide said with only mild reproach. 'No more than you got around to writing home.'

It all became clear then: A boy named Paco, from Zaragoza, who wanted to be an artist, naturally he had to be the one Mariana's uncle wanted to find.

But how could he have written? *Dear father, I have work as a dishwasher in a restaurant in a slum behind the Plaza Mayor. I earn no salary and have no money to buy paints and brushes. . . .*

'I have letters for you, one from Padre Pignatelli and one from your father. And,' in that dry voice again, 'I have some questions. Could you swallow that Aragonese pride long enough to answer them?'

Paco felt his face grow hot again.

'Nicholas Pignatelli claims you have a talent, young man,' Olavide began. 'And Spain needs native painters. Have you been painting?'

A long pause. 'No, señor.'

'Then sketching?'

'No, señor.'

'Could you tell me why?'

After a while Paco said: 'I could. I'd rather not.'

Olavide's eyebrows lifted toward his powdered hair. 'But you want to paint?'

'With all my heart, señor.'

'Splendid. The heart is a good place to paint from.' Olavide took a pinch of snuff from a gold box. 'In a few minutes I'll address my guests here. My words will be in French, which I assume you don't understand. You'll learn it. It's the language of the court. You'll learn other things. The Olavide family will sponsor you.'

'Señor,' Paco said stiffly, 'I could not accept charity.'

'Charity? Who the devil's talking of charity? I want you to master the talent Nicholás Pignatelli has seen. It won't be easy. I want you to find your limits – and then surpass them. Charity?' Olavide laughed. 'You'll be given barely enough for your needs? You'll work. You'll work until you never want to hold another paintbrush in your hand. No, young man, don't talk to me of charity. A time will come when you'll wish the good Lord had been charitable enough to see that we'd never met.'

Pablo de Olavide sat up in bed, a frown on his face, a red flannel cap on his head and on his raised knees a journal called *Correspondance Littéraire,* sent from Paris by a German named Grimm. A friend of Diderot, of Rousseau, and of the patriarch of all the Enlightenment, Voltaire, Grimm had written: 'The world is made up of nothing but abuses which none but a madman would try to reform.'

And certainly the abuses, if anything, were worse in Spain than in France. Why, even Olavide's clandestine reading of the age-yellowed copy of *Correspondance* was a sin and a crime, interdicted by the Holy Office. Was he then, as Baron von Grimm suggested, a madman to fight those abuses?

The frown left his face. He chuckled. He liked the image of himself as a madman, quixotic, tilting at windmills.

There was a tap at the door. Mariana, wearing a soft woolen dressing gown, came in.

She glanced at the journal and made a face. 'Baron von Grimm,' she said. 'One moment he assures you the *philosophes* can do anything; the next he admits it is madness to change what cannot be changed. The French – '

'Are the most civilized people in the world,' Olavide finished for her. 'It's late, my dear, and I refuse to enter into that particular discussion again. Sometimes I regret the education I've given you.'

Mariana sat on the edge of the canopied bed. 'What do you think of him, uncle?'

'Crude but not coarse,' Olavide said promptly. 'Proud but not arrogant. Of course, everything depends on his talent. How did your talk go?'

'He'll accept our sponsorship. Whatever it costs he wants to consider a loan.'

'I like that,' Olavide said. 'The young man has fiber. Why are you smiling?'

'I think he's in love with me.'

'Puppy love,' Olavide snorted. 'How old is he, eighteen?'

'I suppose so,' Mariana said.

'Well, if this puppy love makes him work harder, good. Do you find him attractive, my dear?'

Mariana's eyes dropped. 'He's only a child.'

38

'Spoken like a mature woman of twenty,' Olavide commented dryly, and changed the subject. 'I missed Anton Rafael tonight. Is there trouble between you?'

'I beg your pardon, uncle?' Mariana looked startled.

'Dear girl, I have eyes. Anton Rafael likes to get away from that stuffy wife of his occasionally and play the majo, and if it amuses you to share his masquerade – '

'Rafael had to deliver some sketches to the Academy. He was probably delayed, that's all.'

'In any event, you can now play the maja in earnest. It is the privilege of every maja, I gather, to support the majo of her choice?'

'You're making fun of me, uncle.'

'Hardly. If the boy thinks he's in love with you, all the better. Arrange everything, my dear. A studio, a small allowance, French lessons.'

'Art lessons?'

'No, not yet. He's had a few years under Luzán in Zaragoza. Let him paint what he feels, let him paint what the eyes of an Aragonese *baturro* see in Madrid.'

'Yes,' Mariana said. 'I think you're right.'

Her uncle waggled a forefinger. 'To paint like a rustic from Aragon, yes, but not to think like one. I want you to expose him to the ideas of the Enlightenment.'

'I won't be a very enthusiastic teacher,' Mariana said.

Olavide smiled. 'I'll supply the books and journals, my dear. You can supply the rebuttal. Just see he reads them.'

'He'll read them,' Mariana promised.

'And see that he enters the Academy's competition this year. What's the subject to be?'

'Sirens,' Rafael said.

'Sirens.' The word left a bitter taste in Olavide's mouth. 'With a living, breathing world to paint, what do we have? We have sirens. Well, no matter. He won't win the competition. They'll find his work too crude, I'm sure. But the losing will do him good.'

'He'll compete,' Mariana said, and again her uncle smiled.

'Wrapped him around your little finger, have you? Sometimes it's hard for me to realize how fast you've grown up.' Olavide leaned forward for Mariana to kiss his cheek. 'Twenty,' he mused. 'We really should think of finding a husband for you, my dear.'

'When my uncle wishes, I'll marry.'

'Good night, my dear.'

39

Mariana retired, and Olavide read another page or two of Grimm's *Correspondance*. The ideas of the Enlightenment were not new to him. He had traveled to Paris, to Berlin, to Rome, and counted Diderot and the Encyclopedists among his friends. His visits to the royal palace in Madrid were frequent. King Carlos called him Don Pablo, affectionately and with respect.

Still, although he had read Locke and Adam Smith and David Hume's *An Inquiry Concerning Human Understanding*, he did not understand the ways of a lusty twenty-year-old girl.

In another part of the house, in her own bed, Mariana tossed restlessly. What shoulders for a boy of eighteen! And that deep voice, and that pride – it almost is arrogance, though my uncle doesn't see it.

Those hooded, secret eyes. . . .

Dear uncle, sweet uncle, don't find a husband for me just yet.

CHAPTER THREE

Love and Sirens

THOSE HOODED, SECRET EYES came to delight her, to infuriate her, to make her laugh, to make her cry, to challenge her, to probe the depths of her passion long before she knew it was being tested, to surrender to her, to conquer and dominate her.

She found a garret room for Paco, a large room, sparsely furnished with table, stove, three chairs, and a bed hidden in a curtained alcove. To Mariana it was a monk's cell, but Paco went eagerly to the window, which looked out over the Plaza Mayor, gazed down at the crowds scurrying like ants far below and turned to say: 'Perfect! All I need now are some paints and a brush or two,' and before she could begin to consider the absolutely minimal changes necessary to make his room livable he had whirled her out of it, and down the four flights of stairs, her dueña lumbering and puffing behind, those eyes of his sparkling with the prospect of some paints and a

40

brush or two so that her absolutely minimal changes would have to be forgotten.

Resignedly, she accompanied him to the art shop in back of the San Fernando Academy. The moment they passed through the doorway Paco forgot she was there. He bounced from easels to palettes to brushes to mahlsticks, to sketch pads and chalks and ink and pens, those hooded eyes glowing. He quickly selected canvases and wooden slats to stretch them on.

'Turpentine or naphtha?' he asked no one in particular.

Mariana, who knew something about painting, began: 'I'm told that – '

'Turpentine,' Paco decided, and the quantity he wanted was poured.

'Linseed oil? Or hazelnut oil?' Paco wondered.

'The advantages of – '

'Linseed oil,' said Paco, who had already approached the display of brushes again. 'Maybe just one squirrel, very fine, for delicate work.'

'They tell me sable – '

But he was off again. So much sizing, so much ground, have you a storage cabinet, señor?

'We'll need a cart, Mariana.' The first time he had ever used her name.

Two palette knives, one very broad and heavy.

Where's that cart?

'Paco – ' finally, with a smile – 'don't you think you might buy some paints?'

The hand clapped to head in that now-familiar boyish gesture as the wizened old Basque shopkeeper led them to a pungent-smelling back room, where a heated conversation on the preparation of pigments followed. Paco jumped around the room, examining slab and muller, mortar and pestle, beakers, pipkins and crucibles. The substance that gave the room its pungent smell was cooking at a rolling boil on a stove, and he sniffed at it gingerly. He chose his pigments, which the shopkeeper weighed out and wrapped in little twists of paper – rose madder and flake white and chrome yellow and emerald green and asphaltum and three different kinds of blue.

'I've heard that verdigris is better for – '

Where's that cart?

'It's been waiting half an hour, Paco.'

Her dueña, who had come to Spain from Peru with the Olavides and was called the Indian, helped Mariana climb into the cart. Paco's equipment was loaded next, and then the Indian

41

got in ponderously. There was no room anywhere in the cart for Paco.

'I'll walk,' he said.

He ran.

Sometimes he would disappear for days on end.

Mariana would come, the Indian at her side carrying a case of books and journals, and they would climb the four flights of stairs. Mariana would knock on the door and, getting no answer, cautiously push it open.

Stale eggs on a plate, a fly buzzing at the window, a bare canvas resting on the easel pegs, crusted blobs of paint on the palette, but no Paco.

The next day the same, and the next.

The fourth day, or the fifth, he would be there.

'You can't just go off like that. What about your French lessons? Maître Lachine comes every afternoon.'

'J'apprends le français,' Paco would say. 'C'est très facile, n'est-ce pas?'

Or another day: 'You're like a gypsy. Where do you go?'

'Oh, here and there.' With those eyes distant.

'And the journals I left? The *Correspondance* with the critique of Rousseau's – '

'Oh, that,' Paco would say. 'Rousseau's rejection of original sin is too much for Baron von Grimm, that's all.'

She would sigh, or sometimes she wanted to scratch his eyes out. She had worked for hours over the *Correspondance,* translating the French words Paco might find difficult, and she began to wonder why she bothered. He seemed to grasp intuitively what the French *Philosophes* had to say. In a sort of offhanded manner, as if it hardly mattered.

Or, after another disappearance: 'What about those letters? You promised.'

'Oh, that.' The way Paco oh-that-ed everything exasperated her. 'I've already had answers. My family is well and Padre Pignatelli wrote to say the fellow I stabbed is on his feet again.'

Once she said: 'If I've climbed these stairs once. I've climbed them a hundred times. Every time I'm here I see your canvas empty, your brushes clean, and the same stale paint on your palette. Don't you want to be a painter? What about the Academy? You want to try for a grant, don't you?'

'Oh, that. I applied weeks ago.'

'Then why aren't you working?'

'There's no hurry. I won't win. I'm not ready for the Academy yet; I know that. I'll give them a painting, though.'

'Can't you get some prints to copy? Ulysses, the boat, the sirens on their rocks – '

'There's only one way to paint a siren,' Paco stated flatly.

His sudden interest interested her. 'Yes? How?'

'Naked, on a rock, with her hair streaming over her body. Of course, to paint from the nude is forbidden. But if it's done secretly. . . . Would you pose for me, Mariana?'

'Paco!'

The tone of her voice made the Indian come lumbering in from the hallway.

'You wouldn't pose for me?' Paco said quickly in French, taunting her.

'Paco, stop that. Now.' Her confusion made her own French worse than Paco's.

He knew when to stop. He looked at her shyly and said in a subdued voice: 'I've been working. On the streets. I really have, Mariana.'

He went to the sleeping alcove, parted the curtain and reached under the bed. He brought three large sketch pads to the table.

In pen-and-ink line drawings, and sometimes with the faintest of washes, he had captured the streets of the city.

A corner just off the Puerta del Sol, and a water vendor with her jug and cups surrounded by a thirsty crowd. Just how did they seem thirsty? Mariana could not say, but they did.

Three young majos, who had to be brothers, striding down the center of a street, scowling fiercely from behind three big black cigars, daring anyone to cross their path.

A scrawny beggar in rags, looking more sure of himself than the young dandy in a cab who casually tossed him a coin.

Mariana turned the sheets slowly. She heard Paco take a long breath at the window. Far below, a horse went clopping by.

Crude, she told herself; her uncle might say they were crude. And in a way they were. But perhaps that was part of their strength. They were real, so incredibly real that you could live a life in those sketches.

'Oh, Paco,' she said. 'Why didn't you let me see?'

'I was afraid,' he said.

'They're wonderful. They're so alive.'

And he was so alive, in his old majo clothing, and seemed so unsure of himself, listening to her words of praise. She took two steps, and he two, and their hands touched, and their

43

bodies almost touched and then the Indian, who must have had eyes that could see through a wall, growled something in the hallway, and they drew apart.

Of course, to paint from the nude is forbidden. . . . Would you pose for me, Mariana?

Those words, so lightly spoken, began to dominate her every thought.

In France they painted from nude models. Fragonard did, and Boucher. And what about old Tiepolo, the Italian, who had left his wife at her gaming tables in Venice and brought his beautiful young model Cristina to Madrid?

Would you pose for me, Mariana?

Sometimes those words sent her, shyly, at night, to stand unclothed before her mirror with only the light of a single candle, her red hair down almost to her waist, one taut-tipped breast peeping through, the curve of a hip highlighted by the candle, the supple waist so narrow that she was sure Paco could span it with those strong hands of his. . . .

And the dreams she had! No, she would not let herself dwell on those dreams; how could she help what she dreamed?

Her uncle noticed the change in her. 'Is something troubling you, my dear? You seem – distracted.'

'What? No, it's nothing.'

But it was everything.

One night when she was posing before the mirror with a saucy smile on her lips, the Indian walked in.

Mariana dove for her bed and covered herself to the chin. 'Please don't tell my uncle. He'd never understand. I was only – '

Only what?

The Indian, for once, was not laconic. 'Oh, he would understand. He would understand only too well. There are things I could tell you about your uncle.'

The Indian snuffed out the candle flame. 'To be young and beautiful, and in love,' she sighed wistfully in the darkness.

In love? Was it that obvious?

It was obvious Paco would do nothing about that siren painting. Every afternoon she saw the canvas, still propped on the easel, still blank, accusing them both.

'The idea just won't come,' he would say.

'I told you, get prints to copy. I could borrow some from the Academy if you'd like.'

'Borrow. Who wants to borrow a copy that someone copied

44

from someone else?'

The Indian, in her secret Indian way, almost seemed to become Paco's ally. More and more she would find excuses to leave her post outside the garret room, a mysterious errand that could not wait, or her friend, the dueña of Count This-and-that's daughter, was sick and needed comforting.

Mariana's indecision seemed to exasperate the Indian. One night she said: 'The only thing worse than to be young and in love and doing something about it, is to be young and in love and doing nothing about it.'

Soon the Indian was worrying about Mariana's health. 'Look at you,' she would say, 'you're as pale as a ghost. Your bones show. Who ever found a skinny girl attractive?' She would try to entice her with rich, tempting foods, but Mariana would take a nibble or two of lamb or poke a spoon at her custard, staring off into space.

'Pah, what am I going to do with you?' the Indian would say. 'You eat like a bird, you hardly sleep, the only time you go out of doors is when you visit that boy in his garret.'

One afternoon after Mariana's siesta, the Indian threw the drapes back, letting pale winter sunlight into her room, and said: 'I think the gold dress today.'

'The gold?'

Mariana usually dressed as a maja for her visits to the garret room over the Plaza Mayor.

The gold dress was daring, with a skirt that barely reached her ankles, a tight bodice and a dangerously plunging neckline.

'The gold,' the Indian said firmly, and soon she was helping Mariana into it.

'No hair powder,' the Indian said. 'There's a wind. It would blow all over you.' She combed the long, dark red hair high, pinned it up in back and turned her attention to Mariana's beautiful blue eyes, darkening the brows and lashes, touching the lids with oil. She stepped back and surveyed her work.

'Pale as a mouse in winter,' she muttered, and tweaked Mariana's cheeks so hard that the girl cried out. But when the Indian stepped back a second time she clucked her tongue, pleased with herself. Mariana's cheeks had a good rosy color.

'The black silk cloak,' said the Indian.

'I'm not going to the theater,' Mariana protested.

The Indian paid no attention. 'All in black and gold, like the daughter of a grandee.'

Downstairs, Mariana asked: 'Have you the journals?'

The Indian nodded. She was carrying a leather case.

As they walked outside, the journals seemed to make an odd clinking sound. Mariana decided it was her imagination.

When the Indian put the case on the table in the garret room, it made that odd clinking sound again. She did not remove her cloak. 'My friend, the dueña of Count This-and-that's daughter,' she said, mumbling the name indistinctly as she always did. 'Still sick with her catarrh, and I promised I'd sit up with her.'

Neither Mariana nor Paco said anything. Paco couldn't take his eyes off the neckline of the gold dress.

The Indian smiled. It was only the second time Mariana had ever seen her do so. The first was when Mariana had shown unmistakable signs of puberty. 'Be good children.'

She started for the door.

'Wait,' Mariana called. 'When will you be back?'

'In three or four hours,' the Indian said, and shut the door firmly behind her. They heard her lumbering down the stairs.

The empty canvas stared at them.

'Cold out,' Mariana said.

'Windy.'

Silence.

'Did you sketch today?'

'No.'

Outside, a church bell bonged the half-hour. Others, further off, echoed it.

'Half past,' Paco said.

Mariana felt pale and frightened. The Indian had pinched her cheeks for nothing.

They sat looking at each other as the light began to fade.

'I wish you'd stop staring at me like that.'

'It's a beautiful gown.'

'It's not the gown you're staring at.' She almost bit her tongue. Calling his attention to the low-cut neckline was worse than ignoring it.

She glanced at the case on the table. 'I didn't bother to translate anything this time,' she said brightly. 'Want to try it yourself?'

'All right,' Paco said. He seemed relieved. He brought a pair of candles to the table, bent low to strike sparks from flint and steel, found himself staring at Mariana's plunging neckline and turned away quickly. The candle went out. He fumbled with his tinderbox again. Soon both candles were

46

burning.

Paco opened the case. 'That's funny,' he said.

In the case were a pair of wine bottles, their corks pulled and rammed back in.

'That Indian,' Mariana said in an odd voice, shaking her head. 'She brought the wrong case.' But Mariana knew she had not brought the wrong case.

Outside, the church bell bonged the quarter-hour.

'Quarter of five,' Paco said. He got up.

'Where are you going?'

'Cups. For the wine.'

He poured two cups full, and raised his. 'Health,' he said.

'Money,' Mariana responded automatically, raising her own cup.

'Time to enjoy them,' Paco said. He waited.

Mariana hesitated. The last line of the toast? How could she say it, alone in this room with Paco, with those eyes of his challenging her to say it?

But she would feel more foolish if she didn't. 'And love over all,' she finished hastily.

They gulped their first cups very fast, and their second. A third cup for each finished the first bottle. It was delicious wine, deep and heady.

After a while things got much brighter.

They talked animatedly about the journals that weren't there. What Diderot might have written. Or Baron von Grimm. They laughed a great deal. They began on the second bottle.

The conversation switched to art. Three days until those damn sirens. . . .

Don't say damn.

Fragonard. Boucher.

Who brought them up? Mariana wondered.

She stood, knocking over her empty wine cup.

'I'll pose for you,' she said, and once the words were spoken, her knees felt weak.

'You will?' Paco seemed surprised. 'You don't have to.'

'Don't you want me to?'

'Of course I want you to.' In an uncertain voice. Surprised was too mild a word. Dismayed, rather.

He went to the storage cabinet and took out brushes, pots of paint. He almost dropped his oil jar.

Mariana remained standing near the table. What do I do now? she wondered. Take off my clothing right here? She couldn't. She wished she had never spoken those words.

With a brush Paco pointed to the curtained alcove. Mariana went weak-kneed in that direction, reached the curtains, parted them, and collided with the bed. The curtains fell into place behind her.

She could hear Paco fussing with his paints. She would feel ridiculous undressing.

She would feel more ridiculous not undressing.

Swiftly, before she could change her mind, she took down her hair and slipped the gold dress over her head. She stood there a long moment, the bed crowding her, then removed her underclothes. She began to shiver.

No sound at all from the other side of the curtain.

She couldn't do it.

But again, now that she had gone this far, it would be more ridiculous to stand there, trapped, naked, between bed and curtains.

She parted the curtains high up. Only her pale face peeked out.

Across the room, Paco was fumblingly lighting all the candles he had.

'It's too dark,' he said. 'How can I get the colors right when it's so dark? Perhaps tomorrow,' he suggested, 'if you came earlier. . . . '

She parted the curtains with one swift, smooth motion and stood, arms still raised, head down, hair down, eyes downcast. She heard Paco gasp, heard the tinderbox drop.

And then Paco was beside her.

He touched her bare shoulder. His hand was cold.

She wanted to cry suddenly. She wished the Indian would return, and dress her, and drag her out by an ear. She wished the roof would fall in. She wished she had never met Paco, never brought him home to meet her uncle. She couldn't stop shivering. Under the tent of her hair she could feel her breasts puckering with the cold. Her lips were trembling. Her knees were probably blue.

She wished she had never been born.

Paco's fingertips touched her throat and traced a cold scalding line between her breasts.

'You're beautiful,' she heard him say in a soft voice.

His hand grew bolder. His mouth covered her mouth.

Indian, Indian, please come now, I'm not cold any more, I feel all strange and wonderful, but I won't know what to do, how will I know what to do?'

48

'The sirens,' she protested against his lips, and then she shuddered, and all at once it was simple, so very simple, to arch her body and give him access to its secret places, and she felt tears on her cheeks, his tears, and she began, tentatively at first, and then boldly, to explore with her hands the hard strength of his body as he was exploring the litheness of hers, and finally, gleaming above her face as sooner or later they had to be, were those secret, hooded eyes.

The sirens?

He lit his whole supply of candles and painted in a frenzy, before the Indian returned, while Mariana slept on his bed, her dark red hair spread on his pillow, a sated smile on her lips.

He had no time for an elaborate structure of layers of pigment, no time to underpaint the design in monochrome, no time for the slow painstaking addition of texture, of subtleties of reflected light and shadow, no time for anything he had learned at José Luzán's studio.

He painted impatiently, attacking the canvas with thick gobs of pigment, not pausing to think, troweling his paints on with a palette knife, smearing them with a rag, using blues and grays and blacks, the merest suggestion of a storm-tossed sea and a glowering sky as background for two sirens on a rock, one demure with eyes downcast, the other provocative with arms wide and head thrown back, both with long hair, wet like seaweed, cloaking their bodies.

He stepped back, bleary-eyed. The background was wrong, hardly a background at all. As for the sirens, he could imagine the academicians shaking their heads at that pair of ill-defined creatures sitting on their rock, their drenched hair making them seem part of the tossing sea.

No, he would not win a prize.

To ignore the techniques he had carefully, laboriously acquired was perverse.

Yet somehow, despite their crude execution, they *felt* like sirens.

He felt exhausted.

Most of the candles had gone out.

He could hear wind shrieking over a foam-flecked sea.

He could hear a roll of drums and a tattoo of musket fire, and voices crying out in the night.

He could see a giant with fists that could shatter whole villages.

Suddenly the room was plunged into total darkness.

Sea and musket fire became a roaring in his ears. The giant

4

smote the earth.

He bowed his head and prayed, and he thought fleetingly that his brother Camillo would have been pleased; but then he knew he was praying to no God Camillo would understand.

That you grant me a long life, whoever you are. That you grant me a crowded life, rich in pleasure but also rich in pain. That you grant me patience to paint as they expect, so that someday I can paint as I must. . . .

The roaring mounted in his ears.

'Paco? What is it?'

'I – nothing.' He was at her side, his heart pounding wildly. 'Mi vida. Te amo. Te adoro.'

'Mi corazón.'

He would not paint that way again, abandoning technique in a frenzy of feeling, for half a lifetime.

BOOK TWO

BOOK TWO

UNDER THE GASLIGHT-DAPPLED leaves of the chestnut trees on the Rue de la Paix in Paris in 1824, the old man taps the table leg with his Malacca cane and orders another coffee. He is uncertain about his voice. As he is deaf, he does not know if it is a whisper or a bellow.

He remembers Dr Rodríguez-Pereira and his beautiful deaf-mute nurse trying to teach him. It is a feeling in the throat, Don Paco, Rodríguez-Pereira tells him, and Don Paco places his own hands on the doctor's throat while the deaf-mute Isabel watches. So long ago!

The autumn wind is cold. A waiter emerges with a brazier. The warming glow of the charcoal is reflected from the glass walls on either side of the café.

Seated in the semi-darkness, the Prince of the Peace seems lost in thought. And what, the old man wonders, is going through that mind of his, after the life he's led? Would he, if he could, obliterate months and years of it, like a master painter rubbing out the black chalk lines of his apprentice with a quick stab of his thumb?

No, not the Prince of the Peace, not him. He was one who lived without regrets.

And Don Paco? Hunched over his coffee, waiting, on his lap the leather case with its dueling pistols?

He would change none of it either, not the torment, and not the magic.

He remembers the dark red hair spread on his pillow as if it were yesterday. He remembers the demonic visions.

Madness and genius, the two sides of a coin.

And a voice, the voice of the dark red hair a little later, crying out scornfully, those blue eyes blazing up at him: 'Damned Aragonese peasant rutting like a pig in a barnyard!'

Regret that? Rub it out with the thumb of a master painter?

53

Mariana dead now, so many gone, the old man reflects bleakly; why should I have outlived them all?

I had a few canvases to paint, he thinks. Yes, that was it, I had a few canvases to paint.

Josefa – patient, quiet, competent Josefa of the golden hair, who speaks now in his mind: 'You'll be back, caro, and Madrid will know that you have returned.'

The Apiñani brothers. Four of them surviving the bulls, surviving revolution and war and an alien occupation, and the fifth, dead so young, his blood running over the cobbles of the Puerta del Sol.

The most beautiful face in Spain and a certain arrogant elegance. . . .

And the Prince of the Peace sits there, drinking cognac he cannot afford, his life over but his heart, his murderous heart, still beating.

Always there are the others who touch your life, who hold it in their hands for a moment, who shape it.

Anton Rafael Mengs, who never forgot the boy standing at the kitchen door.

Francisco Bayeu, painter to the king, gruff, pedantic, born middle-aged, the master painter studying his sketch and telling him: 'It's wrong, it's all wrong, this line here is pure chaos, this shadowing too heavy, and yet – it does have something. Why don't you put it in oils, Goya? I really do believe I'd like to see it on canvas.'

And Paco, so young then, works in a cloud of well-being.

Padre Pignatelli, his face haggard, his voice grim: 'Get out of Madrid or you'll wind up a convict in the galleys at Cádiz.'

Mariana's uncle, his friend, his benefactor. But how wrong it all went, and how it changed his life!

Olavide, who later wanted to horsewhip him through the streets of Sevilla. Perhaps, the old man thinks with a chuckle, it is a good thing I did not go to Sevilla.

Olavide, burning with an idea, taking it to the king one morning at the royal palace, insisting he could change the face of Spain.

Don Paco can almost see them, in the palace, at dawn, when the dwarfish, mahogany-faced, kindly King Carlos began his day. . . .

CHAPTER FOUR

The King's Levee

PABLO DE OLAVIDE, usually the most tranquil of men, was nervous.

For one thing, he was not at his best in what he regarded as the middle of the night. Yet he had had to rise before the sun in order to arrive at the royal palace shortly after six in the morning.

For another, the page had ushered him not into the Porcelain Room adjacent to the royal bedchamber but into the Yellow Room next door, a subtle matter of protocol. The closer to the royal bedchamber you waited, the more important your business with the king.

What bothered him most, though, at this ridiculous hour of the king's levee, was the reason for his visit. Only a fool tried to solve his personal problems by resorting to his public position. Yet that was what Don Pablo de Olavide found himself doing this hot morning in August 1765.

He sat stiffly on the edge of a comb-back chair, staring at a piano encrusted with mother-of-pearl. The room was exquisitely neoclassic in a style Anton Rafael Mengs would have approved.

The style would not have been approved by the other two occupants of the Yellow Room. The old Italian court painter Giovanni Battista Tiepolo stood with one elbow on a corner of a gilded writing desk. His halo of fine white hair, surrounding a pinkish bald spot, looked almost like a tonsure. His hand shook as he opened a snuffbox. His son Domenico sat at his side with a resigned look on his face.

They put me in here with painters, Olavide told himself; and who is waiting in the Porcelain Room next door? His friend Count Aranda, perhaps, who had arranged his visit to the king's levee. Aranda was young and bold, a rising star in the royal firmament. And certainly Squillace would be there, the king's first minister, Squillace the Italian, who had done more to weaken the king's hold on his subjects than if he had been the king's worst enemy.

The Olavides, uncle and niece, had spent almost a year in France. Received in Paris by the Encyclopedists, Mariana had charmed Diderot and Baron von Grimm both, and she had become a success at court. They had even gone as house guests for a week to the great Voltaire's place at Ferney on the Swiss border. All of it should have been enough to bring the girl to her senses.

But when they returned to Madrid two weeks ago, Mariana had immediately resumed her affair with young Goya. The Indian, as a dueña, was worse than useless. She encouraged them.

And Mariana, strong-willed as ever, would have no other dueña.

Olavide had threatened to cut off Paco's allowance. But Mariana said: 'If you cut off his money, I'll go to live with him. Openly.'

'But what do you see in the boy? Almost two years in Madrid, and what's he accomplished? He didn't get a single vote at the Academy; he hasn't had a single commission — '

'You've seen his sketches. You know he's talented.'

'Yes,' Olavide had admitted wearily, 'I know he's talented.'

A page in royal red silk stockings came to the doorway of the Yellow Room. Domenico Tiepolo looked up; his father squared a pair of ancient shoulders. The page gave them a disdainful glance and bowed in Olavide's direction.

'His Catholic Majesty will receive Don Pablo de Olavide.'

Olavide made a minute adjustment to his powdered wig, and followed.

The king's hairdresser had placed the royal wig on a plaster head and was smearing it with oil preparatory to powdering it. The king's barber was stropping his razor. The king sat on the edge of his canopied bed in silk stockings and dressing gown, tickling his favorite hound Blanquí's left ear and peering owlishly through horn-rimmed spectacles at a report that, Olavide noticed, bore the seal of Squillace.

As Olavide bowed low, dropping one knee to the floor, King Carlos inclined his own head in a courtesy bow not called for by protocol.

'Your Majesty.'

'It is good to see our Peruvian again,' the king said in a soft, wistful voice. The accent of Naples was very pronounced this morning. In the sixth year of his reign and the fiftieth of his life, Carlos III, former king of the Two Sicilies, was an awkward widower with a shy and self-effacing smile.

The barber approached, testing his razor on the ball of his thumb. Hot towels covered the royal visage, the tip of a long Bourbon nose alone protruding.

'Enjoy Paris?' the king's muffled voice inquired.

'Very much, Your Majesty.'

Towels removed, the royal skin emerged beet-red. The barber stropped his razor once more and set to work.

'And how does Madrid seem on your return?'

'There are many beggars in the streets, Your Majesty,' Olavide said carefully.

King Carlos shook his head. The razor retreated. 'I know, Don Pablo. I know it only too well.' Half-shaven, the royal face looked more lugubrious than ever. 'Fifty thousand new mouths to feed this past year. No rain anywhere. They're leaving the countryside and swarming into Madrid like locusts. And we can't feed them, Don Pablo.'

'Nor should we,' Olavide said flatly.

'You'd have them starve?'

'I'd put them to work, Your Majesty.'

The royal face was dabbed with Italian cologne. 'Squillace urges the same, Don Pablo. But there's no work in Madrid.'

'I don't mean Madrid,' Olavide explained eagerly. 'The countryside. They must go back. A thousand deserted villages. Send them back, sire.'

'They've eaten seed grain to keep from starving. How will they work the land?'

'Import seed from New Spain. Order the towns to lease common land to the peasants. Let them borrow from crown revenues to pay for it. They've got to work the land.'

The royal valet held forth the royal breeches. King Carlos began to dress.

'Have them build roads,' Olavide urged. 'Have them dig canals and plant trees to hold the soil. The drought doesn't have to be a calamity. It could be the best thing that ever happened to Spain.'

If only, Olavide thought, he could make the king understand. Spain was mired in the Middle Ages. Money was hoarded in palace coffers and ecclesiastical treasuries. Landowners stayed away from their land, leaving it fallow, preferring life on the fringes of the court here in Madrid. Any Spaniard who considered himself more than a commoner took pride in idleness. Some of the most adept beggars in Madrid these days were hidalgos who thought begging less demeaning

57

than honest work.

'Import foreign workers,' Olavide said suddenly. 'They'd teach us how to reap a harvest from drought.'

The idea was a bold one. He waited uneasily for the king's answer.

The king's answer was an impish smile. 'We are pleased an earthquake sent our Peruvian to live his life in Old Spain. His ideas are diverting.'

'I'm serious, Your Majesty.'

'Foreign workers? They'd never come. Wages are lower in Spain.'

'They'd come,' Olavide persisted. 'Wages are lower, yes; but Spanish coin has more silver in it. Besides, there's unemployment everywhere in Europe.'

The abnormal climatic conditions that had dessicated the Spanish landscape for almost two years, Olavide had learned in Paris, affected the entire continent.

North of the Pyrenees, north of the Alps, it rained, and rained, and rained.

South of the mountains it did not rain at all.

North of the mountains grain rotted in the drenched fields, and the grain weevil bred in the damp and consumed what little remained.

South of the mountains grain shriveled on the stalks and locusts descended on the fields, stripping them bare.

Returning to Spain, Olavide had seen the migrants moving along the mean roads to Madrid, raising great clouds of dust. They swarmed into the city, crowding into garrets and cellars, whole families sharing a pile of vermin-infested straw. Children of three or four begging soon became a familiar sight, and girls of nine or ten offering their bodies for a few copper coins.

Garbage piled high in any corner, in any courtyard, on any staircase. Refuse squads came with carts and shovels to attack those festering piles, but the people drove them off. Why, anyone knew the beneficial effects of those piles of garbage! When they rotted, their malodorous vapors were a proven antidote to the disease-carrying winds from the mountains.

Every street, every hovel, every cellar in Madrid had its victim of putrid fever, of malignant fever, of intermittent fever, of smallpox. On some streets the groans of the stricken outnumbered the stony silences of the merely starving.

The royal valet set the royal wig on the cropped royal head, and held up a mirror. King Carlos stared dolefully at his reflection. 'Not exactly beautiful,' he said, and when the valet drew back in alarm added: 'No, not the trappings; those are fine as always.'

The king turned to Olavide with a frown. 'Those foreign workers – the idea intrigues me. They'd be Catholic, of course?'

'Yes, Your Majesty.'

'Then our ecclesiastical friends could have no objections. Where would you put them to work? In abandoned villages here in Castile perhaps?'

'No, Your Majesty. The crumbling ruin of an abandoned village is a gloomy place to begin. I'd build new towns.'

'New towns. Yes, I see,' said the king slowly.

From the adjacent Porcelain Room, Olavide heard music. The king's chamber ensemble was late as usual.

'Telemann,' muttered the king. 'Foreign music, foreign ideas, and now foreign workers. What will happen to poor Spain?'

'The Enlightenment will happen to poor Spain,' Olavide said boldly.

King Carlos strode to the doors of the royal bedchamber. 'Tiepolo next,' he told the page, and Olavide thought he had gone too far, was being dismissed with nothing settled.

The king returned. His eyes held Olavide's. 'In a few months,' he said, 'the governorship of the Sierra Morena will fall vacant in Sevilla. Would you be happy with the post?'

There was no area of Spain more backward, no land more difficult, than the mountains of the Morena range.

'I would be honored, Your Majesty.'

'The appointment will be announced in due course. Go with God, Don Pablo.'

The Sierra Morena, a hard land, yes, but a good place to put his ideas to the test, Olavide realized. A challenge for Mariana too, so unlike the idleness of Paris.

Doing good works, and so far from Madrid, she might finally forget her Goya.

CHAPTER FIVE

The Lady of Charity

WHEN PACO AND MARIANA entered the garret room above the Plaza Mayor, one brother and two mirrors were waiting.

Since Mariana's return from France, Paco hadn't seen the

Apiñanis. What he saw now shocked him. Their black majo jackets threadbare, their breeches rumpled and patched, they stood there like three scarecrows. Their eyes stared at Mariana from deep hollows.

'We thought you'd be alone,' Gaspar said at last. He couldn't take his eyes off Mariana.

'We never meant to intrude,' Pascual said, his eyes fastened on the same vision.

Emeterio blinked, and for once said nothing.

'That's nonsense,' Paco told them. 'I'm delighted to see you. Mariana,' he said formally, 'may I present the Apiñani brothers, bullfighters from Navarra? Doña Mariana de Olavide – Gaspar, Pascual and Emeterio. The best friends I have.'

'Enchanted,' Mariana said, and curtseyed.

One brother and two mirrors bowed stiffly.

Their visit was a relief to Paco. These past two weeks, since Mariana had told him she had to go away again, had been difficult.

Sometimes she would subside into moody silences. Their paseos, their drives in her uncle's berlin, their pique-niques in the French manner, disturbed her. They had coachmen, footmen, and the Indian, like a royal escort. They took enough food on their pique-niques to feed half a dozen starving people. And everywhere they went the Madrileños were in rags, their faces gaunt with hunger, their eyes dim with hopelessness.

Sometimes she would talk too much. 'Don't you see?' she would say. 'Can't you understand? Make a success of yourself, become a member of the Academy, and my uncle would – '

Her voice would trail off. She knew she was treading on dangerous ground. Perhaps because he thought it impossible, Paco had never asked her to marry him.

When she went to France he spent a year dreaming of her. But now that she was back he would glimpse a pair of dark eyes veiled by a mantilla, or the curve of an ankle under a daringly short dress, and he would wonder about them, those unknown others he would never know.

Marriage? He wasn't ready. Not yet. And if not Mariana, then someone else. Someday he would settle down, raise a family, become a dutiful provider.

If not Mariana, then someone else.

How he hated himself when he thought that!

But if an artist had the heart of a gypsy, he would argue with himself, could he help it? Then he would laugh mockingly.

And who says, Paco Goya, you're an artist? An artist wins a grant from the Academy, an artist gets commissions. All you have is a room full of sketches.

' . . . very sick,' Gaspar was saying. 'Both of them. Muy malo, Paco.'

'The doctor says it's malignant fever,' Pascual explained.

Emeterio gulped. 'We have no money to pay him.'

Paco sprang to the door. 'Santa Maria, why didn't you say so?'

A strange look had come into Mariana's eyes while they were talking. 'I'm coming with you.'

Hardly any light penetrated the room's drawn shutters. A single candle burned on the battered table, the flame flickering on a stove and a big chest, its drawers open and overflowing with what looked like unwashed laundry.

The doctor sat gingerly on the edge of one unmade bed, holding a handkerchief doused with cologne under his nose. On the other bed, under a damply gray and rumpled sheet, lay Tuertillo and Juanito Apiñani, both of them sweating. Red splotches covered the sallow skin of their faces.

'One house call, but two patients,' the doctor began in a businesslike voice. 'That will be twenty reales, señor.' A small spare man in a black frock coat, he rose from the edge of the bed and approached Paco.

Mariana swept between them and to the window, her face furious. Paco had never seen her so angry. She unhooked the shutters and shoved them open. She glared at the doctor. 'What are you trying to do, suffocate them?'

'Everybody knows that night air, señora. . . . Since it will be night soon. . . . '

'What else have you done to them?'

'Bled them, of course. And a paste of spider web, powdered unicorn horn and virgin's milk for their eruptions,' the doctor stammered, alarmed by the look on Mariana's face.

'I see. They're so weak they can't stand, so you bleed them. As for that paste of yours, spider web even a charlatan like you can find, but there's no such thing as a unicorn, and as for virgin's milk. . . . Is it malignant fever?'

'Yes, señora,' the doctor said nervously, retreating a step before her wrath.

'So you bleed them and then – let me guess – dose them with ipecac to purge them.'

'Exactly, señora,' the doctor brightened. 'I was about to

suggest ipecac.'

'But wouldn't waste it until you were sure they could pay?'

'My supply of ipecac – ' the doctor began, raising the scented handkerchief before his face again.

'They don't need your supply of ipecac,' Mariana stormed at him, 'and they don't need you.' She turned her back to him contemptuously and called: 'Indian!' and the Indian's placid face appeared in the doorway. 'Pay this barber his fee, and fetch Dr Rodríguez-Pereira. Buy meat and vegetables for a good soup, and fresh fruit and milk.' She glanced scathingly at the doctor. 'Cow's milk will do nicely.'

Paco stood there amazed. The Indian left, and the doctor right behind her, and then Mariana set to work, tugging the sleeves of her white dress to the elbow, tidying the room, finding dry, somewhat cleaner sheets for the bed, sending Gaspar to fetch charcoal for the stove and Pascual for water from the well in the courtyard, telling Emeterio to light the stove, setting the bucket of cool water between the beds and with one brisk motion sweeping the sheets down and away to sponge-bathe Tuertillo and Juanito, unmindful of the fact that they were wearing nothing whatever.

'A barber,' she told Rodríguez-Pereira, when he arrived with his deaf-mute nurse Doña Isabel. 'Bled them. Wanted to purge them. Malignant fever, he said.'

Rodríguez-Pereira, who was the youngest doctor Paco had ever seen, examined his patients, peering into their eyes and throats, tapping their chests, taking their pulse and blood pressure. By then the Indian had returned, and a pot of soup was bubbling on the stove. Rodríguez-Pereira touched Doña Isabel's shoulder, and the deaf-mute turned to him with a watching look. He raised his right hand and formed quick signs with the fingers, and the girl poured an astringent-smelling liquid into the bucket of water and began to bathe the two sick Apiñanis all over again.

'It is malignant fever,' Rodríguez-Pereira said after concluding his examination.

Gaspar shuffled his feet and asked in a hesitant voice: 'Are they going to die?'

Neither Pascual nor Emeterio had anything to add.

Rodríguez-Pereira shrugged. 'Two out of every three victims of malignant fever survive, señor, and the rate of cure would be far higher except for barbers – ' he used the word as scathingly as Mariana had – 'like the one who just visited here. He's weakened them with the bleeding.' Another shrug. 'But what's done is done. Wash them in cool water, see they get fresh fruits and vegetables to eat, and whatever you do don't close those shutters. They need fresh air. The body – with the help of Nature – can usually cure itself.'

'Then they won't die?' Gaspar asked more brightly.

'Probably not. There are ten thousand victims of malignant fever in Madrid right now, and half that many of smallpox, and despite the blundering of barbers who call themselves physicians, a surprising number of them survive.'

'Can't anything be done for the rest?' Mariana asked.

'They're undernourished,' Rodríguez-Pereira said. 'They're surrounded by filth, infested with vermin and lice. They can't get work; they live in despair.' He paused. 'Yes, something can be done. Clean the city; give the people food, work, self-respect. But it won't happen overnight.'

'Isn't there anything *I* can do?' Mariana persisted.

'You, Doña Mariana de Olavide?' Rodríguez-Pereira seemed amused. 'You could become a Sister of Charity, I suppose. But if I know your uncle, he'll let you take no vows.'

'No,' Mariana said, meeting Paco's glance, 'I could take no vows.'

'Then a Lady of Charity,' Rodríguez-Pereira suggested when he saw she was serious. 'You'd serve as a volunteer among the poor and the sick. But it's no small thing, Doña Mariana.'

A delicious aroma filled the room. Mariana went to the pot of soup bubbling on the stove. Her eyes were glowing.

The crisis came for Tuertillo and Juanito on the third day after Dr Rodríguez-Pereira's visit. They burned with fever, crying out in terror against demons and witches. Mariana comforted them, saying words of assurance in a soft, soothing voice, bathing them with cool water, giving them what little nourishment they could take.

The fever broke in the evening. They lay spent and drenched in their own sweat and looked at Mariana with gratitude, convinced that her nursing had saved their lives.

Gaspar, Pascual, and Emeterio weren't so sure. They had borrowed a few reales from Paco to purchase at the parish church little slips of paper with the name Maria Madre de Diós written on them, and the little slips of paper were balled tightly and put in water which the sick brothers drank.

'Not that it does any harm,' Mariana told Paco.

The offhand way she said that surprised him. 'I never real-

63

ized you were an unbeliever,' he said. He almost crossed himself.

'An unbeliever? Nonsense. Of course I believe – but not in a slip of paper with something scrawled on it. That's superstition, not religion. Religion is a matter of faith.'

Her faith told her to become a Lady of Charity, as Dr Rodríguez-Pereira had suggested. She went to the Hospital General near the Puerta del Sol and was invested by the Order of St Vincent de Paul. She spent most mornings at the hospital. Afternoons and evenings she wandered the meanest streets of Madrid, disappearing for hours at a time into vermin-infested buildings to nurse the victims of fever and smallpox. Soon her cheeks became hollow and smudges of weariness lay under her eyes. Her dark red hair and slender figure became a familiar sight in the streets behind the Puerta del Sol.

One cold morning at the end of the year, her uncle was waiting in the vestibule of their townhouse as she prepared to leave for the hospital. The sun had not yet risen.

'It seemed the only sure way to see you,' Pablo de Olavide said with a wry smile.

'I have to hurry, uncle.'

'You always have to hurry these days, my dear. Rodríguez-Pereira's told me what exemplary work you've been doing. I wonder if you could do the same work in Sevilla.'

'Your appointment's come through?'

'The king will announce it this morning. Governor of the Sierra Morena. We'll leave within the week.'

'I see,' Mariana said.

'You see? Is that all you have to say?'

'I'm needed here in Madrid, uncle.'

'There's poverty and disease in Sevilla too.'

'And how long will you stay in Sevilla?'

'Through the winter. Then in the spring we'll explore the Sierra to find sites for the new towns. Think of it, my dear: colonists from Bavaria and Switzerland, good peasant stock who revel in hard work – what an example they'll set for Spain!'

'I can't go with you, uncle.'

Her words, when they penetrated his enthusiasm, were like cold water dashed in his face. 'What?'

'I said I can't go with you, uncle.'

'I won't let you stay in Madrid alone.'

'I've got to stay. Don't you understand? It's as important to me as those new towns are to you.'

'I understand you have a convenient excuse,' Olavide said harshly. 'Goya's the real reason you want to stay in Madrid.'

'If you really believe that, you don't understand anything about me at all.'

'You still want to crawl into Goya's bed.'

'That's not true.'

'Isn't it? You can't keep yourself out of his bed.'

'That's a lie!'

His hand struck her cheek stingingly. She cried out, and when he saw the livid imprint on her face and the tears that sprang to her eyes he reached out awkwardly to touch her arm, but she backed away from him.

He looked bewildered. 'Forgive me, my dear,' he said, bowing his head. 'Forgive me. I never should have done that.'

His need to be forgiven, when she knew she was as much to blame, made her bow her own head and say: 'No, it's you who should forgive me, uncle. It's just that – we're so different.'

'And so similar despite our differences. Say, then, that we forgive each other.'

But nothing had been settled, and they both knew it.

'I'm late,' Mariana said after a while. 'I have to go.'

He opened the door for her. 'Mariana?'

She turned.

'You have my permission to remain in Madrid,' he said slowly. 'For as long as you wish, Mariana.'

And she? What could she do? She looked into her uncle's blue eyes, and saw her own eyes there, and knew she had to offer something in return. She came into his arms, and against his chest she said: 'All the while you're gone I – I'll live as if I've taken my vows. Poverty,' she went on, feeling the words stick in her throat, 'obedience and . . . . chastity.'

Paco, she thought, Paco, you'll have to help me. You'll have to understand.

Shortly after the turn of the year, an announcement of the fifth triennial competition of the Royal Academy of Fine Arts of San Fernando appeared on the front page of the Madrid *Gazette*.

The subject of the painting, Paco saw as he read the notice, was monstrously long.

Martha, empress of Constantinople, presents herself in Burgos to King Alfonso the Wise and asks him for a third of the ransom fixed by the sultan of Egypt for her husband the Emperor Baldwin; the Spanish king orders the entire sum given

5

her.

You could fill a whole canvas just writing it all down.

What did he know of Martha, empress of Constantinople? Paco fumed. What did he know of King Alfonso the Wise, and the sultan of Egypt, and the kidnapped Baldwin?

Did they want a painting or a history lesson?

He spent days mulling over his sketches of street life in Madrid, or adding to them in a desultory fashion.

These he understood. Into these he could breathe life.

And if somehow his painting got by the judges? Qualifying candidates, the notice in the *Gazette* said, would present themselves at the Academy at half past eight on the morning of July 22 for a final competition to be announced on the spot and executed there in two hours.

Doubtless another history lesson.

Well, he still had plenty of time. He told himself to relax.

He found it increasingly difficult to relax with Mariana. They would meet after her work and take long walks in the unseasonably warm January evenings. Mariana would ride in no coach, no sedan chair. She would eat only simple food and drink only watered wine. She would cling to Paco's arm sometimes as they walked, and the touch of her would almost make him wild.

'Perhaps it's wrong to see each other now,' she would suggest.

'I have to see you.'

Sometimes he might plead: 'Just tonight? What harm could one night do?'

She would put him off.

One Sunday morning they strolled along the avenue past the Olavide house to the site of the new Alcalá Gate. In fair-weather crowds gathered there to see the marvelous construction. Two million reales had been spent, the project had been abandoned, another million had been appropriated, and the massive gate proceeded in fits and starts. Madrileños all agreed that it would never be completed.

Sundays the site became a fairground. Jugglers and rope-walkers performed; gypsies danced the flamenco, told your fortune, and stole your money in more direct ways. A street of shops in shacks and tents extended beyond the gate all the way to the huge plaza de toros, where no bull had been killed for almost three years.

The poor people of the city, even though they came to marvel at the construction, Paco knew, resented that gate.

Wrapped in their long cloaks and wearing the broad brims of their sombreros low over their faces, they muttered about the cost. The king's Italian minister Squillace – Esquilache, they called him – wanted to transform Madrid into a second Naples or Rome, squandering the royal treasury on a new gate and on the wide avenues that cut through the old sections of the city, burying funds in the elaborate gardens of the Retiro and the foundations of the new summer palace in Aranjuez. And what of the drought, Paco heard them ask, and the bad harvests? What of unused gristmills, because there was no grain to grind? What of a thousand deserted villages, and country people dying of hunger in the streets of Madrid? What of the fever that swept through the city like a scythe? What of the monstrous taxes the people had to pay for Esquilache's new Rome and Naples?

As they made their way through the muttering crowds, Mariana said, 'Listen to them. Did you ever hear anything like it?'

'Madrileños always complain,' Paco told her.

'It's not just the Madrileños. I heard the same kind of talk in Paris. There's going to be trouble, Paco. The people – they're like tinder in a tinderbox, waiting for a spark to ignite them.'

The road ran, unpaved now, past the bullring and east to Alcalá and Zaragoza and beyond to the seaport of Barcelona. If he won the Academy prize he could pay his passage on a swift packet to – where?

To Italy. To Rome, to Florence, to Venice with its canals and palazzos, where the great Tiepolo had been born.

'What is it, Paco? You seem so far away.'

Before he could answer, there was a quick beating of hooves and a rumble of wheels behind them, and a great coach came hurtling by, drawn by four pairs of horses.

The beating hooves receded, the rumble of wheels faded into the distance.

Not this year, Paco thought. And maybe not any year.

As they walked in the hard upland country, the sun warm on their backs, it poured out of him: almost three years in Madrid, and a few books of sketches to show for it; a new competition at the Academy, which he could never win; perhaps some talent as a painter, but the wrong kind of talent.

'You mustn't say that. My uncle thinks you have enormous talent.'

'Your uncle's no Academy judge. I paint the way they taught me in Zaragoza – the way they painted fifty years ago. A hundred years ago.'

'Then take lessons at the Academy. I could speak to Anton Rafael. He'd accept you as a student.'

They had crested a rise in the road, and the city was left behind. A grove of gnarled olive trees grew along the way. A hawk wheeled overhead against the high Castilian sky.

'Your uncle's money,' Paco said bitterly, 'your friend Rafael Mengs – '

'Stop that. Sometimes you're so full of resentment it frightens me.'

Resentment?

Sometimes he was so full of love, like now, when Mariana tried to understand him, to help him. And how did he respond?

Like a stubborn *baturro* from Aragon, who'd eat soap to prove it was cheese.

They walked among the olive trees, not speaking, not looking at one another. Then Mariana was half a pace ahead, and a faint breeze stirred, and he could smell the fragrance of her hair. He had to say something, had to bury his pride.

Mariana looked over her shoulder at him.

'If you – ' she began.

'The only – ' he began.

They both smiled uncertainly, and then her smile changed and she came against him hard.

'Paco, Paco.'

He could feel the frantic beating of her heart.

He lifted her chin with a strong square hand and kissed her savagely, crushing her lips. She began to respond with a wildness of her own, but then she struggled and broke free, stumbling to the ground and rolling over once before he was on top of her, clawing at her skirt.

'Please,' she begged him. 'Please, no, I can't, you know I can't.'

He knew she couldn't, but he also knew he couldn't stop.

'Baturro!' she screamed. 'Damned Aragonese peasant rutting like a pig in a barnyard!'

The contempt in her voice struck through the violence in him. He gazed dejectedly at the ground, the wildness gone as suddenly as it had come. After a long time he turned to face the hatred blazing in her eyes.

But Mariana was crying.

68

CHAPTER SIX

Padre Pignatelli

WINTER AND PADRE PIGNATELLI both came to Madrid in February.

Hard and bitter, winter hurled itself at the city on the winds that howled down from the Guadarrama Mountains. It came late that year, but came more fiercely than anyone could remember.

A blizzard blew down from the north, blanketing streets, hovels, houses, and palaces in white. Roads became hazardous, and soon it was a common sight to see a horse or mule down in the traces, a leg broken, screaming piteously until a squad of police came to dispatch it with a pike or musket fire. Then the people would swarm to the spot with knives and hack the beast to pieces, stuffing the raw bloody meat into their mouths.

Mornings after it snowed, white-shrouded corpses lay frozen solid in the streets and were carted off to the cemeteries to be stacked like cordwood, awaiting the thaw.

Charcoal grew scarce, firewood vanished. Indoors became as cold as out, and the people sat huddled and shivering in tattered cloaks and blankets.

Fires burned on all the hearths in the royal palace and glowed in all the windows, and this the people did not resent. The king, after all, was the king.

Smoke rose from all seven chimneys of the House of the Seven Chimneys, where the hated Squillace lived, and this the people resented bitterly.

It snowed for a week, and a second week. Madrid became a frozen graveyard.

The post coach that brought Padre Nicholás Pignatelli from Zaragoza took two weeks to make the journey it usually made in three or four days.

Padre Pignatelli went directly to the palace of the papal

nuncio in Madrid, where he sat closeted with the nuncio for forty-five minutes, warming his frozen feet at the nuncio's fire. Then the doors of the study were thrown open, and in came one of the king's young firebrand councilmen, Count Aranda. Padre Pignatelli's bland round face hid his surprise. Why would the professed, dedicated to the rule of the Church Militant, consort in matters as grave as this with a layman?

But Pedro de Abarca, Count of Aranda, was no ordinary layman. He had drunk the heady wine of Enlightenment in France; he had studied military organization in Frederick's Prussia; he had already served his king as a lawyer and a general. He numbered among his closest associates Pablo de Olavide, and Padre Pignatelli felt inclined to trust any friend of his good friend Olavide.

Aranda was faultlessly dressed in a dark blue velvet frock coat with gray broadcloth trim. His manners were equally faultless, and when he spoke he spoke briefly and to the point, but with wit. Padre Pignatelli, his backsides unspeakably painful after the interminable coach ride, eased the discomfort with wine and found himself warming to the man.

Their conversation, though, shocked the Jesuit from Aragon. He had never been privy to a coup d'état before.

'Then we're agreed, my friends?' the nuncio said finally. 'Squillace must go?'

Padre Pignatelli nodded his massive head. Though as yet he had no idea what role he would play in deposing the king's Italian first minister, the decision to rid Spain of Leopoldo di Gregorio, Marchese di Squillace, pleased him.

Since the first bad harvest three years ago, the Society of Jesus had favored opening the royal coffers to the poor. Squillace had opposed this extreme measure. Squillace was more interested in parks and palaces, in French modernity and Italian pomp – while the people starved.

'Clearly,' the nuncio said, 'it is God's will. It remains now for us to implement His will – *ad majorem Dei gloriam.*'

'To the greater glory of God,' Padre Pignatelli repeated automatically.

Did he see the faintest of smiles on Aranda's face? The count, after all, was known as a freethinker.

'Perhaps you wonder, Padre,' the nuncio spoke in measured tones, 'what role you will play in this – shall we call it by its proper name? – cabal.'

'Frankly, Your Eminence, I do. I'm only a simple teacher in Zaragoza, as Your Eminence knows.'

70

'Not exactly, Padre,' said the nuncio. 'You're no simple teacher, you are of the professed. And, unless I'm mistaken, your brother Canon Ramón is a friend of the general of the Society of Jesus.'

'They were schoolmates, Your Eminence.'

'A post coach leaves for Barcelona at the end of the week. You will be on it.'

Padre Pignatelli settled his aching backsides a little less uncomfortably on his chair and groaned inwardly. Santa Maria del Pilar, not another post coach!

'From Barcelona a fast packet will carry you to Civitavecchia and Rome,' the nuncio went on.

This time the groan escaped Padre Pignatelli's lips. A sea voyage, and in winter! He invariably became seasick the moment he set foot on the deck of a ship.

'By the time you reach Rome, of course, our plans will be well underway. You will inform the general and the holy father of them in the utmost secrecy.'

'I shall try to live up to the faith Your Eminence places in me,' Padre Pignatelli said in a faint voice. He was still thinking of post coaches and fast sailing ships.

Late that night Pedro de Abarca, Count of Aranda, penned a letter to his friend Pablo de Olavide in Sevilla. His eyes sparkled in the light of a four-branched candelabrum as he sharpened his quill. Olavide, as one of the originators of the conspiracy, would be anxious for news.

Aranda dipped and wrote, dipped and wrote. The candles burned low. His handwriting, like his dress, like his manners, was faultless. The letter covered two pages, then three, then four. He concluded by writing:

And so you see, my dear Olavide, if we are bold we can kill two birds with one stone. Squillace will go, that much is certain. In a month, or two months at the outside, the administration of Bourbon law will be out of Italian and in Spanish hands, where it belongs. Regarding the complicity of the Society of Jesus, we will bide our time. Now we need them, and they need us. This mutual dependence will pass with the passing of Squillace, and the complicity of the Jesuits will be one more nail in the coffin we are building them. If we are patient, in a year or two they will find themselves banished from the Two Spains, as already they have been chased from Portugal and France. Then see how the

71

Enlightenment transforms this peninsula. As you so frequently say, my friend, and as we all so fervently wish, there will be no more Pyrenees.

Padre Pignatelli shut the last sketchbook. The small iron stove in Paco's garret room glowed red for the first time in weeks. The fat Jesuit had arrived carrying a large bag of charcoal. He had also brought gifts from Zaragoza – a wool scarf from Doña Engracia, a gold cross on a chain from Camillo, paints and brushes from José Goya and Tomás, a small image of Maria del Pilar from Paco's sister Rita.

'I see what you're attempting,' the Jesuit said slowly. He was a little frightened by the gift God had placed in Paco's hand. The sketches, drawn in ink or black chalk with an occasional use of wash, were deceptively simple. But with a few bold lines Paco could show the weight of years in a beggar's stance or the proud carriage of a washerwoman, giving her the appearance of a dethroned queen; with a touch of gray so faint it was almost white he could drape winter over the city like a shroud.

'Yes, I see what you're attempting,' Padre Pignatelli repeated, unwilling to make his praise too lavish. But, turning the pages of the sketchbooks, he had grinned, sighed, laughed aloud, exclaimed with delight.

'Has anyone else seen these, my son?'

'Only Señor de Olavide,' Paco said, 'and his niece.'

The padre remarked a slight pause before the word niece, and a faint lowering of Paco's voice. He tried to recall the niece. What was her name? Mariana. Plump, ten years old when he had last seen her, with dark red braids and enormous blue eyes. An orphan, the Jesuit remembered, arriving as a little girl in Spain with her uncle, who had come to Madrid after the great earthquake in Lima. Mariana had been educated by a French tutor, and she would be, dear me, yes, the padre thought, a year or two older than Paco here.

'You have become friends?' the Jesuit asked.

'Señor de Olavide is my patron,' Paco said.

'I meant the girl Mariana.'

'We were friends,' Paco said glumly, and wore his heart on his sleeve so obviously that Padre Pignatelli hid a smile and a laugh behind a hand and a cough, telling himself every young Dante needed his unattainable Beatrice.

'You live in a state of grace, my son?'

Paco lowered his eyes. 'No, Padre.'

The Jesuit demanded sternly: 'You will tell me why you have turned away from the Church.'

'I haven't, Padre. It's just that . . . I don't know.'

Paco could see himself on his knees in the confessional, his lips against the grate, his voice a whisper. 'The other day I almost raped a girl. She's the niece of my benefactor.'

No, he could not put himself through that.

But there was more. His childhood in a home where the Church mattered, his brother Camillo studying for the priesthood, his youth at a Jesuit school, at Padre Pignatelli's school, and now his young manhood in Madrid, exposed to the ideas of the Enlightenment, exposed to Voltaire and Diderot, to Rousseau and von Grimm, for whom faith counted for very little and reason for everything, for whom falling from a state of grace was far less perilous than falling down a flight of stairs – how could he explain all that to his former teacher?

Slowly a wry smile arranged itself in place of the scowl on Padre Pignatelli's round face, and he said: 'It serves me right. I sent you to Pablo de Olavide, after all, and I doubt there's a more blatant freethinker in Madrid. Has he given you books to read?'

Paco looked very uncomfortable.

'French books? Proscribed books? Has he?'

'I'd better not say, Padre.'

'Then you *have* said. And I say good! I'm no Dominican, buttressing my faith with the Holy Office of the Inquisition, I'm a Jesuit. Our founder Ignatius Loyola was a rakehell soldier in his youth, and his first disciple Francis Xavier knew the whores of Paris better than he knew Scripture, and for a long time he resented Loyola quoting the Gospel at him – you recall what Loyola said?'

' "What is a man profited, if he shall gain the whole world, and lose his soul?" ' Paco quoted, pleased that he remembered.

'Yes, and finally Francis Xavier realized the wisdom of it too. Not through faith, my son, but through the finest tool God can grant to mankind – human logic. Isn't that a kind of enlightenment too? Doubt is a healthy thing in these difficult times. There's a spirit of radical change in the air, and where it will lead God only knows. Logic is a perilous gift that can take a man either back to God or down the paths of alienation and despair. But there are some who must use it, whatever the dangers.'

Padre Pignatelli had risen from his chair and stood with his round face red and one plump fist shaking heavenward, as if challenging God to do battle over the dubious gift of human logic.

'Your doubts are just a preparation for a return to faith, to a far stronger faith than if you'd never doubted at all. Accept it when it comes, my son. Your salvation depends on it. The alternative is too terrible to contemplate.'

And Paco remembered suddenly the God he had prayed to the night his siren canvas stood wet on the easel and Mariana's dark red hair was spread on his pillow, a God that Padre Pignatelli would understand no better than his brother Camillo. To that unknown God Paco would give his soul.

CHAPTER SEVEN

'Like Tinder in a Tinderbox'

ON PALM SUNDAY Paco went with the Apiñani brothers to buy a lottery ticket.

Sun warmed the streets, the last dirty patches of snow had melted, church bells rang in the balmy air, and the parishes of Madrid had imported from the palm forests of Elche a quarter of a million palm fronds, more than enough for every man, woman and child in the city.

It was a fine morning to be alive, especially since half the male population of the city had decided, that splendid Palm Sunday, to break the law.

The law, an edict signed by Squillace, prohibited the wearing of broad-brimmed sombreros and flowing capes, garments which most Madrileños thought as necessary as a pair of breeches to cover them decently.

Squillace claimed they covered the identity of criminals.

Having seen that ridiculous edict posted on every street corner, the majos of the city put on their longest and most voluminous capes and their broadest-brimmed sombreros.

The edict, they claimed, was just one more irritating foreign idea from the irritating foreigner Squillace.

From almost every pulpit that Palm Sunday morning came

74

words extolling the virtues of old-fashioned ways. Echoing a pastoral letter from the Casa Profesa of the Society of Jesus, parish priests said that *castizo,* the Spanishness that was the soul of Madrid, was pleasing to the eyes of God.

The king must have sensed something in the air. He spent Palm Sunday with most of his court at the not-quite-completed summer palace in Aranjuez, awaiting Madrid's reaction to Squillace's latest maneuver.

The king did not have long to wait.

For the Apiñanis, Paco soon learned, buying a lottery ticket was no simple matter.

On the eve of Palm Sunday, they had bought a copy of *How to Win in the Lottery,* which had gone through five enormous printings in the three years of the lottery's existence. They had studied the book half the night, which meant Paco had read it to them, for none of the Apiñanis could read. Paco read, and they began to argue. They were still arguing in the morning when Paco returned. Even swaggering outside in their majo capes and sombreros in defiance of Squillace's edict failed to cool their tempers.

'Clearly, we'll have to buy *al ambo,*' Gaspar said.

Pascual's eyes almost popped from his head. *'Al ambo?'* he cried. 'Any idiot knows its an *al terno* day.'

They were referring to the types of lottery tickets that could be purchased.

'Al determinado,' Emeterio insisted, looking at his brothers as if they were insane.

Juanito gazed up at the cloudless blue sky and hummed softly to himself.

They sat at a café on the Puerta del Sol, watching the crowds in their long capes and broad-brimmed sombreros.

A lottery-seller came by. Instantly the brothers were all attention.

'He's the one!' shouted Gaspar. The lottery-seller was an old man with a stubble of gray beard.

Pascual insisted on waiting for a one-legged former bull-fighter who also worked the Puerta del Sol.

'A blind old woman,' Emeterio suggested.

A second lottery-seller came by, and a third. Suddenly Juanito stopped humming. His eyes fastened on the colorful strip of tickets held by a man with a huge wart on his nose. All the brothers sat absolutely still, watching him.

'The winning numbers,' the man with the wart assured

them, 'are right here on this sheet.'

'Quiet,' Gaspar said.

'Hold your tongue,' Pascual said.

'He's concentrating,' Emeterio explained.

Juanito Apiñani hadn't moved. The humming began again, and stopped, and began. Tuertillo crooked a finger at the man with the wart, who came closer. The brothers held their breath.

Juanito delicately touched the second ticket from the bottom.

Tuertillo bought it.

A few moments later the rioting began.

Once the eastern gateway to the city, the Puerta del Sol had become the center and pulsing heart of Madrid.

The pandemonium in that great public square on Palm Sunday was unbelievable. Coaches and cabriolets clattered over paving stones, harness bells jangling on gaily-caparisoned mules; peddlers bellowed their wares with leather lungs; outside every café and chocolatería tables spilled onto narrow sidewalks and the hubbub was punctuated by the shouts of harassed waiters calling inside for coffee, for chocolate, for sherry and mariscos. Crowds ebbed and flowed along the twelve streets that entered the Puerta del Sol, boots and buckled shoes beating a tattoo on Squillace's new pavements. Majos argued with everybody at the tops of their voices.

Then, at noon, all the church bells in the city pealed to celebrate the triumphal entry of Christ into Jerusalem.

In that torrent of sound, no one heard the rattle of drums as a company of Walloon guards in their outdated plumed helmets, ruffled collars, and leather cuirasses marched along the Calle Mayor and into the confusion of the great square.

With them came tailors carrying the largest shears anyone had ever seen.

The Walloons split into detachments, each with its own tailor. The guardsmen stomped along grimly. The tailors looked embarrassed.

The four detachments marched on the four biggest, noisiest, most crowded cafés.

They stationed themselves around the outdoor tables, the hafts of their long pikes smartly smacking the pavement.

The tailors looked more embarrassed than ever.

'We seem to have been invaded,' Gaspar said.

'A brilliant military maneuver,' Pascual observed.

'Run for your life,' Emeterio said with a yawn.

All the patrons of the café laughed. No love was lost in Madrid on the king's imported Walloon guards.

'Everybody-up-command-of-the-king!' bawled the Walloon sergeant.

Slowly, by twos and threes, the patrons of the café pushed their chairs back and stood, grinning expectantly.

The sergeant's plumed helmet bobbed among them. He quickly divided them into two groups, left and right. Paco and the Apiñanis found themselves in the group ranged to the left, which included somewhat more than half the café's patrons. They were tall and short, fat and thin, young and old. What they had in common, Paco realized after a while, was their attire. All wore long capes and wide-brimmed sombreros.

The detachment of Walloons surrounded them, pikes smacking the pavement smartly again.

'Tailor!' shouted the sergeant.

The tailor, a small man with watery eyes and a long nose, dutifully approached the sergeant, who produced a scroll and in a sonorous voice read Squillace's edict.

'Begin with that one,' said the sergeant in his ludicrous Walloon accent, and two guardsmen grasped a majo by either arm and propelled him forward.

The tailor, looking very unhappy, crouched before the majo, who made a horrified face and squealed in a high falsetto: '*My cojones* – he's cutting off my *cojones*.'

Instead, the tailor quickly and expertly snipped with his huge shears at the hem of the majo's cape. No longer amused, the majo began to curse and struggle in the grip of the two Walloons. But the tailor succeeded in shortening his cape before he was released.

'That one,' the sergeant pointed, and another majo was grabbed, and another cape shortened.

'That one.'

Pascual Apiñani shook free of the first Walloon and struck the second in the face so hard that the plumed helmet flew from his head.

A majo caught the helmet, tearing the scarlet plume from its socket. Others tossed the helmet around like a ball. It hit the pavement with a clatter and they stomped on it, kicking it back and forth while the bareheaded Walloon scurried after it.

Someone tripped him, and they stomped on him too, and he screamed.

Suddenly the crowd, in high spirits a moment before, became ugly.

'Down with the Walloons!' a voice cried.

'Out with the macaroni Esquilache!'

'Death to Italy and long live the king!'

'Kill the damned foreigners!'

'Kill. . . !'

Buckled shoes flashed and struck. The fallen Walloon no longer tried to rise.

The guardsmen formed a solid rank and lowered their long pikes to the horizontal.

Even then it was not too late. Even then the full killing frenzy had not gripped the mob. Paco stood among them, watching the flash of sunlight on the triangular blades. He thought it was all over then, thought the crowd would disperse. He saw oily beads of sweat on the sergeant's brow. He wondered if the Walloons would arrest Pascual Apiñani.

And then Pascual grasped the shaft of the nearest pike in both hands and pushed.

It caught the guardsman by surprise. He lost his balance and fell back a step, then stood with both feet planted firmly. Pascual, grinning, hearing words of encouragement on all sides, pulled the pike toward himself. The guardsman suddenly let go.

Only one-eyed Tuertillo saw what was happening. With an agonized look on his face he tried to shove Pascual aside. He was too late.

Pascual Apiñani pulled the blade of the pike into his own body.

His eyes widened in disbelief; his hands tugged at the shaft of the long pike protruding from his belly; his knees buckled, and as he fell Tuertillo caught him.

Clasp knives appeared in a dozen hands.

Other hands grabbed pikes.

Knives struck, and two Walloons dropped. The others, some of them abandoning their unwieldly pikes, retreated.

Tuertillo was kneeling with Pascual's head cradled in his arms, his one eye blinking rapidly. He opened his mouth and said nothing and opened it again and then he could speak. 'He's dead. They killed him.'

Paco knelt with Gaspar and Emeterio beside their fallen brother.

'Dead? What do you mean, dead?' Gaspar demanded.

'He can't be dead,' Emeterio said. 'He can't be.'

Juanito Apiñani, tears streaming down his cheeks, stared at the lifeless body of his brother. Then he brandished his clasp knife high over his head and with a wild wordless roar at the retreating guardsmen.

Paco lunged at him, trying to stop him. But then the crowd exploded across the sidewalk, separating them, and Paco was swept up by that surging, screaming mob as it poured across the Puerta del Sol, and he thought no more of Pascual, dead on the sidewalk, or of Juanito, the tears streaming down his cheeks as he ran; he thought no more of anything.

And those arrogant Walloons in their ridiculous costumes and with their ridiculous edict became three years of bad harvests, became slow starvation, became fever and smallpox that had struck at every family, became a frigid winter without fuel, became the despair of peasants marching on the city to find no work, no food, and no hope.

Paco saw a mounted Walloon captain dragged from his horse, the horse hamstrung and disemboweled with a captured Walloon pike, the captain going down under a dozen hands, a dozen knives.

Then the crowd parted and the captain's head, eyes wide, mouth wide, emerged spitted on the blade of a pike, plumed helmet still in place. Hands tore at the helmet, replaced it with a broad-brimmed sombrero. Pike and severed head and sombrero went aloft.

The mob screamed and danced around it.

The Walloons screamed and died around it.

The mob moved like a single mindless monster. It sent tendrils into shops, and the tendrils looted. It sent tendrils along the twelve streets that converged on the Puerta del Sol, and the tendrils found flint and steel and burned anything that would burn.

Along the Calle Mayor came another company of Walloons. These were no ceremonial pikemen, but musketeers with bayonets fixed to their muskets. They came in three ranks, and the first rank dropped to its knees.

Musket pans were primed and pan covers slid back over priming powder; musket cocks were drawn and clicked into place; steel struck flint, showering sparks into priming pans.

Fifty muskets fired in salvo.

Ten members of the mob dropped.

A hundred took their places, and with knives and pikes and bare hands charged into the second salvo of the musketeers, and ten more dropped, and a hundred more took their places.

79

When the smoke from the third salvo cleared, three ranks of musketeers fell, and the mob had muskets.

The tide flowed along the Calle Mayor toward the royal arsenal.

They stormed the arsenal, and took it; and there were muskets and bayonets for hundreds.

They stormed the Cárcel de Corte near the Plaza Mayor, and opened its gates, and the prisoners swarmed out.

Blood flowed along the new pavements and over the new cobblestones of the city, on the new streets of Squillace.

Until the storming of the arsenal and the Cárcel de Corte, the corregidor's police had managed to avoid committing themselves on the side of the hated Walloon guards. But soon they too saw in the mob a ravening beast and, reluctantly at first, they fought it. The mob split, became many mobs, swarming ant-like along the streets radiating from the Puerta del Sol. The police beat them back with clubs, fired grapeshot point-blank at them from blunderbusses, and fell under their trampling feet.

By late afternoon, without plan, without intent, quite by accident, the mob controlled Madrid.

By nightfall, they had torn down Squillace's street lamps, ripped up his paving stones and converged on his House of the Seven Chimneys, ranging themselves along the iron fence and staring in disappointment at the darkened windows.

'Down with the macaroni!'

'Come out, Esquilache, come out, we want to give you a big black sombrero!'

'Es – qui – laa – che!'

But Squillace wasn't there.

They forced the gates, sacked the House of the Seven Chimneys, and put it to the torch. As they emerged, a bugle blew and a troop of mounted Walloons charged through the broken gates toward the burning house.

Half an hour later, topping every second spike on the iron fence, perched a Walloon head wearing a black sombrero.

By midnight, bands of wild men set out along the Alcalá to sack the houses of the rich. They forced the gates, sprinted across the parks, smashed flimsily barricaded doors, thrust aside terrified servants, and entered with their torches. Soon windows glowed red, and bands of wild men emerged whooping and hollering, arms loaded with jewels and fans, with silver-plate and elaborate clocks, with silk curtains and tapestries ripped from walls, with anything they could carry, anything they could drag.

Paco found himself part of the mob that stormed the royal arsenal. He was numb, he couldn't think; the mob did his thinking for him. The mob shouted; he shouted. The mob ran; he ran. He had a musket, but no ramrod, no shot, no powder. He did not remember how he got the musket. He waved it aloft and ran with the mob. Its madness seized him, its fury infuriated him, its insanity deranged him.

Then outside the arsenal something struck his head. There was a ringing in his ears, and he fell. The musket was torn from his grasp. He lurched to his feet, fell again, dragged himself into an alley and fainted.

It was dark when he staggered out of the alley. His ears still rang; his head throbbed with dull pain. He saw torchlight in the distance and went toward it. A crowd was assembling, and a voice shouted something about the palaces out along the Alcalá, and he ran with that new mob, trying to remember who he was, but he had no name.

A bell tinkled ahead, an acolyte in white, just a boy, his eyes big with fright in the torchlight, came slowly by swinging a golden censer, its incense mingling with the acrid smoke of the torches, and behind the acolyte a priest in white vestments, a very old man carrying the viaticum for the dead and the dying.

The crowd fell to its knees as the Eucharist went by, every head bowed.

Darkness swallowed the acolyte and the priest. The tinkling bell faded into silence. The torchbearing men rose and became a mob again.

Paco remained on his knees. The ringing in his ears grew fainter.

He remembered his name, remembered the Puerta del Sol and Pascual Apiñani dead on the sidewalk, and all that followed.

It was madness, and the madness had touched him. He could feel it, waiting, crouching in the dark places inside him. It was madness, and no one was immune.

He shut his eyes and saw a disembowled horse dying on the pavement, saw a disembodied head held aloft on a pike, saw himself striking with a knife, and a throat spurting blood.

And he saw the mob.

To burn and loot and kill – for what?

To stop in their tracks when a priest passes with the Eucharist, and then begin again as if the priest had never passed, as if the priest stood for nothing – for that?

He began to run, through the smoke, past broken windows and piles of abandoned booty.

The ringing returned to his ears, and inside his head the crouching beast stirred.

'Nada!' he shouted. 'Nada y nada y nada,' he cried, waving his arms in the darkness.

It was all nothing. People nothing loving kindness nothing the priest with his viaticum nothing the city nothing himself nothing and nothing and nothing –

The mob. The Alcalá.

Mariana.

The beast left him. He ran along the Alcalá and saw the glow of torches.

They had pulled down the great chandelier in the white and gold salon, and it lay smashed in the center of the parquet floor. They had smashed the harpsichord too, where once he had seen the Duke of Alba play.

Curtains had been torn from the windows and a halfhearted attempt had been made to set them afire, but the flames had died. Brocaded rosewood chairs and sofas had been slashed, heavy furniture overturned, drawers opened and left hang empty. Most of the gold sconces had been ripped from the walls, but candles still burned in a pair of them.

The servants had fled, even the Indian. The great house was silent. He took a candle and followed the trail of destruction into the smaller salons, into the kitchens and storerooms and then back through the white and gold salon to the hallway and upstairs.

He wanted to call out Mariana's name. But he was afraid – he knew with an irrational certainty that if he spoke her name, if he spoke any word, if he did anything but follow the light of the candle upstairs, he would find Mariana dead.

He explored a bedroom, and another one. Canopies had been pulled from fourposter beds, tapestries from walls, carpets from floors.

The door to a third bedroom hung askew on its hinges. He knew at once it was Mariana's room, the walls pink satin, the pink satin bedspread torn back, a rosewood chest gaping wide, the ripped remnant of the golden gown, Mariana's golden gown, draped over the open lid, a shrine in a deep alcove opposite the bed, its ivory image of the Virgin untouched by

82

wild men who would drop to their knees at the passing of the Eucharist.

As he approached the shrine, a gust from a broken window snuffed his candle out.

He stood in darkness, and something moved in the shrine.

It was on him suddenly, bearing him back across the room, and when he raised a hand instinctively before his face a knife blade tore at his sleeve.

With his other hand he struck out, hitting flesh and bone a glancing blow, and the knife passed under his arm harmlessly, ripping his cloak. He got both hands around a throbbing throat and smelled jasmine.

He remembered saying her name, and she his. He remembered uncertain laughter, not quite hysterical, ending on a cry. He remembered how, without another word being spoken, they sank on the bed together; out of madness passion, out of death life, the madness rising and falling, plunging and lifting and leaving them limp in each other's arms like children afraid of the dark.

CHAPTER EIGHT

Count Aranda

WAITING IN THE POSTING YARD outside the Embajadores Gate, watching the post-office lackeys loading mail chests atop the black post coach that would soon take him south to Aranjuez, Pedro de Abarca, Count of Aranda, felt very satisfied with himself.

He had declined the king's offer to drive to Aranjuez in one of the king's own coaches, telling the king's red-stockinged messenger that he preferred to take the post coach.

'His Majesty will understand,' Aranda had said. 'Tell him I want to get the feeling of the people.'

The feeling of the people, it seemed as the four teams of matched horses were brought up by the grooms, would be restricted to outriders, coachman, and assistant coachman, for as yet no other passengers had appeared, and with a single change of horses the drive to Aranjuez could be made in a day.

Aranda took a pinch of snuff as the first pair of horses went between the traces. His black traveling case containing his court clothing had already gone atop the coach with the mail. He was faultlessly attired for travel in a black and gray striped frock coat, tight gray breeches and a pair of soft leather walking boots. Nothing elaborate, nothing fancy, nothing Italian. Just the height of French fashion.

Aranda smiled bleakly. Even for the former king of the Two Sicilies, the Italian mode was out. Definitely, irretrievably out. Squillace, already on his way back to Italy, had been lucky to escape with his life.

And King Carlos had sent for Pedro de Abarca, Count of Aranda.

As the coachman climbed up on the box, a berlin sped through the gates of the posting yard. Aranda watched with curiosity and then recognition while the footman lowered the step and two women climbed down. Aranda put on his black tricorn hat, walked over to them, swept the tricorn off and bowed low over the younger woman's hand.

'Señorita de Olavide,' he said, 'this is a pleasure. Are you riding with us as far as Aranjuez?'

Mariana curtseyed. 'Further, Don Pedro. We're on our way to Sevilla to join my uncle.'

Aranda's glance took in the Indian. Like Mariana, she wore dark blue for traveling. Her stolid face bore evidence of the riots – a brownish bruise on her left cheek, a jagged cut, partially healed, from left ear to jaw.

'By God, señora,' said Aranda. 'Did the rabble do that?'

The Indian nodded glumly, averting her injured face in the bright early morning sunshine.

'They left her for dead outside the house, Don Pedro,' Mariana said.

'By God,' Aranda repeated.

Mariana's face looked drawn. A sadness shone in her blue eyes, and little wonder, Aranda thought, after what she must have gone through. No, not just sadness. Those eyes seemed – haunted was the only word he could think of. They made her, somehow, even prettier than he had remembered.

The postmaster bowed and pulled at his forelock. 'If Your Excellencies are ready?'

Aranda offered an arm to help Mariana mount. Moments later, the great black coach started with a lurch, passed

84

through the gates, and headed south along the highroad to Aranjuez.

The Indian soon fell asleep, snoring gently. Aranda made a small joke about it. Mariana's smile was wan.

She spoke little, and that surprised the count. He knew her as a gay and outspoken girl whose ideas often clashed with her uncle's and hence with Aranda's own. Spain, Mariana always said, had to find Enlightenment through its own Spanishness.

The more he failed to draw her out on the long coach ride, the more intrigued Aranda became. Her unexpected gravity, her unfamiliar silences, that haunted look in her eyes – he found all of it immensely attractive.

By the time they stretched their legs in the posting yard south of the monastery of Cerro de los Angeles, he was stealing secret glances at her, at the lustrous dark red hair, at the swell of her breasts under her traveling cloak, at the full-lipped mouth, at those blue eyes.

And his thoughts led him in an unexpected direction.

Soon to be the only layman ever to preside over the Royal Council, for he expected the offer of that post rather than the first ministry, Pedro de Abarca, Count of Aranda, was unmarried. The melancholy widower King Carlos, he was sure, would prefer his new president of the Royal Council to have a family. It gave a man balance, Carlos always said. Besides, he was well into his forties; it was time for Madrid's most eligible bachelor to settle down.

Would the king approve of Mariana? Aranda thought he would. The king, after all, held Pablo de Olavide in high regard.

It would, Aranda told himself, be a good if not a spectacular match. Mariana would be grateful. She was no countess, no marquesa, and Aranda might easily have aimed that high. As for her ideas, he could change them. It might even offer some amusement. She was still young. He could, with patient firmness, shape her however he wished.

For the remainder of the drive to Aranjuez he extended himself. He was charming but respected her silences; he was witty but not cutting; he drew her out slowly on those *castizo* ideas of hers and found with considerable pleasure that she had a sound intellect to go with her beauty.

He had all but made up his mind by the time they drew into the posting yard at Aranjuez.

When he reached the summer palace, Aranda learned that the

king awaited him in the new Church of San Pascual. The church had not yet been consecrated, and at first Aranda wondered what King Carlos was doing there. A functioning San Pascual he would have understood. Adversity brought out the king's faith as well as his well-known melancholy.

Aranda blinked as he followed the royal page inside. Though dusk had already fallen, the interior was lighted almost as bright as day by lamps and scores of candles. It looked more like an artist's studio than a church.

Domenico Tiepolo stood before the altar, dipping brushes in turpentine. His father was moving sprightly about the scaffolding above, despite his seventy years, adding some final touches to one of the altar-pieces. It was, Aranda observed, a painting of the Immaculate Conception. Suddenly he smiled. The Virgin looked familiar.

Would Tiepolo dare? Aranda wondered.

His Virgin looked remarkably like Margarita de Oviedo, the same eyes, the same hair and wide cheekbones, Aranda was positive. Yet with a beautific smile instead of a lascivious one, the Oviedo woman managed to look most saintly. Damnably beautiful too, Aranda remembered wistfully. He had once had an affair with the lady.

Margarita de Oviedo had served as lady-in-waiting to Maria Luisa, Princess of the Asturias, the king's daughter-in-law, until her profligate ways had become the scandal of the court. But the royal decree banishing her to a convent, it was rumored, had come too late. The young crown princess already showed signs of having become Margarita de Oviedo's willing disciple.

Perhaps, Aranda reflected, it was not a matter of daring. Tiepolo, with his head in those clouds he painted so well, was probably unaware of the lady's reputation.

Except for the Italian, crouching now on the scaffolding and applying a brush to one corner of his Immaculate Conception, and his son Domenico down below, Aranda at first thought the church unoccupied. But then he saw King Carlos seated in the front pew, absorbed in Tiepolo's work.

Aranda went down the aisle. He smelled paints and turpentine and the fresh cut wood of the new pews until he approached the king, and then he smelled horses. King Carlos had come directly to the Church of San Pascual from his stables, a sure indication that the Bourbon affliction was troubling him.

The king's father and half-brother had both suffered from

86

a melancholy bordering on insanity. To relieve his own moods of deep depression, Carlos, Aranda knew, turned to hunting with his horses and hounds. What with the Squillace riots following three years of drought, bad harvests, and wild inflation, no wonder the king was sunk in gloom.

Aranda doffed his hat, knelt and kissed the royal hand. As he stood, he saw Domenico Tiepolo climb the scaffolding to join his father. The king wore an informal gray coat and tall Córdoba boots.

'Well, Aranda,' he asked at once, 'what do you think of our Italian?'

The abrupt question startled the count. 'Sire,' he began, 'Squillace could hardly foresee – '

The king smilingly shook his head. 'No, no, Don Pedro. I meant Tiepolo's altarpiece.'

Aranda relaxed. They discussed Tiepolo's work for a while. The billowing clouds and vibrant colors that could not be contained by a mere canvas – baroque at its best, said Aranda, which was equivocal enough. Aranda would commit himself to no firm position in the artistic controversy raging at court, not with a sovereign as art-conscious as King Carlos.

'Does the Virgin look familiar?' Carlos demanded.

'Familiar, Your Majesty? A bachelor tends to see something familiar in every pretty face.'

The king did not insist. 'Tell me about the riots, Don Pedro.'

Aranda told him, carefully and in detail, and the king's face grew more and more lugubrious as he listened.

Finally he said: 'I wanted to give them a capital they could be proud of, a capital like Paris or Rome – and how do they thank me? Like babies who bawl when you change their diapers. What are we going to do with them, Don Pedro?'

'Let them alone for a while,' Aranda suggested. 'Let the city's temper cool. It was a near thing, sire. For two days the rabble owned Madrid. It could happen again. Next time they might find a leader.'

'And Squillace? Was he to blame?'

'Squillace was a very competent administrator,' Aranda said smoothly. 'I could wish, though, that his methods had been more – Spanish.'

'And how would a Spaniard have handled it, Don Pedro?'

'Well,' Aranda said after a small show of reluctance, 'marching his tailors into the Puerta del Sol did smack of comic opera, Your Majesty.'

'How would you have done it?'

'With more finesse,' Aranda said.

'Finesse? How do you mean?'

'The sort of subtlety,' Aranda said smoothly, 'employed against Squillace by the Jesuits.'

'Are you suggesting the Jesuits instigated the riots?'

Aranda considered for a moment. 'Certainly no Jesuit led the canaille in the streets. They're too clever to be that obvious, and I can only admire them. As I said, finesse. The well-timed issuance of pastoral letters, sermons in praise of our old Spanish ways on Palm Sunday – '

'Oh, come now, Count. That's absurd.'

And Aranda said: 'Sire, earlier this year the papal nuncio in Madrid sent a Jesuit courier to Rome with a message for the general of the Society of Jesus saying – '

'How precisely did you come by this knowledge?' the king asked sharply.

This, Aranda knew, was the difficult part. A wrong word and he might find himself not in the Royal Council but in the dungeons of the Inquisition.

He looked at the king, and then down at the floor. 'They took me into their confidence,' he said finally.

'What?' demanded the king. 'You knew of this plot and only came to me now?'

'Sire,' Aranda said contritely, 'I have no excuse except to point out that a moment ago Your Majesty said it was absurd. At the time I considered it absurd too.'

'You play a dangerous game, Aranda,' the king said coldly.

'I never dreamed it would end with the rabble running wild in the streets. I merely thought that if there was more to the plot than the elimination of Squillace, I could best serve Your Majesty by remaining in the Jesuits' confidence.'

King Carlos chuckled. 'This is a day for absurdities. How could a freethinker like you be a friend of the Society of Jesus? They'd be insane to trust you.'

'But hardly insane to use me. Am I too bold to assume that Your Majesty will offer my name to the Royal Council as its next president?'

'I might well offer your head to the Inquisition instead,' the king said dryly.

It took some doing, but Aranda managed a smile of appreciation for this singularly unamusing royal joke.

'You'd be the first layman ever to head the council,' the king pointed out. 'What makes you think the Jesuits would approve?'

'They know a layman will be president sooner or later, and they know they can do business with me.'

The king chuckled again. 'Aranda, did you ever read Machiavelli?'

'No, sire.'

'Ordinarily I ask my new councilmen to study him. In your case I don't have to. You could have written *The Prince* yourself.'

'Then Your Majesty is pleased?'

The king ignored the question. 'Tell me, why were the Jesuits so determined to get rid of Squillace?'

'Except for Rome, Spain is all they have left, sire. In Portugal they plotted to assassinate the king, and where banished. The French also banished them for political intrigue. Besides, Spain's always been home to them. Loyola and Francis Xavier both were Spaniards, after all.' Aranda paused. 'Squillace's attempt to modernize Spain at any cost threatened the Jesuits' hold over the people.'

'This whole matter shocks me, Aranda. It shocks me deeply,' Carlos said. 'If what you say is true – '

'It's true, Your Majesty.'

The king rose, his homely features hard and very regal as he said: 'No religious order, no matter how exalted its history, no matter how high it stands before the pope – *no* religious order will usurp power in Madrid while I am king. You've served me well, Don Pedro. You'll have your Royal Council.'

Aranda bowed.

'Maintain your close contacts with the Society of Jesus. Let them believe they have their handpicked man in the president's chair. We'll see, Don Pedro. We'll see.'

Another bow, and Aranda thought the meeting was at an end. But the king had one further question. 'You said they took you into their confidence. Who, Don Pedro? I want names.'

'We met,' Aranda said, 'in the palace of the papal nuncio. The nuncio, one of the professed named Pignatelli and myself. The nuncio sent this Pignatelli to Rome.'

The king's face went pale. 'My friend Canon Pignatelli? I could never believe that.'

'No, sire. I have no idea where the canon's loyalties lie. I meant his younger brother Nicholás.'

A faint smile played across Aranda's features. The closer the conspiracy came to the king, the more decisively he would move against the Jesuits when the time came.

Too bad about the plump Padre Pignatelli. Aranda had thought him an amusing character.

He'd have a considerable surprise in store for him on his return from Italy.

CHAPTER NINE

'You Have the Magic'

A FULL QUARTER OF AN HOUR before eight-thirty on the morning of July 22, a group of six young men, all well-scrubbed and well-dressed, assembled outside the San Fernando Academy of Fine Arts. Those who had watches took them out from time to time to glance at them anxiously. It was doing to be a fine day, they said, but hot. Have you seen the newest *sainete* of the playwright Ramón de la Cruz? they asked. Have you heard, they're fighting bulls again in Sevilla? A boy named Juanito Apiñani's the wonder of the Royal Maestranza; he can do everything but make a bull stand on its hind legs.

There was talk of everything but painting.

It came to a temporary halt when the first two judges arrived at the Academy, the brothers Velázquez-González. They came along the Alcalá arm in arm, studiously ignoring the six candidates on the sidewalk. They knocked, the porter opened for them, they disappeared inside.

Did they seem in good humor? Opinions varied.

With the arrival of the two Academy professors, the talk finally turned to painting. You hardly had to worry about the Velázquez-González brothers. You hardly had to worry about Venturo Rodríguez or Mariano Maella. Felipe de Castro? Forget him. All of them danced to the tune of Academy Director Mengs, a decidedly neoclassic tune.

Francisco Bayeu was somewhat more independent. And, after Mengs, he was the most fashionable painter in Madrid these days. Wander from the neoclassic purity of line and Francisco Bayeu might come to your defense.

Ordinarily, that is.

But not today. Today one of the candidates, yet to arrive, was Ramón Bayeu, Francisco's brother. On the sidewalk outside the Academy they all agreed he would win the three-ounce gold medal and the scholarship. The most anyone else could expect, even if he painted like a Rembrandt, was second prize.

The dark, gypsy-looking Mariano Maella arrived in a cab, climbed down and walked past the candidates as if they didn't exist.

Then the old Italian Tiepolo appeared along the Alcalá, a huge portfolio under his arm. His arrival surprised the six candidates. Tiepolo, though a member of the Academy, would not sit on the board of judges. That, the candidates agreed, was typical. Of all the professors, Tiepolo alone seemed human. But Mengs regarded the Italian as a relic of a bygone age.

Tiepolo spent a few moments chatting with the candidates, a smile wreathing his pink-cheeked face. Finally he asked: 'Which one of you is Goya?'

None of the young men admitted to being Goya. None of them has ever set eyes on Goya, though he was one of the eight finalists.

Receiving word that they had passed the first part of the competition, the six young men had paid a small fee to enroll in the daily classes at the Academy, receiving instructions from Mengs, Maella, and Francisco Bayeu. Even Ramón Bayeu, who worked as an apprentice in his brother's studio, came once or twice and dutifully sat with sketch pad on knee, but his lofty manner seemed more that of a professor than a student.

This fellow Goya never came at all. To add to the mystery, old Tiepolo wanted to see him now.

After the Italian had wished them good luck and gone inside, there was further speculation about Goya. He was deformed or incredibly ugly, one candidate suggested, and hated to show his face in public. He belonged to a religious order and had been refused permission to attend the Academy classes. He was a drunkard. Someone suggested that perhaps he couldn't afford the enrollment fee, but all the others rejected that idea as ridiculous. Anyone in Madrid could scrape together the necessary twenty reales. Why, all it did was cover the cost of materials.

Paco awoke that morning with the sun. He knew from experience that a wave of dizziness would seize him when he swung his legs over the edge of the bed. He hadn't eaten in three days.

The more he tried not to think of food, the more he did. A red pepper and garlic aroma seemed to fill the room which, otherwise, was all but empty. He had pawned his easel, pawned his cabinet, pawned his brushes at the Monte de Piedad, sold his pigments at a loss to the Basque who owned the shop behind the Academy, sold all his clothing except a single pair of breeches and an old frock coat.

He got up. The expected wave of dizziness came and went. He fingered the stubble of beard on his jaw. He had only cold water and no soap. Either hack the beard off, he told himself, or don't go. You can't go there looking like that.

He hacked the beard off, painfully, and washed with cold water from the bucket he had carried up last night.

This being the third day without food, he knew he would feel no hunger pangs. They were bad on the first day and could tie you in knots on the second. On the third day a kind of merciful numbness replaced them.

The breeches fit him well enough, but he had lost weight through the shoulders and chest and the threadbare frock coat hung loosely on his frame. He finger-combed his dark, matted hair. His eyes were sunken and wild-looking. He spilled some water into a jar, the only jar left in the room, and drank it. He flexed the fingers of his right hand. They felt stiff, weak, unresponsive. He tried to imagine them gripping a paintbrush.

Don't go, he told himself. What's the use? You don't stand a chance anyway. It was a miracle you passed the first competition.

The day of that miracle should have numbered among the happiest of his life – the crackling parchment letter from the Academy, the restrained congratulations tendered by Anton Rafael Mengs himself, the offer of a course of instruction for a fee of twenty reales. But when he ran downstairs and outside to find a cab, the porter called after him. A package had also arrived.

From Sevilla.

He tore it open, right there at the porter's lodge, and all the letters he had written to Mariana spilled out in a heap. They were still sealed.

Pablo de Olavide had penned a brief note, with neither salutation nor signature: 'You are to attempt no further communication with my niece. You may consider my sponsorship of you and your career at an end. If you should come to Sevilla, I would take great pleasure in horsewhipping you through the streets.'

Early in July the porter had asked Paco about the rent. Paco knew nothing about the rent except that, until now, he had never had to worry about it. 'How much?' he asked.

'Fifteen reales. First of every month,' the porter said as he waggled a finger threateningly under Paco's nose. 'Or out you go.'

The next day Paco lugged easel and cabinet to the Monte de Piedad. But after paying two months' rent he had nothing left to pawn, and he regretted his haste. What did a roof over his head matter if he had nothing to eat, and no easel, no brushes, no paints?

The Apiñanis could not help him. They had left Madrid a month after Pascual's death.

Gaspar and Emeterio had become sullen, Tuertillo developed an unpredictable temper, and Juanito picked pockets as skilfully as ever but without verve. They never mentioned Pascual, not once, until the night before they left Madrid.

'We'll be on the road at dawn,' Tuertillo told Paco.

'The highroad to Andalucía,' Gaspar said.

There was a pause, as if all waited for the dead Pascual to speak.

Finally Emeterio explained: 'They're fighting bulls again, in the south.'

'It won't be the same without Pascual,' Gaspar sighed.

Emeterio shook his head. 'Madrid's not the same without him either. Everywhere we go, he's there. He – '

'Shut up about Pascual!' Tuertillo shouted. 'He's dead. We're going south.'

All the brothers looked at Paco. 'Why don't you come with us?' Gaspar and Emeterio asked together. Suddenly their eyes sparkled, and even Tuertillo abandoned his foul temper long enough to say:

'We could teach you to fight the bulls, man. In a month you'd be handling a cape like one of Costillares' own peones.'

For a while the brothers rhapsodized about the beauties of the south. It was all stylized, and Paco had heard it all before, but still their enthusiasm was contagious. The salt-gleaming brilliance of Cádiz, they said. Granada with its hidden waters that weep. Silent Córdoba, city of the Moors. Almería the Golden, and Silver Jaén. Huelva, port of the three caravels of Columbus. And Sevilla. Once a man was caught by the enchantment of Sevilla, it became his whole life.

Their talk of the south wove a spell. It stirred the blood of every Spaniard who dreamed of gypsy women and golden sand and groves of orange trees. Paco was tempted.

But no, he had to stay in Madrid. There was the Academy, and the competition, and if he did not paint he would be unworthy of Mariana; if he did not paint he could not live.

The next morning he went with the Apiñanis as far as the Embajadores Gate. He stood a long time near the posting yard watching the four figures plodding south until they crested a rise in the road and turned, and waved, and were gone.

What he came to think of as his canvas of 'Martha, Empress of Constantinople, etc.' did not, after the first flush of enthusiasm, please him. It was a totally derivative painting. He had diligently applied his paints one part Bayeu (background and lighting), one part Maella (ornamentation and costume), one part Mengs (the posed static neoclassic quality), and the eclectic result had pleased the judges but was no more the work of Paco Goya than of the man in the moon.

Now, his face painful from scraping off the stubble of beard, his stomach empty as it had been for three days, his frock coat rumpled, his breeches patched, he almost decided not to enter the final competition. He had too much pride to appear before the Academy judges looking like that.

He wouldn't win anyway.

He paced the small bare room above the Plaza Mayor. He should have stayed in Zaragoza, he told himself, to become a gilder along with his brother Tomás. He should have gone south with the Apiñanis, to seek fame fighting bulls and lay that fame at Mariana's feet.

Almería the Golden, and Silver Jaén. . . .

At eight-thirty he ran downstairs and outside. He had to try, for Mariana.

And for himself.

Anton Rafael Mengs, director of the Royal Academy of Fine Arts of San Fernando, moved through life in a cloud of urbane dislike.

He urbanely disliked all art but the neoclassic, urbanely disliked all his students but Francisco Bayeu's younger brother Ramón, urbanely disliked Madrid, Spain, the Latin temperament, urbanely disliked all conversation unless he dominated it, all women unless he mastered them, all air, one of the candidates suggested, unless he breathed it personally.

He had spent the past several weeks giving lessons to the candidates. While they copied plaster casts or worked from a

94

nude male model seated on a dais in the large studio, he would walk among them, stopping here and there, frowning disdainfully at a sketch, using his thumb to erase a line with a motion oddly like squashing a bug, replacing it with a line of his own, then fastidiously brushing at the two inches of white lace ruffles protruding from his coat sleeve. Slender, arrogant, pretty rather than handsome with his arched eyebrows, long lashes, and soft feminine lips, he was the terror of the Academy.

Seated in his office on the morning of the final competition, resplendent in brocaded silk, he looked more like a courtier than an artist. The contestants had been assigned their subject; they sat at their easels in the studio now. In a few hours it would all be over; Ramón Bayeu would have his medal and his scholarship; second and third prizes would be doled out; the usual little speech about the worthiness of all candidates would be made, and Anton Rafael Mengs would take a well-earned vacation before getting down to the serious business of ousting that doddering old Italian Tiepolo so that he, Mengs, could decorate the new summer palace and new church in Aranjuez.

There was a knock at the door, and the door opened, and panting in the doorway stood a wild-eyed, wild-haired apparition in a rumpled frock coat and patched breeches.

'Señor Director,' he gasped, 'I'm – '

'Goya and late,' Mengs cut in.

' – terribly sorry, but I overslept.'

'I see. You overslept. What should have been the most important day of your life, and you overslept.'

'I hope you'll allow me to – '

'Lessons offered at a pittance, and you don't take them. A scheduled hour for the final competition, and you're late. Tell me, Goya, do you think so little of the Academy?'

'No, Señor Director.'

'Perhaps you thought you could teach yourself to paint?'

'I often sketch in the streets, señor. In fair weather I – '

'Couldn't we then have had your company when it rained?'

Anton Rafael Mengs spoke Spanish with a German accent. He had been born in Bohemia, where his father was a miniature-painter. 'Painting is work, Goya,' he said, his little joke over, 'difficult work which requires relentless self-discipline. Have you any self-discipline at all?'

'I think so, señor.'

'It can be learned,' Mengs went on slowly, stealing more precious moments from the time Paco had left to do his painting. 'I learned it. When I was young, half your age, my father took me to Rome. Every morning he would lock me inside the Vatican galleries with paints, bread, and a jar of watered wine. All day I copied. All day, Goya, every day. Do you see what I mean by self-discipline?'

'Yes, Señor Director,' Paco said, fidgeting.

'The subject,' Mengs told him abruptly, 'is this: 'Juan de Urbino and Diego de Parades, in Italy, in view of the Spanish army, discuss to which of the two should be given the arms of the Marqués de Pescara.' There's an easel waiting for you in the main studio, should you care to begin.'

The wild eyes looked at him. 'Juan de Urbino. . . . Could you repeat it, señor?'

Dryly and even more rapidly, Mengs repeated it. 'The allotted time was to have been two hours. You are now thirty minutes late, which leaves you an hour and a half. Self-discipline, Goya. Self-discipline's the thing.'

Paco bowed and turned quickly toward the door.

'The mode that interests us,' Mengs said slowly, 'is the neoclassic. The greatest art in the history of the world was the classic Greek, and a facsimile of it is what we hope to achieve.'

Paco fidgeted again.

'We are not interested in the exaggerated poses and action of the baroque. We require the noblest of simplicity, a poised heroic quality, a steadfast soul in the midst of passion. You understand? Nature is crude, mere men cruder. We want an improvement on both.'

A gold watch was produced, the case clicked open. With agonizing deliberation Mengs said, 'You have – let me see – one hour and twenty-eight minutes.'

Paco bowed a third time and ran out.

And Anton Rafael Mengs sat there, remembering a night when he had learned something about himself that with luck he would never have had to learn, remembering a boy in the kitchen doorway watching. As if that wasn't enough, the boy had succeeded with Mariana where he, Mengs, had tried and failed.

The boy would not succeed this time, in anything, if Mengs could help it.

'It is the unanimous verdict of the jury,' Anton Rafael Mengs announced less than forty-five minutes after the competition had ended, 'that the three-ounce gold medal, and the scholarship, be awarded to Ramón Bayeu. The jury further recognizes the considerable promise shown by Sebastián Gómez and Gregorio Ferro, and respectively awards them second and third prize.'

Mengs smiled as Francisco Bayeu placed an arm paternally around his younger brother's shoulders. Gómez and Ferro were congratulated, and after the applause dwindled, Mengs said: 'The Academy is pleased with the work – and the worthiness – of all contestants. We are quite certain that among the members apprenticeships will be available for most of them.'

Mengs hung the medal, dangling from its blue ribbon, around Ramón Bayeu's neck and, with a curt bow, left the studio.

Paco looked at the hurriedly-done canvases still wet on their easels. His own canvas, the painting blocked out but incomplete, seemed a travesty of the neoclassic mode urged by Mengs, the figures of the two generals stiff and wooden, the cypress-clad hills of Italy suggested by a few quick brush strokes, the ranks of the Spanish army a forest of upright pikes with a pennant fluttering here and there – all of it executed in a frenzy of haste.

It was, Paco admitted to himself, the worst of the eight paintings.

Now, he knew, it was over. He had deluded himself. He had no talent. Luzán's training in Zaragoza had come to nothing, his years in Madrid had come to nothing; he had let down Padre Pignatelli, he had failed himself; he had no money, he had no food, he would have to beg in the streets; his patron Olavide had abandoned him, Mariana would scorn him; his life had not yet begun, his life was over; there was nothing left, nowhere to go, no hope for today, no dream for tomorrow, nada y nada y nada.

He walked slowly from the building, weak with hunger. The sun was bright, the day hot, the crowds on the Alcalá lively and animated, all of it counterpointing his black mood.

But then, among the people streaming along the Alcalá, he saw a face, a fat self-indulgent face on a man dressed like a peacock, and with a few strokes of chalk he knew he could capture the sybaritic look on that face, and he saw the dark haughty beauty of a pair of eyes half-hidden by a black lace mantilla and he wanted to capture that hauteur, and a milord came racing by, the horse in a fine fluid trot, the driver wearing a tricorn rakishly, and he wanted to capture that too, the superb steed, the jaunty passenger, that and all of it, the

7

world and its beauty and ugliness, and he could do it. He had to do it. Nothing, no foppish Anton Rafael Mengs, no lack of money, no lack of recognition, would stop him. He still had some sketch paper, he still had some chalk. He was weak from hunger but he began to run.

'Young man,' a voice called behind him. 'Aren't you Francisco Goya, the painter?'

He stopped. He turned slowly. Francisco Goya, the painter? Had someone called him that?

He saw a halo of white hair and a pink-cheeked face. 'Permit me to introduce myself,' the man said formally. 'I am Giovanni Battista Tiepolo.'

'Señor,' Paco said gravely, 'everyone in Madrid knows Giovanni Battista Tiepolo.'

Pale brown eyes sparkled at him. 'You seem to be in something of a hurry. I don't suppose you could spare me an hour or so? I know a little restaurant behind the post office where they serve chilindrón chicken.'

'But señor, of course I– did you say chilindrón chicken?'

Paco felt tears spring to his eyes, and for the first time since he reached Madrid his pride deserted him. 'Maestro,' he said tremulously, 'I love chilindrón chicken, I haven't eaten in three days, I. . . . '

Tiepolo linked arms with him and they walked along the busy Alcalá.

The old Italian chuckled. 'You have a decided talent for eating, whatever the Academy judges may think of your talent for painting.'

Paco looked up, dabbing a napkin at a dribble of chilindrón sauce on his chin. He drank another cup of wine. The huge meal and strong wine had eased the sting of defeat. At least he could talk about it. 'Maybe they're right,' he said. 'Maybe I have no real ability at all.'

Tiepolo snorted. 'Do you think an old man like me would have chased you along the busiest street in Madrid just to tell you that Bohemian fraud Mengs was right? He's gone further on less talent than any man in the history of painting, and I suspect he knows it. He surrounds himself with second-raters like himself. He's afraid of real talent. He's afraid of you.'

'Afraid of *me?*'

'Of course he is. Oh, you're crude, your colors are wild, sometimes you all but forget there's such a thing as line, but – '

'Maestro,' Paco said boldly, 'you've always made color

dominate line. Why can't I?'

Tiepolo shook his head impatiently. 'Never mind what I've done. I'm a has-been, and I realize it.'

'A has-been?' Paco cried. 'You're the greatest painter in the world.'

'Oh, I get by,' Tiepolo said with a smile. 'But I know my limitations. I can't master line, and I obscure that shortcoming any way I can – with a certain dash, with a vivid use of color, with a trick of pushing the space of a painting to infinity and bathing it all in an impossibly glowing light. Tricks, my boy, all tricks, and it takes an academic popinjay like Mengs to expose them so that *his* shortcomings go unnoticed.'

'Tricks?' Paco said. 'You paint saints and angels like living people, there's a zest and a youthful vitality – '

'Youthful,' said Tiepolo mockingly, 'is the correct word. Baroque is a kind of artistic adolescence, which may make me the oldest adolescent in the world. But it's finished now. The pendulum's swung to neoclassicism. If I were young I know what direction I'd take. But I'm almost seventy, Paco. Nobody's going to teach me any new tricks.'

Tiepolo set his wine cup down, his pale brown eyes intent on Paco's face. 'Three years ago I saw your sirens. I told myself then they could have been an accident. Then I saw your Empress Martha. It was no accident, and it isn't talent I'm talking about. Talent is not so rare a commodity as you think; it's part of being young.

'What is more important,' Tiepolo went on slowly, 'what is essential, is the magic. There is no other word for it. In a bullring it takes the pain and suffering of a doomed beast and ennobles them. In a theater, in the hands of a Lope de Vega, it lifts human misery out of the depths of despair and onto the rare heights of tragedy. In art it makes a painting live, makes it more alive than life itself. It is magic, and you must be born with it. These old eyes haven't deceived me. You have the magic, Paco. God knows why, but you have it. At rare moments I could almost feel it in my own hand, but I never really had it. You do,' Tiepolo said almost sadly, jabbing a gnarled old finger in Paco's direction with each word. 'You have the magic.'

Paco held his breath. Such words, coming from Giovanni Battista Tiepolo, were far better than having a three-ounce gold medal draped around your neck by Anton Rafael Mengs.

'And I pity you,' Tiepolo said. 'It is a tremendous responsibility, the magic. It will torment you. It's the price you pay.

What will you do with it, Paco? To what use will you put it?'

Paco's first wild elation passed. This talk of magic was too —
too metaphysical, he thought. What would he do with it? Why,
he told himself, it would be a fine thing to start with if it permitted him to eat.

He smiled a shy smile but spoke frankly: 'In a week I'll be
thrown out of my room unless I pay the rent, and I won't be
able to pay it, maestro, because I haven't a copper. Don't ask
me about the uses of what you call magic. Instead ask me how
I can go on living while I paint.'

Paco almost expected an indignant explosion from the old
Italian, but Tiepolo thrust his head back and roared with
laughter. 'That does bring an old dreamer back to earth, now
doesn't it?' he said. 'What you must do, of course, is become
an apprentice.'

'Maestro,' Paco said eagerly, 'if you'd take me into your
studio — '

'My studio? That's the worst thing that could happen to
you. It would set you back five years. I paint baroque. I paint
too wild and too big, and people are tired of pagan gods and
goddesses fornicating on a mattress of clouds.'

'I can't paint in the neoclassic style,' Paco argued. 'It's artificial, it has nothing to do with Spain, it totally lacks, well — '

'Magic?' suggested Tiepolo.

'All right. Magic.'

'How old are you?' Tiepolo asked. 'Twenty? You have your
whole life ahead of you. Before you reject the accepted style,
learn it. No artist has a right to break the rules until he's
mastered them.'

'Then what should I do?'

'I'd say Francisco Bayeu's your man. After Mengs he's the
busiest painter in Madrid. And he's learned to compromise
since he left Zaragoza. Part baroque, which I suspect he secretly favors, part neoclassic, which he has the good sense to
realize is crucial these days — '

'I can't paint like that. It wouldn't be me.'

'Confound it,' cried Tiepolo, 'who cares if it would be "you"
in the beginning? Learning a little technique never hurt anyone. And whatever his shortcomings, Bayeu's a sound craftsman.' Tiepolo scowled. 'Unfortunately, I can't help you there.
Bayeu and I had a falling-out. We're not on speaking terms.'

'Oh, I could apprentice myself to Bayeu if I wanted to,'
Paco said, and explained about the letter of introduction from
Padre Pignatelli.

'What?' demanded Tiepolo. 'You've been carrying that let-ter around for years and never used it?'

'I wanted to succeed on my own,' Paco said lamely.

And Tiepolo, spreading his arms wide, exclaimed: 'God spare me such idiocy! What's the matter with you, boy? No painter ever succeeded on his own. Why, when I was your age I married the sister of Francesco Guardi in Venice. Do you think I loved her? She was as vapid a bitch then as she is now. I leave her behind whenever I can. She doesn't mind; all she cares about are her gaming tables. But I married her because Guardi could help me, and I'd do it again cheerfully.

'Take that letter of yours to Francisco Bayeu. Exploit every opportunity, use every person, live every event, cheat, beg, bully, lie, fornicate – anything. The magic is fair cur-rency for anything you can grab in your two hands.'

'But after all these years, Bayeu's bound to think – '

'Who on God's earth cares what *Bayeu* thinks?'

CHAPTER TEN

7 Clock Street

FROM THE WINDOW of his small third-floor room in the house of Francisco Bayeu at 7 Clock Street, Paco could look out to-ward the royal palace or down across the Campo de Moro to the Manzanares River and the arid hills beyond. It was a splendid view in what was, by middle-class if not noble standards, a splendid house.

Bayeu's parents had died young in Zaragoza, and Fran-cisco was now the head of the family. The responsibility had etched lines in his face and grayed his hair prematurely. He had thin lips and wore a perpetual frown. People said he had been born middle-aged; he had that look about him. His brother Ramón had been his apprentice even before winning the Academy medal, and fourteen-year-old Manolo soon would join him. Of his two sisters, Josefa, then nineteen, had the thin lips of her older brother, hazel eyes and long golden hair. With a nod or a gesture or a single soft-spoken word she would direct the servants, reprimand young Manolo or soothe Francisco's ruffled feelings. Almost without trying, she ran the household. Her younger sister Maria del Carmen, then seventeen, was a plump, saucy-eyed flirt.

Paco soon realized that Francisco Bayeu had taken him on only as a favor to Padre Pignatelli. It was Maria del Carmen who made his life at 7 Clock Street bearable. With those saucy eyes and full red lips, she would flirt with him – surreptitiously at the dinner table, more openly on their walks in the garden, brazenly when they promenaded on the bank of the river with Josefa serving as dueña.

Afterwards Josefa would ask her sister: 'How can you be so shameless?'

But Carmen would stamp her shapely foot and say: 'I'm not being shameless, I'm being friendly. He's very lonely here.'

'Lonely? He ought to be grateful, Francisco taking him in like that.'

Then Carmen would smile, undressing in the bedroom they shared, and stretch her plump body in a feline manner that infuriated Josefa, and say: 'Don't you have eyes, Josefa? He's the most attractive boy I ever saw.'

Paco exasperated Josefa. He was polite to her but distant. He would respond to Carmen's flirting with a jest or a compliment that just missed being outrageously insolent and then, before Josefa could object, he would change the subject.

His apprenticeship was, mostly, drudgery. He would grind the pigments with slab and muller, mixing the medium in slowly. He would stretch Bayeu's canvases and tack them to their frames. He would clean the studio at night and prepare it in the morning after a hurried chunk of bread and a cup of chocolate. He would carefully set out paints, oils, brushes, mahlstick for his meticulous master. He would uncover the model's throne, set out a tray of refreshments for model and painter, and retreat to his room upstairs, which was barely large enough to contain his bed and his own easel. Occasionally he was allowed to share a model with Francisco Bayeu's younger brothers, usually a beggar or washerwoman who earned a few coppers for a morning's sitting. For the rest, Paco copied from plaster casts, reworked his sketches, and spent his free afternoons roving the streets of the parish of San Martín with his sketch pad.

Bayeu would study his work and grumble and erase a line,

improving it effortlessly with his own facile hand, mouthing a few platitudes from Winckelmann's textbook on art.

'Winkelmann's theories have revolutionized painting,' he would say irritably, as if he had no time to explain the obvious to Paco. 'If you don't understand that, there's no hope for you. Haven't you read his book?'

Paco had read it. And read it. And read it yet again.

As nearly as he could interpret – the translation from German was ponderous and pedantic – Winckelmann claimed that since nature was imperfect and any painter even more so, the best you could hope for was a combination of forms that improved on the imperfection of nature, paradoxically through the imperfection of man.

You had to use your mind, not your heart, and you had to use it to cure nature.

Soon Paco knew every line of the ill-conceived and ill-translated book, and came to hate them all.

He argued Winckelmann's theories with Francisco Bayeu who would finally, in exasperation, slam his mahlstick down and exclaim: 'Goya, will you for God's sake shut up? I have only three days to complete this commission for the Duchess of Osuna, and you stand their distracting me with your nonsense about Winckelmann. The German's right. Line, Goya. Line. It's everything.'

And then, before the breach between them became irreparable, it was not Carmen who would enter the studio, but Josefa, moving softly as she always did, inventing an errand for Paco and with the faintest of smiles on her thin lips saying a placating word or two to her brother.

The times when Bayeu did praise his work would give Paco contentment for days. It might be a sketch he had done, in the late autumn, of a Dominican brother rushing across the little plaza to enter the Church of San Martín, the skirts of his cassock flying in the bitter wind, and Bayeu would look at it and say: 'It's wrong, it's all wrong, this line here is pure chaos, this shadowing too heavy, and yet – it does have something. If you haven't improved on nature at least you haven't damaged it. Why don't you put it in oils, Goya? I really do believe I'd like to see it on canvas.'

And Paco would work at his own easel, in a cloud of well-being.

Such instances were rare, but Ramón Bayeu was jealous of them. He couldn't understand how his brother could have a word of praise for a sketch that exaggerated nature so that a

103

stiff autumn wind permeated every line, the wind almost becoming a living entity, bitter, implacable, and somehow outrageous.

Ramón Bayeu, as the months passed, came to hate Paco.

His fourteen-year-old brother Manolo came to idolize him and followed him around like a puppy – which further incensed Ramón.

'Paco,' Manolo told Ramón and his sisters, 'is going to be a great artist. As great as Francisco. You'll see.'

Ramón snorted derisively. Carmen dreamed of Paco living in a house bigger than the one at 7 Clock Street, with ornate carriages outside, footmen waiting while their masters and mistresses sat for Francisco Goya, Painter to the King – and flirted more brazenly than ever.

But it was Josefa who asked permission to enter his room while he was at work. His paintings disturbed her. At their worst, they were hateful. They made her feel uneasy. At their best, they were insolent. Insolent was the only word she could think of. They had a way of – well, she thought, *insulting* nature.

If a thing is ugly, why paint it?

If a thing is beautiful, why search for the single imperfection and mar the beauty?

Paco Goya seemed to delight in doing both.

But his total absorption in his work astonished her, and she began to wonder whether young Manolo's prediction was so farfetched. Her brother Francisco could paint with one hand, nibble a piece of cake held in the other and discuss the state of the Spanish economy, all at the same time. Either Manolo was right, Josefa decided with nineteen-year-old wisdom, or else Paco Goya would become the unhappiest man in Madrid.

As for that scatterbrained Carmen, Josefa mused, how can she find him attractive? He's not tall and slender, but broad-shouldered and stocky. He isn't at all charming, except to Carmen. He's stubborn and opinionated, he refuses to take advice from people who know more than he does, and yet –

And yet what?

He confused her.

Sometimes she suspected that a woman could cheerfully spend her life being his slave. Not herself, of course.

On the first of April 1767, Madrid awoke to find the buildings of the Society of Jesus surrounded by troops of the king. Carriages bearing priests and their hastily assembled belongings poured from the gates.

King Carlos' decree was posted on every street corner of the city:

'For reasons that I reserve in my royal heart, I the King hereby banish the Society of Jesus from the Kingdom of the Two Spains.'

The Jesuits, King Carlos had written to the holy father in Rome, would take ship for Italy to help him do God's work there.

In Madrid six great buildings were evacuated under the muskets of Carlos' soldiers. An enormous crowd assembled outside the novitiate in the Calle San Bernardo, and the king's grenadiers diverted traffic for blocks around. The Imperial College of the Society drew another mob hoping to learn what cabalistic rites went on inside the building. There were rumors that the large wooden chests carried away by the Jesuits contained the bodies of children – even, some claimed, young princes of the realm.

The king's grenadiers seized Jesuit libraries, archives, treasures, and, especially, the secret correspondence between the Society and its general in Rome. Allowing the priests to keep their personal books, boxes, tobacco pouches, and clothing, the grenadiers escorted them to staging points on the outskirts of the city, to await their departure for Italy.

The move came as a complete surprise to Madrid, and it was debated hotly on all sides.

Conservatives muttered darkly about a plot to remove the last force in Spain that stood for the old ways of *castizo,* opening the way to the complete Frenchification of the country.

Liberals insisted that the reasons reserved in the royal heart were good reasons indeed. Hadn't the Jesuits once plotted to assassinate the king of Portugal so that country could be ruled from Rome?

Besides, if their banishment helped bring the Enlightenment sweeping down from the north, why object?

The Dominicans did not object at all. With the Jesuits gone and the Holy Office of the Inquisition already in their hands, they would wield almost as much power as the king.

In the course of a single day, every Jesuit in the city was conducted away by the king's troops.

Every Jesuit but one.

Over dessert that night in the house at 7 Clock Street, Francisco Bayeu said: 'That's quite enough, Paco.'

But Paco persisted: 'I can't believe they were plotting to assassinate the king.' Padre Pignatelli, the only Jesuit he knew personally, was his friend.

Ramón sneered. 'All of a sudden Paco's getting religion. I'd never have believed it.'

'I said that's enough. Both of you,' Francisco Bayeu shouted. All during dinner he had tried unsuccessfully to steer the conversation in other directions. But the more he tried, the more Paco had defended the Jesuits. Ramón, who usually had little interest in politics, seemed determined to goad him on. 'An artist depends on his patrons,' Bayeu told them both. 'The moment he pokes his nose into politics he jeopardizes his career. The king has issued a decree and so far as I'm concerned that's the end of it.'

'An artist's still a man,' Paco countered. 'He's entitled to his opinions. A king can be mistaken, like anybody else.'

Francisco Bayeu leaned forward. His lips were white. 'One more word,' he said coldly, 'and out you go. I mean out. On the street. I won't have that kind of talk in front of Manolo and the girls. It's dangerous talk. It's subversive.'

And Ramón suggested in a taunting singsong: 'Why don't you say one more word, Paco? Just one little word? We'd love to hear it – since you know more than the king.'

The color drained from Paco's face. Carmen was on the verge of tears.

'That's not fair,' Josefa said in her soft voice. 'Stop taunting him, Ramón.'

'Why, I was only suggesting that our political expert here, our ingrate of a *baturro* lout who won't even listen to his betters when they take him in, feed him, clothe him, and try to make a painter out of him, which incidentally he'll never be because he has all the talent of a mule driver – '

Paco leaped to his feet, knocking over his chair. He banged a fist on the table, and a glass of wine spilled in Carmen's lap.

'Now by God – ' began Francisco Bayeu, but Manolo pleaded:

'He didn't mean it. I'm always spilling things and you don't order *me* from the house.'

Manolo's words brought a reluctant smile to Francisco Bayeu's lips, and the tension might have ended then. But Paco looked steadily across the table at Ramón. 'Call me a *baturro* again,' he said. There was absolutely no expression on his face.

Ramón looked at him for a long moment. 'Not only a *batur-*

ro,' he said, 'but the son of a *baturro*. Why, your father couldn't even make a go of the family farm. Some people are born to failure. Your father was one. You're another.'

'Now Ramón, that really is unfair,' Francisco Bayeu said.

That was not enough to mollify Paco, or perhaps he hadn't even heard it. He jerked a thumb in the direction of the dining room door. 'Come outside with me and we'll see who's the *baturro* and who the hidalgo.'

'Hidalgo? Son of somebody? You?' demanded Ramón. 'Why yes, I suppose you are. Everybody has to be a son of somebody. You just happen to be,' he finished with a wide smile, 'an ungrateful son of a bitch.'

Paco pulled Ramón to his feet by his white neckcloth and struck him in the face.

Carmen screamed.

Ramón lurched back against the wall.

In her quiet way, without anyone realizing she had even risen, Josefa moved between them. 'You deserved that,' she told Ramón, 'and Paco deserves an apology.'

'He deserves a hiding. He's going to get one,' Ramón panted. With the back of his hand he wiped his bloody lips.

'Any time,' Paco said. 'Anywhere you say.'

Josefa turned to face him. 'Please stop,' she whispered quickly. 'Please. You almost had Francisco on your side. Fight now and you'll be playing right into Ramón's hands. He wants Francisco to throw you out.'

By then Francisco Bayeu was on his feet. 'I cannot, I will not abide this.' His tone of voice was regretful, his lips a razor-thin line. 'Ramón, you behaved disgracefully. I'll settle with you later. Goya, I know you were provoked but – '

Just then the downstairs maid appeared in the doorway. 'A visitor, Don Francisco,' she said hesitantly.

'Well, and who is it?'

'He wouldn't give his name, Don Francisco.'

'Then send him off,' Bayeu told her irritably.

'Begging your pardon, señor, but perhaps you ought to see him.'

'You know the man?'

'Yes, Don Francisco.' Even more hesitantly.

'Then out with it. Who the devil is he?'

'I very much fear,' said a deep and rumbling voice behind her, 'that he is a fugitive from the king's justice.'

'So you see,' Padre Pignatelli said ten minutes later, 'I had nowhere else to turn.' He was wearing the plainest of frock coats and breeches, and a tricorn hat covered his tonsure. 'Surely it is God's will that I stay here until I can safely contact the papal nuncio.'

'What's so important about seeing the nuncio?' Francisco Bayeu demanded uneasily.

He had wanted to send the rest of the family from the room, but Padre Pignatelli objected. 'Things are being said about the Society of Jesus. Slanderous things. I want you all to hear the truth.'

'Even the children?'

'Most of all the children, Don Francisco. When the Society, in God's good time, is permitted to return to Spain, the children must know we're not monsters.'

'We're only one small family, Padre,' Bayeu said nervously. He kept looking at the door, half-expecting the king's soldiers to force their way in.

'One small family is a beginning, Don Francisco.'

So they all stayed in the dining room while Padre Pignatelli related how he had escaped arrest.

Returning from Rome, he had taken the post coach from Barcelona to Madrid. In a minor accident along the road his Jesuit habit was torn. Thus he entered the city on the day of the Society's banishment in borrowed clothing.

'How can you explain any of that except as God's will?' he asked. 'I'm the only Jesuit left in Madrid, the only one who can disprove the lies that have been spread against us.'

'The king's lies?' Francisco Bayeu asked. He was growing increasingly uneasy.

'The king can be – deceived,' Padre Pignatelli said. 'I ought to know. I was at the nuncio's palace when the Count of Aranda plotted Squillace's downfall.'

'Then the stories of Jesuit plotting *are* true,' Bayeu interrupted.

'Well, as to that, yes and no. I reported the agreement between Aranda and the nuncio to Rome. The general condemned the nuncio for a fool and took the matter to the holy father himself. Pope Clement was shocked. No more meddling in politics – those were the orders he gave me for the nuncio. We are loyal servants of the pope, the Society, and the king. Henceforth politics is a word we don't understand.'

'Isn't it a little late for that, Padre?' asked Francisco Bayeu.

'Not if the nuncio can explain matters to the king. If God wills it, the royal decree may yet be rescinded.' Padre Pignatelli's face sagged with exhaustion. He had lost weight and his jowls hung like a rooster's wattles. 'Well, there it is,' he said finally. 'I'm asking you to hide me for three days. If I can't manage to see the nuncio by then, I'll give myself up.'

Francisco Bayeu looked at the Jesuit's tired face and bleak eyes. He frowned, and stood up and came around the table to rest a hand on the priest's shoulder. 'We're old friends, Padre,' he said, and cleared his throat before going on. 'I wish I could help you. There's nothing I'd – '

Paco heard a pounding at the street door, a shout, a splintering of wood, and seconds later half a dozen of the king's grenadiers in their green and gold uniforms and high scarlet-plumed hats burst into the room.

Behind them stalked a gaunt Dominican brother wearing the black and white cassock of the Holy Office of the Inquisition.

'Which one's the Jesuit Pignatelli?' snapped the grenadier captain, a tall, thin fellow with a pock-marked face.

'I am Nicolás Pignatelli,' the priest said calmly.

Two grenadiers had stationed themselves in the doorway, two at the French windows. The fifth seized Padre Pignatelli by the arm.

The Jesuit shook him off. 'I'll go with you,' he said with dignity, and appealed to the Dominican: 'But not dragged from the room like a common criminal, if my brother in Christ agrees.'

His brother in Christ said: 'Hold him.'

'I want it known,' Padre Pignatelli said, 'that these good people had nothing to do with my coming here, as God is my witness.'

'God witnesses, as we all do,' said the Dominican, 'that you have abandoned the robes of your order to slink through the streets of Madrid in layman's clothing. As for these others, the Holy Office will decide what their role has been.'

'To hell with your Holy Office,' Padre Pignatelli cried, 'if they let the likes of you wear their cassock.'

Paco stood, fists clenched. His head ached fiercely. A pulse pounded heavily in his throat. He could feel the dark wildness stirring inside him.

'Search him,' said the gaunt Dominican, and then he seemed to think better of it. 'No, I'll do it myself.'

He moved in front of Padre Pignatelli, and at the next moment stepped back with a triumphant look on his face and a sealed letter in his hand. He broke the seal quickly and scanned the letter, his hard eyes glittering in the candlelight.

'So this is how the Society of Jesus serves Christ and the king,' he observed mockingly.

'What is it?' the grenadier captain asked.

'Instructions from their general to the Jesuits here in Madrid. Proof of the plot we suspected.'

Padre Pignatelli tried to shake free of the grenadier. 'This is monstrous!' he cried. 'I had no such letter. It's a forgery.'

The gaunt Dominican, almost languidly, struck him across the face.

'Monstrous!' roared Padre Pignatelli, and then he did succeed in breaking free and leaped at the Dominican.

The grenadier captain shoved him back. He stumbled against a chair and fell, a trickle of blood gleaming on his bald pate.

It was, coming after the fight with Ramón, too much for Paco. He hurled himself at the captain, clutched a shoulder, the golden epaulet coming loose in his hand. 'Leave him alone, you have no right to do that, leave him alone!'

He flung the golden epaulet in the captain's face.

'Paco, don't!' shouted Padre Pignatelli, but by then the brief scuffle was over. The captain, with a single backhand clout, sent Paco reeling across the room. Two of the grenadiers dragged him forward.

'Your name?' the captain demanded.

'Francisco Goya y Lucientes.'

'You are part of this household?'

'He's an apprentice painter here,' Ramón said quickly. 'We took him in as a favor to the Jesuit Pignatelli.'

'And what other favors were you prepared to do for the Jesuit?' demanded the gaunt Dominican.

It was Padre Pignatelli who answered. 'No other favors at all. I asked them to hide me. They refused.'

The captain's pock-marked face creased in a frown. 'Striking an officer of the king,' he said, 'a man could draw a term in the galleys at Cádiz for that. But still,' he continued, mulling it over, 'he's young; it was in the heat of the moment.'

'I'd have done it under any circumstances,' Paco said, and Padre Pignatelli gave him a warning look.

'Your trial would be a long one, Paco,' he said carefully, staring at the grenadier captain while he spoke, and suddenly Paco knew what the Jesuit had in mind.

The officer would have to attend the trial, would have to

110

add three or four hours a day to the ten he served routinely. An old soldier would try to avoid that any way he could.

The pock-marked face was still frowning. 'I'll have to take this to higher authority,' the captain said finally. 'If the boy did lose his senses in a fit of passion – '

'It should be clear enough he did,' said Padre Pignatelli.

'Higher authority, yes, you'll hear from us tomorrow – say, at noon?'

It was, Paco knew, like Zaragoza all over again. They wanted him to leave Madrid. But not just Madrid, that wasn't enough, not when he'd struck an officer of the king.

What it amounted to was a drumhead court martial, exiling him from Spain.

Padre Pignatelli was speaking. 'I have two hundred reales,' he said, producing a clinking moneypouch from his sleeve pocket. 'The boy will need legal counsel, of course. May I offer this to him?'

The captain rubbed his cheek.

'Everything the Jesuit has must be confiscated,' said the gaunt Dominican.

'It's only money, after all,' the captain told him blandly. 'And we all know you've taken the vow of poverty.' He took the pouch from Padre Pignatelli, opening the drawstring and in an impossibly short time counting the reales. 'You seem to have made a mistake,' he informed the Jesuit. 'I find only a hundred reales, Padre.'

Padre Pignatelli did not quite smile. 'I never had a head for figures,' he said. 'Then the boy will have the money?'

'The hundred reales,' the captain said. 'For his legal defense. As I said, I'll need a warrant for his arrest from higher authority. He may spend the night here.'

'Here?' said Ramón. 'You can't expect us to be responsible for his whereabouts tomorrow.'

The captain sighed, and the sigh, despite his own predicament, brought a faint smile to Padre Pignatelli's lips. All the captain wanted was his hundred reales and no fuss afterwards, and Ramón's attitude was not calculated to help that.

'Understood,' the captain said. 'He's free until noon tomorrow on his own parole.'

'You saw me search the Jesuit and find this letter?' the Dominican demanded.

'Yes,' said the captain wearily. That would mean a trial too, depositions to be filled out, testimony to give.

'May I have a moment alone with the boy before we go?'

111

Padre Pignatelli asked.

The Dominican objected, but the captain saw no harm in it. In a way the Jesuit was his ally.

Alone in the pantry beyond the dining room, Padre Pignatelli spoke quickly. 'Paco, listen to me. I know what you're thinking. The letter's a forgery, and they'll use it to crucify the Jesuits.'

'To crucify you, Padre. I can't let them.'

'You can't stop them. Your word – against half a dozen grenadiers and a member of the Holy Office? Get out of Madrid or you'll wind up a convict in the galleys at Cádiz.'

'I've got to help you.'

'Don't worry about me. Oh, they'll discredit me, but they can't defrock me, only the general or the holy father himself can do that. And I won't spend much time in prison. They'll give me the alternative of exile.'

'But to lie like that, to pretend the letter – '

'Enough,' Padre Pignatelli said impatiently. 'Promise me you'll leave Spain until this blows over. It won't be forever. A hundred reales can take you from here to Barcelona, with enough left over for your passage to Italy.'

'Italy?'

'Of course Italy. Where else does a student of painting go? Will you promise? God gave you a talent, and I refuse to see your pigheadedness throw it away.'

'Leave God out of this,' Paco said, his voice hard. 'Every time I think of God's work on earth I'll think of that lying Dominican.'

'Don't blaspheme,' said Padre Pignatelli, but he spoke the words mildly.

Paco looked at the face of his friend, at the tired eyes staring back at him so urgently. At last he said: 'When they come for me at noon, I won't be here.'

Padre Pignatelli raised his hand to make the sign of the cross. But then he grasped Paco's shoulder instead. A few moments later they took him away.

Paco remembered the look of satisfaction on Ramón's face, the youthful disbelief on Manolo's, the tears on Carmen's, the very real and surprising sympathy on Francisco Bayeu's.

'Try to get some sleep,' Bayeu had urged gruffly. 'Our coachman will take you to the Alcalá Gate in the morning.'

'But we'd be implicating ourselves,' Ramón had protested.

Francisco Bayeu gave his brother a withering glance and

said nothing.

Manolo had come to the foot of the stairs with Paco. 'Someday you're going to be as great an artist as El Greco. Greater. I know you will, Paco. I know it.' He was crying.

Paco patted him on the back awkwardly and then impulsively embraced the boy. They went upstairs together, Manolo to his room on the second floor, Paco to his on the third. The house was very quiet.

Paco tossed and turned in bed. Zaragoza had been different, he thought. He was ready to leave Zaragoza; the Apiñanis had been right. Madrid was where he belonged.

Madrid was still where he belonged.

Despite their differences, Francisco Bayeu had been a good master. Another two or three years with him would have helped enormously.

The eaves creaked over Paco's head, a faint wind stirred the trees outside, a far-off handclap summoned the *sereno* to open a housedoor. The night was so still Paco could even hear the jangling of the night watchman's keys. Then the distant door banged and the silence returned.

All the familiar night sounds of Madrid, and the silences, and this house which, hardly realizing it, he had come to regard as home, the only real home he had had since leaving Zaragoza – tomorrow it would all be behind him, finished, as dead as Pascual Apiñani, as impermanent as Mariana's love. Life gave so little, gave it grudgingly at that, and then took it all away.

He felt hot tears on his cheeks and immediately hated himself for them. Pascual wasn't just leaving, Pascual was dead. Padre Pignatelli had more than mere exile to face. Paco had to leave, but still he wouldn't change places with a Ramón Bayeu for anything in the world, not for all the security of the Bayeu money and the fame of Ramón's older brother. He was Paco Goya, and Tiepolo said he had the magic. Someday you're going to be as great an artist as El Greco, greater, I know you will, Paco, I know it – and Paco tried to believe it too, lying there in bed, praying again to his unknown God for a long life because part of talent was survival, wiping the childish tears from his cheeks.

He heard the door open softly in the darkness.

'Who is it?' he called hesitantly.

Quick footsteps, and the bed sagging at one end, and then the warmth of her body close to him, her softness against the hardness of him, and she said in a soft voice, that very soft

113

voice of hers, 'It's so unfair, what they're doing to you,' and it wasn't Carmen but Josefa, who knew exactly what to do without ever having done it before, who removed her robe and gave him her breasts, and he made love to her with strength and with pride in the responses he drew from this soft, silent golden-haired girl whose intuition had brought her here to give him back himself. When it was over tears were stinging in his eyes again but he could, and he would, face anything.

Before she left, that soft voice of hers said against his chest: 'It's strange, caro, but once my brother Francisco told me he wished he had struggled; he never really had to struggle at all, everything was always so easy for him. If he'd had to suffer he might have reached greater heights. You'll be back, and the pain you find before you return will help you. You'll be back, caro, and Madrid will know that you have returned.'

BOOK THREE

BOOK THREE

A COLD AUTUMN RAIN drips from the leaves of the chestnut trees on the Rue de la Paix in Paris in 1824. Water sluices down the glass walls on either side of the sidewalk café. The old man sees his wavering image in the glass – the grizzled hair, the cross-hatching of age on the skin of his face, like lines etched in aquatint on a copper plate.

An occasional coach comes rumbling by, coachman cloaked against the rain, horses gleaming wet under the gaslights.

The old man is chilled to the bone. Only half a dozen idlers remain at the café tables, among them the Prince of the Peace. Will he stay all night? the old man wonders. The dueling pistols are heavy on his lap. The Prince of the Peace lifts an ornate watch on its gold chain, looks at the time and shakes his head.

And the old man thinks: Time, time is the enemy, the relentless hours and days, the inexorable months and years, crowding you to your grave. He remembers with a faint smile Josefa's words that first night they were together. You'll be back, and the pain you find before you return will help you. The smile becomes a chuckle. Pain? What did she know of pain? Why, he had all the time in the world then, in Italy. Pain is time running out. Everything else is living.

What does a man remember, fifty years and more later?

In cold weather there is a garret room in Trastevere. In summer he often sleeps on the bank of the Tiber, close by the Castel Sant' Angelo. He develops a cough, and for the English milords on their grand tour – for the English milords frequenting the English coffee house on the Piazza di Spagna – the stocky, coughing, dressed-any-which-way sidewalk artist is a picturesque part of what they came to see. In a matter of minutes, coughing all the while, he can dash off a small canvas of

117

the new pope, Clement XIV, seated awkwardly in papal finery on his white palfrey. He does not sign those canvases. He is less than proud of them. Santa Maria, he thinks, how many of them he painted and sold for the price of a meal and a bottle of wine!

In Trastevere he meets the young Frenchman Jacques Louis David, raging with enthusiasm for the neoclassic. David, who will later paint Marat dead in his bathtub, the note from Charlotte Corday in his hand.

They argue. Gods and goddesses fornicating on impossibly colored clouds are finished, David insists. Line, man. Line is everything.

Tell it to Tiepolo. Tell it to Titian and Michelangelo, Paco says. They almost come to blows. They find a fencing master and work off their aggression in face masks and padded vests.

They meet Giuseppe Balsamo, not yet known as Count Cagliostro, but already claiming to be two thousand years old, already planning his fantastic life as the self-styled Prince of Trebizond, grand master of the Cabala. Il est absolument fou, young David says, and Paco agrees. The madness is contagious, to gull the world amusing, and David and Paco develop a flourishing trade in fake antiquities.

The madness is also dangerous. One moonlit night, to collect the princely sum of an English pound sterling from Giuseppe Balsamo, Paco climbs the dome of St Peter's, all the way from the gallery to the great cross, so sure of himself, so absolutely convinced that time will stretch on forever, that he feels no peril. He stands a moment, tall at the cross, high above the lights of the city, roaring his laughter at the wind. He climbs down and Balsamo hands over the pound sterling, only then telling him that every year more than one of the hereditary workmen of the dome, the Sanpietrini, falls to his death.

Later, when Paco becomes a figura, a legend in his own lifetime, when people point to him thundering recklessly by in his two-wheeled carriage, on his way to the palace to paint the king, they speculate about those years he spent in Italy.

Did you know? Did he really?

Break into a convent in pursuit of a lovely novice?

That's our Don Paco. Fought bulls too, you know.

A novice in a convent? Don Paco smiles broadly, in the rain in Paris. True or not, it is a pleasant story. But there were women, in the streets of Trastevere, among the jaded tourists from England and France. He never lacked for women. He would sketch them first, or paint them, giving their likenesses a sensuality that intrigued them, and for a night, or a week, or a month he would possess them.

Pain, the old man thinks. No, Josefa, living by your wits is not painful.

Failure is pain.

He journeys to Parma, to enter an art competition sponsored by the provincial academy. He will, he decides, be Italian for the competition. His name is Goja in the Italian style, his master's name Vajeu. And the chairman of the committee, a Frenchman named Péchaux who once worked with Francisco Bayeu, never bats an eyelash.

First prize goes to one Paolo Borroni, who takes his medal and promptly disappears forever.

Being second best is pain.

Monsieur Péchaux writes: 'In the second canvas the Academy was pleased to observe the skilful brushwork, the glow in the eyes of Hannibal and an undeniable air of greatness in the general's appearance. Had Signor Goja departed less from the subject of the painting, had he been capable of more truth in the use of color, he would have shared first prize.'

What did they expect? the old man thinks.

Another damned history lesson!

And Paco returns to Rome, sells a few more fake relics and tells Jacques Louis David and Balsamo: 'I'm going home. I'm a Spaniard. I need the feel of Spanish earth.'

Antaeus, Balsamo calls him with a mocking laugh.

His haunting of galleries, of museums, of churches, his daily sketching, all have helped him. He can sense it in the keenness of his eye, in the dexterity of his hand.

He sails from Civitavecchia to Barcelona. The journey is depressing. He hoped to return to Spain in triumph; he has nothing but a small gold medal, second prize in a provincial competition, to show for his four years in Italy.

What does a man remember, fifty years later?

The wide, bare hills of Aragon, and the spires of the basilica rising on the bank of the Ebro. The familiar crowded streets, the smell of charcoal and garlic in the June air. The streets are narrower than he remembers. Zaragoza is no Rome, no Madrid.

His mother opens the door. She is small, Doña Engracia. She looks older. Her face crumples, and she is crying. How thin you are. How tired you look.

It is his sister Rita who is thin, her skin waxen and taut over

119

sharp cheekbones. She coughs rackingly and says little. Her eyes have a desperate look.

Knowing you have very little time left, that is pain.

Camillo is off at the seminary; Tomás works as a gilder with competence and pride. José Goya, looking older too and tired, so tired from a lifetime of work, studies the sketches his son brought back from Italy. In July he displays them in his gilder's shop.

August is searingly hot, and Paco takes long walks in the city and the hills with his friend Martín Zapater. Martín has set himself up in business, supplying the army with grain. He is provincial and self-satisfied. The bleak hills of Aragon are his horizon, and he is content.

Camillo studying, Tomás working, Martín established – and Paco? Twenty-five years old, and he has seen something of the world but accomplished nothing.

One day in August everything changes. The Count of Gabarda visits José Goya's shop. The Gabardas are redecorating their palace; new gilding is needed.

And these sketches? asks the count.

My son, says José Goya. Tomás? asks the count in surprise. No, the youngster. Paco. Did them in Italy. Spent four years studying there, won an important competition. José Goya holds his breath.

Can he also paint, your son? I would like to meet him.

You have the magic, Paco.

Now it must be put to the test.

He paints three large wall panels for the Gabarda palace, biblical scenes, and four small ones. He works slowly, feeling the magic flow. There is a joyousness of spirit in those panels, as if he has taken the brush from the hand of Tiepolo.

The Count of Gabarda is delighted with the work. He is chairman of the building committee of the Shrine of Our Lady of Pilar, and a fresco is needed for the cupola. Paco works three weeks on his sketch, eating little, sleeping less.

What will you charge? the committee asks.

He sits there in a sweat. He does not know what to say. Suddenly the words leap from his lips. It is, he thinks, an enormous sum.

It is far less than his nearest competitor's bid.

From late January to June, every day, Paco climbs the rickety scaffold in the shrine. For Tiepolo, he thinks, disillusioned and dead in Madrid, for Tiepolo, who spoke the right words when I needed them most.

Not line. Color. Color that sings like a heavenly choir.

And his fresco soars in the cupola of the shrine, the chorus of disturbingly pagan angels disporting themselves on billowing clouds, the golden triangle of the Trinity, the inscription in Hebrew of the Name of God – all of it pure baroque.

The notables of Zaragoza come, they look up at the cupola and at one another. Some of them are nervous. The original sketches should have been submitted to the San Fernando Academy in Madrid. Zaragoza, after all, still wallows in what the professors call rustic baroque. Perhaps it was a mistake to approve the commission. Yet young Goya's bid was so low, his sketch so beguiling –

For an unbearably long time they look up at the cupola. Paco waits for a sign, any sign. At last the Count of Fuentes glances at the Count of Gabarda, and both begin to smile.

Overnight Paco Goya is Zaragoza's leading artist.

He receives the enormous sum of fifteen thousand reales. Fifteen thousand, count them, Martín, count them, Tomás, count them, Doña Engracia – spilling coins on his bed in the kitchen – we'll knock out this wall here and build a fireplace, a real fireplace, we'll do this, we'll do that, see how it shines, the silver, the gold –

Now in Paris the old man remembers the boy with his heaps of coins, remembers the commissions that came to him after that fresco, remembers how in no time at all old José Luzán, once painter to the king, was proud to say he taught Paco Goya.

But Zaragoza is not Madrid. To conquer Zaragoza you need competence.

And Madrid? Mere competence won't do in Madrid.

'I have the magic.'

Has he spoken the words aloud? He cannot hear, he does not know. He looks around in alarm. But no, the Prince of the Peace still sits there, watching the rain drip from the chestnut trees.

A cab stops in front of the café. The Prince of the Peace rises to his feet. A waiter rushes out with a huge umbrella, and a woman steps down. She is young and beautiful; she wears a pelisse of peacock blue velvet gleaming in the glow of the gaslights, and Santa Maria! it is trimmed at the collar and hem and down the front with chinchilla.

The waiter escorts her to the terrace of the café. The Prince of the Peace steps forward, a cavalier's smile on his

121

face. He bends over her hand, kisses it. He seats her.

The old man clutches his leather case. *The most beautiful face in Spain, a certain arrogant elegance. . . .*

But still, he nods grudgingly. For the Prince of the Peace, as for himself, whatever else it was, it was always a woman.

For Paco Goya, when he returned to Madrid, it was two of them.

CHAPTER ELEVEN

One Day in Madrid

THE COACHMAN APPLIED his drag brakes and the post coach came to a creaking halt, its three pairs of matched horses pawing nervously. A Dominican friar climbed down, then an elderly couple, and then Paco Goya.

He stood a long moment, breathing the air of Madrid. To leave as a fugitive, slinking from the city at dawn, and to return now, five years later, his success as an artist assured, at least in Zaragoza, money in his pocket – why, the whole city lay at his feet.

And what a city Madrid had become by June of that Year of Our Lord 1772! Paco hardly recognized it.

It was late afternoon, and crowds came streaming past the posting yard from the nearby plaza de toros, animated as Madrileños are only after a good bullfight in which the matadors have fought bravely and the bulls died nobly. Paco picked up his heavy bag and walked out the gates of the posting yard. He stared in disbelief. The three central arches of the Alcalá Gate had been completed, work had begun on the two horizontal gateways; it actually seemed that what everyone sneeringly called Sabatini's Folly would soon be completed. Tents had gone; between the huge gateway and the bullring stood rows of booths and shops where aficionados lingered for a bite to eat or a cup of wine.

An announcement of the bullfight had been tacked to the wall outside the posting yard. Paco glanced at it. *The King Our Lord, whom God protect,* the stylized wording began, and Paco scanned further, the date, the time, the weather permitting – the weather had indeed permitted, it was a fine warm June afternoon –

The second matador on the program was Juanito Apiñani.

Juanito, he thought, silent, shy Juanito, you've not been idle either these five years. He almost wanted to drop his heavy bag and run to the bullring. Perhaps Juanito was still there, in the patio de caballos, slender and unsmiling in his brocaded jacket, receiving the plaudits of his admirers.

But no, that could wait; anyone in Madrid could tell him where Juanito Apiñani, matador de toros, lived.

A cabman on his box looked down at Paco – the expensive fawn colored frock coat, the black tricorn hat, the tight breeches and soft leather traveling boots – 'Cab, Your Excellency?'

The cabman took his bag. Paco climbed up and settled back comfortably against the cushions.

Beyond the gate Madrid was waiting for him. He had written ahead, to Mariana at the Olavide townhouse off the Alcalá, to Francisco Bayeu on Clock Street. A well-earned holiday in Madrid, fifteen days perhaps. Then back to Zaragoza. He had all the commissions he could handle; he had commissions coming out of his ears.

Perhaps Pablo de Olavide would have forgiven him by now. Perhaps he would like to see the boy he had befriended, the boy whose talent had matured.

And Mariana? She'd be nearing thirty, the dark red hair gleaming, the blue eyes flashing, none of the excitement gone.

Paco wanted to share his triumph. He could almost see Mariana's face as the major-domo announced him.

And Francisco Bayeu, master painter? Grumpy, pedantic Bayeu, how proud he'd be of his apprentice!

Josefa?

It was strange, he could hardly understand it. He would dream of Mariana sometimes and in the dream the dark red hair would become golden, and there would be Josefa. Or he would dream of Josefa, quiet, competent Josefa, and the next thing he knew he would sit up in bed and see Mariana's blue eyes.

He gave the cabman an address.

Madrid in 1772 was growing, and growing fast, out beyond the Alcalá and the Retiro. Population, two hundred thousand, living in twenty-one parishes. Sixty-six convents, sixteen colleges, eighteen hospitals, five prisons. Two theaters catered to the tastes of the Madrileños, the Theater of the Cross and the Theater of the Prince. A third, the Caños del Peral, presented Italian opera. Like all things Italian it wasn't very popular in

124

Madrid, although the Count of Aranda, the king's first minister now, enjoyed it. Aranda, who had so cleverly removed the old sombrero and long flaring cape from the streets of Madrid by making them the uniform of the public executioner. No one else wore them now, not even the majos. But Aranda, soon, would go the way of Squillace. He had fought for his Enlightenment ideas too forcefully; his friend Olavide had made a fiasco of the Sierra Morena affair; his star was falling. The Count of Floridablanca waited in the wings for the royal summons. That was the talk at the *tertulias* at every sidewalk café, at the Fountain of Gold, the Angel, the Little Parnassus, and even at the Fonda de San Sebastián, gathering place for the literary and artistic set of the capital. It was the talk, too, in the salons of the nobility and the drawing rooms of the bourgeoisie.

In two Madrid households that June afternoon the talk was not of Aranda's troubles. Paco Goya, twenty-seven years old, who with his paintbrush had taken Zaragoza by storm, was coming.

In the Olavide townhouse Mariana changed her dress for the third time. Would the lavender do? Did he like lavender? She couldn't remember. The white then, with a green bow at the waist. And the white comb, yes, the white comb would take his eyes from the few strands of gray in her hair.

Her uncle had promised. Well, not quite promised. At least he hadn't threatened to horsewhip Paco through the streets when they met. He'd more or less said he'd try to be civil – civilized was the word he had used – and that would have to do. Pablo de Olavide, his niece was well aware, had his own troubles these days.

Perhaps Paco would arrive before her uncle returned. That would help. The widow Mariana de Solis, entertaining a guest with her dueña in attendance – how could her uncle object to that?

'Indian! ' she called out. 'I can't get this comb right. It won't stay up.' Her nervous fingers fumbled with the comb.

'A moment, marquesa,' came the Indian's voice distantly. 'This boy, he won't stand still a minute.'

Soon the Indian appeared, her hair white now, her figure more massive than ever, her black dress neatly starched, and in her hand the hand of a small boy, perhaps five years old, looking uncomfortable in a tiny blue frock coat brocaded with silver, his dark hair already awry though the Indian had probably plastered it down five times by now. He gazed up at Mariana all smiles, and she saw those hooded eyes that looked so strange in such a young face and that almost made her weep.

'You look very nice, Paquito,' Mariana said.

'You smell like flowers, mamá,' the boy told her.

Perhaps, she thought, she shouldn't have insisted on calling him Paquito, as if, perversely, to remind her uncle. It wasn't his name, actually; it was his second name. But that made it even worse. Antonio Francisco de Solis y Olavide. A boy normally received his father's name as his own second name.

'Is he coming soon, mamá?'

'Yes, dear, I think so.'

'Is he nice?'

'He's a very nice man, Paquito.' A look at the Indian's impassive face over the boy's dark head.

'You look funny, mamá.' Paquito scowled, those hooded eyes narrowing. 'Like – like me when I'm scared of the dark. Is he scary?'

'He's an old friend, I told you,' Mariana said somewhat crossly. 'You'll like him. He paints pictures.'

'What does he look like?'

'Oh, you'll see soon enough.' Her eyes again met the Indian's over his head.

'Does he look something like papá?'

Papá, dead more than a year now, had been Antonio, Marqués de Solis. Of an impoverished noble family, he had been sixty when he had agreed to wed Mariana in Sevilla. He had known the child was coming. It did not matter, not in the face of the dowry offered by Pablo de Olavide. In the last years of his life the marqués had treated the boy like his own son. It had even seemed to give him some pleasure.

'Like papá? Oh no, silly. He's much younger.'

'Is he handsome?'

'Well, your mother thinks so.' Her cheeks colored.

'Can he teach me how to paint pictures?'

'We'll see. He's come on a long journey and he'll be tired. So be on your best behavior,' Mariana warned.

'I'm always on my best behavior,' said Paquito with a grin.

'Now hush. I mean it. Your very best behavior. You see, Paquito, he – that is – '

'Your mother means,' said the Indian, 'that she hasn't seen him in so long that he doesn't even know she has a son.'

'He doesn't?' The boy laughed. 'That's really funny. Everybody knows me. What's his name again?'

126

'Paco Goya,' breathed Mariana.

'Paco. Just like me.'

'Yes,' said Mariana after a while. 'Just like you.'

She heard the wheels of a coach crunching over gravel in the driveway and ran to the window.

And saw her uncle climbing down from his landau.

For years now the ceremony of afternoon tea, high tea in the English fashion, had been a daily routine in the house at 7 Clock Street.

Francisco Bayeu would emerge from his studio promptly at five, wearing the smoky gray frock coat that was almost a uniform with him. He had three of them. By then Josefa would have steeped and poured the China tea, and the maid would pass the turrón cakes Josefa insisted on baking herself. The imported blue Wedgwood tea set, pride of the household, went very well with the blue velvet armchairs in the smaller of the two drawing rooms at 7 Clock Street.

That Sunday afternoon an air of tension pervaded the room. Everyone showed it except Josefa, who seemed as calm as ever. Her golden hair bound by a coronet of braids, she wore the same simple green frock she'd worn all day. The barest suggestion of a smile touched her thin lips.

Manolo, the youngest of the Bayeu brothers, was pacing back and forth. 'Shouldn't he have come by now?'

'He'll get here,' Ramón Bayeu said dryly.

'It's after five already.'

'Of course it's after five,' said Francisco Bayeu. 'We're having tea, aren't we?' As the years passed the oldest Bayeu brother became increasingly methodical.

Maria del Carmen, dressed in a pale blue taffeta gown with frilly pagoda sleeves and satin bows, the gown low-cut over her plump bosom, exposing more of it than Francisco deemed fitting, went to the window and returned with a drawn-out sigh.

'By God,' said Ramón, 'you'd think we were expecting a visit from royalty, the way you're all acting.'

'Blood is inherited but virtue acquired,' Francisco Bayeu told him. The painter had a habit, these days, of speaking in aphorisms.

'What's that supposed to mean?' Ramón asked.

'Paco worked hard to earn his reputation. He deserves our respect.'

'You're twice the painter he is. So am I.'

'Self-interest,' pontificated Francisco Bayeu, 'throws all things awry.'

'What's *that* supposed to mean?'

'Why don't you wait and see before passing judgment on Paco's ability? Luzán's written from Zaragoza – '

'Luzán! That rustic baroque has-been,' snorted Ramón.

'He was my teacher,' said Francisco Bayeu quietly.

Josefa poured more tea. Francisco, who had developed a slight paunch that his gray frock coat failed to hide, ate two more of the little turrón cakes. He licked his fingers. 'Delicious, my dear.'

'How long's he going to stay?' Ramón asked.

'Fifteen days, more or less.'

'That's all?' wailed Carmen, fanning herself with a blue and ivory fan. 'Only fifteen days.'

'He has a great deal of work in Zaragoza, I understand,' Francisco Bayeu told her.

Manolo beamed. 'Fifteen days, that's a good long visit.'

'Too long if you ask me,' said Ramón irritably. 'What does he think we are, innkeepers?'

'That will be enough, Ramón. Hospitality – '

' – is its own reward,' singsonged Ramón, and just then they all heard the thud of the doorknocker.

'He's here!' cried Manolo.

Carmen primped her elaborate coiffure. Manolo stood up so quickly that he dropped his teacup. It shattered on the floor.

'Just how many thumbs do you have?' Francisco Bayeu asked, and the maid stood aside in the doorway as Paco walked into the room.

The boy who had left the house at 7 Clock Street five years ago had become a man. His face was broad and leonine. He wore his thick, dark hair loose to his shoulders. His eyebrows too were thick over the dark, secret eyes. His mouth was sensual, his chin bold. He walked with the faintest suggestion of a swagger.

He bowed formally to Francisco Bayeu. 'Maestro.'

'No, no, Francisco will do nicely now. It's good to see you, Paco.'

Carmen dipped in a low curtsey, and he kissed her hand, winking over it at Manolo, whose face had split from ear to ear in a wide grin. Josefa's curtsey was more perfunctory. She shook her head at the maid and gathered up the broken pieces of Wedgwood herself. A curt bow exchanged with Ramón completed the formalities.

'You must be tired, Paco,' Josefa said. 'A cup of tea?'

'Or maybe you'd like a bowl of macaroni, after all those years in Italy,' suggested Ramón.

'Tell us about it,' urged Manolo. 'Tell us everything, Paco. Rome, the Spanish Steps, the galleries – '

'Are the Roman women very beautiful?' Carmen asked over the edge of her fluttering fan.

Josefa shook her head and suggested: 'Give him a chance to relax, why don't you? Your old room's ready, Paco. Let me help you unpack.'

'First I think I'd like that cup of tea, thanks.'

They all sat again, Ramón got a bored look on his face. Carmen chose the comb-back chair closest to Paco.

'Any promising new apprentices, Don Francisco?' Paco asked.

Francisco Bayeu shook his head. 'Two in a career are more than a man has a right to expect. I don't do much teaching these days.'

'We don't take apprentices any more,' Ramón said. 'They just aren't worth the bother.'

'Hardly anyone does, as a matter of fact,' Francisco Bayeu explained. 'Most young painters study at the Academy now. Things have changed since the days of Tiepolo.'

'Tiepolo?' Ramón said scornfully. 'Things had to change. He survived on a reputation made thirty years ago. Forty years ago. They finally got some sense at court. They removed his altarpieces in Aranjuez and replaced them with Mengs'.'

'Surely not while he was still alive?' Paco asked.

'No,' said Ramón, 'they waited until the old man went up to heaven on one of his impossibly billowing clouds. I hear you've painted a few of them yourself.'

There was an awkward silence. 'I've taught the cook how to make chilindrón chicken,' Josefa said brightly. 'At least I *think* I have,' she added with one of those rare thin-lipped smiles that made her face unexpectedly pretty. 'We'll be trying it tonight.'

Paco looked uncomfortable. 'I hope I'll be back in time for dinner.'

'Back?' Manolo asked, disappointed. 'Where are you going?'

'I have an appointment I can't postpone.'

Carmen spread her fan and fluttered it again.

'Do you find Madrid changed a great deal?' Francisco

Bayeu asked.

'No. Far less than I expected.' But Paco wasn't referring to Madrid. He meant the house at 7 Clock Street.

The meeting with the Count of Aranda, Pablo de Olavide reflected as he entered the townhouse off the Alcalá, had gone even worse than he had expected.

How badly he still wasn't sure. Even the Holy Office of the Inquisition itself might be brought in to consider the activities of the former governor of Sevilla.

Aranda, it had become clear in the two hours they had spent together in the count's study, no longer considered him a friend. To put it mildly.

Aranda hated him, thanks at least in part to Paco Goya. No man, let alone the first minister of the realm, likes to be made a fool of. Aranda had brought the matter up only briefly, but it was there, bothering him like a canker.

And now, of course, Mariana would expect him to be civil to this ingrate of a painter. Civility be damned, he told himself. I still ought to horsewhip him.

But there was the boy to consider, his grandson, the young Marqués de Solis so far as everyone knew. Everyone but Pablo de Olavide. Everyone but Mariana. Everyone but the Count of Aranda.

Grandson. He had to be careful, everything was falling on him all at once. That was a secret he intended to keep – especially from Mariana.

Grand-nephew, he reminded himself. Paquito is your grand-nephew.

Had the events in Sevilla five years ago led to the disastrous confrontation today in Aranda's palace? More than likely, Olavide thought bitterly.

There had been an exchange of letters. Aranda had asked for the hand of Mariana in marriage, and the proposal had immensely pleased Pablo de Olavide.

'I won't marry anyone I don't love,' Mariana had said, in Sevilla five years ago. 'I hardly even know Count Aranda.'

'Don't be foolish. It's a superb match for you. One doesn't marry for love. One finds love in marriage afterwards.'

But she would not be swayed, and finally he had blurted: 'You are a wilful, self-indulgent child, just like your – ' His voice had suddenly stopped.

'Just like my what?'

'Nothing. You're going to marry the count if he'll have you,

130

and that's that.'

Aranda arrived in Sevilla a few weeks after Mariana had joined her uncle there. He made no secret of the journey. He had even informed King Carlos that he was going to Sevilla to claim the hand of Pablo de Olavide's niece, and Carlos had beamingly wished him Godspeed.

When he arrived, Mariana became sulky and withdrawn. Her attitude surprised Aranda, but he was a patient man and a man accustomed to getting his own way. Her wilfulness even intrigued him. It dismayed Pablo de Olavide.

'Patience, my friend,' Aranda had advised him. 'She'll come around. Madrid is full of passive, titled little snippets, but they're not what I want in a wife.'

What he certainly did not want was a girl two months pregnant.

Late one night Mariana came to her uncle's room. He was reading Voltaire. He patted the edge of the bed, removed his horn-rimmed spectacles, and said: 'Sit down, my dear. I have news for you, not that it's unexpected. This evening the count asked me formally for your hand in marriage.'

Mariana remained standing. Her face was pale.

'I can't marry him,' she said. She began to cry.

'Sometimes,' said Pablo de Olavide in exasperation, 'I don't understand you at all. He's the president of the Royal Council, he'll be the king's first minister one of these days – he's the finest catch in Spain.' He put on his spectacles again. 'If it comes to that, I command you to accept him.'

'I – I didn't say I wouldn't marry him,' Mariana sobbed. 'I said I can't. He wouldn't have me.'

'What nonsense are you babbling now? Don't you see the man can't take his eyes off you?'

A fresh flow of tears, and a large handkerchief extended irritably by Olavide. 'Wipe your eyes. There. Now what is it?'

Some further sniffling, and a long silence. Finally: 'Send me somewhere. Anywhere, uncle. There are places.'

'Places? What places? Will you try to make some sense, girl?'

'Places where – where I – oh, I wish I were dead!'

Off came the spectacles again. A wryly sympathetic look replaced them. 'Come now, Mariana. Whatever it is, surely it can't be as bad as all that.'

And Mariana said: 'Places where a girl can go to – have a baby.'

Pablo de Olavide sat up straight in bed. Voltaire fell to the floor. Olavide's face felt suddenly as stiff as parchment.

'What did you say?'

'I'm going to have a baby. I'm over two months gone.'

A rafter creaked somewhere in the big old house, and a dog barked outside.

'Goya?'

'Y-yes.'

Olavide clenched his fists. 'So you take a hypocritical vow and stay behind in Madrid,' he said slowly, his voice cold, 'as Paco Goya's whore.'

'No! You don't understand. I wasn't going to, we didn't even see each other, we were never going to see each other again, but – '

'Whore. Just like – ' His voice stopped. He rubbed his eyes. 'Leave me,' he said.

'The count?'

'I'll think of something. Just leave me.'

The next morning he walked in the garden with Aranda. A perfect spring day in Sevilla, he remembered, with the fruit already heavy on the orange trees, the boxwood maze a deep leathery green, the geraniums vividly pink and red. Aranda was walking with a jaunty stride.

'Perhaps in August,' he said, 'when the court goes to the Escorial. A wedding in the cathedral there. The king already hinted he would approve. He considers it a fine match for me. You're very much in his favor these days, Don Pablo.'

They paused by the Neptune fountain. The splashing of the water was loud.

'I'm afraid there'll be no wedding, Count,' Olavide said. Swallows swooped in quick graceful arcs to the pool, skimming the surface of the water before they winged up and away.

'Come now, my dear Olavide.' With a slight chill in the cultivated voice. 'Surely you've had enough time to bring her around.'

'It's not that, I'm afraid.'

'Then what on earth?'

Flatly, Olavide told him.

The cultivated voice then was like the ice that still held the high sierra in its grip. 'And when, my dear Olavide, did you learn of this?'

'Only last night. She told me last night.'

'You know the man?'

'He's only a boy. Who he is doesn't matter.' Afterwards, Olavide would be pleased with himself for that. Despite the bitterness he felt toward Paco, he never revealed his identity. A word from the president of the council could destroy his career forever.

'You knew of the affair?'

'Yes.'

Aranda rudely turned his back and said: 'My dear Olavide, did you actually think I was in the habit of accepting – used merchandise?'

And, his back very straight, Aranda strode away through the boxwood maze.

In its own way the conversation five years later in Madrid was even more painful.

Olavide had come, hat in hand, into the count's study in the Aranda palace near the Retiro. Aranda offered no refreshments. He was reading a document and sat reading it a long time before he looked up and silently waved Olavide to a chair. He put the document down.

'You really have made a botch of things this time.'

'I'm sorry you feel that way.'

'Sorry *I* feel that way? I protected you as long as I could. The king's furious with me.'

'I did what I thought had to be done, Count.'

'Yes, and with undeniable flair. Not that you haven't managed to get yourself into trouble before. I seem to recall the Holy Office once revoked your license to read proscribed books.'

The license had been a long time coming and Olavide had lost it not because of the printed word but thanks to some prints of Boucher and Fragonard. They were nudes and, even worse, the Dominicans of the Holy Office had considered the Bouchers pornographic.

'It was no more than some French prints,' Olavide said. 'You enjoy them yourself.'

'I also seem to recall,' Aranda went on dryly, 'you were unable to keep the Marquesa de Solis out of trouble.' He used the title mockingly. 'Before she became the marquesa, of course. Getting into trouble seems an unfortunate family trait of the Olavides, wouldn't you say, my dear Don Pablo?'

Don Pablo said nothing.

Aranda leaned forward. 'I urged the king to give you a free hand in the Sierra Morena, to appoint you governor of Sevilla itself. To make things easier for you.'

'It *was* easier to – '

'To destroy the whole thing, my dear Don Pablo. To place

my own career in jeopardy, as if making a laughing stock of me over – ' again the mocking tone – 'the marquesa wasn't enough.

'But let us consider the confiscated Jesuit properties in Sevilla, shall we? You recommended giving them to the university and, with my urging, the council approved. Then you changed the curriculum. Modern philosophers, mathematics and – experimental physics, wasn't it?'

'We'd already talked about that before I left Madrid. Given the chance, and we had the chance, there'd be – '

'No more Pyrenees? The trouble was, you wanted to do it all like a race horse at full gallop. I had the Inquisition breathing down my neck in a matter of weeks. They haven't stopped.'

'Almost every university in Spain's accepted the new curriculum,' Olavide pointed out.

'Which makes them angrier still. The Inquisition breathing down my neck, not to mention the Sheepmen's Association.'

'The Mesta? But I couldn't – '

'What you could not do is of no importance. We are considering what you *did* do. You had forty-four new villages and – was it eleven towns, there in the Sierra?'

'That's right.'

'And you barred the Mesta from all of them.'

'The idea,' Olavide said patiently, 'was to farm those lands. To farm them, Count. No farm anywhere in Spain can prosper with the Mesta flocks free to graze on its crops.'

'They're very powerful, the Mesta, not only in the council but at court. Their merino wool's our most important export.'

'Our crops thrived.'

'Yes, yes,' Aranda said in a bored voice, 'you proved you knew a thing or two about farming. That new English plow – what was it called?'

'The Rotherham plow. Light, easy to – '

'Spare me the details. Tell me instead, my dear Don Pablo, what prompted you to exclude every religious group from your forty-four villages and eleven towns?'

'We had parish churches. We still do.'

'Isn't it true you forbade the saying of Mass in those churches on weekdays?'

'I thought Sunday Mass quite sufficient.'

'You thought,' Aranda said contemptuously.

'How could we turn Spain toward the rest of Europe unless – '

'The rest of Europe? Ironic, isn't it, my dear Olavide, that

134

it's a Capuchin monk from Bavaria who's finally denounced you to the Santo, saying your colonies are anticlerical?'

'The Santo? I didn't know.'

'Yes, the Holy Office. Unlike you,' Aranda observed, 'they move slowly. But you'll be hearing from them.'

The news stunned Pablo de Olavide. He had avoided real trouble with the Santo over the matter of the prints, and his license to read proscribed books had finally been renewed. But a second summons by the Holy Office was more than any man could afford.

'That Capuchin monk,' he finally said, 'was a drunken, woman-chasing hypocrite.'

'I don't doubt it. So many of them are. And no doubt you threw him out of the colony?'

'Naturally.'

'Straight into the arms of the Santo. We had a small debate in the council, just a small friendly debate about your activities. It lasted eight days. Among other things it was suggested that a man shouldn't wear two hats, as I have – council president and first minister. It is being most fervently suggested by our mutual friend Floridablanca. Tell me he's not ambitious.'

'Ambitious, yes – but a believer in the Enlightenment.'

Aranda stood up suddenly, and Olavide rose too, the tall count towering over him.

'Just how big a fool are you, my dear Olavide? Floridablanca's support of the Enlightenment is sheer opportunism. He's a natural conservative, that one.'

'As your support was opportunism, Count?' Olavide asked angrily.

'To support an idea is one thing. To allow an incompetent bumbling dreamer to damage your career is another.'

Olavide's face went livid. 'No man can talk to me like that.'

'No? What will you do, call me out to the Retiro at sunrise? Pistols? Swords? Come now, my dear fellow.'

'No, no, I didn't mean that,' Olavide said wearily. 'If you need a scapegoat, I concede you've found one.'

Aranda raised an eyebrow. 'You're finished in Sevilla, Olavide. You'll have a "Yo el Rey" to that effect in the morning. With royal thanks for your fine work, naturally. Not,' he added, 'that it will be extravagant.' He paused. 'And, should the Inquisition decide on a full investigation, expect no help from me.'

The Count of Aranda seated himself again behind his desk

and picked up the document he had been reading. Without looking up he said, 'Adiós, my dear fellow.'

The boy had been sent from the room in the Indian's care, protesting and then bursting into tears. 'I want him to teach me how to paint.'

Olavide had promised him a painting master if he wanted one, and that had placated him somewhat.

Now Olavide told Mariana: 'That's final. He will not set foot in this house.'

'That isn't fair. It was so long ago. Will you make me suffer for it the rest of my life?'

'You brought it on yourself.'

'What about the boy? His own – '

Her uncle raised a hand in warning, chopping at air with it. 'You are never to refer to Goya as the boy's father. Never, do you understand? Antonio Francisco is the Marqués de Solis. The boy has a name.'

'If I married again he'd still have the name.'

'Marry? Goya? He'd consider it a match, that one. Married to a marquesa, the doors of all the noble houses in Madrid open to him – a painter's as much an opportunist as a politician.'

'Uncle,' Mariana said carefully, 'I've never disobeyed you before. Don't force me to now.'

'Haven't you though? I seem to recall a vow, six years ago.'

'That's – different.'

'It's precisely what we're talking about. There's a wilfulness and a weakness in you, Mariana, side by side.'

'You'll never forgive me, will you?'

'You don't want forgiveness. You want license.'

'I'm still young. I want to marry again. I want the boy to have a father. His own father.'

He raised his hand a second time, as if he were going to strike her. But he turned his back and said: 'Whore.' He couldn't stop himself. Too much had happened, his whole world was collapsing. 'Whore. Just like your mother.'

'Wh-what?' Mariana faltered.

'Just like your mother.'

'What are you saying? My mother was your own sister.'

'My sister died in the earthquake in Lima,' Pablo de Olavide said. 'But she wasn't your mother.' He laughed. He couldn't help it – an odd choking sound close to a sob. 'My sister had just taken her vows. She was in a convent when the earthquake struck.'

Mariana's face was very pale. 'Then who was my mother?'

Olavide hesitated. He had blamed Goya for his downfall, which was logical enough. But what about Mariana? Was she any less to blame? His own flesh and blood?

He had climbed the political heights to a provincial governorship, and come hurtling down. Oh, there'd be legal work for the Royal Council; he was a talented advocate and the king knew it, but his career was finished. Except for Goya and Mariana, how far might he have gone? All the way, perhaps. Aranda was as good as out, Floridablanca wouldn't last forever.

Pablo de Olavide, first minister to the king.

Not a chance of it, not now.

'Your mother,' he said through clenched teeth, 'was an actress in Lima. For all I know she still is.'

'She's alive?'

Olavide went on as if she hadn't spoken. 'An unsuccessful actress who would give herself to any man – '

'Stop! I don't want to hear any more! '

' – for the price of a good meal or a gift. She stole when she had to. She drank. It would kill her, and she knew it. She tried to reform. For two years she had just one lover. Just one.'

Suddenly it was as if Mariana no longer was in the room. 'A young fool, an advocate on the corregidor's staff, and after the earthquake, with Lima laid in ruins, certain properties had to be accounted for. The corregidor assigned the task to the young advocate. A matter of jewelry, silver, precious heirlooms. Some she'd received as gifts. Some she'd simply stolen. The advocate still loved her. He covered her tracks. They summoned her to Madrid. He could not account properly. He took the blame himself. He – '

'You? You, uncle?'

Olavide blinked. His eyes gleamed with suppressed tears. 'He spent a brief time in prison, and was pardoned because the king needed his services. But that was later. Before he left Lima, she'd returned to her old ways of life. In the rubble, like an animal.' The tears were flowing then. Pablo de Olavide felt very young and vulnerable, as if it had all been yesterday. 'The advocate,' he said, 'the advocate took their child away with him, to Madrid. The mother had no interest in her, you see.'

Mariana stared at her uncle blankly. She had never seen him lose his composure, his dignity. Now he was crying like a child.

'A lovely little thing, like her mother, the dark red hair, the blue eyes. . . . '

'Oh, God,' Mariana whispered. 'Oh, my God.'

Pity and love, the one corrosive, the other binding, flooded her. She placed a hand tentatively on his shoulder. He clutched her to him.

'I'm not governor any more,' he said brokenly. 'Aranda dismissed me.'

'You're not my uncle.'

'No.'

'My father. You're my father.'

To see him defeated like that, and to learn the truth at the same time; it was too much. Pity and love merged. She'd do anything for him. Anything. For the rest of her life if necessary.

The doorknocker thudded. The white-wigged major-domo entered the salon. 'Señor Goya to see the marquesa,' he said. Olavide had turned his back and busied himself with an arrangement of porcelain on an end table.

Mariana waited a long moment, the longest moment of her life. 'Tell him,' she said at last, 'tell him that the marquesa sends her regrets but does not wish to receive him.'

CHAPTER TWELVE

One Month in Madrid

SOMETIMES THEY DROVE in the open Bayeu landau to the royal gardens of the Retiro, Paco and Maria del Carmen on the rear seat and Josefa, serving as dueña, facing them. Carmen, plump and prettily attired, would laugh when she read the notice displayed prominently at the gateway. Women had to remove their mantillas; men had to wear waistcoats and frock coats, not jackets, capes or greatcoats. Any offending garments could be removed and confiscated by the corregidor's guards. Some days they made quite a collection.

'Well, if they want me to undress,' Carmen giggled, removing her lace mantilla. She looked at Paco archly, as if suggesting that he picture in his mind the rather more complete act of disrobing.

She was a silly little thing, but pretty and pleasant company, exactly what he needed now. Nothing serious, nothing deep, nothing complicated.

He had tried to see Mariana three times, always with the same result. *The Marquesa de Solis sends her regrets but does not wish to receive Señor Goya.*

She was wilful enough to get around her uncle's objections, had she wanted to. Paco was sure of that. It had to be Mariana herself. That Aragonese pride of his would not let him try again.

Sometimes they would stop on the mall and watch a game of croquet while sipping a cup of sherry. Carmen would clap her hands in delight, watching the genteel sport. Then Paco and Josefa would talk in soft voices.

'Something's troubling you, isn't it?'

'Oh, it's nothing. Life doesn't always work out the way you want it to, that's all.'

'I'd listen, if you'd care to tell me.'

'It's nothing.'

Sometimes the three of them strolled on the Paseo del Prado, among the gaily dressed crowds on a hot June afternoon, Josefa carrying a sensible parasol and Maria del Carmen fluttering one of her ornate fans. Manolo accompanied them, striding happily at Paco's side. Of the new fountains in the city, Carmen liked the Apollo in the Paseo del Prado the best, and they often sat there feeling the cooling spray of the water.

'I'd like to be really naughty,' Carmen would say. 'I'd like to come here at night and bathe in the fountain. Like the majos. I mean, just take off all my clothing and jump right in.' She would bat her eyes at Paco. The blue and ivory fan would flutter. 'Wouldn't that be fun?'

And Paco, as he was meant to, found himself picturing the plump, nude body as she plunged into the cold water.

Once Paco suggested a bullfight. Manolo's ears perked up. 'That would be great, but Francisco doesn't approve of them.'

Carmen said: 'I don't know if I could *stand* all that excitement. It would make me wild. There's no telling what I'd do afterwards.'

Paco and Josefa exchanged knowing half-smiles. Carmen's flirting was so obvious. She was a delightful little froth, somewhat empty in the head but decidedly well-endowed elsewhere.

And she made the most of it.

Josefa was anything but a fool. She lacked Mariana's quick brilliance and trained intellect. She had a slower, more earthy intelligence. When she spoke, it was quietly and to the point, and what she said often made sense in an unexpected way.

'I know I ought to hate bullfights,' she said. 'They're barbaric. And yet, I don't know, a good one leaves you feeling all weak and exhilarated at the same time.'

'I go positively wild,' Carmen said.

'Juanito Apiñani's fighting tomorrow,' Manolo suggested hopefully. 'Some say he's the best matador in Spain.'

Paco's face split in a broad grin, and Josefa looked at him. 'That's the first time I've seen you really smile in days,' she said quietly, her hazel eyes glowing with pleasure.

'Juanito and I, we're old friends.'

'You are?' cried Manolo. 'Really?'

'He could probably get us into the patio de caballos.'

Carmen squealed and clapped her hands in delight. Manolo's grin surpassed Paco's.

'Want to go?'

'We'll never get tickets,' Manolo predicted dispiritedly. 'It's too late. Every time Juanito Apiñani fights, it's "no hay billetes." '

'But if Paco uses his influence,' Carmen said.

They were strolling on the Alcalá at the hour of the paseo. A gold and white berlin went rumbling by. Paco turned his head to stare after it.

'Someone you know?' Josefa asked.

'The Olavide berlin,' Paco told her. Perhaps Mariana was inside. His heart began to pound.

'I didn't know you knew them.'

'It was a long time ago.'

She looked at his eyes and away. Her cheeks colored.

'All the influence in the world won't help,' Manolo said, returning to the subject of the bullfight. 'The impresario's a pirate. Give him an extra fifty reales a seat, and then it's a different matter. A one-eyed pirate.'

Again that grin split Paco's face. 'Did you say one-eyed?'

'Yes. They call him Tuertillo, for his one eye. Never any surname. Just Tuertillo.'

They had come abreast of a busy café. Paco found a table. 'Will you wait a few minutes?'

'But where are you going?' Carmen asked as he ordered drinks for them.

140

'To see this one-eyed pirate of Manolo's.'

'Out! Everybody! Come back later, come back next week, come back next year. Everybody out! '

The hangers-on, the would-be banderilleros, the old matadors down on their luck, the mayoral of the bulls that would be fought tomorrow – all of them left the office of Madrid's bullfight impresario, glancing back enviously at the young man responsible for their departure. A bull-breeder unknown to them? A young new fenómeno would bring a reckless courage to the plaza de toros? The door shut behind the last of them and Tuertillo Apiñani came out from behind his cluttered desk.

'Paco! Hombre! By the Virgin of Atocha, it's good to lay this eye of mine on you.' Tuertillo embraced Paco in a bearhug.

He had aged. His bald head looked waxen in the afternoon sunlight streaming through the single window. He had developed a double chin and a middle-aged corpulence that bulged his purple and gold frock coat. His eyepatch was black silk, the tight breeches on his fat legs silk too.

'That Juanito,' he said. 'You should see him. A terror. A marvel. Costillares himself's a pale shadow next to him. Have a cigar.'

He offered one from a cedar box and took one himself, snipping the end delicately with golden clippers. 'From Havana. That's in Cuba. Special order for me. How the devil are you, boy? From the look of you, life's treating you well.'

'They're buying my paintings in Zaragoza.'

'Then they'll buy 'em in Madrid. Some brandy?' He began to pour from a decanter. 'Special reserve, just for me, from the Domecq bodega in Jerez. Come to the fights tomorrow. Juanito's on. I'll give you barrera seats. There a wife? A girlfriend?'

Paco said he needed four seats.

'Done. Right over the patio de caballos. We'll disappoint Señor de Góvez; who cares?' He raised his glass. 'To Señor Money. The best señor is Señor Money, true? I knew they'd be bringing the fights back. Everybody else quit and went into some other business. Couldn't wait. Me, I knew old King Carlos would have to give in. So he says, "Tuertillo, can you run the bullring for me?" and I say, "King, it'll be a pleasure." How long you staying?'

The fifteen days had come and gone. 'A week or two, I

141

guess.'

'Got a place out back of the Retiro. A fornicating palace. Belonged to a count. From Málaga. Still does. He keeps an apartment there; the rest is mine. He's hardly ever in town. I mean a palace, flunkies all over the place so you trip over them if you're not careful. Señor Money's the best, verdad? Look at Juanito up there.' Tuertillo pointed a huge hand in the direction of a painting on the wall. It was a portrait of Juanito Apiñani by Mariano Maella. 'Look at our little Juanito, he's making more money than I am, you wouldn't recognize him. A dandy, an absolute fornicating dandy. Women swarming all over him. Throws gold and silver around like the Duke of Medina Sidonia's own prodigal son. Can't hold onto a copper. Thinks it'll last forever. Maybe it will. Good new boy coming up, though, José Delgado, they call him Pepe Hillo. Takes his alternativa in a year or so and Juanito'll have to watch out, because he'll be one of the great ones. Why don't you paint his picture?'

'Whose?' Paco asked. It hadn't been easy following Tuertillo's rambling monologue.

'Juanito. In action's what I mean. That one up there, he did it like Juanito's on his way to a wedding. His own. That's a laugh. He'll never marry, says there are fifty thousand good-looking dames in Madrid and he wants to have 'em all. One at a time or in any combination they'd care to suggest. That Juanito.' He handed the tickets to Paco, who reached into his sleeve pocket.

'On me, Paco. Compliments of King Carlos' friend the impresario of the plaza de toros of Madrid. See you at the fights, chico. Hasta mañana.'

'Until tomorrow,' Paco said, dazed.

The huge bull came exploding out of the gate and skidded to a snorting stop on the sand halfway across the plaza de toros.

The crowd, over twelve thousand of them that hot Sunday afternoon, leaped to its feet. The bull turned, cat-quick, and galloped toward the barrera, striking the fence with wide-spaced, white-tipped horns as sharp as rapiers, splintering boards and sending them flying with an angry toss of its massive head. This was no mere toro. It was a toro-toro, a bull of bulls, and perhaps it could save the afternoon.

Thus far the afternoon had been a disaster. The veterans Costillares and Juan Romero had caped their bulls indifferently and dispatched them with a perfunctory disdain that brought groans and whistles from the crowd. The bulls had seemed lethargic under the hot Castilian sun, resigned to dying as Costillares and Juan Romero were resigned to putting in a journeyman's work for far more than a journeyman's pay. The old lament could be heard everywhere in the crowd: when there are toros, there are no toreros; when there are toreros, no toros.

You couldn't blame the bulls, they were saying in the grandstand, and perhaps you couldn't blame Costillares. He was Numero Uno now, and knew it; a mediocre performance would soon be forgotten. But grave old Juan Romero of Ronda, son of that Francisco Romero who one hot day in Ronda, fifty years ago, a poor carpenter then, had rushed into the ring and caped a bull away from a fallen horseman, and then, even after horse and noble rider were safe, had, eyes glazed, lips parted, caped the bull past him again and yet again, showing that a bull could be fought on foot, inventing it all but making it look as if he had done it all his life – this son of Francisco Romero you could blame. You could shout imprecations down at him from the safety of the high benches, while he gazed up sneeringly, the bull apathetically killed, Romero's gold-embroidered jacket as neat as if he had just entered the ring, his light buckled shoes not even scuffed, not a single drop of sweat on his long face.

Now the crowd's mood changed. This was a toro-toro, all right. Juanito Apiñani's two brothers rushed around the bull, flapping their big capes, distracting it while the bullring carpenter hammered new boards into place. The bull took a lot of distracting. It was big, and fast, and the hump of muscle, the morillo between its shoulders, the tossing muscle that moved ponderous head and great horns, was swollen with an enormous anger. A black monster of a bull, they said in the crowd, that needed old Francisco Romero himself, not his son Juan and not a cynically cautious Costillares.

A bull that would get Juanito Apiñani, who was young, making money, but still hungry with the hunger that came out of the dirt-poor provinces and made a man risk death with dignity and passion.

Hungry enough now?

After the parade across the arena, after the matadors and their cuadrillas had saluted the president of the bullring high in his box, Juanito Apiñani had marched back across the ring and draped his dress cape on the barrier before a broad-shouldered young man and spoken a few words which only those closest had heard:

'Things have changed for both of us, eh Paco?'

He'd said it with that wolf's grin of his, and the predictable number of fashionably dressed ladies nearby had almost swooned. Juanito Apiñani wasn't much given to talking – the wolf's grin spoke for him, the eyes cold but the white teeth flashing.

He'd bowed and turned and strutted away with that stylized, stiff-legged matador's walk, and the plumply pretty girl seated next to the young man called Paco could be heard to say, fluttering her fan: 'He's beautiful. Madre, but he's beautiful.'

Earlier, while the bullring lackeys had wet down the sand of the enclosed patio de caballos and the picadors walked their nags back and forth, Juanito Apiñani, squaring his shoulders in the tobacco brown, gold-embroidered jacket, had listened a while to the nervous talk of Costillares and Juan Romero and the inane, grinning 'suerte, matador' that was repeated over and over again by the visitors to the patio, and then he had seen Paco come in with his friends.

Juanito went right over to them. He embraced Paco, and that wolf's grin split his face. 'Not just one beautiful lady,' he said, 'but two. Hombre, you've grown up.'

The taller of the two ladies, wearing a black mantilla over her golden hair, awarded his gallantry a thin-lipped smile. The plump one, in a low-cut, bustled, emerald green gown that would give her trouble on the narrow benches of the bullring, curtseyed low and spread her fan in a wide flutter.

The fourth member of the party was a mere boy, his eyes now as big as saucers.

'You like the bulls?' Juanito asked the plump one.

'I *adore* them. You must be very brave.'

'Sometimes I'm so frightened I can hardly stand,' said Juanito Apiñani with that wolf's grin.

The plump one giggled. 'You don't expect me to believe that.'

Juanito shrugged. 'Look at Costillares there. He's killed a thousand bulls by now.' In the slanting afternoon sunlight Costillares stood silent and pale. He was smoking a thin cigar in nervous little puffs.

'But not you,' insisted the plump one.

'No, not me. I eat the bulls for breakfast.'

They talked a while longer, the plump one animated, dividing her attention between Paco and Juanito Apiñani. Then the trumpet sounded.

Now, after the carpenter had made his quick repairs to the shattered fence, Maria del Carmen said: 'You never told me he was so beautiful. The way he moves.'

He was moving out into the center of the ring and with a careless wave of one hand sent his brothers from the arena. Even from this distance Paco could see the looks of uncertainty on Gaspar's and Emeterio's faces. They'd hardly had time to try the bull for their brother. A toro-toro. A real bull. They didn't like it.

Juanito Apiñani spread his cape, stamped a foot on the hard sand and called the bull. 'Ay, toro! Toro, ay!'

And the bull came fast at a sudden spurting gallop.

Holding the magenta cape by its collar, Juanito pivoted slowly, the spread cape swinging in a long, impossibly drawn-out arc that slowed the bull's charge. The bull went by as if galloping through molasses.

'Ay, toro! Toro!'

Back came the bull, and Juanito passed it closer, right horn all but picking the gold embroidery off his jacket.

'Olé!' cried twelve thousand voices.

And Juanito did it again, calmly, as if it were the simplest of matters to control the charge of a wild fighting bull bent on killing him.

And did it again, with that wolf's smile.

Then he rose suddenly into the air, caught not on the horns but between them. Only Emeterio had seen it coming. He was already out from behind the barrier and running across the sand, flapping his cape frantically. The bull, attracted by the motion, turned as Juanito landed heavily on his back and scrambled to his feet.

He waved Emeterio away angrily and passed the bull again, closer. Then he swirled the cape completely around his body and the bull stood stock still. Juanito, turning his back, strutted arrogantly away. The bull, watching him, did not move.

Juanito went to the barrier, where Gaspar handed over a long pole.

Paco could hear Gaspar ask: 'Are you sure, chico?'

'He knows Latin and Greek, that bull,' Emeterio said.

'Costillares was dismal, Romero worse. I want to show them.'

The pole was a Navarrese specialty. The toreros of Ronda and Sevilla disdained it. Or couldn't use it.

Juanito was already running across the sand, holding the long pole with both hands at one end. The bull, no longer transfixed, charged. Juanito kept running. At the last instant, when it seemed bull and man must collide, Juanito leaped up and brought the pole down into the sand directly in front of the bull's massive head. He vaulted high and clear, twisting in midair, bringing the pole up and over with him. Where the bull had seen a man, it now saw nothing.

The crowd, roaring, saw a torero.

Twice more Juanito vaulted over the bull. The crowd was delirious.

A trumpet blared, summoning the picador on his nag. Juanito, caping the bull first to the left then to the right, brought it into position before the horseman. The picador leaned forward and down, driving the point of his pike into the bull's morillo with all the weight of his shoulders.

'What's he doing that for?' Carmen asked Paco. 'I want to see Juanito.'

'To weaken the muscle, to get the bull's head down. Watch.'

She watched – and she screamed. The bull's third charge brought it under the horse, head lifting, horns searching. The horse came up off all four hooves; the pike flew from the picador's hands; horse and rider rose under a single powerful toss of that massive head. Carmen buried her face against Paco's chest.

Juanito flapped his cape, gracelessly now, to draw the bull away from the prone picador. The horse twitched and lay still. Two lackeys rushed out to cover it with canvas. From under it crawled a snake of blood, deep red against the golden sand.

'That's brutal,' Josefa said, her lips tight.

'They have to – '

'I know. Give the bull confidence. Let him know there really is something he can hit. But it's brutal.'

'I love it,' said Carmen in a weak voice. Her face looked green.

Gaspar and Emeterio dispensed quickly with the formality of the banderillas, the barbed sticks used to correct any tendency of the bull to hook in one direction or another. Each in turn came running at an angle that would bring him across the path of the bull's charge, each coming up high at the last instant on his toes, standing straight and planting his pair of sticks in the bull's back. The massive head tossed, the sticks clattered, the trumpet sounded again.

Juanito came over to the barrier above the patio de caballos. He bowed low before Paco and then unexpectedly winked at him. The wink seemed to say: You'll understand, amigo, she wants it so much. And Juanito handed his bicorn hat up to Maria del Carmen.

'I dedicate this bull to the most beautiful lady at the corrida,' he said formally, and bowed again, and walked across the sand toward the waiting bull.

He carried a smaller cape, dark red, and a sword of Toledo steel, its point downward-curving. The wolf's grin was gone.

The cape behind his back, showing it first on one side of his body then the other, he caught the bull's attention. Then he retreated, still moving the cape that way, and brought the bull back with him, slowly, so slowly, toward the barrier above the patio de caballos.

The death would be done for Paco and Maria del Carmen.

He spread the cape along the length of his sword and passed the bull on his right side. The bull rushed by. He repeated it, more slowly. The bull followed the cape, almost languidly. A third time, and the bull came by in a dream.

Paco was on his feet. It was like painting, it was something you either had or did not have. No one could give it to you.

It was magic.

Juanito switched the cape to his left hand, the sword remaining in his right. The lure he offered then was smaller, more dangerous. The bull accepted it. Juanito's feet remained planted on the hard sand. Then he pivoted with an agonizing slowness. He seemed to wrap the bull around his own body.

Those great horns, as wide across as a man's shoulders, red with the blood of the dead horse, passed now to the left, now to the right. They seemed to belong not to the bull but to Juanito Apiñani.

Bull and Juanito became one.

Then a full pivot by the lithe body, the small cape flaring, and once more the bull was transfixed. Juanito, his back to the beast, less than an arm's length away, smiled his wolf's smile up at Maria del Carmen.

'Enough?' he asked.

'Oh, yes. Oh God, yes.'

And Juanito bowed gravely, and stamped one foot delicately on the sand, and the bull looked at him.

Looked, and waited for death.

Juanito raised the sword in his right hand. He held the small cape, the killing cape, in his left, low and unfurled. His left hand moved, the cape moved, the bull's eyes following.

Juanito climbed on his toes and profiled himself to the bull, sighting along the length of the sword.

Bull stood without moving. Man stood without moving.

The beast, Paco thought, the dark beast everyone has to face, outside himself or within, and Juanito doing it for us, taking it all, pain and pity and terror, here, now, with his own fragile body and a blade of Toledo steel.

Taking it away and for a time destroying it so that we can live with it later.

The bull charged, head down, horns searching, seeking the cape.

Juanito did not move at all.

The hump of muscle behind the bull's massive head took the sword, and the steel went in smoothly. Then finally Juanito moved, off to his own left, crossing the cape to the right as the knuckles of his right hand, holding the sword, punched against the bull's hide.

On its back, all four feet in the air, the bull was dead.

And Juanito Apiñani stood over it, arms raised, head down, eyes down, not smiling.

He was always somehow in all the years that followed larger than other men. He would walk into a room and the rest of them would seem colorless, their voices flat, their smiles pale imitations of the dazzling smile of that full-lipped mouth, their eyes showing the message of their hearts while his eyes always remained so secret that I never really knew what he was thinking. He lives life at twice the rate of other men, as if there is never enough time for anything. Of love he gives enough, but not all that he might or all I could dream of. In love, in his love for me, he is strangely reserved. Half a love. I have had half a love from him all these years and that half is far better than all the love I ever could have had from anyone else I might have married. Sometimes alone in the same room with me he is still far away, those hooded eyes unreachable, those thoughts that only he understands, if even he understands them, not for such as me. I don't mind the disappearances and the actresses, the odd, sudden coldnesses and the duchesses, or the way he will listen to an idea of mine and nod that big lion's head and not really hear a word of it. As much as he can be, he is a good husband and a good father, and if it isn't all of him it is still far more than most men can give. I have been lucky. He is one of the special ones. He can create a world from nothing with that magic of his and it is a beautiful world though sometimes frightening. The backgrounds are stark and dreamlike, and at times the dream is a nightmare. It is as if he must get to the heart of things quickly and has no patience with the inconsequential. I know when he wants me, know when he needs me. For I know that in that biggest of men there lurks a small child who can be hurt by the world; and if those are the bad times for him, they are the good times for me, and I will use them selfishly. But he is like quicksilver. I cannot hold him. He is elusive and he eludes himself too because the essence of him is to give a quick, blinding flash of insight to all the rest of us whose lives are so much dimmer than his own. He mocks his own fate and tells me that to be a legend in your own lifetime is nonsense, but he takes a secret joy from it too and does what he can to embellish the legend. He is a giant walking the streets, but sometimes a baffled giant who cries out at all the pain in the world, the cruelty, the injustice, the bloodlust. He loves the bullfights not merely because a matador like Juanito or that Pepe Hillo has some of his God-given magic but because he loves the bulls too. The bulls, he says, are beautiful in their power, and if I argue that it is the power of darkness, he will tell me that darkness too walks the face of the earth. The king dotes on him and he makes little of it, leaving for the palace in the morning with that strange self-mocking smile and saying well, it is time to paint a little ugliness, but at times like that he is transparent – the peasant from Aragon who can tell the king to stand this way or that, move your head to the right a little, sire, the light isn't quite right, and it pleases him. The peasant from Aragon with those shoulders like a wrestler's and the narrow flanks of a boy, and he knows I understand what that powerful body needs – softness now, and compliance; wildness then, and fire. He lives too hard and too much because it is the only way he knows, and I am his haven. It is beyond comprehension except for that. I am a pale thing at his side. His heights are unreachable, his depths unfathomable. I am lucky, and I thank the Virgin for granting me the half of him. He would never understand that. He doesn't believe. It makes him uneasy. The saints he paints are people with dirt under their fingernails. Perhaps he knows a God the rest of us can't understand. Perhaps it is a kind of blasphemy. I don't care. Perhaps he needs no God at all. But he wakes at night sometimes shouting nada y nada y nada out of a nightmare. He is always so alone in a crowd. He always wants to get it over with and move on to something else. That first time after we were married. Those shoulders and flanks and that big heart of his pounding against the un-

149

certain flutter of my own; they were there, there for me in our marrriage bed, but were his dreams elsewhere? Perhaps they were. But I knew. Yes, I knew what he wanted then, and I could give it to him. 'The Earth Mother' is the pagan way he would have put it, though he never talks about it. Lush and fertile as if the marriage bed were a silent woodland glade, sun-dappled, sweet-scented and receiving. I gave him that. I have given him what I could. Has it been enough? I have no way of knowing. He never says. The half of him. The half of him permits me, and I don't even know if it is more than he permits anyone else. But he returns. He comes back. All these years I have had the half of him, and half of him is more than any woman has a right to hope for. So I will take what he gives, and I will thank the Virgin. For I know with a pride and a delight that the half of him is far more than all of anyone else. He has brought his wildness and his magic to my life, and if it goes on forever that would not be long enough.

If Paco had expected Maria del Carmen to spend the evening at 7 Clock Street raving about Juanito Apiñani, he was mistaken.

They sat down to a late supper in the dining room, all of them busily shelling shrimp and dismembering crayfish, and then Francisco Bayeu presented one of his inane riddles.

'Who is the cruel son who tears his mother to pieces, and whose mother by devious ways gradually eats him?'

There were a few half-hearted guesses, but nobody knew the answer.

'The plow,' said Francisco Bayeu with a fatuous little laugh, and Ramón groaned elaborately.

Carmen told Paco: 'I wish I could understand the bullfights the way you can. Have you seen many of them?'

'When I was a boy in Zaragoza.'

Paco didn't want to talk about it. He felt exhilarated, not merely because the triumph had been Juanito's but because the bullfight had deep roots in Spanish earth. It had been part of the people since there was a Spanish people, and some said it went back beyond the limits of history to a distant time before the Romans brought Jesus Christ to Spain. It was religion then, it was a fertility cult; the blood of the bull shed to fructify the soil, the death of the bull to give life to the people. Critics like Nicolás Moratín understood that, and wrote about it. Their writing left the Church less than happy.

Paco knew his exhilaration would pass, knew he would suddenly be left with an empty and dead feeling, and he both looked forward to the moment and dreaded it.

' . . . explain it all to me. I'd be an earnest pupil, I promise,' Carmen was saying.

'What?'

'I wish you'd explain it all to me.'

Francisco Bayeu said: 'I'd rather he didn't. It's a pagan ritual, an embarrassment to Spain.'

'Why should Spain be ashamed of its uniqueness?' Josefa asked in that quiet way of hers, and the question surprised Paco. The implicit answer was that Spain shouldn't be ashamed, an answer that Mariana herself might have given.

Mariana, he thought, and could feel himself plummeting from the heights.

'I'll bet you could paint them,' Carmen said.

'Paint what?'

'Why, the bulls, of course.'

'I never thought about it.'

'I'd love to see you do it. I'd love to see you do anything you loved.'

That familiar exchange of half-smiles passed between Paco and Josefa. Her sister was so delightfully obvious.

'Well,' said Francisco Bayeu sententiously after the coffee had been served, 'to accomplish anything you have to work.' He yawned. 'I have a busy day tomorrow.'

He excused himself, and for a while the younger Bayeus and Paco sat around the table talking. It was late.

'What a beautiful day,' Carmen said, looking at Paco. 'I was hoping it would never end.'

Manolo agreed eagerly, and in his innocent agreement blunted the effect of Carmen's remark. She gave him a spiteful look.

'Well,' said Ramón in an almost perfect imitation of his older brother's sententious tone, 'as they say, since the time of Adam, some warm the oven and others eat the bread. If I'm to warm the oven tomorrow. . . . You will be hungry, won't you, Paco old fellow?'

Carmen tittered nervously.

'Ramón,' Josefa said.

Paco waited for the anger to leave him. He'd return to Zaragoza soon, but he'd be back in Madrid to stay one of these days. He and Ramón were both painters beginning to establish themselves, and their paths would cross frequently.

'Oh, save me a crust or two if it isn't too much trouble,' he said lightly.

Ramón's departure signaled an end to the small supper party. They all retired upstairs except Paco. The predictable letdown, after the exhiliration of the afternoon, was on him. He felt restless and knew he wouldn't sleep. He went into the library, trimmed the wick on the lamp and ran his eyes over the gold-tooled, leather-bound books. He selected the translation of Winckelmann's tome on classic art and browsed through it. The book showed a lot of use. Francisco Bayeu had underlined passages, put brackets in the margins, jotted comments in his indecipherable scrawl.

'I thought I'd find you here.'

Paco looked up and saw Josefa. She was wearing a blue robe, buttoned all the way to the neck, and blue silk slippers. Her hair hung loose. He had never seen it that way before. It fell straight to her waist in a golden cascade.

'Can't you sleep?' he asked.

'I'm feeling a little depressed. I don't know why.'

'It's the bullfight. If it lifts you high enough it has to drop you sooner or later.'

'Oh, that old mystique.'

'It works that way for me, anyway. Even when I was a boy.'

'In a lot of ways you still are.'

He raised a thick eyebrow.

'Really. As much as Manolo.'

'He's a nice boy.'

'I wish we had a few more of him around here. Instead of — oh, never mind. I said I was feeling blue. I suppose the real reason I hoped to find you up was to apologize.'

'Apologize?'

'For Ramón.'

'He was only joking.'

'It was more than a joke. He resents you. And he's jealous of you. He's always had Francisco to show him the way. What you did you did by yourself.'

'I was Francisco's apprentice too.'

'Less than a year. You didn't need him.'

Paco shook his head. 'I'll tell you about that some time. I did need him.'

'I don't think so.'

'Tiepolo thought so.'

'Tiepolo? Really? That's quite a compliment to my brother.'

It hadn't been, not the way Tiepolo had put it, but Paco didn't say that.

'Because Tiepolo was really talented. Even more than

152

Mengs,' Josefa said in that quiet voice of hers.

She asked Paco suddenly: 'What kind of painter do you want to be?'

'What kind? The best I can, that's all.'

'Francisco says you make too little of line, too much of color.'

'Maybe he's right. I don't really know what I'm trying to do. Something totally different. When I find out it'll probably be awful.'

'Oh, I doubt that.'

Paco smiled. He was glad Josefa had joined him here in the library. She was easy to talk to. She asked exactly the right kind of questions for the mood he was in. She always had that way of calming him. In the light of the lamp her thin-lipped face with its wistful hazel eyes was pretty.

They talked for hours. It grew very late and the night sounds of Madrid faded and were gone. Afterwards he could hardly recall what they had talked about. Everything and nothing. Painting, bullfighting, politics, growing up in Zaragoza, life on the streets of Madrid, the life of a maja.

'Sometimes I wish I could live like one.'

'Why don't you try?'

'Oh, I never could. I know I couldn't. But it's nice to dream.'

'They have troubles, like everyone else.'

'They're more alive. They're so – free.'

'Nobody's free.'

'*You* are, inside yourself.'

Her belief in his independence both pleased and embarrassed him, and he tried to make light of it. 'I'm the only one who knows what's inside myself – and sometimes I'm not even sure.'

'That's what I mean. You're such a private person.'

'Instead of private you might say selfish,' he suggested wryly.

'You? No, not selfish. But if you were, an artist has a right to be.'

Again this quiet girl, who for some inexplicable reason was talking far more than she ever had, made him think of Tiepolo.

'Perhaps. If he has the magic.'

'The what?'

'Talent and magic, they're not the same thing. I can't explain it. Tiepolo once tried. The magic is – well, it's part of you and not part of you. It's more than talent. Only the great

153

ones have it.'

'I think I see what you mean. Juanito Apiñani – he had that magic you're talking about, didn't he?'

Paco nodded earnestly, surprised again by the quality of her mind. 'Yes. He did.'

A faint dawn had appeared at the windows. 'Would you look at that?' said Josefa. 'We've spent the whole night talking.'

Paco felt wide awake but calm. He had been high, and then he had felt himself falling, and she had got him through it.

She was seated then beside him at the desk, the Winckelmann face down where Paco had put it. She reached past him to the lamp and turned the wick down low and then out. Only the faint early dawn lighted the room.

He could barely see her. There was no sound. He could smell the oil of the darkened lamp. The loneliness which was the curse of an artist and which made his art possible had left him. He felt comfortable, so comfortable that he wanted to sit there for another day and another night talking to her. The loneliness would return; it had to return; he wanted it to return. But how good it felt to be without it for a while!

'Paco,' she said. 'Paco, I – ' Her voice caught. He waited.

'I'm so tired of Madrid,' she said finally. 'Oh, not really Madrid. The bourgeois life that's so important to Francisco. Running my brother's household. The eternal squabbling, all the time, every day; it isn't just your visit. I'm here, but it's as if I'm not. Did you ever have the feeling life's passing you by?'

'There's never enough time,' Paco said, and wondered if he sounded like Francisco Bayeu then.

'That's it. Never enough to do the things you really want to do. To be yourself. To start living instead of just existing.' She asked abruptly: 'When are you going back to Zaragoza?'

'In a few days, I guess. I hadn't thought about it.'

'Take me with you. I'm twenty-five, Paco. Twenty-five, and I haven't even started living. I don't want to spend the rest of my life with them like this. Take me with you. I'll manage your household for you. I'm really quite good at that at least – '

'Josefa,' he said gently. 'It's the bullfight. It's the first light of morning, when death feels close. You don't mean all that.'

'I mean it. I never meant anything so much in my life. Let me live with you. I'd be good for you. I won't intrude. I'll just – be there when you need me.'

He could say nothing. She had offered all of herself for very little of him in return. And it was tempting. It was more tempting than he cared to admit. She could push the loneliness further back inside him. She could make it go away for a while. He felt a thickening in his throat. He had no words for his gratitude then, and because he had none he turned and kissed her tenderly on the lips.

'Remember that time when you – when you had to go away? You were so young, and so unsure of yourself, it was as if your life had ended before it began. I was good for you then, remember? It's all I remember It's everything I remember. There haven't been any others, ever. There won't be.'

'Don't say that.'

'Please take me with you. I can be there again like that, when you need me. I want to. I want you to be my whole life.'

Someone to share the torment. Someone to share the magic.

'You'd be living outside the Church.'

'I don't care. I don't care about anything else.'

It was tempting. It was so calmingly, soothingly tempting.

'What would you tell your brother?'

'I'm twenty-five. I don't care what I tell my brother.'

'You've got to tell him something.'

'Then you'll – do it? You'll take me with you? Oh, Paco!'

He remembered thinking once, so long ago: *Marriage? Not yet. And if not Mariana, then someone else*. It would definitely not be Mariana. She had made that clear. *He would settle down, raise a family, become a dutiful provider*. The loneliness. To make the loneliness more bearable.

Outside, the first coach of the new day went rumbling by. Paco heard the serving girl's soft footsteps on the stairs.

Josefa was crying.

'Tell him,' Paco said after a long time, 'tell him. . . . No, I'll tell him. I'm going to marry his sister Josefa.'

CHAPTER THIRTEEN

The Royal Tapestry Works

ANTON RAFAEL MENGS, his soft leather boots dusty from the bare earth yard between the dye house and the office of the Royal Tapestry Works, looked up at the feeble trickle of smoke issuing from the dye house chimney, looked at the weed-grown path leading to the factory itself, and finally turned his disdainful eyes on Francisco Bayeu, who was just climbing down from Mengs' landau.

The place resembled a rundown farm rather than a factory, with its dirty whitewashed buildings and broken red tile roofs.

'And like Spanish countrymen,' observed Mengs, brushing fastidiously at a speck of lint on his purple sleeve, 'they've let it go to seed. Look at the place, will you?'

Junk littered the yard – the massive logs of unused looms, some shattered crockery, a few old wagon wheels. The gardener came out of his small hut and gave them a passing glance. He led a donkey away on some unknown errand.

'Hot,' said Bayeu, removing his tricorn and mopping his brow.

'It's going to be hotter for Mynheer van der Goten.' Van der Goten was superintendent of the Royal Tapestry Works of Santa Barbara.

'He's worked with a minuscule budget for years. You really can't blame him. They're down to half a dozen tapestries a year.'

'We'll change that. We'll change everything.'

'It's not the cook who supplies a good meal. It's a well-stocked larder.'

Mengs' eyebrows lifted. He could never get used to Bayeu's aphorisms. 'Meaning, I suppose, that we ought to give van der Goten a bigger budget?'

'And,' Bayeu said, 'some decent artists. His cartoons have been painted by unknowns for years.'

'What decent artists did you have in mind?' asked Mengs in a tone that indicated there was just one, or at most two, in all Madrid.

'Yourself for one,' Bayeu said promptly.

'And you, of course,' Mengs said magnanimously.

Bayeu ticked the others off on his fingers. 'Maella, Luis Meléndez, my brother Ramón.' He paused. He looked at Mengs questioningly. 'And Goya.'

'Goya? Are you serious?'

'He's had fantastic success these past three years in Zaragoza. Last year alone his commissions – '

'Ramón I can see,' said Mengs. 'His talent's grown. But Goya – that smacks of nepotism, Francisco.'

'He'd be just right for the tapestry works,' Bayeu said patiently. 'He's sketched the life of the people since he was a

156

child, and he's lived it in a way you and I haven't. Give him a chance.'

'You'll get no Gobelins out of him.'

'We don't want Gobelins. We want Spanish tapestries. We want genre paintings for them.' Francisco Bayeu cleared his throat uneasily. 'My sister Josefa's going to have a baby.'

Mengs laughed condescendingly. 'Then that explains it, my friend. Why didn't you say so? Goya can use the money.'

'He's earning as much in Zaragoza as we could pay him here. I'd feel easier with Josefa in Madrid when her time comes, though.'

'There is that,' Mengs said. He clapped Bayeu on the back, a rare gesture for him. 'Well, I won't argue with you, Francisco. If you want your brother-in-law, you'll have him. But don't say I didn't warn you.'

A grayness seemed to suffuse Mynheer Cornelius van der Goten, as if he had lived too long in his sunless Flemish homeland. His sparse hair lay plastered against his skull in sweaty gray ringlets. His knee-length smock, possibly once white, was now a dull gray. His mournful eyes were gray too, and a gray stubble of beard covered the gray skin of his face.

Short, podgy, and unkempt, at his best merely nervous, he was in a state bordering on collapse three months after Mengs and Bayeu had first visited the tapestry works. They had expected too much of him, and too fast. They were impatient with delays, angry with mistakes, quick to ridicule anything and everything. Especially that insufferable Bohemian Mengs. Sometimes Mynheer van der Goten wished Mengs had never been born. Sometimes he wished he himself had never been born. On bad days – and this was one of them – he wished both.

He could work with Maella. He could work with Luis Meléndez and Ramón Bayeu. They knew the difference between a tapestry cartoon and a canvas painted for its own sake.

This Goya, though, was another matter. This Goya was impossible.

Van der Goten's voice emerging from all that grayness was surprisingly shrill. Jabbing a finger in the general direction of the three canvases Paco had propped against the wall of the tapestry works office, he said:

'Look at those colors! Look at the confusion! At that infernal blending! My weavers could never reproduce them – never!'

For his first three tapestry cartoons Paco had painted a wild

157

boar hunt, a fisherman, and three leashed hounds. His brother-in-law had suggested the subject matter. 'They're simple, they're not controversial, and Anton Rafael couldn't possibly object to them,' Francisco Bayeu had said. 'Secure your place at the works with them and you'll be able to range further afield.'

'I've already secured my place. As an artist.'

'Zaragoza – '

'Is not Madrid,' Paco finished for his brother-in-law.

'Precisely. The king's taking a real interest in the tapestry works. It's why he appointed Anton Rafael to direct them. Be sensible, Paco.'

Paco stubbornly shook his head. 'I had in mind something more imaginative.'

'I'm asking you to hold that imagination of yours in check. For Josefa – and the baby?' Bayeu urged.

And just then Josefa came quietly into the drawing room at 7 Clock Street. Both men stood up.

'For me and the baby – what?'

Paco relented and set to work.

Now, at the tapestry works, Mynheer van der Goten glared at the three oil paintings, and at their executor, and again that unexpectedly shrill voice issued from the grayness: 'Take them back. Rework them. Simplify them.'

Paco had embellished Bayeu's simple subject matter with a baroque use of color. 'No,' he said. 'I like them the way they are.'

Van der Goten seemed to sink inside his gray smock, his neck all but disappearing. 'Señor, they are really very fine paintings. I'm not disputing that. But as tapestry cartoons they'll give my weavers apoplexy.'

'Ask them,' Paco said.

'I don't have to ask them.' The plump gray van der Goten neck re-emerged. 'Since its founding my family has run the Santa Barbara works.'

'Into the ground,' Paco said coldly.

His three years of success in Zaragoza had given him a confidence bordering on arrogance. He dressed stylishly and drove his own secondhand landau. He and Josefa lived next door to 7 Clock Street, renting the somewhat smaller house from Francisco Bayeu. Paco had spent a small fortune refurnishing it. He kept a staff of four, more than the house required. But, after all, wasn't Josefa going to have a baby? Besides, he was living high and enjoying it. He had lived equally high in Zaragoza, despite Josefa's protests, and he had also assumed his father's debts. He spent every reale he earned and tottered on the brink of debt himself.

Mynheer van der Goten did not know that. If ever he saw an annoyingly self-confident individual, it was this twenty-nine-year-old artist who thought he knew more about tapestry cartoons than he, van der Goten, did.

'I'm telling you they'll give my weavers apoplexy.'

'And I'm telling you to ask them.'

The plump shoulders shrugged under the gray smock. 'Very well, señor. You're wasting my time, and you're wasting my foreman's time, but we'll ask.'

The podgy form waddled from the office and returned a few minutes later. Paco expected the foreman to be an old man in an ill-fitting smock like van der Goten's, a weaver who had spent his lifetime at the Santa Barbara works. But a young woman – hardly more than a girl – entered the office behind van der Goten. She wore a bright blue smock that fell in a straight line from the curve of her breasts to her slender ankles. There was something about her – the dark red hair, the high cheekbones – that reminded Paco of a less refined Mariana.

Without so much as a glance at Paco, she went straight to the paintings. She brushed a strand of dark red hair back from her brow. She was scowling.

'You see what I mean?' van der Goten asked in his shrill voice. 'Not only difficult but impossible. All those colors.'

The girl began to nod.

'Color,' said Paco flatly, 'is what a painter uses.'

The sound of his deep voice turned the girl's head in his direction. 'You painted these, señor?'

'As tapestry cartoons, señorita. They can be done.'

'I haven't seen you here before.'

'They're my first three cartoons.'

'They *are* difficult.' The girl was looking at his eyes. 'But I like them. What's your name?'

'Paco Goya.'

She was still staring at those hooded eyes of his. 'I'm Barbara García. It's easy to remember. You know, Barbara – just like the works?'

Paco swept off his tricorn and bowed. 'Enchanted, Señorita García.'

'Call me Barbara, since we'll be working together.'

'Then you can do them – Barbara?'

159

'I think so. I know I want to try.'

Cornelius van der Goten rubbed his plump gray hands.

'Santa Barbara,' Paco said. 'You won't be sorry.'

She smiled. 'I rarely am.'

CHAPTER FOURTEEN

The Patio de Caballos

IF ALL THAT MATTERED was the quality of the corrida, the last bullfight of the '75 season would not have been memorable. The October day was cool, the bulls lethargic, the gusty wind a danger to the bullfighters because they could not control their capes.

It surprised Paco that Juanito Apiñani, younger than himself, fought as senior matador. It dismayed him that Juanito fought now with cynical caution, doing his Navarrese tricks with consummate grace but keeping a safe distance from the bull, a distance which made the tricks somehow cheap and vulgar. The other two matadors had at least tried, despite the wind. Pedro Romero, young grandson of the great Francisco Romero, fought in the cool, aloof classic style of Ronda. José Delgado, called Pepe Hillo, used his wind-blown cape like a madman bent on his own destruction. The conflict between them was an artistic one; Romero was a bullfighting Anton Rafael Mengs and Pepe Hillo a bullfighting Tiepolo. But neither of them could entirely ignore the wind. They seemed so good because Juanito was so bad. No, Paco told himself, it was not a memorable bullfight.

Still, looking back on that cool October day, he knew he would always remember it as a pivotal one in his life.

'I feel so sorry for Juanito,' Josefa said. 'They made him look very bad, didn't they?' She drew her wide woolen cape more tightly around her. The baby was expected in two months.

'He wasn't trying,' Paco said. 'He's careful these days. A

160

family and bullfighting, they don't go together.'

Josefa squeezed his hand. 'And a family and painting?'

'Well, that's another matter,' Paco said. 'We'd better see him, cara. Would it be too tiring?'

'No. He'll need us now.'

After the traditional last fight of the season, the matadors held court in the patio de caballos, swaggering and talkative if they had been good, grimly silent or ready with excuses otherwise. Juanito Apiñani, Paco knew, would be grimly silent.

They waited a few more minutes in their barrera seats. Paco wanted Josefa to avoid the crowds shoving toward the exits.

'How's your Santa Barbara?' she asked with that thin-lipped smile of hers.

Paco returned the smile. The frankness between them was one of the things he liked best about their marriage. 'Still a flirt,' he said. 'She's a little like Maria del Carmen, you know.'

'Paco,' said Josefa in mock horror, 'you're talking about a married woman. A mother.'

'The important thing,' Paco became serious, 'is that Señorita García said she'd be able to do those tapestries, and she can. They're coming along beautifully.'

'Is your relationship with Santa Barbara coming along beautifully too?' Josefa asked archly.

'She thinks so.'

'And it flatters you.' Said not entirely in jest.

'It means I can paint the way I want to.'

'Despite Mynheer van der Goten?'

'He's always on the verge of a nervous breakdown. The García girl really runs the works.'

'And does she run the painters?'

Paco, in fact, had been flattered by Barbara García's attention. 'I think we can go down now,' he said.

The enclosed patio de caballos, windless but cool, was crowded. The three matadors stood apart, each holding court, each still sweating in his heavy brocaded jacket.

Or, Paco observed, two of them were holding court. Juanito Apiñani stood off to one side with his wife and his three brothers.

'Hombre, hombre,' Tuertillo was saying, 'what's one day? One fornicating day – I beg your pardon, señora.' He always called his sister-in-law señora, possibly because he still couldn't believe that Juanito had actually married. 'There's a whole new year, next year.'

'So you had a little bad luck, chico,' Gaspar said.

'Everybody has a little bad luck from time to time,' Emeterio said.

'It's unfair, caro,' Maria del Carmen told her husband. 'They expect you to be perfect. Nobody can be perfect every day.' She was holding his arm possessively. 'You can do everything they can do. That Romero and that Pepe Hillo. He's a lot of man, though, Pepe Hillo. Look at all the women around him. He's like a magnet.'

'Why don't you go over and flutter your fan?' Juanito suggested coldly.

'Caro, I was only – '

'No, I'm sorry.' The wolf's smile appeared then. 'In fact I'm sorry I entered the ring with him today.'

'Tuertillo's right. There'll be other days.'

'Hola, Paco,' Juanito called as Paco and Josefa made their way through the crowd. Paco punched Juanito's shoulder. 'Some days I paint so bad I'm sure I'm a fraud. It can happen to anybody.'

They chatted a while. An elderly man resplendent in black and gold approached them. With him, trying to look very mature in a bustled gold dress, her masses of black hair piled high on a mantilla-draped comb, was a lovely young girl.

Santa Maria, Paco thought instantly, I'd love to paint that child.

Juanito bowed low and swept the sand with his hat. 'Your Grace,' he said.

The old man said: 'Speaking as an aficionado, matador, I've seen you on better days. But this granddaughter of mine, she says you fly like a bird when you vault over the bull. Pepe Hillo and Romero be damned, she said, though that's not quite the way she put it – '

'It is so, grandfather,' the girl cut in, 'and you scolded me.'

'At any rate,' the old man said, 'she did want to meet you. Juanito Apiñani, may I present my granddaughter Cayetana?'

Juanito bowed even lower, with that wolf's grin big on his face. He kissed the small, offered hand. 'Doña Cayetana,' he said, 'the house of Alba does me great honor.'

'I love the way you smile even more than I love the way you fly,' Cayetana said.

The old man, it finally entered Paco's head, was the Duke of Alba. He remembered his first visit to the Olavide townhouse, when the duke had played Scarlatti on the harpsichord. Fleetingly he thought of Mariana.

162

'In fact I love all bullfighters,' Cayetana said.

'A pox on all bullfighters,' said Tuertillo. 'A pretty señorita like you ought to save some of that love for us poor impresarios.'

Those enormous dark eyes in that young face looked at him coolly.

'Oh, I have a lot of love in me, Señor One-Eye. More than enough to go around.'

The duke laughed uneasily. Paco could almost tell what he was thinking: this one I'd better marry off young.

Cayetana produced a small book and asked Juanito to write something in it. There was an awkward silence. Her grandfather gazed skyward painfully.

'Little lady – ' Juanito began apologetically, and Paco took the little book from the girl's hand.

'What he means is you'd rather have a picture of him.'

Cayetana nodded eagerly. 'Oh, I'd really love that. Who are you?'

But Paco had already taken chalk from his pocket and in a moment sketched a good likeness of Juanito, knees tucked up as he vaulted over a bull. He returned the book to the girl.

She considered the sketch. She considered Paco. 'Sign it,' she said.

Paco scrawled below the sketch: Goya, plaza de toros de Madrid, October 1775.

'I like it, Goya,' Cayetana said, 'and I thank you. But I don't like a man who doesn't answer my questions.'

That arrogance, even then.

'Your Grace,' a voice said.

Pepe Hillo had made his way through the crowd and with a low bow to the duke joined the group around Juanito. He had laughing eyes and a full-lipped, sensuous mouth.

'Hola, Hillo. You were tremendous today,' said the Duke of Alba.

'I was lucky. The wind decided not to bother me. Instead it bothered Juanito here.'

'You're the one who dances,' Cayetana said.

Pepe Hillo glanced down at her. 'A dancing torero is a frightened torero.'

'Oh, I don't mean away from the bull, silly. I mean with him. Like a ballet.'

'In that case,' said Pepe Hillo gravely, 'you're forgiven.'

'You're funny,' Cayetana said. 'When I have my own palace will you come to my soirées?'

'With pleasure,' said Pepe Hillo, even more gravely.

Cayetana looked at the sketch in her little book and at Paco. 'You can come too. I can't make up my mind about you. Am I going to like you?'

'I hope so,' Paco said.

'Perhaps I'll hate you.'

'Cayetana,' the Duke of Alba said.

'Anyway, I'll have my palace sooner than you think. Grandfather's afraid of me.'

This time the duke merely looked skyward again.

'I mean he's afraid if he doesn't find me a husband soon – *very* soon – he'll regret it. You know what? He's right.'

'Cayetana, now that really is too much.' The duke clicked his watch open and cleared his throat. 'We must be going,' he said. 'Convey my regards to Romero, please.'

'It really is a very nice picture,' Cayetana called back over her shoulder as they left.

'What a saucy little bitch,' Maria del Carmen said.

'But somehow quite lovely,' Josefa told her sister. 'Beguiling.'

Twelve years old, Paco thought. Or thirteen at most. Beguiling indeed.

'She'll be a woman, that one.' Hillo smiled at him. 'She'll have Madrid at her feet some day.'

'She already knows it. So does the duke.'

'I'd like to be there when she grows up.'

'You bachelors,' Maria del Carmen told Hillo. 'It's all you ever think about.'

'Well, I think about the bulls when I have to,' Hillo said.

The crowd in the patio de caballos had thinned out. A bull-breeder from Andalucía came over and earnestly began to discuss with the Apiñani brothers the merits of his bulls.

'Next year's crop,' Hillo told Paco cynically. 'Of course they'll be bigger but not too big, and they'll charge faster but not too fast.'

'And if Tuertillo signs for them now,' Paco said, 'he'll get a good price.'

Horns as wide as barn doors, the earnest bull-breeder was saying. Quick as cats. Noble beasts.

'They're always noble beasts until you fight them,' Hillo said.

A price was mentioned. Tuertillo's one eye widened in disbelief.

'Want to meet Romero?' Hillo asked Paco. 'Introduce your

lady?'

As they walked across the sand Paco saw the dark, gypsy-looking Mariano Maella who, like himself, was painting cartoons for the Santa Barbara works. Near him, her back turned, stood a woman holding the hand of a little boy staring up in awe at the tall Romero.

Suddenly the woman turned in profile.

It was Mariana.

Paco barely heard the introductions. The matador Pedro Romero, the painter Francisco Goya. His wife, Doña Josefa Bayeu de Goya. Maella of course you know. I don't believe, Hillo said, I've had the pleasure of meeting this lady.

The Marquesa de Solís, Romero said. Her son, Antonio Francisco, Marqués de Solís.

Bows exchanged with the tall Romero. A hand extended by the marquesa, his lips not quite brushing it. The dark red hair streaked with gray, the face with its fine high cheekbones and blue eyes still young, still lovely. A simple canary yellow frock, a shawl. The hand trembling. The boy waiting expectantly.

'My son Antonio Francisco,' Mariana repeated Romero's introduction.

And the boy turned away from Romero to stare up at Paco. With that broad face and those hooded eyes.

'I remember you,' Antonio Francisco said brightly. 'You're the painter who didn't come that day.'

'He was very disappointed,' Mariana said.

Some small talk with Maella. A joke about van der Goten. A joke about Santa Barbara. Paco had started it, and everyone called her that these days.

The boy's eyes.

A candle, blown out by the wind. The scent of jasmine. Coming together like two children afraid of the dark. Nine years ago.

Josefa would have a baby in two months. Their baby.

'How's Don Pablo?' Paco heard himself saying.

'Fine, he's fine.' In a thin, nervous voice. 'He's not in Madrid much these days. Doing legal work for Count Floridablanca in Andalucía. Contracts for factories.'

Paco said inanely he was very glad to hear it.

There was an awkward silence. Everyone was staring at Paco and the boy. The resemblance was almost uncanny.

Josefa stood there, her face pale, her cape swelling over the life inside her.

Juanito and Maria del Carmen joined them. 'I won't fight Zayaz bulls and that's that,' Juanito was telling his wife. 'Not next year and not any year. I don't like them.' He brightened. 'Why, I remember you. You're the Lady of Charity.' He kissed Mariana's hand.

'It's been a long time, Juanito.'

Maria del Carmen blurted: 'It's absolutely incredible. The boy. The boy and Paco. They – '

Juanito nudged her. She took in the embarrassed expression on all the other faces. She looked at her sister. 'What a fantastic coincidence,' she said lamely. 'But you have to admit they – '

Another nudge from Juanito.

Maella said they'd have to be going. A small supper at Botín's. The boy couldn't stay up all night.

'Will you come and teach me to paint some time?' the boy asked.

The Marquesa de Solis sends her regrets but does not wish to receive Señor Goya. But if she had? If she had?

'He's terribly busy, Paquito,' Mariana said quickly.

'My regards to Don Pablo,' Paco said.

He kept staring at the boy. He couldn't help it.

Bows and more hand-kissing.

One small part of Paco stood outside himself. He wanted to see his own face, would give anything to see it. What a study it would make, if he could capture it – a self-portrait to end all self-portraits. The shock of recognition, the ludicrous, open-mouthed, wide-eyed shock of recognition.

He took Josefa's hand. It was cold, the fingers stiff and unresponsive.

'She's very lovely,' Josefa said that night in their bedroom at 9 Clock Street.

'Considering her gray hair. Say well-preserved.'

'It makes her look younger if anything.'

'Josefa, I – '

'You should have seen your face then, in the patio.' With a brave little smile.

'I can imagine.'

'What are you going to do?'

'Do? Nothing.'

'Surely you have to recognize the boy.'

'You mean legally? That's ridiculous. It's the last thing Mari – the marquesa would want. He has a name. A title.'

166

'You can call her Mariana. Were you very much in love?'

'We were very young.'

'First love is the best love, they say.'

'You sound like your brother.'

'I'm sorry.'

'No. I'm sorry. I shouldn't have put you through that this afternoon.'

'It wasn't your fault. How could you have helped it?'

'I should have told you about her.'

'What difference would that have made? One look at you and I could tell you didn't know about the boy.'

'One look and the whole world can tell whose son he is.'

'Do you want to see them?'

'No. Why should I?'

'You're his father.'

'He doesn't know that.'

'He doesn't have to know it. You can be a – friend to him.'

'I don't think it's wise.'

'I don't think I could love you as much if you didn't.'

'Are you serious?'

He turned on his side and took her in his arms, feeling the weight of their unborn child against him. She stiffened.

'Tell me, the first night you came back to Madrid – was it to her you were going?'

'Yes.'

'Did you see her?'

'She wouldn't see me.'

Josefa moved to the far edge of the big canopied bed. 'And if she had?'

Paco said nothing. He knew what was coming. He knew he had no answer.

'If she had seen you,' Josefa said softly, 'would I now be the Señora de Goya or would – '

'Stop it. There's no sense talking like that.'

'I want to know.'

'I can't tell you. I don't know. It was a long time ago. We're married. You're my wife, Josefa. I love you.'

'And the child?'

He thought she meant Antonio Francisco. 'That's over and done with, cara.'

'I mean our child.'

'Of course I'll love our child.'

'I can't wait.'

'No, neither can I.'

167

'I still think you ought to see the boy. It isn't fair to him if you don't.'

'It isn't fair to you if I do.'

'Let me be the judge of that.'

'I'm not going to see him. That's final.'

'You're afraid. Afaid that you still feel something for his mother. That's why you don't want to become friends with the boy.'

Paco tried a laugh. It sounded forced. 'Well, they always say you'd better humor the whims of a pregnant woman.'

'Now *you* sound like my brother.'

'To hell with your brother.'

'No, you never have liked him, have you?' Josefa said bitterly. 'He took you on as an apprentice, he got you the appointment at the tapestry works – '

'I didn't mean that. I'm sorry.'

'You hate him.'

'I don't have any reason to hate him.'

'You hate Ramón.'

'You mean Ramón hates me.'

'Oh, never mind. You twist everything I say.'

'Josefa, it's been a long day. We're both tired. You ought to get some sleep.'

'You don't want to talk about it.'

'About what?' he asked wearily.

'If you'd seen Mariana that day, who would be lying here in this bed with you tonight?'

Paco tried once more to make light of it. 'Oh, that's no problem. It wouldn't be this bed or this house if it was Mariana.'

'You wanted to. You were going to ask her to marry you. Deny it.'

'I don't know. I just don't know.'

'And when she wouldn't have you, you proposed to me.'

'Now wait a minute,' Paco said. 'I seem to recall it was your – '

'That's hateful. How can you say that?'

He reached out to touch her shoulder. She pulled away.

'Don't touch me.'

'All right. Good.'

He got out of bed. He dressed.

'Where are you going?'

'Out. Anywhere. Nowhere. For a walk.'

'Don't bother waking me when you come back.'

He left the house and walked slowly along Clock Street and down to the river. A cold wind blew across the water. He turned his face to it and let it blow through his hair and sting his eyes.

It was late when he returned to the house. He removed his shoes and climbed the stairs. A single candle cast its feeble glow on the bed. Josefa was awake.

'I'm a great big, silly fool,' she said.

He went to her and knelt with his head on her lap. He could feel the stirring of life, of their child's life, against his cheek.

CHAPTER FIFTEEN

The Midwife

EVERY PARISH IN MADRID had its midwife, an old woman who had attended at a thousand births or more. She was experienced; she was confident; she knew more than any mere doctor. She felt an antipathy toward doctors because increasingly, especially among the upper classes, they were encroaching on her profession.

Paco had urged that a doctor attend the birth of their child, but Josefa scoffed at the suggestion. 'A doctor? I'm not sick. I'm going to have a baby.'

Paco had suggested Dr Peral, the most expensive society doctor in Madrid.

Josefa laughed. 'Paco, please. The parish midwife's a good one. Besides, how could we afford Dr Peral?'

As usual Paco had been spending his tapestry works salary as soon as he got it, and sometimes before. He had bought two small Tiepolo canvases from the great Italian's son, and a set of Rembrandt and Velázquez prints from a dealer. If anyone asked, he always said he owed his art to Rembrandt, Velázquez, and Nature, but he had paid most for the Tiepolos. As Josefa's confinement neared, he would come home with a necklace or a ring or a jewel-encrusted music box. Josefa liked to play the harpsichord. He bought her one, secondhand but still expensive. Like his father, and especially since he had assumed his father's debts, he himself was going into debt.

Francisco Bayeu also opposed calling in a doctor. 'My mother always had a midwife,' he said, 'and her mother, and her mother's mother. Let a doctor cure a cough or set a broken leg. A midwife's for childbirth. Besides, the Bayeu women never have any trouble delivering.'

And Josefa would sit listening, or playing the harpsichord, and telling Paco not to worry.

What worried Paco most was the San Martín parish midwife, a fat old crone named Zárate. For fifty years she had delivered most of the babies of the parish. She was toothless, and she cackled, and her gnarled, stubby-fingered hands were dirty. She wore a filthy black dress and a black shawl. She smelled of dust and disuse, as if someone kept her locked in a closet. She reminded Paco of a slovenly witch and after one of her visits he sketched her from memory.

Josefa smiled when he showed her the sketch. 'Better not let the Zárate see that. You make her look more like a witch than a midwife.'

'Do you feel at ease with her, cara?'

'Of course I do. She's very self-confident.'

Paco almost said too self-confident. He suggested Dr Rodríguez-Pereira, but Josefa smilingly shook her head and he let the matter drop.

The old Zárate woman had been with Josefa since early morning. She had emerged once or twice before noon, all bustle and confidence, ordering the servants to fetch this or that and retreating again into the bedroom. She would not let Paco enter. She waved him off irritably, like brushing at a fly.

She came downstairs once late in the afternoon looking less confident.

Paco turned away from the window. It was beginning to snow. 'How is she?' he asked.

'Your daughter is giving us a little trouble.'

'Daughter?'

'I can always tell,' said the Zárate. 'I never make a mistake.'

'What kind of trouble?'

'A delay. Did I say trouble? There is no trouble.' She waved him away and returned upstairs.

Paco waited with his brother-in-law in the drawing room. Francisco, as usual, admired the Rembrandt and Velázquez prints. He ignored the Tiepolos. A light supper was served. Paco picked at his food, tasting nothing.

Upstairs Josefa screamed.

Maria del Carmen arrived with Juanito. It was then almost midnight. They brushed snow from their cloaks.

'The baby?' Carmen asked.

'Not yet,' Paco said.

Upstairs Josefa screamed again.

It seemed to bother no one but Paco.

'It's the Zárate, isn't it?' Carmen asked.

'Yes.'

'Then Josefa's in good hands. She's the best midwife in Madrid. She delivered my Pepita.'

Another scream from upstairs.

'You should have heard me,' Carmen said quickly. 'I don't think I stopped screaming for five minutes. A man doesn't understand. 'Push,' the Zárate says, and you get so tired you can't. "Push." You try. "Push." You hate her, but then when the baby comes. . . . '

Another scream, weaker.

Paco ran for the stairs. Halfway up he met the Zárate. He merely looked his question at her.

'She's very weak. The baby won't come.'

They stared at each other, long enough for Paco to see the confidence drain from the Zárate's eyes.

'A breech baby. Very difficult. If the señora had more strength – '

'How long have you known there'd be trouble?'

'It's the weather. The cold. A person's hands grow numb.'

Every fireplace in the house was blazing.

'I'm getting a doctor.'

'Doctors don't understand – '

He brushed past her and upstairs and into the bedroom.

The golden hair spread, the face desperately pale, the eyes tear-filled.

As he entered, she clenched her teeth and would not scream. He kissed her. 'I'm getting Rodríguez-Pereira.'

'Hurry.'

He grabbed a cloak, ran through the snow to the stable, harnessed the mules himself, and climbed onto the box of the landau.

He did not know where Rodríguez-Pereira lived. He drove through the deserted streets to the Alcalá. The gates to the Olavide townhouse stood open. The house blazed with light. He heard music. He drove in, leaped from the box, told the grooms to keep the mules ready.

The major-domo barred his way. Paco shoved him aside, entered the grand salon with its brilliant chandeliers, its silks and satins and brocades and curious faces. Pablo de Olavide stood before him, surprised and angry. He saw Mariana across the room. He pushed past Don Pablo, almost knocking him down.

'Where's Rodríguez-Pereira?'

'What? What, Paco?'

'Dr Rodríguez-Pereira? Where does he live?'

She looked at his face and did not ask why. She gave him the address.

Out past the Retiro.

Silks and satins and brocades and angry faces all got out of his path. He ran from the room and past the startled major-domo and outside.

He tossed a few coins at the grooms and was on the box again, using his whip. The landau almost overturned as it swung through the gates.

The snow, falling heavily now, blindingly. The snow, almost up to the hubs of the wheels. The howl of the wind. The crack of the whip. The mules snorting, their breath like white smoke in the night. A wrong turn. A long slewing skid and clinging with all the strength of those great shoulders so that he did not fall from the box. The Paseo del Prado, its broad, tree-lined drives dark. The Retiro.

Rodríguez-Pereira's house. Dark. Pounding on the door. Pounding with both fists until finally a light appeared in a window. A sleepy-eyed servant in a tasseled nightcap. Must see the doctor. Life and death. Hurry, hombre. Hurry.

The doctor at last. A look like the one Mariana had given him. Two minutes, said Rodríguez-Pereira, and in two minutes he and the beautiful deaf-mute Doña Isabel had climbed into the landau.

Another look at Paco's face as he prepared to mount the box. 'Get us there alive,' Rodríguez-Pereira suggested.

They reached Clock Street a few minutes after the parish priest.

'I tried,' the Zárate said. 'How could I help it if it was God's will?'

Rodríguez-Pereira said nothing. Juanito patted Paco's back awkwardly. Francisco Bayeu stood gazing at the fire in the drawing room. He fetched another olive log and put it on.

Paco went upstairs with the doctor and Doña Isabel. Josefa

was barely conscious and as pale as a corpse. Maria del Carmen was crying. Paco could smell incense from the acolyte's censer. The priest was mumbling Latin and sprinkling holy water on the dead infant's brow.

'I want my baby,' Josefa said faintly. 'What have they done with my baby?'

Doña Isabel touched Paco's hand. No, don't go to her, the gesture said. Paco stood back. The deaf-mute went to the bed. She stroked Josefa's temples. Her lovely eyes were huge. Josefa stared up into them. Her head nodded and she was asleep.

Rodríguez-Pereira had examined the dead boy, a tiny, pathetic, shriveled blue thing.

Paco went over. 'Could he have been saved?'

'A breech birth. If you know in advance – and she should have, of course – '

Paco waited.

'God's will be done on earth,' said the priest to no one in particular. 'We can only thank the Lord there was time to baptize the child.'

'Get out of here,' Paco said.

The priest's mouth clamped shut. He left with the acolyte.

Paco faced Rodríguez-Pereira. 'Tell me.'

'She used her instruments like a butcher. Had the child survived – look at the skull. Here, and here.'

Paco could not look.

'There would have been brain damage. It's better this way.'

Paco's mouth was dry. He felt a chill. He couldn't swallow. 'Could you have done it?'

'I think the baby could have been saved.'

'My wife?'

The doctor turned to Doña Isabel. He flashed signs quickly with the fingers of his right hand and she responded with her own fingers and nodded her head vigorously.

'She'll be all right. A week in bed to get her strength back. Perhaps ten days. Then let her have the sun. Can you take her south?'

'I'm in debt, doctor.'

'Well, it's not important. You have a patio? A spot protected from the wind? She'll be fine.'

But it was important. The Zárate instead of the society doctor Peral, instead of Rodríguez-Pereira. It had been easy for them to talk him into it. He was short of funds. He was always short of funds. A small patch of weak Madrid sunlight instead of a healing journey to Almería the Golden, to Silver

173

Jaén, to orange blossoms and the scent of jasmine. . . .

He had to buy his Rembrandts, his Tiepolos. There would be jewels and fine clothing for Josefa. That was the way they had to live.

He would be rich. He would be richer than a painter had ever dreamed of being.

He would have it all. This would not happen again, not to himself, and not to his Josefa.

Or life was nothing.

CHAPTER SIXTEEN

A Little Act of Faith

THE GRAND INQUISITOR climbed the ornate marble staircase of the palace of the Holy Office of the Inquisition to his private quarters. He ordered a bath and, removing his sacerdotal robe, slipped his spare frame into the warm, soothing water. He was a thin man with hollow cheeks and the sunken eyes of an ascetic. He lived luxuriously, as he had ever since becoming a power in the Holy Office.

Almost no one, the Grand Inquisitor told himself, soaking in his bath. He felt a brief, smouldering disappointment. Aranda was safe. Floridablanca was safe.

For now.

Strike high enough and the way would be open for a return to the old days.

In his youth the Grand Inquisitor had witnessed one of the last great Acts of Faith held in Spain. He was then a novice of the order in Toledo, sixty years ago, and the magnificent *auto de fe* had remained one of the memorable experiences of his life.

Of the eight heretics who had been relaxed over to the secular authorities, all but one had accepted their fate stoically. One, a young girl of sixteen accused of blasphemy, had been dragged screaming to what the people called the brazier, the Place of Burning.

The Grand Inquisitor remembered it all as if it had been

yesterday. He loved the euphemism for execution – relaxation. Since no prelate could shed blood, the condemned were given – relaxed – over to the secular authorities for punishment, with the proviso that no blood be shed. Hence the garotte for those who repented at the last minute, followed by burning at the stake. And burning alive for those who did not repent.

It had been a spectacle, in Toledo, when the Grand Inquisitor was young. Peasants had streamed in from the countryside. Booths were set up to supply them with food and drink. The carnival atmosphere was enhanced by the colorful programs handed out, by the ornate dais for the notables who had come to watch, by the slow parade to the Place of Burning, by the long-robed Dominicans and the gentry of the city. The first brand was lighted by a visiting dignitary from France.

Bells clanged, and behind the standard of the Inquisition came the condemned carrying lighted tapers in their hands. They wore yellow robes transversed by the black cross of St Andrew, and tall yellow mitres. Pasteboard dolls of heretics who had escaped into exile were carried by members of the faithful. Others carried the exhumed remains of those convicted after death.

The whole affair, from the ringing of bells, through the solemn parade and the reading of the sentences to the garotting and the burning, took most of the day. The Grand Inquisitor still remembered vividly how the young girl had screamed her innocence and would not repent, how the first flames had licked at her yellow robe, how the St Andrew's cross had writhed at the touch of the fire, how her body had arched against the stake and her face turned black as her soul was committed eternally to hell.

The bonfire in the final light of the setting sun had been a beautiful sight – a demonstration of the power of the Inquisition.

And now? Now there had been no *auto de fe* on the grand scale for years. Now the *auto* was usually held in private – an *auto de fe particular*, it was called officially, an *autillo* in the vernacular of the people: a Little Act of Faith.

There had been few burnings anywhere in Spain during the reign of the Grand Inquisitor. Sometimes he thought he had been born too late. The king's attitude was incomprehensible. Weren't men born with immortal souls? Hadn't the incarnation of Our Lord Jesus Christ yielded to every man the way to the gates of heaven? It was the only way. All other ways led to hell. Knowing this, a man possessed of his sanity would go to any lengths, submit to any discipline, to safeguard his eternal reward. Otherwise he was clearly possessed by the devil and the Santo would help the devil claim his own.

The Grand Inquisitor rose from the soothing water of his bath. Two servants immediately appeared, one to wrap him in a robe of soft merino wool, the other with a decanter of wine chilled by ice from the ice pits of Madrid. He sipped his wine and thought of the coming Little Act of Faith, thought of it sourly when he remembered Toledo sixty years ago.

But still, it had its merits. To strike close to the king, to strike after patient years of investigation, to throw the whole affair in Carlos' face like a gauntlet –

A Little Act of Faith. Almost private, really, with only sixty or seventy invited guests. A cross-section of the nobility, to witness the Santo's powers. Prelates from other orders, to realize their subservience to the Holy Office. And best of all, a few individuals who had particular reason to fear the Inquisition. The Act, as a warning, could save their immortal souls.

There was still the question of the niece and her child. The niece who really wasn't a niece at all but a daughter. A witness had been brought from Lima to testify to the sin of fornication. A sin the girl herself had repeated. The Grand Inquisitor wondered briefly if that testimony should be made part of the official record. No, he thought, probably not. The issues at stake were religious and political. Why complicate them?

The cool wine was really quite lovely. The Grand Inquisitor clapped his hands softly for another cup.

The legend, the living legend of Francisco Goya which would follow him wherever he went and whatever he did, began on a day in April in the royal palace.

Paco walked in a daze, through endless halls, past innumerable colums, led by a pair of red-stockinged lackeys carrying three of his latest canvases. His hair was neatly clubbed and powdered, and he wore his best frock coat. His knees shook.

He passed through the *saleta* and heard the chamberlain announce him in a stentorian voice: 'The painter Don Francisco Goya y Lucientes! '

And Paco came into the presence of Don Carlos, by the grace of God King of Castile, Leon and Aragon, King of the Two Sicilies, of Jerusalem, of Navarra, Granada, Toledo, Valencia, Córdoba, Majorca and Sevilla, of Sardinia, of Corsica, of Murcia and Jaén, of the Algarves and Algeciras, of

Gibraltar, of the Canary Islands, of the East and West Indies, of Terra Firma of the Ocean Sea, Archduke of Austria, Duke of Burgundy, Brabante and Milan, Count of Hapsburg, Flanders, Tirol and Barcelona, Lord of Vizcaya and Molina, etc.

What Paco saw, enthroned beside and slightly above the robust crown prince, was a dwarfish, mahogany-faced, big nosed, weak-chinned elderly man. It was the face struck in all the mints of the realm – the same profile in gold on escudos and doubloons, in silver on reales, in copper on maravedís, a plain face and a rather benign one. Hardly a kingly face, it was almost lost in the grandeur of the throne room. Paco took it all in with his artist's eye, the red velvet hangings embroidered with silver, the great mirrors from the royal works at La Granja, sixteen of them reflecting sixteen Paco Goyas as he approached the throne, reflecting the four gilded bronze lions flanking the steps, reflecting the busts of Homer and Seneca, the score of ornate clocks, the great Tiepolo fresco on the ceiling and the somewhat fatuous smile on the crown prince's somewhat fatuous face as he said:

'This Goya, sire, is choking my Pardo Palace with his tapestries. I can't resist them.'

Paco swept off his tricorn, mounted the steps, kneeled and kissed both royal right hands.

'No, no, cover your head, Goya,' said the king. It was a signal honor. Only a grandee of Spain might routinely wear his hat in the presence of royalty. 'Cover your head because you please the crown prince.'

He had indeed pleased Carlos, Prince of the Asturias, heir to the throne of Spain.

It started with his tapestry cartoon of *The Parasol,* so sumptuous in color, the mysterious source of light streaming up from below to support the figures of a man and a woman against a hazy background. And if the woman with her floppy little black dog and the red ribbon in her hair resembled Barbara García? Perhaps Paco wasn't aware of the resemblance. If Mynheer van der Goten was, he ignored it. He was immensely pleased with the cartoon.

'The light,' he said over and over, his close-set eyes twinkling in his gray Flemish face, 'it's the light. The light supports everything. It has no substance but it's like a wall, that light. This is one for the Pardo Palace, Goya. The crown prince will want it.'

Van der Goten was right. Crown Prince Carlos and Princess

Maria Luisa, visiting the works, fell in love with *The Parasol*, and they wanted others. They wanted *The Kite*, and they wanted *The Man Drinking*, again with that mysterious light from below, the man's face as red as the stream of wine squirting from the wineskin he held at arm's length.

In those first three years at the Santa Barbara works, Paco painted more than thirty cartoons, most of them to be made into tapestries for the Prince of the Asturias. They were baroque. They borrowed from Tiepolo in their vibrant use of color, in the disappearance of intermediate distance, in the lowness of the horizon. But they had Paco's own stamp on them too. He knew Madrid and its people.

Now in the throne room Paco clapped the tricorn back on his head while the king studied his three canvases. He studied them a long time. Like the tapestries which had found such favor with Crown Prince Carlos, they were genre paintings.

'The people,' the king said finally. 'You do know the people.'

'He's a man of the people,' said the crown prince with a fatuous little laugh. 'Poor beginnings, quiet home life, married to a good and unassuming woman – '

'Any children, Goya?' asked the king.

'No, sire,' Paco said. 'Not yet.'

Josefa ran the household skillfully in that quiet way of hers, never intruding on his work, never letting others intrude, but the distance between them grew. No children. He never reproached her for the Zárate and she never admitted they should have had a doctor. Once she echoed the priest who had administered the last rites, saying it had been God's will. Paco, without a word, pushed back from the dinner table and retreated to his studio to paint. Her God was not his God.

They grew to hate the room they had prepared as a nursery – the small empty crib on its rockers, the new walnut furniture, the gay hangings on windows and walls. One day Paco said:

'We're moving.'

'Moving? We can't afford it.'

'I found a place on San Gerónimo. Nearer the tapestry works.'

They moved, and for a time they were close again, furnishing the larger house in one of Madrid's older quarters. The closeness did not last. A month after they had settled into the house on San Gerónimo, Paco brought a cot into the studio. He often ate a quick solitary dinner there and went on painting until he snuffed out the candles and slept. Other nights he would share the big canopied bed with Josefa, and they would turn to each other and have each other in the loneliness both had created. But such nights were rare. For a time, for a time that became months and then years, he lived for his work.

'You please me,' said the king. 'A man dedicated to his profession is a rare thing these days.'

'Dedicated?' laughed the crown prince. 'I'll say he's dedicated. If I were another artist at the works I'd be jealous, sire. The looms are full of Goyas. Why, they're beginning to call it the Royal Tapestry Works of Francisco Goya.'

Once Barbara García had indeed called the works that. And Ramón Bayeu was indeed jealous. Everything about Paco, from his popularity with the crown prince to the way Barbara García flirted with him, bothered Ramón. Still a bachelor, Ramón found Barbara García attractive. Her infuriating response was to call him her little popinjay and tweak his cheek as if he were a child. She had an acid tongue and used it on Ramón. He smouldered. His resentment grew, not against her but against Paco. His time would come, he told himself. That brother-in-law of his was heading for a fall, and Ramón would be pleased to give the final push.

Dedication? Determination, Paco told himself in the throne room. He had his salary of thirteen thousand reales a year and the patronage of the crown prince. He watched the shuttles work the looms, the golden thread, the coarse wool, the patient tying of knots by nimble fingers – and finally, between the huge logs of the loom, a tapestry emerging. He lived with Francisco Bayeu's supervision and suffered Mynheer van der Goten's anxiety. He saw Josefa's lips become thinner, and that wistful look in her eyes, as if she dimly saw a life she would never lead. He painted twelve and sixteen hours a day. He had that trick with light, and his facility grew steadily.

This cartoon, and that, and another – and what the crown prince liked all Madrid would like.

He would have it all. This would not happen again, not to him, and not to his Josefa.

Or life was nothing.

'You please me,' the king said again.

Paco thanked His Most Catholic Majesty. He had meant to speak softly. His voice came out boomingly, like that of the crown prince.

'I would like you to visit the palace galleries,' the king said.

Paco held his breath. The galleries, hung with paintings by

179

El Greco, Velázquez, and Murillo, were jealously guarded. Even Francisco Bayeu rarely had access to them.

'Are you a member of the Academy?'

'No, Your Majesty,' Paco said, his voice hardly more than a whisper now as he dreamed of his immediate investiture in that august body.

'Good.'

'Sire?'

The king smiled his shy smile. 'Everyone at the Academy paints like Mengs. If everyone paints the same way, how will we ever have another Velázquez?' The king paused. 'Velázquez,' he repeated in that soft voice of his. 'You must visit the galleries as often as you can and study Velázquez. Have you had any experience etching?'

'I know the technique, Your Majesty, but – '

'Use it. Copy Velázquez. Copy his portraits. Spanish painters,' said the king in his Italian accent, 'have studied under foreign masters too long. There's a feeling of Spain in your work, of good red Spanish earth. I'd like to see it cultivated.'

Paco bowed. His tricorn fell off, his face flushed, and the king chuckled as he gestured to the waiting lackeys. 'I will keep these,' he said, indicating the three small canvases.

Paco jammed the tricorn on his head and bowed again. This time it stayed in place.

He left the throne room in more of a daze than when he had entered. It did not occur to him until he reached San Gerónimo that his pay for three weeks' work had been a few words of royal praise.

But what words they were – to hear the king hint that he might someday take his place beside the immortal Velázquez!

Then paint, he told himself, and learn to etch, and whatever you do, continue to please the crown prince. Tiepolo's magic, if there was such a thing, if in fact it was anything more than the dream of a disillusioned old man, a dream impossible to realize – the magic could wait.

Manolo Bayeu met Paco in the entrance of the house on Gerónimo. He was pale. He would not meet Paco's eyes. 'There's a letter for you. Delivered by a Dominican messenger.'

Paco felt something plummet inside him. The Santo. The Holy Office of the Inquisition.

Josefa sat waiting in the drawing room, lips drawn tight, eyes terrified, clutching in her hand the sealed letter.

'God knows you haven't done anything to merit an examination by the Santo,' Manolo said. But still he did not look at

Paco. He looked at Josefa. Paco was out of the house so much these days, sometimes even painting at the tapestry works, there was no telling what he had or hadn't done.

'God and the Santo don't always see eye to eye.' Paco even managed a smile.

His fingers were not steady as he broke the dreaded Santo seal. No mere paper for the Holy Office, he observed. Expensive parchment that crackled in his hands. And that precise, careful calligraphy. He took it all in before reading a word. He turned his back. He did not want them to see how his hands shook.

There was no relief in his voice when he said just one word: 'Olavide.'

'Olavide?' Manolo repeated.

And Paco read: 'To Francisco Goya y Lucientes, painter at the Royal Tapestry Works of Santa Barbara: The Holy Office of the Inquisition requests your presence at the *auto de fe particular* of Don Pablo Antonio de Olavide, to be held, by the grace of God and His Most Catholic Majesty, at three hours after noon at the Church of San Domingo el Real on the thirteenth day of October, Year of Our Lord 1778.'

It was, of course, no mere request. It was a summons. See the *autillo* of one heretic and you are not likely to become one yourself. It was more than a summons. It was a warning.

If Paco was not relieved, Josefa was. 'Thank God,' she said. 'I was so afraid that you – '

Paco said: 'I've got to go to her.'

Josefa looked at him. 'Who?'

'Mariana.'

A bailiff in a green coat of military cut opened the door of the Olavide townhouse. He wore an unsheathed sword at his side and a truculent expression on his face.

'This property's been sequestered,' he said in a bored voice.

'I know that. Is the marquesa at home?'

'Just a little warning, friend. We have a book. Your name goes in it if you go inside.'

'Francisco Goya to see the marquesa,' Paco said coldly.

'On what business?'

'I'm a friend of the family.'

The bailiff clucked his tongue as he laboriously wrote Paco's name in his book. 'You mean they have one left?' He called inside and Paco caught a glimpse of the Olavide major-domo crossing the hall. But it was the squat, square-faced Indian

181

who came up behind the bailiff.

'Adiós, Paco. Adiós. I knew you would come.'

'How is she?'

'Not here,' warned the Indian.

The bailiff snickered. 'Are you chattel?' he asked teasingly. 'I might buy you.'

'Your mother's milk,' said the Indian, and the bailiff's face darkened as he let Paco pass.

In the white and gold hall the Indian said: 'She's changed so, the poor thing. Almost overnight.' A servant scurried by on some nameless errand. It was dusk but no lamps and only a few candles had been lit. The great townhouse had a gloomy air, as if all the furnishings had already gone on the auction block.

'Even the de Solis family wouldn't have her. Not that they're rich. But they could have helped her and the boy.' The Indian shook her head. 'If I know them, they're secretly gloating. The marquesa will be left without a copper.' She added: 'So will your son.'

'All right,' Paco said irritably. 'All right. Just take me to her.'

They were upstairs in the boy's room. Here at least there was the cheery light of an olive-wood fire glowing on the hearth.

Mariana was reclining on the bed, the boy seated at her side holding her hand. He got up.

He was tall and lean like an Olavide. My God, Paco thought, he's twelve. I have a twelve-year-old son. Hooded eyes looked into hooded eyes, and Paco found himself waiting for some sign of recognition on the boy's part. But there was none.

'It was good of you to come, Señor Goya. We've had few visitors lately.'

'We've had none,' Mariana said in a flat voice. She wore a black dress and under it the remembered figure was still lithe and young. The blue eyes were puffed from crying. Wrinkles bracketed her mouth.

Her hair was as white as the Indian's.

Paco bowed over her hand. A feeling welled up in him, not love nor even the memory of love. Pity.

'His trial's the day after tomorrow.'

'I know. The Santo invited me.'

She apparently did not hear that. The blue eyes had a vague look, like eyes painted without depth by a second-rate portraitist. 'You're looking well, Paco. Prosperous.'

The boy, the young Marqués de Solis, managed a smile. 'You never did teach me to paint, Señor Goya.'

'Did you really want to learn?'

'Once. When I was little.'

'He wants a military career these days,' Mariana said.

'What else can a penniless nobleman do?' shrugged the Marqués de Solis. 'Either that or take holy orders.'

'Paquito,' his mother said, 'we're not exactly penniless. There's my uncle's – '

'*Autillo*,' the boy cut in, almost savagely. 'There's his *autillo*.'

Mariana's head jerked back as if he had struck her. Her lips were quivering. 'They'll confiscate everything we own.' She began to cry. 'And my fath – my uncle, dear God, what will happen to him?'

'He hasn't been convicted yet,' Paco said.

Those hooded eyes met his again. 'Since when doesn't the Santo convict, Señor Goya?' The question, asked so matter-of-factly, almost made Paco dislike the boy.

Mariana clung to the false hope in Paco's words. 'Every now and then you hear of cases. . . . ' Her voice trailed off. Her eyes looked vague again.

'They'll find him guilty,' the boy said.

Mariana's vague eyes begged Paco for a denial.

But instead he turned to the boy. 'Could I have a few minutes alone with your mother?'

Paquito resisted his exclusion from the grown-up world. 'Anything you say to my mother I ought to hear.'

'If Señor Goya says alone he means alone,' the Indian rumbled.

The boy's maturity deserted him. 'This is my room.'

'Paquito Solis, you'll come with me or I'll give you a why-not,' the Indian warned him.

Paquito's wry smile tore at Paco's heart. 'Forgive me, then, Señor Goya.' He bowed. 'She's always telling me I'm too big for my breeches. Perhaps she's right.'

He left with the Indian.

'He's very mature,' Paco said.

'Oh sweet Mother of God, look at me. Look at me,' Mariana cried. 'I've become an old woman overnight.'

'White hair? What's white hair?' Paco said gently. 'You're as beautiful as you ever were. Truly, Mariana.'

'The sirens,' she said. 'Remember the sirens?'

He said he remembered the sirens.

'And the Indian and those wine bottles of hers?'

He said he remembered the wine bottles.

'You're a famous man now.'

'Not, not really famous.'

'Paco, Paco,' she sobbed, clinging to him. 'If only he'd let us marry.'

He stepped back awkwardly. 'Listen,' he told her. 'They'll confiscate everything. You know that.'

Her eyes were vague again. 'The way you wouldn't borrow a copy from the Academy for your sirens. You were always so proud. Paquito. He's so much like you. He's so much like you I can cry just looking at him.'

He shook her shoulders. He could feel how frail they were. 'Listen to me. Please. They'll confiscate everything. You'll have nothing. I earn twenty thousand reales a year, sometimes more,' he lied. 'It's far more than Josefa and I need. I'll take care of you.'

A wan smile touched her lips. 'I love you for offering it. But we can't accept charity.'

'It's not charity. I took your uncle's patronage for years. As a loan, remember? I want to help. I've got to, Mariana. Not just for you.'

'For the boy?'

'For the boy. And for myself. You know what I'm like.'

'Prouder than a fallen angel.'

Paco found it difficult to talk. She still loved him. Her present was bitter, her future unknown. He was the sweetness of her past.

'Take care of us, Paco. Oh please, God, take care of us. You're strong. You always were. We'll be so alone.'

'I'll take care of you.'

'Will they – relax him?' She said the dreaded euphemism with a shudder.

'There hasn't been a burning in years. The worst he can expect is a few years to repent in a monastery.'

Mariana laughed hysterically. 'A monastery? My father?' She wasn't even aware of calling him that. 'He's been a freethinker all his life. I can just see him in a monastery. He'd go mad.'

'Pablo de Olavide? He'd probably find it damned amusing.'

Mariana's eyes went vague again. 'Don't say damn. Don't blaspheme. You're blaspheming, Paco.'

The poorly painted eyes looked at him. 'Boucher paints from the nude,' she said.

He shook her shoulders, but she remained in the past then. 'And Fragonard.'

184

He kissed her cheek and called for the Indian.
He fled from the boy's accusing, hooded eyes.

Paco sat in a back pew of the little church of San Domingo el Real.

Members of the Royal Council entered and were ushered to their pews. Paco's eyes roved the audience. Seventy, he thought, no more than seventy. The king had not come. The crown prince had not come. No woman was present, not even Mariana.

He recognized Count Floridablanca, bewigged, dressed in scarlet frock coat and breeches, and wearing the sash of the first minister. The count looked nervous.

Finally, under the vaulted ceiling of the church, through the cool dimness, came the Suprema – the supreme council of the Holy Office – led by the Grand Inquisitor himself. A small bell tinkled and three bailiffs in green led the prisoner to a dais before the altar of the church. Paco's gasp was lost in the stirring and whispering all around him.

Pablo de Olavide, his hands manacled and clasped together piously in front of him, was now a bent old man. He wore a long yellow robe transversed by a black St Andrew's cross. On his head stood a tall yellow mitre bearing another twin-armed cross in black. His head drooped; his neck was shriveled; he sat listlessly with his eyes downcast. He looked as guilty as a man could look, and as old. He was not even waiting. He was beyond waiting. He sat there like a dead man.

The recapitulation of the charges, spoken in a monotone by the public prosecutor of the Holy Office and echoed in the vaulted church, did not stir him. The rasp of the notary's pen on parchment, the only other sound, was a sound he did not hear.

At last the Grand Inquisitor stood. He stared a long time at Pablo de Olavide, as if the strength of his will could make the broken man raise his head. Olavide did not move. Count Floridablanca shifted in his seat. The tonsured churchmen in their black and white habits, their hands clasped across their ample middles, looked bored. A few of them were actually sleeping.

A shaft of sunlight from a high window spotlighted the yellow mitre and black cross on Pablo de Olavide's head. Mitre and yellow robe, Paco now saw, were also adorned with crimson flames pointing downward. These signified that the prisoner, by confession and contrition, had avoided burning at the

185

stake.

But at what price to his own spirit?

I've got to paint this, Paco told himself. Someday I've got to paint this.

And if I do? If I do, they'll haul me before their Suprema. I'll find myself wearing the yellow robe and the mitre and the cross. I'll be seated there where he sits.

Was that the curse of Tiepolo's magic?

Was it the warning of the Santo's invitation?

The Grand Inquisitor was speaking of edicts of faith, of the confessional, of Spain's holy crusade against heresy. He spoke for a long time and in a voice as monotonous as the prosecutor's. The single ray of sunlight shifted, left the bent, mitred figure of Pablo de Olavide, advanced over the pews in the Church of San Domingo el Real.

It stabbed into the eyes of Paco Goya.

I'll paint this. I must paint this. But not yet. Not until – until what? Until he was big enough to stand up before the Inquisition?

Was anyone, ever?

How they could destroy a man, a full third of them dozing now, indifferent to that destruction! In the name of their faith? Or their God? To save the prisoner from eternal damnation?

Fat black priests dozing in a dimlit church.

These stay, while Jesuits like Padre Pignatelli are forced into exile.

I'll paint it. I have to paint it.

And to hell with all of them. If necessary, to hell with me.

'Pablo de Olavide,' the Grand Inquisitor intoned, 'because you have been found guilty of heresy on numerous counts;

'Because in your materialism and atheism you entered into correspondence with the arch-heretics Voltaire and Rousseau;

'Because you read books on the proscribed Index without license;

'Because you are guilty of philosophism and naturalism;

'Because in the Sierra Morena you objected to the burial of corpses in the churchyards;

'Because in the same towns and villages of the Sierra Morena you excluded the Order of the Dominican Brothers;

'Because you permitted Mass only on the Sabbath;

'Because you objected to the ringing of church bells to ward off thunderstorms;

'Because you espoused the heresy of the Copernican as-

186

tronomy and advocated its teaching in the universities of Spain;

'Pablo Antonio de Olàvide, for all these reasons attested to in secret session of the Suprema by eighty witnesses, the decision of this court is that you be relaxed over to the secular arm. . . . '

A great collective gasp arose. The crimson flames pointed down, not up; on the sacred yellow sack worn by the prisoner there was no image of the devil with his pitchfork. Surely the euphemism for burning at the stake had been an error, the old man in his black and white sacerdotal robe had made a mistake.

The broken man on the hard-backed chair, who once had been Pablo de Olavide, slumped forward and fell. The tall mitre tilted crazily on his head. Two bailiffs caught him, seated him again. Smelling salts were brought, held under his nose. In the absolute silence his labored breathing could be heard. His eyelids fluttered.

The Grand Inquisitor raised his hand. A scrawny arm emerged from the black and white robe. 'But,' he said, 'because you have maintained that the Faith still burns within you – do you so maintain?'

A faint voice that Paco did not recognize said: 'I do so maintain.'

'As God is your witness?'

'As God is my witness.'

'And because you abjure all your errors, all your heresy – do you so abjure?'

'I do so abjure,' said the voice that Paco did not recognize.

'As God is your witness?'

'As God is my witness.'

'Because the Faith still burns within you and because you abjure all your errors and your heresy, Pablo Antonio de Olavide, it is the decision of the Suprema that you shall not be relaxed over to the secular arm.

'It is the decision of the Suprema, in its mercy and God-granted wisdom, that you be reconciled with the Church. It is the further decision of the Suprema, in its mercy and God-granted wisdom, that you be condemned to the loss of all your property, and one hereby so condemned; that you be banished forever from Madrid, Sevilla, the Sierra Morena, and Lima, and are hereby so banished; and that you be confined for a period of eight years to the Monastery of Montserrat to undergo religious education, and are hereby so confined.'

No sound but the echo of those last words, like a litany. Head and mitre slumped forward.

'Have you any words, Pablo Antonio de Olavide?'

And the voice issued, like death, from below the tall mitre: 'I abjure, I recant, I confess, I thank the Suprema in its mercy and God-granted wisdom.'

A bell tinkled. The prisoner was assisted from chair and dais, his old man's feet shuffling on the cold stone floor of the church.

Nobles and clerics were rising all around him, but Paco sat in his pew.

He felt cold with a coldness that came from within him.

He would remember. And he would paint.

CHAPTER SEVENTEEN

'I Can't Hear!'

DOWNSTAIRS IN THE NURSERY Maria del Pilar, three months old, was crying lustily to be fed. Brush hovering over his palette, Paco could picture the fuzz of golden hair on the pink scalp, the seeking pink lips at Josefa's breast. The delivery had been easy, a matter of a mere two hours at the skillful hands of Dr Rodríguez-Pereira and Doña Isabel. Paco rubbed a hand over the stubble of beard on his haggard face. His lips parted in a tired smile.

The infant's bawling did not disturb him. By candlelight he was applying the final brush strokes to his tapestry of *The Washerwomen*. It was a big canvas, and one of six he would deliver that winter to the Santa Barbara works for the crown prince and Princess Maria Luisa. Over the idyllic landscape stormclouds lowered. Clothes hung on a line tied to the gnarled branch of a tree; one of the women carried a bundle of laundry on her head; one dozed; a pair of them were playing with a lamb. The faces of the women were blurred slightly as if captured almost between breaths. This, he thought, is the way people live. Find them, put them on canvas, hold them in

188

a single instant of time.

But was it any good? Again that weary gesture of rubbing a hand across his face. He was too exhausted to tell. He doted on little Maria del Pilar and there now was a new tranquil closeness with Josefa, but he was working under crushing pressure.

In that winter of 1780, he had three families to support.

Josefa was singing to Maria del Pilar, the *cante hondo* soft but so clear in the night stillness of the house that he could hear the words distinctly. It was an old song, older than anyone could remember, and the sad, haunting Moorish wailing, in Josefa's soft, true voice, quieted the infant.

> Whoever called you Petenera
> Knew not your true name then.
> You should have been called
> The perdition of men.
> Do not wonder who is dead
> When you hear the mournful bell.
> Ask your heart instead –
> Your own remorse will tell.

With the ensuing silence, Paco's pleasure faded. He was tired, he needed a bath, he needed a shave, he needed a long rest. He would get no rest.

The Washerwomen was finished only a little behind schedule. And then? He had done preliminary chalk sketches for a bullfight, for child with tree, child with bird, woodcutters, a ballad singer, a doctor. And *then?* There would be others, without end.

He had settled Mariana and the boy in a small apartment behind the Plaza Mayor. Mariana supplemented the small sum Paco could afford by becoming a modiste in the French manner, but business was slow. Even the Indian's usually stolid face wore a defeated look.

Six months before, his father had suffered a stroke in Zaragoza. One side of his body all but paralyzed, his face drooping lugubriously, José Goya could not work.

Paco had rushed to Zaragoza. One look at the crumbling state of affairs in the Goya y Lucientes household and he suggested they all move to Madrid. There was more than enough room in the house on San Gerónimo. But Doña Engracia had stubbornly shaken her gray head. 'Moving would kill your father. And don't expect an old woman to change her ways,

Paco. Madrid? What would I do in Madrid? I'd be scared to death. Besides, there's Rita.'

Paco's sister was all skin and bones and those frightening bright spots of red burning over her cheekbones. She coughed constantly and sometimes, her eyes wide with terror, coughed blood.

'I can take care of the family,' Paco's brother Tomás had said, and up to a point he could. But there were doctor bills for the elder Goya, doctor bills for Rita, and the third brother, Camillo, now a parish priest in Zaragoza, could offer no help. Most of the burden of supporting the family and paying José Goya's debts fell on Paco's shoulders.

He was now earning over fourteen thousand reales a year. On that sum he and Josefa could have lived in style. But three families. Thirty-five hundred for Mariana and the boy. Another five thousand to Zaragoza. Leaving barely more than five for the Goya household in Madrid. There were canvases and paints to be bought, copper plate and asphaltum and acid and etching tools.

Josefa did not complain. For the only time in her life she put on weight and the thinness left her lips. If they ate more bread and oil than meat and eggs, and if their wine was watered, what of it? Paco would become a professor at the Academy or even a painter to the king. Meanwhile they had sold their fancy furniture and the bare plaster walls were damp, but they had a roof over their heads, and a bed, a table, five chairs, a fry pan, a guitar, and the cheerful nursery, decorated by Paco, in which Maria del Pilar, surely the most beautiful baby in all Madrid, was now sleeping peacefully.

'You are going to be a beauty, little one,' Paco would croon in his deep off-key voice, strumming a chord on his guitar. Josefa would shake her head and pretend to scold him:

'Where are your eyes? She already is a beauty.'

'Just like her mother.'

Paco removed the cot from his studio. They slept together always in the big canopied bed, Josefa waiting up for him when he worked late. She was relaxed when they made love, as if bearing Maria del Pilar had proved her womanhood to her.

And if there were shadows? They would pass like a sudden Aragonese thunderstorm.

Paco had to borrow constantly against future canvases. Mynheer van der Goten had cooperated so far, but grumblingly. He might not cooperate forever.

190

If Josefa had gained weight for the first time in their married life, Paco had lost. His cheeks were hollow, his eyes red-rimmed with lack of sleep. When he wasn't rushing all over Madrid, sketching here, finding a model there, sweeping in and out of the palace galleries, visiting Mariana and the boy, watching the nimble-fingered girls weaving a new Goya tapestry, he labored over his canvases or over the copper plates he could hardly afford while he learned the difficult technique of etching. He wolfed down his meals, telling Josefa between mouthfuls what wonders she could perform with bread and oil and red peppers and garlic, and then he would run upstairs to work on another cartoon.

Sometimes, some frightening times in the dimness of the candlelight, he would see double. Sometimes his hand was not steady. Too much coffee, he told himself. Too little sleep. He had to resort more than he liked to his mahlstick. The frantic pace had to stop.

But it could not stop. Not with three families to support.

Now he applied the final strokes to *The Washerwomen*. No sound stirred in the house, no fire burned on the studio hearth. His hands were numb with cold. He stepped back bleary-eyed and studied the canvas. Damned good, he decided, or else you're damned tired. He'd know in the morning.

He slept fitfully and dreamed that he was running down an impossibly long corridor past countless looms with their great pine logs, past countless nimble-fingered, blue-smocked girls all weaving Goya tapestries, in pursuit of Santa Barbara. He ran, he reached out, he could never quite overtake her; she taunted him with a lewd smile over her shoulder. The corridor gave on a moonlit knoll where the devil waited in the form of a goat. A coven of witches circled him and one by one kissed him under the tail for his magical powers and rubbed his magical ointment in their armpits and mounted their broomsticks to fly off cackling as they sang: 'Without God and without Santa Maria, from town to town. . . . '

One flew down the chimney of the house on San Gerónimo and slashed at Paco's *Washerwomen* with her broom, smearing the wet paint, destroying the canvas.

At least he thought he had cried out.

He sat up in bed. He was sweating. He felt hot and then very cold and then hot again. His head ached fiercely. There was a terrible ringing in his ears.

He looked at Josefa, who sat on the edge of the bed, her

frightened eyes intent on his face. She was saying something.

Paco said: 'I can't hear you.'

He was sure he had said it. But he did not hear that either.

The ringing in his ears faded. He heard a creaking sound, like wooden hinges turning.

Josefa's lips continued to move.

Another chill. He was trembling all over. He could tell Josefa was shouting. He looked at her dumbly. He heard nothing.

'I can't hear!' he cried as loud as he could.

And heard only the creaking of wooden hinges.

He fell back against the pillow and pulled the cover over his head. The ringing and creaking in his ears became the cackle of witches. He tumbled down into blackness.

When he awoke, pale winter sunlight barely penetrated the slits in the shutters.

He saw Dr Rodríguez-Pereira and Doña Isabel. Josefa stood behind them, the back of one hand to her lips. Doña Isabel looked at him with that beautiful, grave sympathy of hers. Rodríguez-Pereira was asking a question. At least from the expression on his face Paco assumed it was a question.

He could not hear it. There was only the ringing, the terrible ringing in his ears.

'I want to see *The Washerwomen,*' he said.

Rodríguez-Pereira took out pad and charcoal and wrote: 'What washerwomen?'

'My painting. Upstairs. I dreamed . . . witches. . . . '

Josefa was gone and back in the time it tood Rodríguez-Pereira to take Paco's blood pressure and thump his chest. She took the pad and wrote: 'The painting is beautiful, Paco. Beautiful.'

Rodríguez-Pereira wrote: 'You have a fever, and you can't hear. What else?'

'Headache. Awful headache,' Paco said, not knowing if he had shouted or whispered.

Scrawled on the pad: 'More?'

'Ringing in my ears. It won't stop. It's driving me mad. And a creaking sound. The witches – '

Josefa and Rodríguez-Pereira looked at each other.

'Witches?' wrote the doctor.

'Cackling. Cackling inside my head.'

The pad again. 'You've been working too hard. Lowers the resistance. Fever, delirium, temporary loss of hearing.'

'Temporary?' shouted Paco. 'How do you know it's tempor-

192

ary? I can't hear, I tell you. I can't hear!'

Rodríguez-Pereira was dispensing powders from three twists of paper. Josefa brought a jar of water and a cup. Rodríguez-Pereira spoke to her, looking serious and self-assured. A very good bedside manner, Paco thought desperately. The powders were mixed in the water, turning it a sickly gray. Doña Isabel raised Paco's head. The touch of her hand was wonderfully soothing.

Rodríguez-Pereira wrote: 'Eight days of absolute rest. Fifteen if you can afford the time. Pay me when you can.'

Paco drank the bitter brew. He slept.

He could not hear the next day, nor the day after that. Except for the ringing in his ears.

On the fourth day, while Josefa was nursing the baby, he got out of bed. His legs wobbled. He hadn't shaved, his hair was wild, his face white and pinched. He still had a fever. He dressed in frock coat and breeches, his warm woolen cloak and a muffler. He mounted the stairs to his studio for his sketchpad and some chalk. He came down again, lurching like a drunkard.

Josefa met him at the bottom of the stairs, snatched sketchpad and chalk from his hand and wrote: 'Are you crazy? Where do you think you're going?'

'The palace.'

'You're sick,' she wrote.

'You don't understand,' he told her, and thought of the long-nosed ugly little man with the kindly eyes and the Italian accent: *There's a feeling of Spain in your work, of good red Spanish earth. I'd like to see it cultivated.*

'You can't go. I won't let you.' In a quick angry scrawl.

'You're wasting your time, not to mention my paper. I'm going.'

'It's raining.'

'I won't drown.'

She stared at him. 'Then shave. Comb your hair. You can't go to the palace looking like that.'

'There's no time,' he said. 'I've got to hurry.'

'You've always got to hurry.'

But she relinquished pad and chalk, and kissed his cheek.

Time and sickness, the deafness, the fear of death when there was still so much to do. No, he thought, she would never quite understand. But she would try. He loved her very much then.

She went to the door with him and gave him the big black umbrella. He would have to walk. He had sold the landau and the mules. He plodded out into the cold wet morning. He began to walk faster.

The custodians of the palace galleries saw an unkempt white-faced, sweating man who needed a shave. They did not recognize the Don Francisco Goya they had often seen. They spoke. He could not hear. They tried to bar his way. He showed them the king's letter, and they let him pass. One of them was assigned to follow him.

And spent the day watching the bearded apparition sketch on white paper with red chalk in a frenzy, making odd clucking noises to himself as he plodded from one Velázquez canvas to another, stood back, came closer and let the red chalk fly over the white paper. Sweat streamed from his face and he rubbed it out of his red-rimmed eyes. The custodian took pity and brought him watered wine. He drank in a single, long, grateful gulp. He went on sketching. He did not stop until the light faded. He was trembling. He had not removed cloak or muffler. Still wearing them, he marched out.

He looked as tired and sick as a man could look. But he was smiling.

The first sound he heard, except for the now faint ringing in his ears, was the scratching of the etching needle on a copper plate.

To prepare the aquatint he had poured powdered asphaltum into a box, blowing it into a fine cloud with a small bellows, then quickly inserting the plate on the floor of the box and closing it so the powder would settle smoothly on the copper. Then he applied heat with a candle to fix the ground to the plate. Aquatint, he knew, would give him the transparent luminosity he sought. Anything else and it wouldn't look like the great Velázquez. Not that he really wanted it to look exactly like Velázquez. He was Goya, after all.

Carefully he scratched the second line. Careful not of its value, not yet, because he could always hammer it out on the reverse side, but to see if he heard it.

Again he heard the faint scratching.

He worked faster. He hardly had to look at the chalk drawing pinned to his easel. He had it all in his head. A few more lines, and a dunking in the Dutch bath for the plate, because those first lines would be the deepest. More lines, the second-

194

ary ones, and another immersion in the Dutch bath. Careful, not too long, or the first will be too deep. There. Then bite again through the soft asphaltum with the etching needle. His fingers flew. Time flew. His hands were stained with acid. His studio reeked of acid.

The ringing had left his ears. The scratching was louder. He thumped a fist against the plaster wall and heard the satisfying sound of it. He laughed and heard the satisfying sound of that. He laughed wildly as he gave the plate its final brief Dutch bath. Removing it, he polished the surface with muslin.

'Josefa!' he shouted, and she came running upstairs in alarm.

'What is it? Are you all right?' Not thinking, she had spoken instead of writing the words.

He took a fresh copper plate and gouged deep scratches into it with his etching needle. 'Listen! Listen to the beautiful noise! I love you,' Paco Goya said.

The nightmare was over. He wanted to live forever.

CHAPTER EIGHTEEN

The Basilica

RAMÓN BAYEU COULD NEVER decide which rankled him more, his brother-in-law's success at the tapestry works or Barbara García's obvious preference for him.

Not that Ramón thought of the girl in terms more serious than a tumble in a convenient bed. She had a pretty face and a lush figure but there was a coarseness in the way she talked and even – Ramón Bayeu was rather fastidious – in the faintly visible pores of her small nose and in the faint woman smell of her after a day supervising the weavers. Ramón, a tidy slender man with nervous, darting eyes, was attracted by those very animal qualities in Barbara García which he thought appealed to him least.

He had planned his campaign carefully – the first warm days of an uncertain spring, the first good bullfight of the new season, the prospect of impressing her because his sister's husband Juanito Apiñani was on the program and they'd be able to visit the patio de caballos.

'I do enjoy the bullfights,' Barbara admitted.

'Then you'll come?'

They were talking in soft voices at the last loom in the long row where – you might have known – the girls were busily weaving Goya's *Washerwomen*. Paco had come and gone in his usual hurry, barely pausing for a word with Mynheer van der Goten before rushing out.

'Well, no one else has asked me,' said Barbara García.

Bitch, thought Ramón.

'And dinner?' she asked.

'We'll make a night of it.'

Barbara flashed her teeth at him. 'My little popinjay is taking me to the bullfights. I think I'm going to like that.'

The day came. Ramón wore a black jacket and scarlet breeches with pink stockings and a scarlet sash – a little gaudy, he told himself, a little painful to his artistic sensitivities, but very much in the majo mode. He met Barbara, as they had arranged, at the Little Parnassus Café. She had refused to tell him where she lived. Probably a mean little hovel she was ashamed of. He'd find out. He was determined to spend the night with her. She wore a low-cut black maja dress and a filmy golden shawl draped over her head and shoulders. No necklace, no earrings, no fan. The expanse of exposed bosom was awesome.

Ramón helped her into his waiting cab. Their drive across the city, with all Madrid heading through the bright afternoon sunlight to the bullring beyond the Alcalá Gate, was a delight.

Everything else was a disaster.

A last minute substitution in the program replaced Juanito with the veteran Juan Romero, father of the great Pedro Romero. Juanito had sprained his ankle on the morning of the fight.

There went the patio de caballos.

The wind was high, the fights poor. Ramón had purchased expensive contrabarrera seats but their tickets had been printed incorrectly or had been printed twice. An argument with two majos twice Ramón's size developed, and Ramón found himself confronted with the option of a fight or a pair of seats high up in the tendido. He settled for the latter. Barbara sighed resignedly, as if to say, 'What can I expect from my little popinjay?'

Her little popinjay was soon waxing enthusiastic about this pass or that of Costillares or old Juan Romero. Barbara, with an unexpected and galling expertise, disputed his judgments. 'No, no,' she said. 'Watch his legs. He's in no danger. He merely makes it look dangerous.' Or: 'You call that a good kill? He was already going out around the horn before the sword started in. Caramba, you could have done that.' A pause. 'Well, maybe not you.'

Ungrateful little bitch, he thought.

Afterwards, when the sun was low, they moved along with the crowds streaming toward the Alcalá Gate. Ramón found a cab which a surly fat man reached just after they did. Ramón began to argue for his rights. The fat man settled the argument by heaving his bulk up into the cab.

And Barbara, unexpectedly, said: 'It's a lovely afternoon for walking.'

They walked a little way and stopped at a crowded booth for wine and tapas.

'Two tintos,' Ramón said, and the sweating, ruddy-faced barman drew the red wine from the bung in the great barrel, banged the cups on the bar and asked: 'A little *tapacita?* A little cover for your cups?'

They decided on pinchitos, skewered cubes of beef heart grilled over charcoal.

Barbara took the chunk of bread off the end of her skewer and bit off some meat.

'It's raw,' she complained. Ramón called the barman.

'That's the way I serve 'em,' he snapped. 'You don't like 'em, you don't eat 'em.'

The barman, like the two men who had taken their seats, was twice Ramón's size. He stared at Ramón truculently.

Another sigh from Barbara. 'I'll eat it raw.'

The barman looked down the front of her dress. The ruddy face grinned. 'For you, little lady, that's different.' He returned the pinchito to the glowing charcoal.

That was the way it went.

They finally found a cab. But then it was dark. Ramón suggested a cellar restaurant that featured flamenco dancers. 'Oh, I'd love that,' Barbara said.

It turned out she knew some of the gypsies in the troupe. They came to the table and dominated the conversation while they passed a wineskin inches from his face and squeezed delicately. A trickle of wine reluctantly entered his mouth.

'Harder,' said one of the gypsies. 'Further. You're abusing the bota, amigo.'

'We can't have the bota abused,' said Barbara.

And Ramón opened his mouth wide, held the wineskin at arm's length and squeezed hard. A jet of wine hit his chin and splashed down the front of his ruffled white shirt.

Much laughter, Barbara's the loudest, and he tried again with more determination and more success. Soon he was squirting fine hard streams of the chalky red wine into his mouth. He began to enjoy himself. He even got a little drunk.

'Going to Zaragoza in the autumn,' he told Barbara.

'You are?' In an indifferent voice.

'My brother and me and,' he added grudgingly, 'Goya.'

'Paco's going too?'

'Isn't that what I said?'

'What are you all going for?'

'The basilica in Zaragoza. A very important commission.'

He waited for her to be impressed. 'Well,' she said, 'don't fall off the scaffold.' She laughed that bawdy laugh he had begun to hate.

He didn't laugh. He drank more wine. Suddenly he was aware that Barbara had left the table. He heard a guitar, and rhythmic hand-clapping, and the clack of castanets.

'Olé! ' someone shouted. 'Olé gitana brava! '

Barbara and the gypsy who had first offered the wineskin were dancing an intricate, and intricately seductive, flamenco. She was not just good; she was magnificent – the hauteur, the arched back, the lowered eyelids, the enticing way she moved her hips, arms raised, hands turned inward, castanets clacking out the staccato rhythm. Soon the gypsy left the small floor. Barbara's heavy-heeled shoes began a slow soft tattoo. It became faster, harder. Her arms remained upraised but the castanets were silent. Faster and harder beat the heels of her shoes. Her eyes were shut, her red lips parted, her face shining with sweat. Her heels thundered, the floor shook.

She stopped suddenly and dropped her arms.

One single enormous olé! filled the small smoke-filled cellar room and then the applause and stamping of feet and banging on tables began.

Ramón's head pounded from all that noise, all that wine.

Barbara and the gypsy returned to the table. He could smell the strong woman scent of her. He wanted her.

The gypsy was smoking a big black cigar. He wore a single gold loop earring in his left ear. He was saying something.

'What?' Ramón asked. He was very drunk.

Barbara leaned over him. He could almost see the nipples of her breasts. The scent, the provocative scent, was very strong.

'Anselmo says he knows a place where they dance all night.'

'A – what?'

'A place,' said Barbara in the slow exasperated tones reserved for a drunkard, 'where they dance all night. Are you coming? I want to.'

'Want wha'?'

'Want – to – dance – all – night.' More slowly, very exasperated.

Ramón pushed his chair back and rose unsteadily to his feet. The room whirled. He saw thick blue cigar smoke hanging in streamers and two Barbaras and a gypsy with a gold earring going in and out of focus. He tottered and sat down again heavily.

When he looked up, Barbara and the gypsy had gone.

He rested his cheek on his forearm on the table. He dozed. A hand shook his shoulder.

'Twenty reales, señor.'

'Twenty? We didn't even have dinner.'

'Twenty reales.' A big man with a leather apron and sleeves rolled up over muscular arms. Today the world had been peopled by big men. Ramón felt in no condition to debate the inflated bill. He paid. He lurched outside.

A clear moonlit night with houses looming crookedly on either side of the narrow winding street. He walked for a while, unsteadily, in one direction and then another.

It took him an hour to find a familiar landmark near the Puerta del Sol.

Every step of the way his fury mounted. Against Barbara at first. She had been taunting him. All day. She knew the evening would end exactly as it had. She'd planned it. Probably she had even joked about it beforehand, with Paco. Ramón could almost see them laughing together. By the time he found a cab his fury was directed not against Barbara but against his brother-in-law.

Paco, with his flamboyant use of color that kept the looms busy all the time. Paco, with that arrogance of his. Paco, who could fall so far because he had climbed so fast.

He'd find a way, Ramón promised himself. There had to be a way.

Francisco Bayeu brushed snuff from his gray frock coat and

ushered Paco into his studio. Propped on the easel, the paint barely dry, was a Crucifixion.

'You like it, as one artist to another?'

Paco had to admit he did like it. Neoclassic in its severity of line, yes – but there was real suffering in the face of the Christ.

'I painted it for you,' Francisco said with his thin smile.

'For me? I don't understand.'

'Cuñado, no man can support his parents and his wife and child on your salary. If you were a member of the Academy, you'd have a teacher's salary, not to mention commissions for portraits. And I can almost guarantee this painting would get you in.'

Paco studied the Crucifixion again. It was unsigned.

'Surely you don't expect me to pass it off as my own work?'

'No, no, of course not. I expect you to copy it. Use it as a model.'

Paco was going to refuse. He wanted to enter the Academy on his own terms. But Francisco had made the offer so earnestly, so guilelessly. And wasn't he doing it, really, for Josefa and the baby rather than for Paco?

'Besides,' Francisco went on, 'there's the basilica commission in Zaragoza. The committee wants me, and it wants Ramón, and it will want you too – provided you're a member of the Academy. I can show you the Count of Fuentes' letter. You're too mercurial, they say in Zaragoza. Too unpredictable. The basilica frescoes have to be all of a piece. If you're accepted by the Academy and if you follow my supervision, that would satisfy them.'

Paco's share of the commission could keep his parents living in style in Zaragoza for three or four years. Two families, Francisco had said. He didn't know about Mariana and the boy. To copy meretriciously this one time would take some of the awful pressure away. It was tempting. He looked at the canvas again. It was too tempting to resist.

All that spring he carefully reworked his brother-in-law's painting. If anything he made it even more neoclassic. Gone was the look of suffering on Christ's face so skillfully accomplished by Francisco Bayeu. Paco painted a Christ so neoclassically steadfast in his passion that all emotion was lost. It was Winckelmann with a paintbrush. It was a lesson in how not to paint.

By the time Paco finished it in July he knew the copy was inferior to the original.

That did not matter. Because he also knew it would, finally, open the doors of the San Fernando Academy to him.

What he did not know was that Francisco had casually mentioned the project to his brother Ramón.

A battered black traveling coach stood outside the apartment building on the street off the Plaza Mayor. Chests, even more battered, were being loaded on top under the Indian's supervision by a pair of footmen sweating in the heat of the late afternoon. Two old nags waited patiently in the traces, nuzzling their feedbags.

'You're going away?' Paco asked. It had been weeks since he had visited Mariana and the boy.

The footmen were struggling under the weight of a large case. The Indian, as solid as a block of wood, got her shoulder beneath it and heaved it onto the roof of the coach. 'To see Don Pablo,' she said. 'He's been ill. His liver. They've given him permission to leave the monastery and take the waters at a spa in the Pyrenees.'

'How's Mariana?'

'If you visited us more often,' the Indian scolded him, 'you'd know.' She shrugged her wide shoulders. 'She has her good moments. Otherwise. . . . ' A doleful shake of the head.

The dim stairway smelled of garlic, olive oil, dampness, and too many defeated lives crowded into too small a space. Paco heard a baby wailing and the voices of a man and woman raised in weary argument. He reached Mariana's door and knocked.

Her appearance shocked him. Her face was wrinkled, her white hair in disarray, her mended frock faded and rumpled. Her eyes had that flat, badly painted look. She could have passed for fifty.

They sat awkwardly on hard chairs facing each other. The once-cluttered little apartment was bare. A roach scurried across the floor.

'When do you leave?'

'This afternoon. As soon as Paquito gets back.' Mariana held a finger to her lips. 'We're not going to the Pyrenees,' she said. 'It's a secret.'

'Where are you going?'

Mariana got up and went to the door. It stood an inch or two ajar. She shut it firmly. 'The Santo has ears everywhere. Everywhere.' She sat down again.

'But we still have friends. Important friends. The Pyrenees.' She laughed, a high nervous sound. 'Who wants to go to the

Pyrenees? It's all been arranged.'

'What's been arranged?'

The flat, badly painted eyes widened with a wild look like that of a snared animal. 'We were wicked, Paco. We were very wicked, you and I. It's God's punishment. The boy has to work, to beg almost. He plays his mandolin at the cafés, for coppers. Every afternoon. We need every copper we can get.' She appraised Paco's stylish clothing. 'Why didn't you send more money?'

'I sent all I could.'

'Well, it's over now. My father's escaped. I told you we had important friends. He's in France. We'll join him in Paris.' Again the finger raised to her lips, again the plea for silence.

'That's wonderful,' Paco said. 'I can't tell you how pleased I am.'

'It's a secret.'

He knew it was no secret. The Santo did indeed have ears everywhere. After two years they were allowing Pablo de Olavide the option of exile. Olavide would be received like a conquering hero in the Enlightenment salons of Paris. Mariana might even find a life, a real life for herself again. And the boy, tall and slim and handsome, would cut a dashing figure in Paris.

They heard a sound on the stairs and Paquito came in. He was lean as a sword and wore a black majo jacket. He carried a mandolin over his shoulder.

'Hola, Don Paco,' he said with a little bow.

'Hola, chico. How goes it?'

'Mother's told you?' Paquito asked.

'Yes.'

'I look forward to France.'

'As anyone your age should,' Paco agreed.

The boy studied his face with a disturbingly objective intensity. 'Oh, I know what you're thinking. The salons, the soirées, the night life. You're wrong, Don Paco. I don't have time for any of that. This is a great opportunity for me, and I intend to make the most of it.'

Paco suddenly felt uneasy in the presence of this boy, his son, who had the grave bearing of a grown man. The hooded eyes, so like his own, continued to study him – now with a tolerant condescending amusement.

'What sort of opportunity?'

Antonio Francisco – Paco could not think of him as Paquito that afternoon – said: 'I wouldn't be at all surprised if the Enlightenment digs its own grave. When that happens the canaille will rise in Paris. They'll rise all over France. They'll give the enlightened nobility more than they bargained for. They could even pull the throne out from under the king. I've been reading, you see. I've – '

'It's a secret,' Mariana said in an anguished whisper. 'A deep secret.'

'Yes, mother,' said the boy, dismissing her with a nod. 'It's a secret, but we're going where the Inquisition can't touch us. That's the opportunity I meant, Don Paco. Because when the Bourbon dynasty ends in France – and it will end – the French will look south across the Pyrenees. There'll be war.'

'Santa Maria,' Paco said, not so much at the boy's prediction but because he seemed so sure of himself and so relentlessly adult.

'You mean, of course,' said Antonio Francisco, 'Santiago and long live Spain. Because I don't intend spending the rest of my life in France. I'll be back. I'll be back when Spain needs me. Do you understand now?'

'Not entirely, Antonio Francisco,' Paco said. He did not understand at all, neither what the boy had in mind nor that this icily self-confident thirteen-year-old, despite the resemblance, could be his son.

'Had I remained in Spain,' Antonio Francisco went on patiently, 'I would have had no choice but to join one of the four military orders. Santiago, Alcántara, Montesa, Calatrava – Pah!' he snorted in unexpected imitation of the Indian. 'They're living in the past, dreaming of the Century of Gold. They don't know how to fight a modern war. They never will. When the time comes, Spain will need leaders, men trained in modern military tactics. I'll be one of them.'

Listening to him, Paco was sure that he would be.

'My grandfather – ' he did not, Paco noticed, refer to Olavide as his uncle – 'will be able to enroll me in the French military academy. I'll study, Don Paco. By Santiago, how I'll learn what the French can teach me! When they cross the Pyrenees I'll be ready for them.'

'I wish you wouldn't always talk of war and destruction,' Mariana said.

'War and destruction is what we'll have. A man's a fool not to prepare himself.'

'You're only a boy.' Her eyes looked normal then.

'I won't be a boy forever.' Antonio Francisco ran a hand through his dark hair and smiled for the first time. 'But here

I've been discussing my own plans, Don Paco, when it's time to say goodbye and – more important – to thank you for all you've done for us.'

'Your grandfather was my patron,' Paco said uncomfortably. 'I did what any man would have done. I wish I could have done more.'

'You'll have my gratitude always. Even in France I'll remember what you've done for us.'

'I was in France once,' said Mariana in a singsong voice.

Antonio Francisco looked at Paco. The boy seemed impatient with his mother's infirmity of mind.

'And I'll take you there again, mamá,' he said finally, relenting, and Paco could have embraced him for that.

The last small case had been carried downstairs. Paco went down with Mariana and the boy. There was an awkward silence as he helped her into the battered black coach.

'Write when you're settled,' he said, and impulsively mounted the step and kissed her cheek. She drew back. Her eyes went flat and vague. *'Baturro,'* she said, 'rutting . . . wicked, wicked, wicked. . . . ' She began to cry softly.

'Take care of her,' Paco told the Indian.

'I will. She's all I have. The boy – frightens me.'

The boy had climbed atop the coach to check the leather straps that held their cases. He came down and shook Paco's hand.

'We'll meet again,' he said.

Somehow, Paco was sure they would.

It all started well. It started beautifully, with Martín Zapater meeting his friend at the posting yard outside the old Roman walls of Zaragoza, Martín looking very prosperous in a frock coat of the latest cut, Martín with a paunch that surprised Paco, Martín with the serious mien of a successful provincial grain merchant, his clubbed hair beginning to recede, his eyes sparkling with eagerness at the long-awaited reunion.

'Professor,' he said with a broad smile, grasping Paco by both arms. 'Let me look at you, let me see the newest fellow of the Academy of San Fernando.'

'I gather you got my letter,' Paco said dryly. But he was immensely pleased to see Martín.

'Well, I got something. I suppose it was a letter. Did anyone ever tell you that for a painter you write a hand remarkably like a stonemason's?'

He released Paco and turned to Josefa. He bent over her

hand and kissed it. 'Doña Josefa,' he said, 'motherhood seems to agree with you. You're as lovely as ever.'

Footmen helped the nurse alight with her charge, the sleeping Maria del Pilar. Martín examined the little pink bundle crowned by a head of fine golden hair. He gingerly poked at a cheek and the baby stirred. 'She looks just like her mother, Martín decided. 'Which, considering the father, is a lucky thing.'

While the post-office lackeys unloaded their baggage Paco asked: 'Did you find a place for us?'

'In the barrio of Boterón,' Martín said promptly with a half-smile. Boterón was the most expensive district in the city, and Paco had written ahead to say that their financial situation was somewhat less than rosy.

'Santa Maria,' he said. 'We can't afford Boterón.'

'Well, if you won't accept our hospitality,' said Martín.

Paco gaped. 'You mean *you* live in Boterón?'

'On the edge of the district, and not a very impressive house compared with the Allué or the Palafox. But we have plenty of room.'

'We couldn't put you to all that trouble,' Josefa said.

'Trouble? Serafina can't wait. Don't you realize that husband of yours has become a figura here in Zaragoza? The crown prince's favorite painter? Of course,' Martín went on, 'the reputation cuts both ways. Nobody's given the tapestry works more problems, I gather. But then he's from Aragon, isn't he? Trouble? With Paco Goya in her house, Fina says, she'll feel the equal of the Señora de Palafox herself.'

By then all the baggage had been assembled and the post office lackeys were waiting for instructions.

'That berlin over there,' Martín told them, and smiled with a provincial bourgeois pride while the baggage was loaded on his own coach. It was old and painted a dull bottle green, but the mules had been groomed until their coats glistened and two footmen climbed down to help with the cases.

Paco recalled the necessity of selling his own secondhand berlin. Martín's pride nettled him. One way to afford your own coach, he told himself, was to save every copper you got your hands on.

But he looked at Martín, his smile so open, his pleasure so real, and took his friend in a powerful *abrazo*. 'Martín, it's wonderful to be back. And even better to see you.'

It was still wonderful that afternoon when he left Josefa to settle into the Zapater house and raced off to the basilica.

Two towers dominated the off-river side of the building, and the great dome loomed over its exact center. The original architect had conceived the structure as pure baroque but Venturo Rodríguez, in renovating it, had managed to impose a neoclassic order which Paco, for once, did not find displeasing.

He went inside. The light was dim and the interior of the cathedral cool. Scaffolding had already been erected under the three domes where the Bayeu brothers and Paco would work. Soon he would climb up to the dome of the Gospel, almost as high as the great dome itself, above the three naves, above the twelve buttresses with their fluted pilasters, above the image of the Virgin in its chapel of jasper and bronze, above the silver steps that climbed to the sacred pillar itself. It was the world he had come from, the basilica that had awed him as a boy even more than the Seo, where once he had chalked a caricature of the bishop – and he would be up there, above it all.

He felt jubilant in the silence of the vast cathedral, young and powerful and sure of his talent. He saw a tired old priest go by in his black cassock, and he had a crazy impulse to dance the jota, the wild dance the Moors had brought to Zaragoza a thousand years ago. He could almost hear the bandurrias carrying the melody and the single guitar striking the rhythm, and the words of a song Doña Engracia had often sung:

> What is it in the jota, mother?
> Mother, what's in the jota
> That makes the old folks cry
> And the young ones laugh?

He wanted to cry, he wanted to laugh. Six months was what they expected. He'd paint in a frenzy, the way you danced the jota. He'd put his Virgin Queen of the Martyrs up there in the dome in four months, in three. He couldn't wait to begin.

He went outside into the bright sunlight. He walked quickly to the Roman wall at one end of the plaza and through the narrow streets to where his parents lived. He ran up the stairs.

The meanness of the Goya y Lucientes apartment brought his spirits tumbling down. Its two rooms seemed, now, small and cluttered. They smelled of medicine and failure. Their bare plaster walls were cracked and damp, and the elaborate brick fireplace he'd had constructed after his return from Italy seemed ridiculously out of place.

His father answered his knock at the door – an old man in robe and slippers, with those lugubriously twisted features, an old man waiting to die and pleased that he had something to do, even if it was only walking the few steps to the door and opening it.

'Paco,' said the twisted mouth, and the tired old voice was raised: 'It's Paco at last!' The words came out haltingly in a strange, thick voice. The stroke had impaired José Goya's speech.

Before they could embrace, Doña Engracia was there, plumper, her hair gray, her nose flatter and broader, her smock patched and frayed.

'You might let a person know when you're coming,' she said crossly, but her eyes were glowing.

Old José Goya settled into his chair, the only cushioned chair in the room. One of his eyelids drooped, his mouth drooped, his head quivered on the stalk of his neck. 'Tell us everything,' he said in that pathetic, thick voice. 'Is it true you're going to paint the dome? You and the Bayeu brothers?' He said their name almost reverently.

'The Virgin Queen of the Martyrs, José,' Doña Engracia said, bringing a jar of lemon water. 'Don't you remember Martín told us?'

'Martín? Martín, yes, of course.' In a vague voice.

'His memory,' said Doña Engracia softly. 'He's so forgetful these days.'

'How's Camillo?' Paco asked. Camillo, quiet, modest Camillo, the parish priest. 'How's Tomás?' Tomás, hawk-nosed and balding, who had taken over his father's trade as a gilder. Paco waited. He didn't want to ask the next question.

'They're fine, fine,' Doña Engracia answered uneasily, wanting to put off the moment herself. 'Tomás works too hard and so does Camillo, but his parishioners love him.'

'We'll find a better position for him,' Paco said. 'I was covered in the presence of the king. He asked me to cover; he was impressed by my painting. We'll find a position that suits Camillo, you'll see.'

'So you wrote two years ago,' Doña Engracia said dryly. 'I seem to recall it was the only letter you wrote that year.'

'We still have it,' said José Goya.

Paco sipped at his lemon water. The smell of medicine, the cracked plaster walls, the ostentatious hearth depressed him. 'How's Rita?' he asked finally.

A silence followed. José Goya sighed. Doña Engracia filled

Paco's cup.

As if in answer to his question Paco heard a wracking cough from the other room. It grew softer and fainter and ended on a choking sob.

'There's no hope,' Doña Engracia said at last in a whisper. 'No hope at all. How long will you stay in Zaragoza?'

'A few months, mother.' He knew what was coming.

'Then you'll be here to bury her.'

José Goya sighed again, his face twisted. Paco went inside to see his dying sister.

The work, high on the scaffold in the dome of the Gospel, began splendidly.

Ramón, Paco later realized, was in no hurry. He had made no comment on Paco's sketch when Francisco approved it in Madrid. He made no comment while the plaster was applied in small sections, nor any comment while Paco sprinkled red chalk through holes in the sketch, to trace the design on the still-wet plaster, nor any comment while Paco painted, quickly, before the plaster could dry, the brush strokes of the fresco bright and crystalline in their intensity.

Ramón could wait. Ramón painted his own fresco at half Paco's speed and twice his brother Francisco's, Ramón working with a kind of limp diligence and Francisco with the sure hand of a craftsman, slowly but with competence.

They would sometimes pass one another below the scaffolding, the smell of wet plaster strong, their hands and smocks covered with paint.

Francisco would make a comment about the speed with which Paco worked.

'I want to give it to my sister as a present. Before she – '

'I know, Paco. I know.'

Ramón would say, 'You're nothing if not fast. Have you an appointment in Madrid?' In only the faintest of malicious tones.

For all Paco's success in Madrid, for all his boasting about being covered in the presence of the king, he still felt ill at ease among the notables of Zaragoza. They reminded him too much of his childhood and his poor beginnings. The Bayeu family, by contrast, had been solidly upper middle class for generations. There would be parties to celebrate the completion of this section or that of a fresco, often at the palace of the urbane Count of Fuentes, sometimes at Allué's big house in Boterón, occasionally at Martín Zapater's house. The count would chide Paco for his speed. 'But I suppose you were that way as a child,' he would say. 'Always racing through life.'

Allué was a dry, caustic man who knew little about art and accepted the opinions of Francisco Bayeu. The Count of Gabarda was now an old man. Of the three, he was, and would remain, Paco's champion. He had discovered Paco Goya, after all, and he was quick to remind people of it in his high, nervous voice.

But when Ramón was ready to act, no one took the Count of Gabarda seriously. His day had passed. It was all Fuentes and Allué and the dashing Palafox, rich, handsome, supremely self-confident, the youngest colonel in the Spanish army.

Palafox who, like Allué, knew little about art.

As for the old Count of Fuentes, seventy years old but still a commanding figure, he was a little embarrassed by what Madrileños referred to as the rustic baroque of Zaragoza. He liked Paco, but liking Paco was not enough. He knew how his brother Nicholás had adored Paco – the good padre dead and buried now in the Papal States – but even that wasn't enough. He wanted to show Madrid that there was another city in Spain.

Ramón Bayeu sensed all this.

And knew it would be useful when the time came.

Paco paid for the funeral with money borrowed against his commission.

In the solemn procession making its slow way behind the bier to the graveyard outside the walls marched two counts, the bishop of Zaragoza, and all the notables of the city. Old José Goya had to be helped along by his sons. Doña Engracia stumbled beside Josefa in a daze. The December day was bright and cold, like the day Rita had died.

She awoke that morning with a sparkle in her eyes. She had no fever. She didn't cough all day. Even the spots of color on her cheeks seemed fainter. Paco, Josefa, and the baby were visiting. It was a crisp, clear Sunday, with the wind whistling across the high Aragonese plateau.

Doña Engracia and Rita both like Josefa. She was shy and unassuming, and she had a way of making Rita forget her illness. She spent the afternoon talking to Rita about Madrid.

'Do you know,' the dying girl said, 'I actually believe I'm going to see it. Madrid. I'll get there someday soon.'

'Of course you will. We'll take you.'

'I haven't felt this well in years.'

Josefa could hear Doña Engracia playing with little Maria del Pilar in the other room. Paco and Tomás had taken their father for his Sunday paseo.

Josefa looked at the sharp bones that all but protruded through the taut, waxen skin of her sister-in-law's gaunt face. 'The zarzuela theater,' she said. 'You're going to love it.'

'Much better than Zaragoza, sister, I'm sure.'

'And the bullfights. And Paco could even take you to the Pardo Palace to see his tapestries there. He's the crown prince's favorite, you know. We'll have a wonderful time.'

'A wonderful time,' Rita repeated. She raised her emaciated arm. 'Come sit by me, sister.'

Her smile then was not that of an El Greco martyr. She was enjoying her Sunday with this good woman, this golden-haired woman who had married her prodigal brother. Her smile was warm and outgoing.

She said: 'I want you to have many children. Boys. I want a lot of nephews.' She reached forward to touch Josefa, who was sitting on the edge of the bed. 'When they're big enough, I'll take them for a paseo in the Retiro Park, I'll get them lemon water at the cafés in the Puerta del Sol, I'll teach them how to dance the jota.' Her eyes suddenly opened wide. 'The jota,' she said again, and then her mouth opened wide and blood gushed out as her head fell back on the pillows.

By the time Josefa cried out for Doña Engracia and the older woman came running, Rita was dead.

Perhaps the talk, the cruel talk, started the day after the funeral. Paco had been unable to sleep that night. He climbed the scaffolding early in the morning. He had a small section of intonaco applied on the left side of the great hemispherical fresco, and among the faces below the figure of St John the Baptist he painted the face of a little girl as an angel in the heavenly choir.

It was the face of Rita as he remembered it from his youth, a healthy, happy Rita.

He did just that one face and climbed down again to join his family in mourning. He told no one why he had had to paint that day of all days.

Has Goya no feelings? they asked in Zaragoza.

The self-centered arrogance of the man. It was all very well to live for your work, they said, but this really was going too far.

It was like dancing on his sister's grave.

One day in the basilica Ramón spoke to Colonel Palafox,

who had come to see the partially completed frescoes.

'Well, if nothing else,' Ramón said, 'Goya certainly has a hand for billowing clouds. Reminds me of poor old Tiepolo.'

Tiepolo had been thoroughly and ruthlessly discredited in Madrid by Mengs, and Palafox knew it.

'Do you think so? Tiepolo?'

'Yes, but he's very good at it. And his women. Look at them, colonel. Did you ever see such a voluptuous heavenly choir?'

'They are rather overblown,' agreed Palafox. He smiled. 'Look at the one floating there above the middle. I wouldn't mind bedding down a girl with a body like that.'

'Neither would I,' laughed Ramón. 'Perhaps he's done too good a job.'

'Too good?'

'Well, too realistic. Rather unseemly for the dome of the Gospel, don't you think?'

Colonel Palafox cleared his throat. 'I'm really no great authority on these matters. Shall I mention it to Allué?'

'No, I wouldn't do that. It's Goya's painting, after all. It is unfortunate, though.'

'Unfortunate?'

'You see,' Ramón gestured to the frescoes he and his brother had been working on, 'there's a jarring note. The basilica's been remodeled in the neoclassic style, after all. So it obviously calls for neoclassic paintings, like Francisco's and mine. But just look at those clouds, and those wild colors and – '

'Yes, and that voluptuous heavenly choir. I really think I ought to bring it to Allué's attention.'

'I don't know. Paco's a fellow of the Academy, same as Francisco and me. He knows what he's doing.'

'If you say so,' said Colonel Palafox doubtfully.

A few days later, Ramón saw Francisco coming down the rungs of the scaffolding slowly with a look of displeasure on his face.

'A bad day?' Ramón asked.

'They'll have to apply fresh intonaco tomorrow.'

'Too bad you don't have Paco's facility.'

'Paco's facility? What do you mean?'

'He never makes a mistake. Or never admits he's made one. He just goes on and on, as fast as his brush can fly.'

'Some people work faster than others. Paco's young. A higer flame brings the kettle to the boil faster, that's all.'

'But if he'd stop to think, stop to consider. . . . ' Ramón let his voice trail off.

'Yes?'

'Compare Paco's fresco with your own. It's marvelous, by the way. I love your use of line. I wish I could do it.'

'If Paco would consider what?' Francisco Bayeu asked, pleased by his brother's compliment.

'Well, it's hard to explain. Paco's Virgin Queen of the Martyrs would have suited the original conception of the basilica, I suppose that's what I mean.'

'But not the new one?'

'See for yourself. It's splendid baroque, but is baroque what we want? It's a bold tour de force of color, but is *that* what we want? Mengs would have been very disturbed by it. There ought to be a unity here. Frankly, I don't see it. Paco's been working so fast he doesn't realize he's struck the one jarring note.'

'I'll have to give the matter some thought.'

Francisco Bayeu gave the matter much thought. When Paco had submitted his sketches in Madrid, Francisco had expressed some qualms about their baroque quality.

'I'll tone them down,' Paco had assured him.

But now Francisco began to think that Ramón was right. Far from toning down the elaborate use of color, Paco had increased it. There *was* a jarring note. Perhaps the basilica chapter wouldn't notice it – certainly Allué wouldn't – but the point was that Francisco did, now that Ramón had pointed it out. And Francisco was responsible for the overall conception of the frescoes. He saw himself as Spain's number one painter, and he was awaiting the day when he would be named first painter to the king, a day which still might elude him if the basilica commission was less than perfect.

But how to mention it to Paco?

For one thing, his brother-in-law, as a new Academy fellow, was more headstrong than ever. For another, he was in mourning for his sister. For a third, the seeds of doubt had been sown by Ramón, and Francisco Bayeu was well aware of the antagonism the two younger painters felt toward one another.

Leave Ramón out of it, of course, Francisco told himself. For the rest, be gentle. Paco's young, and he knows what he owes me. He'll listen to reason.

Paco did not listen to reason.

'That's not you talking,' he said coldly. 'It's Ramón.'

'Ramón has nothing to do with this, cuñado.'

They were strolling around the plaza on a Saturday afternoon. They approached the Seo, Zaragoza's other great church.

'The boy who once chalked the bishop on that wall's come a long way,' observed Francisco Bayeu.

'I guess everybody in Zaragoza knows that story by now.'

'The higher you climb,' pontificated Francisco, 'the further you can fall.'

'Count Gabarda visited the basilica day before yesterday. He liked what he saw.'

'So many heads, so many opinions. And Gabarda's opinion counts least of all, I assure you, Paco.'

'Exactly what is it you want me to do?'

'Tone down your colors. Get rid of some of those billowing clouds. I'll pay for a new intonaco out of my own pocket. Show us more line.'

Paco turned to face his brother-in-law. 'Have you thought of increasing the intensity of your color? That's what fresco's for. Color, Francisco. Color.'

'Times have changed. You have only to look at my work, or Ramón's.'

'I have,' said Paco dryly. 'Every day.'

'If I hadn't given you that Crucifixion to copy, you wouldn't even be here.' Francisco took snuff and went on more calmly, 'Listen to reason, Paco. You're not doing this for yourself. It's an important commission. I'm responsible for it – and we're both responsible to history. These frescoes will last a long time.'

'We're both responsible to nature, too.'

'A painter's task is to bring order to nature.'

'Your task, maybe,' said Paco.

'Then you won't make the changes?'

'I actually believe,' said Paco dryly, 'that you're beginning to understand what I've been trying to say.'

'You've grown too big for your breeches, cuñado.'

The feeling of gloom that had pervaded the Goya y Lucientes household since Rita's death had come, for Paco, at the worst possible time. The eagerness with which he mounted the scaffold every day was tempered by the knowledge that he'd spend the evening with his mourning parents. He wanted to be finished with it all. He was fed up with Zaragoza, fed up with the basilica, fed up with Francisco

213

Bayeu.

'Too big for my breeches?' he asked. 'Maybe. Or maybe too talented for my brother-in-law.'

'You're an ungrateful upstart.'

'Because I insist on sole responsibility for my own work?'

'Insist, do you?' Francisco Bayeu said coldly. 'Then you'll have it.'

After dinner in the Zapater house in Boterón, Martín and Paco sat in the drawing room over cognac and cigars. There was an awkward silence. Two weeks had passed since Paco's argument with his brother-in-law, and he expected another argument now. He did not look forward to it.

Martín cleared his throat uncomfortably. He looked down the length of his long nose at the glowing tip of his cigar. He said: 'Paco, they don't want you to peel the whole thing off the dome and start all over again. Not even Francisco wants that.'

Francisco Bayeu had gone before the chapter of the basilica. 'Goya's work is jarring,' he had told them. 'It clashes with the overall plan developed in Madrid.'

'Tell him to change it,' Allué said promptly.

'It's not that simple. Goya's a successful artist in his own right, you know. He demands freedom from supervision.'

'Even you'd have no right to demand that, Don Francisco,' said Allué. 'Not that there's any danger there.'

'I mean freedom from my supervision, not the chapter's. The chapter, after all, is paying for the work.'

They had adjourned to the basilica to study Paco's work. Some of them even climbed the rickety rungs of the scaffold.

'I'm well pleased with it,' the old Count of Gabarda said, puffing when he came down.

He was the only one who was. Allué and Palafox saw painting through Francisco Bayeu's eyes; the Count of Fuentes, as ever, was disturbed by Madrid's derision of rustic baroque. Paco's female figures were unseemly. His fat pink clouds were old-fashioned. His colors would clash with those of the other frescoes.

They voted, with only Gabarda dissenting, to instruct Paco to alter his work.

'Of course I could be wrong,' Francisco Bayeu admitted.

'We can't all be wrong,' Allué said. 'Tell him to revise it.'

'That's a difficult matter,' Francisco said slowly. 'You see, he was once my apprentice.'

'What my brother's trying to say,' Ramón said smoothly, 'is that now the relationship's changed. They're brothers-in-law. They see each other almost every day in Madrid. It would be very awkward for Francisco.'

'Why are we all standing in awe of this upstart?' demanded Colonel Palafox. 'We agree we want changes; we'll have changes. The chapter will write him a formal letter demanding them. Would that solve the problem, Don Francisco?'

Francisco Bayeu thought that would solve the problem.

It was the formal letter from the basilica chapter that Martín now wanted to discuss.

'They only asked you to mute the colors. And to make the women – uh, somewhat less physically desirable.'

'I won't do it.'

'It really doesn't come to much.'

'You saw my counter-proposal. An objective judge. Two of them. Mariano Maella and any other member of the Academy they'd care to name. I'd pay their way here from Madrid. Let them decide the issue.'

'The chapter turned down that suggestion.'

'Because it would be a slap in the face to them if Maella decided in my favor. They'd deserve it. Their knowledge of art is what Francisco tells them it is – something they're painfully aware of.'

Martín finished his cognac and stubbed out his cigar. 'Chico, we've been friends a long time. I hope I can be frank with you.'

'What the devil do you know about painting?' Paco snapped.

'I'll tell you what I know about painting. You're a better painter than Francisco Bayeu right now. But you'd be a jackass if you made an issue of it. I think Francisco's a little afraid of you. He knows how good you are.'

'Maybe it's time he admitted it.'

'Chico, you're not listening. Give him fresh sketches. Give him what he wants. This one time. He's at the top. He'll be first painter to the king soon. He could hurt you if you make an enemy of him.'

'You said Francisco's afraid. I say you are.'

'Me?' Martín asked in amazement. 'Afraid of what?'

'Palafox,' said Paco flatly. 'He'll be captain-general someday, and you do most of your business with the army. Everybody knows you're my best friend in Zaragoza. You want this to blow over smoothly for your own benefit.'

'Are you serious?' Martín demanded.

'Zaragoza's full of provincial panderers. Tell me you're not one of them.'

'Martín stood up. His face was flushed. 'If anyone else said that I'd throw him out of this house.'

'You could try,' Paco said.

Martin sat down again. 'I'm sorry. I didn't mean that.'

'No, neither did I. I'm just sick and tired of this whole mess.'

'Did it occur to you that Zaragoza's sick and tired of your artistic temperament?'

'Temperament? I thought we were talking about integrity.'

'What's the difference what you call it? You won't listen to me. You won't listen to anybody.'

'As one *baturro* to another,' Paco said with a mocking smile, 'you're absolutely right.'

CHAPTER NINETEEN

Paco Furioso

IF HIS DEALINGS with the chapter of the basilica had, so soon after the death of his sister, brought Paco to the edge of his self-control, if his argument with Francisco had taken him over the edge, if the even more acrimonious argument with Martín had made him wish he'd never returned to Zaragoza, his discussion with Josefa, finally, was too much.

'After all,' she tried to reason with him, 'Francisco's the best painter in Spain.'

'Thank you very much,' Paco said sarcastically.

'That doesn't mean that you won't be, someday.'

'You think Francisco's a genius and I'm just a dauber. That's what it comes down to, isn't it?'

'I like the way you paint. I love it. But sometimes it – frightens me. The way you look for what's ugly or – '

'Let's not go through all that again.'

'Perhaps the trouble is that you really don't like to do religious paintings.'

'If there is any trouble.'

'Everybody from Francisco to Allué's dissatisfied.'

'Did you know the great Rembrandt spent most of his life a pauper? While idiots like his disciple Flinck were making a fortune?'

'I wouldn't want us to be paupers, Paco,' Josefa said quietly.

'No, nor would I. Believe me, we won't.'

'We might, if you went on antagonizing Francisco at every turn.'

'You mean antagonizing Ramón.'

'We're not talking about Ramón.'

'You don't actually believe this was Francisco's idea, do you?'

'Stop shouting at me. You'll wake the baby.'

They were in bed in their room at the Zapater house. Little Maria del Pilar was asleep in the small nursery next door.

'Then listen to reason. We're both working in the tradition of church painting. We're both working with intonaco. Intonaco's a question of color. I understand color. Francisco doesn't.'

'I've seen your fresco, Paco.'

'And?'

Josefa sat up. Her golden braids gleamed in the candlelight. She reached out for his hand. 'Paco, do you believe in God?'

'Do I what?'

'Do you believe in God, in the Holy Virgin, in the Church?'

'Santa Maria, what has that to do with it?'

'Do you?'

Paco considered. 'Oh, there's a God,' he said. He waved a hand vaguely. 'Somewhere out there, I guess. And less interested in what we do than you think.'

'That's heresy.'

'I never said it wasn't.'

'You never go to confession.'

'I never feel the need to confess.'

'Can't you see that your forsaking of the Church – '

'So now I'm an apostate.'

' – doesn't let you see their objections? You make a choir of angels look like – I'm almost too embarrassed to say this.'

'Go ahead. You've said just about everything else.'

'You make a choir of angels look like a group of whores waiting on a street corner. That's the chapter's real objection.'

'Damn it, look at Titian, look at Rubens, look at Tiepolo.'

'Do you want to be a discredited has-been like Tiepolo?'

'Thanks for your confidence in me, cara.'

217

'I didn't mean it that way.'

'No, Martín said some things he didn't mean either.'

'Martín wants you to submit new sketches? I didn't know that. Even Martín. Your best friend. You're as stubborn as a mule.'

'He's not my best friend. All that ended a long time ago. He's a provincial panderer afraid of his own – '

'Stop it. He's the kindest, gentlest man in the world. You're being hateful.'

'I'm being bludgeoned. I can't stand it any more.'

'Then give in. Do what they want; finish the job, and the day you finish it I'll return to Madrid with you.'

'With an apostate has-been of a painter? That would take courage. More courage than the Bayeu family possesses. You didn't know Rembrandt had been a pauper, did you? The greatest painter who ever lived. It frightens you, doesn't it?'

'Your attitude frightens me. No man can paint for himself alone.'

'No, that's true. But if your patron's an idiot, you find a new patron.'

'If you make a mistake, you admit it and correct it.'

'If,' said Paco.

Josefa reached for his hand again. 'I'm sorry. I'm trying to say all the right things, but I'm saying all the wrong ones. I only want what's best for you. How can I prove it?'

'By keeping your long Bayeu nose out of all this.'

'Paco. Paco, what's happened to us? I *have* faith in you. Someday – '

'I'm talking about now.'

'Then make those changes now. You're upset. I know how they've upset you. And coming on top of Rita's death – '

'Tell me I shouldn't have gone up there.'

'Up where?'

'To paint. The day after her funeral.'

'There was talk that – '

'I painted Rita. Rita, do you understand?'

'I didn't know that.'

'You might have looked.'

'You might have let me know. It's as if you – don't want me to be close.'

Close? he thought. Closeness, and love, and mutual dependence – did they help an artist? Did he really have time for love, as Josefa understood love?

'You're shutting me out of your life,' she said. Almost in

218

tears. 'I want to understand you. I try to.'

'Stop trying so hard,' he said cruelly.

And even then she did not cry. Suddenly he felt contrite. She *was* trying. To understand him, to help him.

He said wearily: 'I'll do it. I'll make new sketches. I'll make their God-damned changes.'

'Oh, Paco!'

He felt her weight shift, and came into his arms.

He drew away. 'Not because I ought to. I'm just fed up, that's all. I'll give them what they want. I'll give Francisco his petty little victory. Then I want out.'

'Out?'

It was Josefa who had raised her voice then. Inside, the baby began to cry.

'Out of Zaragoza.' He gestured toward the nursery. 'Away from that. Away from your brothers, who'll still be daubing at plaster after I've done it all twice. Away from – '

'Don't say any more, Paco. Please, not now.' Her mouth was very close. He could smell the freshness of her. He longed for the scent of jasmine, a lifetime ago. He could not have that. He longed for –

For what?

The tapestry works, where he was Numero Uno. Old Mynheer van der Goten wringing his hands. A blue smock, and dark red hair like Mariana's, and the musky smell of her after a day's work.

Then you can do them – Barbara?

I think so. I know I want to try.

Santa Barbara.

Away from Josefa. Finish the work any way at all, return to Madrid, send for Josefa after their tempers had cooled.

'Make love to me, Paco. Please. Now.'

But her body was too familiar to him then, like her arguments. He turned to her, without passion, and then he shut his eyes and thought of Barbara García, and Josefa cried out under him.

The last time he climbed down from the scaffold he did not look back at the fresco. He went straight to Allué and demanded his money.

'You'll be paid when the entire commission's finished.'

'I've made the changes you asked for. I want my money now.'

'There's to be a ceremony, medals to be struck,' Allué told

219

him.

'Gold or silver?' asked Paco.

'Why, silver.'

'Silver. Zaragoza. Of course.'

'You're an insolent fellow, Goya. Too insolent for your own good.'

'Nobody hired my personality.'

'If that's what you had to sell, you'd find no work in Zaragoza.'

'By dint of enormous effort,' Paco said slowly, 'I think I could manage to survive without Zaragoza, Señor Allué.'

Allué's face went pale. 'You'll have your money today.'

It still might not have been too late for them if Josefa hadn't wanted to stay for the ceremony. Paco, relenting, asked her to return to Madrid with him.

'It's only a few more days,' she said. 'I think we ought to stay.'

'No, I'm going.'

'You've earned that medal if anybody ever earned one.'

'I don't want it.'

'They say there'll be a medal for me too,' Josefa told him uneasily.

'For you?'

'Martín let them know I convinced you to submit new sketches.'

'Don't accept it,' Paco said.

'Why not? I'd be proud to have it.'

'Don't you see what they're doing? They want to put me in my place. The Bayeu family, and that upstart Goya. I'm going back to Madrid.'

'I'm staying,' Josefa said.

Paco shoved a dish toward the pile of dirty crockery on the dining room table. A swarm of flies buzzed away.

The house on San Gerónimo was a cluttered mess. He had not stirred from it for a week. He hadn't washed or shaved. He drank more than he was accustomed to – anís with his morning coffee, wine all day, cognac at night. He awoke each morning with a headache. He sketched his own portrait twice, with deep circles under the eyes and a stubble of beard. He destroyed the sketches.

He thought of Josefa in Zaragoza accepting her medal. He hated her then.

Toward the end of the week he dreamed of dark red hair

and that musky scent. All during the next day he couldn't get them out of his mind. He sketched her from memory, but the sketches were as unsatisfactory as those of himself.

He shaved, bathed, dressed in his best frock coat and rented a landau. He drove to the Inn of the Comb and asked for the best room in the house.

'For how long, señor?'

'I don't know. Three days, four.'

He sent out for food and wine, though the inn had its own restaurant. He slept there one night alone. All night he saw the thin smile on Josefa's face as she accepted the medal. All morning, awake, he still saw it.

In the afternoon he drove to the Royal Tapestry Works of Santa Barbara.

There were two Goyas on the looms, a Maella, a Meléndez and a rather tepid hunting scene by Ramón Bayeu.

Barbara García did not see him enter the long, narrow workshop. A strand of that dark red hair down over one eye, a smudge on one cheek, she was scolding one of the girls working on the Ramón Bayeu.

'What he lacks you'll have to make up for,' she said. 'Tighten it, chica. With your spindle. It's to be a tapestry, not a fishnet.'

Paco came up behind them. He gripped Barbara's shoulder and could feel the warmth of her through the thin blue smock.

She turned. She looked down at his strong fingers and then up into his hooded eyes. She knew instantly.

'Now,' he said.

For three days and three nights they did not leave the Inn of the Comb.

They ate at odd hours, a bite or two of country ham, some bread, the legs of a chicken from the kitchen of the inn. They drank wine sparingly. They talked little. They never slept more than an hour or two at a time. They feasted on each other's bodies.

The first time, the scent of her had been maddening. It was everywhere, that muskiness, that young animal scent. He could not wait. He ripped the blue smock from her body and threw her on the bed.

'Oh God, I knew it would be like this,' she cried. 'You're a bull. A bull.'

'I'm using you,' he said once. 'You don't know.'

'Use me,' she said against his mouth. 'God yes, use me.'

There was a sleek firmness to her body. On the warm spring mornings, with sunlight in the room, he would leave her shining with sweat, her mouth slack, her thighs quivering. The scent was stronger then, intoxicating. Sometimes at dusk she would stand at the window, watching night fall on Madrid. He would come up behind her and cup her breasts in his hands. He loved how she whirled, in mock-surprise, with that dazzling smile which quickly became a lewd smile as she said: 'And does my toro want another pass or two with the muleta?'

Her toro wanted another pass or two with the muletta.

The nights were best. In the darkness he would feel a new strength as her legs grasped his and the sleekness of her body moved rhythmically under him holding him holding him moving as he moved waiting as he waited and except for the now familiar scent of her she could have been anyone Mariana a dozen years ago or all the women he knew now he would have the unknown ones waiting the young ones waiting younger that Santa Barbara who was anything but saintly as her legs gripped and her loins moved frantically he would stay with Josefa giving her what she was willing to accept husband father provider seeker after and lover of other women the medal that damnable silver medal and jasmine so long ago and the not-quite-heard *cante hondo* the way the years go hurtling by and a man ages there is never enough time never enough if a man could live a hundred years and feel the strength of his youth flowing in him always the magic –

'Querido, you're hurting me.'

But she did not really mind.

On the fourth morning they both knew, without a word being said, that it had ended.

It was a cold, gloomy morning with rain lashing in at the windows as he sat up in bed and watched Barbara García pad naked across the room to close the shutters.

She was a somewhat long-legged, somewhat pretty, somewhat dull girl with a well-padded posterior, coarse skin, few words, a serviceable body, and a scent, now acrid, that was only mildly objectionable.

She came back to the bed. He touched his jaw and realized he hadn't shaved for three days. They stared at each other. Her hair had lost its luster in those three days. It hung snagged and unkempt down to her shoulders. On her thick neck were faint blue marks left by his teeth.

She waited. Deliberately he bit off the end of a cigar and lit it. 'Three days,' he said. 'You'll have a lot of explaining to do to van der Goten.'

'Oh, I can take care of Mynheer van der Goten. He couldn't run the works without me.'

'Shall I drive you back?'

'You'd better not.'

'I'll give you money for a cab.'

'Good.'

'Barbara – '

'What?'

'Nothing. Santa Barbara.'

She laughed lewdly.

In ten minutes she was gone.

He was whistling a jota as he unlocked the door of the house on San Gerónimo. The first thing he noticed was the musty smell. He'd have to fling back the shutters, air the place out. Then he could get to work.

The second thing he noticed was the pair of letters that had been shoved under the door. He tossed them on the hall table and opened all the shutters on the ground floor. It had stopped raining. The air smelled fresh. Patches of blue showed in the sky. Low clouds scudded past.

He took the letters into the kitchen. Josefa's handwriting. He spent a few minutes lighting tinder in the stove and shoveling in charcoal. Josefa could wait. He ground coffee and filled the pot with water and set it to boil. Only then did he turn to the letters. He broke the seal on the first one and read it.

Dearest Paco,

Today my brothers and I received the silver medals struck by the chapter of the basilica to commemorate the painting of the domes. The ceremony was attended by all the dignitaries of the city, even the Count of Fuentes. I missed you. But more than that, I actually felt guilty when the count himself hung the medal around my neck. You were right, my dear, and I was so very foolish. I should have returned to Madrid with you. I had no business accepting that medal. I wanted to refuse it, and I think at the last moment Francisco knew. It would have upset him terribly. So will you believe me if I say I would have refused it except for that? I love you very much, Paco, and hope you can forgive me.

Francisco and Ramón are on their way back to Madrid. I would have gone with them but will have to wait a few more days until we can be reunited. Maria del Pilar has a fever and a slight sore throat, the poor little thing, and the doctor said we should not travel until she is well. She joins me in sending you a thousand kisses.

Your Josefa

The contrition so evident in that first letter made Paco feel the first vague stirrings of guilt. But how could he have known, he asked himself, that Josefa would have such a complete change of heart?

He opened the second letter. It was very short.

Dear Paco,

I have no words. I cannot write what must be written. I look to God for solace but there is no answer there. All night the doctor tried to scrape the membranes from her throat so that our poor Maria del Pilar could breath. It was diphtheria. She died this morning. She will be buried here in Zaragoza. Come for me. No, I will come to you as fast as I can.

Josefa

He remembered crying out wordlessly. He remembered reading the letter again. He remembered the sound of the coffee boiling on the stove and how he picked up the pot and hurled it across the kitchen. Outside a knife grinder went by playing his pipes. The wind was fresh, blowing through the house.

He found himself in the nursery. He looked down at the little bed on its rockers. He looked at the plaster walls, where he had sketched fanciful animals in red and black chalk. In the bed was Maria del Pilar's gypsy rag doll. He picked it up. He held it cradled in his arms. He hurled it away from him.

Damned Aragonese peasant rutting like a pig in a barnyard. While his daughter was dying.

He went upstairs to his studio. A tapestry cartoon which he had begun before leaving for Zaragoza still stood on the easel. A child on a swing, a golden-haired child as Maria del Pilar might have looked in two or three years.

He slashed at the canvas with his palette knife, destroying it. 'Nada!' he screamed. 'Nada y nada y nada!'

There was a ringing sound in his ears, that terrible ringing sound.

He shut his eyes and saw a cowled witch poking a pin in

Maria del Pilar's gypsy rag doll.

He screamed again and did not hear it. He clapped his hands over his ears to make the ringing go away. It grew louder.

He ran outside.

He lay in an alley in the blacksmiths' barrio. Every bone in his body ached. He remembered a bodega, and too much chalky red wine, and picking a fight with the biggest man he could find, a bull-necked blacksmith wearing a leather apron.

They had stood in the alley, legs planted, pounding each other with clenched fists like hammers until both had fallen.

The ringing in his ears had become fainter. His left eye was swollen shut. He was alone in the alley. A voice shouted above him and a slop pail was emptied, its contents splashing nearby. He tried to get up. A letter. Something terrible.

His right eye blinked open in brilliant sunlight.

He remembered everything; it all came rushing back at once.

He got up carefully, like an old man, and lurched out of the alley. He walked, losing himself in the maze of crooked streets in the blacksmith's barrio. His frock coat was torn and stained with wine and vomit. Passersby, even in that seedy district, gave him a wide berth. Children darted around him, laughing, taunting the strange figure, hair wild, face stubbled with dark beard, one eye swollen shut.

If he had refused to make the changes.

If he had insisted on taking Josefa and the baby home with him.

If Josefa had not waited for her medal.

He walked past a house where plasterers were working. The smell, so like intonaco, made him gag. He fled.

Paint?

How could he ever paint again?

He walked all day. It was over. Everything was over. He had not been true to himself, he had abandoned his integrity; his daughter lay dead in Zaragoza.

He reached the river. Late afternoon, and the water running turbulently with snow melting on the Sierra. Distantly he could see the royal palace.

There's a feeling of Spain in your work, of good red Spanish earth.

Cultivate it? It was all nothing, nothing.

To hurl himself into the rushing water would be so simple. To end it that way. To stop forever the ringing in his ears.

And then, through it, he heard a sound. A guitar. The ringing faded, the notes of the guitar grew louder. He rounded a bend along the dirt path that skirted the riverbank and saw a group of people clustered on a hillock around a blind guitarist. No longer young, the blind man stood staring sightlessly upward as he plucked the sad gypsy melody from his guitar, a rapt expression on his face. A child stood beside him, another pair sat at his feet gazing up in admiration. An hidalgo on horseback looked down over the heads of the crowd. A black water-carrier bent under the weight of the big jug strapped to his back, a rakish tricorn on his head, stood off to one side. Opposite, a herdsman was goading a pair of stubborn oxen along the riverbank.

It all made an intriguing triangular composition, crowned by the hidalgo on horseback. The palace, dimly-seen in the background, Paco decided, was wrong. The scene was in Madrid but not of Madrid.

Aragon then, and a dimly-seen mudéjar building.

What am I thinking of? he wondered. What in the world am I thinking of? He wanted to paint it.

No, not paint it.

He wanted to use the biggest copper plate he had and attack it with his etching needle.

He left a few coins for the blind man. He walked. He walked faster, the chords of the guitar fading.

He climbed the stairs to his studio and saw the destroyed canvas. The ringing in his ears was gone.

He found his biggest copper plate. He had an hour or two of daylight left.

Savagely with his etching needle he attacked the copper, as he had in his deafness. He worked until it was too dark to work and then he lit candles and worked some more.

He was still working when Josefa returned to him in her grief.

226

BOOK FOUR

BOOK FOUR

A BLUSTERY WIND sways the cab as it jounces along the slick cobbled streets of Paris in the autumn night. The rain has stopped. The evening star and a high moon, not quite full, race among the swift-moving clouds.

Napoleon with his foot on an ant heap, the old man thinks: 'These, or mankind! What difference does it make, when seen from Venus or Saturn or the polestar?' And the emperor's boot crushes down.

Once it made a difference to the old man. His humble origins, his Aragonese pride, his driving ambition – How far can I go? Who will stop me, if I have the magic?

And is the Prince of the Peace so very different? Born of a poor hidalgo family in Extremadura, the second of two sons who go to Madrid to join the royal guardsmen? Extremadura, that bleak land on the Portuguese frontier, where the meagre crop is hogs instead of wheat? With the same pride, and even more ambition?

If, the old man smiles, such a thing were possible.

A hundred yards ahead in another cab sits the Prince of the Peace and his lady of the evening. While he lives, for as long as he lives, he will be himself.

The old man clutches his dueling pistols and snorts in grudging admiration as the cab stops outside the Café de Paris. At Chez Flicoteaux the Prince of the Peace could get a good meal for two for forty sous. Or he might have taken his lady to Véry's or Les Frères Provençaux. Expensive, the old man tells himself, but not astronomical. But the Café de Paris. A gold livre, at the very least.

The Prince of the Peace lives to impress. He always lived that way, and for a long time his star soared high, like Venus racing among the clouds, brightest in the sky. To finally flare out, like the brief brilliant trail of a meteor.

They say – his detractors say – that it all began with a handsome face, a well-turned leg and a beautiful singing voice. To reach the queen's bed, perhaps, the old man thinks. But then, the queen's bed was always reachable. Politics, that is something else. Did he become a statesman because he hated mankind? Like Napoleon with his ant heap?

No matter. For a time he set his foot on the ant heap of Spain, as Napoleon set his on the ant heap of France.

While Don Paco remembered two dead children and two vows. He will never be poor again. He will never surrender his integrity as an artist.

He clings to the first vow. The second can wait. Time still stretches before him. Conquer Madrid with your brush first. There is always time. But of course there is not.

A portrait of Count Floridablanca, a most flattering portrait, with a mysterious light emanating from the splendidly dressed, arrogant-faced count himself, and a humble Paco Goya standing before him offering a canvas.

Floridablanca, as tight with his own purse strings as he is with the royal treasury, admits mild pleasure but fails to pay for the portrait. 'The fact that you have painted me will be the making of you, Goya. Be content.'

He is not content. He has already painted his San Bernardino in Madrid's Church of San Francisco el Grande, in competition with Maella and Francisco Bayeu. The painting is close to a masterpiece, close to the magic – contrasting the ardent simplicity of faith with the transitory pomp of the world. But perhaps Josefa was right: her Paco is never really at ease doing churchly canvases. In the last days, on an impulse born of that Aragonese pride, he paints himself into the mighty canvas. All its other figures are intent on the saint himself. The face of Paco Goya stares out boldly at the viewer. There in that palace of a church where the Divine Majesty receives the homage of the earthbound ones.

He wants more. He spends a summer at the country estate of King Carlos' brother the Infante Don Luis, a happy-go-lucky man who has access to everything and wants little, while the painter has access to little and wants everything. Living luxuriously, drunk with delight, Don Paco tosses off portraits with astonishing speed – fifteen of them. The portraits please the infante, and among Don Paco's rewards is a gold and silver dress for Josefa, made by the royal wardrobe mistress at a cost of thirty thousand reales.

'Come every summer, Don Paco,' says the infante, his enormous Bourbon nose hooking over a wide smile. 'If you have the time. All Madrid will want to be painted by you now.'

And Don Paco, before he leaves the infante's estate, secures the position of confessor there for his quiet brother Camillo. Two Goyas are on the rise.

Now, in Paris, the Prince of the Peace alights from his cab offering an arm to his lady. Together they pass through the glittering gaslit entrance of the Café de Paris.

The old man waits. He is cold and hungry. He considers. Go inside, have a fine meal yourself. Unlike the Prince of the Peace, you are no poor man.

Will he see you? Possibly.

There is nowhere he can hide, if he does.

The restaurant is large, crowded, noisy. The old man is seated. Their tables are not close, but for an instant it seems that the Prince of the Peace stares straight at him. He waits for some sign of recognition, but there is none. He orders oysters and sole and a bottle of Sancerre. His French is coming back. The words slip more easily from his tongue.

He had to learn French a second time, then, after his summer with the infante. The court speaks French, after all.

He paints Mynheer van der Goten just before his death. A good portrait and an honest one because he has nothing to fear from van der Goten. The close-set eyes, the pointed nose with its flaring nostrils, the large fleshy mouth, the double chins, the grayness of the man. He paints the architect Venturo Rodríguez, director of the San Fernando Academy. He is more careful there.

Which is the illusion and which the reality? Van der Goten painted as he is, or Venturo Rodríguez as he would like to be?

Illusion is everything to a Spaniard, the old man knows. The Prince of the Peace taking his lady to the most expensive restaurant in Paris, like the impoverished hidalgo whose home is a hovel to which no one is ever invited but whose clothing tends toward the spectacular. How typical of a Spaniard to clothe unpleasant reality with an illusion. . . .

The oysters are served, and the bottle of flinty-dry white wine in its ice-filled urn. The old man sips suspiciously at the wine while the waiter hovers attentively. A small indifferent nod, though the wine is delicious. The waiter beams and pours carefully.

No man can be cynical unless he is sentimental. That is Jovellanos, Spain's great writer-statesman. Or no man can be sentimental unless he is cynical. Jovellanos with those dichos

231

of his. Jovellanos who would one day bring Paco Goya roaring in his deafness out into the arena.

Was it cynical to have affair after affair, and then return to Josefa? Or sentimental? Or merely that Aragonese pride?

Any man, Madrileños said, who loves his wife is a fool. He was doing what everyone else did. The affairs meant nothing.

The wine is suddenly too cold. It chills him. He shivers.

Hair black, almost too black to paint, a certain arrogant elegance that could make a man cry out in delight –

Or enslave him –

An illusion, surely. A very Spanish illusion. No woman could be that beautiful.

But she was.

Santa Maria, she was my life.

Illusion or reality, what difference does it make? The illusion, for Francisco de Goya y Lucientes that summer of 1786 when they met, was one of enormous success.

CHAPTER TWENTY

Three Guests

EVEN IF IT WAS the product of a rather jaded taste, the Duchess of Osuna loved the park at the rear of the Alameda, her summer estate beyond the northern outskirts of Madrid. Here was mystery: the green labyrinths of boxwood, the leaping, shimmering fountains, the curving allées, the Grecian temple on an artificial hill, the miniature fort (defending nothing) that came abruptly into view, its silent brass cannon pointing at a serene blue sky.

Doña Maria Josefa Pimentel y Borjia, Condesa-Duquesa de Benavente, twice a princess, eight times a duchess, was the least jaded of women. Married to her first cousin Pedro, ninth Duke of Osuna, she had given her husband free rein in designing the park, and her own pleasure in it surprised her. He was a rotund man with jovial eyes, a round face, and a sensuous mouth supported by double chins.

The Duchess of Osuna was all Toledo steel.

Far from pretty, her face commanded attention, not to mention obedience. Long, fine-boned, with cold gray eyes, a slash of a mouth and a hard, pointed chin, it was like a matador's sword. Uncorseted, her figure was firm and strong as a man's. Determined to excel in everything, she usually succeeded. Seated astride and galloping across the plain or urging her mount up steep cliffs, she could outride most men. Sometimes she would disappear for days on end, sleeping where she could, eating what was available, rubbing shoulders with anyone who might cross her path.

She was too much woman for the pleasure-seeking man she had married, and Don Pedro wisely never questioned these disappearances. She collected protégés the way Crown Prince Carlos collected clocks. Among them were the playwright Tomás Yriarte and the bullfighter Pedro Romero. If she slept with either, or both, no one could prove it. No one dared cross her. The author of a satirical song about the Duchess of Osuna drew a year in prison.

Not that she was vindictive. She had no time to waste on revenge. But she valued her privacy. It was she and not the duke who administered their vast estates. It was she who joined and then, despite her sex, dominated the Economic Society of Madrid.

If she had any weakness it was her insistence on patterning herself after Marie Antoinette, outdoing the French queen with the amount of frills, ruffles, and ribbons she wore. They emphasized the boniness of her, and the strength, and the very unladylike steel.

The duchess, on a flawless summer afternoon in August 1786, had just completed her guest list for a performance of Yriarte's latest play in the little theater at the Alameda. She paced the terrace between the wings of the building impatiently. Don Pedro was drinking his afternoon chocolate, and chocolate for her spouse meant an hour or so lingering over pastries. She wanted to read the guest list to him. It held a few surprises, as the duchess herself always did.

At last Don Pedro appeared, patting his stomach under the brocade of his waistcoat.

'Well, and is it finished, my dear?'

'For an hour and a half,' she said dryly, and began to read from the list. The duke nodded his head, his double chins quivering. Suddenly he raised an eyebrow.

'Did you say Maria Luisa?'

'Yes, of course. Why not?'

'The crown prince won't come with her. He'll be too tired from the hunt.'

'So?'

'She's an outrageous flirt.'

'Aren't we all?' demanded the duchess with a faint smile.

'*And* she'll drink too much despite that liver of hers, and wind up making a fool of herself.'

'So?' asked the duchess again.

'King Carlos is old. She'll be queen one day soon. Don't make an enemy of her.'

'Why,' said the Duchess of Osuna sweetly, too sweetly, 'I make an enemy of no one.'

She continued reading the list and was soon rewarded with another raised eyebrow.

'Surely I misunderstood. You didn't say the Alba?'

'Cayetana? Of course. Why not?'

'Maria Luisa detests her.'

'That should make the party interesting,' the duchess predicted, and resumed reading the list in her deep contralto voice. 'And some bullfighters, I think. The ladies of the court love bullfighters.'

'Yes, don't they,' said the duke a little uncomfortably.

'Juanito Apiñani, Pedro Romero, and Pepe Hillo,' said the duchess, sandwiching her current favorite's name between the other two.

'Do we need all three of them?'

'Well, I suppose we could drop Juanito. He's a bit passé.'

'No, no. We'll have the three, though Romero can be pretty grim.'

'I'd say grave rather than grim. And you'd be surprised how that gravity of his appeals to the ladies.'

The duke did not say, 'Would I?' He sighed. Romero had been no surprise. Romero was a frequent visitor at the Alameda. Too frequent.

The duchess' third surprise was the painter Francisco Goya y Lucientes.

'Goya? Really? I wouldn't have thought him ready.'

'You like his painting well enough.'

Paco, that year named a painter to the king and already sub-director of painting at the Academy of San Fernando, had recently finished a family portrait of the Osunas. It hung on the white and gold wall of the ballroom of the Alameda, showing the softness of the duke, the steel of the duchess, and the distance between them. The children looked like porcelain dolls.

'I suppose so,' said the duke. 'But don't you think him a little – gauche?' They were speaking French, as they usually did.

'He won't spit on the floor,' said the duchess in that outspoken way of hers, 'and I rather doubt he'll fart in public.'

The duke coughed uncomfortably. Since the arrival in Madrid of the foul-mouthed singer La Caramba, it had become fashionable for highborn ladies to shock their men with frank talk. In private, of course. But still, the duke never could grow used to it.

'Besides,' Doña Maria Josefa went on, 'he's enormously talented, and he has presence.'

'Two hundred pounds of presence,' said the duke spitefully.

'Yes, he has been putting on weight. A fine figure of a man, as is my very dear Don Pedro.'

Which ended the duke's objection to the third controversial guest.

The first guest was, at that moment, traveling in royal splendor in her black coach emblazoned with the coat of arms of the Prince of the Asturias. She was only going to Segovia, but attended as she was by two countesses, her footmen, her detachment of royal guardsmen on fine white steeds, she might have been crossing from one end of Spain to the other.

Doña Maria Luisa de Parma y Borbón, Princess of the Asturias, soon to be Queen of the Two Spains, was then just thirty-five years old. She looked older. Most of her teeth had fallen out and the gold and jeweled false set fitted poorly; she had an addiction to rich food and strong drink which gave her, as the French said, a liver (and gave her face a greenish cast); and her dissipation did not end at the table. If the Duchess of Osuna collected protéges the way Prince Carlos collected clocks, Princess Maria Luisa collected bedfellows even more assiduously.

But what else could she do? she thought as the coach raced along behind its team of six perfectly matched horses. Don Carlos, her dolt of a husband, was more interested in hunting or in wrestling with the stableboys than in lovemaking. Maria Luisa was a sensual woman and, if she lacked the icy sangfroid of the Osuna or the incredible beauty of Cayetana de Alba, she was, after all, a princess. She could choose her bedfellows, and would go on doing so. Let Carlos have his hounds, his insufferably ticking clocks, his asinine wrestling matches. . . .

Suddenly the Countess of Pizarro screamed.

Outside the window of the coach a horse had reared, almost throwing its rider. His bicorn hat flew from his head as he hung precariously from one stirrup. The Countess of Matallana cried: 'He's going to be killed! '

The boy – he was no more than eighteen or so – grasped the horse's thick mane and lashed its flank with his whip. He clung perilously, and then brought the horse under control with a final slash of his whip and a powerful tug at the reins. Doña Maria Luisa watched, fascinated. He was a horseman to match the Osuna, she thought enviously. She always felt uncomfortable and awkward mounted side-saddle on a horse, and rarely rode. The envy faded. In his red, white, and blue uniform, the boy was beautiful. He had fine auburn hair, and those white buckskin breeches fit his lovely muscular legs like a second skin.

Maria Luisa decided that she felt faint.

'I could use a cordial,' she said, and the Countess of Pizarro poured the sweet blackberry brandy. She sipped. Coach and outriders, after the mishap, were now advancing slowly across

236

the plain. The handsome boy rode silhouetted against the high Castilian sky.

'See if he's all right,' the princess told the Countess of Matallana, and the countess opened the window and beckoned to the guardsman.

'Shall we halt a while?' she asked.

'No, madame, I beg you not to,' said the boy in a wonderfully melodious voice and, unexpectedly, in passable French. 'And I apologize for my ridiculous clumsiness. I ought to ride a donkey after this.' He bowed his head.

'Nonsense,' said Maria Luisa, 'you're a fine horseman.'

Another bow from the saddle. 'It is kind of the princess to say so.'

'Are you new with the Guards?'

'Not exactly, Your Highness,' said the boy in a shy voice. 'I joined six months ago.'

'Where are you from?'

'Extremadura,' said the boy, again shyly. Extremadura was not exactly the center of the universe.

'Some of our finest men come from Extremadura,' said the Princess of the Asturias. 'Where did you learn French? You speak it beautifully.'

'Hardly that, madame. I learned it at the barracks, from French émigrés.'

'Then you learn quickly. What other talents do you have?'

'I sing,' said the boy, more boldly. 'I play the guitar.'

'Yes? Then you must sing and play for me one day.'

'I would be honored, Your Highness.'

'What's your name?'

'Manuel,' said the boy.

'And your surname, Manuel?' Now that his face had been at the window of the coach for some time, the boy looked tantalizingly familiar.

'Godoy,' said the youth.

'Now that really is too much of a coincidence,' Maria Luisa replied a little breathlessly. 'We recently had a guardsman called Luis Godoy.'

The boy hesitated. 'He's my brother. There was a scandal . . . with a lady-in-waiting . . . Luis is no longer with the Guards.'

Maria Luisa admired the boy's tact. It had been no lady-in-waiting, but herself. The guardsman Luis Godoy had been discreetly exiled.

Maria Luisa smiled, showing her gold teeth. 'I'm glad you

237

had your little accident, Manuel Godoy. Otherwise we might never have met.'

The two countesses exchanged glances.

The boy bowed again, dug in his spurs, and raced off to join the outriders.

The second controversial guest on the Duchess of Osuna's list, Doña Maria Teresa Cayetana Manuela, etc., etc., to a total of thirty-one names, Duchess of Alba, Countess of Huéscar, Marquesa of Oropesa, was crying.

The shutters were closed and the vast bedroom at the Alba summer palace of Piedrahita was almost dark. Under the blue velvet canopy of her high bed, Cayetana tossed restlessly, naked in the heat of the late afternoon, her curly black hair spread in disarray on the pillow. Despite her tears, she was incredibly beautiful – the huge, dark eyes under arched black brows, the classic nose, the creamy whiteness of her skin, the enticing full lips – it was, Madrileños said, the most beautiful face in Spain. They could only guess at her body, or dream about it. It would not have disappointed them: the same creamy skin, the firm, pink-tipped breasts, the waist that a man could span with his two hands, the flat belly and rounded haunches and long slender legs; it was a body to drive a man wild.

Any man but her husband, Cayetana told herself.

Don José Antonio Alvarez de Toledo, Marqués de Villafranca and now, through marriage to Cayetana, thirteenth Duke of Alba, had left his wife's bedroom ten minutes ago. She had enticed him there; enticing was often necessary with the duke. She liked making love in the lazy hours of the afternoon. Afternoon or night, Villafranca would, much of the time, make excuses instead of love. He was a pale man, effetely handsome, nobly inbred. He loved poetry and music (he maintained a lively correspondence with the Austrian composer Haydn); he had a mildly trenchant wit and a kindly disposition. He adored his wife.

Adoring her and satisfying her were not the same thing, thought Cayetana.

Villafranca had joined her in the bedroom and drawn the shutters. He had undressed with his neat, graceful economy of motion while she stripped off her dress and her underclothes as fast as she could, tossing them anywhere. She was in a fey mood. She wanted to frolic, but the duke was not one to frolic, at lovemaking or anything. A very earnest man, cul-

238

tivated, charming – and languid. So languid.

He had embraced his wife with a sigh. He had barely been able to perform the necessary act – a quick and partial penetration by his limp little thing, a few moments of agitated motion, another languid sigh, and it was over. He dressed with the same neat graceful economy of motion and left Cayetana's bedroom, almost tiptoeing out. At the door he blew her a kiss. She could see his face then. He looked relieved.

No doubt, she thought, he's in the conservatory now, playing the violin. With passion.

He never brought passion to her bed. He never had, not even in the beginning. They had been married thirteen years, half Cayetana's life. He was well-meaning. He tried to please his wife because he knew that that glorious body of hers needed satisfaction. But she needed more – a kind of restrained brutality, something Villafranca could never give her.

Thirteen years, she thought.

Cayetana de Alba, even at thirteen, had been the commoners' favorite noblewoman. Often she could be seen on the streets of Madrid clothed as a maja. She had a madcap sense of humor. Once, shortly after her marriage, she left the family's Buenavista Palace dressed in gypsy rags to wander unattended through the blacksmiths' quarter. She returned triumphantly with a handful of copper coins.

'I can always earn my way, you see,' the thirteen-year-old girl told her husband with an arch smile.

He told her her little joke was unseemly.

Her father died when she was seven. She could still remember the church and the black-lined casket and how small her father had looked in it. She could remember the two rooms in the ducal palace, draped in black and white baize, where her mother received condolence visits, the visitors perched uncomfortably on white straw seats. She remembered most of all the dazzlingly white gloves of the pages who lighted the Mass and the vigil.

Her mother had remarried, still in her thirties, Marianita de Huéscar she was called. She had been as lovely as her daughter and had won the heart of a wealthy confirmed bachelor.

Her mother was dead now too. She had no one. No one.

Perhaps if they'd had a child, she and Villafranca –

But no child had been born to them.

She had loved her grandfather most, that crusty old duque-general. He understood her. His restrained arrogance matched her youthful exuberance. He died of dropsy a year after her

239

marriage.

Twenty-six, she thought.

Like a bird in a cage, fluttering its wings helplessly against delicate golden bars.

She knew that Villafranca, that wan, well-intentioned, urbane man, would not mind an occasional affair, and she had them. He never quite said it – he could not, he had too much pride – but they removed the burden of her passion from him.

The latest was the bullfighter Pepe Hillo. He was in love with her wildly, as wildly as he fought the bulls. She did not know what love was. The cool, distant relationship, passionless but tranquil, with Villafranca? The excitement of the bullring beyond the Alcalá gate, screaming herself hoarse for Hillo, all the while gripped by a terrible fear that he might be hurt? The wild abandon in his arms afterwards?

Love? What did she know of love?

Sometimes she believed she loved places more than people. The sheltered valley here at Pidrahita, or the sanctuary of Doñana in Andalucía, with its dazzling salt marshes and the call of a wild sea bird, a call which seemed to say I'm free I'm free I'm free –

At last, in her canopied bed, she slept fitfully and dreamed of her own death.

Once a gypsy in Cádiz had looked at her hand and gravely shaken her head. The gypsy never knew she was telling the fortune of a young duchess.

'Live, child. Live while you can. You'll see no old age.'

With those dark gypsy eyes probing into her eyes as if reading the secret of the day of her death.

She cried. She was sixteen then, married three years. Villafranca was at the ducal palace studying the score of a new sonata. He was not to be interrupted at his music. She could not go to him in her terror. She wandered the streets of the city. She went down to the harbor. She met a fisherman, just a boy really, and shared his wine and his bed with him. It was the first time. He had been awed by her beauty, clumsy, eager but hard, beautifully hard like tempered steel.

That night she had wept in Villafranca's arms. He never knew why.

You'll see no old age.

There had been others. Brief affairs for an incognito duchess. They had meant nothing.

Until Pepe Hillo.

She awoke with a start. In her dream she had fallen and fal-

240

len and fallen and become smaller and smaller and smaller, until she was no longer there.

Tonight she would go to Hillo.

And the third guest?

Paco Goya, as the Duchess of Osuna had observed, had put on weight. But at forty he was solidly built rather than fleshy, and his massive shoulders could carry that weight, even if it sometimes did leave him a little breathless rushing up a flight of stairs.

He stepped down from his landau at the royal palace – a fine coach but rather conservative with its two mules and black leather seats. His new coach, a rakish birlocho complete with Italian coachman named Luigi and a pair of spirited horses, was on its way from Barcelona. He couldn't wait. Any day now and he'd be racing through the streets of Madrid in style. Eyes would turn. That's Goya. Painter to the king. Look at the man. Dressed like that, and the coach and horses! And he began just like you and me. Decorating the Alameda for the Duke of Osuna these days.

Paints all day and all night. All night? The cognoscenti knew how. They had seen Paco's latest self-portrait, a cocky smile in those hooded eyes and on those full lips, and that strange hat with candles all around the brim to light the canvas.

Always painting?

Well, maybe. But if so he can squeeze forty hours into every day, because when was the last time you saw him squiring La Caramba herself about town? I did last week. And the week before. Caramba! And the week before that. That arrogant, sexy La Caramba, who somehow manages to seem subdued on his arm.

If Cayetana de Alba was the commoners' favorite noblewoman, Paco Goya, painter to the king, was their favorite man about town.

He dressed rather too elaborately, his frock coat brocaded like a bullfighter's, his doeskin breeches tight over muscular legs, his tricorn hat worn at a jaunty angle. As if to say, look at me, and I dare you to do better.

That afternoon he was dressed more conservatively in tan frock coat and black breeches. The tricorn sat squarely on the powdered wig that court protocol called for. He'd had some difficulty stuffing his long dark hair under the wig.

He waited while two palace lackeys took the draped canvas

from his landau. 'Careful,' he said in his deep and rumbling voice. 'That's a portrait of the king.'

'Yes, Your Excellency.'

They were careful. They followed him up the broad staircase to the first landing, where Paco turned right and continued up the narrower stairs, their balustrades adorned with marble lions. This brought him into the Hall of Guardsmen, where he was asked his business.

'Francisco Goya to see the king,' said Paco offhandedly, as if Francisco Goya saw the king every day. The guardsman saluted and let him pass.

He strode rapidly through the Hall of Columns, sculpture-filled and at this hour of the afternoon crowded with petitioners waiting hopefully for a moment in the royal presence, a moment that Paco would not have to wait for at all.

The king had sat for him – or rather stood – just one hour, at the Casa del Campo across the Manzanares River. After that a model had donned the royal hunting garb.

'Don Paco,' the king had said, 'I'm an old man, I was never pretty, I'm certainly not pretty now. I want you to paint me as I am. Once Mengs, God rest his soul, painted me like a waxen image of a king in a suit of armor. Armor, for heaven's sake! It was a good painting, I suppose, but it wasn't me.'

The lackeys were carrying a painting of an old man, never pretty and certainly not pretty now. Paco began to wonder if he had gone too far. Did the king really want to see himself, at seventy, a homely, stoop-shouldered, bowlegged old man?

Five minutes later Paco was sure that the king did not. A mistake, he told himself. Surely his painting had been a mistake. He wouldn't be the first painter to the king whose tenure lasted just long enough for one portrait.

There he stood in the *saleta,* surrounded by mahogany consoles and elaborate clocks and gold candelabra held by gilded Winged Victories. And there stood King Carlos, dressed most royally now, and on one wall hung the Mengs portrait of the king, all red velvet and armor and a Grecian column and the king holding his scepter. Carlos himself, the flattering correctness of the Mengs portrait, the knowledge of how he had painted the king – all convinced Paco that Carlos would take one look at the canvas and send him packing. The king he had painted was no king at all.

Sweeping off his tricorn and bowing, he kissed the royal right hand while the lackeys propped the large canvas against the wall on which the Mengs hung.

'A fine day, Don Paco,' said the king.

'Perhaps, Your Majesty. You haven't seen the portrait yet.'

The king glanced from Paco's face to the Mengs and back again. He chuckled. With a wave of his hand he ordered the lackeys to undrape the canvas.

He stood some distance from it. His keen eyes, deepset now in wrinkled folds of skin, studied the painting. He scowled.

What he saw was an old man wearing an ill-fitting slate gray hunting coat over a yellow waistcoat with the royal blue silk sash crossing it, and a pair of high soft leather boots. He held a white glove in his bare right hand instead of the Bourbon scepter and his gloved left hand gripped the barrel of a flintlock musket. At his feet lazed a white dog. A faintly impish smile sparkled in his eyes. He wore his black tricorn at a rakish angle.

The king took a step closer to the canvas. He took another step, and another. The closer he came, the more his face resembled the face Paco had painted. By the time he stood at arm's length from the canvas, king and portrait bore identical impish smiles.

They were the same man.

'Yes, Don Paco,' said the king at last with a sigh. 'I really must have a new coat fitted, don't you think?'

'Your Majesty is not pleased?'

'And would you be pleased with this face, a handsome young fellow like you?' demanded the king testily.

Paco could think of no adequate answer.

'Look at Mengs' portrait,' said Carlos with a fierce scowl.

Obediently Paco looked.

'It's very much in the tradition of royal portraits, sire.'

'As yours is not?' Still with that fierce scowl.

'I – suppose not, sire.'

'You suppose not? Indeed it *is* not.'

Paco said nothing. It's going to be bad, he thought. It's going to be worse than I expected.

But the impish smile returned to Carlos' eyes. 'And thank God for that. It's an honest portrait.'

A bow, and a feeling of weakness in the knees. Paco wanted to rush home and tell Josefa and Doña Engracia. But the king, unexpectedly, wanted to talk.

'I imagine we can keep Count Floridablanca waiting a few more minutes,' he said. 'A sherry?'

'Why, thank you, Your Majesty.'

The king sat wearily and waved Paco into a chair. Sherry was brought on a silver tray.

The king sipped. Paco sipped. The king said: 'Floridablanca never did pay you for that portrait of his, did he?'

'No, sire.'

Was there anything that escaped the attention of this bent old septuagenarian of a king? Paco wondered.

'Well, no matter. You'll be a rich man soon. Prince Carlos loves the way you paint. Though someday that honesty of yours may be too much for him.'

'I hope not, sire.'

'I'll never know in any event. I'll be long dead.' The king snorted. 'They have me dead already, damn them all.' He seemed surprised by his own mild profanity; he shook his head and crossed himself. 'The court. Always currying favor with the crown prince, as if I'd been put to rest in the vaults of the Escorial already. I'm tired, Don Paco. I'm tired of counts and dukes and marqueses fawning before my son, and I could do without his impatience. He's almost as eager to be king as Maria Luisa is to be queen. Still, who can blame any of them? I'm a dour old man. They'll bring life to the court, or she will. He'll hunt all day and they'll dance all night. He'll be a far more popular monarch than I've ever managed to be. But I've done what I could for Spain.'

Paco, listening to the ramblings of the disillusioned old man, was astonished that he could feel pity for a king. It taught him something about Carlos, who had never really been popular, no more with the commoners than with the nobility, and it taught him something about himself. If his awe of the king could give way to pity, there were no circles in Madrid in which he would not feel free to move.

'Horses,' said the king, his mind wandering.

'Sire?'

'Two superb white horses, perfectly matched. Brought from England by King George's ambassador as a gift for me. But he took one look at the king, and one look at the crown prince, and decided he wasn't sure which Carlos the gift was intended for. Do you know what I told him?'

'No, sire.'

' "I'm old, I don't ride much these days; give 'em to Prince Carlos." So the ambassador bows and scrapes and smiles and goes to Carlos with his damned horses.' The king crossed himself again. ' "Two superb white steeds for Your Highness," he tells the crown prince. "A gift from King George." And the

244

Prince of the Asturias, God bless him this once, says, "Yes, my father the king told me to expect them." Which I had.'

Carlos eased himself out of his chair. Paco stood.

'I've enjoyed this talk, Don Paco. The court, damn them – ' no crossing himself this time – 'listen with a glazed look in their eyes. When will the old curmudgeon shut up? When will the old curmudgeon have the decency to die? When can we dance on his grave?   '

Paco said nothing. His pity had become embarrassment.

'How difficult, how incredibly difficult it is to find an honest man. Or an honest painter.'

The embarrassment became pleasure.

'Court appointments are in the crown prince's hands these days,' said Carlos. 'I want him to make decisions. It's not his strong point. What will you do when he names you first painter to the king? Because one day he will.'

'I'd be honored, Your Majesty.'

'Be honest instead. A dishonest artist is as bad as a dishonest politician. Do you realize Spain's produced only two great painters in all her long history? And one of them, come to think of it, was born Greek. Yet El Greco painted from the depths of the Spanish soul, Don Paco. A religious man. A very religious man. Are you?'

'To be honest, sire, I – '

The king waved the answer aside with a bony hand. 'And Velázquez. Pride, the pride of empire in the Century of Gold, wouldn't you say?'

'With perhaps a touch of cynicism, sire.'

'Exactly. With a touch of cynicism. That's good. The pride that goes before a fall needs a cynic to interpret it, and Velázquez was that man. And you? Not the religious mystic and not the proud cynic – what sort of Spain will you paint?'

'Wouldn't that depend on Spain, Your Majesty?'

The king turned on him sharply. 'Then open your eyes and keep them open. You'll see a time of turmoil, of despair and anarchy, of pigheaded politicians leading us into wars I've tried to avoid. You'll see the dark side of the Spanish soul emerging, the bloodlust of the bullring spilling into the streets of Madrid. You'll see the land ravaged. You'll see a time of madness. Will you paint that?'

An old man at the end of his reign, Paco thought, at the end of his life, all his hopes unrealized, all his illusions shattered, naturally his thoughts would turn to gloom and madness. And yet –

King Carlos sounded anything but mad.
'Will you paint it?'
'If I see it.'
'You'll see it,' said Carlos.

CHAPTER TWENTY-ONE

A Certain Arrogant Elegance

JOSEFA COULD HEAR the Italian coachman Luigi shouting instructions to Paco in that excitable voice of his. Every few
minutes the new coach, the high, black, two-wheeled, rickety-
looking birlocho, would go thundering by drawn by two fine
dappled horses and spewing a cloud of dust along the unpaved
river road.

They were living that summer in a small house with a
walled garden on the edge of the Manzanares with a good
stretch of country on either side where poplars and willows
grew.

Josefa was sitting in the garden with two-year-old Javier
who was proudly stomping back and forth on his little legs, as
if he too were learning a new means of transportation. The
boy, with his long face and fair hair, looked more a Bayeu
than a Goya. Paco spoiled him terribly, and so did Doña Engracia, who had been living with them since the death of José
Goya.

The old woman came into the garden. 'Well, and has he
broken that fool neck of his yet?'

Josefa laughed. 'Not yet, mother. I really think he's master-
ing it.'

'He's rich. He's richer than his father ever dreamed possible,
the Good Lord rest his soul. What's he need that two-wheeled
contraption for? We have a landau in the stables, and a gilded
berlin. We have a coachman and three servants and a brace of
mules and I can't keep track of what else. He's always buying
things. A two-wheeled – what do they call it?'

'Birlocho, mother.'

'Birlocho. To break his neck in.'

In her early sixties, Doña Engracia looked older. Her face

was as creased and puckered as a shriveled apple.

'For his image, mother. There are only three birlochos in all Madrid.'

'His image? Then I'd suggest he eat a little less. He's putting on too much weight. His image,' the old woman snorted.

Javier toddled up to her and hugged a leg under the long black dress. 'G'ama,' he said, and Doña Engracia smiled and forgot all about the two-wheeled coach that came hurtling back and forth along the river road dragging its cloud of dust.

His image indeed, thought Josefa. Though she had kept her youthful good looks, there was an expression of sad resignation in her clear hazel eyes. The house on the river was small; Paco's studio was half a mile away. She hardly ever saw him these days.

The medal, she thought. That awful, spitefully given and foolishly accepted medal. Had it started then? Was it all her fault? It had dealt Paco's pride a terrible blow, and he had been distant ever since.

One night last spring when Paco hadn't returned home at all, she had been unable to sleep. Taking the medal from its velvet-lined box, she had gone outside and hurled it into the river. For being a Bayeu, she had thought bitterly. But I'm not a Bayeu now. I'm the Señora de Goya. How I want to be the Señora de Goya in more than name!

She had cried herself to sleep that night. Paco never learned what she had done with the silver medal, so foolishly accepted so long ago in Zaragoza.

The symbolic act hadn't helped. She had the house to take care of, and their son. Paco had his friends.

Not that he wasn't busy working. Ever since his summer with the king's brother Don Luis all the nobility wanted him to paint their portraits. Most of them had to wait. Paco had reached the point in his career where he could pick and choose, and he reveled in it.

He also reveled in his new life.

The rather too elaborately dressed man about town. Friend of the banker Cabarrús. He had painted Cabarrús' portrait and the portraits of all the other directors of the Banco Nacional. It was to them now rather than to Martín Zapater that he turned for suggestions about investing his money. Josefa had no idea how much he earned. His salary as painter to the king came to fifteen thousand reales, and he often earned almost as much for a single portrait. The Duke and Duchess of Osuna had paid him an enormous sum to decorate the walls of

247

their summer palace. It was rumored that Villafranca, Duke of Alba, wanted him to do his portrait. With Spain's two leading noble families behind him, how far might he go? Santa Maria, thought Josefa, they would become rich beyond her wildest dreams.

And she would see less and less of Paco.

The play at the Alameda tonight, with all Madrid there including the Princess of the Asturias. Paco would go, in that new birlocho of his. Josefa would stay home. And all the highborn ladies would cluster around, fluttering their fans, begging him to paint their portraits.

How different from her brother Francisco, Josefa thought as the coach came by again with Paco at the reins. Francisco, austere, still a bachelor with simple tastes, given to mouthing platitudes, director of painting at the Academy – he worked as hard as Paco did and never dreamed of the high life though the doors of all the ducal palaces in Spain were open to him.

Wasn't Francisco the better painter?

She no longer knew. Madrid no longer knew.

Madrid, particularly Madrid society, was not interested in scenes of domestic tranquility. A wife was someone you left at home. A wife was a convenience, like a comfortable chair beside the hearth, like well-worn slippers.

Was it Venturo Rodríguez who had introduced Paco to the king's brother? Or Count Floridablanca? It hardly mattered. Both their wives liked Paco, as the Duchess of Osuna did, and only Santa Maria herself knew who else.

Paco, lately, had been squiring around that foul-mouthed singer La Caramba. Squiring her around, thought Josefa. She would never allow herself to imagine Paco in bed with another woman.

The affair with La Caramba was ending. Josefa could tell. Even more interest in the child, if that were possible, a pleasanter disposition in his rare appearances at the dinner table, an increased ardor in bed with her. But there would be others. There would always be others. Paco wanted to grab life, all of life, and shake it in his two strong talented hands.

The medal. Always it came back to the medal. Josefa could accept Paco's infidelities if she blamed herself.

And Paco? Once he had told her: 'Since you can't live forever, there's only one way to live. Crowd everything into the years you have '

If nothing else, Paco was trying.

To crowd forever into sixty or seventy years.

Now, sweaty but with a broad smile on his face, he came in through the garden gate. 'Nothing to it,' he said. 'Luigi's a good teacher.'

The Italian coachman bowed. 'Thank you, Excellency.'

'No, I thank you, Luigi. I'll be taking the birlocho out to the Osunas' this evening.'

'Perhaps I'd better come,' Luigi suggested. 'Begging your pardon, but you had a little trouble on the turns, Excellency.'

Paco shook his head and casually tossed Luigi a few reales. 'Have yourself a night on the town. Find yourself a maja. Far better than waiting in a carriage park all night.'

'As Your Excellency wishes,' said Luigi with another bow.

Find yourself a maja, thought Josefa. And how many times had Paco done precisely that?

But still, despite it all, on their Sunday paseos she would see heads turn and hear voices say, 'That's Goya, painter to the king,' and her own head would swell with pride. Her brother Francisco, for all his success, could walk from one end of Madrid to the other without being recognized.

And there were the rare moments when Paco would take her in his arms after some particularly difficult work and say, 'Cara, you make it all possible. You're the whole world, right here.'

She lived for those moments. They gave her atonement for the medal, so blithely, so stubbornly, so ruinously accepted.

Paco lifted little Javier high, hurled him, caught him under the arms. The boy screamed with delight.

'What's that he's wearing?' Paco asked Josefa.

The boy was wearing a red silk suit with wide pantaloons.

'The suit you bought him last week,' Josefa said.

'Buy him others. Every color of the rainbow. We're not exactly poor.'

'Rainbow,' repeated the precocious boy. 'Buy me a rainbow.'

Doña Engracia made a noise that sounded like grrmph.

'Paco,' said Josefa, 'you're going to spoil him.'

'Good. It'll give him self-confidence.'

'Or self-indulgence.'

'There's no security in an artist's life, cara. Get him everything. Live high while you can.'

'And make a pauper of yourself one of these years,' warned Doña Engracia. 'Or kill yourself in that contraption out there. See if we care. I'm only your mother. Josefa's only your wife.'

Paco planted a big smacking kiss on her wrinkled cheek.

249

'Care or don't care, I still love you, Doña Engracia.'

'Oh, you.' With a reluctant smile.

'There. That's better, mamacita. Come to think of it, you could use some new clothes yourself. There's a Parisian modiste who works for the Osuna – '

'I have three black dresses and they are quite enough, thank you,' Doña Engracia said firmly. '*I* don't have to impress anyone.'

'A rainbow,' Javier said. 'Buy me a rainbow.'

In his bottle green, gold-brocaded frock coat, a white carnation in his lapel, Paco sat high on the black birlocho, urging the horses on, grinning as he passed a landau or a berlin drawn by mules on the road to the Alameda. He risked taking one hand from the reins to wave. Hands waved back.

It was a beautiful evening, cool for September, with the sun setting and a lingering mauve light on the few scattered clouds in the west.

The birlocho swayed from side to side every time Paco shifted his weight. He felt he was flying, a *baturro* boy from Aragon flying high in Madrid, on his way to visit a duke and a duchess. Perhaps, he thought, Cean Bermúdez would be there. Cean Bermúdez, the most influential art critic in Madrid. And who else? Why, everyone. Everyone that mattered. He flicked the reins and, on the narrow road, boldly raced past an elaborately gilded berlin. On the door he saw the coat of arms of the Duke of Alba.

After that he had the road to himself. The sky darkened. He debated stopping to light the sidelamps, but he knew the road well. He had been this way dozens of times. A single sharp right turn to come, another quarter of a mile and he'd be there.

He pulled back on the reins for the turn. The dappled horses, at full gallop, surged powerfully forward. He pulled back with all the strength of his shoulders, but still approached the turn too fast.

He could feel the two-wheeled coach tipping to the left, and then tipping further, and then going up on one wheel, and suddenly he was off the box, the reins torn from his hands as he hurtled through the air.

Baturro boy flying high in Madrid –

The coach tumbled into the ditch alongside the road. A horse whinnied. He could see the spokes of the wheel flashing, faintly mauve in the cloud-reflected sunlight. He landed hard on his side and rolled over and over. The ground, the still-

250

bright horizon, the dark sky went flashing by. Pain lanced agonizingly through his left leg.

For a few moments he remembered nothing.

Then he found himself seated in the ditch. He took in great gulps of air. He felt something moist trickling from his clubbed and powdered hair. He raised a hand and touched blood. One sleeve of his bottle green frock coat was torn from elbow to cuff. He was covered with dust. He tried to stand. The pain lanced through his leg worse than before. He tried again.

Gritting his teeth, he stood.

He spent a few seconds cursing the two dappled horses. They stood, still in the traces, their legs trembling. The coach had fallen on its side. He braced his one good leg and heaved. He succeeded in lifting the coach partially, but then it fell back.

Light as a feather, Luigi had said. Luigi, he thought, ought to try lifting it.

And then he laughed. I could have been killed, he told himself. He laughed wildly. He found his tricorn hat and used it to dust himself off. The trickle of blood on his forehead had stopped. He wiped at the blood with a silk handkerchief.

The laughter trickled off too.

How can I go there looking like this? he thought.

How can I not?

He heard hoofbeats and saw the glowing sidelamps of an approaching carriage. Drawn by four mules, it slowed to a stop.

It was the Alba berlin.

The footmen jumped down. 'Is Your Excellency all right?'

'I think I'm still alive,' he grumbled.

They set their shoulders to the birlocho, two lithe young men. They could not budge it. The door of the berlin opened and one of the footmen rushed over to put down the step.

Cayetana, Duchess of Alba, climbed down.

'Who is it?' she asked.

'A stupid imbecile who thought he knew how to drive this contraption,' Paco said.

'What stupid imbecile?' asked the Duchess of Alba.

One of the footmen brought a lamp.

'Why, you're bleeding.'

'It's nothing.'

The lamp was close to his face. He could see her only as a dim, shadowy figure.

'Goya, isn't it?'

251

He admitted his identity.

'You don't have to snap at me.'

'I'm sorry, Your Grace. It's the horses. I would very much like to kill the horses.'

Suddenly Cayetana de Alba was giggling. 'If you could see yourself. You look like a chimneysweep.'

'Very funny. Your Grace.'

'I'm sorry. I shouldn't have. . . . ' She made an odd strangling sound. Paco realized she was trying her best not to laugh.

'What is that coach, anyway?' she asked.

'Birlocho. Only three in Madrid. I'm beginning to wish there were only two.'

This time he joined in her laughter.

'Get it out of the ditch,' she told the footmen.

'We tried, Your Grace. We can't.'

'Are you still going to the party, Señor Chimneysweep? *I* would. Make quite an entrance.'

'Or a quick exit, when the Osuna gets a look at me.'

'Why don't we find out? You can ride with me.'

'No,' said Paco firmly. 'I started out in this thing and by God I'm going to get there in this thing.'

Laughter again. He liked the sound of it. He wished he could see her better.

'What? On its side?'

He hobbled to the coach and heaved with all his strength. It teetered for a moment and settled upright on its wheels.

'You're very strong.'

'Only when I'm angry.'

'And very funny.'

'Only when I'm angry.'

'Then I must learn how to make you angry.' She came closer and he could smell her perfume. Jasmine. Like Mariana. 'Remember a day in the patio de caballos?' she asked. 'Years ago. I was a little girl. My grandfather brought me.'

He remembered it vaguely.

'Juanito Apiñani was fighting. You sketched him for me. I said then I didn't know whether I was going to like you or hate you.'

'Yes,' Paco said, grinning. 'I remember now. Have you made up your mind?'

She mounted the step of the berlin.

'Oh, yes. I've made up my mind,' she said.

Ripples and eddies and tides of color swirled through the

ballroom of the Alameda.

Madrid society, aping the French, dressed in a wild extravagance of hues and tones. The mocking names given to even the most minute gradations of color were even more extravagant. From brown to purple the range of hues included young flea, old flea, flea's head, flea's back, flea's belly, flea's leg and consumptive flea. In the range from yellow to green, colors were called kitchen sink, street filth, nymph's leg, monk's belly, Carmelite's belly, poisoned monkey, moribund monkey, merry widow, sad sweetheart, resuscitated dead man.

The Duchess of Osuna herself, seated on a dais to greet her guests, wore a striped and embroidered transparent silk summer coat with satin collar, bow and facing in nymph's leg green. Her silk gown was moribund monkey with darker braid and tassels and a fringed sash of deep green. It was a flowing feminine costume on a knife-blade of a woman.

The men, if anything, were even more elaborately dressed. The duchess' portly husband wore a habit à la française; his silk embroidered summer frock coat was sad sweetheart, his waistcoat a shade or two lighter, perhaps poisoned monkey, his hair powdered, clubbed and held in back with a black velvet ribbon. A white silk cravat, a lingerie shirt, two watch fobs, a felt tricorn fringed with ostrich feathers which he carried under one arm, fawn breeches, silk stockings, buckled black kid shoes, and a ceremonial sword completed his costume. He had taken longer to dress than the duchess.

When the major-domo called out: 'Her Grace Doña Maria Teresa Cayetana, Duchess of Alba,' into that sea of finery came Cayetana wearing the simple black skirt and gold blouse of a maja. Her thick and lustrous black hair hung loose almost to her waist and her enormous dark eyes sparkled as she went straight to the dais to kiss the Osuna on both cheeks.

'I'm sorry I'm late. There was an accident on the road.'

'I hope nothing serious, cousin,' said the Osuna in her deeper voice.

The members of the oldest grandee families of Spain, perhaps a hundred of them, called one another cousin. They had the right to call the king cousin too, a right which they rarely exercised.

'Serious?' said Cayetana. 'Oh no, it was rather amusing.'

'You didn't pass Don Tomás on the road by any chance?'

'Yriarte? No. Isn't he here?'

'He's never late for one of his own performances. I'm a little concerned.'

'Oh, he probably stopped to dally with a maja.'

'Cayetana, can't you ever be serious?'

'Who has the time to be serious, cousin?'

Cayetana left the dais just as Princess Maria Luisa was announced. As ever, the Alba's timing was perfect. With a secret little smile she curtseyed and swept by the false-teethed, sallow-faced, plump Princess of the Asturias. No one noticed the princess.

In a matter of seconds, her fan fluttering – it was a gift from Pepe Hillo – Cayetana found herself the focus of a group of courtly admirers. Pepe Hillo shouldered his way through, bowed and boldly said: 'Hola, cara.'

'Cara, matador? Surely you must mean some other maja.'

Pepe Hillo's round, handsome face darkened. Madrid society knew of their liaison, but Cayetana always pretended it was a secret. Pepe Hillo was a passionate and passionately jealous man.

He put on and swept off his tricorn in an exaggerated bow. 'Sometimes we bullfighters can't keep track of our majas, Your Grace.'

Cayetana rewarded him with a smile and a 'touché, matador' before turning to Cean Bermúdez. 'Don Agustín, have you seen the Goya panels yet?'

Agustín Cean Bermúdez, the doyen of Madrid's art critics, who could make or break a painter with a favorable or an acerbic paragraph in the Madrid *Gazette,* nodded eagerly. He was a tall man whose protuberant eyes almost seemed to pop from his head when he was excited. His eyes were popping considerably now.

'The man could be a genius,' he said.

'Well, is he or isn't he?'

'There's nothing he couldn't do, Your Grace. Nothing. He's already demolished the tyranny of line with those short brush strokes of his, and nobody uses color better. But he's – restrained. How old's the man, forty?'

'I would have thought younger,' said the Duchess of Alba. 'He looks younger.' She had said somewhat more than she wanted to say. Her fan fluttered. Pepe Hillo watched her closely, the way he watched a bull before the kill.

Bermúdez's eyes popped again. 'Damn me – begging Your Grace's pardon – the man could be the equal of Velázquez or El Greco. It's infuriating.'

'That he could?'

'That he won't let himself. It comes too easily on him. He

needs something to goad him – anger, perhaps.'

'Anger? It's funny you should say that.'

'Why, Your Grace?'

A small smile touched that perfect mouth. The fan snapped shut. 'No reason, I suppose. I really don't know much about painting.'

She took Pepe Hillo's arm. 'Now bullfighting, there's another matter. I could spend forever in the plaza de toros – with our Hillo fighting. Are you angry when you face the bulls, Hillo?'

'I'd better be. Because, believe me, they're angrier.'

Bermúdez excused himself to greet his hostess. Cayetana and Pepe Hillo found themselves alone for a moment.

'I didn't realize you knew Goya,' Hillo said.

'Oh, I hardly know him. In fact, we just met. Stop sulking. I don't like it when you sulk. Goya's a friend of yours, isn't he?'

'We meet occasionally. At Juanito Apiñani's. He's a lusty fellow.'

'Who? Apiñani?'

'Goya.'

'Well, you lusty fellows ought to have something in common.'

'Something, yes. Not someone.'

'You seem determined to put ideas into my head.'

'That wasn't my intention.'

'I'm very suggestible. You ought to know.'

'All right. All right. Goya and I are friends. Good friends. I'd like to keep it that way, cara.'

Her fan tapped the sleeve of his brocaded jacket. 'Isn't that up to you and Goya?'

'Perhaps,' said Pepe Hillo, and then the princess and her two ladies-in-waiting approached them.

'Cousin,' said the beautiful young duchess to the dowdy princess, 'you look positively ravishing this evening. Doesn't she, Hillo?'

'And you, my dear, look like a delectable little tidbit of a maja.'

'To the manner born, you know,' said Cayetana.

Hillo stifled a laugh. He bowed to the princess and kissed air an inch above her plump hand. 'When will you dedicate a bull to me, Hillo?' she asked.

'The next time I fight, and with pleasure, Highness.'

'He's quite a man, our Hillo,' said the princess. She has

some difficulty with her false teeth. She made a sucking sound. 'As you ought to know better than anyone, my dear,' she said and swept off with her ladies-in-waiting.

'Why, that frowsy, hypocritical, royal bitch,' said Cayetana. Then she smiled radiantly. 'But I do *so* love her teeth. The poor thing hates to dine in public, you know. I really do feel so sorry for her.'

'I'm sure you do,' said Pepe Hillo. 'Cat.'

'Not a nice little kitten, all purry?'

'Cat and you know it.'

'And you love it.'

'Yes,' said Hillo, and it was all right between them again.

Except that Cayetana realized she was waiting impatiently for the arrival of Paco Goya.

A liveried servant stood before the dais on which the Duchess of Osuna still sat. He was pale. He cleared his throat. 'Your Grace,' he said at last. 'There's someone to see you.'

'Who is it, Diego?'

'From the Santo,' said the servant Diego in a frightened whisper.

'The Inquisition? How extraordinary.'

The duchess rose and strode rapidly through the ballroom, an artificial smile on her narrow face. She saw the Princess of the Asturias and her ladies-in-waiting sipping champagne – that marvelous new wine all the rage in Paris – from silver goblets. The princess caught her eye. 'Where's your Yriarte, cousin? We're all awaiting his play most eagerly.'

Was the princess' tone faintly mocking? Was there a glint of triumph in the small, close-set eyes?

The Osuna fanned herself. 'He'll be here.'

'Of course he will, my dear. No playwright is ever late for one of his own performances – unless he's met with a catastrophe. Let's hope nothing has happened to your Tomás.'

Dressed in green, the messenger of the Holy Office of the Inquisition was seated in the antechamber. He rose and bowed. 'Your Grace.'

'What do you want?' snapped the duchess. Under Carlos III those who could call the king cousin had little to fear from the Inquisition.

'The playwright Don Tomás de Yriarte sends his regrets, Your Grace, but he is unavoidably detained. Naturally, Your Grace will be discreet about this matter.'

256

'The Santo is holding Yriarte?'

'He has business with the qualifiers, yes, Your Grace. A matter of possible heresy. I remind Your Grace again that in such a situation discretion is essential.'

It was so essential, in fact, the duchess knew, that even those brought before the qualifiers had to keep their fears secret until the charges were formally lodged or dropped.

In that case, the arrival at the Alameda of this fellow made no sense at all.

Unless someone outside the Holy Office, and more powerful than the Holy Office, had sent him.

To put the play on without Yriarte was one thing, but to go ahead with the performance while he underwent the ordeal of the qualifiers was quite another. It was unthinkable.

The Osuna turned her back rudely on the green-clad messenger and returned to the ballroom.

Maria Luisa? she thought. Would she dare? She spent half her time in bed with her guardsmen – only the prince remained ignorant of that fact – and the other half trying to outdo, or undo, her social rival, the Duchess of Osuna.

But would she dare bring the Holy Office into it?

The duchess, in a cold rage, joined her in the middle of the vast room, where the princess was still sipping champagne.

'Delicious, cousin,' she said, raising her silver goblet. 'How you managed to import it before Carlos, I have no idea.'

The duchess didn't want to accuse her openly. She knew it would be a mistake. The ultimate power, of course, lay in the hands of the princess. She could, if her hand were forced, banish the Osuna from court. Revealing the secrets of the Santo would be reason enough. But for once the duchess's sang-froid had deserted her.

'If Your Highness would allow me a moment in private.'

'Why, of course, cousin.' Sweetly. Too sweetly.

Calm, thought the Duchess of Osuna. You must keep your calm. But she knew she had lost it.

The princess finished her champagne in an unladylike gulp. She seemed eager.

'The library?' suggested the duchess.

The two women began to make their way through the crowd.

Just then the major-domo announced: 'His Excellency Don Francisco de Goya y Lucientes, painter to the king.'

The major-domo sounded somewhat baffled.

Into that glittering, crowded ballroom limped a disaster of a man.

Paco had cleaned himself off as best he could. But, his clubbed hair undone and hanging loosely almost to his shoulders, his fine brocaded frock coat torn and still dust-covered, his breeches stained, a fresh trickle of blood oozing from his hairline, he brought a dead silence into the room with him.

For a moment he regretted coming. It was a blunder. He would, he already had, made a fool of himself. It was the Alba's lighthearted urging that had spurred him on. He hated her then.

He bowed low before duchess and princess. 'A small matter of an overturned birlocho, Your Grace,' he brazened it out in his deep voice.

'And have you reprimanded your coachman?'

'I'd have given him hell, Your Grace. Except that I was driving myself.'

'I suppose,' said the Osuna, suppressing a smile, 'we ought to think of a name for the current color of your frock coat.'

'Over-enthusiastic driver?' suggested Paco.

The duchess threw back her head and laughed. Suddenly there was laughter on all sides. For years Goya had had a reputation as a reckless driver.

The duchess felt wonderfully, delightfully amused. Not that Goya was being a buffoon. He had too much presence for that. His sheepish smile and then his shrug and his own roar of laughter were just exactly right, as was his assertion that nobody in possession of his senses would miss an evening at the Alameda.

'Would he, Your Grace?'

'Obviously, *you* wouldn't.'

The duchess had almost committed a terrible blunder, and inadvertently Paco Goya had prevented it. She would remember, and remain in his debt.

The guests stood around the ballroom talking in subdued tones. The talent of Paco Goya, they said. The daring of Pepe Hillo. That one-eyed rascal Tuertillo and the prices he charged for a good barrera seat. The biting wit of Cañuelo, editor of that if-as-and-when newspaper *El Censor,* if it was still publishing and if Cañuelo wasn't in the hands of the Santo by now. Champagne was sipped, and commented on.

Conversation became more desultory. The party needed a spark.

It was supplied by Cayetana.

'Shall I shock them, cousin?' she asked the Osuna.

'Do you ever do anything else?'

'Not if I can help it. Are there musicians?'

'Waiting in the theater.'

'Fetch a guitarist then.'

The guitarist came, and Cayetana produced a pair of castanets. 'Can you play a seguidilla?' she asked.

'Of course, Your Grace.'

'In the taverns of Madrid,' said Cayetana, 'they've recently made some changes. The same rhythm. But slower at first, more seductive. And then faster.'

The guitarist's eyes widened. 'The bolero, Your Grace? You'll dance the bolero here?'

'Why not? Isn't this place as good as a tavern?'

The guitarist struck a chord and found his rhythm. The sound, at first familiar and then not familiar, brought the Osuna's guests gathering around.

'Slower,' said Cayetana. 'As if you wanted to put them in a trance.'

The guitarist tried again. Cayetana smiled a sleepy cat-smile, raised her arms and clacked her castanets once.

Then she began to dance.

Slowly at first, her movements languid, as if she had just stirred from bed. For each step a clack of her castanets. Then, at a signal to the guitarist, imperceptibly faster, that wonderfully lithe body moving with a still languid grace as she went from man to man in the room.

And then faster, and more seductive. A pause here before a marqués, there before a count, and a haughty glare or sometimes a look of open invitation in those enormous dark eyes. A pause before Cean Bermúdez, who flushed to the roots of his hair, his eyes popping, as the castanets clacked and the supple body seemed to stalk him.

A simple rhythm, thought Paco – just three steps, really, repeated over and over, subtly, seductively. But the way she danced it! Not just with her feet. With all of that glorious body, thighs thrusting against black skirt, breasts heaving against gold blouse as the tempo increased, waist bending like a willow in the wind. All of love was in that dance – from first coquetry to indescribable ecstasy to ultimate disillusion.

Still the tempo increased. Faster and faster she whirled. Her eyes became glazed. In a trance, in the same trance that held every man in the room in its spell, she danced.

She whirled before Paco. He could see beads of sweat on her upper lip. He could smell the faint woman scent of her through the jasmine. She suddenly plucked the white carnation from his lapel and placed the stem between her teeth. The castanets clacked at his ear.

Then she leaped.

She was on a table, still dancing, still in a trance, alone now, dancing for herself for the sheer pleasure of it. Faster and faster in a swirling gold and black blur of motion, her skirt swinging wide, her beautiful legs daringly exposed, her steps smaller and smaller, her arms dropping slowly to her sides, her head tilting forward and down, the castanets stilled, that mass of raven-black hair cloaking face and breasts, and it was over. She had made love to every man in the room.

Silence. For a long time silence. And then a swelling roar of bravos.

Cayetana went to Paco and replaced the carnation. She was only a little breathless.

'Good?' she said.

'Not bad,' he said, his voice thick.

'They've been doing it in the taverns for months.'

'Not like that.'

'No. Of course not. But it's still fun. Take me some time?'

Then Pepe Hillo was there. 'Magnificent, cara.'

'Why, thank you, Hillo.'

'Paco,' the bullfighter said. The two men bowed formally.

Cayetana left them. 'Let's dance, all of us,' she urged the Osuna. 'The evening's young. It's glorious.'

The orchestra was brought from the theater. They danced. They danced until morning.

His ankle swollen and aching, Paco watched the stately quadrille, and the even more stately contradanza, the men and women lined up in two long rows, advancing and retreating in slow pantomime of the eternal war between the sexes. He watched the less restrained fandango and the not at all restrained seguidilla.

Soon he found his eyes seeking out Cayetana.

They never said another word to each other that night.

He never stopped watching her.

Santa Maria he kept thinking, duchess or not, I've got to have that one.

CHAPTER TWENTY-TWO

In the Year the King Died

CARLOS III DIED on the fourteenth of December, 1788. His body lay in state for several days in the royal palace before the funeral cortege made its slow way to the Escorial, where the kings of Spain were entombed. All along its route, flowers were strewn in the path of the black coach carrying the bier. A king is always more beloved dead than living.

Then forty years old, the Prince of the Asturias was proclaimed Carlos IV, King of the Two Spains. But the night his father died it was not the new king but his wife Maria Luisa who convened the ministers of the realm.

The year of mourning, she said, would be cut short by the coronation of her husband the following September. December was no time for a coronation in Madrid, when a snowstorm could destroy the glory of the event. She also proposed that, as it had been King Carlos' dying wish, Floridablanca would remain on as first minister. She proposed it, not her husband. The word quickly got around that any 'Yo el Reys' issued by Carlos IV in his broad childish handwriting would be issued *to* the new king by his wife.

In the year the king died, Frederick the Great of Prussia was also laid to rest.

Berber pirates captured a Spanish brigantine laden with gold and silver from New Spain.

What else happened, in the year the king died?

Maria Luisa hastened to order a new wardrobe from Paris.

Haydn, the Duke of Alba's favorite composer, produced lieder for Central Europe's overfed blonde princesses, and continued his lively correspondence with the duke.

The duchess remained what she was at heart, a maja.

Grain was in short supply in France, and bread riots erupted on the streets of Paris. The French treasury collapsed into near-bankruptcy in the year the king died, and his royal cousin Louis XVI convened the States-General for the first time in nearly two centuries.

The new Spanish ambassador to Paris sent dispatches telling of the alarming spread of republican ideas.

In Spain too bread was scarce. The Catalans rose in the streets of Barcelona, and had to be put down by troops from Madrid. Seven ringleaders were hanged.

Maria Luisa's gowns arrived. They cost the Spanish treasury more than the funeral of her father-in-law.

All the chancelleries of Europe looked with interest toward Madrid. Wise and wily, Carlos III had given his potential enemies no advantages they could exploit. His bland, lukewarm son, hiding behind the gowns of Maria Luisa, would be another matter.

Manuel Godoy, that handsome young guardsman from Extremadura, was commissioned a lieutenant.

Lieutenant Godoy cultivated French mannerisms, aping the émigrés among the guardsmen. He neither liked nor trusted the French, but Maria Luisa preferred speaking their language. It was the language of love, she said, and before long they were speaking it in her royal bed. The new King Carlos resumed his hunting parties.

The new queen soon realized she did not like her first minister. Floridablanca was old, he was cranky, he was vacillating – and he was the first member of the court to discover she was cuckolding her husband with a Guards officer more than fifteen years her junior. When Madrid laughed at the anonymous pamphlet ridiculing Floridablanca, Maria Luisa laughed too. Soon there was an armed truce between the count and the queen. He would conduct affairs of state. She would dispense patronage.

In the year the king died, the Inquisition did not remain inactive. Cañuelo, publisher of *El Censor,* was forced to adjure. So was Tomás de Yriarte.

But newspapers aside from the official Madrid *Gazette* continued to appear in Spain. There was the *Correo de Madrid* with its long letters almost as bold as the anonymous pamphlets; there was the *Diario de Madrid,* which popularized the ideas of the French Enlightenment in a way they had never been popularized before.

Both newspapers were eagerly awaited all over Spain. They passed from hand to hand, and for the first time the lights from the north reached any townsman who could read.

Meanwhile, the Dominicans busily prepared a new Index of proscribed books, the first in fifty years.

The edition of the Index would contain three hundred and fifty pages with double columns and small print. Luther was proscribed. Calvin, Erasmus, Rousseau, and Voltaire were proscribed. The works of Dante, Petrarch, Boccaccio, Macchiavelli, and even Cervantes had to be expurgated. *Robinson Crusoe* was forbidden. Astronomers like Tyccho Brahe and Johannes Kepler were forbidden. The sun, after all, still rotated around the earth, and the center of the earth was Madrid.

Jovellanos and Cabarrús, the incorruptible judge and the astute banker, disagreed. Let's have Rousseau, they said. Let's have Voltaire. Spain needs them.

Floridablanca vacillated.

Maria Luisa bided her time.

And Paco Goya painted. He painted portraits of the new king and queen without number. He painted furiously. Every noble family in Spain wanted those portraits, and following the lead of the Osuna, most wanted Goya to paint them.

The king is dead, long live the king, they said in Madrid and in the provinces. In September there would be the coronation, fireworks, singing and dancing in the streets, parties at all the great ducal palaces. It was a glorious time to be alive.

And, in an obscure French garrison town an as yet unknown lieutenant, born twenty-nine years before in Corsica, went about his duties. Antisocial and reserved, he studied the campaigns of Caesar while his fellow officers drank and reveled and ridiculed him.

His name was Napoleon Bonaparte.

'So that's the way you do it. Delightful, Goya.'

'Surely Your Grace knew.'

'I never really believed it,' Cayetana de Abla said.

Night had fallen on the Street of Disillusion, where Paco had his studio. He was thinking of buying the entire building – a good address and far roomier than the house on the river road. Or, he had been thinking that until the Alba's unexpected arrival. A knock on the door, and she had breezed past him, dressed in maja black and wafting the scent of jasmine. Palette in his hand, he wore matching tan frock coat and breeches. Not even an artist's smock. And, of course, that flat-brimmed hat with candles on it.

On his easel stood an unfinished portrait of Villafranca, the duchess' husband. He had already roughed in the litheness of the man, and the odd ethereal quality of his face. The right el-

263

bow leaned on nothing, and would eventually lean on a harpsichord. The hands were far enough apart to hold a musical score. At the moment they held nothing.

'Your Grace likes it?'

'I'm not sure yet. Will he be holding music?'

'A score of Haydn's.'

'Naturally,' said the Alba. She sat, uninvited, on the red damask sofa opposite the easel. Between them, draped, stood the model's throne. On a sideboard was a pot of coffee and Wedgwood cups and saucers. Paco put down his palette and brush.

'No, please paint. I'd like to watch.'

'I've done all I intended to do tonight.'

'Will Villafranca have to sit any more?'

'No. I already have the face.'

'You make him look – languid.'

'But intelligent.'

'Oh, he's intelligent. Might I have some coffee?'

Paco poured two cups.

'I love the name of this street,' she said. 'There's a wonderful legend that goes with it.'

'Something about a duel, wasn't it?' Paco stood leaning against the model's throne, balancing cup and saucer in one hand.

Cayetana laughed. 'That's almost my husband's pose.' Her enormous dark eyes met his. 'But not so languid. Yes, a duel. Two cavaliers, fighting for the love of a woman. A shade passes between them, and propped against the wall they see a horrible vision – a mummy.'

'The woman they were fighting over.'

'Gruesome, isn't it? But very Spanish. Would you fight a duel over a woman?'

'I haven't used a sword since I was in Italy. And only foils then. Besides, I'm too fat.'

'I'd have said solid. Nothing that a day or two a week with a fencing master wouldn't take care of.' Cayetana leaned forward. 'Would you do a sketch of me? Just a quick study?'

'Now, Your Grace?'

'If you keep calling me that, we'll never get to know each other. Of course now. I live for now. Besides, it's to be a gift. A peace offering. I was very wicked to Hillo tonight.'

Paco got a pad and some red chalk. He hovered over the seated duchess. The chalk moved over the paper in quick, deft strokes.

'Don't you ever get tired?'

'I don't have time to get tired. I'd rather get rich.'

'Which I gather you are.'

'By my lights, Your Grace. Not yours.' Paco went on sketching.

'Cayetana.'

The red chalk flew. The candles on Paco's hat highlighted the duchess' fine cheekbones. He handed her the sketch.

She studied it, her face impassive. 'I don't how much about art, of course, but. . . . ' Her voice trailed off, as if she wanted him to pick up the thought.

'But?' he merely repeated.

'I'd have said this was a sketch of a woman somewhat more sensual than I.'

Paco shrugged. 'It's a game I play.'

'You mean, putting ideas into their pretty little heads?'

'Something like that. Cayetana.'

She looked away from him. 'Will five hundred reales be enough? I'll have it sent in the morning.'

'No charge, Your Grace. If you can give Hillo a gift, I can give you one.'

'Then sign it.'

Paco took the sketch back and scrawled his signature with the red chalk.

'Hillo's a terribly jealous man,' said the duchess with a faintly mocking smile.

'Surely you don't mean of me?'

'Ever since that night at the Alameda. He can tell.'

'Tell what? We haven't even seen each other since then.'

'A pity,' said the duchess.

'And you wanted me to sign it to make him more jealous?'

Cayetana studied the sketch again. 'Not just sensual. I'd say this is the likeness of a woman the artist would like to sleep with,' she said flatly.

Paco felt a thickness in his throat. 'As you said, you don't know much about art.'

'But a lot about men. Have you dreamed about me, since the Alameda?'

'I never remember what I dream,' Paco said.

'When it suits you, you don't. You're an arrogant man, Goya.'

'Yes, Your Grace.'

'You don't understand. I like arrogant men. Unless they get possessive, like Hillo.'

'I can't blame him. I could feel possessive – about you.'

'That's better. That's much better.'

'You want to make Hillo jealous.'

'It's a game *I* play.'

Paco took the sketch back. 'I'm not sure I want to be used.'

Cayetana looked at him, her eyes hard. 'I said I liked arrogance, but there are limits.'

'Yes, Your Grace.'

'That's arrogant too, and you know it.'

Paco shrugged again.

'Please let me have the sketch?'

'Of course.' He returned it to her.

'When will you finish the portrait?'

'After the coronation, probably. I've done a thousand portraits of our smiling King Carlos and – '

'A thousand and *one* portraits of our toothless Queen Maria Luisa,' Cayetana laughed. 'They've kept you pretty busy, haven't they?'

'I like money.'

'Do you like the queen?'

'She's a good sitter. Very proud of her arms and neck. Paint them like marble, and she's happy.'

'And then of course,' said Cayetana sweetly, 'there are her teeth.'

'And there's a cat sitting in my studio.'

'That's what Hillo calls me.'

'My mistake then. A kitten, but with claws.'

'Have you ever slept with the Osuna?' Cayetana asked abruptly.

Paco gave her an exaggerated shocked look. 'Do you think I'd say?'

'Hillo would boast, among his cronies.'

'I have no cronies. Just friends.'

'She really likes you.'

'As a painter.'

'For rather different reasons, she has the same kind of husband trouble I have.'

'You can stop right there,' Paco said coolly. 'I'm not your confessor.'

'There's that arrogance again. Come here, Goya.'

'No. I never make a mistake with a duchess, Your Grace.'

'Under certain circumstances I rather fancy I'd like you to call me that after all. I said come here.'

'And I said no.'

She stood swiftly and in the same motion came into his arms. He could feel the sketch paper crinkling behind his back, and the shape of her breasts against his chest. His arms circled the supple waist. He breathed the jasmine in her black hair. He kissed her. She cried out against his mouth, and moved two steps backwards until they fell across the sofa.

Then she went slack in his arms like a puppet.

'And how many little majas have you taken on this sofa?' she asked.

His hand moved from waist to breast. She slapped at it, not hard. 'Not here,' she said. 'And not now. I won't be one of your majas.' Then she began to laugh, in control of herself again. 'That hat. That crazy hat. You're still wearing it. There's wax in my hair.'

'I'm sorry. Your Grace.'

'I'm not. How the man can kiss! Like an Indian savage.'

'The only Indian I ever knew was hardly a savage,' Paco smiled. 'I rather liked her.'

'Of course,' Cayetana said promptly. 'The Olavide dueña. I always wondered who that young Marqués de Solis reminded me of.'

'I talk too much.'

'Hardly. When I was a little girl I thought Mariana de Olavide the most beautiful woman in Madrid, after my mother. Mariana and Marianita. They made quite a pair. Did you ever know my mother?'

'No.'

'She was very lovely. Like your Mariana.'

'Like her own daughter.'

'Kiss me again?'

Paco shook his head. 'I like to finish what I start.'

He picked up the sketch and handed it to her. It was only slightly creased.

They heard footsteps on the stairs. The door burst open and Pepe Hillo stood there, filling the doorway.

'I saw your coach outside.'

What he saw, inside, seemed quite innocent. They stood at arm's length, Paco wearing the candled hat and Cayetana holding the sketch.

'A peace offering, see?' Cayetana said brightly, giving him the sketch. 'I was very foolish, Hillo. Will you accept this as an apology?'

Hillo looked at the sketch, his eyes narrowing.

'Don't you like it?' Cayetana asked him.

'Too well, maybe.'

Paco picked up his palette and returned to the portrait of the duke.

'Goya – ' Hillo began.

Cayetana scolded him: 'Never interrupt an artist at his work. He was furious with me. He did this only because it was for you, he said.'

Paco did not turn to face Hillo. He liked the man, and felt a little sorry for him.

Arm in arm, the duchess and the bullfighter left the studio.

From the city hall, in finery two centuries old, emerged the mayor of the city, the corregidor, and all the grandees of Spain. In solemn procession, led by drummers, buglers, and mace-bearers, and followed by a platoon of light cavalry on chestnut horses, they brought the fluttering red and gold standard of Castile, symbol of the monarchy. It was ten-thirty in the morning, the twenty-first of September 1789.

The coronation procession made its stately way to the Plaza of the Arsenal, across from the palace. A platform had been raised in the plaza, draped with velvet, with floral arrangements and tapestries. When the dignitaries had taken their places, the royal pair emerged from the palace in gold-brocaded velvet, led by guardsmen on prancing white horses. King and queen knelt on the platform, hands joined, facing the vast sea of faces between the plaza and the palace. It was a fine flawless blue-skied day, warm but not hot. Carlos wore a fatuous smile on his thick-featured face; his queen's smile was one of triumph. She had come a long way from Parma.

A great chant went up from the crowd outside the iron fence of the Plaza of the Arsenal. 'Castile, Castile, Castile! For the King Don Carlos!'

The mob pushed forward to see the royal couple, now crowned, rise. Carlos, officially His Most Catholic Majesty King Carlos IV, stood and waved his right hand over his head.

At that signal, lackeys at the palace end of the plaza began to toss silver and gold coins into the air. The crowd turned its back on the platform and rushed in a wave toward the palace.

Coins, hundreds of gold and silver coins, spun and flashed in the sunlight.

It was an ancient tradition, and a happy one, the new king distributing largesse to his new subjects.

But the bread shortage, the ruinous inflation – before long the crowd became a shouting, screaming mob that fought tooth and nail for gold escudos and silver reales. The corregidor sent his light cavalry to disperse them.

Soon blood seeped into the dry, hard earth of the plaza of the Arsenal.

'They're like animals,' Maria Luisa said to her husband.

The animals did not hear. The animals kept fighting for gold and silver.

'Stop the largesse!' shouted the king. Those were the first words he spoke after his coronation.

The palace lackeys retreated up the palace stairs with their bags of coins. The crowd rushed the gates. The gates shook.

King Carlos IV shook his head slowly. He did not understand. He would never understand.

Maria Luisa understood. It wasn't largesse the people needed. It was a firm hand wielding a whip.

But that of course must wait.

For eight days and eight nights the standard of Castile would flutter from the main balcony of the palace. Carlos' standard? thought Maria Luisa. Or mine?

She watched the crowd gradually disperse. If she heard the groans of the injured, if she saw the blood in the plaza or the horsewhips lashing down on the mob, she gave no sign. The canaille, anyway, forget so easily.

Three days of revelry, of pomp, of homage would follow the coronation. All for her.

All for her. Maria Luisa caught a glimpse of Lieutenant Manuel Godoy on the edge of the crowd, so handsome in his red, white, and blue uniform. She had plans for that one, as she had plans of a very different nature for that doddering old fool Floridablanca.

Animals, she thought again.

Two months before, in Paris, the canaille had stormed the Bastille.

Given to wild flights of fancy at her best, jaded and bored at her worst, Cayetana felt at loose ends the night of the Alba coronation ball. The king and queen would come, carried directly into the ballroom in their sedan chairs; the king and queen would stay an hour; the king and queen would go. The guests would dance, they would eat, they would drink a little too much and flirt a little too much and gamble a little too much in the gambling rooms below the ballroom. They would still be there in the morning, rumpled and sweaty in their finery. The night would cost her more than half a million reales, and though she could easily afford it she thought the money poorly spent. She'd rather be at the theater, seeing her favorite La Tirana perform. Or in the plaza de toros, watching Hillo. Hillo, she thought, my God, yes, how that man flirts with death; but how insufferable he could be in a ballroom, how suspicious, like that night in Goya's studio – and why, she thought, should she be thinking of Goya? She virtually alone among the grandees had not commissioned him to do a royal portrait for the event. She hadn't even seen him since that night. One little kiss, but it disturbed her. He disturbed her.

He had no flaws that she could see, no touch of a bird with a broken wing. He was not – what was the word? – *manqué*. Cayetana liked to collect strays. Hillo never understood that, and quite accidentally it did not matter. Hillo faced death on golden sand under a high blue sky, and that was enough. I give myself to him, she thought, because tomorrow or next week or next month he may be dead. The thought thrilled her.

But not tonight. Tonight Hillo's possessiveness did not even anger her. It bored her. She could see it in his eyes. Why are you dancing with that one? they seemed to accuse her. Or fluttering your fan – the fan I gave you – at that one? Your husband keeps you in a cage with golden bars. I take you out of it. Isn't that enough?

It wasn't enough tonight. Nothing was enough tonight.

Sometimes Cayetana de Alba hated being a duchess.

Why, right now, she could be out on the streets, a maja, squirting a hard stream of chalky red wine into her mouth from a wineskin, dancing the bolero on a tabletop, her skirts high, her spirits soaring, a thousand men, real men, paying her homage not because she was a duchess but because she was a woman.

'Your Grace.'

'Oh, it's you. Goya. Good evening.'

'Good or bad, it's hard to tell,' he said. 'I haven't slept for three nights.'

'Has anybody?' Cayetana felt her heart beating fast. He'd had the boldness, the effrontery, to come in a short majo jacket and sash. He cut quite a figure in them too. Tight breeches and soft leather boots, and that dark hair of his, unpowdered and hanging free almost to his shoulders.

'I took your advice,' he said.

'My advice? What advice?'

'A fencing master, twice a week.'

She looked at him again. He had lost considerable weight,

but his shoulders still bulged the majo jacket.

'Maella,' he observed, studying the portraits of the king and queen mounted on the long wall of the ballroom between gold sconces. 'It isn't easy making that pair look pretty. Maella's managed.'

'Do I detect a note of injured pride?'

'Santa Maria, no. I got sick and tired of seeing my own king and queen everywhere I went. Maella's a refreshing change. Besides, it gave me time to finish your husband's portrait. That's why I'm here. It's ready any time you want it.'

'*That's* why? You were invited.'

'I was invited everywhere. I went everywhere. I saw all the same faces. I heard all the same talk.'

'You too?' said Cayetana.

'No more grand ballrooms after tonight. Not for another ten years at least If another footman offers me another glass of champagne, I'll – '

'Throw it at him?' Cayetana laughed. 'I know the feeling.'

'You'll forgive me if I don't stay? I'm not exactly dressed for it anyway.'

'Neither am I.'

'You're the loveliest maja in the room.'

'I'm the only maja in the room.'

'In Madrid then. I could prove it to you.'

'Could you then?'

'But of course it's impossible. You wouldn't dare.'

Her dark eyes narrowed.

'Your Grace,' he said.

'I wouldn't dare what?'

'To leave with me. In half an hour. I want the streets tonight. I want wine from a wineskin. I want skewered meat grilled over charcoal. I want – '

'You too?' Cayetana heard herself saying again. Her voice had been too eager, and she added: 'I'd have thought you'd be honored to be entertained by every grandee in Madrid.'

'Being honored and enjoying yourself aren't the same thing. Half an hour,' Paco said.

'The king and queen haven't even arrived yet.'

'I always thought you liked to shock people.'

'Goya, are you a little drunk?'

'I've been drinking. For three days. Like everybody else. I'm never drunk.'

She could feel it, like something tangible, the way he was dominating her.

'Can't we wait until after they leave? They'll only stay an hour.'

'No, Your Grace.'

'Then – meet me somewhere?'

'Where?'

'The Plaza Mayor. Where the stairs go down?'

'Good.' He bowed and left her.

The effrontery, the absolutely insufferable effrontery of this upstart –

It delighted her. It was exactly what she needed, tonight.

A full moon rode high and bright over the Plaza Mayor, dimming the stars. If Paco turned and walked down the flight of stone steps, he could go along the Street of the Knifemakers to the restaurant where he had once worked as a dishwasher. He wondered if the same ill-humored fat man owned the place. He went back twenty years and more and saw Mariana sitting there with Anton Rafael Mengs. Mariana, her hair white now, in France with their son. Mengs dead and buried in Rome.

He turned his back on the steps and looked across the broad moonlit plaza. Wooden tendidos had already been put up for the coronation bullfight, and rickety platforms had increased the size of third-and fourth-story balconies overlooking the plaza. The place would be jammed, Paco knew, and even the surrounding rooftops would hold thousands of spectators. Inevitably some skylights and some platforms would collapse. A corrida in the Plaza Mayor could be as dangerous for the spectators as for the bullfighters. Still, it was something special, a bullfight in the old tradition of Madrid, before the great plaza de toros had been built outside the Alcalá Gate. Paco wondered how Juanito would fare. It was said in Madrid these days that Juanito Apiñani was a has-been, and Paco felt concern for his friend. That wolf's grin was more a grimace on Juanito's face now. He fought compulsively and without pleasure. He drank a great deal.

Cayetana was late. It did not surprise Paco. It would not have surprised him if she never came. Suggesting the assignation with the effrontery he knew would appeal to her, he had been all but quaking in those soft leather boots of his. His blasé attitude toward the parties in the ducal palaces had been a pose. Every time he went he had crowed inwardly. The *baturro* from Aragon, he would think. They talk about you in all the salons of Madrid as much as they talk about Hillo.

They talk about you when you drive thundering through the streets of Madrid. They talk about that clever candled hat and the fine money-producing patronage of the Duchess of Osuna and the knowledge, shared by all Madrid, that you are the new king's favorite painter.

The one thing they do not talk about is the real and sometimes frightening insecurity you feel. This you hide. You take pains to hide it. Your life these days is like a dream, a beautiful dream, and you pray it will never end. You're the most facile painter in Spain. You can do more, you can do better. But doing better, or trying to do better, might not please your patrons. Paint Carlos and that sow of a queen the way they really look? The king with his fatuous smile of an apprentice baker with one drink too many, the frumpish queen whose little pig eyes dart this way and that, to this man's crotch and that, wondering whom to invite to her royal bed next, while fat Carlos snores in his own bed, bone-weary from the hunt? Yes, of course, paint them like that just once and you'll be back in Zaragoza teaching the *baturros* which end of a paintbrush to hold.

Paco listened to the crackle of fireworks far off. A distant rocket soared high and burst in a spray of color over the rooftops. The Plaza Mayor was almost deserted. A drunk lurched by, a bloated wineskin slung over his shoulder. On impulse Paco bought the skin and the drunk staggered happily down the steps to the Street of the Knifemakers. Paco held the wineskin at arm's length and squeezed. A hard jet of chalky red wine hit the back of his throat and he bit it off cleanly.

'Bravo,' said Cayetana de Alba.

She was there suddenly at his side, a shawl over that dark hair of hers. She had come out of nowhere, like a dream, like the dream Paco wouldn't give up, not for a little while longer, and possibly not for anything.

Wordlessly he offered her the wineskin, and she took a stance with it, feet apart, arms extended, and squirted a stream as hard as Paco's own into her mouth. She bit it off casually. Not a drop of wine spilled. The wineskin exchanged hands twice more. He was very careful not to touch her. She seemed equally careful not to touch him.

'I used to work down there,' Paco said.

'Where? On Knifemakers? You had a studio there?'

'I was a dishwasher in the restaurant down there.'

Cayetana laughed. 'Sometimes when I was a little girl my grandfather used to take me there to eat. He loved the place.

Perhaps our paths crossed.'

'I didn't stay very long. I was fired.'

'For being insolent?'

'Something like that.'

'Then what happened?'

Paco waited a moment. He said: 'Mariana de Olavide happened.'

Again Cayetana laughed. 'It's you that's the cat. Always landing on your feet.'

She removed the shawl, holding it in both hands like a bullfighter with his cape. She took half a dozen running steps out into the plaza. 'Ay, ay, toro!' she called, and stamped her foot.

It was that kind of night from the very beginning. A little talk, a little discovery, and then they played. It seemed the most natural thing in the world for Paco to put his head down, to place a hand on either ear, fingers extended, and charge at her. He even snorted – a poor imitation of a bull's snort – as he rushed, light-footed, in the moonlight. Cayetana stood, feet planted close. She swept the shawl to one side and Paco followed the lure, feeling inanely pleased that he could move so quickly. She called and he came by again, and a third time. A child's game. You be the bull. I'll be the bullfighter. He felt reckless and lighthearted and very young. The fourth time, her leg moved, and Paco was a wise and crafty and speedily-learning bull. He swerved into the movement and caught her around the waist, harder than he had intended. They fell together. He could feel the litheness of her under him and smell the jasmine in her hair.

'I've been gored,' she cried. 'Terribly, perhaps fatally gored, and my peones are rushing me to the infirmary and – are you going to sit on top of me all night, Goya?'

He helped her to her feet. She brushed herself off. They looked at each other.

'Let's go watch the fireworks,' she said.

But first they stopped at a café to fill their wineskin. Paco heard a voice in the crowd: 'That's Goya over there, painter to the king.'

Goya, not the Duchess of Alba.

The recognized painter and the unrecognized duchess, hand in hand, left the café. They heard music from the direction of the Puerta del Sol, and the fireworks were again forgotten.

Four bands played, lamps lit the terraces of the cafés and glowed in the windows of the post office, and ten thousand people were dancing in the great square. Ten thousand people and five thousand wineskins, filled again and again from the casks in the wineshops.

'It's not the Gate of the Sun,' Cayetana said solemnly. 'It's the Gate of the Moon, and they're a coven of witches, all the brujas in Spain, waiting for the Queen of the Witches to dance for them.'

'There's no Queen of the Witches.'

'Just you watch.'

It was like the evening at the Osunas', only more so.

Cayetana danced, and at first those closest to her stopped their own dancing to watch, and then those further, and the four bands came and played together while Cayetana, alone on a cart then in the very center of the Puerta del Sol, danced the bolero. Sinuously slow at first, and then faster, and men brought torches, and there in the torchlight her face gleamed, her eyes glowed, her legs flashed and every man in the vast crowd wanted her. She leaped down, she was among them while they clapped out the rhythm and made love to her with their eyes, while the wineskins passed swiftly from hand to hand, while they shouted for more and she gave them more, tireless in the moonlight, and Paco stood, holding a wineskin at arms' length, feeling the wine go down, not tasting it, seeing Cayetana and her coven of witches, feeling the same jealousy Pepe Hillo must have felt as she lingered too long before a man in a short majo jacket, feeling it again as she danced a tight, small-stepped circle around another, feeling it wrenchingly as a tall majo reached out and grabbed her, drawing her close before she could pull away, skirt swirling, black hair flying, smiling back over her shoulder as she fled, still dancing, the Queen of the Witches in the moonlight with a small invisible doll of Paco Goya and a pin stuck in it for every suggestive gesture and for every time her dark eyes met a man's in stylized invitation, and then she was back, back in front of Paco and ending the dance as she had ended it at the Osunas', like a bullfighter after the kill, head bowed, arms dropping slowly to her sides, and he was drunk then with the wine and the wild free magic of her as she lifted her head and shook the strands of black hair from her face and gravely in the torchlight kissed him full on the mouth and took his hand and they ran.

It was that kind of night, and more. He remembered the fireworks in the Retiro Park, the acrid smell of the powder, the crowds, the rockets bursting, the flashing pinwheels spinning like liquid fire, the ear-splitting thunder of it all, and another wineskin, and another, and then the din was behind them; they were running through the streets again, dark silent streets and then torchlit streets and more crowds, and there was the great Neptune fountain on San Geronimo, the water all golden in the lantern light, and by then the night was cool, the night had given way to the faint glow of false dawn. Majos were there, daring each other to plunge in and he remembered Cayetana saying they were all nothing but timid little boys afraid to get their feet wet and she ran past them and through the spray and into the cascading water, arms widespread, teeth flashing white, long dark hair plastered to her head and shoulders as she reached the statue of Neptune and clung to it with one hand and then returned, teeth chattering now, drenched blouse clinging so that Paco could see the outlines of her breasts, skirt clinging to the perfect legs revealing more than any dance could reveal, and again they were running, Paco's jacket around her shoulders. We have to run or I'll freeze to death, she said, and they ran while the false dawn faded into darkness again, the busy streets, the empty streets, the occasional coaches rumbling by, the tired sagging faces of all-night revelers, the sky brightening again as they reached Paco's studio on the Street of Disillusion.

Soon her drenched clothing was steaming on a chair before the hearth. She sat on the model's throne huddled in a woolen robe.

'Cold?'

A shake of her head. 'No, I'm warm now. What a night! They'll be wondering what happened to me. They always wonder.'

'Do you tell them?'

'No.'

'Not even Villafranca?'

'No. You mustn't call him that. The Duke of Alba.' She was a little drunk, bundled shapelessly in Paco's woolen robe. He brought a towel and dried her hair.

'The duke. I'll remember that, Your Grace.'

'I'm sorry. I didn't mean it that way. It's just – sometimes I feel so sorry for him. He got more than he bargained for when he married me.'

Paco leaned down and kissed her lips. He turned her body against his and could feel the shape of her through the coarse wool. After a while she brought her hands up against his chest.

'Aren't you afraid?' she said.

'Of what? Of the duke? Of Hillo?'

'Of me. Of us. I know I am.'

'Afraid?'

'I could fall in love with you. Not like Hillo. Not like the others. It would be – I don't know.'

'I'm half in love with you already,' he said.

'Half?' Her smile was sad. 'Maybe that's what I'm afraid of. Or maybe I'm afraid I could hurt you very much, Goya. I don't want to.'

'Let me worry about that.'

'And I think you could hurt me. I don't want to be hurt. Once a gypsy told me I'd die young. I have no time for pain.'

He tried to take her in his arms again, but she stood and went to the fire and stared at the flames.

'I wouldn't be faithful to you,' she said, her back turned. 'A time would come when you'd hate me.'

'I could never hate you.'

'Believe me. I know.'

'I'll take the chance.'

'I don't want you to. Or perhaps I do. Too much.' She turned and lightly traced the shape of his mouth with her fingertips. 'Cean Bermúdez told me a strange thing. He said you needed – anger.'

'Anger?'

'To find your greatness as an artist.'

'We're not talking about art.'

'I wouldn't want that anger directed at me. And sooner or later it would be. You don't know me well enough. I'm not even sure I know myself. I'm all impulse, Villafranca says. His beautiful little animal. He's very patient with me. Would you be?'

'A man's patient with a wife, not a mistress.'

'I'll never be anyone's mistress.'

'Hillo?'

'*He* thinks I am. But he doesn't own me.'

'No man could ever own you.'

'That's better. That's much better. You'll have to remember that. Except – ' She shook her head.

'Except what?'

'You couldn't be owned either, could you?'

'No. Life's too short.'

'You see? We're back where we started. I don't want to be hurt. I own Hillo, but Hillo doesn't own me.'

'That's very convenient. For you.'

Firelight danced on her face. It was very warm in the studio. She stared up at him a long time. 'You know what I want to do?' she said at last.

'What?'

'Take off this robe. Let you make love to me. As the end of a glorious evening. As the beginning of nothing. Would you take me – like that?'

'No, Cayetana.'

'What?' Mockingly. 'Don't you find me attractive?'

'You're the most beautiful woman in Spain. I don't have to tell you that.'

'You see?' A little sadly. 'You want what you can't have. It's what makes an artist. Or a man.'

All night he had known he would take her to his studio, and had known she would come willingly. He could have her now, right now. On her terms. The end of a glorious evening. The beginning of nothing. The most beautiful woman in Spain. Suddenly the night seemed a dream he could hardly recall and he was very much in love. Not like the shy first love with Mariana, so long ago, and not the comfortable but incomplete love with Josefa, the family love, with their child, in the cozy house on the river road, the love that had almost been destroyed in Zaragoza but had remained, somehow, like a banked fire.

Cayetana.

A love that could be a man's whole life. Or his death.

'Well?' she said.

He wanted to rip the robe from her with one brutal tug of his hand.

'I'll take you home,' he said.

CHAPTER TWENTY-THREE

The End of a Matador

FROM HIS SUITE on the upper floor of Sebastián Martínez's villa in Cádiz, Paco looked across the red tile roofs of the city to the harbor.

Andalucía!

Orange trees lined the avenues of the city and palms grew along the quay, their fronds clattering in the fresh November breeze. Beyond them, anchored beside the mole, three-masters, frigates, and brigantines bobbed on the tide, tall masts swaying against the deep blue of the sky.

Though now, in 1792, Cádiz had surrendered some of its trade monopoly with New Spain to other cities, it was still Spain's principal port. Sebastián Martínez, treasurer of the Council General of Finance, spent half the year there to oversee the arrival of gold and silver from Mexico and Peru. High-cheekboned, ruddy-faced and sparkling-eyed, he had sat patiently for his portrait. Painted against a plain background, dressed in a fancy blue coat and a frilly white neckcloth, he stared happily at Paco from the canvas as if to say, 'This is the best portrait you've ever done.'

Quite likely it was. Paco owed it to the man. Ten thousand reales for the work, and a holiday in Andalucía to boot.

Paco began to clean his brushes. He smiled contentedly. Ever since the coronation no portrait painter had been in more demand than Goya. And if he neglected the tapestry works, what difference did it make? Let the Bayeus and Maella and the others keep the Santa Barbara looms busy. True, there had been some unpleasantness. His salary as painter to the royal household was partly for cartoons. But a man grew tired of tapestry cartoons, and he had painted over sixty of them. He had also painted fat King Carlos a dozen times since the coronation and toothless Queen Maria Luisa as often. Except for them, he painted not what he wanted these days but whom he wanted. Madrid society claimed it was more difficult getting your portrait done by Goya than it was buying a pair of barrera seats at a fair price from that one-eyed rascal Tuertillo.

Santa Maria, Paco told himself, gazing out the window and watching the smaller coastal boats, great eyes painted on their prows, slip in and out among the frigates, I'm rich, I'm famous, I'm in Andalucía, all expenses paid – who cares if Francisco Bayeu had to smooth the ruffled feathers of a minister or two because I'm just a little weary of tapestry cartoons?

He was a figura as much as any bullfighter. And he relished it.

Sebastián Martínez had expected Paco in October, but he had set out a month earlier with Pepe Hillo and Juanito Apiñani in Hillo's big traveling coach.

The rivalry for the favors of Cayetana de Alba remained under the surface and, perversely, made closer friends of Paco and Hillo. It was as if Hillo had to learn everything he could about the man who one day might win Cayetana away from him. But the rivalry between Hillo and Juanito Apiñani for the hearts of the aficionados had become intense and strained the friendship between the two matadors.

Pepe Hillo had already established himself as one of Spain's two leading matadors. Perhaps he was still chasing Pedro Romero, grandson of that Francisco Romero who had started it all, but he would catch him in time.

Meanwhile there was Juanito Apiñani to dispose of.

Bullfighting is not a sport in which a man competes against a bull. Bullfighters compete against one another.

It was Juanito's bad luck to be the last champion of the passé style of his native Navarra.

It was Hillo's very good fortune to be the champion of the gay, romantic style of Sevilla.

Tall, not slender but quick on his feet, and with an almost oriental cast to his handsome features, Pepe Hillo over the years had become condescending to Juanito.

'Amigo,' he would say, 'in Sevilla we run with the bull, we dance with the bull, we become one with the bull. We don't vault high over his horns and look down on his tossing muscle, we don't make an enemy of him. We love the bull and give him a beautiful death.'

'In Navarra,' Juanito would say stubbornly, 'the bulls are fast and can turn as quick as a cat. You can't dance with a bull like that.'

'Yes, our Sevilla bulls are bigger,' Hillo would admit happily. 'And stronger, and more dangerous.' And he might pull up his shirt to reveal a horn scar, crescent-shaped, under his ribs. 'They do this.' And another one, long and jagged, high on his left thigh: 'And they do this – if you're not careful.'

'I'm careful.'

'Which takes the joy from it, amigo.'

The joy of the corrida had been taken from Juanito Apiñani. Since the coronation bullfight, in which he had fared a distant third behind Hillo and Pedro Romero, he had fought with talent but without alegría. Often cushions and wine bottles rained down on him, and he had somehow to flee the ring quickly while still maintaining his dignity. A matador without dignity is nothing.

A man without dignity, Paco had thought on the journey down to Sevilla, is nothing.

Each morning before they started out with fresh horses Juanito's hands shook. Two or three cups of anís with his coffee would stop the shaking – until lunch, when he downed a bottle of chalky red wine.

The contest would be a travesty in Sevilla, where Pepe Hillo had been born and had first learned to fight the bulls.

Gaspar and Emeterio Apiñani reached Sevilla a few days before their brother. They wore long faces when Juanito arrived.

'It's bad, Juanito,' Gaspar said.

'It's a catastrophe,' Emeterio said. 'The style of Sevilla. That's all you hear in the streets.'

'I might have a surprise or two in store for them,' Juanito said, but his voice lacked conviction as he unbuckled the straps of his black traveling case.

'What's that in there?' Gaspar asked.

'Are you out of your head, chico?' Emeterio asked.

Juanito had produced the costume he would wear for the bullfight tomorrow: padded jacket and tight breeches of sun-bleached suede. His only concession to color was a broad crimson sash.

'Scarlet and silk!' cried Gaspar.

'Gold brocade, silver buttons! Silk stockings!' cried Emeterio. 'Hillo will look like a peacock next to you.'

'Since when,' asked Juanito, 'can a peacock fight the bulls?'

There was a pathetic quixotic quality to the old *ante* suit. For years in Madrid Juanito had wisely abandoned the less flamboyant costume of Navarra. Now he insisted on it. Hillo, in peacock blue one day, bottle green the next, scarlet for a third fight, rarely wore a suit of lights more than once, and then only in the provinces where it hardly mattered. Cayetana de Alba's own modiste designed his costumes at a cost of six or seven thousand reales each.

'We'll get you a real suit of lights,' Gaspar said. 'There's still time if we hurry.'

'Brocaded gold,' suggested Emeterio, 'with linen lining.'

Juanito uncorked a bottle of cognac. 'I'm fighting in *ante* tomorrow,' he said. He was still drinking, staring moodily at nothing, when his brothers retired for the night.

Paco stood in the callejón – the alleyway between the two

fences separating the arena from the spectators – to witness the debacle.

The afternoon was hot, the sky that incredible Andaluz blue, the tiers of benches packed with Sevillanos ready to shout themselves hoarse for Pepe Hillo.

The shouting began even before the bullfight, high up in the cheapest seats on the sun side of the old royal riding ring of Sevilla with its Moorish arches and columns.

'Ee-jo! Ee-jo! Ee-jo!' ten thousand throats roared in the dialect of Andalucía, and Gaspar Apiñani gave Paco a doleful look.

'Juanito won't have a chance,' he said.

'As far as they're concerned he's not even here,' said Emeterio.

In deference to their brother the other two Apiñanis wore old suits of faded *ante*. By contrast Hillo's peones, now folding their capes neatly across the top of the barrera, looked like grandees.

'Just where did you bumpkins come from?' one of them asked the Apiñanis. Gaspar and Emeterio looked down at the sand and did not reply.

The bulls wore the fluttering green and white ribbons of Espinosa de Arcos, big Andaluz bulls that stood as high as a man's shoulders. Their wide upward-curving horns were twice the length of a Navarrese bull's. They were ponderous animals that would turn slowly and attack from a distance. Gaspar had complained at the sorting earlier in the day that they would let Pepe Hillo construct his fight like an architect designing a cathedral.

'Slow and voluptuous, like a fat woman making love,' Emeterio said in disgust. 'Juanito needs a small, nervous bull, a virgin he can seduce.'

At the sorting the mayoral – the ranch foreman – crumpled six strips of paper and tossed them in a Córdoba hat. On each he had written the name of one of the bulls. Gaspar drew first, and then Hillo's chief lieutenant, and then Gaspar again, until all six bulls were selected. Paco could tell that the Apiñanis were nervous. Juanito, who had stayed up half the night drinking cognac, had gone right to work on a bottle of anís in the morning.

Now in the callejón Paco wet his lips anxiously. He had seen his friend fight the bigger Andaluz bulls in Madrid, but then Juanito had accommodated his style to them. Now, with the wrong kind of bulls, he wanted to prove a point. As stub-

282

born as a *baturro,* Paco thought.

If you were clever enough, and Juanito was, you could accommodate yourself to anything.

To pretty compositions for tapestry cartoons, facile but hardly your own art at all.

To patrons who wanted flattering portraits.

To – why did he suddenly feel envious of Juanito?

Juanito would fail. Hillo's own Sevilla, the partisan crowd, the bulls tailor-made for Hillo – Juanito had to fail. And yet, he would go out there this afternoon doing exactly what he wanted and in the way he wanted to do it. There was something glorious in the gesture.

I'll paint as they expect, so that someday I can paint as I must. . . .

But someday became next week or next month or next year. Or maybe never.

Juanito fought with the same quick grace that Paco had always seen, fought the big, long-spined, massive Andaluz bulls as if they were nervous little Navarrese animals hardly longer than they were tall. He turned quickly, swirling his cape. He taught the bulls to turn quickly with him. He passed them close, scorning the horns that could disembowel him, letting the huge shoulders brush his chest, waving the picador away after a single lance had been placed in a bull that needed four or five to bring the great head down, instructing his brothers to put in the barbed banderillas quickly, just one pair each, even though the bulls needed correcting because all had a tendency to hook to their right.

The first bull tossed him twice. Still light on his feet and lithe, but never a strong man, Juanito sailed through the air and landed heavily while Gaspar and Emeterio rushed out flapping their capes. He waved them away, as contemptuously as he had waved the picador and his nag away. The horse had not even been gored.

Juanito dropped to his knees to pass those first two bulls, then leaped up, pivoting, to kneel again as the bulls came rushing by in the opposite direction. Four times, and five, and six. Then a swirl of his cape, and a bull fixed in place, and an arrogant strut to the barrera for his vaulting pole, the Navarrese specialty.

The bulls charged from a long way off. Juanito ran to meet them, dropping the end of the pole and rising high between the horns and then over the horns and then landing like a cat where Gaspar was waiting with another cape.

In the callejón a slow smile spread over Paco's broad face. He has it, he thought, he really still has it. The magic.

And the crowd?

The crowd didn't see it.

The crowd wanted only Hillo, Hillo with that impossibly slow cape of his, Hillo with the long swooping breath-holding passes and the way he seemed to flow with the bull, to orchestrate the bull, to dominate the bull, and then suddenly stroke its muzzle or take the tip of a horn between his teeth while the bull stood there, its wide-spaced eyes seeing nothing.

That was magic too, Sevilla magic, neither better nor worse but different. The crowd loved it. Their 'olés! ' shook the old Moorish ring when Hillo fought.

When Juanito fought there was silence. Or, worse, conversation. They did not hiss and whistle in contempt. They hurled no cushions or bottles. They waited while the outré figure in *ante* performed the ritual as well as he ever had. They were indifferent. They wanted Hillo.

Even at the kill.

Juanito killed receiving the bull, citing the beast with a flick of the wrist that moved the scarlet muleta and then waiting, profiling himself to the bull, up on his toes, Toledo steel an extension of his arm, while the bull, following the lure of the cape, galloped suddenly forward, spurting like blood from a severed artery, to take the sword into its own back while Juanito crossed the cape from left to right and then, only then, moved to his own left, clearing the bull's right horn by a scant inch as his knuckles punched the bull's back and the bull fell.

The crowd talked. The crowd drank beer. The crowd ate sausages. That was one way to kill a bull. That was how they killed in Navarra. But this was Sevilla. They wanted Hillo, who killed the bull with flying feet.

Hillo, profiling as Juanito had profiled, holding the muleta low as Juanito had, and then raising it to see that the small eyes followed, and then dropping it again, and then going up high on his toes, arm and sword one, and then running at the bull, the bull planted and the man on flying feet and the sword going in with the strength of the man's arm instead of the weight of the bull's back, and the bull dropping like a stone as Juanito's bull had dropped, except that then Hillo smiled radiantly while Juanito had remained impassive.

And thirty thousand Sevillanos rose to their feet screaming.

Before Juanito's final bull, Gaspar urged: 'Kill him *volapié*, chico. Flying feet. They expect at least that.'

'Stand like a statue and they'll ignore you,' Emeterio said.

Juanito looked at them. He was sweating and cold now in his suit of *ante*. The late afternoon sun was low and the arena in shade.

'No, they don't like the old ways,' he said.

'Well then?' Gaspar asked.

'Do what's expected of you, chico,' Emeterio pleaded.

For the briefest of moments that wolf's grin appeared. 'I'll give them something new.'

Gaspar and Emeterio shook their heads.

Once more Juanito entered the arena. Once more, on the biggest bull of the lot, he refused to slow his cape. He could have, Paco knew. He could make a fourteen-hundred-pound bull pass like a bull in a dream. He refused. Navarra with its masculine *ante,* Sevilla with its effete silks. He wanted to prove something. He wanted to show them, once and for all. Where Hillo, and Hillo's style of fighting, reigned supreme.

It was impossible.

Again a single lance from the picador, again two sets of cursory banderillas, again the zigzag Navarrese cape work with a bull too big, but somehow Juanito managed it. Again the pole-vault, twice, three times, four, while the crowd buzzed with conversation, guzzled beer, and ogled the señoritas fluttering their fans impatiently near the president's box.

And the kill? Juanito's something new?

He cited the bull, raising the muleta in his left hand and watching the eyes follow it, then dropping it slowly. He went down with it, to his knees. He continued to cite from his knees. Incredibly, he profiled from his knees, the bull's great head and wide horns looming over him. Then he rose in a smooth graceful motion off his knees and flowed forward and up, the sword rising with him in an arc that carried it, just as he reached his full height, to the killing place between the bull's shoulders, disappearing to the hilt as Juanito crossed the muleta to his right, the bull's horn ripping the *ante* from his leg as his knuckles punched home and the animal tottered and bellowed once and started to turn and fell dead.

Ashen-faced, Gaspar and Emeterio watched. Paco couldn't believe it. He had never seen a more dangerously executed kill nor, in the tantalizing smooth rising-from-the-knees slowness of it, a more beautiful one.

The crowd actually stirred itself. There was a polite smattering of applause that quickly faded.

Juanito had given them everything. An apotheosis. It should

have been that.

For the crowd it was nothing.

'Ee-jo! Ee-jo! Ee-jo!' they chanted as the mules dragged the dead bull across the sand, one horn gouging a furrow, and Pepe Hillo stepped out into the arena to await his final bull.

Paco watched his old friend enter the callejón, face grave, eyes bleak, the wolf's grin a rictus.

'I showed them,' he said in a very soft voice.

Gaspar and Emeterio said nothing.

'The crowd,' Juanito said. 'I showed them, didn't I? What's the matter with them?'

'Sevillanos,' Gaspar said.

'Hillo has them in his pocket,' Emeterio said.

And Paco, finally, placed a hand on his friend's shoulder. 'You were magnificent, Juanito. Truly.'

Gaspar gave him a clay water jug, but Juanito brushed it angrily aside. 'I want cognac.'

And Paco stood there thinking: If the old doesn't work, the best of the old, done with style and daring, and if the new doesn't work, the unexpected, done with an astonishing bravery, then what can you do?

The rabble – all the way from the highest grandee to a beggar on a street corner. They never understand. Never.

If you were smart enough, if you were cynical enough, you gave them what they wanted. Or you ended up like Juanito Apiñani, who stood in his old *ante* suit, sweat- and blood-stained, drinking cognac from a bottle, hearing the crowd scream for Hillo.

If a bullfighter was smart enough, and cynical enough.

Or a painter.

CHAPTER TWENTY-FOUR

The End of a Painter

EVERY CAPTAIN OF A SAILING SHIP returning from New Spain with specie looked forward eagerly to a visit from Sebastián Martínez. The florid-faced treasurer of the Council General of Finance was a collector of Mexican art objects. At least, the captains joked among themselves, he called them art objects. The captains called them junk and were astonished that Martínez paid good silver reales for them. Every three-master, every frigate, every brigantine brought back its quota of heathen junk for Martínez, and every captain stuffed his purse with an extra two or three hundred silver coins in the process.

'They think I'm God's biggest fool,' Martínez told Paco with a gleam in his eye. 'Have a look. What do you think?'

It would have been impossible for Paco not to have a look. Every nook, corner, and cranny of the villa became a repository for the art of New Spain. It overflowed into the cellar and ran upstairs into the attic. It cluttered the grand salon and the drawing room and stared at Paco from every wall of his second-floor suite.

'A man doesn't have to be an Academy professor to recognize real art,' Martínez said, 'and he doesn't have to study in Rome or Madrid to produce it. These people are primitive. They're heathen. I've been there, and I know. Have a look, Don Paco.'

He was always saying have a look. 'See these golden nose ornaments,' he would say, and from under a table in the drawing room he'd pull out a box full of the crescent-shaped things. 'They're sacred to the god of pulque. Do you know what pulque is?'

'No, Don Sebastián.' Sometimes Paco could sympathize with the ship captains.

'The god of drunkenness. Can you imagine it? A god for souses?' Martínez laughed. 'Oh, they're heathen, but still. Have a look at this.'

This was a stucco mask of a face, the nose long and high-bridged, the face covered with red and black stripes. 'That's the old god of souses himself. A bit of a nose, eh? He almost *looks* drunk.'

The stucco was hard as stone, the red and black stripes richly glazed. The vividness of the colors surprised Paco. He doubted that he could produce them on his own palette.

Martínez owned boxes of jade ear plugs shaped like flowers; his tables groaned under the weight of crudely turned yet somehow arresting pottery; a great stone calendar slab was set into the floor of the grand salon.

'The signs of the zodiac, heathen style,' he told Paco. 'Have a look. Tell me they're not art.'

But art they were. They had a primitive strength. Their execution seemed simple, but the more Paco studied them the more complex he realized they were. The color red predominated.

'Red for immortality,' Martínez explained. 'They're not all that primitive if they believe in a life after death.'

'Perhaps,' Paco said, 'that's a sure sign that they are.'

Martínez did not comment. Like Paco, and like almost every freethinker in Spain, their old beliefs cast into doubt by the Enlightenment, he usually kept his thoughts on such matters to himself.

Three days after the portrait had been completed, Martínez led Paco into a room off the salon. The ruddy-faced treasurer's eyes were sparkling more than usual. 'The pièce de résistance,' he told Paco. 'I'd give up the villa and my house in Madrid before I parted with these. Have a look.'

Paco had a long look. Lining the walls of the room were great stucco figures of heathen gods. Again the stucco was hard as stone. Some of the god-figures wore stucco head-dresses in the shape of feathers. A motif of serpents adorned the heads of others.

It was art, all right, art of considerable quality. It had a vitality that made much of the statuary produced in Madrid seem effete.

Half a world away, in Mexico, Paco thought, savages who ran around half-naked, savages with no real education, savages with no art tradition that went back to the Greeks and Romans, to the Renaissance, patiently built and painted these stucco figures. No worry about this school of art or that. No need to please a patron, except the god himself.

Paco felt envious of those unknown artists half a world away. And felt impatient with his own career.

In their heathen way, those savages had the magic.

Perhaps because they were heathen.

Perhaps because they cared only for their art.

Paco could not see those unknown artists fawning before a Floridablanca, painting themselves sycophantically into the portrait offering a canvas for the great man's scrutiny. He could not see them accepting a commission merely because the word would spread and it would lead to other commissions. He could not see them mistaking facility for genius.

But then he remembered Juanito, after the bullfight in Sevilla – Juanito, who disappeared for three days, drinking himself sick. His brothers found him in an alley off Sierpes. He had been beaten and robbed. One eye was swollen shut and he had lost two teeth.

'I'm through,' he kept saying. 'I'll never fight the bulls again.'

Gaspar and Emeterio did not believe that. Juanito had reason to despair then, but he'd get over it.

'You'll fight again, chico,' said Gaspar.

'You'll make Hillo look like one of his own peones,' said Emeterio.

Paco did not share their optimism. Juanito meant it. He would wear neither *ante* nor a suit of lights again. By being true to himself he had destroyed himself.

The unknown artists in Mexico with their integrity in a simple world, or Juanito with his in a complex one.

And Paco Goya, who often boasted that all he needed was a small house, a copper pot, a stove, a few chairs, and his paints. The small house had become a mansion on the Street of Disillusion and Paco was caught in the trap he had set for himself.

That afternoon a letter came for Paco. 'By private messenger,' Martínez told him. 'In the Alba livery, I think.'

'The Alba?' Paco reached for the letter eagerly.

Discreetly, Martínez left the salon while Paco broke the seal. The message was short.

Dear Goya,

Cean Bermúdez tells me that you are in Cadíz painting Sebastián Martínez's portrait. I'm spending a few months here at our estate in Sanlúcar de Barrameda and, as it's so close, I thought you might like to paint me as well. It would seem a shame if you left Andalucía without doing so.

The duke, who is returning to Madrid today, conveys his warm regards, as do I.

María Teresa Cayetana
Duchess of Alba

Paco rushed into the anteroom, where Martínez was waiting. 'Where's Sanlúcar?'

Martínez suppressed a grin. 'There's Sanlúcar near Sevilla, and Sanlúcar de Barrameda at the delta of the Guadalquivir. A day and a half's drive from here.'

'Sanlúcar de Barrameda, yes,' Paco said. 'A day and a half?'

'Around the bay and then up through Puerto Real and Puerto de Santa María to – '

'Only a day and a half?'

'Or two, in this kind of weather.' Again that suppressed grin. 'Hadn't you noticed it's raining?'

Paco looked out the window. A steady downpour fell on the red tile roofs of Cádiz.

'The road will be a quagmire,' Martínez said. 'Possibly you ought to wait until it lets up, my friend.'

The duke, who is returning to Madrid today, conveys his warm regards.

'No, I'd better not wait. An important commission, Don Sebastían.'

'From the Duke of Alba?' Martínez emphasized the word duke slightly.

'From the duchess,' Paco said. 'Wants me to do her portrait.'

'Cayetana de Alba,' said Martínez in a wistful voice. 'It makes a man wish he were a painter'.

'Can I rent a coach here?'

'Take mine,' Martínez offered. 'I won't be needing it. And, of course, anything I can do to help you paint the Duchess of Alba, I'd be pleased to do.' This time he placed faint emphasis on the word paint.

Paco wondered briefly if there had been talk. It had been a long time since he had disappeared from the coronation ball with Cayetana. But then, Madrid society lived for its delightful little scandals.

'Tell her man I'll leave tomorrow. Perhaps the weather will change.'

'Would it matter?' asked Sebastían Martínez.

A few minutes later the Alba servant galloped off.

The weather seemed to show promise in the morning.

Paco left shortly after dawn in the Martínez traveling coach. A fresh wind blew across the narrow isthmus that connected Cádiz to the mainland, and low, scattered clouds raced overhead.

'Only a fool would drive to Sanlúcar on a day like this,' Paco had heard the coachman tell one of Martínez's servants before they set out. 'It's going to rain again, I can feel it in my bones.' He was bundled in a woolen cloak and wore a slouch-brimmed hat over his unhappy face.

They drove south across the isthmus to San Fernando, the coach swaying in the wind. By mid-morning it had begun to rain. They passed through the deserted streets of the village and headed north along the coast road toward Puerto Real, palm fronds rattling angrily in the wind.

Shortly after noon the coach came to a stop. The coachman's face appeared at the window. Paco, huddled in a woolen cloak himself, was half-frozen. The door opened and the coachman hurled his drenched bulk inside.

'We've got to sit it out, Excellency,' he said. 'There's an inn this side of Puerto Real.'

For no reason except that he couldn't, he wouldn't wait, Paco said: 'No, I've got to get there tomorrow.'

The coachman shook his head.

'A hundred reales more,' Paco offered.

'I wouldn't sit up there on that box in this rain for five hundred,' said the coachman. 'We'll spend the night in Puerto.'

It could, Paco knew, rain in Andalucía in November for days on end. Weeks on end.

'Then five hundred reales,' he said.

The coachman hesitated.

'And I'll share the driving.'

'Can you handle four spirited horses?'

'In Madrid I usually do my own driving,' said Paco, not bothering to mention his reputation for recklessness.

'Don Sebastián wouldn't like it.'

'Five hundred reales,' Paco repeated.

The coachman mulled it over. Paco could almost see what was going through his mind. These rich, crazy Madrileños. Why, five hundred reales was close to a year's salary.

'Maybe,' the coachman said, 'for five hundred reales we won't have to mention it to Don Sebastián.'

Paco climbed outside. The wind almost swept him off his feet. Clapping the coachman's hat tightly on his own head, he mounted the box, released the drag brake and took the reins in hand. Before they had covered half a mile he began to shiver with the cold.

They made Puerto Real an hour later. Through the driving rain Paco could dimly see the bodegas lining both sides of the road. A cart came by in the opposite direction, loaded with casks of the dry, heady manzanilla wine of the region. The carter, sodden and miserable-looking, cast a surprised glance at Paco sitting hunched over on the box of the traveling coach. It was the only other vehicle they had passed all day.

Paco reined up and hailed the carter. 'How's the road on the other side of town?'

'Na,' said the carter in his incomprehensible Andaluz. 'Casi na'.'

Nada. Nothing. Almost nothing.

291

'Difficult?'

The carter laughed, as if to say difficult was putting it mild-ly, and drove on. Paco and the coachman held a brief consulta-tion.

'There's a decent enough inn in town, Excellency.'

'I'd hoped to reach Puerto de Santa María today.'

'Road's not paved. Be hub-deep in mud. There's nowhere to stop along the way, if we have to.'

'Let's give it a try,' Paco said, his teeth chattering.

'You give it a try. I'm staying inside.' The coachman slammed the coach door shut. Paco returned to the box.

Rain splashing off the wet-sleek backs of the horses. Rain hurling itself at his face. Rain drenching his woolen cloak and running in two steady streams from the coachman's hat. A gust of wind that blew the hat away. Paco grabbing for it and almost tumbling from the box. The rumble of wheels on cob-blestones replaced by the plopping of hooves in mud. Paco had never felt so cold in his life, not even that first winter in Madrid. His left ear began to throb with pain, deep inside, and he heard a faint buzzing sound. The mud deepened. The horses, struggling now, could barely pull the heavy load along. His fingers grew numb. He could not feel the leather of the reins. His right ear began to ache, and he shuddered with a sudden enormous chill. But he felt exhilarated. Exalted. He even managed a smile. The duke was on his way to Madrid. He was on his way to the duchess. Braving the elements, brav-ing everything like a crusader seeking the Holy Grail five hundred years ago. Five hundred years he had been up there on the box, freezing to death, feeling the wheels slide and slip, the horses getting nowhere at all. He felt cold and sick and heard the wind call Cayetana, Cayetana, Cayetana, and the rain lashed down on him and the road curved and he drove straight off it into the ditch, the two lead horses down, the coach rising on two wheels before it settled back into the mud.

Paco climbed down stiffly from the box. The coachman came out and surveyed the damage. 'End of the road,' he said in disgust. 'What'll I tell Don Sebastián?'

'I'll pay for the repairs.'

The right front wheel had rolled a few yards off. It lay on its side in the mud. The road, what passed for a road, was de-serted. Dusk was only a few minutes off.

'We can't stay here,' the coachman said bitterly. 'But if we don't, gypsies'll strip the coach bare by morning.

'There are no gypsies. There isn't anyone.'

292

'There'll be gypsies. They have a sixth sense.'

'Then I'll pay Don Sebastián for the coach.'

'It must be nice to be rich,' replied the coachman in his bitter voice. 'Can you ride?'

Paco said he could ride.

'We'll take the horses on to Puerto de Santa Maria. Give me a hand.'

The downpour increased. By nightfall they had managed to unharness the horses. The coachman had cut harness leather short for reins and long for leads. He put his knife away and mounted. He leaned down and grudgingly offered a flask of brandy. 'Have a swig. You'll need it.'

Paco drank and returned the flask. For a brief moment the brandy warmed him. Then he was cold again. He heaved himself astride one of the horses. He clung to the reins with one hand and to the lead with the other. No saddle, no blanket. He had all he could do to keep his seat on the broad, slippery back, let alone lead another horse.

They turned and set out through the storm toward Puerto. The wind blew in their faces. The going was slow and treacherous. At first they could see little, and then they could see nothing. They rode slowly through a wet, black void, knee to knee. The horses floundered in the mud. The night grew colder.

Cayetana, the wind shrieked. Cayetana, Cayetana. Mockingly now.

They reached an inn on the outskirts of Puerto at midnight.

A bed. Sunlight streaming in through the shutters. Three faces peering down at him. The coachman. A fat fellow in a dirty white shirt with a blue stubble of beard on his jaw. A third face with the grave mien of a doctor with unpleasant news.

The doctor's mouth moved. The fat fellow gesticulated, and his mouth moved too.

Paco heard nothing.

He tried to sit up. He could not sit up. He heard a creaking sound in his ears, like dry wooden hinges turning. He tried to move just his right arm. Then just his right hand. He tried to move a finger. He felt a wild animal terror. The doctor's face blurred, and there were two fat fellows in dirty white shirts, and the coachman went in and out of focus. The sunlight at the window faded, like the light of a lamp when you trim the wick too low.

He could not hear. He could not move. He could not see.

293

He sank down into the terror.

Time stretched in darkness and silence. He lay there, not sleeping, not moving, not anything. Just the creaking in his ears. He burned with fever. His body ached as if he had been cudgeled from head to toe.

A long time later, movement. The dreamlike sensation of being carried along a dark, endless tunnel. And then something soft under his feverish head, and a jouncing under his body. Minutes? Hours? Days? He did not know. Again he tried to lift a hand, again just a finger. He could not.

Sebastián Martínez poured sherry from a crystal decanter into three glasses. His usually sparkling eyes were bleak. He looked his question at Cayetana and at Dr Peral, Madrid's most prominent physician. Peral had just come from the sickroom. He had driven down from Madrid at Cayetana's request after Cádiz's best doctors had diagnosed the case as hopeless.

Martínez's questioning look drew no reply from Dr Peral. 'Well?' he asked at last.

'The man should have been dead ten days ago. Two weeks. He has the constitution of a horse.'

'Or a tremendous will to live,' said Cayetana. 'Is there any hope at all, Don Felipe?'

Peral sipped his sherry and shrugged. He was a tall, stout man in his late forties, physician to the royal family and most of the grandees of Spain. He had probing, arrogant eyes and a mouth that wore a perpetual sneer, as if he had seen too much not of human misery but of human folly.

'Who can say? If he's lived this long, he may go on living.' Peral took snuff daintily. 'The constitution of a horse and the will to live, yes. But I fear they won't be enough.'

Cayetana looked at Martínez. There were tears in her eyes.

'What is it, doctor?' Martínez asked after a while.

Another shrug. 'Paralysis. A general paralysis of the nervous system. How his heart keeps beating, how he continues to breath, I don't know. He's blind, he's deaf, he can't move a muscle. I don't even know if he can think. There's no way to communicate with him.'

'And no hope? No hope at all?' Cayetana asked again.

'That depends on what you mean by hope, Doña Cayetana. What if, miraculously, he remains alive? He'd be a vegetable. Far better if he died.'

Peral's probing eyes searched their faces. Nobody spoke for a long time. At last the doctor cleared his throat and said:

'You're both intelligent people, or I wouldn't suggest this.'
Again that searching of their faces. 'It would be simple. It
would probably be for the best. I could – ' another clearing of
the throat – 'put him to sleep. He may be suffering terribly,
down in there where no one can reach him. I could give him
peace.'

Sebastían Martínez hurled his glass across the room. It shattered against a stucco mask of the pulque god. 'By Christ, no! '
he cried. 'The man took such a joy in living. Why, he – '

'What he's doing now is not living, Don Sebastián,' said
Peral softly. 'He'll never paint again. Never. The best he could
hope for – and even that would be a miracle – is a chair in the
sun and someone to spoonfeed him the rest of his life. If you
call that living.'

'You'll give him no easy death, Don Felipe,' Martínez said.

'As you wish, of course, my dear Don Sebastián.'

Martínez turned on him savagely. 'You know something?'
he said, and his voice sounded like that of an angry child.
'You're wrong, Señor Society Doctor. He'll live. He'll live to
paint your portrait.'

Peral took snuff daintily again and slowly shook his head.

Cayetana de Alba was crying softly.

Deep inside where no one but himself could reach through the
darkness and the infernal creaking he waited and lived a life in
those weeks and month a longer life than he had lived before
the body growing thin and the face gaunt but the mind living
that life removed from life and struggling every day every
hour every minute if I can move just one finger once or even
open an eye but the eyes did open unseeing Juanito who had
failed because he had to succeed by failing and Cayetana waiting in Sanlúcar is Josefa here now has it been a week or a year
does Javier know I can feel things a hand under my head and
they turn me someone turns me to change the sheets I suppose I am at the villa in Cádiz or Santa Maria perhaps it's the
Alba estate and her hand have they given up have they sent
for specialists or a priest move a finger try again no nada y
nada y nada perhaps this is death nobody ever came back to say
what it was like so maybe it is like this but it could have been
so different things you wanted to paint for yourself short savage strokes attacking the palette Mariana's hair spread on
your pillow in France now and simple-minded their son frightens the Indian learning war from the French so he can return
and fight the French someday if you tried if you only had really

wanted to try your hand at God's gift Padre Pignatelli called
it but God doesn't care He made the world and went away
take it all back erase the facility and tapestry cartoons to
please a crown prince now a king fatuous fat man cuckolded
by his toothless lady if lady is the word how Cayetana revels
in her toothless ugliness I could paint her that way I can feel
the gentle touch of a hand but it will go away there is never
enough time and perhaps now no time at all to please the
pretty society people stuff my purse with their silver and gold
for what Juanito had the magic once Pepe Hillo has it now
and I never found out about myself Sebastián Martínez's
heathen even they had it Santa Maria they did unable to read
or write naked savage living for their art because art is life
what do you believe in yourself isn't it too late to ask the
creaking the creaking in my ears is driving me mad never to see
a sunrise or hear a voice a sweet voice crying out in love Mariana Josefa Cayetana never feel a woman under me never smell
pigments and oil and turpentine never maybe I'm dead I might
as well be dead but if I had the chance the chance to do it all
over again a fornicating phony Tuertillo would say if he understood what this hand of mine that now I cannot feel
might have done a talent abused the magic never explored perhaps this is the punishment and I deserve it to have an opinion
and not be able to voice it to have a life and not be able to live
it to think you have the magic and not be able to discover it
nada y nada y nada never mind the pretty people paint for
yourself and now it's too late but the ideas chasing one another through your brain Olavide at his trial and maybe a few
others to enhance the composition a few lost recanting others
fat black priests in a dimlit church you have the magic Paco
said the old man who almost had it himself and you've got to
live got to move start with one finger one finger one finger
creaking in his ears and he wanted to scream but he could not
scream.

In the spring they took the emaciated body, for he was hardly
more than that, back to Madrid. It could do no harm. They
thought it only a matter of time until he died. Josefa had developed a congestion of the lungs and could not travel. They had
written warning her of his condition, but she refused to believe
it. She cleaned his studio and got his paints ready and his
brushes, and redecorated the room where he would recuperate.

Once, in the big black traveling coach that might have been
his hearse, he moved the fingers of his right hand.

CHAPTER TWENTY-FIVE

Popular Diversions

MANUEL GODOY, knight commander of the Order of Santiago, lieutenant-general of the Spanish Army, Duke of Alcudia, father of Maria Luisa's daughter Princess Isabel, found his status at court so awesome that he hardly could believe it.

Twenty-four years old and from a family of poor hidalgo pig farmers in Extremadura, Godoy dispensed royal patronage for the queen.

His mother had become a lady-in-waiting to Maria Luisa. His father served a brief term as royal treasurer before retiring to Extremadura on a fat pension. His friends held office everywhere.

Floridablanca, first minister of the realm, feared him, hated him, fought him and, this very night, if Godoy's guess was right, would fall from power.

For the oddest of reasons.

Floridablanca, according to Godoy's spies in the palace, had finally taken the king aside and told him what all Madrid already knew. Godoy could almost picture the scene.

'And why, sire,' Floridablanca might have said, 'are the Duke of Alcudia's quarters just one floor below the queen's, right under her bedroom?'

King Carlos might have been playing with his clocks, watching the cleverly constructed German ones send little porcelain figurines dancing out to mark the hour. Or he might have been cleaning his guns for the next day's hunt. He trusted the cleaning of his guns to no one but himself.

'Why? They have business together. I can't be bothered with the petty details of patronage, my dear count, and neither can you. We have bigger fish to fry. Ha-ha-ha. Let the queen and her little general – ' her little general was six feet tall – 'take care of those onerous details.'

'At night, Your Majesty?'

'Day or night, what difference does it make?'

'And why, sire, did the queen have a secret staircase constructed between her quarters and Godoy's?'

'A secret what? Staircase?'

'I can show Your Majesty.'

'No, if you say there's a staircase, there's a staircase. The halls are drafty and it's a long way around from – why are you looking at me that way?'

'Don Carlos, no man can govern who is a laughingstock.'

'Are you in some trouble, Count? If there's anything I can do to help – '

Floridablanca sighed. 'I wasn't referring to myself, sire. What I'm trying to say – '

'Trying to say? Ha-ha-ha. Be decisive. Say it.'

And finally, apparently, Floridablanca had said it.

The king looked at him, the enormous jaw thrust out, the beady little eyes blinking, the sensuous lips quivering. 'A slander! A monstrous slander! Who told you that? He'll get the garotte!'

But Floridablanca, a careful, thorough man, had gathered his evidence over a period of years. He could prove his case, and did.

The royal jaw seemed to retreat, the eyes blinked faster. The royal lips were flecked with spittle. 'And how long has this been going on?'

'Since before you were crowned, sire. Even your father knew. He had hoped her accession to the throne would curb Her Majesty's – appetites. I fear it's increased them.'

'*You* fear? What about me? What am I to do?'

'Get rid of him, sire. Exile him from Madrid. His control of patronage has made him a rich man, you know. You could use that as an excuse.'

'He's such an attractive, even-tempered young man,' the king said petulantly. 'Only yesterday he sang for me in that beautiful voice of his. I like the lad.'

Floridablanca said nothing.

'What does he see in that ugly old frump of a Maria Luisa?'

'Don't underestimate her, sire. A most voluptuous woman. And, she's ambitious. So's Godoy.' Floridablanca paused. 'There are two questions, sire. First, who is to rule Spain? You, or the queen and her – bedfellow?'

'I,' said Carlos in a querulous voice, 'am king.'

'Second, how can you rule if they're making a laughingstock of you? I'm sorry to put it so bluntly, Your Majesty.'

The fat king mulled it over. He hated intrigues; he hated unseemly disturbances. Maria Luisa had the temper of a fishwife, an Italian fishwife from Parma. Besides, she was clever, far cleverer than he. This business of being an absolute monarch was tiresome. Maria Luisa handled so many of the petty details.

But to fornicate with a swineherd from Extremadura? It was too much.

'Godoy is finished,' the king told Floridablanca. 'And you'll have your reward, Count.'

'I only want what's best for Spain.'

Would Floridablanca have mentioned Princess Isabel? Probably not, Godoy told himself. But who except the king would be blind enough to miss the resemblance between Godoy and his daughter – the same auburn hair, the same nose and full-lipped mouth, and even at the age of three that lovely, melodious voice? The king spluttered and boomed. The queen's voice was hoarse and nasal, as if she had a perpetual cold.

That hoarse and nasal voice now said accusingly: 'Some nights I'm almost surprised to find you here, Manuel.'

The queen had just entered his quarters through the secret staircase. She wore a purple dressing gown embroidered with gold.

'Some nights I'm busy elsewhere,' Godoy said flatly.

The queen's heavy bottom settled on a Louis XIV chair. She was wearing her gold teeth tonight.

'As, for example, with Pepa Tudo?' she demanded. The gold teeth clicked, biting out the name of her rival.

'Rumors,' said Godoy blandly. 'I have enemies.'

'And friends. Too many friends, Manuel.'

Godoy thought it wise to hold his silence. Maria Luisa was right about Pepa Tudo. When this business with Floridablanca blew over, Godoy would resume his affair with her. She had a wonderful body and knew how to use it, and with that dark hair and those big dark eyes, she bore an uncanny resemblance to the Duchess of Alba.

If this business with Floridablanca blew over. Godoy had packed an emergency bag. He was ready to flee the palace and the capital if he had to.

'Nervous?' Maria Luisa asked.

'No. Why should I be?'

'Carlos wants a word with me tonight. He sounded angry.'

'Floridablanca?'

'No doubt. The vacillating old fool doesn't give a damn who I sleep with. But he's afraid of me. And of you. He wants to cut us down to size. But he'll fail.'

'What makes you so sure?'

A lewd smile. 'I have ways. Come here, Manuel.' She patted her lap with a plump hand, and he obediently dropped on his knees before her and placed his head there. She fondled the auburn hair. 'Don't I have ways?'

'Your Majesty is a very attractive woman.'

'From the neck down, Manuel,' the queen said. 'As for this face of mine – '

'It has character.'

'And no teeth.' She exaggeratedly clicked the false ones. Godoy, his head on her lap, winced.

'And the cleverest mind at court.'

'Since when does a man make love to a mind?' Maria Luisa asked.

She was fishing for compliments. It was, Godoy realized wearily, her prelude to lovemaking. He thought of Pepa Tudo. He felt the plump royal hand stroking his chair.

'A man makes love to a real woman,' he said.

'After we get rid of Floridablanca,' she asked abruptly, still stroking his hair, 'what do you think will happen?'

'Aranda?'

Aranda had returned from his post as ambassador to France after the revolution.

'Yes. Aranda again, probably. For a while.' The plump hand, surprisingly strong, grabbed his chin and jerked his head up. The queen's eyes looked at him archly. 'Aranda won't last. He's too old, and too arrogant to suit Carlos.' The gold teeth flashed. 'And how would my Manuel like to be first minister?'

'Your Majesty, I – '

'You will be, one day. If you can keep your hands off little diversions like Pepa Tudo. I won't be anybody's fool, Manuel. One in the royal family is quite enough.'

Once again he said nothing. Sometimes, with Maria Luisa, he felt he had to walk a tightrope like a circus performer.

She pushed his head aside, as if it were an inanimate object, and stood, stretching voluptuously. His cheek rested for a moment on the brocade of the Louis XIV chair, and then he stood too. He hated her then. But he was the calmest of men. Nothing ruffled him. Nothing.

'Turn all the lights up, Manuel. I like to watch when you make love to me.'

He obediently went around the room adjusting the wicks in the oil lamps. Maria Luisa had disrobed. Under her sallow, ravaged face, her full breasts gleamed like white marble. Firm like marble too. She was not soft, that one, not in any way.

'Let me undress my little general,' she said, and he submitted to that.

As ever, she was very artful in bed. He could almost forget her unfortunate, her very unfortunate, face.

The king could not.

'How could an ugly old frump like you,' he spluttered, 'have an affair with a swineherd right here in the palace? It – it's monstrous. Deny that it's monstrous!' he shouted.

'I deny everything. Where did you hear such ridiculous nonsense? I want to know who's slandering me.'

'Everybody in Madrid's slandering you.'

'I want names.'

'You deny it? You actually deny it?'

'Look, you,' the queen said scornfully. 'If I were having an affair with General Godoy or with anyone, of course I'd deny it. And if I weren't having an affair I'd deny it too.'

'I have proof.'

'Proof,' she scoffed. 'A devious man can prove anything in any of a hundred ways. Believe me or believe that old shit Floridablanca. Take your choice.'

'I wish you wouldn't use language like that. And Floridablanca has nothing to do with it.'

'I can't accept that.'

'I can't accept a queen who's a promiscuous whore.'

Cry? Not yet, she thought calmly. Attack first, and then reason, and then resort to tears if you must. Carlos was in a state. She had the advantage. She intended to keep it.

'What did you call me?'

'Whore. You're a whore.'

She slapped his face, three times, quickly, as hard as she could. His head jerked back. Tears sprang to his beady little eyes. The heavy rings on her fingers had hurt him.

'How dare you!' he bellowed. He sat down on the edge of the canopied royal bed, resting his big jaw on his hands. 'How dare you strike the king!' The eyes blinked. A single tear rolled down his cheek. He looked ludicrous. 'I'll send you packing.'

'All right,' she said. 'When?'

'When? When what?' He gave her a dazed look.

'Return my dowry; give me a royal escort. I'll return to Parma. In a week, shall we say?'

She turned away from the bed and walked toward the door.

'Wait!'

'What do you want from me now? A denial? I've already given you that. Apparently you take Floridablanca's word over mine.'

'I didn't say that.'

'What did you say?'

'I don't know. Leave me alone.'

'I thought you wanted to talk. While we're at it,' she went on glibly, 'there are a few business matters we ought to discuss. Have you seen Martínez's latest report on the trade with New Spain?' Carlos never read his reports. They confused him. 'Two hundred thousand ducats less than anticipated for the fiscal year. For one thing,' she went on in a rapid-fire voice, 'there's the British blockade. For another, the Berber pirates. Last month they sent a flotilla up the Guadalquivir and sacked a dozen towns after they'd captured a frigate returning from New Spain. Martínez says – '

The King's jaw had sunk further into his large, powerful hands.

'Spare me the details,' he told her. 'Attend to it. Have Martínez attend to it. You know I have no head for figures. Why can't we sink the British fleet?' He brightened. 'Yes. Sink them and be done with them.'

'They,' said Maria Luisa, 'have a hundred and sixty ships of the line. We have sixty.'

'Then build more ships.'

'We don't have money to build more ships.'

'Then ally ourselves with France. Of course. The French, sworn enemies of the British, why didn't I think of it before?'

'With the Republicans, who've made a prisoner of your cousin Louis? We can't do that.'

'Then ally ourselves with the British instead of the French. Godoy's been in favor of that all along. Ask Godoy if that new French ambassador, what's his name – '

'You refused to recognize the new French ambassador.'

'What? Yes. Yes, so I did. On Godoy's advice. Or was it Floridablanca's?'

It had been Maria Luisa's.

'Don't mention that man's name to me,' she said.

'So we're back to that.'

'Isn't it why you sent for me?'

'*You* said Floridablanca advised me of your – little pecadillo. I didn't.'

From whore to little pecadillo. She was making progress. Carlos couldn't govern Spain without her and he knew it.

Maria Luisa, when she had to, could be a splendid actress. She sat down beside the king on the edge of the bed. 'He's nasty,' she said. 'He's a nasty old man who once – '

'Yes?'

Maria Luisa began to cry.

'Who once what?'

'Last year when the court went to the Escorial and I stayed behind because I. . . . Never mind. It isn't important. I wish you had more faith in me, that's all.'

'I do have faith in you.'

'Last summer when you went to the Escorial, Floridablanca stayed behind too. That sanctimonious Count Floridablanca of yours.'

'Of course, I remember now. The French ambassador, a treaty – '

'Which was impossible to execute, and Floridablanca knew it. A very convenient excuse.'

'An excuse? For what?'

Maria Luisa wiped away her tears with a scented handkerchief. She held tightly to her husband's hand. 'Maybe I will feel better, getting it off my chest. Your nasty old Floridablanca, he – he tried to seduce me.'

'Floridablanca? He *what?*'

'And I refused him. That's why he hates me. That's why he fed you those hateful lies about me. Don't you understand? He wants to destroy me. Destroy our marriage.'

Maria Luisa began to cry again.

The king began to laugh. He laughed until his massive body shook. He held his sides and went on laughing. Maria Luisa wondered if she had gone too far. But Carlos said: 'My dear, my dear, forgive me. It's just that – Floridablanca! How amusing! He's almost seventy. That old goat! '

And he went off into peals of laughter again. His face turned red. Tears streamed down his cheeks.

'I never want to see him again,' Maria Luisa said.

That sobered the king. 'I need him. I couldn't get along without him.'

'Could you get along without me?' she asked. 'Either Floridablanca goes or I go. Right back to Parma.'

'You don't mean that.'

'I never meant anything so much in my life. Do you need him more? Or me? Make up your mind.'

They talked, they argued, they talked some more. The king was bewildered; Maria Luisa was firm. They embraced, they cried together, they made love.

At three o'clock that morning a stunned Count Aranda was awakened and summoned to the palace, where the king and queen, both their faces blotched from crying, informed him that the first minister's portfolio once again was his.

For a few months, Maria Luisa told herself triumphantly

Once his vision returned and he was strong enough to sit up in bed or sometimes on a padded chair Josefa placed by the window, he began to read the illegal political pamphlets then circulating in Madrid. The young poet Leandro Moratín brought them, carrying them under his arm as casually as a loaf of bread. The art critic Cean Bermúdez hid them in a copy of the official Madrid *Gazette*. Sebastían Martínez and Carbarrús the banker came to the Street of Disillusion with the illegal pamphlets tucked between the sheets of an investment porfolio.

None of them stayed long.

Paco talked little, sometimes in a hoarse shout, sometimes in a whisper. His visitors wrote their comments on the pad Josefa always left at his side, and if a word displeased him he would hurl the pad across the room with a snarl, and the visit was over. It usually happened within the first few minutes.

Even Josefa, patient Josefa, had no success with him. Dr Rodríguez-Pereira had left a set of sketches of the hand symbols he used to communicate with the deaf-mute Doña Isabel, and Josefa painstakingly went over them with Paco. Soon she mastered them. He didn't.

He grew a beard beneath his gaunt cheeks. He could not be bothered with shaving. His thick, dark hair was streaked with gray now, and unkempt locks tumbled down over his broad forehead and half hid the ears that could not hear. Deep creases bracketed his mouth. Only his eyes, burning with a preternatural glow over puffy dark circles, showed the will to live that had taken him this far along the road to recovery.

Those burning eyes, with a look of sadness and intense curiosity, always returned to the pamphlets.

They told of Count Aranda, seventy-five years old now and first minister, falling asleep at a meeting of the Royal Council, his head nodding slowly, his chin finally coming to rest on the white silk ruffles of his shirt while the fate of Europe, or certainly the fate of Spain hung in the balance. A sudden snore disturbed the meeting, but nobody paid any attention. Maria Luisa ruled Spain. Her Manuel Godoy ruled Spain – Godoy, who wore the Order of the Golden Fleece and the grand cross of St John of Jerusalem on the elaborate, gold-embroidered uniform of a captain-general, the highest military rank in Spain.

Why, didn't everyone know that Godoy could trace his ancestry to the old Gothic kings? His name proved it. *Godo soy*. Goth I am. No wonder he had climbed so fast, the anonymous pamphleteers wrote. And wasn't it wonderful that Spain, in her time of troubles, found in this twenty-five-year-old paramour of the queen a Gothic king of old, a full grandee now in 1793, to help?

'There will be, there can be, no war,' Godoy insisted at the meetings of the Royal Council, while French Republican troops massed across the Pyrenees.

How could Spain go to war? If Spain did, that very considerable part of the royal treasury which went to furnish Godoy's new palace, not a small palace at all, would find other uses.

Such as the casting of artillery pieces for the northern frontier. All those forts, all those high mountain passes, and only six hundred artillerymen to defend them. Oh, there were twenty thousand cavalry, but the Royal Council seemed unaware of what the pamphleteers knew: cavalry charging into French artillery would quickly be blown to pieces.

But when Dr Guillotine's famous cure-all sent the royal head of Louis XVI tumbling from his shoulders, Madrid clamored for war. How dare the French behead the cousin of King Carlos of Spain? Wasn't England already fighting the French? Weren't the Prussians and Austrians and Swedes and Russians mobilizing to wipe out the disease of French Republicanism? The Church, led by the Dominicans, filled the royal coffers with money to fight the Republic. The grandees of Spain contributed more than their share. Even the blind beggars of Madrid tithed themselves, and their contribution was not small.

War? As long as the French don't attack, Godoy insisted, there'll be no war. The king named him Minister of Justice and Foreign Affairs. With the king's blessings he appropriated old Jesuit estates which until then had been crown land. The newest of Spain's grandees became the wealthiest.

Count Aranda, the pamphleteers wrote, was awakened one autumn day to be informed of his retirement as first minister. The queen allowed him to sleep on as president of the Royal Council, with all his honors intact.

Twenty-five-year-old Manuel Godoy became first minister. The queen visited him openly in his new palace, or his mansion in Aranjuez.

When he wasn't sleeping with Pepa Tudo, who so strikingly resembled the beautiful Duchess of Alba.

The king visited him frequently too. Soon it was the king who went to Godoy's levee, not the other way around. The king who by now had to know Godoy and Maria Luisa were lovers. Even Carlos, the pamphleteers wrote, was not that stupid. Not quite.

The king still delighted in wrestling with stableboys and guardsmen. To show his prodigious strength? Or because he enjoyed the bodily contact?

The king couldn't seem to get enough of Godoy, the pamphleteers snickered. Perhaps the first minister had *two* royal lovers.

France declared war in March 1793. A few minor garrisons were overrun in the Pyrenees, and the French Republicans sent arms and gold across the border to the restive Catalans.

War? A declaration, Godoy said. Just a declaration and several minor skirmishes.

As social arbiter of Madrid, Queen Maria Luisa had two rivals. The older of the pair, the Duches of Osuna, no beauty herself, kept the rivalry on an intellectual level the toothless queen could tolerate. But Maria Luisa's younger rival was a different matter.

Cayetana, Duchess of Alba, enjoyed the game for the sake of the game. She looked every inch a queen, as frumpish Maria Luisa did not, and people began calling her the uncrowned queen of Madrid. Everywhere she went, crowds gathered. Often she would leave her landau or berlin for an afternoon stroll, dressed in a simple maja costume while her ladies-in-waiting wore elaborate gowns. Cayetana did not have to dress like a queen to look like a queen.

Late one afternoon Maria Luisa sent her lord high steward, the Duke of Medinaceli, with a message for the strolling Cayetana. Medinaceli, accompanied by an escort dressed in the family livery, seemed very embarrassed.

'Good afternoon, Cayetana,' he greeted her. It was indeed a

306

lovely spring afternoon. Commoners, urchins, beggars – all followed happily in Cayetana's wake, to catch a glimpse of her beauty.

Cayetana caught the tone of the duke's voice at once. 'What have I done this time?' she asked.

'Why, er, nothing.'

'Then would you like to stroll with me? I thought through the Retiro.'

'I can't,' said the Duke of Medinaceli. A pause. 'And neither can you.'

'Neither can I? Whatever are you talking about?'

'She wants you off the streets.'

Cayetana smiled a ravishing smile. 'Surely you're joking.'

'Her Majesty says it's unseemly for you to promenade like this.'

'Like what?'

Medinaceli waved a hand vaguely. 'Like this. With all Madrid at your heels. As if you were – soliciting.' A quickly raised hand. 'Forgive me, Cayetana. That's what she said.'

'That jealous bitch!'

'Shh! They'll hear you.' Medinaceli nervously adjusted his powdered wig.

'Queen Maria Luisa,' said Cayetana clearly, 'is a jealous bitch.'

The crowd tittered.

'My God, Cayetana, have you lost your senses?' gasped Medinaceli.

And a melodious voice behind them said: 'Her Grace is right.'

They turned and saw Manuel Godoy, First Minister Godoy, resplendent in his gold-embroidered uniform. He swept off his bicorn and bowed.

Medinaceli's bow was even more correct. Like Cayetana and himself, Godoy was now a grandee of the first rank, but the old nobility was forever cutting him. He would, as the French put it, *tutoyer* them, and they would respond with a stiff and formal 'Most Excellent Señor.'

'It's a case of jealousy, plain and simple,' said Godoy. 'Cayetana's too beautiful. The queen resents it.'

With Cayetana, Medinaceli had been embarrassed. With Godoy he was annoyed. 'I have strict orders,' he said, 'to take the duchess home.'

'I,' said Godoy with a bland smile, 'have a sudden impulse to escort Cayetana wherever she'd like to go.'

He offered his arm. Cayetana looked at the two men. 'Why, thank you, Don Manuel,' she said.

'My orders – ' Medinaceli began, feeling ridiculous.

'Tell the old bag you couldn't find her,' Godoy suggested.

The crowd laughed. Medinaceli stood his ground. ' – are the queen's orders.'

Godoy put a hand on his shoulder. 'I like your livery,' he said, indicating Medinaceli's waiting escort. 'Have you noticed mine?'

Medinaceli flushed. Recently, King Carlos had issued a 'Yo el Rey' allowing Godoy's staff to wear the royal red stockings. This all but made Godoy a part of the royal family.

'Would you tell the king,' Goloy asked blandly, 'that *he* couldn't take Cayetana for a stroll?'

Unsure of his ground, the elderly duke retreated. Soon his carriage rumbled off.

'Thank you, Don Manuel,' Cayetana said.

He tucked her hand under his arm more snugly. 'The pleasure's mine.'

That night they shared a dinner for two in the private dining room of Godoy's palace.

The man intrigued Cayetana. In a few short years he had climbed from nowhere to first minister. Via the bed of the queen, of course, but still. He was handsome, he was charming, he had that beautiful voice.

The small, elegant dining room, its walls decorated with Goya tapestries, glowed in the soft candlelight. The partridge, well-hung from last year's hunting season, was delicious. The wines were French.

'Don't tell anyone,' Godoy said jokingly. 'One shouldn't drink French wines these days. But just try this Burgundy. Look at the color. Savor the fragrance. And then sip.'

Cayetana tossed the wine down in a long, healthy gulp.

'You're a strange one,' Godoy said.

'I do what I want. What's so strange about that? The wine's marvelous.'

The cognac was even better. After Godoy dismissed the servants, he poured it himself with loving care and heated the snifters over a candle. 'Try that fragrance.'

Again Cayetana tossed the drink down.

'You rush through life as if you want to live two lives at once,' Godoy said, shaking his head in amusement.

'Two? At least three or four,' Cayetana said, and mentioned

308

the gypsy's prophecy. 'I'll see no old age. I don't mind. I'd hate to grow old and ugly.'

They had more cognac and more talk. Cayetana knew what the first minister wanted, of course. Sooner or later they all wanted that from her. They knew about the languid duke.

'Like to see some sketches?' Godoy offered.

Cayetana bit her tongue to keep from laughing. He was so predictable. Erotic sketches, no doubt. To arouse her. It had probably worked with the likes of a Pepa Tudo. Daring nudes kept by the daring Manuel Godoy.

'Why not?' she said.

Godoy unlocked a cabinet and returned to the table with half a dozen small sketches. Red and black ink and a faint wash, Cayetana observed. The rather over-lush body of the actress La Tirana.

She recognized the style at once. She felt an unexpected twinge of jealousy. La Tirana had posed nude for him – and what else?

The poor man. People said he would never paint again.

'At the height of her powers as a woman, wouldn't you say?' Godoy asked.

'At the height of his powers as an artist,' replied Cayetana.

'You know who did them?' Godoy asked in surprise.

'Naturally. It has to be Goya.'

'You impress me,' Godoy said.

'Goya and I, we're old friends.' The thought of Goya so ill saddened her.

'I'll tell you one thing,' Godoy said. 'He'll paint again, or die trying. He's like you in a way. Wants to crowd everything into a lifetime. I admire that in a man.'

'And in a woman?' she heard herself respond with automatic coquetry. Would Goya ever climb out of that invalid's chair of his?

'Even more in a woman, Cayetana.' He was hovering over her, carefully pouring more cognac.

Would Goya ever be able to shock people again with that *baturro* arrogance of his?

She felt Godoy's hand on her hair. Would Goya come down to Sanlúcar after all? To recuperate far from the frantic pace of the city?

Godoy's hand lifted her long, dark hair and she could feel his lips brush the nape of her neck. Her boatman, she thought, could take them across to the sanctuary of Doñana, where they could picnic and walk among the dunes and watch the sea birds. Where they could dally for a while, on a warm afternoon, in a secret glade that she knew. The prospect made her shiver.

Godoy misunderstood. She was off in a dream. She hardly knew he was there. Emboldened, he reached inside the bodice of her black maja dress.

She stood suddenly and moved away from him. She had lost interest in the game. She never thought of herself as immoral: conventional morality bored her. She had briefly considered Godoy as a potential lover, a pawn in the game with Maria Luisa. But now Godoy bored her too. She regretted coming here. She wished she were home in bed, dreaming of Goya. And then making the dream happen. He'd need her now. An eagle. An eagle or a hawk, with a broken wing.

'The lady's gone off somewhere,' Godoy said with a wry smile.

'What?'

'Have I offended you?'

'I've been offended before.'

He bowed. 'It wasn't my intention.'

They stared at each other. A faint smile still lingered on his lips, but his eyes were hard.

'Would you have your coachman take me home, Don Manuel?'

'It's early. You're a very attractive woman, Cayetana.'

'That's news,' she laughed. 'But compared to Maria Luisa, who wouldn't be?'

'Now you're making fun of me.'

'It's a game I play.'

His triumph over Medinaceli, the intimate dinner, the wine, the cognac – all had inflamed him. 'I can think of other games.' He took her in his arms and kissed her. She struggled, one hand sending the crystal cognac decanter flying from the table. It shattered on the floor.

'Why,' she said sweetly, no longer resisting, 'I think Maria Luisa's little guardsman is going to rape me. What fun!'

He released her. 'Too good for me, are you?'

She yawned elaborately. 'It's strange *you* should say that, Most Excellent Señor.'

'Don't call me that. I want to hit them, when they call me that.'

'And will you hit me then? I wouldn't enjoy that at all.'

He glared at her. 'You share the bed of any popular bullfighter,' he shouted. 'What's wrong with me?'

This was a new game. Manuel Godoy had a reputation as the most even-tempered of men. She had managed to infuriate him.

'There's a difference,' she said. 'You see, I invite them.'

'The queen was right all along. You're nothing but – '

'Naturally. The queen is always right. You ought to know.'

'I will not be made a fool of.'

'Your reputation's intact, Most Excellent Señor. We're quite alone.'

He backed off. His pride could take only so much. He even managed a rueful smile. 'Perhaps I've been too hasty. Would you forgive me, and let me hope there'll be another time for us?'

'There are always other times.'

The smile became less rueful. 'Then I'll be patient. Tell me – what can I do to make you change your mind?'

She waited a moment, pursing her lips in thought. 'Oh, that's easy. They say the war is going poorly.'

'The war? What's the war to do with it?'

'When the captain-general marches at the head of a victorious Spanish army through the streets of Paris, I'll become his devoted slave.'

He turned away from her. He kicked the shards of broken crystal under the table and called for his coachman.

CHAPTER TWENTY-SIX

More Popular Diversions

Dr RODRÍGUEZ-PEREIRA'S COACH pulled up in front of the house on the Street of Disillusion. He helped the deaf-mute Doña Isabel alight. Josefa herself opened the door for them.

'Any change?' Rodríguez-Pereira asked. He looked younger than his fifty years. Doña Isabel, in a simple white dress, looked as ageless as ever.

'He sits all day. He won't talk to anyone. His friends have given up. They don't come much these days. He sits reading those pamphlets of his, over and over.'

'Now, Doña Josefa,' Rodríguez-Pereira said urbanely, 'you're not supposed to tell me about the pamphlets.'

They went inside and upstairs to the sickroom. It was a summer morning, not yet hot, but all the shutters were drawn. Paco sat on his padded chair with a stack of pamphlets on his lap. An oil lamp burned on the table at his side.

Rodríguez-Pereira threw the shutters back. 'What a beautiful day!' he cried, beaming as he faced Paco and formed the words distinctly with his lips. 'What a splendid day to be alive, Don Paco. Though I imagine those pamphlets of yours have it otherwise.'

'Don't understand,' Paco shouted.

Rodríguez-Pereira took the pad and wrote quickly: 'You ought to read more cheerful things. Like de la Cruz's *sainetes*. They've been bound and published, you know.'

Paco snorted. 'The older de la Cruz gets the more gloomy he becomes. So he writes comedies.'

'A man sees the follies of mankind, if he lives long enough,' wrote Rodríguez-Pereira.

'They're all mad,' Paco shouted in his loud, hoarse voice.

'Who?'

Paco waved an arm. Rodríguez-Pereira was pleased with the easy articulation of the movement. 'Everybody. The king. The queen. Aranda. Godoy. The French. Their insane Robespierre. My friends, wasting their time coming here. You. Me.'

'I?'

'To think you can cure me. Waste of time.'

'Strong as a bull,' wrote Rodríguez-Pereira. 'You should have died last year.'

'Then I'll die this year.'

'You'll live to be eighty.'

'Who wants to?' Paco bellowed. 'Will I ever hear again?'

'No.'

'Will I ever sleep without having nightmares?'

'That's up to you.'

Paco snarled, turning his face to the wall.

Rodríguez-Pereira wrote, and shoved the pad at him. 'Self-pity can destroy a man.'

'I'm already destroyed. I'll never paint again.'

'Show me your hand. No, hold it out in front of you. Steady as a rock. You could paint right now.'

'From a cripple's chair?' shouted Paco. 'I have to see life to paint it.'

'You could get up today if you wanted to.'

Paco gripped the arms of the chair tightly. His broad shoulders flexed.

'Try.'

'I can't.'

'You're afraid.'

'Me? Afraid?' In a roar.

'Afraid to leave this room stone deaf. Afraid of that voice. You shout. You whisper. You can't tell the difference yet. You could learn. Hand symbols too, if you wanted.'

'For deaf-mutes,' snarled Paco, and Doña Isabel, watching his lips, smiled at him.

'Afraid people will make fun of you. Afraid society won't accept you any more,' Rodríguez-Pereira wrote on relentlessly. 'You're a coward.'

'Get out of here,' snarled Paco.

'Throw me out,' wrote Rodríguez-Pereira.

Paco laughed harshly. 'I wish I could.'

'Get up and try.'

'Up? Don't be a fool.'

'I would have thought,' wrote Rodríguez-Pereira, 'that an artist of all people, with his imaginary world to fall back on, could cope with the disillusions of reality. You're deaf. So what? Stop feeling so sorry for yourself. Get up, get out, see the world – don't just read about it. And paint.'

'I can't walk, you fool. I'll never walk again.'

'You could have been on your feet three months ago.'

'Get the hell out of here!'

'Your tantrums don't impress me at all, Don Paco,' said the doctor. He did not write; he spoke slowly and distinctly, forming the words carefully with his lips.

'Tantrums? You don't know what it's like.'

'Doña Isabel knows.'

Doña Isabel, so frail, with that serene smile on her lips.

'You're the fool,' said Rodríguez-Pereira. 'You could have been blind. You're only deaf. Maybe you're even lucky. You don't have to hear the idiotic things people say.'

For a moment Rodríguez-Pereira thought Paco would smile. He didn't. 'Only deaf,' he said bitterly.

'You almost had the voice right that time.' Rodríguez-Pereira stood over him. 'Put your hands on my throat. Here. And here. That's right. Now – '

He felt the pressure of the big square fingers tighten. He saw the maniacal glow in Paco's eyes and the ghastly smile that showed dirty teeth through the unkempt beard. He heard a sound of laughter rumble up from the throat. The laughter bubbled away.

'I could kill you, you know,' Paco said in a flat voice.

Rodríguez-Pereira gazed steadily into the madness of those eyes. 'It's a question of vibrations,' he said, ignoring the fingers digging into his throat. 'The vocal chords vibrate, you see. Feel it. Now I'm shouting! Now I'm speaking normally. Now I'm whispering. See? Now put your hands on your own throat. Try it.'

But the strong hands remained where they were, tightening. Rodríguez-Pereira did not try to break their grip. Doña Isabel touched Paco's forehead under the stray locks of thick, matted hair. He was sweating. His fingers tightened. Josefa cried out. Doña Isabel stroked his forehead. Soothing. So soothing.

Through the window he could see a chestnut tree, the leaves stirring in a faint breeze. The infernal creaking in his ears had quieted. He cocked his head to one side. He could not hear it at all. He released Rodríguez-Pereira. He put his hands on his own throat. 'Now I'm shouting!' he shouted. 'Now normal. Now whispering.'

'Exactly,' said Rodríguez-Pereira.

Tears stood out in Josefa's eyes.

With unexpected strength Rodríguez-Pereira grabbed Paco's arms, heaved him to his feet, and stepped back.

Paco tottered. Sweat beaded his brow and ran down the creases of his emaciated cheeks. He bellowed at the doctor. He took one uncertain step after him. And another. Rodríguez-Pereira retreated slowly across the room, retreated from the preternaturally glowing eyes, the groping hands with their long, dirty fingernails. Paco took a third step. He clutched the window ledge to keep from falling. Two more lumbering steps. Waves of vertigo swept over him. He could not keep his balance.

'Dizzy?' asked Rodríguez-Pereira in a hoarse voice. His throat ached.

'Not so dizzy that if I get my hands on you – '

'You're walking, you great fool. Walking. Of course you're dizzy. The inner ear, the deafness, the vertigo, they're all of a piece. You'll have to learn to compensate. It won't take long.'

'I'm walking!' shouted Paco.

'You're shouting.'

'I'm walking.'

'That's good. That's better.'

An enormous smile suddenly wreathed Paco's face.

He reached Josefa. He clung to her. The tears were bright on her cheeks.

'Woman!' he cried. 'Where's my razor? This beard itches. I'm starving. I want chilindrón chicken. Call the maid. I'm filthy. Have her draw me a bath, hotter than hell.'

'Yes, Paco.'

'Where's Javier?'

'In school.'

'Get him. I want him to see how his father can walk.'

'He'll be home soon, Paco.'

'Get my studio ready.'

But in the weeks that followed he didn't set foot in his studio. He walked around the house. He climbed the stairs up and down, strengthening his legs. Soon he took short walks in the neighborhood. His appearance had changed so much that no one recognized him. Before long he would disappear from dawn to dusk. Walking. Just walking. He took no sketch pad. It was as if paper and chalk were inside his head, as if somehow they had replaced his lost hearing.

One day he told Josefa: 'I'm going to see Juanito. What's the matter with the man? He sits around the house all day sulking.'

'Maria del Carmen says he's retired.'

'Retired? A man retires when he dies.'

Paco swaggered out of the house that day without his cane. He walked briskly to Clock Street, where Juanito and his family were living. He pounded on the door impatiently and brushed past the sour-faced servant who opened it.

'Juanito! Where the hell are you, hombre?' he called. 'Indoors on a day like this!'

The four younger Apiñani children swarmed all over him. 'It's Uncle Paco, it's Uncle Paco.'

Maria del Carmen, matronly plump now, brushed back a stray lock of hair. 'Your uncle's not a well man,' she scolded. 'Stop jumping all over him.'

Paco caught most of what she said. He had grown more adept at reading lips. 'Who's not a well man?' he thundered. 'Where's Juanito?'

'Upstairs.'

'Hey, you, Juanito!' Paco shouted. 'Come on down, chico.'

315

'You won't recognize him,' Maria del Carmen warned. 'He's in a terrible state.'

'In a what?' Paco had missed the words.

'Terrible state. Drinks all – '

'We'll fix that. Juanito!'

Juanito Apiñani came slowly down the stairs. The four younger Apiñani children went outside to play, as if the sight of their father frightened them.

And well it might have. Juanito's hair, gray now, hung limply to his shoulders. His eyes were bloodshot, his white shirt wine-stained, his gait uncertain. The once-slender figure had gone to fat. His belly jiggled as he descended the stairs. Under the wiry gray stubble of beard, his skin was an unhealthy sallow color. When he shook hands Paco could feel how his fingers trembled.

'So, chico,' Paco grinned.

'They said you'd never walk again.'

'More slowly,' Paco said, with that mannerism of cocking an ear that could not hear.

'They said you'd never walk again.'

'Me? I'd been working too hard. Just taking a little rest.'

'Want a drink?'

'Not with you, chico,' Paco said, and saw the meanness in Juanito's eyes. 'You drink too damn much. You'll kill yourself.'

Juanito shrugged. He led Paco into the salon. Maria del Carmen was about to follow. Paco shook his head warningly. Juanito took a bottle from a scarred and stained table, pulled the cork, tilted his head back, and started to drink.

Paco struck the bottle from his hand. Wine splattered both of them. The bottle hit the floor, rolled but did not break.

'What the hell do you think you're doing?' Juanito cried.

'Saving your life, maybe. When's the last time you were out in the open air? The sunshine.'

Juanito shrugged again.

'Dumb bastard,' grumbled Paco. 'Want to leave Carmen a widow?'

'I'm finished. What difference does it make?' Juanito said in a listless voice.

'Makes a difference to her. And the children.'

'I'm all washed up.'

'Look, chico. Is it the bulls?'

'I'll never fight again.' Juanito glanced at the bottle.

'Good. Accept it. Your brother Tuertillo knew when to

316

quit.'

'I've quit, all right.'

'Go to work for Tuertillo. He'd have you.'

'I tried that. Seeing all the new kids coming up, it made me sick.'

'Then buy yourself a café. You're Juanito Apiñani. In a month you'll have every bullfighter and aficionado in Madrid for customers.'

Juanito laughed. 'I couldn't buy a loaf of bread. Francisco lets us live here. No rent. Tuertillo sends money from time to time. I've got debts. I could wind up in debtors' prison.' Another shrug. 'Who cares?'

'Everyone but you, apparently.' Paco felt an impulse to laugh wildly. He hadn't worked in almost a year, but it looked as if he'd have a second family to support again. 'I'll buy the café for you,' he said.

Juanito brightened for a moment. Then he said: 'I couldn't let you.'

This time Paco did laugh. 'You think I'd be doing it for you? I like a place to go afternoons. There isn't a café in Madrid I give a damn for. I mean a real bullfighters' café, not a phony one for the phony aficionados. A place a man can go with his friends, and maybe a back room where they could talk without the Inquisition breathing down their necks. Could you run a place like that?'

'I don't know,' Juanito said.

'You couldn't. Not looking like that. You need some color in your cheeks, a sparkle in your eyes. And either get thin again so they recognize Juanito Apiñani or get so fat they recognize Tuertillo's younger brother. Nothing in between. You need to look like you enjoy living. Right now you look like a walking dead man. See what I mean?'

Again Juanito brightened, and again the brightness faded. 'I couldn't let you buy it for me.'

'I'm not even sure I want to, chico. Not yet. Prove you could handle it first, then we'll see.'

'How?'

'We're taking a trip,' Paco said. 'We've both been cooped up too long. How soon can you start?'

'Are you serious?'

'Tomorrow,' Paco said firmly.

'Where to?' Juanito asked, and this time the brightness remained.

'I'll get us a couple of mules. We'll just go. Not Juanito

Apiñani the matador and Francisco Goya the painter. Just a pair of gypsies. Spain!' Paco cried, the idea building in him while he spoke, his voice louder and louder, his grin broader and broader. 'Maybe up to the Asturias or out to Extremadura. I want to see where that ignoramus Godoy comes from. I want – '

'Paco, amigo, you've changed.'

'I almost died. I want to live. Come with me. You'll be doing me a great favor, Juanito. Just the clothing on our backs, two old saddle mules, a few silver coins. We'll live off the land. We'll prove we're still alive. Well? What do you say? You'll come back ready to run the best café in town.'

'You're doing it for me.'

'Idiot. I'll come back ready to paint the way I've never painted before.'

The strength of the man, the new awesome strength of him, was too much for Juanito. 'Carmen,' he called, and his wife came in. 'Paco and me, we're taking a trip.'

'Alone? The two of you?' Maria del Carmen asked in alarm.

'Alone. The two of us, woman,' Paco said firmly. She looked at him and saw what was in his eyes.

'When?' she asked.

Paco waited. Juanito said: 'Tomorrow. At dawn.'

Before Paco left the house he gave Carmen a purse stuffed with silver reales.

They named the mules Manuel and Maria L. The latter, as if mindful of the fact that it had been named for a woman, and a toothless one at that, proved the more balky of the two. But it would follow the road half a dozen paces behind Manuel, and if Paco sometimes had to dismount and walk, leading Maria L by the reins, what did it matter? They had no real destination.

Working their way west they chose the narrowest, meanest roads they could find. These often led to tiny villages – a widening in the road, a few crumbling hovels, a small adobe church – that appeared on no map drawn by the royal cartographers. They camped in fields or on the rocky, dessicated hillsides, taking turns cooking over an open fire whatever Juanito had been able to steal during the course of the day's journey. Soon Juanito's jiggling belly melted away, and he became lean and hard. Both their faces were burned brown by the strong summer sun, so that they looked like gypsies. Juanito returned to his laconic ways and Paco, after all, was deaf. They would go sometimes for days without talking. Looking.

Just looking.

They saw a Spain that could have, that very likely had, existed in the fourteenth century.

One day they reached a village with an inn, where they spent a few of Paco's silver coins for a bed of straw and a meal. Paco wanted to talk, to try out his voice and his ability to read lips. They drank beer at the inn, and soon swineherds came in, staring at them suspiciously. Their suspicion faded when Paco offered beer. They drank to the health of Manuel Godoy, the first minister.

'Swineherd just like us, eh?' said the first man.

'Understand pigs and you'll understand people,' said the second. Both smelled of the barnyard.

'From Badajoz?' the first man asked them.

'No. Madrid,' said Paco.

'Madrid.' With an exchange of glances as if he had said St Petersburg. 'What brings you here?'

'The king's work,' lied Paco. Both swineherds crossed themselves and regarded him suspiciously again. 'The war, you know,' Paco went on, improvising.

'The war?'

'To learn how the people in the provinces feel about the war,' Paco elaborated.

'What war?'

'Who are we fighting now? All that France to the north?'

Paco had the notion that they could name no other country. 'Yes, France,' he said.

'What for?'

'They declared war on us because the king tried to rescue Louis XVI. Then the sans-culottes guillotined him and – '

'The what?' asked the first swineherd.

'Did which?' asked the second.

'Louis who?' asked the first. He pronounced it in the Spanish manner: Luis.

Fifty miles west of Madrid, Paco thought, and they had gone back five hundred years. The name of the dead French king, the revolution that had forced a constitution on him, deposed him, and finally killed him, Dr Guillotine's replacement for the headsman's axe – all of it was the talk of Madrid and all of it unknown here.

'I'm surprised you haven't answered the call to the colors,' he said, 'two strong young fellows like you.'

'The army? They'd have to drag us in shackles.'

Two mugs of beer thumped on the table. 'You wouldn't be

recruiters?'

Paco denied it. The two swineherds remembered an important errand and left, not quite running.

'I don't think,' Paco said, 'we're going to fare very well against the French.'

The town was called Fountain of Flowers, a real town with cross streets and three churches. Paco could see neither a fountain nor flowers anywhere. Dun-colored buildings stood high on a dusty escarpment over a dry riverbed. Manuel and the balky Maria L had climbed all day along the winding track to get there. The wind was hot. They passed other travelers on foot or riding donkeys. All the travelers seemed in a hurry. Paco hailed one of them, an old man dressed in rags.

'What is it?' Paco asked. 'Why all the people? Market day?'

The old man looked at him as if he were insane.

'Second Holy Week,' he said.

'Second what?' Paco thought he had misunderstood.

'Holy Week. You from Badajoz?'

Everybody always thought they were from Badajoz. Once you left Madrid and headed west, Badajoz seemed the limit of most people's horizons. Paco wondered where the people of Badajoz would think they came from.

'Badajoz,' he said. 'That's right.'

'City. Too big. Too much hurrying about. No time for Second Holy Week.'

'The Lord died for us only once,' Juanito said.

The old man bared toothless gums. 'Don't you sin more than once a year, in Badajoz?' he said, and walked on.

They reached the main street of Fountain of Flowers just in time for the procession. Women, old men, and children crowded the balconies on either side of the street. Soon the procession, following priests with tapers and a great wooden figure of Christ bearing his cross, made its slow way from the town hall to the biggest of the three churches. Many of the penitents, barechested but wearing pointed black hoods that covered their faces and dropped to their shoulders, carried huge crosses. Their bare feet shuffled along the unpaved street, raising clouds of dust, and Paco could hear the clanking of chains on their ankles. They carried whips, and when they reached the center of town, they began to whip themselves. A young woman in white leaned far over a balcony as they passed, and then another, and soon all the women were leaning perilously over the low iron railings. A spot of red sud-

320

denly appeared on a white dress, and the woman smiled. Another spot, and then a crimson splotch. The men continued to whip themselves. Sharp pieces of glass affixed to the tips of the leather whips glinted in the sunlight. The flagellants advanced, never breaking ranks, whipping themselves rhythmically with every second step they took. The Christ disappeared into the church, and the priests. The flagellants followed them. The dust settled. Splatters of blood alone remained on the empty unpaved street.

Carts and boards and old covered wagons, their canvas tattered and bleached white, formed a barrier for the makeshift bullring. The town was smaller than Fountain of Flowers – a cluster of hovels, a single plaza entered and left by the single narrow road.

At a signal, the bull was released from its cage, a monster of a bull with huge forequarters and a long sway-back.

'Eight years old if it's a day,' said Juanito in a shocked voice. 'Fought hundreds of times, probably. Look at those horns.'

Broad around at their base as a man's upper arm, they were the largest horns Paco had ever seen. The left one was splintered.

'Going to be a slaughter,' Juanito predicted. 'Let's get out of here.' He hadn't wanted to come anyway. He seemed determined to keep his distance from the bulls.

Paco shook his head, and they stayed. He wanted to see everything.

That monster of a bull gored three young boys during what passed for a corrida. The boys would rush out, gamely smiling, stripped to the waist, and using their shirts as capes. The bull never followed the lure. It stood planted on all four hooves and waited. Then when a boy, goaded by the crowd, came too close, the great head tossed, the boy went flying, and the bull was after him. Two of the victims had a chance to live, depending on the ability of what would pass for the local doctor – a veterinarian, if that. The third died in the ring screaming, tossed and caught again, and then down on the sandy ground on his back, the bull over him, bellowing, the head rising and falling, the horns at first impatiently digging into the ground and then one of them catching the boy under the chin and raising him high and tossing him a third time and catching him so that he hung head-down from the splintered horn as the bull galloped to the barrier and the boy's skull

321

struck the hub of a wagon wheel and split open like a ripe melon.

This, only this, enraged the crowd. They jumped the barrier with butcher knives and rusty old swords and began to hack at the bull. They swarmed all over the huge sway-backed beast, scores of them. The bull sank to its knees, tongue protruding. Paco saw the look of impotent rage on Juanito's face, but he felt nothing. He was just watching. Just watching, as he had watched the flagellants, shackled and whipping themselves, spraying the pretty white dresses of their pretty Extremadura women with blood.

The bull died. The knives went on hacking. A furious fat man stood near the cage that had held the bull, jumping up and down, red in the face, shouting soundlessly. Someone gave him a purse and he weighed it on the palm of his hand and suddenly smiled.

They would eat well in the village that night, all but the two injured boys. All but the dead one.

Paco felt nothing. He told himself it would be different if he could hear. But he would never hear again.

The dust of the road. The barren plateau of Extremadura. The mean-faced, small-eyed, undernourished pigs, surprisingly pink because they had no mud to wallow in. The swarms of flies. The emptiness of the landscape. No trees, no hovel, no house, hardly a road. It was like the highlands of Paco's own Aragon. The days, one after another the same, Juanito riding, Paco leading Maria L, starting from nowhere and going to nowhere. Extremadura, that rugged land on the Portuguese frontier. And then finally the city, the only real city they saw on their strange journey.

Badajoz. No wonder Godoy left, Paco told himself. A few dusty plazas, a few church spires over the low dun-colored buildings, the people, like people in any border town anywhere, hostile to foreigners.

But it was a city of some size. It had a Hospital General and a madhouse.

They reached it early in the afternoon, a brutally hot day. They found a fountain with a meagre trickle and washed the dust of the road from their faces. They drank the tepid water.

'Where does a man go to get cool?' Paco asked a woman filling a clay jug.

She heard the alien accents, the accents of Aragon and Madrid, the other end of the world, and made the sign to ward off the evil eye. Balancing the jug on her head she walked off quickly, casting one furtive glance back.

A man came, a one-legged man hobbling with the aid of a crutch, and Paco asked his question again.

'On Sundays?' the man said.

'Is this Sunday?' Paco asked.

'Church. It's cool in church.'

'Anywhere else?' Paco thought of the flagellants. The last place he wanted to go was church.

'Well, as it's Sunday,' the one-legged man said, and cackled like a rooster.

'As it's Sunday what?'

'They open the madhouse. To visitors. Used to be an old fortress. Walls a yard thick. It's cool in there.' Again the rooster cackle. 'Good for a laugh or two. Diverts a man, it does. You gypsies?'

'No.'

'They wouldn't let gypsies in.' Another cackle. 'Or maybe wouldn't let them out. I'm going. You coming?'

Paco and Juanito looked at each other. 'All right,' Paco said.

As the rooster had predicted, it was cool in the madhouse. They paid a copper coin each for the privilege and climbed upstairs to a gallery. Narrow, with a flimsy wooden barrier, it went around three sides of the main room. It was crowded with gentry dressed in their Sunday best, men and women both. They stared down, they pointed, they nudged one another; they laughed and stared down some more.

It took Paco's eyes a while to adjust to the dim light that entered through a grated window high on the opposite wall.

The floor, huge slabs of flagstones, was littered with inmates. Littered was the only word Paco could think of. They sat, they reclined, they lay stretched out, their bodies flung across one another. Most of them were naked. Some wore tattered remnants of clothing. One wore a tricorn hat and nothing else. Another stood in a rigid arrogant pose, wearing an Indian feather headdress and a leather apron. He extended a hand in a regal gesture, and a man in a black cloak kissed it. Two powerful men, their bodies glossy with sweat, were locked together, wrestling. A man in a once-white shirt was opening his mouth and, Paco realized, probably singing at the top of his voice.

What they all had in common was the look of madness in their eyes.

Where had Paco seen that look before?

For a moment he couldn't remember. And then he saw Josefa, bringing him a mirror and soap and his razor, hoping he would shave. In the mirror he had seen those same eyes.

He heard the creaking of hinges in his ears. Suddenly he wanted to run.

But then he looked away from the floor of the madhouse to the gallery of spectators, the gentry of Badajoz, here on a Sunday afternoon to enjoy themselves.

The same blank madness was in their eyes.

He looked down again. He saw the keeper, big-nosed, wild-haired, naked to the waist like the flagellants and carrying a whip. The same look of madness gleamed in his eyes.

They're all mad. Godoy. Aranda. The king. The queen. The French. You. Me.

The creaking in his ears grew louder. He wanted to run and keep on running. Whatever afflicted him he would never cure.

Juanito tapped his shoulder. He turned. Juanito was talking. He became aware that the gallery had almost emptied. The last few spectators were rushing for the stairs.

'What is it?'

'Fire,' someone said.

'Where?'

Juanito shrugged.

They ran for the stairs.

Smoke poured from the windows of the Hospital General of Badajoz. An occasional tongue of flame tinged the smoke red. People were shouting frantically, screaming, running about aimlessly. Flames billowed and roared at the door. A man tried to rush out. The fire caught him. An instant he stood there, back arching, mouth opening, clothing on fire, hair on fire, then he fell back. From a low window burst out several men. Then they disappeared in the smoke and for a terrible moment Paco thought they were lost too. The smoke roiled, blue-gray, tendrils of flame coiling in it. The men got through. They kept running. A crowd had gathered. Paco recognized some of the spectators from the madhouse. The men were stripping off their frock coats. Some of them darted in through the low window. Flame climbed the walls of the hospital. Flame touched the roof, dancing over the tiles. Smoke poured out of every window. Soon the shape of the building seemed to dissolve. You could no longer see the windows. Just the smoke, black against the sky. A man appeared through it, carrying a child in his arms. Another carrying a baby. And then two using a sheet as a stretcher to bring through the smoke a man wearing a loincloth. Nobody could go near the door. There no longer was a door. They used the windows. The same people who had diverted themselves at the madhouse rushed blindly through the smoke now, forgetting the danger to themselves. All of it in total silence, the silence in which Paco Goya would spend the rest of his days. Suddenly he was running through the smoke himself. A wave of heat buffeted him. He reached a low window ledge and climbed over it, groping. He was aware of Juanito at his side. Dimly he could see a long room, rows of beds. Arms were raised in supplication. At the far end of the room flames leaped. He found an old man and lifted him. The old man seemed to weigh nothing. He ran with him to the window. He could not breathe. He carried the old man through the window and coughed and took a gulp of smoke-filled air and went back. A woman. Her head against his shoulder, her red eyes looking up into his face beseechingly, her mouth screaming soundlessly. He brought her out. He went back. And back. And back again. It might have been minutes. Or hours. He coughed rackingly and went back. His eyes streamed tears. He saw Juanito carrying a child under each arm, stumbling, getting up, reaching the smoke at the window, dissolving in it. A bed. Another man too weak to move. Lift him, hurry. A ceiling beam falling in flames across the bed. More flames, flames in the ward now, spilling liquidly across the floor. He could not find the window. His arms were lead. He wanted to drop the man he held. He had to find the window. The man's hand clutched his shoulder. Someone else grabbed him. They ran with the man to the window and outside. The last few patients were carried and pulled and dragged through the window. What had been a window became a curtain of flame. Again he wanted to go back. Someone held him. He struggled. Juanito. A shake of the head. 'It's all we can do, chico.'

It was all anyone could do, and more than he had dreamed anyone would do. He wanted to cry out with the wonder of it. That they should risk their lives, all of them, the same vapid faces with their mad eyes at the madhouse. That they should rush through the smoke, into the flames, to bring the victims out. That they should do this thing that had to be done because people were dying in there. No heroics. Just the doing of it. He felt outside himself. Suddenly he felt everything.

The roof collapsed. A wall buckled outward, split open, began to fall. He stood there staring. Juanito had to drag him out of the way.

They stayed that night at the best inn Badajoz had to offer. Juanito slept like a dead man. Paco did not sleep at all. The drop of the gleaming blade and the rolling of the French king's head into a basket, the revolution on the other side of the Pyrenees that would be perverted, liberty, equality, and terror, Robespierre's terror of the pamphlets, the war that hadn't come to the provinces, the flagellants whipping themselves with glass-tipped whips, the white dresses of their women splattered with blood, the village bullfight where a boy had died for no reason at all, the maniacal hacking and cutting of the still-living beast, the Sunday diversion of watching lost souls in a madhouse – that would always be, in France, here in Spain, anywhere.

As there would be catastrophes, like the fire.

And men to strip off their Sunday coats and plunge through smoke and flames to save a life, any life.

All night he lay awake with his elation. The world was mad, and beautiful in its madness.

He could hardly wait for dawn. He woke Juanito early.

'I'm starving,' Juanito said.

'Later.'

They went outside and after much searching found a shop that had some paints and brushes.

'Have you canvas?' Paco asked.

'Used to. No call for it. There's a portrait painter comes down twice a year, but he brings his own.'

They left the shop. 'I've got to paint it.'

'Paint what? Can't it wait till breakfast?'

'Find me something to paint it on. Anything flat.'

'Wood?'

'Copper plate, tin. Anything.'

Juanito appeared an hour later in the courtyard of the inn with a small sheet of tin plate, barely a foot and a half long and a foot wide. 'Something like this?'

Paco just glanced at it. A coach came. A coach went. He never saw them. 'Get me a table, hombre.'

'Can't we have our breakfast?'

'Who needs breakfast? A table.'

Juanito shrugged in resignation and entered the inn and came out lugging a low table. He set it down in the courtyard. Paco put the tin plate on it.

'How about something to eat now?' Juanito asked hopefully.

Paco wasn't looking at him. He stood back from the table, studying the sheet of tin. It lay horizontally. He turned it vertically. He scowled and muttered to himself. Juanito went inside to eat.

All day Paco worked. He had it in his hand, and he knew he had it. He could feel it leaping from his fingers like flame.

The magic. Tiepolo's magic.

He painted quickly. The flame-shot smoke hanging like a pall, like death. A rhythm to it, and a violence. Line? The neoclassic purity of line? No. Let it flow, the figures woven together, huddled in a mass under smoke and flame. The decorative baroque? Impossibly billowing colors? No. The light. The firelight. Let it glide. Over the victims. Over their rescuers. Waiting to engulf them. The blackness above. No background. Short harsh strokes here. Avoiding death. Cheating it, almost. Death in the hanging blue infinity of the smoke. So. A lightness to it, but a terror. Hurry. They had to hurry. Paint it all of a piece, flat on the tin plate, an instant in time, a fight against death, an affirmation of life.

The magic of life.

He finished painting *The Fire* in the gathering evening shadows of the courtyard. Juanito came and looked. 'Chico,' he said. 'My God, chico.'

Paco stretched wearily. He had stood hunched over the low table all day.

Juanito stared at the painting.

'We're going back to Madrid,' Paco told him.

He bought the café for Juanito, and then he locked himself in his studio. Word got around somehow. He's painting again. Goya's painting again. Noblemen and their ladies arrived in fine carriages, begging to have their portraits done. Godoy came. He was as much in demand as a portrait painter as before. More. He had come back from death. A *figura*. A legend in his own lifetime.

Josefa sent them all away. Later. Next month maybe. Not now. Now he was painting for himself.

The Procession of Flagellants. The Village Bullfight. The Madhouse. with its somber grays and those eyes, those wild eyes, reflecting the madness he himself had managed to survive.

Then back, back to the destruction of a man, his benefactor Olavide, and back to the flight of Mariana to France, with their son – Santa Maria perhaps he's in the French army now, he'd be old enough, fighting this little war they don't know of in the provinces, learning with that cold frightening logic of his, waiting for the bigger war that had to come, when he would fight against the French – back to all that in the tribunal of the Inquisition, all in blacks and browns and muted yellows, the penitents wearing their tall mitres with the St Andrew's cross, their hands clasped piously, their eyes dead, the fat black priests watching smugly there in the dimlit church.

He did ten paintings in all at the end of that year, and sent them as a gift to the Royal Academy of San Fernando.

He called those paintings *Popular Diversions*.

BOOK FIVE

BOOK FIVE

IT IS DIVERTING, the old man thinks, seated in the glittering crowded silence of the Café de Paris in 1824, to remember how his star and the star of the Prince of the Peace flashed high in the Spanish firmament at the same time.

Diverting?

Ironic, he tells himself, watching the tail-coated waiter bring a silver tray of pastries to the prince and his lady.

Things are never what they seem, or never what you hope. Not for the swineherd from Extremadura, and not for the *baturro* from Aragon.

The war, the dress-rehearsal war for the real war that will come later, goes poorly for Spain. French troops occupy Catalonia and take the fortress city of Pamplona. The king hunts, the queen fumes over Pepa Tudo, Godoy sues for peace. The treaty is signed in Basel, in a little house with a garden. Spain loses half an island in the Caribbean and pays a yearly indemnity to the Republic, money the French will use to cast new cannon for the terrible war to come. Godoy agrees to an alliance with France, and that alliance can have only one result.

War with England.

From the time Don Paco begins to paint again until Napoleon's downfall, Spain will hardly know a year without war.

For this, for this incredible stupidity, Manuel Godoy is named Prince of the Peace. In royal processions a herald precedes him carrying a two-headed mask of Janus, one to look back on the glory of the past and one forward to the greater glory to come.

And that Most Excellent Señor, Don Francisco de Goya y

Lucientes, painter to the royal household, is the irony any less for him?

One night, peacefully in his sleep, his brother-in-law Francisco Bayeu dies. The Royal Academy of San Fernando elects Don Paco to replace him as director of painting. But how can a deaf man teach? He tries. The silent questions come winging from all sides, and he can't read every pair of lips at once. He fumes, he storms, he becomes as tyrannical, as contemptuous, as Anton Rafael Mengs himself. His students tremble at the approach of his heavy footsteps. Each day he enters the Academy promising himself he will be kind and gentle, remembering how Mengs once terrified him. But it is no use. Five minutes in the studio and he is ranting. One boy shows considerable talent, and Don Paco is particularly hard on him. Mengs, all over again. History moves in a circle. There is no escape.

One day the talented boy bursts into tears. His name is Asensio Juliá. He will be a painter, he vows, and to hell with that tyrant of a director Goya. The lesson stops. All the students are watching. Asensio Juliá hurls his palette to the floor and leaves, the tears running down his cheeks.

And Don Paco, contrite after it is too late, resigns as director of painting. Someday, he tells himself, he will do something for Asensio Juliá. The irony again. Mengs, after all, took him into the tapestry works.

But now he is a figura; they mention his name in the same breath with El Greco and Velázquez, and the Academy cannot simply let him resign. They appoint him honorary director of painting.

A title, he thinks now, in Paris in 1824, about as meaningful as Prince of the Peace. Honorary Director. For life. Perhaps now, in exile, he still holds the title. It amuses him to think so.

Francisco Bayeu dies in Madrid and, as suddenly, Villafranca, Duke of Alba, dies in Sevilla. An epidemic of fever, not particularly virulent, but the languid duke succumbs.

Cayetana retreats in mourning to her estate in Sanlúcar.

Two women. Josefa and the duchess. The death of a brother and the death of a husband.

One death gives Paco the coveted post of director at the Academy, which he cannot keep.

The other death gives him, for a time, that certain arrogant elegance, which no man can keep.

In the Café de Paris the old man leans back, cigar clamped between his teeth. The red velvet plush of the walls, the glittering gaslight, the gaily dressed diners whose chatter he cannot hear – and the Prince of the Peace staring across the room at him.

Recognizing him. He is sure of it now.

The leather case of dueling pistols falls to the floor. He retrieves it. And the Prince of the Peace watches that too, not quite smiling.

CHAPTER TWENTY-SEVEN

Only Goya

JOSEFA WAS NOT SMILING at all when Paco came rushing into the house on the Street of Disillusion.

'They voted today,' he shouted. 'Eight votes for Gregorio Ferro. Ten for me. I'm the new director.'

He hugged Josefa, dancing her around the room. 'I'll make changes,' he went on eagerly. 'I won't be a tyrant like Mengs, nor – '

'Nor what?' Josefa asked, pulling away from him. 'Bookish and unimaginative like my poor brother? Is that what you were going to say?'

Paco shook his head. But it was what he'd been thinking.

'You said it often enough when he was alive. Why stop now? All he did was take you in, give you your start, intercede for you when that temper of yours got out of hand. And when he's dead, you get his position. Do you expect me to dance the jota?'

Josefa smoothed her black dress, sat down, and rang for the maid. 'Some tea? You look tired.' Tea had always been Francisco Bayeu's favorite drink.

Paco wanted champagne. 'Yes, I'll have a cup of tea.'

They drank the tea in silence. The tray of turrón cakes, which Francisco Bayeu had loved so much, remained untouched.

Bayeu seemed to be there in the room, between them.

With every sip of tea, Paco felt his elation dwindling. He couldn't blame Josefa. Running in like that, shouting the news; it was his own fault.

'Ramón,' Josefa said.

'What?'

'I said Ramón. Somehow it would have been fitting if they'd named him director. As a tribute to his older brother.'

'I studied under Francisco too.'

'And you're a better painter than Ramón, I know. But still.'

'The Bayeu name,' Paco said, all his elation gone.

'All right, yes. The Bayeu name. What's wrong with that?'

'Nothing's wrong with it. But even Ferro's five times the painter Ramón is.'

'Let's not go into all that again. You never liked Ramón.'

'He never liked me.'

'Sometimes I wonder why you married me. You hate my whole family. Except Manolo.'

'Manolo's one of the best religious painters in Spain,' he said placatingly.

'Religious. You use the word so contemptuously.'

Santa Maria, he thought, what does she want from me?

'Listen, cara,' he said, 'I didn't want to tell you this until I'd finished it. I've been painting a portrait of your brother.'

She looked up in surprise. 'Manolo? I didn't know he was sitting for you.'

'Francisco. From a portrait I did a few years ago. As a tribute to him.'

'I'd love to see it.' With warmth in her voice.

They climbed the stairs to his studio. The unfinished portrait of Francisco Bayeu stood on the easel. Gray, the grayness of the man, more even than the grayness of Mynheer van der Goten. The gray wig, the pale face, the gray frock coat of Francisco Bayeu sitting stiffly on a brocaded armchair, a paintbrush in his right hand, a harassed, defeated look in his eyes, the tight, thin, unflattering line of the Bayeu lips. Josefa studied it for a long time.

'I can finish it in a day or so,' Paco said, his enthusiasm returning.

'Don't.'

Her face was averted. He hadn't seen her lips, but she turned on him savagely then. 'Don't you dare. Look at it. The eyes. You make him look mean.'

'Not mean. Tired from overwork,' Paco tried to explain.

'And the mouth,' Josefa went on. 'So prim and – unforgiving. Is that how you saw Francisco? After all he did for you?'

'We had our differences, but I liked your brother.'

'Not if your so-called tribute is any indication. It's hateful.'

Paco cocked his head to one side in that deaf gesture. 'What? I didn't understand you.'

'Isn't that deafness of yours convenient? You only understand when you want to.'

'That's not true,' he shouted. 'I really didn't hear you.' Hear. To use the word hear, even now. He felt isolated, alone. Josefa stood in front of the portrait, close to him, but she seemed a

336

long way off. Like the rest of the world. He tried to remember the sound of her voice. He could not.

'Or at least change it,' she said more reasonably after a while. 'Soften the mouth. Make the eyes – I don't know.'

'They're Francisco's eyes. Are you trying to teach me how to paint?'

'Nobody could ever teach you a thing. I'm surprised you didn't go to one of your little actresses with your triumph. Tell me *that's* not true. Tell me you didn't understand. One of your little actresses,' she cried. 'With a bottle of champagne and a bouquet of roses.'

There had been no little actresses since his illness. 'Are you serious?'

'It's the talk of Madrid. Don't you think I have ears?'

'Meaning I don't?'

'No, no.' Wearily. 'I didn't mean it that way. Do what you want. You always do what you want. Finish the portrait. I don't care. You always get your way. With Francisco, even after he's dead. With the Academy. With me. With your little actresses.'

Later that day a letter came from Sanlúcar. He recognized her handwriting at once.

Standing precariously in the prow of the flat-bottomed boat, his neck craned so that he could look back at the duchess, Brother Basil asked: 'D-does Your G-grace m-m-mean that?'

Brother Basil had been a lame mendicant friar when Caye-tana de Alba found him and took him into the household some years before. He had a clubfoot and a simple mind, and he stuttered. Though he had a morbid fear of water, he would die cheerfully to please Cayetana. She made him the butt of jokes from time to time, but had still given him the only happiness he had ever known.

'Of course I mean it,' cried Cayetana over the howl of the February wind and the steady slap of water against the sides of the boat. 'In weather like this we'd better propitiate the gods of the sea.'

'That's p-p-pagan,' stuttered Brother Basil. He almost lost his footing in the prow of the boat while the four oarsmen dipped and rowed. Far ahead across the choppy water at the mouth of the Guadalquivir, he could barely make out the low silhouette of the sanctuary. The boat had just left the little landing stage at the foot of the hill on which the town of San-lúcar stood. Brother Basil wished he were back in the palace on the heights above Sanlúcar. Or in Madrid. Or in the Sahara Desert. Anywhere but here.

He raised a hand, almost lost his balance again, and muttered some Latin mumbo-jumbo to the non-existent sea gods whom Cayetana pretended she wanted to propitiate.

'Louder,' she shouted over the wind. 'They can't hear you.'

Brother Basil screamed and stuttered in Latin. What he said was: 'This madwoman will be the death of us all yet.' He could have his little joke too, since she made him risk his life. Cayetana understood no Latin.

'Thank you, Brother Basil. As you can see, already the ocean's calmer.'

'It's not the ocean, Mama-Grace,' said the little Negro child who was seated comfortably on Cayetana's lap. 'It's only the river.'

No one in Madrid – or in Sanlúcar for that matter – knew where the six-year-old black child had come from. Some said that Sebastián Martínez had given her as a gift to the duchess. Three years ago, Cayetana had drawn up papers to adopt her. Maria de la Luz, she insisted, was her own daughter now. She treated the child with warmth, but like a lapdog. Not that she didn't have one. Cowering at her thigh, the little bichon frise, looking like a drenched white mop with tiny legs, whimpered piteously at every sway and lunge of the boat. Cayetana stroked the tiny soaked head. 'There now, Don Carlos,' she purred, 'we'll be across before you know it. I'll take care of you, I promise.'

She watched Brother Basil seat himself awkwardly. It had begun to rain. The farther shore approached slowly, and after a while through the rain she could see the high square tower of the great hunting lodge that had belonged to her dead husband. It would be a mess, she knew. Villafranca had never liked to hunt and the lodge in the sanctuary of Doñana had long since fallen into disrepair. The Sanlúcar palace staff had been there for two weeks now, trying to restore some order.

It would be a good place for the duchess to think things out. Madrid, to understate it, hadn't worked. She had spent too much of her life in mourning – for her dissolute father, for her mother, for her grandfather, the crusty old duque-general she had loved so much, and now for Villafranca. She lacked the temperament for mourning. A month or two in black – black suited her well, it set off the creamy whiteness of her skin beautifully – she could take. But a year? A year without parties, without flirtations, without the promenades that made the

338

queen so jealous, without a man – it was too much.

Perhaps, if she had been in Sevilla when Villafranca had died so suddenly of the fever, it would have been easier to accept. But she'd been in Madrid, at the theater, the night the messenger had come. She set out by fast traveling coach for Sevilla the next day at dawn. They had already buried the duke when she got there. It was as if he hadn't died at all. Or hadn't lived. Or both. He was buried just a few months before his fortieth birthday.

Leaving a very young and very alive widow. June, she thought. June 1796. Eight months ago. She had returned to Madrid. 'We share your grief, Cayetana,' the queen had said. 'And it will be so dull without you. A year of mourning. No parties. No dancing. No promenading.'

Possibly Cayetana could have done it. But, living, she had never seen a great deal of her husband. And she had never seen him dead at all. It was as if he had just gone away for a time.

It worked for two months. And then she went to the bullfights outside the Alcalá Gate. In black. Hillo was fighting.

'No more bullfights,' the queen told her the next morning.

On a fine day in November, she strolled through the Retiro. Could she help it if she was so attractive? As always, she drew crowds. Again she wore black, with a simple yellow sash around her slender waist to set it off. Yellow was her favorite color.

'Cayetana, what am I going to do with you?' the queen said a few days later. 'No more promenading. It's most unseemly.'

'I need fresh air, Dr Peral said.'

'You have a garden.'

And in the garden, she had a palace. In January she invited a few friends – a very few old friends – to a small soirée. Even the queen could not object to that. But one thing led to another, the soirée became a dinner party, the group of a few old friends became a hundred people who danced until morning. Cayetana wore a black gown. But she carried a fan, Hillo's fan, and how much fun it was to flirt with a fan if you knew the stylized gestures! Cayetana knew the stylized gestures. She had even invented a few of her own.

This time the queen did not summon her to a private audience.

A few days later a fire of mysterious origin all but gutted the Alba palace. Cayetana had no doubt who was responsible. Maria Luisa, after all, couldn't banish her from court while she was in mourning. That would make the queen more unpopular and Cayetana more popular than ever.

'My dear Cayetana, this is a bad time for you, isn't it?' Maria Luisa commiserated the next day. She did not mention the all-night dancing at all. 'The death of your poor husband, the Lord rest his soul, and now your palace in ruins. Can we do anything to help?'

'I'm going to the country,' Cayetana said, knowing it was what the queen had wanted all along. A very unofficial banishment.

'Where? Piedrahita?' The Alba palace at Piedrahita was just a day and a half's drive from Madrid.

'No, Doña Maria Luisa. Sanlúcar. I really want to get away by myself.'

She took just her household staff, a single lady-in-waiting, and Brother Basil to amuse her. And of course, her child Maria de la Luz. For a while, to her surprise, she found it restful. But after two weeks she wanted to scream.

It was then that she thought of the hunting lodge in the sanctuary, of the old boatman who knew all the secret waterways through the swamps, of the deer and wild boar, of the shifting sands when the waters of winter receded, of the call of the gulls, I'm free, I'm free, I'm free –

And then that she thought of Goya.

Would he come? He had painted the duke again, the year before he died, and had done a fine portrait of Cayetana herself, in a white dress with a red sash, the little mop of a bichon frisé at her feet in the gardens behind their Madrid palace. For some of the sittings Goya had brought his son Javier along to see the ducal palace and the ducal couple. If the father was careful to keep his distance, the eleven-year-old boy was not. She was kind tò Javier; she treated him like a nephew; she gave him presents. She sent presents to Doña Josefa too, that silent, never-seen wife of Goya's. Could the queen object, now, if she invited Goya to the sanctuary to paint her? They were friends, just friends.

Poor Goya, with his deafness, and that way he cocked his head to one side, as if hoping he could hear. An eagle, an eagle with a broken wing.

But with the arrogant, soaring strength of an eagle, and that look – fleeting, but she had seen it – of restrained brutality in those hooded eyes of his.

Goya. Goya would be exactly right. She wrote him, and posted the letter quickly, before she could change her mind.

But why should she want to change her mind? She didn't know. There was something about him, something that frightened her. Deliciously.

The night after she posted the letter she had that dream again. She was falling and falling and falling, and she became smaller and smaller and smaller, and then she wasn't there. She sat up in bed trembling.

Goya would come. He had to come.

He couldn't wait to come. He dropped everything. He asked the king for a leave of absence, giving a minor recurrence of his illness as an excuse. He even wrote to Sebastián Martínez to say he was coming. He would spend a few days in Cádiz, and then he would resume his interrupted journey – Santa Maria, he thought, five years ago – around the bay and through Puerto to Sanlúcar and the sanctuary of Doñana. Perhaps, he thought, Martínez would give him the loan of the same surly coachman. He would let the coachman do the driving.

An oarsman leaped from the boat and made the lines fast at the small landing stage in the sanctuary. Paco felt the late February wind blowing through his loose hair, gray-streaked now. It was a fine day, the tall aloes on the shore blowing in the wind, the umbrella pines deep green against the incredible blue clarity of the Andaluz sky. The shore stretched flat in either direction, but he could see low hills in the distance, and an old square stone tower looming above the pines.

Cayetana wasn't at the landing stage, though he had sent a note ahead from Cádiz. He climbed out of the boat and stretched his legs and walked along the beach. A flock of gulls rose and soared away against the sky, that blue Andaluz sky. What a place to paint! he thought. He watched the Alba lackeys unloading canvases and his easel and paintbox from the boat and saw a horseman galloping out of the pines.

Not a horseman. A woman, mounted astride, her black hair flying in the wind. Cayetana.

She reined in and dismounted and walked toward him along the beach. Three hundred yards separated them, then two hundred. She began to walk faster. She was running. Then, closer, walking again, color in her cheeks, a smile on her lips, but an unexpected look of – was it fright? – in her dark eyes.

'You're here,' she said. 'You're really here.'

'Only five years late,' he said, thinking: God, she's beautiful.

341

'How long can you stay?'

'A few months.'

'That's a hundred years!' she cried, too quickly for him to read his lips. He cocked his head to one side in that strangely vulnerable gesture, and then her eyes were sparkling.

'Come,' she said, taking his hand. 'I want to show you everything.'

A second horse was waiting among the pines, a groom holding the reins. Cayetana led her own stallion there, and they both mounted. She turned to face him. 'Let's see if you can ride, Goya. Race you to the lodge.'

She galloped off.

Cayetana's idea of showing him everything was to rush from place to place on the sprawling, rundown estate – for it had once been far more than a hunting lodge – hurling comments over her shoulder as they rode or babbling on without pause for breath as they walked, so that he missed half of what she said. But her enthusiasm was contagious and Paco found for once that his deafness did not bother him. She smiled, she gestured, flinging her arms wide or nodding vigorously or shaking her head sadly; she mounted, she dismounted, she walked, she ran, she grabbed a lantern and skipped down the steps to the cellar of the square stone tower, where once prisoners had been kept, and shook a pair of rusty manacles threateningly at him before she burst out laughing; she raced up the steps to the dovecote at the top of the tower where, even if Paco could have heard, her words would have been lost in the cooing of the doves; astride again, she raced him to the corrals where yearling and two-year-old bulls were kept, fighting bulls that in the ring at Sevilla or Madrid would wear the straw and white colors of the Alba ranch.

They returned to the wooden shack next to the landing stage, and soon they were eating squid and tiny fish fried tail-in-mouth and drinking flinty white wine.

Cayetana licked her fingers. 'The stables,' she said. 'They'll give you an idea of the size of the place in the old days.'

They mounted and cantered side by side to the old stables. 'Stalls for two hundred horses,' Cayetana said. 'We only use twenty or so these days.'

The paddock was sandy and weedgrown. Only the posts of the old fence remained. Hitching their horses to one, they entered the vast, dim, hay-smelling stables.

'The old kings,' Cayetana said, 'the Hapsburg kings, used to come here for the hunting. It's been in the family for centuries. But the Bourbons like to hunt closer to home, and Villafranca preferred hunting for new sonatas. My grandfather used to love this place.'

'The Hapsburgs,' Paco said musingly. 'All the way back to the Hapsburgs.'

'Upstarts,' Cayetana told him. 'There were Albas long before any Austrian king ever set foot on Spanish soil. And Osunas too.' She smiled impishly. 'Did you ever sleep with her?'

'You asked me that before.'

'Did you?'

'That's an interesting rivalry the two of you have.'

Again that impish smile. 'You're not supposed to say that. Men have gone to prison for saying it. Did you?'

'Go to prison?'

An imperious stamp of one small, soft-leather boot. 'Sleep with the Osuna. What was she like in bed?'

'I don't remember.'

'You don't remember what she was like in bed?' Cayetana asked, amazed.

'I don't remember whether I ever slept with her.'

'Beast.' She smothered a laugh. 'You know what I like about you? You're independent. You're almost as independent as I am. And as stubborn. And you love life. You want to squeeze everything in. Don't you? Isn't that your secret?'

'I have no secrets. I'm an open book.'

'I'd like to turn the pages. A figura, that's what you are. Come here.'

He thought of that other figura, Pepe Hillo. He shook his head.

'Stubborn, you see?' That first time, in the dimness of the rundown stables, she came to him. He remembered undressing her clumsily, his heart pounding in his throat. Remembered the sweet-wet smell of hay overwhelming the jasmine in her hair. Remembered her face going slack as he touched the silk-smooth skin of her. That, the way the arrogance left her face, always afterwards, when he dreamed of her. When he had lost her, and won her back, and lost her again –

She pulled him to a great yielding mound of hay. They sank into it.

'Love me, Goya,' she said, and he saw those words on her lips. 'Now, just now,' she said, but then her lips were against his throat and those words he did not see.

Her bedroom was straight out of Moorish Africa – the columns and arches, the intricate stonework, the mosaic designs, the silken cushions strewn about, the small recessed leaded glass windows, the enormous canopied and curtained bed that, long ago, had been found in Córdoba.

'It's five hundred years old,' she told him. 'Maybe six. The last caliph slept in it. Every night he had a new virgin, the story goes. As if he were already in paradise. That's a most pleasant religion, Islam. For a man. Do you feel like a caliph, Goya? I'm sorry I can't be a virgin every night.'

'Or every morning. Or every afternoon.'

A little laugh, not at all lewd. 'We do manage to spend a lot of time here, don't we? The rain.'

It had been raining steadily for weeks, the wind-whipped, palm-clattering, stay-indoors rain of a late Andaluz winter.

They stayed indoors. They stayed in that caliphate bedroom, Cayetana in a filmy wisp of silk nothing cinched at the waist with a pink sash that met filmy pantaloons. Harem pants for a houri, she called them, for Goya's submissive little houri. He loved the weightlessness of them, and how easily they could be shed and how, afterwards, her cheeks would be all rosy and how her eyes would look at him, the dark violet of them giving way to black again, to desire, to an eager acceptance of the wildness that never left him all the time he was there with her, or to that strange look of mingled pity and joy when he hadn't understood something she said.

'I adore you,' he told her once.

'You musn't. I don't want to be adored. Love me – just love me now. Adore the moon. Adore the sunset. You can't hold them in your arms. Love me. I can be reached. I'm attainable.' A sulky pout on the beautiful lips then. 'I'm so damned attainable.'

In her arms, for a while in her arms, he could forget the challenge and the warning.

He came to learn, by feel, by sight, by scent, every curve and hollow of her body. There was no angularity anywhere. She was all smooth roundness, yet firm, the breasts round but firm, the haunches firm, the legs that held him with a surprising strength, the little ridges on her spine, so faintly, so wonderfully downy to the touch, like silk, the silken embrace of those smooth rounded arms, the scent of her, a round, firm, almost palpable woman scent, the way her features always went slack at the end – he would rise on his elbows to watch the change, the wonder of it, the arrogance gone, the elegance remaining, the complete female surrender of it.

I'm so damned attainable. But it was raining, and they were together. For a while yet they were together.

'Mama-Grace, don't you like me any more?' Maria de la Luz asked one day at lunch.

'Of course I like you, dear. I love you.'

'You hardly ever play with me,' the little Negro girl persisted.

'Your Mama-Grace has been busy,' said Tadea, Marquesa de las Fuentes, Cayetana's lady-in-waiting. Young and tall, boyishly lean, small-breasted and narrow-hipped, the marquesa had a pert, pretty face with laughing eyes, and a know-it-all manner. She couldn't have been more than twenty. She dressed elaborately in the latest fashions. She seemed to have three gowns for each day of the week. The gowns, white, pink, blue, yellow, set off Cayetana's black. The pert, pretty face set off her beauty.

The pert, pretty face gave Cayetana a knowing look. She knew where and how the duchess had been busy.

'Would you like to walk on the beach this afternoon?' Cayetana asked Maria de la Luz.

'It's raining, Mama-Grace.'

'Not hard. We could collect seashells.'

'Oh, good. Can Brother Basil come?'

Brother Basil glanced up from his plate. 'I'll c-c-come. G-god knows I need the exercise.'

'Did he tell you?' Cayetana asked.

'Blasphemy. Th-that's blasphemy,' warned Brother Basil.

The Marquesa de las Fuentes laughed. The way her duchess played with a man, even with this lame stutterer of a friar. How droll. She wondered how her duchess played with Goya.

'And Don Carlos too?' persisted Maria de la Luz. The little bichon frise, a red ribbon in his hair, stirred on Cayetana's lap and barked. She fed him a small morsel of crayfish.

'Of course. We'll make it a seashell-hunting expedition.'

'And Tadea and the Señor de Goya too?'

'Yes, dear. All of us. After your siesta.'

And two more, two unexpected guests. They crossed from Sanlúcar shortly after lunch and were announced by the major-domo. Young captains in the Order of Santiago, they had been friends of the late duke.

Handsome, thought the Marquesa de las Fuentes. Especially the one called Domingo. So tall, and that smile – and see the

345

way the duchess is looking at him. We do always have the same taste in men, Cayetana and I.

Later, after Maria de la Luz's siesta, the one called Domingo was striding ahead with Cayetana and the little girl, stooping occasionally for seashells. It had stopped raining. The April sun was warm and a golden light shimmered on the waters of the Guadalquivir.

Behind them, on the other captain's arm, walked Tadea, Marquesa de las Fuentes, long-legged, smiling pertly, beguiling the captain, and all the while wondering what that duchess of hers was up to. Did she want to make Goya jealous? She always said she hated jealous men. Goya, a notebook under his arm, brought up the rear with Brother Basil. The little bichon frise was everywhere, yapping ecstatically at everyone's heels.

Brother Basil, hands clasped behind his back, brown robe billowing in the fresh, warm breeze as he limped along, high forehead puckered in concentration, was stuttering on and on about the baseness of the world. Paco stomped at his side in stony silence, every now and then turning his head to catch a few words of the friar's impassioned monologue.

' . . . the p-pomp and glory of the world is t-t-transitory, my friend,' he was saying. 'To lead a good life in the eyes of G-god, that's what counts. I sometimes wish – '

'What do you wish, Brother Basil?' Paco glanced at Cayetana, strolling a hundred yards ahead of them, her arm linked with Domingo's.

'Th-that the duchess would understand that. She has a g-good heart. K-kind and warm, but – you're not listening, Don Paco.'

'I can't listen,' he said flatly. 'I'm deaf.'

'A man shouldn't t-take the afflictions of the Lord as hard as you do. The Lord moves in mysterious ways.'

The ways of a woman, the ways of Cayetana, Paco decided, were far more mysterious than the Lord's. Look at her. The first man who comes along. But he's young and dashing in that uniform, and he's glib and charming – all the things I'm not. How old is he, thirty? A casual flirtation with the widow of his old friend on a warm April afternoon, why should it disturb me? I can't let it disturb me. I'll lose her. I'm fifty; I have a son who'd be old enough to flirt with Cayetana himself and another son she treats like a nephew, and I'm deaf as a stone.

Don't try to hold her, he told himself. Try, and you'll lose her. She's like the mists that hang over the swamps of the sanctuary at dawn. Like the mists when the bright morning sun

346

burns them away. She means nothing to that captain with his smooth chatter, and he nothing to her.

Perhaps, he rationalized, as Domingo spread his cloak on a grassy slope and Cayetana reclined on it with the captain at her side, she's testing me. Like a tienta for those two-year-old bulls of hers. A thrust of the lance, and the mayoral says bullring or slaughterhouse. Hillo hadn't been able to pass that test. Hillo's jealousy, finally, bored her. You must never do that. You must never bore her.

As he approached the grassy slope, he found his notebook in his hand. He did not look at their faces. He did not want to see what they were saying. He took out a red crayon and began to sketch, and by the time he did study their faces he was so absorbed in his work that he hardly minded the smug smile on Domingo's lips or the coquettish sparkle in Cayetana's dark eyes.

'It *is* a pity you can't stay longer, Captain,' she was saying.

'Just overnight, Your Grace. We're already due in Sevilla.'

'Overnight, I see.' With a calculating look, the coquetry gone.

The red crayon flew over the paper and Cayetana looked up. 'Are you drawing a pretty picture, Goya?' Not the words, but the expression on her face stung him. Almost as if she were talking to Brother Basil.

He had captured the young not-quite-innocence of the two reclining figures, the uncertain parry and thrust of them.

'I never draw pretty pictures any more,' Paco said. 'I draw what I see.'

'And does that always give you such a long face?'

'Didn't understand,' Paco grumbled. But he had understood.

Propped on an elbow, Domingo said: 'I admire your work tremendously, Señor Goya. I always have. Why, we young fellows are astonished that an old buck like you has so much energy.'

'Don Paco's full of energy,' Cayetana said.

Playing us off against each other now, Paco thought. Don Paco. She never called him that. Goya. Only Goya.

'Might I see what you've done, Don Paco?' she asked sweetly. He hated her for that. He handed her the notebook.

'An interesting sketch,' she began, and then Maria de la Luz came up and snatched the notebook from her hands. She studied it, tongue protruding in childish concentration.

'Does Mama-Grace have a new boyfriend?' she asked.

'Maria de la Luz!' cried Cayetana.

Domingo managed an urbane laugh. 'I'd be pleased to buy that sketch, Don Paco,' he said.

'Notebook work,' Paco said coolly. 'It's not for sale.'

That night, Paco was not invited to the Moorish bedroom. He waited, he fumed, he paced restlessly through the ground-floor rooms of the lodge. He told himself it didn't have to mean anything. He wasn't invited every night.

Tadea talked with him. He was grumpy and uncommunicative. He wished she would leave him alone. Instead, his brusqueness seemed to intrigue her. It was a long time before he could excuse himself and climb the stairs to his own quarters.

After a while he got out his paints, lit a dozen candles, and did a quick canvas. Cayetana in her lacy black dress and a mantilla, holding a fan, a smile on her lips, every curve of her body coquettish, her back turned to a cavalier who stood in profile. He worked rapidly. He finished the painting before dawn.

It was then that he realized the face in profile over the trim figure of the cavalier was his own face.

Twenty years younger.

'Tired?' Cayetana asked. 'You didn't come to me last night, or the night before. Or the night before that. I missed you, Goya.'

She was reclining on a chaise longue in that odalisque costume. She looked more desirable than ever. He wanted her. He stood with his back to the door. Five steps and he would be at her side. He did not move.

'Goya. If you could see your face. Like a little boy whose mother told him he couldn't have any sweets.' She settled herself more comfortably on the chaise. 'You can have all the sweets you want.'

He didn't want to say it. He knew he shouldn't say it. He said 'Like the captain?'

She had begun to smile. Her face froze. 'That was a mistake,' she said coldly.

'What was? Me saying it? Or you and the captain?'

'Stop that. You don't own me. Nobody ever will. I've told you that from the beginning. You knew what you were letting yourself in for. Isn't it enough that I love you?'

'You have an odd way of showing it.' He wished he could stop. But the words came tumbling out.

'Do I? You're beginning to sound like Hillo.'

'Did you sleep with the captain?'

She laughed then, and he wanted to hit her. 'Did you sleep

with the Osuna?'

'Cayetana, I won't be made a fool of.' Trite, he thought, hating himself, the old lover with no claims, fighting to hold his love and perversely saying all the wrong things.

'Nobody does it for you. A man makes a fool of himself.'

He turned stiffly and opened the door. So it was over.

'Don't go,' she cried. 'Please.' But he wasn't looking at her. She threw a slipper. It hit the door near his head, and he turned, expecting a final scathing remark.

She was removing the wispy silken nothing. There was no arrogance now on her lovely face.

'I don't want to be adored. I told you that. Just love me. Just forgive me and love me now. Please? I couldn't stand it if you went away.'

The sunlight lasting longer every day. The call of the wild geese coming north from Africa with the advancing spring. The stilt-legged storks, brief visitors, who would build their nests that summer in Denmark or Sweden or Frederick's Prussia. No, Frederick was dead. Paco was alive, more alive than he had ever been. Racing on the strand with Cayetana. Walking at dusk along the beach, watching the fading light on the river, Cayetana at his side – the blues and golds and reds with a new clarity, like colors he had never seen before but knew he could paint now. Taking a picnic in the flat-bottomed boat, the bent old boatman poling his way through the uncharted waterways of the sanctuary. The way the sands shifted, all but covering a tree one day, exposing the gnarled roots the next. The vultures with their long necks and wide-soaring wings and ridiculously tiny heads, beautiful in their ugliness, not there at one moment and then mysteriously there the next to squabble and peck and leave bones that would bleach white in the Andaluz sun. The timeless lore of the sanctuary, a million miles from Madrid and a fat cuckolded king and a lustful queen and Godoy who ruled them both, and east across the Mediterranean the triumphant campaign of a young French general in Italy. All of it a million miles away.

Soon their days filled the pages of his notebook. He sketched in red and black crayon and in India ink – Cayetana asleep on a chair with the dozing Maria de la Luz on her knee, Cayetana at her morning toilette, Cayetana tearing her hair in a rage at one of her servants, Cayetana reclining on her chaise longue in that odalisque costume.

'You make me look so – pagan,' she said once, flipping

through the pages.

'You are.'

'Brother Basil would agree. He spends his time trying to save my soul.'

'It isn't possible.'

'To save my soul? Am I that wicked?'

'To save anybody's, if there's such a thing as a soul.'

'Now who's the pagan?'

'I want to paint you, Cayetana.'

'You mean a formal portrait?'

His hooded eyes looked at her. 'Nude.'

She wasn't shocked by the proposal. She just laughed. 'Oh no you don't. A season in the sanctuary? Goya's little pagan conquest? So you can show it off to your friends?'

'You know me better than that. For myself.'

'I'm in enough trouble with the queen as it is,' Cayetana told him. 'Could you imagine what would happen if she found out? A duchess, posing nude for a painter to the royal household? She'd banish me from court. It's impossible, Goya.'

He'd been dreaming of that portrait. Of two portraits, really, matched, one of her dressed as a houri, the beautiful face seductive and inviting, the other nude, the wonders of that sleek body and a smile like the Giaconda's on her lips.

'Yes, Your Grace,' he said.

'Now you're angry.'

'No. Only disappointed.'

Childishly, he took his revenge by sketching Tadea. She loved posing for him. He sketched her asleep, the pert, pretty face in repose. He sketched her adjusting a garter. He sketched her with a look of childlike pleasure on her face as she emerged from her bath with a mirror in her hand.

'Not a bad body,' she said, eyeing him steadily. 'It won't go to fat when I get older. I'm lucky. I can eat like a pig. Sweets, anything.' She held the pose in unspoken invitation. 'Do you like it, Goya?'

He shut his notebook and turned. In the doorway Cayetana was smiling. She tossed a towel at the marquesa. 'Dry yourself, Tadea. You'll catch cold.'

Frequently she reminded him that her year of mourning was almost over. More and more she spoke of Madrid. 'I feel as if I've been away forever,' she said. 'Why, I almost miss that toothless old fool Maria Luisa. I want to feel pavement under my feet again. I want to shock people.'

The arrogance remained on her face then even after he had made love to her, as if her impatient desire to leave the sanctuary was a desire to leave him too. He himself was part of her banishment, like a plaything she had taken along to make it bearable.

One day he posed her on the beach against a background of the umbrella pines of the sanctuary. They compromised on her costume. Black for mourning, yes – but touches of color. White at the throat, and a long-sleeved golden blouse under the mantilla, a vivid red sash at the waist, high-heeled shoes of silver and gold bright under the black skirt. A restrained tension in the rhythm of her pose, the lovely body half-turned but the beautiful face staring straight ahead, thick dark brows arched over the arrogant eyes. An imperiousness in the way her right hand pointed down at the sand, as if she expected someone to kneel there in homage. He painted two rings on the fingers of that hand. On one was written Alba, on the other Goya. Light and shade under the deep blue Andaluz sky, light and shade as Rembrandt might have used them, increased the strange tension that dominated the portrait. Had Rembrandt, he wondered, ever known such a love?

It was a large portrait, more than life-size. She posed three times on the beach, and then he worked alone at the lodge.

'Can't I see it?' she would ask as the work progressed.

'Not yet.'

He worked all day, every day, and she took long walks by herself or with Maria de la Luz. Once, while he was working on the eyes, he felt a hand on his shoulder. Tadea stood behind him, the smile frozen on her pretty face when she saw his fury.

'Get out of here!' he cried. His hands were trembling. He had almost had that invitation and that arrogance in the eyes, and a subtle sadness too. *I'm so damned attainable.* Tadea had spoiled it for him, as the world would spoil it. Other places, other times, other people – her search for fulfillment was like his own search for the raw, crude stuff of life itself. She could never be fulfilled, and he could never have enough of living.

Two weeks after she had first posed, he put his palette down and cleaned his brushes. He had put everything of Cayetana into that portrait, and everything of himself.

She had gone out with Maria de la Luz. He waited in the great hall of the lodge. The little girl came in first and went skipping upstairs with Don Carlos at her heels. Then Cayetana stood before him. She just glanced at his face and said: 'It's finished.'

'Yes.'

'May I see it now?'

He nodded.

He waited in the doorway, in the warm May sunshine. After a long time he felt a gentle touch on his arm. He turned and saw her. The arrogance was gone from her eyes. Her face was slack, as if they had just made love.

'Goya,' she said. 'Oh, Goya.' She was not the woman of the portrait then. She looked like a little girl. 'You wouldn't – give it to me?'

'No.'

'I'll think of it as a gift, anyway. The best anyone ever gave me. It only needs one little change to make it perfect.'

'What kind of change?' he asked, surprised.

'Just a little thing. You'll see.'

She went upstairs and returned wearing the costume she had worn for the portrait.

'Could you find the exact place where I stood when you sketched me?'

He thought he could, and they went outside together. They found the spot, and she posed there. 'Like this?' she asked.

'Yes.' He wondered what she had in mind.

She touched the sand with one silver and gold shoe. 'And you signed the painting here?' In the sand, below her right foot, he had signed his name, as if she had written it herself with the toe of her shoe.

He nodded, waiting.

Her foot began to move. It traced his signature in the sand: Goya. And then, slowly, another word before it.

Only Goya.

CHAPTER TWENTY-EIGHT

The Virgin of Rocío

ALMOST A THOUSAND YEARS AGO, when the Moors swarmed up from Africa to conquer and occupy Andalucía, they turned churches into mosques and smashed all the images of Jesus and

352

the Virgin. Graven images were an abomination to the one God whose name was Allah the compassionate and merciful. He was not compassionate and merciful to the idols of an alien religion. Bands of soldiers roved the countryside to destroy them.

In the church of the little town of Almonte, a few miles from the sanctuary, stood a small stone image of the Virgin. One dark night, hearing that the caliph's soldiers were coming, the people of Almonte took their little Virgin deep into the woods of the sanctuary and hid her in the hollow trunk of an old oak tree, where she remained safe from the caliph's soldiers. Years became decades, and decades centuries, and Spaniards came down from the north to rid their land of the Moors. By then the people of Almonte had forgotten where their ancestors had hidden the statue of the Virgin. But the mosque became a church again.

One day a little girl playing in the woods chanced upon the old oak tree and found the Virgin in the hollow. She ran back to the town, and soon a delegation went out with much pomp and rejoicing and brought their Virgin back to her church.

In the morning, the Virgin was gone.

A few days later the little girl returned to the oak tree, and found the Virgin in her hollow. Again a delegation brought her back to the church, and they locked the church for the night.

Again in the morning the Virgin was gone.

This time the entire town went to the old oak tree, and found the Virgin once more in her hollow.

They decided it was a miracle.

'That old oak tree,' the people said, 'hid our Virgin from the eyes of the Moors for hundreds of years. Our little church is no longer her home. She belongs here.'

But the mayor of Almonte wanted her for the church, and again they lifted her from the hollow. Tears at once appeared in the stone eyes of the Virgin.

The mayor surrendered to the miracle, the Virgin remained in her home, and in time a shrine was built around the old oak tree. From nearby towns and villages, once a year on the day the Virgin wept, pilgrims came to the shrine. Soon they came from all over Andalucía, and then from as far as Madrid. Processions on horseback forded the Guadalquivir where the water was shallow. Ornate coaches drawn by elaborately caparisoned mules brought the nobility. Peasants came on foot. The pilgrimage to the Virgin of Rocío became, after Santiago de Compostela in the north, the most famous pilgrimage in Spain.

A village sprang up around the shrine, with small houses and streets lined with orange trees. Except for one week of the year, no one lived in that village. Then the pilgrims arrived, and then there were displays of horsemanship, and feasting, and the village became alive with excitement. The climax came when the Virgin was carried on a float from her shrine through the streets of the village. Men from all over Spain vied for the honor of carrying her. Soon they fought for the honor. Men would rush at those carrying the float, fists flying, to take their places. All in good fun, of course, but not without bloodshed. When the fighting threatened to get out of hand, someone would shout: 'Viva la Virgen del Rocío!' and for a while all would be peaceful. But soon they would go at each other tooth and nail again. Somehow, the Virgin managed to make the trip in one piece.

The pilgrimage occurred in late May, less than three weeks before the end of Cayetana's period of mourning.

'What's three weeks?' she asked Tadea. 'What's three weeks?' she asked Brother Basil.

'Th-three weeks,' said Brother Basil, 'is how long you m-m-must wait.'

'But I've hardly ever missed the pilgrimage, not since my grandfather started taking me. I'm not going to miss it now.'

'The queen – ' began Tadea.

'Is in Madrid. You'll love the pilgrimage, Goya. Have you ever seen it?'

'The only other time I was in Andalucía, I had a small problem.'

'Then you absolutely must go. What an experience! The old duque-general used to lead the procession. He was a magnificent horseman, but he'd always dismount and get rid of his coat and tear into fellows half his age, sending them flying so he could help carry the Virgin. What a man he was! What a pilgrimage it is! Why, if I didn't go, he'd haunt me from the grave. I *have* to go.'

They all went. They crated the portrait and returned across the Guadalquivir to Sanlúcar. Only a few days remained before the pilgrimage. Most of Cayetana's household staff had idled the spring away in the palace on its hill above Sanlúcar. Now she put them to work. Now they got the carriages ready, polishing brightwork and oiling leather, covering the seats with new brocade. Now they designed an elegant riding costume for the duchess, and the seamstresses stayed up all night sewing it.

354

Now they measured Paco, and with gray cloth and black leather fashioned a costume for him too. Now they hardly had time for a quick meal or a catnap of a siesta.

Thirty-three confraternities would assemble for the pilgrimage and Cayetana said she'd be damned if a single one of them would outdo the Albas.

Paco saw little of her in those few days before the pilgrimage. He slept late. He walked on the heights above the town with Tadea, looking across the roofs and the river to the tower of the sanctuary. He went down to the seashore with her and sketched fishermen mending their nets.

Sketching on the waterfront the day before they departed on the pilgrimage, he shut his notebook when he saw that Tadea was talking. 'I'd better warn you,' she said. 'I've been to Rocío with Cayetana before. You won't recognize her.'

He pretended not to understand. 'In her new riding costume?'

'The last day of the pilgrimage, when men fight to carry the Virgin, everybody drinks too much and – '

'I never drink too much,' he said. He would remember those words, later.

' – everybody just, well, lets go. The final day of the pilgrimage, it's like the last day of the world. Don't be that sure about yourself. Don't be that sure about anything. Or anyone. I like you, Goya. I don't want to see you hurt. Will you fight to carry the float?'

'Maybe. I can take care of myself.'

Tadea shook her head slowly. 'I don't mean hurt that way.'

Paco picked himself up off the hard ground and went roaring back into the fray. It was twilight, torches were lit, a great throng lined the main street of that one-week-a-year village of Rocío to watch the Virgin's return to her shrine. Her progress was slow. She stood, a small, primitive stone statue, tottering every time the float was disturbed.

It was disturbed often. Men leaped at it, shouting and cursing and shoving the bearers aside to take their places. Fights ended as soon as they had started, men tumbled away, came back, were knocked away again, stood panting with bloodied lips or blackened eyes and then launched themselves at the float again.

For a while Paco thought he wouldn't participate. You're beyond all that, he told himself. You should have been here twenty years ago. He stood at Cayetana's side, watching,

355

laughing, moving with the crowd that followed the slow advance of the Virgin. With a count from Sevilla, a fine horseman, she had led the procession that forded the Guadalquivir. Then, with Paco, she had attended every party in every miniature house in Rocío. They drank sherry and manzanilla, they talked, they danced, they never found the time to sleep.

All the men were half in love with Cayetana. Without even trying, she reminded everyone that she was the most desirable woman in Spain. No one had risen to challenge her. No one ever would. Even the other women at Rocío didn't resent her. In her own way, she dominated the pilgrimage as much as her grandfather the old duque-general ever had.

'Are you just going to stand there?' she had asked Paco with a mischievous smile. 'The old duque-general carried the Virgin in his sixties.'

And Paco laughed, at himself, at her, at this solemn religious rite that had become, over the years, a boisterous brawl. He felt young. She always made him feel so wonderfully, gloriously young. He removed his Córdoba hat. 'If Your Grace will hold this,' he said with a small bow. He removed his short gray jacket. 'And this.' He stood at her side a moment longer in white frilly shirt and gray trousers tucked into riding boots. He squared his shoulders and took a deep breath.

The float was just passing in front of them, a mob carrying it, another mob attacking them. He launched himself forward and grabbed someone and heaved and for a moment got both hands on one of the carrying poles, a wide grin splitting his face until something struck his back and he tumbled away, hit the ground hard, got up, and hurled himself back into the melee. Drunken faces, wildly swinging arms, the float heaving like a boat on an angry sea, and again he was clutching the pole with one hand and fending off a pock-marked face with the other. Fingers tore at his shirt, ripping a sleeve away. He swung around. Something hit him. He was down again and up and grappling with a one-eyed fat man.

'Tuertillo,' he said in amazement, and the oldest of the Apiñani brothers embraced him, winked his one eye, ducked and propelled his head, bald and hard as a cannonball, at Paco's middle. They went down together and got up laughing.

'Chico, what the devil are you doing here? They said you were sick in Cádiz or somewhere.'

'Use that head of yours on me again and I'll be sick in Rocío. What are *you* doing here?'

'We all came down. Juanito even shut the café. Got here

356

this morning. All of us – Gaspar, Emeterio, Romero, Hillo.'

'Hillo?'

'Wanted to show those fornicating young dandies what we old men can do with a Virgin. Where'd she go?'

And Tuertillo lumbered after the retreating Virgin of Rocío.

After she had been placed, miraculously undamaged, in her shrine for another year, Paco tried to find Cayetana. He visited all the little houses where they had attended parties during the week but saw her nowhere. He walked the crowded streets of Rocío and watched the fireworks shooting into the now-dark sky, exploding into brilliant sprays of color. He saw the bands playing, saw the young men, faces battered, clothing in tatters, a tooth missing here, an eye swollen shut there, drinking and grinning and shouting silently. *Salud, dinero y amor – amor sobre todo*, their lips said. The women, elegant in their riding costumes, clustered about the Rocío warriors. Appraisingly, but with a wildness in their eyes, as if they had taken part in the fighting too. Flirting became less covert. Paco could feel the tension. Occasionally a couple ducked away into the pines behind the small houses. Men would fight again that night, and not for the honor of bearing the Virgin to her shrine.

He did not find Cayetana. He saw Juanito. 'Party,' Juanito said in his laconic way. 'Romero and Hillo borrowed a place here. Come on.'

The toylike house was jammed. Several casks of Domecq brandy stood in its single room. Someone had already hammered in bungs, and the brandy flowed freely. Pedro Romero dispensed it. Tuertillo dispensed it. A man wandered in with a wineskin and everybody laughed and he tossed the wineskin aside and began drinking brandy. Someone gave Paco a cup. They were all there, the Apiñanis, Romero, Costillares. All of them except Pepe Hillo.

He drank the brandy and had a second cup. Someone handed him a third and a fourth. He drank, his head began to whirl, he didn't see Hillo anywhere.

'You painting these days?' someone asked. It was Gaspar.

'Might as well ask if he's living these days,' Emeterio said.

They laughed. Paco did not laugh. He had another cup of brandy. The lamplight flickered and danced, cigar smoke hung heavy in the room, Romero opened the door and a fresh breeze blew in. Suddenly Paco realized he was very drunk.

He went outside. The street was less crowded. Lamps hung in front of every house. He walked, reeling a little. The dark

357

and the light. In the light peering rudely into faces. He opened doors and looked into toy houses and drunken faces and then was outside again. A large white dog followed him, tail wagging. A woman he had never seen before said something he did not see and looked at him invitingly. He shoved her aside and kept walking. He reached the end of the street, where the oak forest abruptly began, where the shrine stood, where the narrow road led to Almonte. He stood for a while at the shrine, lamplit, heaped with flowers. He turned and walked back. Some of the lamps had gone out. A group of men carrying torches came trotting by. He thought they were singing.

He reached the middle of the town and saw them, just outside the cone of light shed by an oil lamp.

Cayetana and Hillo. Standing tight together in each other's arms.

He stood absolutely still in the darkness. He was instantly sober. He watched them. He did not breathe. He seemed to stand outside himself and watch himself. Something went away from him, a mingled joy and sadness.

I'm so damned attainable.

He felt numb. He could not move.

They shifted in each other's arms. Cayetana stood with her legs wide, her hands clutching Hillo's hair. He towered over her, leaned down and locked his mouth on hers. Her hands dropped from his head to his flanks, pulling him hard against her.

Only Goya.

Traced in the sand with a silver and gold shoe, and in an hour or two the waters of the Guadalquivir, rising with the tide, would have washed it away.

They went, hand in hand, between two toy houses and into the warm waiting darkness beyond.

He walked the length of the town. Only a few lamps remained lit. A drunk lay sprawled near the shrine. He walked back, through the dark. He felt a hand touch his arm.

Tadea. Pert and pretty and so unexpectedly astute. 'Sooner or later it had to happen,' she said.

'You saw?'

'Yes, Goya. And saw that you saw.'

Lithe and small-breasted and narrow-hipped. Not a woman. A girl. He wanted her.

He took her up in his arms and carried her among the pines.

CHAPTER TWENTY-NINE

The Lovers of Ugliness

EVERY TUESDAY NIGHT in the private room of Café Apiñani, the Society of the Lovers of Ugliness met.

It was not really a back room, as Paco had first envisioned it, but a brick-walled cellar below the café. The society was a burlesque and a mockery. Its members had sought beauty everywhere and instead found ugliness. One day the young poet Leandro Moratín asked Bernardo Yriarte, whose brother, seeking beauty, had died of syphilis, 'Why don't we form a society?' Like most of those who would become members, Moratín thought himself the worst kind of cynic. Actually, like most of them, he was a romantic.

'What kind of society?' Yriarte asked.

'For the love and preservation of ugliness,' Moratín said promptly, and they launched the society that very week.

Though a secret passage led from the cellar room of Café Apiñani to the flea market, the society had little to fear in those early days. The desultory war with England meant that things French could be admired again, and openly. Young men of good family walked the streets of Madrid wearing the red bonnet of Revolutionary France. Moratín wore one himself. Noblewomen wore the tricolor ribbon. And many a priest complained that even the whores of Madrid would rather talk of the fall of Robespierre or the rise of General Bonaparte than sleep with you. The Society of the Lovers of Ugliness wondered how the priests knew.

In that year 1798 the enlightened element in Spain found encouragement. Godoy, having blundered into the war with England, needed all the help he could get. Newspapers other than the official *Gazette* came off the presses again, and the anonymous pamphleteers were not badgered by the Inquisition.

One cold night in February, the lawyer Meléndez told the

society: 'I have a Godoy story. They're going to make Pepa Tudo a countess.'

Mostly, the society talked politics. And talking politics meant talking Godoy.

'What?' everybody but Cabarrús the banker gasped.

'It's true,' said Meléndez. 'Godoy promised the queen he'd stop sleeping with Pepa if she got the title.'

'Actually,' said Cabarrús dryly, 'Godoy's a little tired of Pepa Tudo. He's hoping the title will get her off his back.'

'Or him off her back,' offered Bernardo Yriarte. Rumor had it that Godoy liked making love in the manner of dogs.

'Seriously,' went on Cabarrús, 'Godoy has plans for himself. He wants to marry.'

'You're joking!'

'No. Maria Luisa would stomach a wife more easily than a mistress. And Godoy's aiming high. He wants to marry royalty. Old King Carlos' niece the Countess of Chinchón seems the likely candidate.' The society always referred to Carlos III as old King Carlos, and Carlos IV as fat King Carlos.

They speculated about the coming marriage. The Countess of Chinchón was a pale, timid sort. Godoy, who became grosser in mind and body every year, would destroy her. For once the society did not laugh.

Until Jovellanos, who had recently been recalled from exile to receive the portfolio of minister of justice, announced quietly: 'I have a Godoy story too. Or maybe it's a Maria Luisa story.'

A word of praise or a smile from their Jovino, as his friends called the minister of justice, could make any man's day. But gossip? Gossip from the lips of Jovino was almost unheard of. As if in apology he said, 'It really is quite amusing.'

Nobody doubted it at all.

'The queen, as you know, has a new lover. Trying to make Godoy jealous, I suppose,' said Jovino. 'Anyway, the fellow's name is Mallo, and he's a guardsman.'

It was agreed on all sides that both fat King Carlos and toothless Queen Maria Luisa enjoyed wrestling with guardsmen.

'Mallo's been living high, buying horses, uniforms, jewelry. Well, one day fat King Carlos asks Godoy: "Who's this fellow Mallo?" "Just a guardsman, Don Carlos," says Godoy. "But confound it, Manuel, where's he getting all that money?" "Oh," says Godoy with a straight face, "he's sleeping with an ugly old woman who steals her stupid husband's money." Fat

King Carlos laughed until his sides split. In fact, he thought the story so amusing, our fat king did, that he told it to Maria Luisa.'

The meeting broke up with laughter. Then Juanito Apiñani came downstairs with a pitcher of wine. 'Paco's here,' he said.

'Goya?' asked Cean Bermúdez. 'Really?'

'He ought to have some Godoy stories if anyone does,' said Cabarrús. 'Isn't he redecorating the Admiralty Palace for Godoy?'

'Is he?' Cean Bermúdez asked. 'I didn't think he was painting at all these days. Last time I went by the studio that apprentice of his – what's his name, Asensio Juliá? – said he was etching. You should see the studio. A garret, a bare wood table, and a few boards.'

'If he's working at all, I'd be surprised,' said Leandro Moratín gloomily. 'The last time I saw him he was dressed like a gypsy and hadn't shaved in a week. What's the matter with the man?'

None of them knew what was the matter with the man. He had joined the society and attended exactly one meeting. He had rented the little studio on San Bernardino Street and when he wasn't painting in Godoy's Admiralty Palace he would retreat there.

'He has a portfolio with him,' Juanito told the Lovers of Ugliness now.

Cean Bermúdez's eyes popped. Those etchings Asensio Juliá had mentioned? Possibly. The last time Goya had worked in secret he'd painted his *Popular Diversions*. Masterpieces all of them. 'Bring him down, Juanito,' Cean Bermúdez urged. 'What's he waiting for?'

'What he had in that portfolio,' Juanito said. 'He's not sure it's ugly enough.'

'We'll forgive him if it's beautiful,' said Jovino dryly.

In a while Paco came down the stairs, a small slim portfolio under his arm. He had lost weight. His face was gaunt and the stubble of beard on his cheeks unexpectedly gray.

'Asensio Juliá claims you've been etching,' Cean Bermúdez said.

'Can't understand. Write it,' grumbled Paco.

Impatiently, Cean Bermúdez wrote it.

'Yes, I've been experimenting some with etching.'

'As an antidote to working for Godoy?' Cabarrús asked.

'Write it.' And it was written.

'Nothing wrong with Godoy. Or working for him. We've

become friends,' Paco said defensively. Take rides in his coach. Dine together. Talk. You'd be surprised. He's no fool.'

'Isn't he?' asked Sebastián Martínez. 'Fighting a war with England and paying France an indemnity at the same time?'

Martínez, like the rest of the society, felt of two minds about post-Revolutionary France. The Enlightenment could produce wonders; it had. But the French Directory had turned the country into an armed camp, and anyone who objected received a shave from Dr Guillotine's famous blade.

'Godoy's caught between England and France,' Paco said. 'Same as Spain's caught.'

'Will you for God's sake stop talking politics and show us what you have there?' Cean Bermúdez pleaded.

'No damn good, for all I know. Sometimes I have to etch. I can't explain it.'

They all gathered around while Cean Bermúdez opened the portfolio. At first they were disappointed. Just four thick sheets.

'Paper's from India,' Paco said. 'Takes a better print, but it's expensive. Too damn expensive.'

That would make an amusing story for the society, Jovino thought, if Paco hadn't been a charter member. He was as rich as any man in the room except Cabarrús.

The first print showed a man, who might have been Paco himself, paying court to a beautiful woman who bore an unmistakable resemblance to the Duchess of Alba. Blank-eyed, she seemed to be fending him off. At her feet romped two little dogs. The dogs seemed to be enjoying themselves far more than the man who might have been Goya and the woman who might have been Cayetana.

The second showed an old hag watching two young women pluck the feathers from a helpless little creature, half bird, half man. Above them hovered fantastic beings, again half bird, half man. One of them resembled the bullfighter Hillo, one of them the painter Goya. On a tree between them, with the legs of a vulture but her own torso and face, perched the Duchess of Alba.

The third reduced the fantasy to mere wish-fulfillment. A woman, clearly the duchess again, her face grief-stricken, leaned against a wall supporting the dead figure of a man who had to be Hillo. At his feet lay a sword.

Fantasy dominated the fourth plate completely. In the foreground leered a witch, her eyes fastened with unholy glee on a serpent and a toad fighting. In the background loomed a square tower. Reclining, wearing two heads in profile, was the duchess again. Butterfly wings topped the two heads, and a man who might have been Goya gazed soulfully into one of the faces as he clutched the duchess' arm to his chest. Holding her other hand, his own two heads on her lap, was Pepe Hillo. Behind them, a finger to his lips for silence, kneeled the lame Brother Basil.

Cean Bermúdez shut the portfolio. For a long while no one said anything. No one knew quite what to say. Madness, genius, a heart worn on a sleeve, revenge – what were these things?

Sebastián Martínez finally broke the silence. 'It would seem our Paco's had himself quite an affair.'

'Write it,' Paco said.

'Never mind.'

Cean Bermúdez could hardly control himself. Afterwards, Jovino would have enjoyed relating how, for a while, he actually feared that this time his eyes *would* pop from his head. But Cean Bermúdez was a member.

'The light and the dark,' the art critic finally managed to gasp. 'Good God, man! How did you manage it? Dürer could have done it, perhaps. Or Rembrandt. No one else.'

'Mixture of acid and drypoint,' Paco grumbled. 'Dürer,' he scoffed. 'Rembrandt. Hah!' he snorted, hiding a pleased smile.

A second silence, an uncomfortable silence, followed Cean Bermúdez's outburst and Paco's reply. Then the lawyer Meléndez said: 'The Duchess of Alba won't exactly be delighted if you put these on the market. She could sue – or worse.'

'Who says it's the duchess? Does the duchess have two heads? Besides, they're not for sale. Did I sell the *Popular Diversions?*'

'They're hanging in the Academy,' Moratín pointed out.

'These etchings won't hang anywhere.'

The lawyer Meléndez sat back in his chair, relieved.

Jovino opened the portfolio again. 'What a pity,' he said. 'These aren't anywhere near – '

Paco slammed the portfolio shut. 'Nobody's asking you to like the things. I'm not sure I like them myself.'

'That's not what I mean. I was going to say they're not anywhere near complete.'

'They say all I wanted to say.'

'That you had a love affair? And the woman, whoever she

363

is, was unfaithful? You believe that's unique? Think, man. At court they live like pigs wallowing in mud. The Church is corrupt; asses like your friend Godoy take the pulse of a sick country and prescribe the worst kind of medicine: war. The government's full of self-servers, there's superstition and cruelty everywhere – and you sit there smugly complacent because you've had your petty little revenge on an unfaithful woman.'

'That's enough!' Paco shouted.

But it wasn't enough for Jovino. 'A genius,' he said softly. 'A timid genius with magic in his fist. Are you going to stop there? When with that etching needle of yours you could hold up a mirror to the follies of the world?'

'*Mierda,*' Paco rumbled, getting up to leave. 'I don't have to listen to this.'

'No, you don't.' Still softly. 'You're deaf, after all. Perhaps that does isolate a man. Perhaps you really can't get outside yourself. It's a shame.'

'Don't understand.' Paco held out a pad. 'Write it.'

'Stop hiding,' Jovino said more sharply. 'You understood. I'd love to see fifty prints like that. A hundred. Show Spaniards to themselves. Show people to themselves. The folly, the unmitigated stupidity of a government that – '

'When an artist enters politics,' Paco said, 'he stops being an artist.' He began angrily and ended with a baffled look in his eyes, as if he had been through all this before. Francisco, he thought. He sounded like Francisco Bayeu then. He even managed a smile. Josefa would have been pleased. But suddenly, perhaps because he had reminded himself of Bayeu, all that Jovino had said made sense. Too much sense.

'If you're afraid,' Jovino said bluntly, 'then that's a different matter.'

Paco missed that. He could see the images forming in his mind. Fantastic, even more fantastic than these four plates. The inconstancy of women, yes – but more, so much more. The folly of men, the venality of petty officials, the insanity of living in a fourteenth-century world on the eve of the nineteenth. Spain, he thought. Poor Spain. Hold up a mirror, Jovino had said.

Jovino's eyes held his, waiting for an answer. 'At least consider it,' he urged.

'There's nothing to consider,' Paco said, and Jovino shook his head and shrugged.

But Paco went on: 'An artist has the right to delve into his own imagination, doesn't he? Like a man cleaning out his attic? Why, there's no telling what he's liable to find. That's not politics at all, is it?'

'No,' said Jovino with a broad grin. 'Of course not.'

'Of course, you know the sort of device I have in mind,' Manuel Godoy told Paco after they had finished lunch in the Prince of the Peace's new palace. 'They work on a spring. You pull a lever and the first painting slides into the wall, revealing the second. In the blink of an eye.'

'Won't the Princess of the Peace object?'

Godoy had been married to the former Countess of Chinchón for five months. They were expecting a baby.

'Her?' Manuel Godoy sneered. 'She does what I tell her to do.' The sneer was only mildly offensive. The prince, just past thirty, no longer resembled the slim young guardsman who had captured Queen Maria Luisa's fancy. He was sybaritic, but frankly and even ingenuously so. Women petitioners usually came to the palace – it had been the old Admiralty building – at night, and often left in a disheveled state. Men saw in Godoy an open, even a charming man, slightly stout now, the reddish hair beginning to recede, a man who lacked the subtlety of poor old Aranda or the indecisiveness of poor old Floridablanca, a man who took naive delight in his uniforms and his decorations, a man who seemed to say, 'Here I am, all the way from Badajoz. God knows how I got here.'

Where he was, at the moment, was a good question.

Some months before, fat King Carlos had reluctantly accepted his resignation as first minister. But every day court functionaries and ministers of the Council of State arrived at either of his two palaces to receive orders from the Prince of the Peace.

Maria Luisa had forced his resignation, he had told Paco once while they drove through the streets of Madrid in his ornate open coach. Pepa Tudo was the reason. 'Either you get rid of that slut,' the queen had warned, 'or I get rid of you.' He had not got rid of that slut. He seemed to find the situation amusing.

'First,' he said, 'they appointed one Saavedra to take my place. But did you see this Saavedra writing "Yo el Reys" for the king to sign? Maria Luisa does, or I do. Then they appointed one Urquijo. So far as I know, he's still around, but nobody sees much of this Urquijo either.' He had laughed and slapped Paco's knee. 'One Saavedra and one Urquijo together

365

don't make half a Godoy, now do they?'

The only thing that rankled the Prince of the Peace was that the grandees of Spain, united against the upstart Godoy, had sided with the queen. 'The Osunas and the Albas and their ilk,' he said, 'they don't think I'm good enough for them. Me, the Prince of the Peace.' But then he had smiled. If he took childish delight in his uniforms and his decorations, he took a more mature delight in being virtual dictator of Spain without holding any political office at all.

'The odd part of it,' he told Paco now, in the Admiralty Palace, 'is that I *am* going to get rid of Pepa. I've given her two children, same as I gave the queen. So neither of them ought to complain, eh?' He offered cigars, and the two men sat smoking and sipping French cognac.

His egotism, if it hadn't been so childlike, would have been insufferable. But Paco found himself intrigued by the man, and by the commissions he had proposed.

'When do you want me to start on those two portraits?' he asked. The second portrait, the one revealed by pulling a lever, would be a nude. Except for Velázquez's Venus hanging in the palace galleries, nor a single painting of a nude woman existed in Spain. And Velázquez's Venus lacked sex appeal. At least by reputation, a lack of sex appeal was not one of Pepa Tudo's shortcomings.

'What's wrong with right now?' Godoy asked, and shouted: 'Pepa!'

A servant wearing the royal red silk stockings came running in. 'Fetch the countess,' Godoy said mockingly. Pepa Tudo had received her title.

Soon she appeared in the dining room. 'Your Highness?' she said. With some mockery too. An interesting relationship, Paco decided. Perhaps Godoy would have more trouble breaking it than he thought.

And then he looked at Pepa Tudo. He had never seen her before, but had heard that she resembled Cayetana.

She wore a high-waisted Roman dress of embroidered linen, a chain necklace, drop earrings of gold and Roman sandals. The high waist of the dress made her appear slimmer than she was. The short Titus hairdo emphasized the coarseness of a face that otherwise would have been beautiful. The dark eyes knew too much. The lips were too full, too blatantly sensual.

Still, Paco thought, holding his breath, with an arrogance in those eyes instead of the jaded look, with longer, darker hair, with an elegance instead of that overt sensuality – she could

366

have been Cayetana's sister. Change the curve of a cheekbone here, alter eyes and mouth – she could have been Cayetana's twin.

'You know Señor de Goya?' Godoy asked.

'We've never met, but everybody knows Señor de Goya.'

'He's going to paint you.'

'Oh, I'd like that.' For the moment no longer jaded. Everybody who was anybody sat for Don Francisco de Goya. Noblewomen especially.

'Twice,' said Godoy.

'Twice?' squealed the new countess. 'That's wonderful!' Then she frowned. 'Why twice?'

'Once with your clothing on,' said Manuel Godoy.

Paco looked from one to the other, to read their lips. That face, he told himself, so much like Cayetana's. Except for the coarseness. Too bad about the coarseness.

'I'm not sure I'm going to like what comes next,' said Pepa Tudo.

'Don't you like your body, cara? I love it. You ought to be pleased that I want a keepsake. To remind me what a real woman's like when I sleep with the princess.'

'She is a gawky little thing, isn't she?' said Pepa Tudo. 'And the queen's a fat old thing. Poor Manuel.'

Godoy ignored that. He turned to Paco. 'What kind of pose, Don Paco?'

The etchings hadn't been enough. Recently he had seen Cayetana in the bullring screaming herself hoarse for Pepe Hillo. She had greeted Paco coolly, like an old acquaintance. With that arrogance.

'A harem costume,' Paco found himself saying. 'A wisp of a bodice, filmy pantaloons, a red sash at her waist. Reclining on a chaise longue, Don Manuel. For the first painting.'

'And the second?'

'Same pose. No clothing.'

'I'm not sure I follow.'

They spoke, then, as if Pepa Tudo no longer stood listening.

'The first pose all sultry desire. Seductive.'

'Waiting,' said Godoy, 'for me.'

'Yes, that's it. Waiting for you.'

'And the second?'

'Afterwards,' said Paco flatly.

'How clever. How very clever, Don Paco! You see the first painting, you pull the lever, and in the blink of an eye Pepa's been laid.'

'Manuel!' cried Pepa Tudo, pretending dismay. But Paco saw that the idea had begun to intrigue her too. Those knowing eyes, that coarseness of expression on a face that otherwise so resembled Cayetana. . . .

At first Paco was determined to play up both the resemblance to Cayetana and the coarseness of Pepa Tudo. Godoy, he knew, was not the sort who could keep those paintings secret. How fitting, if the lecherous Prince of the Peace owned two paintings, apparently of Cayetana, and apparently of a Cayetana coarsened by his lechery. Or *was* she the duchess? Hair longer than Pepa Tudo's but not so long as Cayetana's, darker than Pepa Tudo's but not so dark as Cayetana's. No background to detract. Just a muted brown. A green velvet chaise longue, two big pillows. And, for the nude painting, not a glorified goddess, and certainly no mere anatomy lesson. Provocative, the eyes drawing you to them like magnets – that is, if your own eyes could tear themselves away from the voluptuous body. Pepa's body? Or Cayetana's? Similar, Paco thought as he proceeded from sketching to oils. Pepa's slightly longer in the legs, Cayetana's slightly longer in the waist, that lovely silken distance from breasts to navel to legs, the hips flaring suddenly, the thighs firm and rounded.

Pepa? Or Cayetana?

He wanted to sully Cayetana. To spoil her. To make her look cheap and tawdy in her resemblance to Pepa Tudo.

Then let Godoy's privileged guests ogle – and wonder.

He'd paint Cayetana out of his mind, destroying her a little in the process.

Except that he couldn't do it. A figure running toward him across the beach of the sanctuary of Doñana stopped him. Lazy afternoons in that Moorish bedroom stopped him, and moonlit nights. Her tenderness to Maria de la Luz, her madcap sense of humor, the way she rushed through life, as if each moment would be her last – all stood in the way.

The more he tried to coarsen, to cheapen Cayetana with his paints, the less he could. The more he studied a breast, or an arm, or a leg, or a knowing eye of his model, with what he thought an icy detachment, the less detached he became.

Not toward Pepa Tudo. Toward Cayetana.

By the time he finished the two large canvases he knew what he should have known all along. He was still in love with her.

The paintings showed it. They were a paean to Cayetana's beauty and desirability. All his longing, all his disillusion, flowed from his fingers and his brush. And with them, some-how, flowed new hope. What they had shared could not end.

He did not paint Pepa Tudo. He painted Cayetana.

Pepa, unaware of her own vulgarity, did not realize this. If Señor de Goya had realized her somewhat – somewhat! – it merely served to show how her beauty had affected him.

Godoy knew better. 'They're beautiful, Goya,' he told Paco. 'But they're not Pepa.'

'Don't understand.'

'The hell you don't. We both know who she is. You devil! Did you really spend a season with her in Andalucía?'

Paco pretended to misunderstand. 'Fifty thousand reales for the two of them,' he said.

'Oh, you'll have your money. You've more than earned it. But did you?'

'Not a copper less,' Paco said.

Soon a carpenter came to mount the paintings in the library of the Admiralty Palace. With that clever device.

A few weeks later, the lawyer Meléndez told the Lovers of Ugliness: 'Now our Paco's really gone too far.'

'What's he done now?' asked Leandro Moratín the poet.

'The prince,' explained Cabarrús the banker, 'invited us to a private little dinner party. Meléndez and me.'

'What's Goya got to do with it?' asked Cean Bermúdez. 'Was he there?'

Meléndez explained about the paintings. The harem cos-tume on top and then, with the pulling of a lever, the nude.

'Who is she?' asked Bernardo Yriarte.

Meléndez shook his head. 'That's where Paco's gone too far. Godoy's a born exhibitionist. He'll show that nude every chance he gets.'

'A nude's bad enough,' Cabarrús said. 'But what a nude! More desirable, if that's possible, than the real thing.'

'Who *is* she?' Yriarte cried.

And, together, Meléndez and Cabarrús said: 'The Duchess of Alba.'

Before long Paco realized the paintings had been a mistake. Not that he feared Inquisition; with Godoy as his patron he felt secure. The Holy Office might gently rap the knuckles of the painter to the royal houschold, but he stood in no real danger.

The duchess did. Godoy, that ingenuous egotist, might

boast that if Cayetana had posed for those paintings she had also shared his bed. A bed that every tart in Spain from Pepa Tudo on down had shared.

He went to Godoy and offered to buy the paintings back.

'Not on your life,' Godoy said.

'Then double. I'll give you a hundred thousand reales for both.'

'They're not for sale at any price,' said Godoy.

'At least the nude. A hundred thousand reales for the nude.'

'What?' asked Godoy in feigned surprise. 'For a portrait of Pepa Tudo?'

Paco ignored the sarcasm and offered a higher figure.

'You're wasting your time, Don Paco. The paintings stay here. I wouldn't exchange them for King Carlos' throne.'

Josefa saw little of him in those final months of the eighteenth century. He seemed three men, or four, each of them abandoned to a frenzy of creative activity. He was everywhere at once – rushing up to Toledo to do a church commission, painting the queen's portrait sitting astride her favorite horse Marcial, painting one Urquijo, that first minister in name only, painting Dr Peral, finishing the huge allegory of Spain, Time, and History for Godoy's palace, painting six witchcraft scenes for the Osuna summer residence.

In the allegory, Time loomed powerfully, a broad-shouldered God-like figure with a scythe in his hands. Time was the enemy, the relentless enemy whose swinging scythe no man could avoid. And the witches, gathered around the devil while they struck pins in the images of children, the witches that so deliciously shocked people in the Osuna drawing room? They were no strangers to Paco. He knew them. He had lived with them in the terrible silence after he was stricken in Cádiz. The creaking in his ears became their cackling. They still came to him at night, if he allowed himself a few hours of exhausted sleep, and sometimes they spoke, the only voices he ever heard, and they said, 'Work, work now and live now. Beyond the grave is nothing.' Witches? He scoffed at his own nightmares. Witches did not exist. He was too enlightened to believe in witches. And too enlightened not to believe what the voices said.

Josefa led her lonely, isolated life on the Street of Disillusion. Canvases of Velázquez, Correggio, and Tiepolo hung on the walls, and prints of Rembrandt and Wouwerman. For the purposes of their joint will the contents of the library had been assessed at fifteen hundred reales. Chairs and sofas were covered with gold damask, and Paco's own still-lifes decorated the dining room. Josefa's collection of jewelry was worth more than fifty thousand reales. Why complain? They were wealthy, their home far more sumptuous than her brother's old house on Clock Street; she was married to a man whose fame grew every day.

But life was passing her by. Paco rarely appeared, even at night. Or, if he did return, late, from the studio on San Bernardino, his hands reeking of acid, he would hurl himself exhausted into bed.

And there was Javier. She did not know what to do with Javier. Fifteen now, their son, slender like a Bayeu, with no hint of his father's strength. Javier was – indolent. School hardly interested him. He dressed modishly in the latest French fashions and moved in a circle of effete young dandies.

'What are your plans, Javier? After you finish school.'

'Hard to say.' With an attempt at worldliness in the indolent voice. 'Travel, perhaps. There's so much to see.'

'Your father would approve of that. But afterwards?'

A shrug. 'Paint, perhaps.'

Spare me another painter in the family, Josefa thought. But she had no real worries there. Paco had equipped a small studio in the house for Javier, but the boy never used it.

'Or perhaps become father's agent. Travel, sell him abroad, you know.'

She didn't know. Francisco de Goya needed no agent. Why, only recently, he had painted the French ambassador's portrait, and the ambassador had returned to Paris with it, most pleased. Paid a fortune in gold livres.

No, Paco needed no agent. Perhaps he needed no one. Yet – he could ignore her for months on end and suddenly, after he finished a canvas, the house would be full of flowers and the sound of his laughter, a giant's laughter, and then his warmth would overwhelm her. He was a man who had to love but was afraid of love, something she never understood.

'I thought these diamond earrings would suit your new *merveilleuse.*'

'They're lovely, Paco. My new what?'

'Hasn't it come yet? A gown. French. Designed by the Osuna's own modiste.'

And soon the gown came, far more than a gown and marvelous indeed, with a white silk lingerie bodice, a cashmere shawl, a blue velvet bonnet, clocked silk stockings, blue kid slippers. A gown? Why, it was an entire wardrobe.

'Paco, can we afford it?'

'We're rich.'

'Are we?' He earned a fortune. And spent a fortune.

'And if we were poor,' he said, 'you'd still have it. All this ugliness in the world, and I'm married to you.'

All this ugliness in the world –

Godoy's wife, nineteen years old and pregnant, sitting stiffly for her portrait with a look of bewilderment and defeat in her eyes, a nervous tic jumping spasmodically on her cheek so that it was difficult to paint her. Arms folded primly across the swollen belly that carried Godoy's child, while Godoy appointed Pepa Tudo her first lady-in-waiting, Pepa Tudo who kept her suite in the Admiralty Palace and received Godoy every night.

Or the goings-on at the royal residence at San Ildefonso, where Paco painted the queen again, dressed as a colonel of the Guards, on her horse Marcial. He did the horse, and then Maria Luisa sat astride a wooden contraption indoors while he sketched her. Her lover Mallo, who had been promoted to a chamberlain, often came to watch. The queen, her crafty little eyes glittering in her sallow face, would soon tire of sitting astride the wooden horse. She did not tire of Mallo. He would help her down, his strong young hands lingering on her waist, and the glasslike eyes would narrow with desire, the heavy lips would part moistly to reveal golden teeth. All of it as if Paco wasn't there at all. One day Crown Prince Fernando came to watch the sketching. The sixteen-year-old heir to the throne could always be found lurking somewhere or other around the San Ildefonso palace, in a corner, in a dark corridor, like a spider. He resembled a spider too, with his bulbous head, his squat misshapen torso, his spindly legs. His father was king. One day he would be king. Meanwhile, he did nothing, read nothing, worked at nothing, played at nothing. Except hatred. He hated his father, hated his mother, hated Mallo. Most of all he hated Godoy. An anonymous pamphleteer wrote that he even hated himself, that ugly, stunted boy who one day would rule Spain.

'You make the queen look fat, Goya,' he said.

Paco continued sketching, with Crown Prince Fernando staring over his shoulder. A fist struck his shoulder.

'I said you make her look fat,' shouted Fernando.

Paco turned, the chalk still in his hand. He drew a red streak on the prince's face, from ear to jaw – accidentally, of course.

'Clumsy oaf!'

'Sorry. Didn't understand.'

'Idiot! You heard me.'

'Begging Your Highness' pardon, but I'm deaf.' Paco quickly and diligently rubbed at the royal cheek with a paint-stained rag. The line of chalk smeared, the prince's face retreated.

'Get this jackass out of here,' shouted Fernando, 'and keep him out.'

Mallo helped Maria Luisa down from the wooden horse. She looked at the sketch. 'Fat? I would have said imposing. I'm an imposing woman.'

'Fat, fat, fat. You let them all make a fool of you. Mallo, Godoy, this painter fellow.'

'If the chamberlain,' said the queen with rare dignity, 'would be good enough to escort the crown prince to his quarters.'

Fernando ripped the sketch from its board and tore it in half and in half again.

'Did you enjoy doing that?' Paco asked. 'Is it more amusing than learning statecraft, Your Highness?'

'You're finished here,' Fernando said. 'You too, Mallo.'

Mallo smirked. Paco calmly tacked another sheet to the board. Fernando grabbed for it. A tack pricked his thumb, drawing blood. 'Out!' he screeched. 'Out, both of you!'

Maria Luisa grasped the lapels of his blue frock coat and shook him. 'You're not king yet, you worthless little turd,' she said, all Parma fishwife then. Spittle flew from her lips. Her false teeth clicked. 'You're not even a man. You're hardly even human.' Shaking him so hard that his powdered wig fell down over one eye.

She released him. He edged out of the room, sideways, like a spider scurrying along its web. 'I'll be king sooner than you think, you fat old whore,' he vowed, and slammed the door.

Maria Luisa's gold teeth gleamed. 'What a hateful little monster,' she said.

A mother and her son. The queen of Spain and the crown prince. The country had to suffer them both, Paco thought grimly as he finished tacking paper to board.

Often after he painted at San Ildefonso, fat King Carlos invited him to the music room. Carlos enjoyed playing the violin. He played terribly, but he loved to have an audience. Even if the audience, in this case, couldn't hear.

'And how did it go today, Don Paco?' The bow sliding soundlessly along the strings, the violin tucked against the quivering double chins.

'Not bad, sire.'

A jovial smile. 'Call me Don Carlos. Not bad! You're too modest, Goya.' The bow slid, the music Paco couldn't hear – it was just as well, he thought – continued. 'Maella's retiring, you know.'

Mariano Maella was first painter to the king.

'The queen's glad to see him go,' said the king, laughing his fatuous laugh. 'Maella paints too placidly, she says. No fire, no *cojones*. All he wants to do is please. See what I mean? a diligent fellow in Spain these days. Enlightened, that's the way you paint me. *Cojones.*'

Paco knew what was coming. He held his breath.

'You'll get a letter from Urquijo later this week, Goya. Naming you first painter to the king. A man of the people. Poor beginnings. I like that, ha-ha-ha. There's opportunity for a diligent fellow in Spain these days. Enlightened, that's the thing. Oh, we have our – what was that?'

Paco, of course, had heard nothing.

The king put down his violin and lumbered from the music room. Curious, Paco followed.

Around a turn in the corridor, dimly lit by oil lamps now, was the doorway to the queen's suite. Paco saw a figure running from it and away along the corridor. Mallo, he was almost certain. Then the queen appeared in the doorway. She was crying. Her nose was bleeding, her hair a mess, her cheeks bruised. Her robe hung loose, revealing dead-white skin from throat to navel. She saw the king and Paco, raised a hand and pulled the robe tight around her.

'My dear, my dear – what is it?' asked the king.

The queen, evidently, had been beaten. Not gently.

A blank stare, a wiping away of tears, and then a look of cunning in the tear-filled eyes.

'Where'd she go?' cried Maria Luisa. 'If I get my hands on that clumsy little fool – '

'Who?' demanded the bewildered king. 'I saw some fellow – '

'That eyesight of yours,' said the queen with more composure. 'It was one of my maids. Didn't you see her, Don Paco?'

'Don't understand,' Paco said.

'One – of – my – maids. Didn't you see her running off?'

'I saw someone. It's dark out there, Your Majesty.'

'One of my maids. A bath. I was having a bath,' the hoarse voice went on, improvising, growing stronger, more sure of itself. 'She held out the towel and tripped. Knocking me down. Struck my head. I could have been killed. Clumsy little fool.'

Carlos accepted the story, as he always accepted all her stories. He placed an arm about her shoulder and gently, solicitously, led her back inside.

Paco had seen Mallo; he was sure of it. An argument? A fight? Had Mallo actually beaten the queen?

In the days that followed, rumors flew through the San Ildefonso palace and then, when the court returned to Madrid, through the royal palace itself. Mallo beat the queen. Mallo beat the queen regularly. Mallo was a man, a real man. He had a violent temper. At first she accepted the beatings stoically. And then began to enjoy them.

Soon all Madrid knew of it. Except the king. Or perhaps the king pretended not to know. It was so much simpler to ignore personal problems. Or problems of state. Or a son who hung around the palace doing nothing. Just hating.

All that ugliness.

Sometimes the new first painter almost thought it a blessing to be deaf. He could retreat into the lonely silence and, at night, with his etching needle and his acid attack that ugliness on a copper plate. Or sometimes dream of Cayetana, sometimes find beauty, just a little beauty that he could, that he had to, give the world.

Tadea gasped when she saw the duchess. 'Are you going to a masquerade ball?'

'In the afternoon? Of course not.'

Cayetana wore a frayed black woolen dress, an equally frayed shawl over her hair, and rope-soled shoes. No jewelry, no make-up. She had darkened the skin under her eyes with soot. On the floor at her feet was a laundry basket.

'Where *are* you going – dressed like that?'

'To the Fountain of the Fan, of course. To wash some clothing.'

Cayetana had been living, that autumn, in the Moncloa, the Alba *palacete* – little palace – that stood on the northern outskirts of Madrid. She found the rebuilt and redecorated Buenavista Palace too big and gloomy, she said. The Moncloa, hardly more than a country house, stood nestled among poplars and willows not far from the Manzanares River. It was cozy, she said. Cozy was a word Tadea had never heard her use before. Ever since she had broken off her affair with Goya, Cayetana had been subdued. Quieter. Pensive. Less madcap. Except for the song, of course. The song was Cayetana at her madcap best.

Those rare times she visited the royal palace that autumn, her reception at the hands of the queen was frigid. There were problems with her husband's estate. The queen sided against Cayetana out of spite, and Cayetana had little patience for the legal battle. But she could fight Maria Luisa's spite with her own. For the first time in her life, politically.

The queen had forgiven the Prince of the Peace his affair with that slut Pepa Tudo. After all, he had made a suitable marriage; he had produced an heir to his unique title and he all but kept Pepa under lock and key in the Admiralty Palace. The queen could almost pretend her rival didn't exist.

But the grandees were determined to rid Spain of Godoy. Cayetana shocked them by attending one of their secret meetings at the Alameda. Cayetana, interested in politics? She never said a word until the end of the meeting. After a few minutes she stifled a yawn. The grandees spoke on and on about British blockades, about indemnities, about taxes, about a French general named Bonaparte and a crown the Prince of the Peace coveted in the south of Portugal. Enough rope, they said. Give Godoy enough rope and he'll hang himself.

'In about twenty years, maybe,' Cayetana told the grandees.

They smiled condescendingly. Their beautiful little Cayetana knew nothing about politics, of course.

'Make a fool of him,' she said. 'Of him and the king both. It isn't the queen who's kept Godoy in power. There were times she would have scratched his eyes out. It's the king. "I can't govern Spain without my Manuel," ' she said, in a surprisingly good imitation of the king's voice. 'What you have to do is make the king hate Godoy – and make them both look ridiculous.'

Cayetana went home and wrote a song, its lyrics set to the tune of a martial air composed by her late husband. She invited the grandees to a little party at the Moncloa and sang it. They laughed. That Cayetana, they thought, always playing. Playing politics now. But what a delightful, what a spiteful little song.

Wherever they went, the Alba servants sang her delightful little song.

Soon every majo and maja sang it, and every merchant

forced to pay the taxes that went to decorate Godoy's two palaces, and every bored night watchman in Madrid. Soon the restless soldiers in their garrisons, waiting to fight the unreal war with England, sang it. Soon you heard it in every café, and echoing along all the streets of Madrid at night. The tune was simple, easy to remember, and it was daring to sing it in your own imitation of the king's atrocious singing voice. Because, the lyrics made clear, it was a song meant to be sung by the king.

> Who is there when I am away?
> > Godoy!
> When I depart, who will stay?
> > Godoy!
> Whom do I give more power and sway?
> > Godoy!
> Who rules in Spain today?
> > Maria Luisa!
> And who rules Maria Luisa?
> > Godoy!
> I'll tell you what gives me joy:
> To wear the crown, to be the king,
> To ride and hunt, to fiddle and sing
> And never do a single thing
> But leave it to
> > Godoy!

Before long a copy of those seditious lyrics appeared mysteriously on the king's desk. He read them, and read them again and said: 'Yes, the Madrileños always have had evil little minds, haven't they? He hummed the catchy tune, and laughed fatuously.

The queen fumed. Soon the song became so popular that just humming the melody was enough to bring the words to mind. And one line had been omitted from the copy that found its way to the king's desk. The line that went:.

> Who is the sire of my youngest boy?
> > Godoy!

It was a hard fact to hide, since the Infante Francisco de Paula bore an amazing resemblance to the Prince of the Peace. Maria Luisa's spies went everywhere, and soon they learned where the song originated.

It was then that the queen began to think Madrid would be a far pleasanter place if Cayetana never showed her face in it. If she were banished permanently. Or even. . . .

Now, at the Moncloa, Tadea said: 'Well, dressed like that, they won't recognize you.'

'Who won't?'

'Anybody,' said Tadea with a frown on her pert face. Cayetana hadn't been going out much lately, and Tadea assumed she was afraid. That song. Tadea had heard at the palace that the queen knew who wrote it. 'Just as well, under the circumstances.'

Cayetana laughed. 'You mean because of the song? Why, I'm the toast of Madrid. Leandro Moratín told me he wished he'd written it. I'm a poet, Tadea.'

'The queen's furious.'

'Most Parma fishwives are furious most of the time,' said Cayetana, humming her song, setting the basket of laundry on her head and taking a few experimental steps.

She left the Moncloa through the servants' entrance and soon made her way through the crisp autumn sunshine along the path that led to the Fountain of the Fan, the basket of laundry on her head. Before long she fell into step with other washerwomen.

'Is he there today?' Cayetana asked one of her new companions.

'Every day,' the woman said. 'Haven't you seen?'

'I'm new here.'

Near the river, not far from the Fountain of the Fan, stood the new little Church of San Antonio de la Florida. For some months now, the Alba washerwomen, who often preferred the conviviality of laundering at the fountain, had returned home late, sometimes with only half their work done. Finally Cayetana had asked them what the trouble was.

'The new church,' one of them admitted.

'The first painter to the king,' explained another. 'Don Francisco de Goya. He's decorating it.'

'We hide in the doorway and watch. You should see him. Rushing up and down the scaffold like a monkey. Using brushes, sponges, rags, his hands. And the pictures!'

'You like them?'

'Oh, yes! They're beautiful, Your Grace.'

Cayetana, being Cayetana, had to see for herself.

What would Goya be like now? she wondered. They say he

works all day. They say he's etching nights in a garret. Wild
things. None of his friends, not even Cean Bermúdez, will tell
me what kind of wild things. As if they're afraid. They say
he's grumpy, but as full of energy as a little boy. They
say. . . .

'Well, dearie, if you're new here, you're in for a treat. Who
do you work for?'

'The Alba.'

'You're lucky,' said the older woman. 'It's said she's a good
mistress.'

'What?' cried Cayetana. 'If I do anything wrong, she beats
me.'

The older woman clucked her tongue and hummed that
song about Godoy. They reached the Fountain of the Fan
and Cayetana diligently set to work scrubbing her laundry.
After an hour or so, a coach bearing the coat-of-arms of the
king came thundering by.

'That's him,' said the older woman. 'The painter. Comes in
the king's own coach every day.'

'Can we go and see him now?' asked Cayetana.

'Not yet. Give him time to get wrapped up in his work. If he
sees us, he rants and raves.' The older woman snorted. 'Not
that I believe it for a minute. I think he's secretly pleased.'
She slapped a wet shirt on the stone and began to knead the
water from it. She set it on a bush in the sunshine to dry. 'I
think we can go now. Will the Alba beat you if you're late?'

'I'll sneak in,' said Cayetana.

Soon half a dozen washerwomen made their way along the
riverbank to the new little church. It was hardly more than a
country chapel, Cayetana saw as they approached.

'You came just in time,' the older woman told Cayetana.
'He's been painting since June. Almost finished. Maybe he's
grumpy, but he loves the people, you can tell. Wait till you see
the – what do you call them again?'

'Frescoes,' said Cayetana.

The washerwomen walked past the royal coach. Coachman
and footmen greeted them mockingly, pretending to be dazzled by their beauty. Cayetana tried to assume the shuffling
walk of the other washerwomen. But even with her face
smudged, her beauty was not hidden. Soon the mockery gave
way to open admiration.

'You are a pretty little thing,' said the older woman.

'Actually,' said Cayetana with what she hoped was a raucous laugh, 'I'm a duchess in disguise.' The coachman and

footmen, hearing her, bowed and scraped, mockingly again, and it was all right.

The washerwomen crowded into the doorway of the church, Cayetana and her new friend bringing up the rear. They saw scaffolds rising high toward the dome and spandrels, and paint-pots and brushes and rags and open sacks of lime everywhere. A short young man in a dirty smock was busily mixing colors on a trestle table. Cayetana recognized Asensio Juliá, Goya's apprentice.

But where was Goya himself?

She caught a movement out of the corner of her eye, and saw a figure high up on the scaffolding, rushing back and forth. He was using no brushes then, no rags, no sponges – nothing but his bare hand, as if the color had to flow from his own being onto the dome of the little church. A touch with his fingertips here, a rubbing with his palm there, then he ran agilely along the narrow planking, back to his colors, or to get a sponge, or a rag on a stick or, occasionally, a brush as big as a housepainter's.

Cayetana caught her breath. He had painted an iron balustrade around the dome and, behind that railing, the world.

All in a pearly light, crowded, impossibly crowded, and not at all saintly. Or perhaps, in its own exuberant Goyaesque way, more saintly than the dome of the Sistine Chapel.

The single saint depicted was San Antonio de Padua, bringing back to life a dead man to exonerate the man accused of his murder. San Antonio resembled a simple Spanish monk, gaunt and ascetic. Cayetana's head swam as she looked beyond him, her eyes slowly taking in the full circle of the dome. There, there behind that painted railing, was Spain – all of Spain surging over the dome: beggars in rags, toothless old crones, majas, gossipy matrons, highwaymen with sinister faces, silly young things swooning with emotion, an ecstatic monk or two – a hundred living, breathing men and women pushing and jostling each other around that balustrade to see the miracle of San Antonio resuscitating a dead man while a peasant in a huge sombrero spread his arms wide to hold them back, so realistically, thought Cayetana, that she could almost hear the peasant shouting: 'Give him room!'

Then she heard another voice: 'We'd better go. He usually stops around now. He's furious if – '

'No, I'm staying.'

Vaguely, she became aware that she stood alone in the door-way. She saw Goya rushing along the planks high above her

380

head, his smock paint-smeared. She wished she could see his face. She had to see his face. That a man could bring the world to life like that, with his two strong fists and some pigments. . . .

See? See now? What he's painting? The culprit, the real murderer – smeared on with rag, formed with a brush, high-lighted with Goya's bare hand – a slouch-brimmed hat low over his face, trying to slink away unnoticed through the crowd. In ten minutes, where he had not existed, he was there. And somehow the hundred watchers behind the iron railing seemed to push and jostle even more – to see him, to stop him? Every minute as the afternoon light changed the fresco seemed to change. It had a life of its own. It lived and moved there in the dome. It was a world more real than the world itself. And so human, so sensuous, so full of the joy and the wonder of life. The colors, the pearly gray tones, how they sang for a man who could not hear!

Who, it was said, had become a recluse full of hate.

Hate! Again Cayetana caught her breath. She felt as if Goya had made love to her. Life – and love of life – that was what he had created there in the dome.

She backed into the shadows of the doorway. He was coming down. In a hurry, always in a hurry, even on that rickety scaffold. He reached the floor. His eyes – she had never seen his eyes like that. They glowed like two lamps in his face.

Asensio Juliá craned his neck and gazed upwards. For a long, a very long time.

'Well?' Cayetana heard Goya ask. 'Are you going to stand there all afternoon? It's finished, I'm hungry, I'm thirsty, let's get out of here.'

Asensio Juliá did not speak at first, and when he did, his voice caught. 'It's glorious. I have no words, maestro.'

Goya stretched the tired muscles of his shoulders. 'Maestro?' he said, his voice gruffly gentle then. 'I don't feel like a master today I feel like – ' He gazed upwards too. 'I'll show you what I feel like,' he cried, and swiftly mounted the scaffold to the dome again.

Rags, brushes, paints, his body blocking the balustrade near the figure of the saint, both hands moving, now deftly, now furiously; and a sound, an echoing sound high in the dome, of his laughter.

He did a little jig. He came down dancing – dancing was the only word Cayetana could think of – though now anybody could dance down a scaffold without breaking his neck she had no idea. Goya managed it. He could manage anything.

What he had done, she saw, was paint a pair of street ur-chins, one climbing the balustrade, one sitting astride it, watching the saint.

'Them,' he said to Asensio Juliá. 'I feel like them today.'

And, graying hair and all, he looked like a little boy who had worked a miracle, or at least come to see one.

Cayetana left quickly. She felt young and reckless and more alive than at any time since –

Since when?

Ever.

Except for the weather report, the first page of the *Diario de Madrid* for Wednesday, February 6, 1799, comprised only a single item.

The weather report said it had been cloudy yesterday and predicted it would be cloudy today, no surprise in Madrid in February. It also said the sun rose at 7: 59 in the morning and would set at 5.01 in the afternoon.

The remainder of the page contained an announcement.

Don Francisco de Goya y Lucientes, first painter to the king, honorary director of painting at the Royal Academy of San Fernando, was offering to the public a series of eighty prints etched in aquatint and drypoint on copper plate.

These *Caprices*, as the series of etchings was called, would be placed on sale beginning February 7 at a small shop on the Street of Disillusion. The shop ordinarily sold perfumes.

A complete set of the *Caprices*, it said in the *Diario*, would sell for one ounce of gold or 320 reales, making it possible for commoners to own works of the renowned Goya, whose can-vases commanded fees as high as twenty thousand reales from the nobility. Three hundred sets had been printed. They would be sold on a first come, first served basis. It was suggested that all those interested should hurry to the little perfume shop.

It was suggested that a little perfume shop seemed an odd place to sell a set of etchings.

The Lovers of Ugliness had canvassed every bookshop in Madrid, but none would handle the prints. They were, the proprietors said, of a surpassing ugliness. Worse, they were dangerous. They stuck pins in everything. Nothing had es-caped the artist's abuse. Not even the sanctity of marriage. Not even the Church. Not even the government. Besides, complained the booksellers of Madrid, there were nudes here and there. See that withered old witch teaching a sexy young witch how to ride a broomstick? They looked, perhaps long-ingly, at the sexy young witch. If this Goya wanted to fight the Inquisition, that was his own affair. The booksellers wanted no part of it, thank you very much, señores.

So the *Caprices* went on sale in a perfume shop. Why? Because the proprietor had fallen into debt and had been saved, some months before, by a gift from Señor Goya, whose house stood nearby on the Street of Disillusion.

All those interested did indeed hurry to the little perfume shop. But not to buy. Only to gawk at the prints. They were afraid to buy, as the booksellers had been afraid to sell. Each day when the shop opened, a pair of Dominicans could be seen pacing back and forth outside.

The Duchess of Osuna, that woman of Toledo steel, came galloping up to the shop on the third morning. She handed the reins of her horse to one of the startled Dominicans and said, 'I won't be a minute,' and went inside to order in a clear voice four sets of the prints.

Each of the Lovers of Ugliness also purchased a set. They argued among themselves the merits of the eighty plates. Jovellanos preferred sick Spain, an old man lying in bed, with Dr Godoy, in the form of a jackass, taking his pulse and prescribing for him. Naturally, nobody said the old man was Spain and nobody claimed the jackass doctor was Godoy, but Jovino had no doubts.

Cabarrús the banker, who was unhappily married, favored the print showing a man and woman chained back to back trying vainly to break loose.

Leandro Moratín, who had had an unhappy affair or two himself, fancied the Duchess of Alba prints.

The lawyer Meléndez preferred the etching which Moratín, who had written the captions, called *The Sleep of Reason Produces Monsters*. A man who might have been the artist himself slept at a desk in the foreground, and behind him the monsters hovered waiting to pounce.

Cean Bermúdez, pop-eyed with enthusiasm, praised the daring Inquisition scenes. That expression of utter defeat on the faces of the penitents – how had Goya managed it with his etching needle?

All agreed that, in those eighty plates, Paco and Goya had captured the dark and savage heart of Spain – sometimes with reluctant humor, sometimes with terrible despair.

Jovino's mirror, they all remembered. How Goya had made use of that mirror!

On the fourth day they saw Cayetana de Alba, for once dressed as a duchess, enter the shop with her lady-in-waiting. The Alba berlin attracted a huge crowd to the narrow street.

She went right to the bald perfume seller behind the stacks of prints and demanded: 'Which ones are me?'

Meléndez realized he was holding his breath.

'You, Your Grace? said the bald man. 'I don't understand.'

'Never mind,' said Cayetana impatiently, and began to go through the prints herself.

Meléndez did not begin breathing again until he saw the smile on the duchess' face. 'Look at this one,' Cayetana told Tadea with a laugh. 'Or this. How easily he can take his revenge! Am I really such a flirt? Or this one. That's Goya behind me, isn't it? It has to be. But young enough to be his own son. Silly! Doesn't he realize he's the youngest man in Madrid? He always will be, even if he lives to be a hundred. We'll take two sets,' she told the relieved proprietor, whose bald head was covered with sweat.

An hour later what the Lovers of Ugliness had feared all along happened. The two Dominicans stalked into the shop.

'Five complete sets,' said the younger one.

'To be delivered to the palace of the Holy Office,' said the older one.

The proprietor bowed, sweat dripping from his pate.

He even forgot to ask for payment, but Meléndez didn't. 'That will be five ounces of gold,' he said, 'or sixteen hundred reales.'

They paid with a pouch containing five ounces of gold.

Soon word spread that the Holy Office had purchased five sets of the prints.

The crowds stopped coming to the Street of Disillusion. Less than thirty of the three hundred sets of prints were sold. They were, after all, the people decided, too ugly.

Paco had given Asensio Juliá a few days off. Young Asensio, who had helped him press the twenty-four thousand prints from their copper plates, was exhausted. Paco, though, was charged with energy. Ugly? Well, at least they recognized themselves, the corrupt ones, the venal ones, the practitioners of the seven deadly sins and a few others that no one had bothered to catalogue.

The smell of acid and ink filled the garret on San Bernardino, the floor was strewn with discarded prints, the press needed cleaning, the plates had to be packed and stored.

384

Ugly? he thought again, his sleeves rolled up as he began to polish the press with an oil-soaked rag. Of course they're ugly, they're the sleep of reason, they're the dark night of Spain. He smiled, a wicked smile almost. Fat King Carlos wants a group portrait of the entire royal family, all twelve of those Bourbon monsters. I'll show them what ugly can be.

He wasn't sure if he had spoken the words aloud. Sometimes, when alone, he had begun doing that. He glanced up from the press and saw Cayetana in the doorway.

He gripped the edges of the press to keep his hands from trembling.

'Am I really a witch on a broomstick?'

'That one wasn't you,' he said.

'Maybe it should have been.'

Don't let it start again, he thought. She's restless. Had a fight with Hillo or something. Don't let it start again. Don't.

'Well? Are you going to invite me in? Or throw me out?'

He did neither. He just went to her and took her in his arms.

'Ink. You're getting ink all over me.'

'Do you care?'

'No. All of a sudden I love ink.'

'So there you are, my boy!' shouted King Carlos, clapping a hand on his son's shoulder. Fernando, heir to the throne, winced. His father's affectionate clout had almost knocked him over. 'What are you doing skulking out here? We've all been waiting for you.'

It was a warm spring day, the first spring of the nineteenth century, and the royal family had assembled at the summer palace of Aranjuez. Fernando had been skulking in the gallery, then under construction, that would extend from the summer palace to the new palace of the Prince of the Peace. Skulking was the only word. He lurked among the pillars or, if someone came along, darted spiderlike behind one.

'You mean Goya's been waiting,' he said in his shrill voice.

King Carlos chortled. 'Don't you like making history? Art history in this case. You can make political history when I'm dead and buried, ha-ha-ha.'

Fernando gave his father a cold-eyed stare. He resembled Maria Luisa then.

'Yes, art history,' repeated Carlos with the enthusiasm he usually reserved for his hounds, his clocks, or his violin. 'So far as I know it's unique. What a way to greet the new

25   385

century? Frederick never did it in Prussia, nor King George in England, nor that nymphomaniac Catherine in St Petersburg.'

The idiot, Fernando thought contemptuously. Catherine of Russia, a nymphomaniac? Well, maybe she did have her affairs, but compared to Fernando's own mother she was a nun in a convent.

'They couldn't attempt it anywhere else,' King Carlos went on. 'Tell me, who do they have? Nobody in England since Reynolds and Constable died. Tiepolo's son in Italy? A tired old man. In Prussia? Third-rate daubers. David in France?'

'There's no royal family left to paint in France,' Fernando said flatly.

'By God, there's a royal family in Spain!' cried Carlos, more enthusiastic than ever. 'That's the point, my boy. A royal family that will last forever, and a painter with the talent to immortalize us all on canvas. What a brilliant idea! That mother of yours, she has a brain in her ugly old head.'

Another wince from Fernando. All right, all right, he thought. We're none of us exactly beautiful. Why dwell on it, you fat old fool? Why commission that deaf Aragonese peasant to put us all on one gigantic canvas? It's never been done before, and it shouldn't be done now, certainly not by Goya.

The number of sitters had grown from twelve to thirteen while Paco made his preliminary studies during the winter and early spring. Maria Luisa was considering a match between Fernando and Princess Maria Antonia of Naples, so the young girl had to be included. This troubled King Carlos, Fernando remembered.

'Thirteen?' he had said. 'Thirteen's unlucky.'

'Then leave her out,' Fernando said quickly. They had met once, and the sixteen-year-old princess had been unable to hide her horror. She was a tall and regal girl, and the top of Fernando's bulbous head hardly reached her shoulder. The sight of his pigeon-chested torso and spindly legs almost made her faint.

'It's not a portrait for today,' said the king. 'It's one for the ages. As she'll be your wife, she ought to be included.'

'The engagement's not official. She doesn't belong in the family portrait.'

'Don Paco will find a compromise,' the queen said. 'Won't you, Don Paco?'

'I could paint her in profile, with her face averted,' Paco suggested. This pleased the queen. Maria Antonia of Naples was a pretty girl.

But the king was still frowning. 'That leaves us with thirteen, and thirteen won't do.'

'I'll paint myself at work in the background,' Paco said, and received the same sort of royal clap on the shoulder that had just victimized Fernando in the gallery.

'What's he need us all for now?' Fernando asked his father. 'He's been sketching and painting for months.'

'The composition, my boy. He can't have us standing any old way.'

'He's a deaf, conceited clod,' said Fernando. 'I hate the man.'

'Save your hatred for our enemies,' Carlos advised. 'God knows Spain has plenty of them.'

It was bad enough, Fernando told himself, to be forced to spend the entire spring at Aranjuez with the family. The family had rarely assembled, all twelve of them, in one place together. It was even worse to be at the beck and call of Goya. Not only couldn't you order him around, you couldn't even disagree with him. He simply pretended not to understand. With that arrogant way of cocking his head to one side.

'But my blue suit will look all wrong against the green wall,' Fernando had protested during one of his sittings. Or standings, rather. He had to suffer the ignominy of remaining on his feet while the deaf man sat comfortably on a stool. Move your head that way, Highness. The right arm somewhat more bent at the elbow. There. No, you're moving, Highness. Stand still.

As if he were a model Goya paid by the hour.

'I'll wear my brown velvet,' Fernando had said.

'Your father will be in brown velvet. Stop moving, Highness.'

His father. Someday he'd show him. Someday he'd show them all. His sister and youngest brother didn't even belong in the portrait. Godoy was *their* father. And the queen – to his face she'd tell him how dumb he was. 'Don't you know how to read? Why don't you read? We gave you a good education. What's the matter with you?'

Or: 'No, no, Fernando my boy,' his father would say. 'That's no way to jump a horse. Can't you do anything right? Let's try it again.'

Or Godoy, insolent and insufferable: 'Yes, dear boy, that is indeed your mother's bedroom I just left. We were discussing matters of state. Why don't you try it sometimes instead of lurking around the corridors of the palace?'

The one thing he could do was lurk. Bide his time. Someday he'd show them. Everybody from his fat, foolish father with his insanely ticking clocks to that deaf boor of a first painter with his stinking turpentines.

You're moving, Highness.

He'd move. Oh, he'd move. When the time was ripe, he'd move against them all, he vowed as he walked along the gallery with Carlos' fat arm draped affectionately over his shoulder.

Posing the twelve members of the royal family in front of the dark green wall of the grand salon, Paco said: 'This won't take long. I have sketches and oils of all of you, and that miniature of the Italian princess. Now we have to put you in your places.'

Was that, Fernando asked himself, the imperial "we"? And put you in your places?

'Over there, Highness. Further to my left. No, that's too far. Thirteen's an unlucky number, as your father said, and you'll hide my own head.'

I'd like to break your own head, Fernando thought.

'There. That's almost right.'

'I'm the heir,' Fernando protested. 'Why put me all the way off at one edge of the painting?'

'The middle's for the king and queen. No, leave a little space. You're too close to Isabel.'

To that at least Fernando did not object. His so-called sister Isabel was Godoy's child.

'One more step to my left, Highness. Have to leave room for Maria Antonia.'

Fernando, fuming, took one more step.

'And now, Your Majesty,' Paco addressed Maria Luisa while he sketched silhouettes quickly, 'if you'll hold the Infante Francisco de Paula's hand? He looks so lonely, standing there. And perhaps your other hand on the Infanta Isabel's shoulder. Good. That really is excellent.'

Maria Luisa's jeweled teeth flashed.

'Don Carlos, I believe you're a bit too close to the queen. Could you move to my right, please?'

The king obeyed, and that also didn't bother Fernando. It placed his father further from him. As ever, King Carlos stank of the stables and sweat.

But after obeying, the king scowled. 'Won't that make the Infante Francisco de Paula seem to – separate us? We're very close, Doña Maria Luisa and I.'

'In life, of course,' said Paco. 'But a king stands by himself, doesn't he?' Not that Carlos would stand by himself in the portrait. Crowded in behind him, as Paco went on sketching, were his brother Antonio, sometimes called Antonio the Idiot, and a few lesser members of the family.

The Bourbons all stood stiffly, waiting, while Paco's chalk flew. He quickly untacked the paper from its board and rolled it.

'Let me take a look at that thing,' said Fernando.

'Just a sketch. To get the composition, Highness. You'll see the painting next month. Life size.'

'For the ages. For all the ages down through history,' said King Carlos happily.

'You'll paint it here in Aranjuez?' demanded Fernando.

'Obviously. It will be eleven feet wide, Highness.'

'Eleven feet wide,' repeated Carlos. 'An epic canvas.'

'I'd like to watch you working,' Fernando told the painter.

'Don't understand,' said Paco, cocking his head to one side.

'I want to watch you working!' shouted the heir.

A look of intense regret crossed the painter's strong features. 'If only you could, Highness. I'd like the company.'

'Why can't I?'

'Very complicated work. Thirteen figures. Fourteen, counting myself. The slightest interruption and it goes wrong. Sorry.'

Soon the rest of them filed from the grand salon, past the dull green wall that would be the background for the group portrait. Fernando stood there a long time feeling almost physically ill. Alone with his hatred.

The sickroom was big and airy, with bright sun streaming in past the open shutters. Flowers were heaped everywhere, and Cean Bermúdez brought an armful of carnations himself.

Jovino smiled wanly from the bed. His long, aristocratic face was pale, almost gray, but he wore a silk robe and, though the hour was early, he had already shaved.

'I'd give my eyeteeth to go,' he said.

'What does Dr Peral say?'

'I stay here. And take his foul-tasting powders for another

week.'

'And then?'

A shrug and a game smile. 'I pack a few books and go into exile again. Back to the Asturias.'

'You're sure?'

'Godoy's sure.'

'They might at least wait until you've recovered.'

'Nerves. It's just nerves.' Jovino grimaced, one hand clutched to his stomach. 'I've been working too hard. I almost look forward to exile. Get a good rest.'

Jovellanos, as minister of justice, had run afoul of the Inquisition. The Dutch consul in Alicante had committed suicide earlier that spring, and the royal governor had sealed his papers. But the Dutchman had been a suspected freethinker and, ignoring the royal seal, the Santo had broken into his house, searched through his books and papers and confiscated the lot. Jovino had journeyed to Alicante to demand their return to the widow. He won his case, and the enmity of the Dominicans. The trip and the legal battle had exhausted him, and on his return he had sent for Dr Peral. Managing a friendly smile despite his perpetual sneer at the follies of mankind, Peral had prescribed a sedative. Apparently it hadn't been enough. The stomach pains began the very next day.

'Are you all going?' Jovino asked. All meant the remaining Lovers of Ugliness, except for the lawyer Meléndez. For his own part in the Alicante affair, he had already been sent into exile.

'Godoy said I could invite a few friends. He rather looks forward to this too, you know.'

'An unpredictable man, Godoy. Sometimes I almost think Goya's right. The prince is nobody's fool.'

It was typical of Jovino, Cean Bermúdez thought, that he could find words of praise for the man who was cooperating with the Santo to exile him.

'He didn't give you any help.'

'He couldn't. I knew I was going too far. But the poor widow's case was just. The books alone were worth fifty thousand reales.'

'That integrity of yours – ' began Cean Bermúdez, but Jovino waved the remark aside.

'Do you think Goya's really done it?'

'He won't say anything. He just grins. Smugly.'

'Will he get away with it?'

'I'll feed them so full of technical jargon, they'll convince themselves the painting's beautiful.' Cean Bermúdez got up to leave. 'Take care of yourself, old friend.'

'I'm in good hands. There's no better doctor in Spain than Peral. Give Goya my heartiest congratulations.'

They shook hands and Cean Bermúdez left the sickroom. On his way downstairs he passed Dr Peral coming up.

'How's the painter today?' asked the doctor. As ever he was dressed impeccably. As ever he was sneering.

'In pain.'

'We'll take care of that.'

Everyone was on time for the unveiling of the portrait of the family of Carlos IV, except Carlos himself. The king was still hunting.

Godoy was there, for once accompanied by the Princess of the Peace. All the members of the royal family had assembled, talking among themselves or occasionally with Cean Bermúdez and the other Lovers of Ugliness. Prince Fernando, wearing the brown velvet he had wanted to wear for the portrait, stood off to one side glaring at the artist.

Goya, Cean Bermúdez remembered, had told the Lovers of Ugliness just what an accomplished skulker the prince was. 'It takes talent,' he had said. 'Real talent. There are probably twenty different ways a man can skulk, and the crown prince knows them all.'

These past few months, Goya had changed. He seemed younger somehow. He laughed a great deal. He walked with even more than his accustomed swagger. It was rumored, Cean Bermúdez recalled, that he had resumed his affair with the Duchess of Alba. Lucky Goya, thought the doyen of Madrid's art critics.

Finally, just before noon, the king arrived. He was out of breath and his face was flushed. Ignoring everyone else, he went straight to Paco. 'What a day!' he boomed. 'Two stags, more rabbits than they could cook in a week – I'd have stayed in the saddle all day, except for this momentous occasion, Don Paco.'

'Your Majesty won't be disappointed,' Paco said, bowing. He went to one side of the canvas. Asensio Juliá, his face pale, stood at the other side. The royal family moved forward, jostling one another in their eagerness – rather, Cean Bermúdez thought, like Paco's Madrileños watching the miracle in San

391

Antonio de la Florida. All except Fernando, who remained in a corner of the grand salon. Paco nodded to Ansensio Juliá, and with a flourish tugged at his end of the cloth. Asensio pulled at his end with trembling hands.

Afterwards, Cean Bermúdez would remember, there wasn't a sound for a full two minutes. Not a word, not a whisper, not a rustle of silk or brocade.

His own eyes bulged. You must not laugh, he remembered telling himself. But he could feel it welling up inside him, the need to roar his laughter, to explode with it.

Not that the huge painting wasn't beautiful. It was monstrously beautiful in its absolutely unrelenting ugliness. Again he had to stifle that wild urge to laugh. Don't look at the king, he warned himself. Or the queen. Or Fernando. Or any of the others. Look at the canvas. That's what they expect from you. Study it gravely. Don't – even – smile. Not yet. And then, finally, the right kind of smile. It took a supreme effort of will to control the expression on his face. Grave, considering, an occasional small nod.

There they stood before him, in all their royal finery, the Bourbon rulers of Spain.

A family of fishmongers, he thought, dressed in costume for a masquerade ball. Or a troupe of amateur actors playing royalty in a back-country theater. It hit Cean Bermúdez like a blow to the face. As if, he thought, the curtain had gone up unexpectedly after the play – a very bad play – and the actors were still milling about gracelessly before their curtain call. The king, off center to the right, his bulky brown-velvet figure half hiding his idiot brother Antonio. The queen, off center to the left, her face a study in malice and depravity but her hands and those gross arms protecting the two bastard children sired by Godoy. Fernando's tall and regal fiancée, her face averted. Staring at the queen? In horror perhaps? Fernando, his round torso thrust forward in the pale blue suit, so that he looked like a pregnant spider. Cean Bermúdez returned his gaze to the queen, nodding again in the uneasy silence, feeling the wild laughter inside him. The fat figure royally loaded with jewels, jewels even in the false teeth, the head drawn back like the head of a viper ready to strike. Then down to Francisco de Paula, holding the queen's hand, a miniature Godoy, pretty, too pretty, and the reddish hair like his father's, the somber yet sly eyes like his father's, the resemblance as uncanny as it was intentional. To Fernando's left, peering over a thrust-back shoulder of the crown prince, his younger brother Carlos stood in shadow, forever in shadow. Between Fernando's puffed-up figure and the averted face of his Italian fiancée was the head of Maria Josefa, the king's elderly sister. With her long nose, pointed chin and protuberant eyes, she looked like a witch. Back to the king, his fat vapid face squatting over the dazzling Order of the Golden Fleece hanging around his neck. And finally Goya himself, standing in the shadows at his easel behind Fernando, a not-quite-mischievous look on his dimly seen features as he diligently painted the family of Carlos IV from behind, as if he could not stand the sight of them head on.

Cean Bermúdez expected truth in the huge canvas, and in that truth, some beauty. But there were limits. To paint them all in their frozen-faced ugliness, to spare nothing, to make the royal family look as grotesque as it was –

The king took a step forward, his face expressionless. 'Yes, Don Paco,' he said. 'Yes, I see.' Not angrily. In a confused voice. It was no more what he had expected than what Cean Bermúdez had expected.

Godoy stood impassively, his somber, sly eyes the same eyes as those of little Francisco de Paula in the portrait. Cean Bermúdez noticed he was holding a small package, gaily tied with a bright blue silk ribbon.

Before anyone but the king could speak, Cean Bermúdez took a deep breath and managed an enthusiastic smile.

'By God,' he said, 'I always thought the man a genius, and this proves it. Look at the composition! A lesser painter would have posed Your Majesties and Highnesses in a stiff row, like toy soldiers. But our first painter? Magnificent! In two groupings, two gracefully correct groupings despite the thirteen figures – or fourteen if you count the painter himself. And see how modestly he remains in the background, so as not to detract from the royal splendor? Two groupings, yes, and Your Majesties a little way apart because each of you has his own work to do for the realm – how absolutely correct, how fitting! Notice the source of light, that mysterious source of light, there below to the left, a most regal radiance highlighting every face from below. Observe the way it enhances the white gowns of the women and the regal splendor of Your Majesty's suit. Observe the brilliance, the consistency, the weight of royalty, the harmonious union of all the figures. But observe the warmth too. Warm shades dominate the entire canvas, as you can see, the warmth of the royal family working for the Spain they love so much. But not a strident warmth.

Understand. Yes, understand. And the golden light giving a tonality to the ochre shadows, as if to show that the golden reign of our king will lead Spain out of the dark shadows of its time of troubles. A masterpiece! An absolutely unbelievable masterpiece, painted as only Goya could have painted it. Your Majesty said this would be a momentous occasion, and as ever Your Majesty is correct. I feel privileged, awed – even humbled by the effect of this mighty canvas. Words – why, words simply fail me.'

Cean Bermúdez mopped his brow. Words had indeed not failed him, and he hoped they had not failed Goya. The art critic waited, and soon the members of the royal family began to speak among themselves.

'A – well, a powerful figure of a man. He makes me that,' said the king, still in a confused voice.

'And your frump of a wife,' said Maria Luisa with a reluctant smile, 'still manages to look regal. Most regal. I never was exactly beautiful.'

'The golden reign of King Carlos,' his elderly sister said.

'Spain's time of troubles, yes,' said the king. 'There's symbolism there. And an honesty. I do wish you hadn't painted me quite so red in the face, though, Don Paco.'

'Often Your Majesty posed fresh from the hunt,' Paco said.

'It's a healthy, ruddy complexion,' added Cean Bermúdez.

'Outdoor living, that's the thing,' said Carlos, staring again at his own face in the portrait, and its pitiable effort to live up to the resplendent uniform festooned with medals. Did he see it? The mockery? Cean Bermúdez wasn't quite sure. He said hastily:

'And the modesty of Your Majesty, as if you find all those medals a nuisance, as if they don't do justice to your real character. An open, warm-hearted, unpretentious monarch who exerts all his efforts on behalf of his people but would rather – '

' – rather be among them,' the king finished for him. 'It's no easy thing, wearing the crown of the Two Spains.'

'And the portrait shows that too,' Cean Bermúdez pointed out. 'Careworn but earnest, weighed down by the affairs of state when, like any good and – may I use the word simple, sire? – yes, when like any good and simple man you'd love to spare some time for recreation but can't. It's all there in that magnificently rendered face. Spain's lucky, sire, and I'll write that when I report the unveiling of the portrait in the *Gazette*.'

Fernando emerged from the shadows with a furious look on

his face. 'Talk,' he said in his shrill voice. 'Clever talk to pull the wool over their eyes, señor.'

Cean Bermúdez feigned surprise. 'What do you mean, Highness?'

'Tell me how he's made *me* look regal. A – pouter pigeon, that's what he's painted there.'

A pregnant spider, Cean Bermúdez thought again. He said: 'A pouter pigeon? But Highness, if your shoulders are drawn back regally, as they are, then naturally that thrusts your torso somewhat forward. Naturally it – '

'Somewhat? This painter fellow's made a fool of me. He's made fools of us all.'

'Don Fernando,' said Cean Bermúdez gravely, 'I'm afraid you haven't studied the portrait. The figure of yourself most of all.'

'I've had enough of it. When I'm king that painter fellow – '

'That's precisely what I mean. When you are king. See how Goya foreshadows it so masterly? As if, despite the noble reign of your father, Spain can't wait. Study it again, Highness. Look at your shadow.'

'My what? Shadow?'

'Certainly. It's the longest, richest, deepest shadow in the entire grouping. Do you know why?'

'Because the light's behind me.'

'And why is the source of light behind you? That's no accident. It's genius. You cast the longest shadow because you represent, in your person, Bourbon history still to come. You stand for the future.'

Fernando looked again. The deep brown shadow cast by his figure was indeed the longest.

'Magnificent symbolism!' cried Cean Bermúdez in what he hoped was an ecstasy of delight. 'Your Bourbon Majesties of today, and the Bourbon Majesty yet to come – Crown Prince Fernando. Making the canvas a living entity that moves through time in the person of the crown prince. That final brilliant touch of your royal shadow, Highness, only Goya could have done it. The future. The glorious future's there in your shadow.'

'Lucky Spain,' said Godoy dryly, and turned to Paco. 'I'm sure,' he said, 'that the royal family will reward you for this wonderful canvas. But first, as a friend of the family, may I give you this little token of my esteem?' And, handing his giftwrapped package to Paco, he moved his lips very quickly to say something Cean Bermúdez couldn't hear.

395

Godoy's approval of the canvas, following as it did the art critic's lavish praise, seemed to dispel any further doubts anyone might have had. Or perhaps Cean Bermúdez's long speech gave the royal family time to examine with malicious pleasure not their own images but those of the relatives they so heartily disliked. How, finally, could they object to their own likenesses without appearing foolish, since the likenesses were so good?

Fernando, glancing from his mother to the portrait and back again, said with an evil little grin: 'Interesting, isn't it? How your eyes and teeth have the same glitter. Almost as if they're false eyes.'

His mother said: 'Yes, and you with your shoulders pulled back for once, actually standing tall like a man.'

And the king's sister said: 'Dear Carlos all red and sweaty from the hunt, it is so in character.'

And Carlos: 'Notice how our Goya so realistically included that patch of lupus on your temple, Maria Josefa.' His sister suffered from skin tuberculosis.

Soon they were all so pleased in pointing out deformities in one another that they forgot about the deformities in themselves.

Finally, even Fernando relented. 'That shadow,' he said grudgingly. 'I see it now. Things to come. When I'm king. Yes, when I'm king.'

Later, when all the Lovers of Ugliness were on their way back to Madrid in Cabarrús' travelling coach, Paco said:

'They had me worried for a while. Did you see their faces when we first pulled the cloth? You saved my neck, Don Agustín.'

'Oh, I just gave them enough time to realize how much they hated each other,' Cean Bermúdez said.

'Santa Maria, what a speech. You almost had me believing it.'

'But not Godoy.'

'No, not Godoy. I think he enjoyed the whole business almost as much as we did.'

'What did he tell you when he gave you that box?'

Paco smiled. 'That if I kept on painting like that, I was going to need it.'

'Need what?'

'His gift.'

'Yes, but what was it?'

And Paco, still smiling, said: 'A set of dueling pistols.'

CHAPTER THIRTY

The Death of the Bull Barbudo in the Bullring at Madrid

THE BULL'S NAME was Barbudo, and he wouldn't charge.

Well, thought Pepe Hillo, offering the cape while Barbudo stood before him pawing nervously at the sand, we all make mistakes. That morning Hillo had ridden out to the corrals where the bulls were kept, had taken one look at Barbudo, and told the other matadors, 'That one is for me.' With the retirement of Pedro Romero two years before, Hillo was the unchallenged Numero Uno. If he said a bull was for him, nobody argued.

Hillo wished that someone had. Barbudo, who in the corrals had seemed such a noble beast, had shown his true colors once the toril opened and he came galloping out onto the sand of the bullring beyond the Alcalá Gate. Barbudo had made a full circuit of the ring before any of Hillo's peones could stop him with a flapping cape, and had returned to the gate and butted at it with his horns, trying to get inside. From the Peñaranda ranch, of a carefully bred strain of fine Andaluz fighting bulls, Barbudo was *manso* – cowardly.

The crowd, in an eager holiday mood, did not understand this. The crowd saw a splendid specimen of animal, sleek, black, wide-horned, confronted by a cautious Pepe Hillo, resplendent in a scarlet silver-brocaded jacket, tight brocaded breeches, and silk stockings, who would be paid two thousand reales for his day's work there in the hot May sunshine. Two thousand reales – why, a Madrid craftsman had to work three years to earn that much. Surely Hillo, who was Numero Uno, could perform miracles with that bull of bulls for two thousand reales.

The crowd called mockingly to the man who had been their

hero not five minutes before. 'Go back to the slaughterhouse in Sevilla, you seller of oil and wine!' they shouted.

Hillo's father had dealt in oil and wine in Sevilla and Hillo, called José Delgado in those days, while he helped with the modest family business, had first learned his skills as a matador in the Sevilla slaughterhouse. For a few copper coins any boy could practice on the beef cattle there, using an old jacket as a cape, and for a few more he could use a rusty old sword to do the killing while the killer of beef cattle lounged nearby, sledgehammer at his side and a wineskin in his hands. Costillares, the greatest matador in the days of Pepe Hillo's youth, had found him using a torn jacket as a cape in the slaughterhouse in Sevilla, and the rest was history.

Now Hillo was a rich man. Now he consorted with nobility and even with King Carlos who, unlike his father, enjoyed the spectacle of the bullfight. Now everywhere he went people stood in awe or tried to touch him, for luck. Now he was a figura. Now he had two mistresses, both of whom he kept in style – the young and virginal-looking Concha and the womanly-wise Carmelina, and any maja in Madrid would sleep with him if he so much as crooked a finger at her. Now he had forty-seven years of living, thirty of them as a matador, and thirty horn-inflicted scars on his body, any one of which might have killed him. In the early days it was said that if you wanted to see Pepe Hillo fighting the bulls, you had better go at the first opportunity, because he fought like a wild man, and he would not survive long. They used to say that about Juanito too, he thought. Now it was said that Hillo was indestructible. Even the use of ashes and horse dung on his wounds in those early days in the makeshift bullrings of Andalucía had failed to kill him. And what bumbling doctors couldn't do, no bull would do either. Hillo, they said, would die peacefully in his sleep, after fighting bulls into his seventies as the great Francisco Romero had done.

When the bull Barbudo refused to charge the cape, but only pawed the sand and let his tongue hang wet and gray and heavy from his mouth, when the crowd became ugly and began throwing things, Hillo, at first, hands on hips, gazed up contemptuously. He had suffered all this before; he had survived cowardly bulls, which were more dangerous than brave bulls because they were unpredictable, and he had certainly survived the likes of fifteen thousand Madrileños who were now casting aspersions not only on Hillo but on his ancestry. He would be no hero here today. Tomorrow at the corrals he would keep his mouth shut and the luck of the draw would give him a good bull. Tomorrow he would be a hero.

But then, with that look of contempt still in his eyes, he saw in the barrera seats beside the toril gate Cayetana, as beautiful as ever, and not watching him and the cowardly bull Barbudo at all, but engaged in animated conversation with Paco Goya.

Hillo could feel the blood leaving his face. A year? No, a year and a half. Cayetana and Paco Goya, together as once Cayetana and Pepe Hillo had been together.

In the beginning, Hillo had gone to Tadea. 'It is Goya? he had asked.

Tadea said it was Goya.

'She'll get over it,' Hillo said. 'She always comes back to me.'

Tadea had given him a strange, sad look. 'I don't know. She's – different. I think,' Tadea had said slowly, 'that she's in love, really in love for the first time in her life. They – did you know he bought a house in the country? On the other side of the Manzanares. They go there often. A big house on a hill with a well and a garden and from the terrace you can look across at the palace. Do yourself a favor, Hillo. Forget her.'

He had tried. With Concha. With Carmelina. With all the others, so many nameless, faceless others. He had not been able to forget Cayetana. Grudgingly, he still liked Goya. He knew how to live, that one, he had the same zest for life that Hillo had.

And, thought Hillo, now in the bullring, the same taste in women.

He saw that Cayetana and Goya were watching him.

'Butcher it, Hillo,' Paco called down from the close barrera seats. 'It doesn't want to fight. It's meat.'

Even that, Hillo thought, again grudgingly. Fifteen thousand idiots telling me what I can do in the milk of my mother, and the man who stole Cayetana from me? He understands the bulls.

Goya was right. To butcher Barbudo, to make no fight of it because Barbudo wanted no fight, was the sensible thing. Hillo felt a grin freezing on his face, the wide wolf's grin of Juanito in his good days.

Butcher it?

He'd be damned if he would. He'd show that helpful understander of bulls what a real figura could do.

Again he tried the cape, and again Barbudo pawed the

399

ground and refused to follow the lure.

Hillo, still grinning like Juanito Apiñani, thrust his hips forward and offered his body as a lure. The hooting crowd instantly became silent.

Barbudo spurted forward.

'Olé! ' fifteen thousand voices screamed.

Paco felt Cayetana's fingers tighten on his hand. 'Why's he doing it? He shouldn't.'

'Because the crowd was ugly, because we're sitting here together, and because he's Pepe Hillo.'

He could speak of Hillo that way now, with admiration. The rivalry had ended. Cayetana had chosen. The wonder of it was still sometimes too much for him, even after a year and a half. She had walked into the garret room of San Bernardino, and walked back into his life. To stay. The wildness had gone from her. She preferred privacy now, just the two of them in the old farmhouse across the river. A fire on the hearth at night, the flames dancing in her eyes, the joy dancing in his heart, the feel of her body in his arms. She even liked to cook for him, a scowl of concentration on her face as she bustled about with pots and pans. She was not a very good cook.

'Well, it's something like a leg of lamb,' he would say.

'With a bad case of some fatal disease. Can't I do anything right?'

'A thing or two, I think.'

'Goya, you're supposed to love me for my mind and because I'm a duchess and a grandee of the first order and – '

'Yes, Your Grace.'

'But it's nice to know you like my body. Come here and like my body.'

Sometimes Paco would bring a bound copy of one of Moratín's plays, and they would divide the roles between them and rush from room to room in the old farmhouse to find the proper setting as they played a scene. They did the love scenes with exaggerated histrionics and told themselves how much better they could manage without the script, and proceeded to do so.

They never invited anyone else to the house across the river. They would spend two days a week there, or three, and the days would be hours, and the hours minutes. They never had enough time to say all the things they wanted to say to each other.

And in the world, the world down there across the river?

They would meet at a soirée or a dinner party and be most circumspect. Don Paco. Your Grace. But they couldn't hide what was in their eyes.

'Did you see the queen last week at the Osunas'? A very knowing bitch, our Maria Luisa. But she doesn't *really* know. She can only guess, like the rest of them. And they're baffled. I used to flaunt my lovers like a new diamond necklace or a Paris gown.'

He laughed. 'Who would want to flaunt a fat old deaf man?'

'Well, you have put on a *little* weight. But you're not old. You're a little boy, deep down inside where nobody gets to see you – except me. You also happen to be the bravest man I ever met.'

'Cayetana, you're talking nonsense.'

'Painting not what people hope to see of themselves but how they really are. Even the king and queen. Or those etchings. They really are horrible, you know. I love them.'

'Even when I stuck a few pins in you, Your Grace?'

She kissed him. 'Say it again.'

'Your Grace.'

'I never really felt like a duchess before. I was just playing at being a duchess. You make me feel like a queen.'

'What? Like Maria Luisa?'

'Maria Luisa! I ought to challenge you to a duel. If I were a man, I would.'

'I have some dueling pistols.'

'You do?'

'Godoy gave them to me.'

'Did you know he once tried to seduce me? I don't think he's ever quite got over the fact that the answer was no. Did you ever go to bed with Tadea?'

'The answer to that specific question is no.'

'But you made love to her?'

'Yes. In Rocío.'

'I deserved it.'

'What makes you think you had anything to do with it?'

'Where *are* those dueling pistols?'

He did not like talking about what she called his bravery. It wasn't bravery at all. It was necessity. He had to paint what he saw as he saw it, or he would never lift a brush again. Bravery? Just that dangerous Aragonese stubbornness. He had yet to hear from the Holy Office about his *Caprices*. He would hear.

Now, in the bullring, he thought of Hillo's very different

26

kind of bravery. Hillo, in the lengthening afternoon shadows, provoking the bull with the lure of his body until the bull learned to follow the cape.

By the time Hillo's picador Sánchez Fat Eye had ridden into the ring on an old blindfolded nag – Sánchez who had been with Hillo through the thirty years of his career and understood the bulls as he did – Hillo knew that he had taught Barbudo a few lessons in the art of tauromachy. The bull was still *manso,* still a coward, but even in his lack of courage he had learned to follow the moving cape because Hillo had taught him that the cape was the enemy. Even with a brave bull, a real toro-toro, that did not last. Soon Barbudo would become frustrated and shorten his attacks into angry tossings of his head because the bright moving enemy was nothing he could hit. Then it would become impossible for Hillo to perform the ritual with the smaller cape, the muleta, the killing cape, and instead of the slow, close-to-the-body passes, he would have to chop with the killing cape, an effective way of preparing Barbudo for the death he would receive, but one lacking in emotion. That was what the horse was for. The horse offered Barbudo a target he could hit, an enemy he could punish.

The first time Hillo brought Barbudo in to where Fat Eye waited astride with his lance, the horse escaped injury. Leaning down from the saddle, his huge shoulders set, Fat Eye drove the lance into Barbudo's tossing muscle and held those horns away. But Barbudo could feel the weight of the enemy in the strength of Fat Eye's shoulders and the stinging pain of the lance, which weakened his tossing muscle and lowered his head so that, later, Hillo could go in over the horns with his sword. The second time, Barbudo went in under the lance, great head tossing, and the horse whinnied and tumbled on its side, Fat Eye still astride with one leg trapped under its weight while Barbudo, in pain but triumphant now, attacked the fallen horse with short savage thrusts of his horns, the horse helpless and dying, the rider helpless and waiting for his matador to take the bull away with a bright swirling motion of his cape, but his matador was thinking of Cayetana.

Then Hillo heard a shout, either Gaspar or Emeterio Apiñani – they served as his peones now – and it was not he but Gaspar who took Barbudo away from the dead horse and trapped rider. The crowd did not like that. The crowd expected Hillo to perform his own *quite,* his own removal.

Bullring lackeys ran out with a canvas sheet to cover the

dead horse. The second picador came riding in from the patio de caballos and Hillo caped Barbudo toward him.

In a barrera seat opposite the toril gate sat the eminent society physician Dr Peral. On his lips, as usual, was that faint sneer that seemed to say he had seen too much of the folly of mankind. Even his own folly.

He loved the bullfights, though. He could get away from it for a while at the bull fights. A most pagan ritual. The risking of a life to give a death for the pleasure of fifteen thousand clods who didn't know a bad bull when they saw one and didn't know a preoccupied bullfighter either.

What was the matter with Hillo? He couldn't seem to concentrate. His mind was somewhere else, and when you face three quarters of a ton of wild fighting bull, *manso* bull in this case, you could not afford to let your mind wander.

Peral felt something inside him, something which he feared and hated and perversely loved, quicken. A stirring of it, just a little stirring, almost like that first time when he had not understood it. A rich man. A grain merchant named Váldez, it had been. Not an old man, but his life was over. He had fallen and broken his back. He could move his head and his arms, nothing else. Soon the ability to move his arms would go. He was in terrible pain. Peral, not asking the family, certainly not telling the family, had administered a fatal dose of an opiate. Knowing he was committing a sin, but for the good of poor Váldez. In a few minutes it was over. Peral, commiserating with the family, could hardly contain that feeling, that unexpected, not-yet-understood elation.

A feeling of power. In his hands, like a bullfighter, he held the gift, the merciful gift, of death.

Soon, in hopeless cases, and if he thought the family sufficiently enlightened, he might suggest it. Obliquely, of course. So that they might have misunderstood. Sometimes they misunderstood, or pretended to misunderstand. Sometimes they said nothing, but simply left the sickroom while Dr Peral prepared his gift of mercy. And administered it. Like God. Not that there was a God. But if there were, and if He had been merciful. Like Dr Peral. The fact that he enjoyed it at first disturbed him. And then disturbed him less. And then he told himself he was not exempt from the follies of mankind, and he lived with it, fearing and hating and loving this strange desire to give the gift.

Once he had suggested it less obliquely. That had been a

mistake.

An invitation. From the Holy Office. The marble corridors of the palace of the Inquisition. He wondered what the qualifiers wanted with him. He kept his nose out of politics and religion. He was a doctor.

It wasn't the qualifiers. It was the Grand Inquisitor himself, fat, surprisingly young, and with those deceptively gentle eyes.

A shared bottle of wine. A fire on the hearth. A cozy chat. Perhaps, he had begun to think, the Grand Inquisitor had a small medical problem.

'You kill people,' the Grand Inquisitor said, those gentle eyes looking at him.

He almost choked on his wine.

'It is a mortal sin, Dr Peral. I gather you are an unbeliever?'

Those pale gentle eyes knew everything. Peral nodded.

'Then the fact that it is a mortal sin is of no consequence to you. But the fact that it is a crime is of considerable consequence. Another cup of wine?'

Peral spilled some of it getting the cup to his lips.

'I offer you exile. Leave Madrid in the morning. Leave Spain.'

Peral said nothing.

'Or I offer an alternative. The rack, the water torture, the driving of a wooden wedge into a man's rectum – these are devices we have had to abandon in this age of enlightenment. A pity, as they are very effective means of learning the truth. Pain, impossible pain, is a little death, you see, which shows a sinner the bigger death to come. How do you kill people, Dr Peral?'

He did not even bother to deny it. 'An opiate.'

'No. That wouldn't do as a temporary death. Have you any other suggestions?'

He made a few suggestions. He knew at once what the Grand Inquisitor was after.

'Small doses, controlled doses, administered in food perhaps? So that the patient survives but gets a taste of pain that is a foreshadowing of death?'

'It can be done,' Dr Peral said. He had another cup of wine. His hand was steadier.

'From time to time we'll call on you, when the qualifiers are confronted with a particularly stubborn situation. You understand?'

He understood. From time to time the qualifiers called on him. As an experiment, it was interesting. Like driving that wedge, he thought. A little pain, and then a little more, and the concomitant weakening of the individual's will. He learned, over some years, the exact dosages. Soon, to his horror, and then not to his horror, he came to look forward to his visits to the dungeons below the palace of the Inquisition. It was, the Grand Inquisitor told him, far more effective than the rack or the water torture had ever been. It simply came upon the victim, like God's punishment. It terrified him, and he talked.

The Grand Inquisitor offered payment. Peral took no payment.

Then Godoy sent for him, Godoy who like the Holy Office had his spies everywhere.

'Mallo,' said Godoy.

'What?'

'The chamberlain Mallo. The queen's tired of him. He has some compromising letters. He won't return them. Tell me, Peral, you're a man of medicine. If he were to suffer a small illness, a small but most painful illness, do you think he might give those letters back?'

Peral said he did not know.

'I'm afraid,' said Godoy with a faint smile, 'that I am being most unoriginal. I offer you two alternatives. The first is exile. Do you understand?'

Peral understood. Mallo took to his bed for a week with a fever and a terrible gnawing pain in his stomach. Peral never learned what happened to the letters. Godoy sent for him occasionally after that, the Grand Inquisitor more frequently.

The pain, like a foretaste of death, Peral thought, in the bullring, watching the two Apiñani brothers take the barbed shafts of their banderillas and test the points on their thumbs. Soon those barbs would pierce the hide of the bull and the shafts would clatter as he tossed his head from side to side trying to rid himself of the pain. Was it the same for the bull? A foretaste of death before the inevitable death in the arena?

Was every goring that Hillo had received a small death too? Had the idea ever crossed his mind while he waited on the sand, rinsing his mouth with water from a clay jug?

Interesting to think that it might have. Interesting to see how distracted Hillo appeared. Dr Peral took snuff and watched Gaspar Apiñani darting gracefully across the sand, banderillas held high, toward the bull.

Hillo, watching the same activity, did not like what he saw.

Not only was the bull Barbudo *manso,* but he hooked to the right. That would make the kill difficult. Hillo would have to escape to the bull's right after he went in between the horns with his sword. He wondered why more bulls were right-horned than left-horned. Like people, he thought. Like right-handed people.

He told Emeterio where he wanted the second pair of sticks placed, and Gaspar where he wanted the third. He stood against the fence, took another mouthful of water and spat it onto the sand. He glanced up at Cayetana. She was watching Emeterio as he went up on his toes to place the fourth and final pair of sticks. Hillo tried to catch her eye but couldn't. He walked along the fence to where his swordhandler and Sánchez Fat Eye were waiting behind the boards. The muleta was folded nearly across the top of the fence.

'Hooking less?' Hillo asked.

'Not enough less,' said Sánchez Fat Eye.

Hillo reached over the boards. 'Let's have it.'

He grasped the hilt of the sword and yanked the blade free with a quick motion. The soft leather scabbard, empty, seemed to writhe like a snake on the top of the fence before it hung slack. With his left hand Hillo grasped the red serge muleta, the killing cape.

'Be careful, maestro,' said Sánchez Fat Eye. 'That *manso* almost got me. Concentrate on what you're doing.'

Hillo grinned, and again the feel of it on his face reminded him of Juanito in the good days. 'Barbudo will make sure I concentrate,' he said, and walked along the fence until he stood below the president's box. He saluted with his sword.

He wondered to whom he should give the *brindis* – the dedication of the killing. To the fickle mob? Not today, he told himself, no thank you. To the fickle Cayetana? He almost thought he would. A fine ironic gesture. But as he walked along the fence and reached her, he changed his mind.

With a casual toss he sent his hat swinging in Paco's direction. 'I dedicate the killing of this bull,' he said formally, 'to Francisco de Goya y Lucientes, first painter to the king.' A pause. 'Because we both know how much alike we are.'

And, spreading the cape with the point of his sword, he waved Gaspar and Emeterio from the arena.

Cayetana watched Hillo test the bull with three quick right-handed passes, the muleta spread by his sword. The third was a high pass, a confidence-giving pass, and Barbudo reared on his hind legs as he rushed past Hillo and then upwards, searching for that elusive cape with his horns. Hillo called him back and finished the series with a chest pass, fixing the bull in place, turning his back and strutting away. The crowd roared.

Hillo's *brindis* had surprised Cayetana. As he'd approached them, she had expected to receive the dedication of the killing herself. How many bulls had Hillo dedicated to her? She no longer remembered. She wasn't disappointed, though. The unexpected dedication to Goya had been, somehow, fitting. Perhaps it meant that Hillo and Goya could remain friends after all. But whether they did or not, she had chosen. God, yes, she had chosen her man. Gruff and sometimes surly in his deafness, and with those wild ups and downs of his and pretending to hate more than he really did all that was detestable in Madrid, in Spain, in the world. Pretending? She wasn't entirely sure. As close as they were, sometimes she hardly knew what he really thought. He would retreat into the silence of his deafness, retreat even from her. Other times he would say, with a suddenly boyish smile on his craggy face, as if he didn't quite believe it, 'I have the magic.' He tended to say it when he believed it least of all. It was a talisman for him, those words. The most talented man in Spain, and he could even doubt that. But not her love. She must see to it that he never doubted her love. Who would ever have believed that the scatterbrained Duchess of Alba would become an anchor for a man who lived his life like a ship on a stormy sea?

Or, in a way, like a dozen Pepe Hillos all in one. Because there on the sand in the form of the bull Barbudo was the dark soul of Spain, the dark soul of mankind, and Hillo now was fighting it and would kill it, for this afternoon, for this day. Goya fought it always, with those paints of his, with his etching needle. Goya could kill it for ten years, or a hundred, by exposing it, by holding it up to ridicule. Hillo could battle only a bull. Goya could take on a king.

My, thought Cayetana, isn't our scatterbrained little duchess getting philosophical? Why, if she spoke those thoughts aloud, people would mistake her for the Osuna. That wouldn't do at all. But her deaf man knew. Her deaf man knew that his pretty little fluff of a duchess had a mind. He had discovered it and held it up for her own inspection. He had cultivated it. He had made her twice the woman she had ever been. He had – completed her, as a matador completes the ritual of the bullfight with the muleta, the killing cape, as Hillo was – doing now, preparing the bull for the sword. Preparing him for death.

Cayetana shuddered suddenly. Death was always so close. And it had nothing to do with a young girl's visit to a gypsy fortuneteller in Cádiz. It just happened. As it would happen to the bull Barbudo.

Hillo felt the faena, the final act of the ritual with the red serge killing cape, grip him.

He executed a linked series of natural passes, muleta in his left hand, sword hand on his hip as he slowly pivoted and led the bull with the cape, the horn an inch from his thigh, banderillas whacking his side, the rich life-smell of the soon-to-die Barbudo thick in his nostrils and the Barbudos came galloping by again.

Another series, he decided, another half dozen natural passes, so that the crowd that had hated him fifteen minutes before would leap to its feet in a frenzy of bloodlust and love, love of Pepe Hillo, whose courage became their courage, love of Pepe Hillo, who took the disappointment and the meanness out of their lives for a brief time with the killing of the bull.

'Olé!' the crowd shouted, and they loved him, and he hated them. Fickle, he thought. Like a woman. But he loved the bull, he loved all bulls, and at this particular moment he loved the black bull Barbudo who followed the cape obediently, forgetting he was *manso,* forgetting that dangerous tendency to hook to the right, forgetting the wild free years on the range, knowing no past and certainly no future but performing with Hillo the ritual of death for fifteen thousand idiots whom Hillo could forget now in the wild slow consuming grace of the faena, performing it for Cayetana too, whom he could forget, performing it for Paco Goya who had received the *brindis,* and whom he could forget because he was alone with Barbudo in a world they shared for a brief moment that made everything almost worthwhile.

He moved backwards, body zigzagging, cape zigzagging, Barbudo following, to bring the killing to Goya. Or to Cayetana. Let them decide. He was doing it for himself.

Barbudo stood, all four legs planted. Hillo raised the cape and lowered it. The eyes followed the movement, head and horns went up, went down. He let the cape dangle from his left hand. The eyes held steady. He brought his right arm back and then forward and profiled along it and the blade of Toledo steel.

No sound. No sound anywhere in the arena.

Flying feet. The style of Pepe Hillo. Not the bull ponderously charging the sword and the death, but the man bringing both to him.

At the last instant something made him glance up at Cayetana. Her eyes had narrowed, her lips were parted slightly. She was beautiful, impossibly beautiful, and in that instant everything changed for him. He had been deluding himself. Concha was nothing, Carmelina nothing but a brief unsatisfactory forgetfulness; the bulls were nothing, the bull Barbudo was nothing but an animal he had to kill to amuse the fickle crowd and the lost Cayetana, the forever lost Cayetana. Over the fence he saw a look of apprehension on Sánchez Fat Eye's face and heard Gaspar Apiñani cry out, and he went up on his toes very quickly and without grace as he brought his eyes back to Barbudo and saw what they had seen, that the bull had begun to move, the bull was coming fast, very fast, and he would have to receive him instead of killing him on flying feet, ironically killing what he suddenly and with finality knew would be the last bull or the last anything of his life, not with the technique of Hillo but the all but abandoned technique of Juanito Apiñani, who had known when to quit whereas he, Hillo, had not.

He passed the cape low to his own right and for a moment thought he was wrong as he felt the blade going in smoothly, not hitting bone, felt his knuckles punch the hide of Barbudo at the killing place, the sword all the way in, his own body swinging to the left as he ran clear, but then he knew he had not been wrong, because Barbudo, dying, already dead on his feet but for a few seconds unaware of the death, hooked to the right, and abruptly Hillo was up on a horn, dangling, and then he was in the air and falling and caught on the horn again, and he felt the shock but not the pain, the pain would come later except that there would be no later, and he knew that the horn had taken him low in the belly that first time, and the second time, still with no pain, higher, he could feel his ribs splintering as Barbudo staggered a few steps with the enemy impaled, the enemy who was gripping the base of the horn with both hands as they fell together, the enemy who tried to see Cayetana but could not see her nor would ever see her again, the enemy who died on the sand of the bullring at the same instant Barbudo died.

CHAPTER THIRTY-ONE

The Gown

EVERY DAY a dry searing wind blew down from the Sierra, and even at twilight the paseos of the city remained deserted. After dark, Madrileños emerged from the ovens of their homes to the griddles of the city's streets. Friends passed each other blank-eyed. Strangers glared. Fights erupted for no reason at all, knives flashing in the glow of the city's oil lamps. It was the heat, everyone said. It was the shortage of water, with the level sinking lower in the city's wells every day. It was the price of grain, so high now that even a family accustomed to a diet of bread and oil could hardly make ends meet. It was Napoleon Bonaparte's Grand' Armée ravaging the north, living off the land and driving refugees into the capital. It was a summer, that summer after Pepe Hillo died, when nobody joked about Madrid's climate. Nine months of winter and three of hell? That summer the gates of hell opened, and the flames spewed forth, and the Madrileños sweated, their eyes bloodshot and gritty with dust, their bodies festering with sores, their nostrils full of the stink of the city's sewers.

The court moved early to Aranjuez. It was a wise move. Angry crowds gathered at night in the stifling heat outside the royal palace, shouting across the high iron fence to the impassive guardsmen. The king was a fool or a coward or both, they said. Godoy was a mockery of a generalissimo who had fought Portugal on Bonaparte's behalf but could do nothing about the French regiments encamped in the north. The queen was a fat old slut. The guardsmen did not disagree.

The king, the anonymous pamphleteers wrote, hunted in the cool royal preserves while Godoy, resplendent in his new white and gold generalissimo's uniform, wrote ineffectual protests to First Consul Bonaparte. The first consul's brother

Joseph usually replied in the ambigious language of diplomacy. The French army stayed.

The queen eagerly awaited a gown from Paris. Bonaparte had promised it as a token of his esteem. In return, the pamphleteers asked, for Catalonia? Or only the Basque provinces?

Soon the pamphleteers found a new name for Godoy. They called him the Choricero – the Sausage Maker. Didn't they raise pigs in Extremadura and grind them up for sausage meat? Wasn't Godoy a sausage maker of a diplomat? Putting Spain through a grinder in that hot summer of 1802 and presenting the finished product to Bonaparte?

The Sausage Maker hardly emerged from his palace in Aranjuez. Those rare times he did, the people of the sleepy little summer capital were ready with the song, Cayetana's song. Everyone from the grubbiest urchin to old men trying to keep cool in the shade of the plazas and arcades sang it. Godoy grew moody and querulous. It was the heat, he said. It was Joseph Bonaparte's evasive answers, he said.

But it was Cayetana's song.

Cayetana herself had lost interest in the song. She had better fish to fry.

'I'll have Maria Luisa dancing on a hot skillet,' she told Tadea.

They were sitting in the garden of the Moncloa *palacete* at dusk. With a rustle of skirts, Maria de la Luz came out to join them. Twelve years old now, the black girl was tall and gawky. Cayetana dressed her like a duchess and treated her like a precious little doll.

'Doesn't Mama-Grace like the queen?'

'Mama-Grace loves the queen. The queen is going to make her very happy.'

'Could you push me on the swing, Mama-Grace? It's so hot inside.'

The girl ran to the swing suspended from the branch of an old oak tree, and Cayetana began to push her – higher and higher until Maria de la Luz's mouth opened in a wide shriek of delight. Tadea smiled, watching them. Cayetana seemed happy and animated.

The duchess had been so unlike herself since Hillo's fatal goring – pensive and subdued, dwelling on the subject of death. 'It was always somehow unreal, until Hillo,' she told Tadea once. 'Tapers burning, and white gloves, and straw seats for the mourners. Or my husband, dying in Sevilla. He just went

411

on a trip and didn't come back. But Hillo, right there, right in front of my eyes. For the first time it was real, horribly, finally real.

'If only I believed in something. My mother was very religious. Even the old duque-general, going to Mass every day of his life. But I – I don't know. Hillo said the bulls were all the religion he ever needed, and Goya doesn't believe in anything but that magic of his.' She shuddered. 'Nothing. Just nothing forever. I don't want it to be like that. Like snuffing out a candle and you aren't there any more.'

It terrified her. She told Tadea about her dream. 'I fall and fall, and I get smaller and smaller and then I just – go away. Every night, the same dream. I hate it. I hate to go to sleep.'

She hardly slept at all. Tadea and Goya tried everything, but it was as if she'd had to mourn for Hillo, whom she no longer loved, because she hadn't mourned her husband, whom she'd never loved at all.

They tried picnics in the country, or riding hard along the river road until Cayetana was breathless and exhausted. They took her to the taverns where gypsies danced the wild bolero. She sat gazing into her wine cup and waiting until they took her home.

One night she disappeared. She was gone a month and returned to the Moncloa wearing gypsy clothing.

'Goya was frantic,' Tadea said. 'Where were you?'

'Out. In the country.'

'Alone?'

'With gypsies. Kettlesmiths.' A brittle, nervous laugh. 'I helped repair kettles in every village in Castile.'

Goya, Tadea remembered, had been more than frantic when Cayetana returned.

'You can't go off like that,' he shouted.

'Why can't I?' With that same brittle laugh.

'It's dangerous.'

'You don't own me. I come and go as I please. If you can't accept that, we'll stop seeing each other.'

'Do you want that?'

What started as another laugh became a choked cry. 'I don't know what I want. Just leave me alone. I want to live. I want to live while I can.'

A few weeks later she disappeared again. She returned to the Moncloa with Pedro Romero, who had come out of retirement to become Numero Uno now that Hillo was dead. He stayed three nights. After that there was a young general named Antonio Cornel. Soon Madrid society was whispering about their affair. Cornel lasted a month.

Again Goya came storming in. Cayetana wouldn't see him. 'She needs time,' Tadea told him. 'She's still in love with you.'

Goya laughed harshly. Tadea knew he was the least patient of men. He stopped coming to the Moncloa. What he did with his time Tadea never learned. Brooded, perhaps. Remembering. Wistfully Tadea herself remembered a night in Rocío. To have a man like that, a real man, and throw him over for the likes of a General Cornel, it made no sense.

But they were alike, Goya and Cayetana. There was never enough time for either of them.

Soon others came to take Romero's and the general's place. For a few days, for a few weeks.

No painting was signed with the name of Francisco Goya that year.

Cayetana lost weight. Her eyes darted nervously this way and that, as if the death she feared was lurking just beyond her vision. She had no time for Brother Basil and no time for Tadea and no time for Maria de la Luz.

Until her mysterious project, whatever it was, Tadea thought now in the garden of the Moncloa. Writing letters to Paris, scowling over a line, crossing it out, writing another, a lovably wicked gleam in her eyes, then waiting impatiently for the return post. She began to joke with Brother Basil again. She began to play with Maria de la Luz. If she had any more casual affairs, Tadea wasn't aware of them.

'So it's to be a Minette,' she said one day, grinning.

'What's a Minette?' Tadea asked.

'You'll find out.'

Now in the garden Brother Basil joined them. 'A c-caller,' he said. 'Shall I t-tell him you're b-b-busy, Doña Cayetana?'

'Who is it?'

'F-french. D-d-difficult to pronounce, F-french names. A Monsieur Le – '

'Leroy!' cried Cayetana as she gave Maria de la Luz an enormous push, almost sending the swing up and over the branch.

With a whoop Cayetana started to run from the garden. She called back over her shoulder: 'Come and see me heat the oil.'

'What oil?' Tadea asked.

'To fry Maria Luisa.'

'Who's Leroy?' Tadea asked.

'Leroy and Minette hate each other,' Cayetana said by way of explanation.

'Who *are* they?'

'Minette's the most famous couturière in Paris. Leroy used to work for her.'

They went together through the French windows into the drawing room where the most curiously dressed man Tadea had ever seen was waiting. She knew that in Madrid, as in Paris, fashions were changing. Some men even wore skintight full-length trousers of elastic stockinet or nankeen imported from China instead of breeches, but this Monsieur Leroy was really too much. Despite the heat of the summer evening he wore a suit of deep yellow, almost golden nankeen. His coat hung open to reveal a black silk cravat and a waistcoat of pale smoky gray piqué with golden ball buttons down the front. On his arm rested a narrow-brimmed straw hat, its tall crown circled by a gold silk cord fastened in front by a gold buckle. At first Tadea thought Monsieur Leroy had a neck as thick as Maria Luisa's, but then she noticed the edge of a white linen cravat peeping out from under the black silk one. Over both stood the stiffly starched white points of his shirt collar. Monsieur Leroy, a diminutive birdlike man, sat perched on the edge of a chair, one nankeen-trousered leg crossed over the other, revealing a yellow and white striped silk stocking and a glossily black flat-heeled shoe. Despite the heat, despite coat, waistcoat, two cravats and that stiffly starched shirt, he managed to appear cool.

'Madame,' he said, and again, 'madame,' rising and bowing twice.

Tea was served. Cayetana could hardly contain herself. When the serving girl left, she asked: 'You have the pattern, Monsieur Leroy?'

'But of course, madame,' said the little Frenchman in a simpering voice.

'I'll need six of them,' Cayetana said.

Monsieur Leroy's mouth pursed like a rosebud just beginning to open. 'Naturally, madame, if it is six that you require, the price must be six times what I quoted in our correspondence.' The birdlike Frenchman named a figure that made Tadea think Cayetana was going to build a new country house or two.

'Agreed,' she said with a radiant smile. 'On two conditions.'

'Which are, madame?'

'First, that they're ready in time.'

'If we hurry. . . . You have skilled seamstresses?'

Cayetana said she had skilled seamstresses.

'And the second condition, madame?'

'That they follow the pattern exactly but are more elegant.'

'But of course, madame,' chirped the birdlike man. 'I am no mere Minette. I am Leroy.'

'You're certain it's the identical pattern?'

'Madame,' said Leroy, 'would I have come all the way to Madrid otherwise?'

It was very hot inside the royal berlin as it rumbled through the Embajadores Gate and into Madrid.

An army of guardsmen had made the journey from Aranjuez, not that Maria Luisa thought she would need them. Madrileños were like children. Offer them a spectacle and they quickly forgot their troubles.

The coach had made good time. There would be daylight enough for a fine paseo, a royal paseo on the fashionable Recoletos, as in more pleasant days. A dozen coaches were strung out behind the royal berlin, a dozen more would join them from the palaces and townhouses of Madrid. The paseo, a grand ball at the royal palace – a triumph, an absolutely guaranteed triumph.

Maria Luisa rode alone in the white and gold berlin. Even her ladies-in-waiting followed in one of the other coaches. No one had seen the Minette. She had entered the coach in Aranjuez wearing a cloak, despite the heat. Never mind the heat. Never mind anything. Let the people, even the nobility, make their evil little remarks about Carlos, about Godoy. They'd see royalty today. Let them talk of deposing Carlos. Let that skulking little monster Fernando – how she hated her son! – plot a palace revolution. She'd show them a queen.

The gown would awe them. It already awed her. Seeing it for the first time, fondling it, holding it off at arm's length, she was hardly able to believe her eyes. And now wearing it – a perfect fit, slimming somehow, an impossibly elegant creation, it almost made her feet beautiful.

Maybe she wasn't as witty as the Osuna, she thought, as the coach went rumbling through the hot deserted streets. Certainly she lacked the Alba's beauty. Her eyes narrowed with hatred, as she remembered the beauty, staring at her, insolently nude, from the hidden Goya painting Godoy had finally shown her. God, she told herself, I'd give half the kingdom for a body like that. Her teeth flashed in a fleeting smile.

415

Carlos' half. She had never deluded herself. She could accept the wit of the Osuna. Wit was of no great importance to a woman anyway. But the Alba's face? The Alba's body? Half the kingdom. And the other half if she could destroy her rival.

Well, she would destroy her a little today, in a way that only a woman could understand.

The gown. The magnificent gown. She could feel the silk of it caressing her now. Dowdy? They always said she was somewhat dowdy. That was the best they said.

She would not be dowdy in the Minette, strolling casually along the wide promenade of the Recoletos. She couldn't wait to see the look on the Alba's face.

That gown, that absolutely unbelievable gown, made Maria Luisa feel regal for almost the first time in her life.

A simple coiffure, Titus-cut for the occasion. Very short, very Parisienne. She dabbed at her face with a cologne-scented silk handkerchief. The Titus cut, a touch of eye shadow, no rouge (Minette had written that rouge was going out of fashion in France, the pale look was favored), no strings of pearls, no clusters of precious stones, just the single enormous diamond, El Estanque, on a simple silver chain.

And the gown.

Maria Luisa could feel the drag brake catching hold. She looked out the window at the brassy sky, the parched trees lining the paseo. A footman opened the door. She glanced past him. She saw the Osuna, her hard face looking harder still over too many frills and ribbons. She saw the Medina Sidonia. Lavender and an enormous bustle, how passé. She saw Tadea, the Alba's lady-in-waiting, and her heart leaped. She hadn't been sure that Cayetana would come. The little whore had ignored royal invitations before. Not this time. How very pleasant.

The footman let down the step, and Manuel Godoy, in his white generalissimo's uniform, offered an arm. She watched his eyes, thinking of those paintings of the Alba he owned. He had not denied sleeping with her. Maria Luisa had asked him once. Taking snuff, he'd said: 'Don't all of us, sooner or later?'

She had liked the reply. She liked even more the widening, now, of those gravely sly eyes. He said: '*Formidable,* Doña Maria Luisa. You look like a goddess.'

She was impatient with his gallantry. 'Help me down, Manuel.' Barely touching the white sleeve of Godoy's uniform with her fingertips, she began to walk. Like walking on air. The gown. The incredible silver gown. She felt young and beautiful and desirable.

She pretended to ignore the admiration, the envious glances, the murmurs of surprise and approval. Magnificent. Regal. Even the way she walks.

The gown made her feel witty. Words came tripping lightly off her tongue, clever pithy little remarks that got a chuckle from a captain-general, a rumbling laugh from the Archbishop of Toledo, smiles and courtly bows from half a dozen dukes and marqueses. Minette, she thought, that wonderful Minette, if only I'd found her twenty years ago. She even felt grateful to Bonaparte and forgot for a while the indignity of his troops. She walked on in a dream.

And saw Cayetana.

The little whore of a duchess had come dressed as a maja, in simple skirt and bodice, with a wide yellow sash around her waist. Ordinarily, it would have infuriated Maria Luisa, as if Cayetana were saying, 'I can dress any old way and still be the uncrowned queen of Madrid.'

But not today. Was there a faintly crestfallen look in the little whore's dark eyes as she curtseyed and for once remembered to kiss the extended royal right hand?

But then why was the Duke of Medinaceli smiling, an odd sort of smile which he tried to hide behind his hand, and why did the archbishop explode into laughter that became a strange choking cough, the archbishop's face turning red as Maria Luisa's eyes met his, and why did the captain-general who had thought the queen so clever a moment before stand suddenly rigid, his lips quivering? Everywhere Maria Luisa's glittering eyes darted she saw the same thing – the grandees of Spain smirking, poking one another and then looking quickly away.

Maria Luisa stared past Cayetana.

'I had no idea,' the Duchess of Alba said sweetly, 'that Your Majesty used Minette.'

Behind her stood the little black girl Maria de la Luz and five of the Alba's lesser ladies-in-waiting, all of them, Maria Luisa was well aware, hardly more than serving girls.

All wore identical costumes – the shimmering brocaded silver, the intricate embroidery, the long, elegantly tight sleeves, the standing lace Medici collar framing the deep decolletage, the long silken train falling – rippling like molten silver – from the left shoulder.

27   417

Maria Luisa's costume, but somehow more elegant. And worn by five slim young girls and that awkward black child.

All curtseyed low. All formed a line, one behind the other, to kiss the royal hand.

Maria Luisa felt pale and fat and withered and old. Everyone was looking at her. Even among the trees that lined the paseo she saw faces rudely smiling – the canaille come to watch the royal paseo. Finally, inevitably, someone burst into laughter, and then the laughter was everywhere, all around her, filling her ears, filling the world, stripping Maria Luisa of that splendid gown so that she stood naked before the grandees of Spain.

Somehow she got through the hand-kissing, the six identical gowns rustling before her, one after the other. Her knees felt weak. Her head began to whirl. The heat of the sun beat down on her. Pretend to swoon, she thought. The heat. It's the only way out.

Pretense was not necessary. Maria Luisa heard a raucous, most unqueenly cry escape her lips. Then she fainted.

No lights glowed from the windows of the grand ballroom of the royal palace that night; no music drifted out into the sultry hot darkness. The ball was canceled.

It seemed a shame, Cayetana de Alba said. The queen's sudden indisposition, the long journey of so many grandees from Aranjuez. Something had to be done.

All night two orchestras played at the Alba palace.

That Cayetana, everyone said. From the outside her palace looked like a condemned building. Hardly in use at all since that mysterious fire after poor Villafranca's death. But now? Now the tables groaned under the weight of roast lamb and suckling pig and chickens and fried and poached fish; the champagne flowed from two hundred magnum bottles; lavish decorations festooned the walls and hung from the ceilings. Cayetana drifted everywhere among her guests, eyes flashing, a guileless smile on her lips. She had never looked more lovely. They asked her to dance the bolero. She danced it, still dressed as a maja. Her five lesser ladies-in-waiting circulated among the grandees in their Minette gowns. Even Maria de la Luz received permission to stay up late. Her first, her very first, grand ball.

Shortly before dawn torches were lit on the tribune and one of the orchestras played a fanfare. Cayetana mounted the tribune. Cheering and applause greeted her.

'Cousins,' she said, 'the hour's late and this really is a gloomy old barn of a palace, don't you think?'

Glances were exchanged. What was the madcap Alba up to now?

'The last time I was terribly naughty, remember what happened? The queen set fire to my palace.'

Shocked glances. The queen? Well, there had been rumors. And Cayetana had disappeared for a season. But to accuse the queen of arson?

'I don't think that's fair,' Cayetana said. 'Why should Doña Maria Luisa have all the fun? It's my palace, and if it's to be burnt again, why don't we do it ourselves?'

Joking. Naturally she was joking. She wouldn't dare.

Everyone looked around. Uneasily. There wasn't a liveried servant to be seen in the vast ballroom, and the members of the two orchestras were carrying their instruments out through the wide French doors.

Cayetana went to the edge of the tribune and seized a torch. She brandished it over her head, the flames leaping.

'Well?' she cried. 'There are torches and lamps for everyone. What are we waiting for? Haven't you ever wanted to burn down a palace?'

She touched her torch to a curtain hanging behind the tribune. Through the open windows, from the far end of the garden, her guests heard the first notes of a seguidilla.

Flames licked at the silken curtain, and leaped, and spread. For a moment Cayetana stood silhouetted against them. She danced to another curtain with her torch.

'For the queen!' she cried. 'As her loyal and obedient servant.'

Flames licked at the second curtain, and climbed.

Soon the wall tapestries began to smoulder. A count, and then a marqués, and finally the old Duke of Medinaceli himself grabbed a torch and set another fire.

The gesture, someone said. The absolutely outrageous, impossible gesture. To top off the social triumph of her life with this. The Alba's mad, of course, unpredictably, deliciously, exquisitely mad. They all loved her for it.

And danced in the garden while fire consumed her gloomy old barn of a palace, the flames rising to meet the dawn.

Manuel Godoy cantered his horse through the predawn darkness toward the Alba palace.

He had to reason with her, he thought. He had to persuade

419

her to apologize, down on her knees if necessary. And then to stay out of the queen's sight. A self-imposed exile to one of her country residences. For at least six months. Perhaps a year.

He had never seen the queen's eyes like that. Never heard her voice like that.

The eyes looked at him. The voice said: 'I want Peral.'

'Peral?'

'For her.'

The questioning look froze on Godoy's face. 'I don't understand.'

'Don't you? How did you get those letters back from Mallo? Why did Jovellanos go into exile like a lamb? They say he's sick and feeble now, in the Asturias. They say he'll be a long time recuperating. I want Peral.'

Maria Luisa was pacing back and forth in the anteroom of her suite at the royal palace. She was still wearing the Minette. She reached up suddenly and ripped the magnificent shimmering train from her shoulder. She turned on Godoy savagely. 'I could strip you of all your titles just like that.'

He knew she could, knew that Marie Luisa and the king, with their backs to the wall, might yet find a most convenient scapegoat in the Prince of the Peace.

He tried to reason with her. 'Cayetana's a flighty little thing without a brain in her head. Harmless and – '

'Don't mention that whore's name to me. You call what she did today harmless? She's made me a laughingstock. I won't be able to show my face in public for weeks. Harmless? With that song of hers? "Who is the sire of my youngest boy?"' the queen squawked. ' "Godoy!" You call *that* harmless?'

Maria Luisa's fury, then, was contagious. For one fleeting moment he thought he would summon Peral. But then he remembered Jovellanos. The queen had not been misinformed. Very sick, dangerously, almost fatally sick. Peral, of course, was insane. He liked it. He liked doing it. Controlling the dose, seeing how far he could go, watching the pain, enjoying it. But Jovellanos was a strong man, and Cayetana de Alba, for all her verve, was frail. She didn't weigh a hundred pounds.

'He's the Alba family physician,' Maria Luisa was saying. 'Visits routinely, doesn't he?'

'He's doctor to all the grandees,' Godoy admitted.

Her head drew back on the thick neck. 'Get him.'

'Sleep on it,' he urged. 'As a favor to me. In the morning – '

Her head shot forward. 'You'll be on your way back to Badajoz, Señor Sausage Maker, in the morning. That, or Peral.'

She would hear no further argument. Godoy returned to the Admiralty Palace and brooded. Badajoz for him, or Peral for the Alba. Besides, if he refused, Maria Luisa herself could summon Peral. Still, he couldn't do it. He ordered a horse saddled and, shortly before dawn, was cantering through the dark silent streets toward the Alba palace.

From a long way off he could see the flames. He urged his horse to a gallop. As he approached, he saw that the entire building was ablaze. He couldn't believe his ears; he heard music. He galloped through the open gateway and reined in hard, his horse rearing. They were dancing. On the lawn, under the great old trees. They were sipping champagne. They were laughing.

He dismounted and led the horse. He looked for a familiar face. He saw old Medinaceli, the queen's lord high steward, dancing in a circle with another man and two girls wearing Minettes. He called, and Medinaceli danced in his direction. Unsteady on his feet. A little bit drunk.

'Never had so much fun in my life.' Medinaceli lurched against Godoy's shoulder, his wig askew. 'Never set fire to a palace before.'

'Never what? *You* did it?'

Medinaceli giggled and hiccupped. 'All of us. Cayetana's idea. The queen was going to do it anyway, she said.'

'She said that publicly?'

'Privately, Most Excellent Señor. All cousins, you know. The grandees. The old grandees.' With faint emphasis on the word old. 'Said it, and did it. Before the queen could. Magnificent gesture. The old duque-general would have been proud of her.'

Medinaceli essayed a small bow and went dancing off.

An apology? Now? Crawling on her hands and knees all the way from Madrid to Aranjuez wouldn't be enough.

Godoy mounted and reached full gallop as he passed through the gateway. He still wouldn't do it, he told himself. Let Maria Luisa do it herself.

He slept a few hours, fitfully, and was awakened late in the morning by his chamberlain.

'A courier, Your Highness. From Paris.'

He brightened. He had couched his last letter to Bonaparte most diplomatically. A masterpiece of persuasiveness. Perhaps

Bonaparte would finally realize the impossibility of maintaining those French garrisons in the north. Present that diplomatic triumph to Maria Luisa and she might forget all about the duchess.

Bonaparte's own seal, Godoy observed. Not his brother Joseph's. That was good. A good sign.

He opened the letter. His fingers tightened on the stiff paper.

Letter? Just an angry one-line scrawl. *Is the king of Spain tired of reigning?* With Bonaparte's signature below.

Godoy sat without moving. She could, she very likely would, strip him of all his titles the way she had ripped the train from the shoulder of that gown.

He waited an hour. He waited another hour. What did he owe the Alba anyway? The way she had rejected him once, with that casual arrogance. And that song, that damnable song.

He went to the wardrobe and got out his generalissimo's uniform. Just to look at it. To touch it.

And finally to wear it, when he went calling on Dr Peral.

CHAPTER THIRTY-TWO

A Gift for the King,
A Gift for the Queen

I HAVE ALWAYS BELIEVED,' said the fat, gentle-eyed man, 'that suckling pig roast on a spit is a dish fit for a king. Don't you agree, Señor Goya?'

Paco looked across his gold place-setting and the damask tablecloth into those gentle eyes. 'It's a damned hot day for suckling pig – begging Your Eminence's pardon.'

The gentle eyes almost disappeared into folds of fat as his host smiled. 'For a mild profanity? I'm quite accustomed to mild profanity. Times are changing, Señor Goya. We could have a simple salad instead.'

'No, the pig will be all right,' Paco said.

'Splendid. And I thought a Valdepeñas wine. We Dominicans have a little vineyard in – you do like Valdepeñas?'

'I prefer Cariñena,' said Paco. 'It's an honest wine.'

His host laughed a gentle laugh. 'Of course. You *are* from Aragon.' The fat man shut his eyes and formed a tent with his fingers over the gold plate, his arms emerging from the sleeves of his black and white cassock like two fat white slugs. 'I've looked forward to this little luncheon. I've always admired your work, Señor Goya.'

'What do you want?' Paco asked bluntly. He was thinking of Cayetana – Cayetana disappearing for a month, Cayetana and Pedro Romero, Cayetana and General Cornel. The Grand Inquisitor was just a fat man with a taste for heavy food and strong wine on a day too hot for either.

He ignored Paco's question as three green-liveried servants brought the suckling pig, its aroma filling the small private dining room in the palace of the Inquisition, and two bottles of wine. He told a footman to bring the Cariñena and said: 'We keep a well-stocked wine cellar.'

Below the hall of judgment, Paco thought. Next to the dungeons.

He wondered if this was the way Pablo de Olavide's Little Act of Faith had begun, so long ago – no sequestering of his property, no bailiff at the door, no denunciations by paid informers, just a tête-à-tête luncheon on a hot July afternoon, a servant cutting the suckling pig in half with a single stroke of the cleaver, another going to fetch a bottle of the guest's favorite wine while the Grand Inquisitor mumbled a benediction.

He watched the fat man eat, the plump dimpled hands using knife and fork with eager dexterity. A sheen of sweat soon covered the round cheeks and sagging double chins. A hand picked up a bone and strong teeth gnawed on it. Paco thought of Cayetana dressing Maria de la Luz and five ladies-in-waiting in the queen's Minette and then burning down the Buenavista Palace. Would he have tried to stop her if he'd been there? He didn't know. Nor did he know if he would ever swallow his pride and see her again.

He had painted nothing, etched nothing, drawn nothing all year. And he had learned that eighteen-year-old Javier would be no consolation in his old age. Javier played at being a señorito, a man about town. He wanted to travel, he said, to broaden himself. Paco cheerfully would have given him the money, but so far Javier had stirred himself no further than Zaragoza for a visit with his grandmother.

Solace in his old age? Santa Maria, he thought, I'm not old.

What's fifty-six? He looked at the Grand Inquisitor, the eyes hidden now in their folds of fat, the hands slick with grease, the strong teeth crunching. That's old. That fat, jowly hound of a Grand Inquisitor sniffing out heresy. . . .

What's a life without Cayetana?

He imagined her in another man's arms, and he glared across the table just as the Grand Inquisitor said:

'I have always maintained that an artist's responsibility to the community increases with his talent. Don't you agree, Señor Goya, as first painter to the king?'

'What are you getting at?' Paco snapped. He had been bored, bored for months by the daily routine of paseos and pamphlets, by Javier's dull, disappointing personality, by Josefa hovering over him solicitously, catering to his every whim, hoping he would return to his studio. At least he found the Grand Inquisitor mildly diverting. He wondered how soon his rudeness would ruffle the fat man's urbanity.

Laughter, only slightly forced. 'I like a forthright man, Señor Goya. So many who come here are reluctant to speak their minds.'

'Who can blame them? They're terrified.'

More laughter, more forced. 'Their terror is not justified. We are no destroyers of men. We are savers of souls.'

'It is my soul you wish to save today?'

'I wish,' said the Grand Inquisitor not quite angrily, 'to discuss your work.'

'An artist always likes to discuss his work.'

'Shall we start with your so-called *Popular Diversions?*' asked the Grand Inquisitor.

'They're not so-called. I named them that.'

'Then the naming is a profanation, considering the subject matter. Do you find a procession of flagellants diverting?'

'It seemed to divert the onlookers, when I saw it in Extremadura.'

'And the Inquisition scene. Do you find a trial for heresy diverting?'

'People are invited. I was invited once. Someone here must consider it a diversion. Using the word loosely, of course.'

'I would have said a lesson.'

A servant brought lemon ice. Paco watched his portion melt into a little yellow puddle.

'You almost make the priests look evil.'

'Evil? Santa Maria, no! Industrious.'

'Some of them are sleeping.'

'Long hours doing God's work, Your Eminence. Sometimes I fall asleep over a canvas or a copper plate myself.'

'You make the penitents look tragic.'

'Aren't they?'

'Not if they repent.'

A servant brought a bowl of peaches. The Grand Inquisitor skinned one, cut it, speared half with the point of his knife and thrust it into his mouth.

'We are,' he said, 'willing to forgive you those so-called *Popular Diversions*. Do you know why?'

Paco said he did not know why.

Another peach was flayed and consumed. 'Because, whatever their moral shortcomings, they are art.' The Grand Inquisitor leaned forward across the table. 'I wish the same could be said for your etchings called the *Caprices*.' The eyes were no longer gentle. 'We own five sets, Señor Goya.'

'Paid for, I hope?'

'With five ounces of gold,' said the Grand Inquisitor, mopping his face.

'Then I'm in your debt. They didn't sell very well, those etchings. I've often wondered why. They drew quite a crowd at first – including a pair of Dominicans who were there every day.'

The Grand Inquisitor reached for his goblet and emptied it at a single gulp. 'I resent your attitude, Señor Goya.'

Paco felt the first thin edge of fear, and found it stimulating.

'Those etchings have no redeeming artistic merit whatever. None. I believe twenty-seven sets were sold, including the five we bought?'

Paco said the figure was correct.

'The Holy Office will assume the responsibility of purchasing and destroying the twenty-two outstanding sets, Señor Goya. Who owns the plates?'

'I do.'

'They must be destroyed. They are monstrous. There is a world of heresy and sin in those etchings.'

'There's Spain in those etchings.'

The Grand Inquisitor heaved himself ponderously to his feet and tinkled a little bell. A servant appeared with a portfolio of the *Caprices*. A fat hand gestured, the table was cleared, the portfolio placed on it.

The Grand Inquisitor opened the portfolio. 'Heresy and sin,' he said. 'Look at the eighth plate. That's rape. Or the twenty-third. That's the Inquisition again. Can you tell me why the caption says "See the result"?'

'The result of heresy, Your Eminence. See the way the victim's hands are clasped? He's clearly repenting.'

'Did you say victim?' asked the Grand Inquisitor.

'When a man is accused, he always thinks himself victimized. We all see the world through our own eyes, Your Eminence.'

The fat face was mopped again. The fat fingers turned the prints. 'Plate twenty-four. I'd like to hear your interpretation.'

'The victim – that is, the accused, Your Eminence – is riding on a donkey to the burning place.'

'We don't have those any longer. We don't burn people.'

'No, of course not. It's historical.'

'Your priests look gleeful. The crowd's a group of fiends.'

'The priests won their case. The crowd's enjoying the spectacle.'

'Your donkey looks saner than your priests.'

'It's interesting that Your Eminence should think so.'

'Plate forty!' shouted the Grand Inquisitor. 'Why is the doctor a donkey?'

'Because some doctors are jackasses. Doesn't Your Eminence agree?'

'We have determined that he symbolizes the government, and that the patient is Spain.'

'What an ingenious interpretation,' Paco said. 'Why didn't I think of that myself?'

'Plate fifty-five.' The Grand Inquisitor's hands were trembling as he turned the prints. 'Is that the queen you're ridiculing?'

'That gawky old crone, the queen? Of course not. The queen's an ample woman.'

'Plate sixty. A nude and monsters.'

'Exactly,' said Paco brightly. 'Because nudity is monstrous.'

'Plate sixty-eight. Another nude.'

'A witch, Your Eminence. Equally monstrous.'

'Plate seventy-five makes a mockery of the holy sacrament of marriage.' Sweat dripped from the double chins onto the mockery of the holy sacrament of marriage.

'I draw what I see, Your Eminence. Don't some people make a mockery of marriage?'

The fat face turned pale. A fat hand slammed the portfolio shut and mopped the gleaming tonsure.

'It has been decided,' said the Grand Inquisitor, 'that these uncompromisingly heretical etchings indicate heretical tendencies on the part of their designer. How many sets were printed?'

'Three hundred, Your Eminence. I seem to have miscalculated their appeal somewhat.'

'They found few buyers because they are an abomination. You will deliver the unsold copies along with the plates. They will be burned.'

'What's fifty-six? Paco thought again. Not old. Old is bowing before cant and hypocrisy. Old is admitting that a frightened public and fat priest know more about your art than you do. Old is painting and etching for them instead of for yourself. Old is surrendering.

And the alternative? The game he had played with the Grand Inquisitor, baiting him, making the conversation slip like quicksilver through his fat fingers – a game so like the game Cayetana played with the queen – was over. The thin edge of fear, which he had found so stimulating, suddenly opened like a chasm at his feet. The Grand Inquisitor was right, of course. The etchings stuck pins in everything. If he refused to surrender them, the alternative was a Little Act of Faith, years of exile in a provincial town or monastery, possibly even prison.

The Grand Inquisitor was seated again, his fat backsides filling the chair, his face as smug as the faces of the fat black priests in the dimlit church.

'We will give you a week to deliver them,' he said.

Paco remained standing. He shook his head.

The gentle eyes looked at him. 'In deference to your reputation and your patrons,' the fat man said, 'I arranged this luncheon. You could have been brought here under – less pleasant circumstances. I had hoped to avoid that. I still do. Will you reconsider?'

'No, Your Eminence.'

'It takes not only humility but courage to admit a mistake, Señor Goya. God knows you're no humble man, but it never occurred to me you lacked courage.'

'If you want the plates, send a bailiff.'

The fat man shut his eyes. 'You will be given one week to change your mind,' he said softly. 'Those etchings are the product of your heresy. Delivering them will be your penance. Mild under the circumstances, don't you agree?'

'Send a bailiff,' Paco said.

The Grand Inquisitor tinkled his bell, and a green-liveried

427

footman appeared.

'Show Señor Goya out.'

Cayetana shrugged back into her blouse, aware of Dr Peral's eyes on her. She had not bothered to turn her back while fastening the bandeau that bound her breasts. Peral, after all, was a doctor, and probably beyond the age when such things mattered. But he did have an odd look in his eyes. Lecherous? She couldn't believe that, although the thought amused her.

'Well,' she laughed, 'will I live?'

'You're too thin, Doña Cayetana.'

'It's the heat. I don't have much of an appetite, I'm afraid.'

'Still, you ought to put on some weight.'

'I didn't know you liked your women fat, doctor.'

Peral's perpetually sneering lips managed a smile. 'Always the coquette, aren't you?' He rummaged in his case and brought out some packets of powder. 'Not eating enough and would I be right in assuming not sleeping enought?'

'No, I – I'm afraid to sleep,' Cayetana said, the bantering tone gone.

'Afraid?'

'I have nightmares. A grown woman. Silly, isn't it?'

'Who knows why we dream what we dream?' Peral said. 'But it's not silly if you can't sleep. It's a serious matter, my dear.' He placed the powders on the night table near Cayetana's canopied bed. 'These should help.'

'I hate taking medicine.'

'It's hardly medicine. Just something to make you sleep more soundly.'

'Without those nightmares?'

'Without those nightmares.'

'Good. I'd like that.'

'One powder every night then, in a little water.'

Every Tuesday night, the Lovers of Ugliness would drift one by one into Café Apiñani and have a cup of wine with Juanito before going down to the cellar room.

It amused the former matador that not all bullfighters like himself but the leading intellectuals of Madrid used his café for their *tertulia*. It amused him that the snatches of conversation he heard while bringing pitchers of wine downstairs were seditious. Not that he understood why the Lovers of Ugliness should be so appalled by the court and the government. To be governed was an unfortunate necessity, like paying taxes or growing old. Who sat on the throne hardly mattered to Juanito. Someone had always sat there; someone would always sit there, puffed up with his own importance and ruling Spain for his own benefit. What difference did it make if King Carlos was a do-nothing king who let the queen decide that – what was the word? – a *rapprochement* with France had to be sought? Or that Crown Prince Fernando wanted to depose his parents and rule in their stead – Crown Prince Fernando, who hated France even more than he hated his mother or the Prince of the Peace? Life in Madrid would go on, with every Spaniard thinking himself the center of the universe (after God, of course), whatever happened in the royal palace. Life in Madrid would certainly go on, whatever the Lovers of Ugliness decided down there in the cellar room. But their talk did amuse Juanito all the same.

His amusement turned to awe those rare Tuesdays, like tonight, when the Duchess of Osuna joined the Lovers of Ugliness. She came, usually alone, a long-faced, long-boned woman, her strength made all the more apparent by the profusion of ribbons and frills she always wore. She usually shared a cup of wine with Juanito before going downstairs, striding like a man, with a man's confidence in his ability rather than a woman's confidence in her appearance, and Juanito never understood how she still managed to convey an aura of femininity. He could almost imagine her fighting the bulls.

Tonight the Osuna hadn't even paused for the customary cup of wine. 'Is Goya here yet?' she had asked Juanito. Paco had already arrived, and the Osuna hurried for the stairs.

Juanito waited five minutes, filled a pitcher of wine from one of the great barrels behind the bar, and went down after her. Half a dozen of the Lovers of Ugliness sat around the long plank table, their faces glum. The Osuna was saying:

'A bailiff from the Holy Office came to the Alameda and demanded to buy my four sets of the *Caprices*.' She looked, Juanito observed as he poured the wine, very angry.

'Did you sell them?' Paco asked.

A hard smile. 'The Holy Office doesn't tell me what to do. But does it mean what I think it does?'

The members of the Lovers of Ugliness all began to talk at once. The gist of it was that all had been visited by a green-uniformed Inquisition bailiff on the same errand. None of them had sold their sets of the *Caprices*.

'It means what you think it means,' Paco said.

Juanito saw shocked expressions all around the table. Paco

himself looked like a bullfighter who had just caught a glimpse of the *manso* monster he had drawn in the day's lot.

'They took you before the qualifiers?' demanded Cabarrús the banker.

'Not yet. Just lunch with the Grand Inquisitor. It wasn't even a very good lunch,' Paco said. He passed a case of cigars around. The Osuna took snuff instead. She sneezed, not daintily. 'They've summoned me to appear before the qualifiers on Friday.'

'Good God,' cried Cean Bermúdez.

By then Juanito had filled all the wine cups. He climbed the stairs slowly with his pitcher of wine. Not that it was empty. But on a hot night like this the Lovers of Ugliness would be thirsty. He'd have an excuse to return soon.

Serving drinks and *tapas* at the bar upstairs, he wondered what Paco had done to be called before the Inquisition. Paco, he knew, was an avid reader of the illegal pamphlets circulating in Madrid. Perhaps he had been caught at it. These days, Juanito almost wished he could read. Not that he cared about politics, but the pamphlets were full of scandal too. Juanito wondered if Paco would escape the wrath of the Holy Office. Hardly anyone ever did.

Gaspar and Emeterio came in, shouldering their way to the bar. Since Pepe Hillo's death, they served as foremen of the staff of bullring lackeys in the plaza de toros outside the Alcalá Gate. Not much to do, but the pay was good. Tuertillo had taken care of his brothers the way Paco had taken care of Juanito. Juanito enjoyed his café as much as he had enjoyed fighting bulls in the good days. Well, almost as much. He wished the could do something for Paco. He told his brothers what he had heard downstairs.

'Then Paco's in for it,' Gaspar said, shaking his head.

'Once you get an Inquisition summons,' Emeterio said, 'it's the big horn. Right here.' He touched his groin.

'I can't let this happen to him,' Juanito said.

'You?' asked Gaspar. 'You'd better hope it's not that *tertulia* downstairs causing the trouble.'

'You could be implicated,' Emeterio said.

Since Hillo's fatal goring, Juanito's look-alike brothers had become cautious men.

'Take care of the bar,' Juanito told them. Of the Apiñanis, he alone was still slender, though his hair was gray and his skin creased and leathery. He filled the pitcher of wine to the top again and went downstairs.

'It's a question of integrity or freedom,' Cean Bermúdez was saying. 'You can't have both.'

'An artist's integrity *is* his freedom,' the poet Leandro Moratín pointed out.

The Duchess of Osuna gave him a withering glance. 'That's easy to say – when your work hasn't been condemned by the Santo.'

'Hasn't it?' Moratín asked. 'If Paco won't surrender the plates, I'm as guilty as he is. I wrote the captions, after all.' He looked at Paco through the blue strands of cigar smoke hanging in the still air of the cellar room. 'I ought to face the qualifiers with you,' he said.

'That would help enormously,' the Osuna told him. 'Two Little Acts of Faith instead of one. A heroic gesture's the last thing we need now.'

Juanito filled the empty wine cups slowly. 'What bothers me,' the Osuna said, 'is the *Popular Diversions.*'

'They didn't bother the Grand Inquisitor,' Paco said.

'That's what I mean. They should have. They've been hanging in the Royal Academy for years. Why were they ignored? Why did they call you in for the *Caprices*? How many sets were sold? Less than two dozen, wasn't it? You didn't exactly inundate Madrid with them.'

'I will try,' said Paco gravely, 'to select material for my next etchings more in keeping with popular taste.'

'That's not funny.' The cold gray Osuna eyes held his. 'You're in trouble. What about the *Diversions*? Why not them?' she demanded. 'Just the Inquisition scene alone should have been enough to earn your Little Act of Faith.'

'Art,' shrugged Paco. 'The Grand Inquisitor was willing to overlook it in the name of art.'

'You mean he liked the *Diversions*?' the Osuna asked, amazed.

'He said they had artistic merit.'

'So do half the books on the Index,' the Osuna scoffed. 'That's not the answer.'

'There's a difference,' said Cean Bermúdez. 'The *Diversions* hang in a musty hall in the Academy, but the *Caprices* circulate. They're like seditious pamphlets, those etchings – even if only twenty-two sets were sold. They pass from hand to hand.'

Juanito stood with his empty pitcher. The Osuna glanced at him and raised an eyebrow. He went upstairs.

'Friday,' he told his brothers. 'He's going before the qualifiers on Friday. It's those etchings.' Juanito paused. 'We could hide him,' he said finally. 'Take him to Navarra. There's a place I know in the mountains above Pamplona – '

Gaspar and Emeterio exchanged cautious glances.

'The Inquisition's everywhere,' Gaspar said.

'They'll drag you before the qualifiers yourself,' Emeterio predicted.

An hour passed. Except for the *tertulia* downstairs, the last customers had left Café Apiñani. Juanito stood behind the slate-topped bar, brooding. Something he'd heard downstairs was bothering him. He couldn't put his finger on it, but it was there. A way out for Paco, who had stubbornly taken his stand like a bull in a *querencia,* who would not destroy those etchings, if that was what the Santo wanted him to. And the Lovers of Ugliness? Except for the Osuna, Juanito decided, they weren't very practical. They were full of clever talk, but they wouldn't be able to help Juanito's friend at all. Like peones, he thought, fluttering their capes uselessly at the bull in his *querencia* because the bull wasn't going to come out, not unless you went in after him, and then maybe, with luck. . . .

What was it he had heard? An answer, a solution, and they had passed right over it. Anxious, cape-fluttering peones when what you needed was the good wrist of a matador capable of dominating the bull. Dominating the situation, turning it around somehow so that the Inquisition was powerless to act. But how? Juanito went back over the conversation he had heard downstairs. He tried to recall every word, the way he had often tried to recall every movement of a bull while his peones flapped their capes and ran him so that afterwards he, Juanito, would be able to construct the perfect faena.

'I have a feeling they were almost onto something,' he told his brothers. 'I know they were. A way out.'

'Only they didn't see it?' Gaspar asked.

'And our brother who can't even write his name did?' Emeterio asked.

'Juanito,' Gaspar warned him, 'ever since that *tertulia* started meeting downstairs, you've been getting some strange ideas.'

'Have a cup of wine,' advised Emeterio. 'Calms the nerves.'

Juanito leaned an elbow on the bar and his chin on his hand and began to brood again.

'Maybe he wants to ask his friend the Grand Inquisitor to grant Paco a pardon,' said Gaspar.

'Or his friend the king,' suggested Emeterio.

'Funny,' growled Juanito. 'Very funny.' He almost hated

his brothers then. A pair of fat, frightened, middle-aged ex-bullfighters who. . . .

He raised his head. He looked at Gaspar and Emeterio. 'The king,' he said suddenly. He could feel the old, remembered wolf's grin large on his face.

'Take care of the bar,' he said, and headed for the stairs. He was still grinning. He called back over his shoulder: 'Drinks on the house for everyone?'

'Generous, isn't he?' Gaspar said.

'We pulled down the shutters half an hour ago,' Emeterio said.

Juanito rushed downstairs. Cigar smoke hung more heavily in the air. Faces looked glummer. Juanito came into the room whistling.

'There's no question,' the Duchess of Osuna was saying, 'that the etchings are heretical, and seditious.' She sighed, a very feminine sigh. 'Goya,' she asked, 'could you at least try to be contrite with the qualifiers?'

Paco cocked his head to one side in that listening gesture, pretending not to understand.

'It could cut your sentence in half,' the Osuna told him. 'I'd say the best we can hope for is three years in a monastery.'

'Santa Maria,' said Paco. 'And the worst?'

'Six in a dungeon,' the Osuna said flatly, and looked up to see Juanito hovering over her shoulder grinning.

'You find this amusing, Apiñani?' she snapped.

'I was just thinking, Your Grace,' Juanito said. 'What are those paintings of Paco's called again?'

'What paintings, Apiñani?' In a peevish voice.

'The ones hanging in the Academy.'

'You mean the *Popular Diversions?*'

Juanito nodded. 'Who owns the Academy?' he asked.

The Osuna looked up at him impatiently. 'Why don't you bring us some more wine, Apiñani? No, make it cognac. We can use it.'

'Who owns it, Your Grace?'

'Would you kindly stop grinning like that? Nobody owns the Academy. The state owns it.'

'Then it belongs to the king, Your Grace?'

'As it's the Royal Academy,' Cean Bermúdez offered, 'technically it's the property of the king.'

'And some of those paintings were as bad as the etchings?'

'From the Santo's viewpoint, certainly,' the Osuna said. She gave Juanito a peculiar look. She would grasp it before the others did, he told himself.

'And they left Paco alone then? The Inquisition?'

'That's a different matter, my good fellow,' Cean Bermúdez explained condescendingly. 'The Holy Office doesn't give a damn – forgive me, Your Grace – about a few paintings hanging in a dark hall at the Academy.'

'That's true,' said Juanito, feeling the grin huge on his face, 'and I'm only a tavern-keeper, but – '

'Then bring the cognac,' Cean Bermúdez cut him off.

'No, let him talk,' the Osuna said. 'I want to hear what he has to say.'

What Juanito had to say could be said very quickly. The Lovers of Ugliness had belabored the problem for hours. Juanito was finished in less than a minute.

First Sebastián Martínez smiled, and then Moratín Cabarrús the banker chuckled. His eyes popping, Cean Bermúdez began to laugh.

Paco sprang to his feet. He wanted to embrace his old friend. With a few words Juanito had barred the road to exile, opened the dungeon door.

'Goya,' said the Osuna, pushing him aside not gently, 'you will kindly wait your turn.' Her smile matched Juanito's wolf's grin. 'Apiñani,' she cried, taking him in a great hug, 'you're a fornicating genius.'

Sometimes, sitting up in bed, Cayetana would send Brother Basil or Tadea to fetch the prints of Goya's etchings. She would study those of herself – the two-headed coquette in Sanlúcar or the birdlike creature with her face – and smile. With what malicious glee he must have used his needle, etching her out of his life one line at a time. She couldn't blame him. She deserved it.

But still, he had come back to her. No, she thought. She'd gone back to him. For a time.

Would it have lasted, if Hillo hadn't died like that, looking up at her before the bull charged? She no longer knew. She wondered if he would ever forgive her, this second time. Could she just walk into his studio again, as if nothing had happened?

Walk into his studio. She sighed. She hadn't left her bed in days. It was a summer fever, Dr Peral said. And the pain? The pain, deep inside her, like a knife twisting? The pain would go away, Peral assured her.

She slept all night and most of the day. She awoke exhausted. She had no appetite. She had lost more weight. The fever was sapping her strength. Peral plied her with medicines, but they didn't seem to help. Peral visited every day now. Sometimes the pain made her scream.

This morning had been worst of all. She had wanted to comb her hair, make up her face. She asked Tadea to bring a mirror.

'I'll comb your hair for you,' Tadea said quickly.

'No. Bring a mirror.'

Reluctantly, Tadea brought it. For a shocking moment Cayetana looked at her face in the glass. Gaunt, so frighteningly gaunt. The skin deathly pale, drawn tight over the sharp points of the cheekbones, the big dark eyes deep-sunk, the lips parched and cracked.

'Tadea, my God, Tadea – what's happening to me?'

Peral would come in the afternoon.

In the courtyard of the Little Royal House of the Workman in Aranjuez, the stableboy struggled mightily not to win. He had King Carlos in a good hold and it would have been an easy matter to dump him on his royal backsides, but the stableboy persevered. With considerable effort, he allowed Carlos to get a leg behind his leg and throw him. He hit the cobblestones lightly and let out an enormous groan. He hoped he looked thoroughly beaten. The king, crouching, his arms wide, stood over him, glaring and then smiling.

'A noble effort, my boy,' chortled Carlos, who was sweating in the heat of the late afternoon. He helped the stableboy to his feet and gave him a gold doubloon.

A smattering of applause from the twenty or so noble spectators, and the stableboy retreated with his gold coin.

Carlos flexed his muscles. 'A man has to keep in shape,' he said modestly in his booming voice. 'Even a king, ha-ha-ha. Shall we have some tea?' Tea was served under one of the loggias of the courtyard.

Tucked away among the ornate Chinese plantings of the Queen Street Gardens in Aranjuez was the Little Royal House of the Workman. Little only in contrast to the summer palace itself and built of the same dun and ochre stone, with courtyard, loggias, and a few dozen rooms, it was King Carlos' favorite retreat. He could walk in comparative privacy in the gardens and pretend to lead the bucolic life. He could forget the cares of state – Don Carlos loved best of all to forget the cares of state – and imagine he was no more than a provincial nobleman with a small holding in the countryside. That the countryside had been architected out of the barren Castilian plain, that its rows of trees and boxwood hedges and ornamental glades and hidden fountains were tended by a flock of thirty gardeners, did not spoil the illusion for Carlos. The Little Royal House was still no palace, and he thought it suited his modest and outgoing nature.

His mood, during the serving of tea, was expansive. The hunt had stimulated his blood, the wrestling match had satisfied his ego, and there was enough of a breeze and enough shade in the loggia to make the afternoon comfortable. Carlos almost wished he could live the rest of his days there in the Little House like a retired grandee of the second rank. He could even, for a while, forget that skulking, plotting, ugly son of his.

He finished his first cup of tea and had another. He related an old joke as if he had just thought of it. His friends – simple people, really, despite their ancient titles – laughed appreciatively. Don Carlos gobbled pastry, licking the crumbs from his lips. He was feeling better and better. He wished the summer would never end. He could forget that gloomy city Madrid, in the summer. Perhaps, in the evening, he would play the violin for his guests.

A traveling coach drawn by six fine white horses came clattering in between the gates and over the cobblestones of the courtyard. Gold and black, with the escutcheon of the Dukes of Osuna. The flabby, aging duke himself? Carlos wondered. Or possibly the duchess? They were rarely together. He hoped it was the duchess. Even if Maria Luisa didn't, or perhaps because Maria Luisa didn't, he enjoyed her wit.

Behind the coach, drawn by a pair of mules, came a small van. The coach braked to a stop, and Carlos' own footmen rushed out to help its passengers alight. The duchess – and Goya. An unlikely pair, thought Don Carlos, the tall, lean Osuna in her frills and ribbons and the stock first painter in a fawn-colored traveling suit and a high-crowned straw hat. Though years ago, Carlos remembered, there had been rumors of a liaison.

And the third member of the party? Slender, wearing a straw hat almost as high-crowned as Goya's, pop-eyed – it was Cean Bermúdez the art critic.

Carlos shook his head with a laugh as Cean Bermúdez prepared to kiss the royal right hand. 'We're informal here in the Little House,' he said. 'Pretend I'm not the king, ha-ha-ha.

436

Pity you missed the wrestling match.'

'Yes, it is a pity,' said the Osuna with a twinkle in her hard blue eyes.

Don Carlos looked past them. The small van piqued his curiosity. A gift? Still seated on the box was a familiar figure. It took a while for Carlos to recognize the former bullfighter Juanito Apiñani. 'You, Apiñani! Join us, hombre, have a cup of tea.'

Juanito climbed down from the van. The king spent half an hour discussing bullfighting with him. Carlos did most of the talking. Every now and then he would cast a glance at the van parked behind the traveling coach in the middle of the courtyard.

Finally he asked: 'What do you have in there, a bull? Ha-ha-ha.'

'Just a few old copper plates, sire,' Paco said.

'Old what? Copper plates?'

'And a few thousand prints taken from them, Don Carlos,' the Duchess of Osuna said. 'Our Goya is being very modest.'

The royal hand clapped the painter's shoulder. 'I like a modest man. They're etchings then?'

Cean Bermúdez cleared his throat. 'They're etchings,' he said, his eyes popping slightly. 'Which is like saying Michelangelo's frescoes in the Sistine Chapel are a ceiling.'

Don Carlos nodded and smiled vapidly. He never could understand intellectuals. They always talked around things.

Cean Bermúdez went on talking around things. Dürer, he said. Rembrandt. And now Goya.

'Has he done something special?' the king asked.

'He's always doing something special, Don Carlos,' the Osuna said.

'Eighty plates,' said Cean Bermúdez, 'and five or six thousand impressions can be taken from each one. They're priced at an ounce of gold the set.'

Don Carlos smiled and jabbed a finger at Paco's chest. 'Goya, you'll be a rich man.'

Paco shook his head. 'No, sire, at least not from these etchings.'

'The etchings,' said Cean Bermúdez smoothly, 'as often happens with great works of art, are a little ahead of their times. They haven't sold very well, though in future years I have no doubt that they will.'

'Which gives us a problem, sire,' said the Osuna. 'You see,

recently there's been interest in these etchings among foreigners, particularly Frenchmen. Quite a few sets have been resold to members of the French diplomatic corps.'

Don Carlos beamed. 'Spread the word. I say spread the word then. Let the French see what a genius our Goya is.'

Again Paco shook his head. 'I'm in my fifties, sire. I hate to think that after my death – '

'You're young, you're still young, Goya,' protested the king.

' – most if not all the sets might fall into French hands.'

'Spain,' said Cean Bermúdez, 'would lose a great treasure, and I'm not merely referring to the ounce of gold per set.'

The ounce of gold per set, though, impressed Carlos. What had they said, six thousand impressions? That was a lot of money.

'We must keep these wonderful etchings in Spain,' said Cean Bermúdez. 'Their artistic value is incalculable.'

'Yes, of course. I can see that.'

'Besides, sire,' Paco said, 'there's a matter of conscience. You see, I etched these plates while on salary as painter to the king.'

'Goya feels,' said the Osuna, 'that they really ought to be regarded as royal property. He wants to present the plates and prints as a gift to the royal printing works.'

Don Carlos was no reader of books, but he did know that the royal printing works lost money every year. Those damnable illegal pamphlets, he thought, that's what everybody's reading these days.

'Both to guarantee Spanish ownership of a great work of art,' said the Osuna, 'and to help the royal printing works turn a profit. Our Goya's being very generous.'

A second clap on the shoulder from the royal hand. 'What sort of prints are they, Goya?'

'Juanito,' Cean Bermúdez said, 'would you bring a set?'

Juanito went to the van and returned with a portfolio. A place was made for it on the tea table, and Cean Bermúdez turned the plates swiftly as he spoke of symbolism and fantasy, drypoint and aquatint, illusion and reality. The king saw monsters and the commission of monstrous acts.

'Some of them, why, some of them – ' he began.

'Are repelling, sire?' Cean Bermúdez said quickly. 'Because they get to the truth of what the French Enlightenment has done to Spain? Because they indicate how a political perversion can contaminate any country it touches? Your Majesty

438

is most perceptive. In that regard, they're meant to be repelling. Which may be one reason why the French are so determined to get their hands on them.'

'No!'

'I'm very much afraid so, sire,' said Cean Bermúdez. 'If you'll look at this plate. . . . ' And he was off again, talking of light and shade, sins and sinners, aesthetics and ethics. Dürer and Rembrandt again, and an Englishman named Hogarth, all the while turning the plates very swiftly.

'You think,' Don Carlos asked, 'the printing works will be able to sell a few sets?'

'Ten years from now, those plates will be pressed flat,' said Cean Bermúdez. 'Six thousand impressions, sire. I can almost guarantee it.'

Don Carlos wouldn't admit that he hardly understood Cean Bermúdez's vocabulary, let alone the meaning of the plates. But if only half the six thousand sets were sold, they'd keep the works going for years without the need of a subsidy from the royal treasury.

'They're a gift?' he asked.

'For all practical purposes, sire. But since they were not done expressly for the royal works,' Cean Bermúdez said smoothly, 'conceivably there could be a problem regarding their ownership some time in the future. We had a document drawn up to make the transaction binding and legal.'

The document was placed on top of the now-shut portfolio. It was, Carlos observed with pleasure, as legal documents so often weren't, mercifully short. It merely said that King Carlos IV agreed to purchase – the king paused at the word purchase, until he saw that the price was a single gold doubloon, the amount he had given the stableboy for a wrestling match – that King Carlos agreed to purchase from the first painter his set of etchings called the *Caprices,* all plates and prints to be used by His Majesty and the royal printing works as they saw fit.

'You sign here, Goya,' said the Osuna. 'And you, sire, sign here.'

A most gratifying gesture on Goya's part, thought the king. Keep them out of foreign hands, French hands, and an ounce of gold per set. . . .

He sent for a pen and blotting powder.

Paco signed first, and the king after him. What with the hunt, the wrestling, the good talk about bullfights with the famous Apiñani, and now the gift of the etchings, it was a most pleasant day, Don Carlos told himself.

He invited the company inside to hear him play the violin. Pity Goya couldn't hear, he thought. Such a generous fellow.

Dr Peral climbed into his landau with a thoughtful expression on his face. The coach, a new convertible model Peral had imported from France, was conservatively black, but rakish in appearance with its leather hood folded back now. He told his driver to take him to the *palacete* of the Moncloa. The driver did not have to be told. Every day at that hour of the afternoon Peral visited the stricken Duchess of Alba.

Peral was worried. He knew nothing whatever about the poison he had been administering in minute doses to the duchess. In his previous work for the Inquisition and the Prince of the Peace he had usually resorted to arsenic or a drug a colleague in New Spain had sent him. Arsenic was comparatively simple. His skilled hand could control the dosage and, after a while, the victim even seemed to build up some resistance. The drug from Peru had given some trouble at first, but now he felt reasonably confident administering it. He preferred it to arsenic, and the Holy Office preferred the results. It brought pain; it paralyzed the nervous system gradually and eventually paralyzed the victim's will as no mere physical torture ever could. Henceforth, Peral promised himself, he would only use the drug from Peru.

He wished he had used it on the Duchess of Alba.

The new drug had been sent by a colleague in Italy. It came from India, the Italian colleague had written, and that had disappointed Peral. He had thought he'd be getting one of the ancient Borgia poisons, and the idea had intrigued him. India? He knew nothing about India.

And nothing about the Indian drug he had prescribed for the trusting Cayetana de Alba, except that he had begun very much to fear its effects were irreversible. Lately he had administered nothing but a placebo, but that had not arrested the rapid deterioration of the duchess. She grew weaker every day. She seemed to age a year between his daily visits. Her blood pressure was feeble, her nervous responses slower, her ability to take nourishment almost nil. She could hardly sit up now without help, and the pain was with her always.

Peral decided he had been a fool to use the unknown drug. Letting a situation escape his control disturbed his orderly mind. Not that the queen worried him. Their meeting had been brief and to the point.

'I want to employ you as the Santo and Godoy have,' Maria Luisa had said.

He had looked into her crafty eyes, paused a moment and then denied nothing. She knew.

'Who?' he asked, and she told him. Peral had felt the excitement, the almost sexual excitement, at once. He had never been called on to poison a woman before.

'How far do you want me to go?' he asked the queen.

'I want the little bitch to suffer as much as you can make her suffer.'

'There are always risks, Your Majesty,' Peral had said. He wondered, now, why he had said that. Usually the risks had been minimal. Had he decided, even then, to use the unknown drug from India?

'What kind of risks, Peral?'

'A large enough dose of poison would be fatal to anyone,' Peral had explained. 'Smaller doses, controlled doses, are somewhat less predictable. An amount sufficient to make one man gravely ill might only slightly indispose another.'

'I want her more than slightly indisposed.'

'Yes, I understand that. But – '

'I have faith in you, Peral.'

'What if she were to die?' Again an unexpected question, almost as if his lips had formed the words of their own accord.

'I'd wear black,' said the queen. 'Madrid itself would mourn for a time. She's very popular.' A long pause. 'Too popular.'

No, in the event that the worst happened, he had nothing to fear from the queen.

But there was still an untidiness about the situation. Peral was surprised how rapidly the mysterious Indian poison had worked. Hardly a week. Like a sudden illness striking fatally in the prime of life. No more Asian mysteries, he promised himself. Stay with what you know, if they need your services again. He hoped they would need his services again.

But meanwhile there was the Alba to worry about. If he had been employed in his capacity as a healer instead of a poisoner, would he have considered the possibility of dispatching her mercifully? Giving the gift of death to one who had no hope and was suffering too much?

He had brought the gift with him, that massive dose of an opiate which he had used with mercy on other occasions. It would kill her in minutes, painlessly. She would simply drift off into sleep.

As his convertible landau drove along the tree-lined lane

that led to the Moncloa, Peral felt his excitement growing.

Tadea was waiting in the carriage park for him. The marquesa was almost crying. 'She's worse, doctor.'

He knew that the routine of paseos and pamphlets, of Javier's disappointing personality, of Josefa's solicitude, had ended. He could thank the heresy-hunting Grand Inquisitor for that, and his old friend Juanito who had surprised the Lovers of Ugliness with his shrewdness, and the Duchess of Osuna and Cean Bermúdez, who had overwhelmed the king with their glib talk. He felt gloriously young and alive when he returned to Madrid. He wanted to work again, really work. A series of bullfight etchings. An outre landscape he had once dreamed of, a fantastic city perched on a rock as if carved from the stone itself. A portrait of Josefa. Santa Maria, he thought, I've never even tried to paint her. Just a few sketches over the years. She's almost the only woman left in Madrid I haven't painted.

He wished, though, that she had been more enthusiastic when he related the events of the past few days. She had grown pale at the beginning and then crossed herself piously. She had listened in silence, absolute silence until he had finished, and then she said: 'You're lucky.'

'That's all? Lucky? If you could have seen fat King Carlos earnestly trying to make sense out of the *Caprices* – '

'I wish you wouldn't call him that.'

The humor of the situation escaped her entirely.

He felt like crowing or pounding his chest or laughing until his sides split. He felt ten feet tall and twenty years old. He left the house, walking for a while in the heat of the afternoon, jauntily, his stick hitting the pavement with every fourth stride, his tall-crowned straw hat worn at a rakish angle, a cigar in his mouth, a smile on his face for every passerby. Most of them recognized him. He was Goya, first painter to the king. He was Goya, first painter to the world.

Twenty minutes after he set out, he began to walk faster. He knew, then, where he was going.

She would understand. She always courted disaster herself and escape it, living life on the peaks and ridges instead of in the valley where everyone else merely existed. She would always understand the boy who once had stood on the dome of St Peter's in Rome, roaring his laughter. She was very much like him. He told himself that it was foolish to have waited so long. Forgive her? She was arrogantly, elegantly, gloriously alive. She was flesh and blood and beauty in a world of shadows. Forgive her what? Her recklessness? Her unpredictability? She was a caprice, etched with a wonderful sharpness that made every other woman he had ever known seem flat and drab. You've been a fool long enough. Go to her.

He reached the river road. Ahead he could see the gate-posts of the Moncloa.

She felt sleep pulling her down. Usually she welcomed it. The slow drifting off, the surging random memories – Goya and that ridiculous two-wheeled coach of his, Goya playing bull-fighter with her in the Plaza Mayor, Goya in the sanctuary forgetting his deafness in her arms, always Goya she thought dreamily, the only man she had ever really loved, and opened her eyes and saw Dr Peral's hovering over her. Always Goya? No, that wasn't it. What had she written in the sand with the toe of her shoe? Only Goya. Yes, she thought. I wonder, if I sent for him would he come?

Sleep enveloped her suffocatingly. She tried to fight it off. She tried to scream. It was different. A different kind of sleep. Something terrifying like the dream, that recurrent dream, but she wasn't dreaming now, it was happening, happening as she had always dreamed it would, she was falling and falling and becoming smaller and smaller and wished oh God she wished she could see him one more time Goya that leonine head and those hooded eyes with a pride in them the equal of her own but she was falling and becoming smaller still and she tried to cry out his name Goya and a hand grasped hers Dr Peral's cold hand Goya I will never hurt you again I was wrong we don't have to hurt each other that first time you kissed me I was afraid you would own me but now I'm afraid you won't falling and falling and smaller and smaller until finally she wasn't there.

Paco immediately recognized Dr Peral's convertible landau in the carriage park. As his own birlocho once had been, it was the talk of Madrid.

He felt a sudden foreboding. He began to run. He thought he saw Tadea's face in an upstairs window, but it disappeared. He reached the door and the door opened and Peral came out, walking slowly, a grave expression almost hiding the sneer on his lips. The two men looked at each other.

Paco's heart was pounding. He didn't want to ask the question.

'Is the duchess ill?'

Peral removed his hat and shook his head and said something slowly.

'What?' Words. He hadn't understood them. He did not want to understand them. He cocked his head in that listening gesture.

'I'm terribly sorry,' Peral said. 'The duchess died half an hour ago.'

BOOK SIX

BOOK SIX

THAT SHE WILL NEVER DANCE AGAIN. That those dark and lovely eyes will never see another sunrise or a summer storm or the changing beauty of the sanctuary, her sanctuary, where the wild sea birds call I'm free I'm free I'm free. That the whimsy and willfulness of her are no more. That that certain arrogant elegance is gone. That she *isn't*.

No, the old man tells himself in Paris in 1824, you must not cry. But his eyes are stinging. His vision blurs. He has shed no tears, not once, in all that time.

No tears? There was a night, at Café Apiñani. . . .

A party of late diners comes boisterously into the restaurant. They are well-dressed and young, and the sleepy waiters stir themselves. Tables are brought together, velvet-collared topcoats and tall beaver hats taken from the men, embroidered cloaks and frogged redingotes from the women. There is banter and laughter, the young faces looking inane to Don Paco as he broods over his coffee.

But he envies them their youth. Life is a new book to them, its pages still uncut by these men with their mustaches and trimmed beards, who will stay up all night for a late supper at the most fashionable restaurant in Paris. Except for side whiskers, his own face is clean-shaven. He does not belong in Paris in 1824. He does not belong anywhere. He is a relic, whose life ended on a hot July day twenty-two years ago.

The party of late diners is seated between him and the Prince of the Peace. The young Frenchmen are all Gallic gestures and flashing teeth. That France is a defeated country means nothing to them. He is glad he cannot hear their ridiculous

447

chatter, or the popping of champagne corks.

He longs suddenly for the arid uplands of Aragon, for the bustling streets of Madrid. He longs for his youth, for that book with its smell of fresh printer's ink, with its uncut pages.

He remembers the rumors after Cayetana's death – the song, the gown, the fire. Has she been murdered? Maria Luisa puts Godoy in charge of the investigation. Nothing comes of it. She died a natural death. A sudden summer fever. That eminent physician Dr Peral was there at the end.

And Don Paco lives a death of five years, days that drag interminably, a void, an emptiness, nada y nada y nada. It is time's final trick. There is never enough time, unless you squander the months and years doing nothing. And then there is too much.

He buys a big house, with an interior patio and fountains where Javier and his bride can join them. But the young Señora de Goya cannot endure her father-in-law's brooding or his unpredictable temper. The arrangement lasts a few weeks; the new house is deeded to Javier.

Don Paco paints occasional portraits. Not very inspired work. He charges extra for full length, for props, even for hands. And pity the sitter who does not remain still as a statue. Goya rages, he throws his palette. Once a critic writes that the touch of the master is gone. Meeting him on the street, Don Paco removes his own bolívar hat and crushes it down over the offending critic's ears. 'Señor Critic, learn to respect a head strong enough to wear this hat.'

Still a figura, a legend in his own lifetime. That much is habit, that much remains.

But too much of him has died with Cayetana. Nothing stirs him from his lethargy for five years.

How can he know, then, that his greatest work still lies ahead of him?

For a while he reads his pamphlets more assiduously than ever. Fernando, that skulking crown prince, comes of age. He plots to depose his father, to kill his mother and Godoy, while the Prince of the Peace dreams of a regency after fat King Carlos' death. They squabble like a family of fishmongers. They conspire like inept Borgias.

And across the Pyrenees, Napoleon Bonaparte watches. He covets Spain, his exposed flank beyond the mountains, where the waters of the Atlantic and the Mediterranean meet. He sends his brother-in-law Murat with an army, at Godoy's invitation. The Prince of the Peace still dreams of a throne in Portugal as his reward.

Don Paco paints him, puffy-faced, double-chinned, fat-thighed, in yet a new generalissimo's uniform, seated in an armchair on a stylized battlefield, bedecked with medals and wearing a look of complacent depravity on his face. So sure of his place in history is Godoy that the portrait pleases him.

Bonaparte settles the dispute between fat King Carlos and skulking Prince Fernando by sending his own brother Joseph to rule as king in Madrid.

The Lovers of Ugliness, weary of corruption in the royal palace, welcomes this romantic, incompetent scion of the Enlightenment. They speak out. They write. But Napoleon, crowning himself emperor in Notre Dame while the pope stands humbly by, overreaches himself, making war on England, on Prussia and Russia, on Spain, all at the same time. The British will sink his fleet at Trafalgar. His Grand' Armée will be crushed at Vitoria and Moscow and Waterloo.

How ironic, the old man thinks, that this small, arrogant, unhappily-married, snuff-taking Corsican with his dreams of empire brought me back to life.

He needs something to goad him – anger, perhaps. That was Cean Bermúdez, so long ago.

The mountains above Zaragoza. The guerrilla leader who learned in France how to fight the French. 'We're as bad as they are,' Paco tells him.

Hooded eyes look into hooded eyes. 'That's not enough, Don Paco. We have to be worse. The victims have to become executioners. You'll see.'

In Madrid at first he courts death. And because his courtship is too strenuous, death, like a too ardently pursued woman, refuses him.

Grim old man stalking about the battlefields with his sketch pad.

That too is part of the legend.

Except for Juanito, his friends are gone. The Lovers of Ugliness, their constitution thrown in their faces by King Fernando, exiled to France. The other Apiñanis, finally realizing their dream of Almería the Golden and Silver Jaén, breeding bulls in Andalucía.

His life is finished. Nada y nada y nada.

Leocadia, he remembers. Leocadia in his arms in a blanket roll in the guerrilla camp, her young breath on his cheek.

He is not too old for that. He is never too old for that.

449

The next day he sees mutilated corpses. And the next month. And the next year.

All at once he is back in the Puerta del Sol, Pascual Apiñani's blood running over the cobblestones, and he remembers the words of the good king, the first Carlos. *I see the bloodlust of the bullring spilling over into the streets of Madrid.*

It spills over, and it fills Don Paco with rage. Suddenly he is working again, as he has never worked before. Art from carnage, life from death, a testament of disaster as long as men have eyes to see. In the house across the river, called the House of the Deaf Man then, the house he bought for Cayetana.

'Do you think he's quite sane, Doña Leocadia?' Javier asks.

'He's the sanest man in Madrid, you fool.' Leocadia, with that acid tongue of hers.

'These paintings are the work of a madman,' Javier insists in a shocked voice.

'You,' says Leocadia, 'should be so mad.'

Is Leocadia right? Or Javier?

Witches and monsters populate the world of his sleep and threaten his waking hours. He is very close to madness, there in the House of the Deaf Man. It feeds the magic. So does the grief that will never leave him. So do the disasters.

Now, in the Café de Paris, a tall figure looms over his table. He looks up. The hooded eyes narrow. It is the Prince of the Peace. A mocking smile on the sensuous lips. A small bow.

'May I sit?' he asks.

'Sit.' One hand clutching the dueling pistols.

'This is somewhat awkward for me, Don Paco,' Seated then, and coming directly to the point. The Prince of the Peace was never one to waste words. 'I seem to be embarrassed for funds. I'm short half a gold livre.'

No request for help. Just the statement.

How fitting, Don Paco thinks, that the executioner should pay for the condemned man's last meal. He tosses a few coins on the table.

'Send the woman home in a cab, Don Manuel.'

'Yes, I thought you would want that.'

The Prince of the Peace takes the coins, stands, bows again, returns to his own table. Don Paco calls for his bill.

He sees the prince in earnest conversation with his lady. Her lips form a thin line, and he remembers the look of disapproval on Josefa's face. The second of May, 1808.

That Cayetana was dead, and that he wanted to die, then, five years later. How could Josefa understand?

The day Bonaparte's Mamelukes, turbaned, savage, stormed into the Puerta del Sol.

CHAPTER THIRTY-THREE

Dos de Mayo

JOSEFA SAT PRIMLY, hands clasped in a pious attitude, a coronet of braids binding her faded golden hair, a silk shawl draped modestly over her shoulders. She stared at her husband, across the room, palette in his left hand, paintbrush in his right. He liked to paint portraits from a distance. He could see the subject all of a piece that way, he said.

She heard shouting, men running over cobblestones, occasionally the quick thundering tattoo of a galloping horse. It had been going on all day, that hot second day of May 1808. She was terrified. She tried not to flinch, the wistful eyes watching her husband as his own hooded eyes studied her. She clenched her teeth. Her lips made a thin line, primly together like her folded hands. She could feel them trembling.

'Try to relax,' Paco said irritably. 'It's no terrible ordeal, sitting for your portrait.'

That he should have chosen this of all days to have her sit for him, she thought. The servants had been in and out of the house all morning, breathless with rumors while Paco mixed his colors.

'Besides,' he said, relenting with a smile, 'it's high time I painted you.'

Josefa nodded. There he stood, with his back to the window, the light streaming over his shoulder, the good north light, oblivious to the tumult in the streets.

She had seen his preliminary sketches. She hardly had to sit for him, she realized. He was painting from memory really, the Josefa of twenty years ago. The first, the only portrait he ever did of her.

She heard a troop of horsemen galloping by. A bugle sounded, peremptorily. Paco went on painting.

'You're moving.'

'Sorry.'

All day, the rumors. The royal family had gone to Bayonne, where the Frenchman Bonaparte, the emperor Napoleon, would decide who ruled in Madrid.

Only Antonio the Idiot, King Carlos' brother, remained at the palace, Don Antonio and the thirteen-year-old Prince Francisco de Paula, not the king's son at all, as everyone knew, but Godoy's. Josefa didn't like to think about those things. And even the crowd, today, chose to ignore the fact that the boy was a bastard.

French traveling coaches had come to the Plaza of the Arsenal, the servants said. To take Antonio the Idiot to France. To take the young prince to France. To leave not a single Bourbon in Madrid.

Or perhaps, the servants said, as fresh waves of angry Madrileños took to the streets, to murder them.

Paco knew nothing of this. He had stopped reading those pamphlets of his. Since painting Javier, a dandified señorita with a fancy walking stick, since deeding the big house to him, he had retreated further into himself.

Five years, Josefa thought, while Paco dabbed a thick brush at his palette. Five years of not caring. It was as if he had decided that his life had ended. Or, worse, that he wanted it to end.

He had aged. His face was fuller, but more lined. His dark eyes, deep in their hooded sockets, gazed out on the world with a curious sadness. He spoke little. More and more he did not trouble himself to read lips. People always spoke the same nonsense, he said. Why bother?

She remembered how he had come storming back from the illness that had almost killed him. The long journey with Juanito, and the lean, hard Paco Goya who had returned, consumed with the need to work. He had painted better than he ever had before. Or since.

Now the soft, flabby, sad-eyed man said, without anger: 'Can't you keep still? What the devil's going on out there?'

Her eyes had been drawn to the window again. The narrow street echoed with the sound of clattering hooves. A horse whinnied.

Paco went to the window, paintbrush still in his hand. He leaned on the sill, his grizzled head far out. Josefa got up quickly.

'Who are they?' he asked. 'They're not French.'

Josefa looked down and saw green-uniformed horsemen carrying long lances. Polish lancers, the servants had said. Napoleon recruited his army from half of Europe. Even from Africa. It was rumored that his Egyptian mercenaries, the turbaned Mamelukes who had won him his empire, were waiting at staging points on the outskirts of the city. She shuddered. Napoleon the emperor, Napoleon the antichrist, with his infidel Mamelukes, sweeping like a scythe through Spain, as the Moors had a thousand years ago.

'Polish cavalry,' she said.

People stood pressed in doorways along the street, watching the lancers pass. Across the way a man leaned out a window and shook his fist. Suddenly, from above, red roof tiles came hurtling down. Josefa saw two men on the rooftop, prising tiles loose and throwing them.

A boy rushed out of an alley with a rusty sword. A horse reared, a long Polish lance flashed in the sunlight, the boy was impaled. His scream was silenced by the thundering hooves. He was trampled. Josefa cried out and turned away.

'The fools,' Paco said. 'Roof tiles. A rusty old sword. Did you see that boy? The look on his face?'

She nodded dumbly. It was the look on his own face that terrified her. The sadness had fled his eyes. Rage, rage born in an instant had replaced it. She remembered the preternatural glow in his eyes when Dr Rodríguez-Pereira had pulled him out of his invalid's chair. Madness. A madness that still made him cry out in his sleep at night, a single word, a single name: Cayetana.

'I'm going out.'

She followed him downstairs. He got his heavy walking stick and his tall beaver hat. He stomped to the back door.

'It's too warm for the beaver,' she said. She began to cry.

Manuel Godoy, Prince of Nothing, Generalissimo of Nothing, Duke of Nothing, his once-dazzling white and gold uniform tattered and sweat-stained, his face sallow and puffy, languished in a cell in the Cárcel de Corte.

He had a few books, he had a set of Goya's *Caprices*, he had enough money to bribe the warder to bring him real food instead of slop, and even a bottle of wine, not very good wine, each day.

Well, he thought with a strange perverse pleasure, he had come from nowhere, he had had his day, his day was over. He could hear the angry crowds in the nearby Plaza Mayor, and musket fire. He had miscalculated. A simple miscalculation. First Junot had slipped across the border with twenty thousand troops, and then Murat with a hundred thousand. He had arranged it. He had opened the frontier posts to them. He had needed them. King Carlos' reign was over. It would be Fernando, he had thought. Or it would be Godoy.

It would be neither. It would be the emperor Napoleon.

A brief meeting with General Murat. Handsome, sure of himself, married to Napoleon's sister Caroline.

'The British have occupied Portugal,' Murat said, that night in the Admiralty Palace. Murat had stalked in with a riding whip. He stroked it. He slapped his thigh with it. 'That changes things, Don Manuel.'

'I can clear the British out of Portugal for you.'

'You Spaniards have no army worthy of the name,' said Murat with a deep-throated laugh. He looked around the ornate grand salon of the Admiralty Palace contemptuously. 'But you do manage to live well. A few of you. A very few.'

'I can put two hundred thousand men at the emperor's disposal.'

Another contemptuous glance, this time at Godoy himself. 'They'd get in the way.'

'I can – '

'*You'd* get in the way.'

'The emperor deceived me with his promise.'

The riding whip lashed out, a gentle reprimand that left a red welt on Godoy's plump cheek.

'The emperor wants Spain,' said Murat. 'The emperor will have Spain.'

Godoy, who had worn his generalissimo's uniform for the occasion, reached for his dress sword, drew it. Cayetana de Alba and now this Joachim Murat. Twice in his long career he had lost his temper.

The whip lashed out again, the sword clattered on the floor. 'Look to your own safety,' Murat advised him calmly. 'By this time tomorrow Madrid will know you opened the frontier to me.' Murat bowed mockingly and left.

The Admiralty Palace staff slipped away the next morning. Godoy spent the day packing. There might be safety for a time in Aranjuez. All day crowds gathered on the other side of the high iron fence that surrounded the Admiralty Palace.

Murat's soldiers kept them at bay.

At nightfall Pepa Tudo came to him. Her pretty face wore a haughty expression, almost regal, as if she had learned from those paintings of Goya, paintings that weren't Pepa Tudo at all. 'It's over,' she said, 'isn't it?'

He nodded. He could see torchlight through the window, could hear an occasional angry shout. Most of the mob had dispersed.

'We had a time of it,' she said.

An hour later Murat's soldiers left. A dozen Madrileños, armed with knives and sticks, broke in. They were drunk. They pulled down tapestries and smashed furniture. They called him Sausage Maker and spat in his face.

They bowed before his wife, the timid Countess of Chinchón, who was royalty. Three of them escorted her to her suite. 'Stay there, little princess,' they said.

They stripped Pepa Tudo naked before Godoy's eyes and raped her. They took turns, two of them holding Godoy, all of them having their way with Pepa Tudo on the floor of the grand salon. Her screams and struggles became weaker. Once Godoy broke free and shouted hoarsely and with a single blow of his fist broke a man's jaw. The man fell and got up, his mouth agape and bloody. He looked at Godoy. He looked at Pepa Tudo. He beat her about the face with his stick. He kept on beating her while the others shouted, 'Hombre, hombre, wait!' He killed her.

Godoy fled upstairs to the attic. It took them an hour to find him, hidden in a carpet. They dragged him out and downstairs. They beat him with their sticks.

'French-lover!' they cried. 'Antichrist!'

The corregidor's police came. They took Godoy to the Cárcel de Corte. He would be safe in prison.

A few days later Murat visited him. 'You'll have a pension in France,' he said. 'From the emperor. For your cooperation.' He smiled, that handsome brother-in-law of Napoleon Bonaparte. 'It won't be large.'

On the second of May, Godoy was still waiting. A pension in France, he told himself. Not large. It was still better than being a pig farmer in Badajoz.

Unlike Godoy, fat King Carlos had been offered a munificent pension of thirty million reales, and a more than princely estate at Compiègne, if he would abdicate in favour of his son.

Carlos who, in the five years Paco Goya slept, saw floodwaters wash away towns and villages, and earthquakes devastate the south. Carlos, whose ministers reported plague from Barcelona to Cádiz, pernicious fever in Castile, yellow fever in Andalucía, famine everywhere. Carlos, who ignored appeals to the royal treasury and never understood why bread was scarce in Madrid, why money did not circulate, why it was too dangerous for him to pass the winters at the royal palace, where angry mobs roved the streets, screaming for food, attacking the coaches of the nobility, sometimes cutting the traces and dragging out a grandee on the Alcalá or the Recoletos and clubbing him to death.

Carlos, who played his fiddle and fiddled with his clocks while Maria Luisa, old and hideous in her debauchery, lusted after the dashing young General Palafox. Carlos, who never wanted to be king and who was pleased with Bonaparte's thirty million reales and his estate at Compiègne.

And that skulker of a crown prince Fernando? Bonaparte let him skulk two weeks on the throne in Madrid before sending him under imperial escort to exile in France.

If the enlightened Spaniards' rallying cry had been 'No more Pyrenees,' Bonaparte's became 'No more Bourbons.' Bonaparte, that child of revolution, was no lover of royalty. Except Europe's new royalty, the emperor Napoleon and his family.

Not that the fate of the last two Bourbons in Madrid would be the gibbet or the guillotine. They would be sent to France to join fat King Carlos in exile.

'The Spanish affair,' Murat confidently wrote his brother-in-law on the eve of the second of May 1808, 'is finished.'

But Madrid, crowded with refugees from the flood- and fever-ravaged countryside, thought otherwise. The Madrileños had lived through a decade of treaties with England, treaties with France, abortive wars with both. Everywhere they saw betrayal. They were, they said in every café and chocolatería, well rid of fat King Carlos. They were of two minds about Fernando, since nobody really knew what he was like. They were, except for the few champions of the Enlightenment like Leandro Moratín and Cabarrús the banker, of a single mind about the French.

They would not trust Murat, or his Polish lancers, or his turbaned Mamelukes, with the life of the meanest beggar in Madrid.

They would certainly not trust Murat with the lives of old Don Antonio the Idiot or young Prince Francisco de Paula, who, everybody conveniently forgot on that second day of May, was the son of the hated Godoy.

So the French coaches drew up to the royal palace, flanked by Polish outriders, and the people gathered in the Plaza of the Arsenal to watch. Soon doddering old Don Antonio appeared on the staircase. He was trembling. The people forgot that he always trembled, that he was afflicted with palsy. He looked terrified.

Francisco de Paula, with the handsome face and crafty eyes of Godoy, emerged next. He paused on the stairs, blinking in the bright May sunlight. He looked at the coaches and the waiting Polish lancers. He turned back and climbed two steps higher on the broad granite staircase. Perhaps he had forgotten something. Perhaps he wanted to say a final goodbye to an old servant. One of Murat's lieutenants grasped his arm. He tried to break free.

They dragged him, resisting, to the nearest coach.

'They're going to kill him!' a woman in the crowd screamed.

The crowd surged forward. A boy no older than Francisco de Paula darted between the legs of a Polish horse and with a kitchen knife cut the saddle girth. The horse reared, the startled lancer fell. The crowd was on him.

Just then the battalion of French cavalry that would provide a royal escort to the border entered the Plaza of the Arsenal. They saw the mob swarming over the coaches. Their captain gave the order to fire. Twenty people fell, but there were thousands. An artillery caisson rumbled into the plaza, and the whiff of grapeshot that had brought Napoleon to power in Paris was tried in Madrid.

The smoke cleared, another dozen Madrileños died. Screams filled the plaza.

The city rose, as one man.

Murat sent for his waiting Mamelukes.

Paco made his way through narrow side streets and alleys past the Plaza Mayor to Café Apiñani. Juanito would know. Juanito, who always said: 'Me? What's politics to me? I'm not interested in politics.' Juanito, just by listening in that café Paco had bought for him, knew as much about politics as any man in Madrid. Not that he cared, of course.

A few old men, regulars at the café, were playing dominoes at their corner table. Juanito stood with his arms folded on the bar. He looked up in surprise when he saw Paco, the wolf's grin on his leathery face. He had aged well, Juanito. He was as lean as when he fought the bulls.

'Chico,' he said. 'I thought you'd gone to Zaragoza or Cádiz or somewhere.'

'I don't go out much.'

'A wine?'

'Beer.' It had been a long walk. He was thirsty. He drank the beer and had another.

'What is it, Juanito? What do the people want? I'd welcome the French.'

'Bread,' said Juanito. 'Bread to fill their stomachs. That they would appreciate.'

'The Enlightenment,' Paco said. 'Napoleon can bring Spain into the nineteenth century.'

He felt a hand on his arm. It was one of the old domino players. He had a wiry stubble of beard on his face. 'Your pardon, señor. You mentioned that man's name? The antichrist? You spoke favorably of him? I have a certain interest,' said the old man. 'My son died with the fleet at Trafalgar. Fighting for your antichrist against the British.'

He bowed his head in Juanito's direction. 'Forgive me, Don Juanito,' he said, and made a hacking sound in his throat and spat on Paco's dusty shoes.

'Now they send an army to occupy the land,' said the old man. 'That is our thanks for Trafalgar. For my son.' A gnarled hand reached out to strike Paco. Juanito caught the wrist and turned it aside.

The other domino players were on their feet. They ignored the disturbance at the bar. They crowded around the door. Paco saw soldiers rushing by wearing blue uniforms with white epaulets and red bandoliers and black hussar hats. They carried rifles, bayonets fixed in place. The old domino player spat again, through the doorway.

A mob had gathered at either end of the short street. The French took their stand in the middle. The mob hurled paving stones. The hussar-hatted soldiers formed four ranks, two facing in either direction. They held their fire. The paving stones fell short. Paco took a step out into the street. He wanted to see them better, these Frenchmen, these soldiers of Napoleon. Juanito grabbed his arm and yanked him back.

At one end of the street the mob suddenly parted and Paco saw mules. Men prodded them with goads and lashed at them with whips. The mules bared their teeth and snorted. The domino players retreated inside the café. Paco remained in the doorway.

Suddenly the mules stampeded into the street. The soldiers fired at them. The mules came and came, thirty of them. Forty. The soldiers dropped their rifles and began to run. The mules were on them and over them, mouths foam-flecked, rearing and bucking and striking with their hooves. The blue-coated figures went down. Mouths opened in silent screams. The striking hooves made no sound. Paco stood there, watching. Again the rage was in his eyes. A hussar hat tumbled away, a head split open. Blood ran between the cobblestones. The mules went through, the mob parting to let them pass at the far end of the street. All the soldiers were down, like discarded dominoes, grotesque on the cobblestones. One of them was still alive, arms twitching, legs twitching, the hussar hat still on his head.

The old domino player who had spat on Paco's shoes went outside. He opened a clasp knife and sawed at the Frenchman's throat. The blade was dull. He sawed and sawed until the blood came spurting, and then he walked slowly along the street, his head high.

Paco was outside too. The other domino players had gone. Juanito was pulling down the shutters of the café and locking it.

'Go home, chico,' he told Paco.

Paco wasn't looking at him. Juanito grabbed his arm again. 'I said go home, man. Hurry.'

'I've got to see this.' There was a roaring in his ears. He shook Juanito off. He walked in the direction the mules had taken.

Madrileños took to the rooftops, to the streets, to the parks and plazas, to fight the French with what weapons they had, what weapons they could improvise. To fight General Murat, Napoleon's brother-in-law, who led the army of occupation – Murat, like a god on his white charger, in his green velvet coat and high red leather boots, the white egret plume on his hat blowing in the wind.

Everywhere Paco went he saw madness, like the madhouse in Badajoz all over again, where the gentry went for amusement on a Sunday afternoon, without the catharsis of the fire in the hospital.

The people had knives and sticks, paving stones and roof-tiles.

The French had sabres and muskets, rifles and artillery.

461

Children used slingshots to tumble Polish lancers from their horses. Old women waited in dim alleys, dressed in black, their bodies coiled like springs, and came darting out with butcher knives.

Murat's Mamelukes galloped into the city from their staging points, herding the mobs along the broad avenues that converged on the Puerta del Sol – the Mamelukes, white-turbaned, with enormous mustaches and broad sashes and wide pantaloons, riding wildly and swinging their sabres over-head and screaming their Moorish battle cry that Paco could not hear.

Kitchen knives gutted horses, the Mamelukes fell, the people fell on them. The air became murky with dust and gunsmoke. Sabres lopped off arms, lopped off heads.

Fat old man walking through death, even through the carn-age in the Puerta del Sol. Nothing touched him. Not a sabre, not a bullet, not a hurled paving stone.

Nothing? Wasn't that the café where Pascual Apiñani had died, where now, among the overturned tables, a Mameluke sabre cleaved a head from crown to jaw? Wasn't that where he had run after Juanito, Juanito crying wordlessly, brandish-ing a knife overhead, until the madness had seized him too and he forgot Juanito and ran with the mob – the sacking of the townhouses along the Alcalá, and Mariana in his arms, two children afraid of the dark? Was Mariana alive or dead, in Paris?

Cayetana was dead. Santa Maria, yes, Cayetana was dead.

A dismounted Mameluke struck with his sabre, and a man at Paco's side tumbled to the ground. The Mameluke stared at Paco, teeth flashing under the bristling mustach. Paco waited. Now, yes, let it be now, it might as well be now as any other time.

But a priest, his cassock tucked up, his two small pale hands gripping a ridiculously large old sword, came rushing up, and Paco saw his lips form the word antichrist as he struck the Mameluke with the flat of the sword and the Mameluke fell, turban sailing off his head to reveal a bald pate oozing blood.

'Antichrist!' cried the priest again, and ran off.

And all day long the man who had heard no sound for fif-teen years and more, except for the creaking in his ears, the cackle of witches, sometimes rarley in the night Cayetana's voice, heard the rattle of musketry and the tatto of drums. And a surf, a surf beating on a distant shore, why should he

462

hear that, this man who could hear nothing?

By nightfall it was over. The Mamelukes and Polish lancers, the chasseurs and carabiniers, had prevailed against the mob. Slowly the dust and green murk settled on Madrid, settled on the entrails of disemboweled horses steaming in the hot dusk, settled on the corpses that lay where they had fallen, settled on the madness.

Murat's soldiers led away all Madrileños found with muskets or swords, to face French firing squads.

Weary, dust-covered, a bloody bruise on his forehead, numb with the madness he had seen, Paco Goya returned slowly to the Street of Disillusion. A squad of torch-bearing soldiers stopped him. He answered their questions contemptuously, as if to say, Take me too and be done with it, can't you see I died five years ago?

They let him pass.

And that night, unable to sleep, the sound of musket fire loud in the ears that could not hear, he saw a giant, looming over a landscape where people, carts, covered wagons were fleeing. The giant, whose massive fists could crush whole villages, smote the earth.

All at once, without knowing why, Paco Goya wanted to live.

CHAPTER THIRTY-FOUR

The Disasters of War

ANTONIO FRANCISCO, MARQUES DE SOLIS, former captain of infantry in the Grand' Armeé and aid-de-camp to General Murat, focused his spyglass on the city of Zaragoza. It came abruptly into sharp detail – the spires of the basilica, the almost dry bed of the Ebro under the scorching midsummer sun, the dun-colored brick buildings with holes punched in them as if a giant had struck with his fist, the rubble where Napoleon's artillery had leveled entire streets, the fires that still burned here and there, the pall of smoke that hung over the barrio of Pilar, where General Verdier had concentrated his cannon and mortar fire, hoping to open a breach for his waiting Polish lancers.

'Weiss! ' Antonio Francisco called, and the bullnecked German, a solidly built man of fifty, came puffing up through the defile between the two ridges of the hill where Antonio Francisco stood. The hill, shaped like a gigantic tooth, was called the Molar. It loomed above the arid Aragonese plateau, behind Verdier's lines.

Isidoro Weiss clicked his heels, a somewhat ludicrous Teutonic gesture for a man wearing rope-soled shoes. He saluted smartly, an equally ludicrous gesture for a man who needed a shave, whose shirt was in tatters, and whose commanding officer led a force of fifty guerrilleros who had done very little so far but watch the bombardment of the city.

'The captain wishes?' Isidoro Weiss asked.

The captain wishes he had five hundred men, or five thousand. He wished he had more muskets. He wished he had some light cavalry to assault Verdier's slow, mule-drawn supply wagons. He said: 'How long can the city hold out?'

Weiss shrugged and showed the dirty palms of his hands. 'Who can say?' he asked. 'For saltpeter they wash the streets. For carbon they burn hemp. They manufacture their own gunpowder and bullets. Mules, dogs, cats they eat. I know.'

Isidoro Weiss knew, all right, thought Antonio Francisco. Weiss had worked for the grain merchant Zapater in Zaragoza, slipping through the French lines and foraging for food. Zapater, provisioner to a beseiged city, had sent his German out once too often. Weiss, with three men and half a dozen donkeys, had stumbled onto Antonio Francisco's camp in the defile between the two fangs of the Molar.

'They expect me in Zaragoza,' Weiss had said.

'You're staying,' Antonio Francisco told him.

He had a deep, cold voice, Antonio Francisco. He was a tall, broad-shouldered man with cold hooded eyes and a black beard that did not quite hide the scar that ran from his left ear to his jaw. The scar was a memento of Austerlitz, where a wild-riding Cossack had almost lopped off the head of the French Captain de Solis while Napoleon had routed the Russian General Kutusov.

Weiss had looked into those hooded eyes and listened to that voice. 'I have a wife in Zaragoza,' he said.

'I have fifty men here. You could betray us. You'll stay. Or die.'

The cold voice had sent a chill down Isidoro Weiss' back. He knew he was very close to death. 'Yes,' he said in his German accent, 'I'll stay.'

'You're lucky,' said Antonio Francisco. 'There'll be a slaughter, when the Polish lancers enter Zaragoza.'

Weiss suddenly smiled. He began to laugh. 'Leocadia. My wife. She's been threatening to leave me. I've left her instead. What will I do for you?'

'You know Zaragoza. You know Palafox. Will he fight in the streets when the French break through?'

'From house to house. From the rooftops. He'll fight.'

'Good,' said Antonio Francisco.

'And you'll come down to help him?'

'Fifty men, with half a dozen muskets?' A harsh laugh that was no real laugh at all. 'No, I won't come down. If Palafox fights, the French will be careless with their supplies and ammunition stores. I need guns. I'll get them.'

Now on the Molar Antonio Francisco heard the boom of an artillery piece. He trained his spyglass on the barrio of Pilar and saw a house come lazily apart and float upward, one wall disintegrating, roof rising like a hat lofted by the wind, chimney going high and dropping slowly through a sudden spurt of flame into a churchyard.

'How long?' he asked again. It was late July. The siege of Zaragoza had been going on for two months.

Weiss scowled. He asked for the spyglass and studied the city. 'In Boterón we were living,' he said, pointing. 'There is very little left of Boterón. The Zapater house, gone. The Palafox.'

'How long, German?'

Again Weiss gave that shrug, almost a *baturro* shrug.

Antonio Francisco grabbed the spyglass from him impatiently. From inside the city a mortar thumped, and behind Verdier's brickwork bastion a brass cannon flew apart in a burst of smoke and flame.

'I asked how long, German?'

'A week. Two at the outside. See, there in Pilar? They'll breach the walls. The Polish lancers will ride through.'

'Good,' said Antonio Francisco.

Weiss looked away from him uneasily, and Antonio Francisco could tell what he was thinking. I've got to get away from this one. This one isn't human. This one looks for death, if death can get him what he wants. What he wants is to kill Frenchmen. With a band of fifty irregulars, guerrilleros, little war makers. This one is mad. This one, some of the fifty irregulars by now must have told Isidoro Weiss, had been a captain in the Grand' Armée. Speaks French like a Parisian. Served as Murat's aide-de-camp and deserted the day before Murat entered Madrid. Came to Zaragoza because that was where the fighting was. Stubborn. More Arangonese in his ways than Zapater or that young General Palafox. Fifty guerrilleros. The French, when they find them, will leave behind fifty corpses. I've got to get out of this.

The German could go, Antonio Francisco told himself. After the siege of Zaragoza. The fighting will shift to the west. It has to shift to the west, toward Portugal, when the British General Wellesley crosses the frontier. I'll have a thousand men by then. Two thousand. And guns. Yes, guns. I know how to fight the French. The ambushed supply column. The poisoned well. The bomb in a café.

He had not learned how to fight the French at their military academy, although he had earned his commission there. He had not learned how to fight the French at Austerlitz, where Napoleon's tactics had prevailed over those of the gross and senile Russian Kutusov. He had learned how to fight the French on the island of Haiti, where he had received his captain's epaulets. That general of color, Toussaint, showed him how to fight them. Artillery determined the actics of the Grand' Armée, and no one had devised a way to transport artillery swiftly. The Grand' Armée fought well, but it crawled. Toussaint knew this. Fight them with irregulars. Stab and run. Strike when they are busy elsewhere. Jab at them. Prick at them. And disappear. Terrify them. No place is safe. No time is safe. But they will, as Antonio Francisco had seen in Haiti, turn in their fear and wrath against the civilian population. For every French soldier killed, ten civilian hostages taken and shot. Let them. That would preoccupy the French. To have them preoccupied was a good thing.

Antonio Francisco telescoped the spyglass and pocketed it. Let the French destroy Zaragoza. Let its people be full of hate. Then he would find recruits.

He felt a vast impatience with the slowness of the French siege, with the stubbornness of the Aragonese inside their city.

Let it end soon.

He remembered his mother, in her last years, in the mad-house in Paris, before she died, and the enlightened Republicans who came to watch and to laugh. He had visited her once, after the military academy. She hadn't recognized him. He had never gone again.

His business was killing Frenchmen.

'Did you see them before they died?' Paco asked. 'Did you speak to them?'

He stood with Martín in the ruins of what had been the barrio of Pilar. Whole apartment buildings had been leveled. Jagged stumps of wall stood silhouetted against the brilliant blue Aragon sky. No more shells were falling on the barrio. There was nothing left to hit. Across the street a building gaped, its façade sheered off cleanly, surgically, revealing dim halls and cluttered staircases and a dozen rooms that would never be lived in again. Here a bed hung precariously over the street, there a kitchen table stood with chairs still around it, dimly on a far wall on the second floor Paco could see a wooden madonna. Men and women plodded by, sweating in the heat of the late afternoon, hauling carts full of broken bricks. They dumped them at the far end of the street, where children, stripped to the waist and burned dark by the sun, were constructing a barrier. A dead donkey lay in a court-yard. Three women with butcher knives were flaying it and hacking off meat. The children turned every now and then to watch them, their eyes big in gaunt, hungry faces.

Martín Zapater shook his head slowly – Martín, tall but stooped now, long-nosed, his eyes deep-sunk and bloodshot from lack of sleep, his voice hoarse from a lifetime of cigar smoking and the acrid gunpowder stench that hung in the air, his chest sunken under his sweat-stained frock coat. He wore a black armband on his sleeve. His wife Serafina had died early in the siege.

'Amigo,' Martín said slowly, 'it was all over in an instant. A direct hit by an artillery shell.'

The apartment that had been the Goya y Lucientes household had looked out over the courtyard where the donkey was being butchered. The building had been reduced to rubble. Martín's letter had brought Paco from Madrid, first in a post coach and then on muleback and finally on foot. In all that expanse of upland country it was no difficult matter to slip through the French lines.

'It's certain they were inside?'

467

The hand tightened on his shoulder. 'It wasn't certain when I wrote you. The bodies were dug out later.'

Doña Engracia, in her eighties, had died in the bombardment of the city. Paco's brother Tomás had died with her.

'I wanted her to stay in Madrid, you know,' Paco said quietly. 'Years ago, after my father died. She tried it a while. Too much bustling about, she said. Too much noise. And the streets weren't safe at night. So she came home to Zaragoza to die.'

He shut his eyes and could see Doña Engracia over her cooking pots, and smell the aroma of good chilindrón chicken.

He waved his arms in a vague motion that took in the ruins of the barrio of Pilar. 'This,' he said. 'This because the people murdered a few French soldiers. When will they learn? You can't fight Napoleon with kitchen knives and paving stones.'

'Murdered?' gasped Martín. 'What do you mean, murdered? Those soldiers were tyrants. We had to fight them.'

'King Carlos was a tyrant. So was Godoy.'

'That's finished.'

'Spain's finished.'

'They raped women. Little girls. They dragged nuns from their convents. They took hostages on any pretext and shot them.' Martín's voice rose in anger. 'Are you telling me we shouldn't have resisted?'

Paco said nothing at first. Doña Engracia dead, Tomás dead, the fanatic heroics that had kept Verdier and the might of the Grand' Armée at bay for two months, the people rising everywhere –

'Heroic idiocy,' he grumbled. He remembered the second of May, not yet three months past, and women and children hurling themselves on the Mamelukes.

'Idiocy?' roared Martín in his hoarse voice. 'You're the idiot if you think – '

'I don't know what I think. I saw French soldiers hanging from trees on the road from Madrid. I saw a mob take a man, a Spaniard, and stake him face down on the ground and shove a hot ramrod up his rectum until he died screaming.'

'A collaborator,' said Martín coldly.

No more Pyrenees, Paco thought. Pablo de Olavide and those proscribed books of his. What had it all meant, finally?

'We're no better than they are,' he said.

Martín turned on him hotly. 'Did we invade France? Or what about you? It's easy to call King Carlos a tyrant now. Did you call him that when you painted him? Or Godoy?'

468

'That was different. Art and politics – ' Paco stopped abruptly. He thought of Francisco Bayeu.

But Meléndez the lawyer, or Cabarrús the banker, even Leandro Moratín and Cean Bermúdez. All the old Lovers of Ugliness except Jovino. How could they all be wrong?

'Murat brought the draft of a constitution to Madrid,' Paco said. 'It's a document that could never have been written in Spain,' he tried to explain, more for his own benefit than Martín's. 'One common law for all. An independent judiciary. Freedom of the press. Freedom of speech. The Inquisition abolished.'

'Words,' said Martín. 'A pretty piece of paper. I can show you Murat's real constitution.'

He led Paco from the rubble of Pilar to the plaza in front of the Seo. The cathedral had miraculously survived Verdier's cannon fire. Paco saw, at almost the exact place where once he had chalked a likeness of the bishop, an Order of the Day affixed to the wall like a bullfight poster.

'They put that up before the siege,' Martín said. 'Before the people rose in the streets. Verdier's infantry. It's like a talisman. Nobody will dare rip it down now.' Someone had scrawled diagonally across the announcement in red chalk a single word: *mierda.*

The order read:

The city will be *disarmed.*
All those bearing arms *will be shot.*
Any street in which a Frenchman is killed *will be destroyed.*
Any meeting of more than eight persons will be regarded as seditious and *dispersed by gunfire.*
The authors or distributors of libelous or seditious printed matter *will be regarded as British agents and shot.*
For every Frenchman attacked twenty hostages *will be taken and shot.*

By Order of the Emperor Napoleon
and Joachim Murat, General, Grand' Armée

Paco turned away from the wall. Very concise, he thought. Excellent Spanish.

Mierda. Slashed across the order with that baturro arrogance.

French ideas and French artillery. Voltaire and Diderot, had they made Napoleon and Murat inevitable? What, really, could Martín or Palafox or the people of Zaragoza have done?

What could they do now? Blind heroics, a few more days of starvation, a few shells left for their pitifully few guns, and then the carnage.

'We can't hold out much longer,' Martín said. 'They'll come through Pilar. The barriers won't stop them.'

'And then?'

'We'll throw them out again. Palafox has organized all the ablebodied men in the city into detachments. Women too. Children. He wants to meet you, by the way.'

'Me?'

'To paint. To commemorate the siege.'

Paco smiled reluctantly. 'I had a little trouble about some painting once, with a Palafox.'

'His father. The basilica,' said Martín, and it was all right between them again. 'You always were a stubborn bastard. The worst *baturro* of them all.'

Paco snorted. 'I can just see it, what he wants. General Palafox on a charger, gallant, his cavalry lined up behind him with their standards fluttering in the wind. It's not that kind of war. Maybe Velázquez could have done it. Not me.'

He recalled the things he had seen on the road from Madrid. That, not Palafox on a charger, was war. It would be like no war ever fought before by people who called themselves civilized.

Antonio Francisco knew, finally and with a sense of elation, that it was time to leave the Molar.

He could hear the roar of a cannon and the angry shrieking whine of a shell speeding toward the ruins of the city. He could see the Polish lancers assembling. Distantly through the clear air he could hear the bugle calls. They would ride. They would ride today. A small detachment of guards would remain behind with the supply wagons, with the rifles and muskets, with the good French sabres, sharp as Toledo steel, with the mules and donkeys.

Booty for a man whose business it was to build an army and kill Frenchmen. There would be refugees. Through his spyglass he could already see them streaming from the city, long lines of them winding slowly into the mountains. Among those refugees he would find men, and turn them into soldiers.

Two peasants in dirty white shirts, their faces caked with dust, muskets slung across their backs, climbed through the defile, dragging the German Weiss between them.

'This one,' one of the peasants said. 'This one was trying to

470

slip away.'

They let go of Weiss. The German dropped to his knees. 'Don't kill me,' he pleaded. 'What is it for you, to kill me?'

Antonio Francisco looked at him, his hooded eyes like chips of ice.

'Don't kill me,' the German whined again.

One of the peasants unslung his musket. His lips parted to reveal dirty, crooked teeth. He was grinning.

'No, hold him,' Antonio Francisco said. 'Until dark.'

Weiss groveled at Antonio Francisco's feet. 'I won't give you any trouble. I'm going back to Germany,' he said. 'I've had enough of Spain.'

Antonio Francisco's mouth smiled. His eyes remained ice. 'Hold him until dark, then let him go.'

He opened the spyglass and focused it on the barrio of Pilar. He saw the Polish lancers galloping through. He stood in the defile between the two fangs of the Molar, hating. Hating Weiss and the stupidity of the peasants he had to turn into soldiers. Hating the citizens of Zaragoza who had withstood the siege so long. Hating the French.

He liked the Polish lancers, though. They had begun his war for him.

By midnight it was over.

In the light of the guerrilleros' torches, Polish corpses lay strewn on the rocky ground. Antonio Francisco and his fifty men had taken them by surprise. The sentries first, a silken cord for their necks. The supply wagons had been drawn up in a circle. Within it, in the clear still night, someone had been singing. An unfamiliar song, a song of the steppes, Antonio Francisco had told himself, if they had steppes in Poland. Maybe it was Russia. Yes, Russia. He had listened a while, with his fifty men waiting. It was a nice song.

Inside their circle of wagons, the Poles had built a fire. They were drinking wine and clapping a rhythm for the song of the steppes if that was what it was. They were glad that they had been chosen to remain behind with the supply wagons.

Antonio Francisco and his men slipped in among the wagons. The singer died first, a musket ball in his throat. The Poles scattered for their lances and rifles. They ran silhouetted against the fire. They died silhouetted against the fire. Antonio Francisco's peasants killed them hot-bloodedly, in a rage against these despoilers of their land, their Aragon. Spain? Spain meant nothing to them. Not yet. He would teach them,

471

and others like them. Spain meant everything. The war would give him years of the teaching. Antonio Francisco himself killed coolly and with a detached competence. He used his French sabre deftly, a matador of men. He accounted for six of the lancers.

He did not want the wagons. He did not want the gun carriages. The wagons and gun carriages moved too slowly on this terrain, like the Grand' Armée itself. He wanted the mules, and the fine long quick-firing rifles of the French. A man could fire three shots or four a minute, with those rifles.

They assembled the mules in a train and filled their pack saddles with ammunition, with grain, with goatskins of wine. They took two hundred rifles. They set fire to the covered wagons. Soon the pack saddles were full. They found a wooden box of grenades. I will teach them, Antonio Francisco thought again. To be riflemen. To be grenadiers. To be killers of Frenchmen.

A few of his men were drunk on the wine. In the glow of the burning wagons they began to mutilate the corpses. At first Antonio Francisco thought it was a bad thing. And then he knew it was a good thing.

Let them remain hot-blooded with rage; let them hack at the bodies now, stripping them, dismembering them, cutting off their dead manhood, to learn that the French are meant to be slaughtered.

Antonio Francisco waited while his men had their way. He saw his mother's face, in the madhouse in Paris.

He fought back the pity and the remembered love. He looked again at what his men were doing. In the firelight a rare smile touched those hooded eyes.

The village of Fuendetodos, where Paco Goya had been born sixty-two years before, had not changed. He could hardly believe it. The same parched stubble of wheat on the bare low hills, the same dusty street with its mean dun-colored hovels, the same little church where he had painted the reliquary cabinet for Padre Gerónimo. Fifty reales. An artist's pay.

Martín looked at the cherubs on the doors of the cabinet in the cool dim interior of the church. 'Well, I suppose they were worth fifty reales, more or less,' he said.

Paco opened the doors of the cabinet and saw his Santiago. He jumped back in mock horror. 'Don't tell anyone I ever painted this.'

The banter, the joking, was forced. They had left the city

with the last wave of refugees. Women and children and a handful of old men. Palafox's army, or what passed for Palafox's army, was already fighting from house to house, from roof to roof. defending the city with their blood.

'What do you mean, old?' Martín had demanded when he was told he must leave. 'I brought the city food. You couldn't have held out without me.'

Palafox was limping back and forth, a musket ball in his thigh. 'Someone will have to lead the refugees. Someone will have to keep them alive. Find them food. We'll throw the Poles out. Then you'll come back.'

Palafox was less than thirty. Fear was a word he did not understand. Paco had changed his mind, had painted him on a charger with the look of a hawk in his eyes. It was not what he had intended to paint. It was Palafox, but it was not his war.

The refugees, under Martín's leadership, had taken three days to reach Fuendetodos. After the reliquary cabinet Paco had walked the distance in a day.

They were in the churchyard now, a hundred of them, weary, their bellies empty. They were drinking from the well. The citizens of Fuendetodos watched them silently, these women and children and old men, these city people. The war had not come to Fuendetodos. It probably never would.

'I really believe,' Paco said, 'that Palafox *will* throw them out. What will you do?'

'Go back. You?'

'I don't know.'

'Why not finish your life in Zaragoza? The war will move elsewhere.'

Finish your life. The words brought a scowl to Paco's broad forehead. He felt his sixty-two years, after the three-day march to Fuendetodos. He had allowed himself to become flabby. The years of doing nothing.

He realized then that in those three days he had not thought once of Cayetana. Not once.

'I don't know,' he said again, waving a hand vaguely. 'There's something, I have a feeling. . . . That it's just beginning for me.'

'Beginning? What?'

Again that vague waving of a hand. 'Santa Maria, I'm tired, I ache in every bone. I'll find out. Don't ask me now.'

A woman approached them. Tall and strapping, she had black hair, a narrow, high-bridged nose, and eyes as dark as

473

Paco's own. There's a striking one, Paco thought. A faint smile touched his dust-covered face. He still had an eye for the women.

'Martín,' she said, and Paco turned to watch her speak. 'A column. Fifty men, perhaps, and mules. Coming from the south.'

'French?'

Her face contorted. She spat on the ground. 'French, or those fornicating Poles, how should I know? We could ambush them, where the road enters the village.'

'With what?' Martín asked. 'With what, Leocadia?'

'With anything,' she said scornfully. 'With our bare hands. Where are your *cojones*, man? Didn't you want to stay with Palafox and fight? Has the fear got to you?'

'I'm supposed to keep these people alive.'

Another scornful look, and then an appraising one cast in Paco's direction. He had marched those three days with his head down, setting one foot grimly after the other. He had not seen the woman until now.

'Who's the fat man?' she asked.

Paco bristled, but then she smiled at him. 'No offense. You're fat, I call you fat. That's the way I am.'

Martín looked amazed. 'You don't know Don Francisco de Goya?' he asked.

'Goya? You're Goya?' Her face softened and suddenly she seemed almost shy. 'Hombre, what you have done. I've seen it in Zaragoza. I've seen it in Madrid. San Antonio de la Florida. The beauty of it.'

'Francisco Goya,' said Martín, 'this is Leocadia Weiss.'

Paco bowed over her hand, a small courtly gesture. Her eyes flashed fury. 'Don't call me Weiss. That stupid clod of a bullnecked German fornicator of goats,' she shouted. 'He's finished. He no longer exists. How I put up with him all those years I'll never know.'

The words came spitting viperously from her wide mouth. Paco missed too damn much. Being deaf has its advantages.

She took Martín by the shoulders with her strong hands and shook him. 'Well, are you going to fight them?'

'Why don't we wait and see who they are?' Martín said, trying to maintain his dignity.

They were a band of guerrilleros led by a tall bearded man with a scar on his face. They came slowly into the village leading a train of mules loaded with booty. Each man had a rifle, and other rifles had been roped to the pack saddles on the mules' backs. They wore tattered peasant smocks and trousers and rope-soled shoes, except for the bearded leader who wore what once had been a uniform, possibly a French uniform. It was so covered with dust it was difficult to tell.

The villagers regarded the guerrilleros sullenly as they made a run for the well.

'Stop,' shouted the tall bearded one. 'The mules drink first.' In a hard, cold whiplash of a voice. He unslung his rifle and looked around. The villagers disappeared like lizards into crannies in a wall. The refugees remained where they were. The guerrilleros waited.

After the mules had drunk, the bearded one went to the well and hoisted a bucket and spilled its contents over his head. He turned. The cooling water was good and brought a white flash of teeth through the beard. Paco saw the startling blue of those hooded eyes. He took a step forward. As blue as Mariana's. And the broad face, the leonine face, the thick head of hair, the chilling confidence in his manner –

'Antonio Francisco,' Paco said.

The bearded one looked at him. A smile touched those hooded blue eyes, and the ice left them.

'It's Goya, isn't it?'

Paco could only nod dumbly.

The younger man took him in the briefest of embraces and then stiffened and backed away.

'Once I told you we would meet again, Don Paco.'

He was shaking. He hoped Martín and the others did not notice. Five years. Five years of nothing. It wasn't death he had been waiting for. It was his son.

Napoleon, seated astride a bay gelding, felt the cold wind knifing through his cloak. Ahead of him loomed the high cliffs of the Somosierra, and beyond the mountains the road to Madrid. Behind him was the seacoast and the road back to France. He removed a glove and reached under the cloak and his green tunic to his waistcoat pocket. He removed a gold snuff box. He saw the reconnaissance party come riding back. The captain galloped up and saluted His Imperial Majesty.

'Eight or nine thousand men hold the pass, Majesty. No infantry attack will take it.'

Napoleon shifted impatiently in his saddle and took snuff. They had told him the Piedmont campaign was impossible too. They had told him Zürich was impossible. And Austerlitz.

He had put his older brother Joseph on the throne in Madrid and Joseph had reigned exactly nine days. Junot and Murat were bogged down. Napoleon had crossed the frontier to take charge of the Spanish campaign himself. You had to do things yourself, finally. You understood them better. They meant more to you. You could see the beauty of them. Spain now, Russia later, the flanks of the continent. The rest would be easy. The empire would extend from Gibraltar to the Urals. Spain was a delay. A small delay.

He cracked his whip, and the bay gelding reared. 'Light cavalry,' he said. It was late afternoon, a bleak November day in 1809. Damn the Spanish irregulars, he thought. More a thorn in his side than Ruffo's irregulars had been in Italy. You kill ten and a hundred rise. Guerrilleros. Little war makers. He would bring them a big war.

He sent his aide-de-camp for the captain of Polish lancers, a new company of them, fresh recruits never before tested in battle. Fewer than two hundred men.

'Take the pass,' he said, 'and you'll come back a brigade general.'

The Pole saluted. His men mounted and galloped off.

Napoleon watched the lancers reach the snow in the high mountains. Their horses floundered but continued to climb. He heard gunfire. His officers assembled the infantry. Let the Poles take the pass and the infantry could follow.

The infantry followed just before dusk.

Napoleon's bay gelding carried the emperor to the top of the pass at nightfall. The Spaniards had been routed. He saw the campfires of the Polish lancers, of the infantry.

He would put Joseph back on the throne himself. The road to Madrid was open.

The road south from Sevilla was the last hope, Jovellanos knew. In Cádiz the revolutionary junta might be safe. A peripatetic government, he thought grimly. A most peripatetic government, this junta that he commanded, while King Joseph sat on the throne in Madrid.

Cádiz, reached by a narrow neck of land, could be easily defended. If they could get to Cádiz. And if, one day or one year soon, the British would finally come. Jovino sighed. A handful of old men, and a handful of firebrands from New Spain, with no army to escort them. The last hope of Spain? He wondered. Perhaps he took himself too seriously. In defeat

476

men dream big dreams. Some were even dreaming of bringing Fernando back from exile, after the war.

He smiled haggardly. After the war, if the war ended the way they wanted it to end, they would get that deformed tyrant Fernando. Still, perhaps he was wrong. The guerrilleros had taken to calling him Fernando the Desired. They dreamed of Fernando's return the way Jovino dreamed of writing a constitution for Spain. To make Fernando a constitutional monarch. It would not work. Nothing would work.

Goya, Jovino thought. Even Goya. Painting Fernando from memory, looking regal and heroic astride a black horse. Goya continued to amaze him. The man, with his wild swinging ups and downs, had lived five lives already. Here he was in Sevilla now, sixty-three years old. No, sixty-four. And lean and hard. Marching with that bearded one they called, with a fine Spanish irony, Captain France. Captain France, who had trained an army in Aragon and honed it in the Gredos Mountains and the Guadarrama, and taught it to attack swiftly and melt away in the mountains like snow in a spring thaw. Well, Captain France might take them through the French lines to Cádiz. And then again he might not. No one told Captain France what to do. The hardest, coldest man Jovino had ever known. Odd how he resembled Goya. Despite that beard and the ice-blue eyes. Almost like father and son. Goya in the Gredos Mountains with him, and now here in Andalucia Goya, as grim as the ironically named guerrilla leader himself. Goya with his sketch pad, stalking across the battlefield like a force of nature.

It was cold in the convent in Sevilla where Jovino had been living. He got up and kicked the olive logs on the hearth into flame. Captain France came in.

No greeting. He never wasted words. 'We're finished in Andalucía. Except for you, we'd be marching north,' he said. 'How soon can you leave for Cádiz?'

'Tonight. Right now.' Jovino smiled. 'And my thanks, captain.'

'Thank Goya.'

He had seen it all, since Zaragoza. He had put it all on paper with his red crayons. Compulsively. There was no word for what he was doing. He did not think it was art. Horror is not art. Brutality is not art. Slaughter is not art. Rape is not art.

He had told Antonio Francisco, in Fuendetodos, what he

477

had told Martín in Zaragoza: 'We're as bad as they are.'

Hooded eyes looked into hooded eyes. 'That's not enough, Don Paco. We have to be worse. The victims have to become executioners. You'll see.'

Martín's prediction had proven correct. Verdier's troops were driven from the city. The refugees were planning to go back.

'Imbeciles,' said Antonio Francisco. 'Verdier will attack again. He won't be thrown out a second time.'

On a hot August morning Martín had assembled his people. Antonio Francisco supplied them with meagre provisions. Leocadia and a few others came to him. 'We want to go with you.' The rest were men, and not young. But some of Antonio Francisco's guerrilleros were no younger.

'You? A woman?'

'You'll have to live off the land. Weiss worked for Zapater. He taught me. I can find water. I can find food where no food can be found. Caramba, hombre, don't you see I can help?'

Antonio Francisco shrugged. 'Then come.'

They had raided the camp of the French, after Palafox had routed them, and they had half a dozen horses. Antonio Francisco mounted. Paco walked over. 'Where will you go?'

'The Gredos. Or the Guadarrama. Above Madrid. Napoleon's supply wagons have to use those passes, and his dispatch riders. They won't find it easy.'

'Take me with you.'

'Why?'

'I don't know why. I have to see it.'

Antonio Francisco looked at the flabbiness of the man. 'You'll need a horse, then.'

'I don't want a horse.'

On the long march to the Gredos the flabbiness melted. The round face seemed to narrow, and became more lined. But the eyes looked younger.

When they reached the Gredos Mountains, Antonio Francisco's fifty irregulars had grown to five hundred. When they were there a month, a thousand.

The first raid was very bad. Paco almost left then. He went with Antonio Francisco and fifty riflemen to a concealed place among the rocks above a narrow valley and a stream where poplars and willows grew. A small detachment of French cavalry came riding through the valley, heading north. A dispatch on its way from King Joseph in Madrid to Paris. King Joseph was one, Antonio Francisco said, who sent many dispatches.

'Soon he'll need a whole company as escort,' Antonio Francisco predicted, waiting among the rocks above the valley. 'And then a battalion.'

When the detachment passed directly below them, Antonio Francisco gave the signal. His men began to fire. Horsemen darted back and forth. They could not see their attackers. Some of them plunged into the stream. Others fired blindly. It was over in a few minutes. Those figures down there Paco thought, that look like toys. They're men dying.

'This is why it will take a company next time,' Antonio Francisco said.

He led his men down from the rocks. Most of them left their rifles behind. They had sabres and coils of rope.

Paco watched them hacking at the toys. Cleaving them from crotch to throat. Decapitating them. Butchering arms and hands. Blood flowed into the stream, reddening its waters. Ten men. He never knew ten men had so much blood in them. That first time he was sick. But he watched. He had to watch.

He saw the guerrilleros taking the toy parts of toy men and roping them to the branches of the willow trees that grew along the stream – a head here, a pair of fettered arms there, a torso, still crossed by its bandoliers, there.

They rounded up the horses. 'The French pass often this way,' Antonio Francisco said.

Am I mad? Paco thought. He was sitting with his sketch pad on his knee. He hadn't even been aware of it. With his red crayon he had drawn the dismembered corpses hanging from the branches of the willow trees in the valley alongside the stream.

Leocadia returned from the village with her mules. The men with her looked dispirited and hungry. They shook their heads.

'We'll get no more food there,' Leocadia said. 'I wouldn't drink the water either, captain. The French have come and gone.' Which meant the French had probably poisoned the well.

Paco went with Antonio Francisco, riding for once, to see what was left of the village. A few guerrilleros trailed behind them.

The village had been leveled, every house reduced to heaps of dun-colored stone. Snow covered the ground in patches. The people had been taken to the little central plaza and massacred. Bodies, already frozen stiff, were heaped near the well. An old man and a very old woman who had somehow escaped the French came out of the rubble screaming. They shook their fists.

'You! You! This, because we fed you!'

Antonio Francisco looked at the corpses. He looked at the old people. His face showed nothing. 'Bury them and be silent,' he said, and wheeled his horse around.

Paco could not like this man, his son. Nor could he hate him. The thirteen-year-old boy calmly predicting the apocalypse haunted him. Now the boy was a man, now he was the Horsemen, all Four Horsemen of the Apocalypse in one – Pestilence, War, Famine, Death. He killed with a coldness. It was his work, and he had become proficient at it. He ate on the run. He had no time for women and very little time for talk.

Once: 'How did your mother die?'

'She died in Paris.' And Antonio Francisco turned away to look at the fire.

Whole battalions were escorting dispatch riders through the mountains by then. Battalions that had to be taken out of the line forming in the west, where the British General Wellesley was preparing to cross the Portuguese frontier.

In a daze Paco walked the streets of Sevilla. It was early morning, only a few hours after the junta had taken the road south to Cádiz. By then Antonio Francisco's guerrilla band was a real army, five thousand men armed with French weapons, even a few mortars. But no artillery pieces. Artillery was for the Grand' Armée. Artillery made the Grand' Armée crawl.

Now those mortars were thumping, a steady pounding sound that Paco could not hear, pinning the Grand' Armée down in the center of Sevilla while the junta made its escape. Buildings burned like torches on Sierpes, that narrow, twisting street that was the pride of Sevilla.

They were dying in the streets, Frenchmen and Spaniards alike. They ran from the blazing buildings and were cut down by rifle fire while the mortars sent explosive shells looping in from the suburbs to strike in great bursts of flame. A small church was hit, and the shock wave buffeted Paco, knocking him down. He got up and in the rubble of the churchyard saw coffins broken open and mouldering corpses exposed. A few nuns ran past him silently screaming. French soldiers in gaudy uniforms and hussar hats pursued them, cornering them against one wall of the church, the only wall still standing. The nuns were still screaming. The hussars threw them on the ground and began to rape them. An officer came at a gallop and dismounted and Paco could see his face when he shouted: 'There's no time for that.' He mounted and raced away. The hussars looked at the nuns and drew their sabres. The nuns were on their knees praying. A priest came running from the ruins of the church, wielding a knife. He grabbed a hussar hat from behind and lifted the man's chin and drew the knife across his throat in a quick slash. A second Frenchman decapitated the priest with a single stroke of his sabre. Then they fled, leaving the nuns as they were, praying.

At noon Paco reached what was left of the central markets. Half the arcades had crumpled into rubble. Corpses were piled everywhere. Some of them had been there a long time and had begun to decompose. Even the city's gravedigger had taken up arms against the French. A boy of five or six, a handkerchief tied around his face against the smell, was methodically searching the bodies. He found a gold watch and a purse. He saw Paco and gave him a ferret-eyed look and darted away into the rubble.

Paco suddenly came face to face with a French soldier in a high hat and tricolor uniform. His left arm was in a sling, the sleeve bloody, his eyes bloodshot from gunpowder and fatigue. The hat was tall, narrow, brimless. A grenadier, of course, thought Paco objectively. No brim on his hat so he could throw the little bombs more easily. They stared at each other.

Sevilla, that could be a man's whole life. Or his death.

Paco wanted to live. He understood the meaning of the magic finally. To show this. That one power-mad man could cause such disaster. That an army could follow him blindly, for the glory of their nation. That the people could rise from fire and blood with an unspeakable barbarity of their own. That men could do this to one another. That the follies and bestiality he had etched in the *Caprices* were a foretaste of what men could do, and would do, in the name of God or in the name of No God as long as they lacked –

Lacked what?

A feeling of it all. Of living in this world, not my little valley in its fold of mountains, not my city, not my country, not my leader, not my king, not my emperor, not my life, but all of us here, now, accidentally sharing a generation, a time in history, a memory of all the dead past that still lived, all the past mistakes, a hope for all the future still to come, a feeling of humanity.

Any other way was madness.

To show that. To etch it. To attach the copper plates with the savage knowledge that he was right. This I saw. And this. And this. And all the other things I still must see. That men could do these things.

The Disasters of War.

The grenadier stood three paces away, bloodshot eyes fixed on him.

And if he kills me? Then I can't. It will die with me. The etching needle untouched, the copper plates unscratched, the Dutch bath waiting forever. And my son, who does not know he is my son, who does not understand his hatred, who will never see, never learn, never stop hating, who will find other enemies if we defeat the French? No I cannot die, this is not my time to die. I have to show him.

The grenadier with his good arm awkwardly drew his sabre.

A horseman came riding up, the horse reared, the hooves struck, the grenadier fell.

Antonio Francisco leaned down from the saddle. 'Mount behind me,' he cried, and his strong arm helped Paco climb astride.

'I've been looking all over Sevilla for you,' Antonio Francisco said, but Paco did not see those words.

An hour later the last of the rearguard abandoned Sevilla to the French. What was left of Sevilla.

The British General Wellesley, created Duke of Wellington after the battle of Talavera, drew up his army between the French under King Joseph and the Portuguese frontier. East of the French, waiting in the mountains, was Antonio Francisco with his five thousand guerrilleros. Far to the south, safe in Cádiz, Jovellanos and his junta wrote their constitution. It borrowed from the French constitution that had been perverted by Napoleon, and borrowed from the constitution of the young American republic, that as yet had been perverted by no one. There were South Americans with the junta too. They looked to the north and they called themselves liberals. It was a new word in politics. It would be the word of the future and the meaning of the future. It was why men were dying now. If Fernando would accept it. The people wanted Fernando. They did not understand a country without a king.

Antonio Francisco advised Paco against it. Leocadia berated him, Leocadia who had become, quite without realizing it, his protector. He certainly needed protection, she thought. Plodding across Spain with the guerrilleros, stalking across the battlefields with his red crayons. All he cared about were his drawings. He showed them to no one. She often brought him food because he forgot to eat. Sometimes she accompanied him when he took paper and crayons and went off for a few hours or a few days. More than once she saved his life. But this time? This time was of a surpassing ridiculousness.

'Do you want to die?' she demanded. 'If you want to die so urgently I'll get a gun and shoot you. Weiss was a coward. You don't have the sense to be afraid. I don't know which is worse.'

'I'll die when I die,' Paco said. 'Dying is nothing.'

'The idiot wants to paint Wellington,' Leocadia said. 'The idiot wants to cross the French lines and report at Wellington's tent and say, "I've come to paint your portrait." '

'He'll liberate Madrid soon,' Paco said. 'I want his portrait hanging there when he comes.'

'Do you think the French will care what you want when you try to slip through their lines?' Leocadia asked. 'Or the first British sentry who sees you, if by some miracle you get through?'

'I'm going,' Paco told her. 'Tonight.'

Antonio Francisco looked at him. 'I'll give you an escort.'

'I don't want an escort. A mule maybe.'

'Give him a spavined old nag and call him Don Quijote,' said Leocadia.

'A patrol,' said Antonio Francisco. 'To scout the French positions. They'll take you through and back.'

'I'm not coming back.'

Both of them looked at him. For almost three years he had been with the guerrilla band that had grown into an army. The guerrilleros loved him. Nuestro pintor, el Sordo. Our painter, the deaf man. Marches with the best of us. Faces death with a few red crayons. Never saw him carry a weapon, not even a knife. He fears nothing. We fight a war. He draws a war.

Sometimes, but with smiles, they demanded him. They had to match his bravery. They would miss him.

'What do you mean, you're not coming back?' Leocadia asked.

483

'That's why I want a mule. I'll do some preliminary sketches of Wellington, then make my way to Madrid.'

'There'll be fighting in Castile,' Antonio Francisco said.

'I'll get through first. Paint the portrait in Madrid. Have you a leather saddlebag for my drawings?' he asked Antonio Francisco.

'Nuestro pintor the idiot,' said Leocadia.

But an hour later in the dark she came to Paco's blanket roll. 'Wake up,' she said, shaking his shoulder.

'Is it time?'

'That depends.' She spread the blanket and got in beside him. 'A real man. I haven't made love to a real man in years. One like you, never. Idiot.'

He left with his mule half an hour later than planned. Leocadia did not say goodbye. She was sleeping in his blanket roll, a faint smile softening her hard handsome face.

Arthur Wellesley, Duke of Wellington, Duke of Ciudad Rodrigo, grandee of Spain and knight of the Golden Fleece, who spoke no Spanish and who spoke English only when absolutely necessary and then in the briefest of monosyllabic grunts, awoke with the dawn and called for his batman:

'Holmes!'

'Suh!' said Holmes, parting the flaps of the command tent, standing rigidly at attention and offering a quivering salute.

'Tea,' said the Duke of Wellington, and Holmes disappeared for that important brew.

Wellington dressed himself, concentrating on the simple task. Arthur Wellesley, then forty-three, turned to everything he did as if it were the most important thing in the world. One thing at a time. The next thing in its own time and its own place. The wound in his left thigh, for example. It had begun to itch. Itching was a good sign. Perhaps the dressing could be removed. He'd see the surgeon later. Reluctantly. He hated physical contact of any kind. He hated social contact. Military encounters were a different matter. Like the battle, there on the plains of Salamanca. He had routed the French under King Joseph. He snorted. King Joseph indeed. Napoleon's older brother. King first in Naples and then in Madrid. Did it mean he knew military tactics? It did not. Wellington had taught him a lesson in military tactics. Damme, he thought, but it's cold for July. Or maybe I have a chill. Infernal Spanish climate. But I've opened the road to Madrid. Damme if I haven't.

Joseph's army still intact, though. What do I do now? No orders to march on Madrid. No orders for anything. I only have one army. It needs a rest. Lord knows I need a rest. Back to Portugal, perhaps. Back across the frontier and then we'll see. There's no hurry about Madrid. Let those guerrilleros harry King Joseph a while. Pack of terriers yapping at his heels. I crossed the frontier to defeat Joseph, and I defeated him. Worry about Madrid later. One thing at a time.

Shave? He stroked his cheek. Bit of a stubble. Got to shave twice a day if I want to look decent. Must have a chill. Bit of a cold sweat now.

Arthur Wellesley slipped into his red coat trimmed in blue and gold. Hell with shaving, he decided. Where the devil's Holmes? Want that cup of tea.

'Holmes!' he shouted.

The batman appeared with a silver tray. Everything in its place. Pot of tea. Pot of water. Cup and saucer. Serviette. Good man, Holmes.

Holmes made room for the tea service on the table inside the command tent by pushing aside a few dispatches, a map, the duke's gilded, walnut-stocked pistol. He poured the tea. Wellington belted on his sword. Never use the damn thing. Feel naked without it, though. Holmes returned to his attitude of rigid attention. He knew you never spoke to the duke while the duke took tea. He knew you never spoke to the duke at all unless the duke invited your conversation. A young man, he had a puzzled expression on his face.

'Damme, Holmes. What is it?'

'An old Spaniard on a mule, Your Grace,' said Holmes uncomfortably.

'A what?'

'Francisco de Goya the painter, Your Grace. He *says*.'

'Goya? Well, is he? Or isn't he?'

'I really couldn't say, suh.'

The Duke of Wellington sipped his tea. He disliked painters. He disliked musicians. He disliked actors. Too much imagination, the lot of them. Too much temperament. That painter, what was his name, Lawrence? Did my portrait once. Couldn't get the sword right. Had him do it three times. Infernal nuisance. Talked too damn much. Every subject under the sun. All that yammering.

Goya thought. Been around a hundred years, I swear. They say he's the best painter in Europe. The Duke of Wellington scratched his itching thigh. He poured more tea.

'He wants to paint Your Grace,' said Holmes.

'No more portraits,' said the Duke of Wellington.

The tent flaps parted and a stocky gray-haired man carrying a sketch pad stalked in. He looked old, except for the eyes. Deep-set, hooded, they were still the eyes of a very young man. He wore a shirt that had once been white, torn at one shoulder and frayed everywhere. Gray wool trousers and rope-soled shoes, torn. A dirty big toe showed through. He needed a shave and he needed a bath. He said nothing at first. Just studied Arthur Wellesley the way you study an exhibit in a museum. Then he began to speak in Spanish. Deep voice. Just missed being harsh.

'What the devil's he saying?' asked the Duke of Wellington.

Holmes translated: 'He would have been here yesterday, except for the battle.'

'Damme, you mean he came through the battle?'

Holmes and the man who claimed to be Goya yammered at each other in that ridiculous language. Holmes was looking in the duke's direction while he spoke, and a strong square hand turned him around.

'The man's stone deaf,' Holmes explained. They went on yammering. 'Rode his mule right through the French lines,' said Holmes, and the Duke of Wellington laughed, a single bark like a rifle shot. The French. Right through their lines. He liked that.

'Then he, uh, rode his mule right through our lines.'

'Nonsense,' said the Duke of Wellington.

More yammering in Spanish.

'Well, through the artillery battalion, actually, suh. He insists on painting – '

'Insists, does he?'

The Duke of Wellington finished his second cup of tea. He was wondering how long it would take to regroup his British and Portuguese forces and retreat back into Portugal.

'He needs just one hour, Your Grace. To draw you. Says he'll paint the portrait in Madrid. Says it will be hanging there when you arrive.'

'We're not going there.'

Get there someday, though, thought the duke. Maybe this year. Maybe next. Who the devil knows? The P.M. Have to wait in Portugal for orders from the P.M. Madrid eventually. Good to have the portrait waiting. Fitting. If he's Goya.

'Ask him to prove he's Goya.'

The young-eyed old man cocked his head to one side while Holmes spoke. Holmes' eyes widened. He coughed into his hand, an amused little cough.

'Well?'

'He says, Your Grace, well, he says, prove you're Wellington.'

Cheeky bastard, thought the duke. Ought to throw him out.

But Goya, if it was Goya, had seated himself on a camp-stool, propped the pad on his knee and began to sketch with a red crayon. He made an impatient motion with his left hand. Head a bit more that way, not quite straight on. The Duke of Wellington moved his head. The crayon moved. No talk, at least, thought the duke with relief. A deaf man, and Spanish.

Goya spoke, and Holmes listened.

'Suh, he wants to know how soon you'll be in Madrid.'

Again that laugh like a rifle shot. 'Tell him I'm a soldier. He's a painter. Leave it there.'

Holmes spoke Spanish. Goya looked at his face. Goya's full lips drew down at the corners. He asked a question.

'This year, Your Grace? He wants to know, will it be this year?'

The Duke of Wellington gazed straight ahead vacantly, his face haggard, the wound in his thigh aching dully. Goya was staring at him, frankly unimpressed by the dazzling red coat, the medals, the conqueror of King Joseph.

'No orders,' said the Duke of Wellington, suddenly disliking the man. 'I have no orders about Madrid.'

Holmes translated. Goya sneered. He said something in Spanish and Holmes turned pale.

'What's he say?'

'I'd rather not repeat it, Your Grace.'

'Damme! What?'

Goya said something else. Holmes loomed over him menacingly. With his left elbow he impatiently nudged Holmes away. He couldn't see the duke. The crayon went flying over the paper.

'Well?' said the Duke of Wellington.

Holmes became paler still. 'The word in Spanish is *manso*, Your Grace. A bullfight term, I believe. I'm not sure what it means.'

Holmes was a bad liar. It showed on his pinched, pale face.

'Tell me.'

'A bull that refuses to charge,' spluttered Holmes. 'A bull – begging Your Grace's pardon – that you might say is, uh, somewhat less than brave.'

'What else?' asked the Duke of Wellington coldly.

'Well, the rest of it really was quite untranslatable. He said if you failed to take Madrid because you were, uh, *manso,* he would like to, uh, do something in the milk of your mother.'

Goya looked up. His deep-set eyes, dark and hot with anger, met the duke's somewhat vacant eyes.

'*Cobarde,*' he said softly. '*Cobarde.*'

Holmes' nostrils flared. He loomed over Goya again, and again Goya pushed him away.

'That's no bullfight term,' said Holmes in a flat voice. 'The man's called you a coward. Shall I thrash him?'

The Duke of Wellington's eyes narrowed. He stood and drew his sword. Goya reached for the pistol on the table, grabbed it up and pointed it at him, cocking it.

Abruptly Wellington laughed that rifle shot of a laugh. He returned the sword to his side. 'Spaniards,' he said. 'Small wonder King Joseph's had a rum go of it.'

Goya put the pistol down and resumed drawing.

'I'll take Madrid, Holmes. When my orders come. Tell him.'

Holmes told him, in a cold voice, and Goya said: 'Less bad,' and Holmes translated that.

Quite a fellow, thought the duke. Rides through the French lines on a mule, *and* our lines. Middle of a battle. Biggest battle of the war. No awe for me. Hero of the day. Just a subject he wants to paint. Madrid. Damme, now I really want to go there. What the devil's the matter with the P.M.?

In a while Goya showed the sketch to the duke. At first Wellington didn't like it. No knight in shining armor. No look of eagles in the eyes. No respect. Just a tired man of forty-three in a fancy uniform, his hair plastered to his temples with sweat, his cheeks shadowed with beard stubble, his eyes a bit vague with fatigue. But it's me. It's me right now. Suddenly the Duke of Wellington liked the drawing very much.

'Damme, yes,' he said, and came around the table to shake Goya's hand.

'Madrid?' Goya said.

'Madrid,' nodded the Duke of Wellington, and then the painter took his hand in a powerful grip.

CHAPTER THIRTY-FIVE

The Year of Hunger

So MANY PEOPLE DIED the year Paco Goya returned to Madrid that King Joseph ordered two new cemeteries built. It would be called, by those who survived it, The Year of Hunger.

Spain had to feed the Grand' Armée, and the armies of England and Portugal waiting indecisively on the Portuguese frontier.

Spain had to feed itself, and food tricked into the capital. Guerrilla bands cut most of the trickle off for themselves.

Madrid waited for Wellington. Paco did the portrait in fits and starts, and in mounting disgust for the general he had risked his life to see. Finally, it hung at the Academy of San Fernando, ready for Wellington's triumphant entry into the city. Wellington did not come.

Paco went out often, and saw a city dying. Wellington. Indecisive bastard. Duke of Nada.

Every day the high, two-wheeled carts came through the streets, drawn by scrawny donkeys. They jounced over the cobbles and dug furrows in the unpaved lanes. They stopped here and there, on the streets, to collect a corpse. Every day they were full of their grisly cargo, with emaciated limbs sticking out the side and the bodies piled high. Every day they made the trip to Joseph's two new cemeteries.

Children hurled themselves half-dead into the streets, lurching about with their bellies bloated from hunger as they begged for charity. They searched the garbage dumps for a vegetable rind or a moldy biscuit or a hard crust of onion bread. They stripped the trees of chestnuts and acorns. Soon they were eating bark.

Paco walked, his eyes probing restlessly. The nobility remained behind the high fences of their townhouses. He did not visit them though all their gates were open to him. He turned them away when they came to commission a new portrait. I'm retired, he said. There's nothing more for you here; there's nothing more for me anywhere.

Except the walking and the seeing and the waiting. He saw men and women chasing cats and dogs to slit their throats and take them home to the cooking pots. Soon they were chasing rats. Finally they stayed off the streets. There was nothing for them either.

The sewers overflowed, and the foul stench of sewer gas, the smell of corruption and death, hung over Madrid. Cholera and typhoid struck the starving population.

One out of every ten Madrileños died that year.

For every one that died, three refugees came in from the countryside. Napoleon's troops were burning farms and villages to keep food out of guerrilla hands, and the guerrilleros would put to the torch any village that harbored or provisioned the Grand' Armée. Both sides took and shot hostages. Both mutilated and quartered and decapitated them and hung them like laundry set out to dry on trees. As a warning it was very effective. As a means of swelling the population of Madrid it was even more effective.

Those who lived dreamed of Fernando, exiled in France, Fernando the Desired, who would return to Madrid one day in glory and give the people back their lives.

His years with Antonio Francisco had hardened him. He could not live through more than he already had. Death? Death was nothing. It had brushed his shoulder a hundred times. He had no fear, except the fear of not being able to complete his work. Still, he was not ready to etch the *Disasters of War*. He hid the drawings in the house on the Street of Disillusion, the house with its bare pantry and Josefa suddenly a gaunt old woman with withered cheeks and white hair. He went for days without talking to her. He went for days without talking to anyone. He sold a painting or two and bought food. Just enough to keep them alive. He felt guilty.

A letter came from Javier, who was in Cádiz. A child was born, a boy. Mariano. He was a grandfather. He went out to drink wine with Juanito, but before they could raise their cups to the new Goya, Juanito spoke of Fernando the Desired. Paco called him an idiot and left the wine on the bar.

The fear of not being able to complete his work. But what work?

Perhaps the *Dos de Mayo*, he thought. The terror in the horses' eyes, the bloodlust in the Mamelukes', the fury in the

490

people's. Perhaps he should paint that. But he wasn't ready
for that either. He had seen too much and felt too much. The
parts and pieces of it, somehow, had to come together. Napoleon, whose ambition could devastate a continent. The French,
who made the earth run red with blood. Antonio Francisco,
who did the wrong things for the right reasons. The victims,
determined to outdo their oppressors. The bloodlust of the
bullring spilling over.

A landcape. Dark gloomy clouds, blue-black and ominous,
like death in the sky. People fleeing on foot and in wagons,
cattle stampeding across the bare, ravaged earth. A single
donkey, saddled, waiting with patient stupidity for doom.

Doom in the form of a giant, the giant of Paco Goya's
dreams, the giant of Mariana sleeping with her red hair spread
on his pillow, nothing lasts, nada y nada y nada, the beast in
us all, no one is immune. The giant towering massively into
that death of a sky, his face fiercely bearded, his powerful
body nude, his fists ready to strike. Fists that could shatter
whole villages.

He painted that, all of it on a single canvas, slashing his
anger on with a palette knife, gouging his rage with his bare
hands, painting it all in one frenzied attack, like the final
battle of a war without end.

He did not name the painting. Later it would be called *The
Colossus.*

The French colonel was named Hugo, no relative of that
General Hugo who led the Grand' Armée's division in Guada-
lajara. A small, soft, fussy man, Colonel Hugo had once shot
fifty hostages because a captain of dragoons was stabbed to
death at the zarzuela theater. He looked like a shopkeeper.

Rubbing his plump, dimpled hands together, he said: 'Señor
de Goya, Señor Maella. The first painter to the king and the
former first painter to the king. This is a genuine pleasure for
me.'

He had summoned them to the royal palace and met them
in the anteroom of the palace galleries, a dim room with a few
chairs and a scarred old oaken table.

Mariano Maella was then in his seventies. His sight was going. He peered owlishly at Colonel Hugo through thick spectacles.

'The emperor has a museum in Paris,' Colonel Hugo explained, his Spanish decent enough, his face pink and smiling.
'The emperor likes trophies. Did you know that he brought an

491

obelisk that dates from the time of the pharaohs back from the Egyptian campaign?'

Mariano Maella shook his white head. Paco grunted.

'We require, señores, a representative selection of Spanish art through the age for the emperor's museum. We could think of no men better able to select it than you.'

'I'm almost blind,' Mariano Maella said.

'Don't understand,' Paco growled. 'I'm deaf as a stone.'

Colonel Hugo smiled a shopkeeper's smile. His pale blue eyes looked at Paco. 'Deafness should be no handicap, señor. How long will you need to make the selections?'

'Weeks,' Mariano Maella said.

'Months,' Paco said. He thought of the treasures, Spain's history in art, the Grecos, the Velázquezes, beyond the door that led to the gallery. Bonaparte wanted them. As trophies.

'I have a few names,' said Colonel Hugo. 'El Greco, Velázquez, Murillo, Zurbarán.'

'Greco wasn't Spanish,' Mariano Maella said, looking at Paco.

'Really?'

'He was Greek,' Paco said. 'Besides, he's been discredited in art circles. Figures too elongated. Tall saints with heads the size of oranges. Too damn religious, everything he did.'

'No, the emperor is not a religious man, that's true,' admitted Colonel Hugo. 'Then Velázquez, of course.'

Mariano Maella and Paco looked at each other again. 'If what the emperor wants to see is the triumph of Spanish arms, then certainly Velázquez is his man,' Paco said. 'No French painter ever showed French glory the way Velázquez painted the glory of Spain.'

'I see,' said Colonel Hugo. 'Murillo?'

'A drunkard. Fell to his death from a scaffold in a church. Painted like he was drunk too. But of course we have no idea what the emperor's tastes are.'

'I rather like Murillo,' said Mariano Maella.

'I don't,' said Paco. 'Zurbarán, now there's a man who could paint.'

'I never cared for him,' said Mariano Maella.

They began to argue about the merits and defects of the two painters.

Colonel Hugo cleared his throat. 'You will have three weeks,' he said. 'Select, shall we say, two dozen representative paintings. A few of your own, of course. I leave the choice to you. Three weeks, señores.'

Three weeks later, Mariano Maella and Paco had let their argument assume monumental proportions. They could agree on nothing except a few second-rate canvases which, Paco had to assume, had found their way into the galleries by mistake.

'Then three more weeks,' Colonel Hugo said, slightly exasperated.

When the time came, the two painters were still at an impasse.

'Perhaps outside the galleries,' Colonel Hugo suggested. 'Could that be the problem? Your Bourbon kings were no judge of great art, after all, any more than ours were.'

Paco agreed with that assessment. The Academy, he said. The Santa Barbara works. The houses of the nobility. It would, of course, take months. If the emperor wanted the very best.

Wellington had returned to Spain with his allied army, massing his troops in the north near Vitoria. It might, Paco and Mariano Maella knew, be the decisive battle of the war.

'You can't have months,' shouted Colonel Hugo. It was the first time he had raised his voice.

The two painters said they would hurry.

They finally selected a few second-rate canvases attributed to Velázquez, a Zurbarán and a Murillo, neither one a masterpiece, some early and indifferent Maella and Goya tapestry cartoons, and a dozen tepid canvases by Ramón Bayeu, who had died some years before.

'Who is this Bayeu?' asked Colonel Hugo.

'What?' said Paco in a shocked voice. 'You never heard of him?'

Both painters went into rhapsodies about the works of Ramón Bayeu. A genius. A second Rembrandt, the critic Cean Bermúdez had maintained. A second Rembrandt, the first painter to the king and the former first painter to the king solemnly agreed.

The colonel looked at the canvases, which had been put on display for him at the San Fernando Academy. He nodded slowly. The Bayeus, if done in Ramón's lukewarm style, were neoclassic, and the neoclassic school dominated painting in France.

The colonel asked if they could be shipped this week.

Mariana Maella laughed. 'Surely the Señor Colonel is joking.'

'Crates,' said Paco. 'Individual crates for each canvas. Packing material, skilled artisans. Three months, four. If we hurry.'

The colonel told them to hurry.

493

Dr Rodríguez-Pereira looked like a fashionable old gentleman who in peacetime might have taken his daily paseo on the Recoletos. He wore long white side-whiskers that curved in toward his jaw, a tall narrow-brimmed hat and a beige suit. With Doña Isabel, he spent more and more of his time at the Hospital General.

One day he banged his walking stick on the door of the house on the Street of Disillusion and demanded to see Paco.

'What's the matter with you, man?' Rodríguez-Pereira came right to the point.

'Nothing's the matter with me.'

'You're not painting.'

'I don't need the money.'

'Congratulations,' said Rodríguez-Pereira dryly. 'What's your charge for a portrait these days?'

'Twenty thousand reales, I suppose. Nobody can pay that kind of money. Except the nobility. And the French.'

'Paint them,' said Rodríguez-Pereira.

'What kind of man do you think I am?' Paco shouted.

And Rodríguez-Pereira told him quietly: 'In a word, selfish.'

Paco got up to show him the door.

But Rodríguez-Pereira thumped his stick on the floor and said: 'Twenty thousand reales for what? A day's work? Two? And you won't do it. The sick need money. The starving need it. The war casualties need it. But you sit here doing nothing because you won't paint a few Frenchmen or a count or duke or two.'

'French-lovers,' growled Paco. 'Collaborators.'

'My patients at the Hospital General aren't collaborators. There's no medicine for them, and very little food. Do you think they'd care where the money came from?'

'I'd care.'

'Not if you didn't keep a reale of it. Think of the good you could do, man.'

It was an argument Paco could not win. Soon it became known that Goya was accepting sitters again. He painted a whole new generation of Osunas. He painted actors and actresses who performed for the French in the theaters of Madrid. He painted two French generals. He painted rapidly, with all his old facility. He was tyrannical with his sitters, more so than ever. No conversation. No refreshments. Don't move a muscle. He discovered after the first few portraits that his eyes had dimmed. He had spectacles ground, and they perched low on his broad, flat nose while he worked. The French generals especially wanted to talk. This was the great Goya, after all. He told them to shut up.

With his brushes, with his palette knife, with a delicate split reed of his own invention, he put his impression of his sitters directly on canvas, in one sitting. He eschewed backgrounds. There was an at first unintentional and then intentional faint blurriness to his work, as if he had caught his sitters between breaths, between heartbeats. He began to like what he was doing. Soon he could almost forget whose portraits he was painting. Almost, but not quite. His years with Antonio Francisco had taught him hatred.

After a few weeks he grumblingly handed the money over to Rodríguez-Pereira. The old doctor was startled by the sum. 'It can keep the hospital going for six months,' he said.

'I can't help feeling like a traitor,' Paco said sourly. 'Look at this.'

This was a ridiculously ornate medal, the Order of Spain, which King Joseph had presented to him. Madrileños called the medal the Eggplant. Bulbous, over-large, it did resemble that vegetable.

'I'll never wear the damn thing,' Paco said. 'I'm through. I'm disgusted with myself.'

'You could,' said Rodríguez-Pereira cautiously, 'give us another six months for the hospital.'

Paco merely grunted. Doña Isabel's smile became angelic.

Rodríguez-Pereira thumped the floor with his stick and asked: 'Have you an hour to spare?'

'I have all the time in the world. I told you I'm through.'

They drove in Rodríguez-Pereira's berlin to the hospital. Sunlight barely penetrated the grim old brick building. It stank of unwashed bodies and sickness and death. A few tired nurses were making their rounds. Thin mattresses covered the corridor floors, and on each lay a mutilated war veteran. They reached out supplicatingly to Rodríguez-Pereira.

The wards held old people and children. 'Famine hits the very old and the very young worst of all,' said Rodríguez-Pereira. The children had distended bellies and big eyes that stared without hope at the doctor. Two men came by carrying a dead girl on a stretcher.

'They're all as good as dead,' Paco said in a shocked voice.

'You'd be amazed what money can do. What food can do, and medicine. The French will sell, for a price. We can save half of them now. Maybe more.'

Doña Isabel made hand signs to Rodríguez-Pereira. He

nodded.

'Even the hopeless cases,' he said. 'Waiting to die in terrible pain. We can ease the way for them, with money for opiates.'

They went back along a dim corridor, past the war veterans. A soldier whose legs had been amputated above the knees looked up at them. One of the stumps was festering. Paco could smell it. The soldier's eyes were wide with terror. Doña Isabel knelt and touched his forehead. The terror faded. He smiled up at her weakly.

At the end of the corridor they reached a large room that held a single patient. Here at last there was sunlight streaming in through big windows.

A shriveled mummy of a man lay on the bed. He looked very small. His eyes were glazed in a face as puckered as a walnut. Even his bald skull was creased and furrowed. He saw Rodríguez-Pereira and raised a hand like a hawk's talon. His dry cracked lips began to move.

'Hopeless case,' said Rodríguez-Pereira. 'Cancer of the bowel. Terrible pain. We can give him opiates now, thanks to you.'

They approached the bed. 'I think you know him,' Rodríguez-Pereira said softly. 'Didn't you paint him once?'

'Who is it?' Paco couldn't take his eyes from the shriveled walnut of a face, from the sunken eyes living deep inside with their pain. He had a feeling that something momentous was about to happen.

They were standing at the side of the bed. 'Adiós, Dr Peral,' Rodríguez-Pereira greeted the dying man.

The lips moved. Paco watched them intently. 'Adiós? There is no God. There never was.'

Doña Isabel stroked his forehead. A hawk talon brushed her hand away. Dr Peral gasped. He tried to sit up. He could not.

'You'll have opiates tomorrow, doctor,' Rodríguez-Pereira said.

The lips moved. They tried to form words.

' . . . anyone to kill me?' the lips said.

Paco watched. He had to watch.

'Out of my misery,' the lips said.

Rodríguez-Pereira shook his head gently, but looked at Paco and formed the words: 'The worst part of it is, sometimes I think he's right. He knows what he has. He wants a swift death. Who can blame him?'

'Did it myself,' said the dry, cracked lips. 'If they needed it. The gift.'

Peral brushed Doña Isabel's hand away again.

'Can't anyone?' asked the lips.

'You'll have opiates. No more pain, I promise.'

Peral mumbled deliriously. Paco could not read his lips and then suddenly he could.

'Did it. When hopeless. So easy. When not hopeless even. Only trying to help. Got out of hand. Can't anyone – ?'

'Easy, old fellow,' Rodríguez-Pereira said. He looked at Paco. 'Seen enough?'

'No.'

'For the Santo,' said the lips.

Rodríguez-Pereira tugged at Paco's shoulder. Paco leaned forward over the bed.

'For the queen and Godoy,' said the lips of the dying man. 'The gift. I killed. Kill me. Now.'

The mummy that had been Dr Peral tried to sit again. Cords stood out on the stalk of a neck. The head fell back.

'Easy. So easy. The gift of death.'

'We'd better leave,' Rodríguez-Pereira said. 'He's delirious. He doesn't know what he's saying.'

'The duchess,' said the lips, and Paco felt himself freeze in an attitude of rigid attention.

'For the queen and Godoy. Pain. Wanted her to suffer,' said the lips. Very softly. Paco could read them. Doña Isabel could read them. Rodríguez-Pereira could not hear the words Doña Isabel turned away.

'Poison. From Italy. No, India. Weaker every day.'

Paco leaned over the mummified face. 'What duchess?'

'India,' said the lips. 'Couldn't control. *I* killed. Kill me. Now.'

Paco shook the fleshless shoulders. 'What duchess?'

'Borgia poison . . . thought. . . . '

'Who was she?' Paco asked, unaware that he was shouting.

'Most beautiful in Spain,' said the lips. 'Thinner every day. Weaker. Nothing to be done.'

Again Paco shook the fleshless shoulders. Rodríguez-Pereira tried to pull him away.

The eyes, sunken deep in the mummified head, became crafty. 'I tell. You kill?'

'Yes,' said Paco in a whisper. 'Yes, yes.'

A third time the man who has been Dr Peral tried to sit. He rose on his elbows. Spittle flecked the dry, cracked lips.

'The Duchess of Alba,' he said, and fell back and was dead.

CHAPTER THIRTY-SIX

Josefa

IT WAS ALL THE PALM SUNDAYS in all the cities where men celebrate the triumphal entry of Christ into Jerusalem, in all the years they have ever celebrated it.

Bells pealed wildly, so wildly from every church in the city that all the birds of Madrid rose from all the trees to flutter and wheel in great flocks against the sun-scorched blue Castilian sky that hot, windless summer day in 1812.

French carriages and the carriages of the nobility drove hard for the Toledo and Embajadores Gates before the roads were closed to them.

General Hugo and his twenty thousand picked troops protected their hasty departure, General Hugo whose son Victor would one day remember and write of what he had seen that day when the Duke of Wellington entered Madrid by the Segovia bridge.

Every window and balcony in the city was decked with the red and gold of Spain and the Union Jack of England. Redcoats marched to fife and drum.

The women of Madrid hurled themselves at the closed ranks of Wellington's soldiers, offering wine and fruit and palm fronds and laurel crowns and flashing smiles and invitations for the night.

A mob surged around Wellington, covering his boots, his sword, his hands, his horse with kisses.

Wellington himself, impassive, the quintessential Englishman untouched by what he called this Mediterranean madness, made his slow way toward the center of the city, his eyes, vague as Goya had painted them, glancing uneasily at those who rode with him in their own improvised uniforms, the guerrilla chieftains.

The triumph had been theirs as much as Wellington's, though neither the victorious duke nor the vanquished Grand' Armée would admit it. They had harried the French in the Gredos Mountains, in the Guadarrama, in the Picos de Europa, in the high passes of Andalucía, everywhere that guerrilla bands could strike and run and strike again. Most of them had *noms de guerre,* and these names were known to every Madrileño as once the words of Cayetana's song had been known.

Behind Wellington rode those called the Shepherd, the Doctor, the Priest, the Grandfather, the One-Arm.

At his left, in a flamboyant uniform that managed to dim Wellington's own red coat, astride a coal black horse, came the Shoemaker, who had kept General Hugo's army at bay in the Guadarrama for years. At Wellington's right, in his tattered French uniform, rode Captain France, most famous guerrilla chieftain of them all, that Captain France who had darted like a will-o'-the-wisp through all the provinces of Spain, that Captain France with his fierce beard and scar and hooded eyes.

Many of the guerrilla chieftains had never seen Madrid before. The size of the city awed them. The crowds made their horses shy. The cries of joy and the frantic shouts surprised them. Until that day they had not known they were heroes. They had done what had to be done. Above the clamor of the brazen bells, above the shrill of fifes and the roll of drums, above the tumult of a city released from the conqueror's yoke, above the shouts of *Viva Velintón,* they heard, like thunder, *Vivan los guerrilleros!*

Some of them almost wished they were back in the mountains.

Captain France did not. He was coming home.

On the eve of their march into the city, he had grudgingly been granted a brief interview with Wellington. The Englishman had been ill at ease until an aide had informed him that Captain France had studied in Paris and was not only an hidalgo but a man of title in Spain, a marqués.

'What's your name?' Wellington had asked. 'Your real name?'

'Captain France will do.'

Those strange, hooded eyes, where have I seen eyes like

499

that before? Wellington thought. 'They tell me you're a marqués,' he said.

'Whoever they are, they talk too much. I'm a Spaniard.'

They were speaking French. 'And now that it's over, Monsieur le Marquis?'

'The hating stops. The killing stops.'

'And you Spaniards plow the soil and prune your vines, is that it?' Wellington asked dryly.

'Now we get a constitution, and a parliament, general. Your brother's with the junta in Cádiz, isn't he?'

'Sir Henry's the king's ambassador to the so-called revolutionary government, yes.'

'What do you mean, so-called?' The eyes went cold.

'The people want Fernando, my dear fellow.' In that dry English voice.

'Of course the people want him. We were fighting for him, in a way.'

'Are you truly that very naive? As king, Fernando will be a worse tyrant than his mother.'

'He'll accept the constitution. He has to. We did it all for him.'

'My dear fellow. He'll tear up that pretty piece of paper and throw it in your faces.'

'You're wrong, general.'

'You'll see.'

Now, riding at Wellington's side, the Segovia bridge behind them, the crowds pushing from all sides, the smile, the glorious freedom smile on every face, Antonio Francisco was thinking: The hating, the killing are finished. A man can let himself be human again. But he remembered the hacking of bodies, the burning of towns, the poisoning of wells. Hatred and killing, pursued too long, became a habit. Even Goya he remembered. Horrified at first. And then it was just something to draw with those red crayons of his.

Wellington was different. Wellington fought a war with no more passion than a priest who lacked the calling. Wellington had told him, at the end of their brief interview: 'Soult still has an army in the field, you know. He may fight yet.'

'And you?'

'Orders, my dear fellow. It all depends on orders.'

Wellington, the conquering hero, with that tepid islander blood in his veins, could understand neither hatred nor love the way a Spaniard could.

We need more than Wellington, Antonio Francisco thought.

And we need more than a constitution. Spain is even less ready for a constitution than France was. Passion is a good thing. Passion is living. But we're too damned passionate. We need a leader. Someone to rally around.

The coldness left his hooded eyes. A woman reached up to embrace his boot. He almost smiled.

We need Fernando. Fernando the Desired.

At the last minute, as a gesture he could not resist, Paco had included his portrait of Fernando, bulbous head, pouter-pigeon torso and all, as one of the paintings to be sent to Napoleon in Paris. Now, fittingly, he thought, it was the last of the paintings to be uncrated. The last because, with luck, Santa Maria we are going to need that luck, we won't have Fernando any more than Napoleon will have his portrait.

All day the carpenters had been carefully uncrating the paintings. They weren't masterpieces, any of them, but they would stay in Madrid. They belonged in Madrid.

Paco watched the last nail prised loose, and there was Fernando's ugly face staring at him.

Mariano Maella grinned. 'That one you should have sent. As a gift.'

All the paintings, the Zubaráns, the Murillos, the Goyas, the alleged Velázquezes, the many Rámon Bayeus, were stacked against the wall of the courtyard in the San Fernando Academy. It was good, even, Paco thought, that the Bayeus hadn't gone. His joke. His little joke. He hadn't told Josefa.

Paco was feeling good. The day before, he had stood with the crowds lining the Segovia bridge, watching the triumphal march. Antonio Francisco had ridden at Wellington's right hand. His face had seemed less brutal. The ice had left his eyes. Perhaps, finally, he could lead a normal life.

And Javier. Now that the war was over, Javier would return from Cádiz, Javier who would never amount to anything, but at least there was the grandchild. He had never seen the boy Mariano.

He had not allowed himself until now to think about Godoy. Godoy and Cayetana. Peral murdering Cayetana for Godoy. The thinking would come later, and the deciding. Peral surely had suffered enough. God, if there was a God who cared, had seen to that. And Godoy, in exile in France? Might as well be in exile in Turkey or India. India, where the poison came from. Santa Maria, I'm too old, I'll never go to France, I'll never go anywhere, there's nothing to decide.

But he remembered the numbness, the complete emptiness, there in the hospital. Rodríguez-Pereira had had to lead him from the room. Rodríguez-Pereira had not known why. Paco had seen the lips moving. Doña Isabel had seen them. Rodríguez-Pereira had heard nothing.

'Is it Peral? I had no idea you were that close.'

'It's nothing.'

If Antonio Francisco had taught him hatred, what was there to teach him mercy and forgiveness?

How many Frenchmen had died, slowly, tortured, how many corpses had been mutilated, how many Spaniards told to bury their dead and be silent because a night had ended as it had, with two children coming together afraid of the dark, with the birth of a life?

No, there had been enough killing. Madrid, here, now, is my life. I must get to know Antonio Francisco. I must spend more time with Josefa, she's been waiting all her life for it. I want to be the doting grandfather to little Mariano. What's Godoy to me now in all that France to the north? I'm an Aragonese peasant, an old *baturro*. All that France to the north, I'm even beginning to think like one. . . .

He smiled. He felt as much at peace with himself as he ever could. It was the last time he would smile for years.

A hand on his shoulder. He turned and saw Juanito.

'It's Josefa,' Juanito said.

Juanito drove him home in an open landau, through the heat of the afternoon and the frenzy of the still-celebrating crowds.

'Bad?' he asked, just the one word.

Juanito nodded and tried to speak and did not speak.

He asked no further questions. Let her live. She had to live. I've been a bad husband to her. There's still time. There are things we can do together, a shared life. I ask for nothing else, whoever you are. Just that she lives.

Maria del Carmen, fat now, her gray hair in a bun, wearing black as she had for years, stood at the side of Josefa's bed.

Josefa's eyes were open vacantly. A faint smile, a forever smile, touched the thin dead lips. Scattered on the bed were several plates of the *Caprices*. Her hand clutched one, the two-headed likeness of Cayetana.

As if trying to understand her man in the final seconds of her life.

CHAPTER THIRTY-SEVEN

Cafe Apiñani

HIS STUDIO REEKED OF ACID. Acid stained his fingers. Acid ate through the sleeves of his smock, leaving them ragged. Acid seared his soul.

He was etching again, returning as he often did in despair to his copper plates and etching needle, his Dutch bath and box of asphaltum. He saw nothing else, felt nothing else, lived nothing else. Soult was on the march. Wellington left the city, and the French returned. The deliverance of Madrid had been a dream, a brief dream, but Paco Goya was hardly aware of that. His face was haggard, his hair wild, his eyes had that preternatural glow. He worked twenty hours a day. There was always a jug of wine at his side, and it sustained him. It had an acid taste.

The plates, the finished plates, were stacked on a shelf. The ideas for the scratching of the needle he could not hear burned their way into his brain. More plates waited to be done. He worked on them through the second French occupation, unaware that it was worse than the first. The hated minister of police, whom he had painted for the hospital patients, returned from Aranjuez to institute a reign of terror against the liberals. Most of the guerrilla chieftains went underground.

His knowledge was of other horrors. Josefa's death had liberated him to etch those horrors. Not hatred, but love and understanding, he had thought at the Academy, as she lay dying at home. Nothing now. All foolishness. Men are human, but mankind is a beast.

He attacked the plates with a relentless savagery. He attacked the French who had brought the apocalypse across the Pyrenees and he attacked the Spaniards who responded with a brutality of their own. He attacked Napoleon and he attacked

503

Antonio Francisco. He had no plan, no focus, no direction. He fought the beast with his etching needle and his acid. He fought the callous indifference of a God who did not care. Stark black and white in a world gone mad. The beast in us all, no one is immune.

People made nations and nations made war.

A mouldering corpse rising half out of the grave while fiendish faces loom above, rising from the grave long enough to scrawl what he had found below, a single word, a terrible truth – *Nada*.

Old people at the well, dirty patches of snow on the ground, the corpses piled high. *Bury them and be silent.*

Refugees streaming from Zaragoza, a mother dragging a child looking back in terror. *This I saw.*

A tree. Fettered to it a nude corpse, his genitals hacked away. Fettered to it a headless, armless torso. Fettered to it a pair of arms. High on a branch a man's head. *Great deeds – against the dead!*

Corpses in a heap, a single figure still alive, hemorrhaging from the mouth. *For this you were born.*

The single standing wall of a little church and a hussar officer preventing rape because he needs his men for more carnage. *There's no time for that.*

Villagers watching with smug approval while a stripped and bound collaborator receives a heated ramrod up his rectum. *Populacho.* The mob.

The dumping into a common grave of mutilated dead men. *Charity.*

A rope around a man's neck, tied too low on a tree, his mouth a rictus of terror, and two French soldiers pulling at his legs while a third braces himself against the tree and kicks at his back so that the rope will slowly strangle him. *¿Por qué?* Why?

A high-wheeled cart and against a dark wall the grave-diggers lifting the white body of a beautiful girl in among the other dead. *Cartloads for the cemetery.*

And madness in a bat-winged monster with an avariciously human face sucking the blood from a dead man. *The results.*

A wolf, the ferocity in man, sitting on his haunches while the populacho watches him write on parchment with a quill: *Mankind, you yourself are to blame.*

He knew those etchings would not be printed in his lifetime. It did not matter. Other eyes would see them.

Would it help? He did not know. It was a thing he had to

do; it was why he had been afflicted with a deafness that freed him from human company when he had to be free, that isolated him, that gave him the wild strange dreams and the madness so like reality.

Once Asensio Juliá came to the studio. Paco had finished a dozen plates, and Juliá, a gentle man, was shocked. 'Maestro,' he said, 'maestro, why must you etch such things?'

He had to turn Paco around and say it again so Paco could see the words. The older man looked at him. For a long time he said nothing. He made a vague gesture. Go away, I have work to do. The younger man waited patiently, and at last Paco Goya said in a very soft and almost gentle voice, his eyes looking sadder than Asensio Juliá had ever seen them: 'Don't ask me why I etch them. Ask men why they do them.'

The proclamation, affixed to the wall directly across the street from Café Apiñani, stared at Juanito accusingly. Every day he saw it, and every day he told himself, Me? – I'm not interested in politics.

He had not been interested in politics when he had offered sanctuary to the guerrilla chieftains either, after Wellington led his army back into the field and King Joseph returned to Madrid. It happened, though, that the tunnel that led from the cellar room of the café to the streets of the flea market was, well, Juanito told himself, available. It also happened that the guerrilla chieftains' lives would be forfeit if King Joseph's army found them. Juanito hid them in his tunnel and somehow found food for them. If sometimes they slipped out to ambush a French patrol or throw a bomb into a restaurant full of French officers, could Juanito help it? All he was doing was offering them a place to sleep.

The proclamation, however, was a severe test of Juanito's indifference to politics. Such proclamations had been affixed to walls all over Madrid soon after Wellington had won the final battle of the war at Vitoria and the French had fled north across the border, soon after Fernando the Desired had returned to the royal palace as King Fernando VII. The proclamation was no problem in the beginning. Juanito could not read. But one day Captain France came and took Juanito outside and read it for him.

That was after Captain France had gone north with a delegation from the Cádiz junta to meet Fernando the Desired at the border, his veteran guerrilleros coming out of hiding from God only knew where to form a guard of honor for the liberal politicians who had written the Constitution of 1812. Captain France had even shaved off his beard for the occasion. Juanito was startled when he saw him. Except for the man's height and the scar on his face. A coincidence, of course, because the Good Lord could manufacture just so many types of eyes and noses and lips, but still the resemblance was uncanny. Then Juanito remembered a day long ago in the patio de caballos, and a little boy holding Mariana's hand. How had he been introduced? The marqués of something or other.

'Captain, are you a marqués?' Juanito had asked before the guerrilla chieftain left for the border to welcome Fernando the Desired.

'What difference does it make?'

'I was just curious.'

'A marqués,' said Antonio Francisco, 'will be just like anyone else under the new constitution. High time, don't you think?'

'I'm not interested in politics,' Juanito said.

The marqués, if he was a marqués, came back from his long journey to the border looking very subdued. He had not thanked Juanito until then for the long months in the tunnel. He thanked him and said: 'That cellar room of yours, is it available for meetings?'

Most of the Lovers of Ugliness were in exile in France. Juanito missed their talk and laughter. Amusing talk, even if the subject had so often been politics. Juanito said the room was available.

'The constitution,' Antonio Francisco said with a baffled look in his eyes. 'We presented it to the king. Very formally.'

Juanito did not understand constitutions. He waited.

'The king shoved it in his pocket without reading it. Then he placed the members of the junta under arrest Then he gave my guerrilleros each a little silver medal for our work against the French and told us to disband.'

'What did you do?' Juanito asked.

Antonio Francisco shrugged. 'We were going to disband anyway. Our work is finished. We defeated the French, we forced Bonaparte to send us back Fernando.' The eyes looked more baffled than before. 'Why did he arrest them, the liberals of the junta? They were the government. Holding Spain together for him.'

Juanito, of course, did not know why. 'The room is yours whenever you want it,' he said. 'Wine on the house, Don Antonio Francisco.'

'How did you know my name?'

Juanito had remembered the introduction in the patio de caballos. 'I don't know. I must have heard it somewhere. Do you know Goya?'

'Do I know Goya?' Antonio Francisco laughed. 'He marched with the best of my guerrilleros. You should have seen him stomping through the mountains in a pair of rope-soled shoes. Drawing those pictures of his. He's amazing. How old's the man?'

'Old enough to be your father,' said Juanito.

Their eyes met. Antonio Francisco shrugged and said: 'Yes, I suppose he is old enough to be my father.'

A few weeks later the proclamation appeared all over Madrid. The vast majority of those Madrileños who could read seemed to approve of it, Juanito observed. They read, and nodded, and sometimes cheered.

Antonio Francisco came and had a glass of wine and said: 'Come outside. You can't read, can you?'

Juanito admitted without embarrassment that he could not read.

At the top of the proclamation in black ink was a cross. Antonio Francisco read the words under it, his voice harsh:

'The Constitution of 1812 is declared null, evil and noxious. Its authors and adherents are guilty of crimes against the State and the Crown will be punished.

'The Holy Office of the Inquisition, abolished by the anti-christ King Joseph, is restored to its full properties and powers.

'All periodicals except the Madrid *Gazette* will cease publication. Publishers, printers, distributors, and readers of such periodicals are guilty of crimes against the State and the Crown, and will be punished.

'The writing, printing, distribution, and reading of pamphlets of any nature, unless authorized by the Crown, is likewise prohibited.

'All those suspected of collaboration with the French will be tried by a Tribunal of Rehabilitation. It is the duty of every loyal Spaniard to report evidence of such collaboration to the tribunal. Those failing in this duty will be adjudged as guilty as the collaborators themselves.

'By order of His Most Catholic Majesty Fernando VII the Desired.'

Juanito scratched his head. 'Why's he still called the Desired?'

'It's his official title,' Antonio Francisco said.

A few men wearing blacksmiths' leather aprons came along the narrow street. They stopped before the proclamation. One of them could read, and did so. The others nodded approvingly. 'Death to the constitution!' they shouted. 'Death to liberty! Long live the Inquisition! Long live Spain and the king!'

As they left, Antonio Francisco shook his head. 'The people. We fought and died for them. We fought and died for Fernando. The Desired,' he said with a terrible scorn. 'It's what the people want. They don't know. They don't understand.' Plaintively then: 'Juanito, why don't they understand? Can't anybody make them understand? He'll be more a monster than Bonaparte.'

'The Pyrenees,' Juanito said. 'I guess they're a pretty big mountain range.'

The scar was livid against the tan of Antonio Francisco's face. Juanito expected his eyes to look like two chips of ice. But they were gleaming with suppressed tears.

If Antonio Francisco had taught himself hatred, rationally, coldly, so that he could go about the business of killing Frenchman, His Most Catholic Majesty Fernando VII the Desired had learned hatred effortlessly. He had learned it from his toothless whore of a mother and his fat, fatuous, fiddling father; he had learned it from the overdressed, preening upstart Godoy; he had learned it from the guards at the chateau of Valençay, where he had spent his exile in France, the guards calling him Prince the way you call a dog Prince; he had learned it from those idealistic fools in Cádiz who had thought they could foist a constitutional monarchy on him; and he had learned it from the guerrilla chieftains who had marched insolently with the junta to present the constitution which he pocketed without reading and abrogated in an instant.

He was still young, barely thirty years old. He had a long reign ahead of him. Spain would tremble.

Fernando, on a cold autumn afternoon in 1815, was waiting in the Hall of Tapestries in the royal palace. The man he had sent for was late. He had a tendency, an insolent tendency, to be late.

Turn your head to the right, Highness. No, to my right, not yours. That way. Now you almost have it. Don't move. That really is very good, Highness. As if Fernando were a model paid by the hour. Deaf lout!

508

Observe the shadow, Your Highness. You cast the longest shadow in the portrait. Had he said that? No, it had been his friend, that critic fellow with his glib talk. While he stood by, pretending not to understand when it suited him not to understand.

He would understand now. The tribunal had sentenced him to death by the garotte. In absentia. He had ignored the tribunal's summons. Too much the figura, too much the national institution, to be bothered by the mechanics of his own demise. At Fernando's orders, the tribunal had not insisted on his presence. A deaf man, a deaf old traitor, Fernando had said, could offer no valid defense. The case was clear. As clear as the case of that guerrilla chieftain called the Shoemaker who had been making inflammatory speeches about the need for a constitutional monarchy. A few hours of persuasion in the dungeons of the Cárcel de Corte had revealed the man's real name, Juan Martín. A few days of persuasion would reveal where the other guerrilla chieftains were hiding. They were a menace. They had done their own thinking too long.

But first the Señor Painter. I have a few scores to settle with the Señor First Painter. Odd that the minister of police should recommend clemency, exile instead of death. Have to look into that one of these days.

It is going to be, Fernando told himself, a most pleasant audience. And, thinking that, he heard the major-domo called out:

'The Most Excellent Señor Don Francisco de Goya, first painter to the king!'

Fernando watched the painter come in. Stocky and still strong, with those broad shoulders bulging a well-tailored gray suit. Carrying a walking stick and swinging it jauntily. Eyes sad but surprisingly young in the broad, leonine face. Hair mostly gray now, but he doesn't look his age. He'll never look his age. He'll die before he has the chance to.

Fernando did not ask him to sit. The majo-domo shut the door softly behind him.

Look at him, Paco thought. *El Deseado*. The Desired.

Fernando wore a suit of tobacco brown velvet, as if to remind Paco that he had once refused to paint him in that color. He wore a fringe of bangs over his bulbous forehead to hide the prematurely receding hairline. His eyes were small, dark, close-set. They darted from Paco to the tapestry-covered walls and back. The tapestries were biblical scenes.

509

'You'll notice,' said Fernando, 'that none of your tapestries hang here, Don Paco. Our father always liked them. We always found them too flamboyant.'

Paco glanced at the wall-hangings. 'Second-rate work,' he said mildly. 'Cartoons by José de Castillo, copied from Italian paintings. There's no accounting for taste, sire.'

'Desired,' said Fernando. 'You're to call us that.'

Paco shrugged. '*Deseado,*' he mumbled.

'Your case,' said Fernando, 'was referred to the Tribunal of Rehabilitation.' He sat on a high gilded armchair. His spindly legs dangled to the floor, one buckled shoe tapping impatiently. The chair was too big for his misshapen torso. It made him look like a hunchback.

Paco stood before him, swinging his walking stick.

'Stop doing that. Stand still.'

'Sire.'

'*Deseado.*'

'*Deseado,*' mumbled Paco.

'The tribunal found you guilty on two counts,' King Fernando said.

'Santa Maria, guilty of what?'

'Collaboration with the French, for one. You painted for the French during the occupation.'

Paco remembered Dr Rodríguez-Pereira and the hospital. He wouldn't give this misshapen tyrant the satisfaction of an excuse. 'I was first painter to the king. Joseph was king. I painted.'

'The antichrist Joseph awarded you the Order of Spain.'

'The Eggplant? I never wore the thing. Ugliest decoration I ever saw.'

'We consider that irrelevant,' said Fernando.

The imperial we, Paco observed. The little monster's learned a thing or two from Napoleon. 'What?' he asked, cocking his head and tapping an ear.

'We consider whether or not you wore it irrelevant!' shouted Fernando.

'It wasn't irrelevant to me. I wouldn't have been caught dead with that damned thing hanging around my neck.'

Fernando smiled. It was not a pleasant smile. 'You'll be caught dead with a garotte around your neck, Don Paco.'

He waited to feel fear. He did not feel it. He had lived a long life and, all things considered, a good one. What difference did it make now? 'You said two counts, sire. What's the second?'

'Consorting with the guerrilleros.'

Paco's eyes widened. This time he really thought he had mis-understood. 'I'm sorry, I must have missed that.' He put on his spectacles and peered at Fernando's soft, fleshy lips.

'We said consorting with the guerrilleros.'

'Funny. That's what I thought you said. What's wrong with consorting with them? They gave you back your throne.'

'We took back our throne. They wanted a constitution, like the traitors in Cádiz. They're enemies of the state.'

'Enemies? I thought they were heroes.'

A smug smile settled on the big-browed, big-jawed, long-nosed, sunken-mouthed face of the young king. Santa Maria, he's an ugly one, thought Paco. Like to paint him that way. He's no fool, though, like his father. Couldn't pull the wool over those eyes.

'We have one of them in the Cárcel de Corte right now,' the smug face said. 'The one called the Shoemaker.'

Then Paco felt fear. The Shoemaker caught, the Shoemaker probably undergoing torture – could the Shoemaker tell them where to find Antonio Francisco? He had to find Antonio Francisco himself, had to warn him.

He said: 'You ought to give him a medal. He pinned down General Hugo's army in the Guadarrama for years.'

The smug smile vanished. Fernando leaned forward. 'In the case of the first painter to the king Don Francisco de Goya, the tribunal recommended death by garotte. The case was referred to the minister of police. In consideration of your past services to the Crown and your age, he recommended exile. The case was then referred to us. What are we going to do with you, Señor Painter?'

No change of expression on the big leonine face. Even the young eyes remained sad, but Paco laughed. He couldn't help the single bark of laughter, oddly like the Duke of Wellington's rifle shot of a laugh.

'The minister of police? He must have liked the portrait I did of him.'

'We have refused the recommendation of clemency. No flattering portrait can save you now, Señor Painter.'

No, Paco thought. No flattering portrait could save him. But the two huge paintings he had labored over all summer were something else again. They had to save him. He had to walk out of here and find Antonio Francisco.

'The garotte!' shouted Fernando. 'You'll get the garotte.'

'Not,' said Paco calmly, 'unless Your Majesty is more a fool than his father was. I've brought you a gift. Or rather, brought

Spain a gift. Had them brought, actually. Biggest canvases I ever did. Twelve feet across, the pair of them.'

'Paintings? It's a little late for that, Don Paco.'

Paco said nothing. He swung his walking stick.

After a while Fernando asked: 'Where are they?'

Paco jerked his thumb to the left. 'In the big corner room.'

'The audience chamber?'

'Is that what it is? Crowd in there. Dukes, counts, a general or two. Some priests. Looking at the paintings, last I saw. Never made a sound, any of them. Just looked.'

'You left the paintings there? At a meeting of the Council of State? How dare you! '

Paco shrugged. 'Walls are covered with red velvet, sire. Sets off the paintings rather well, I thought.'

Fernando regained his composure. He even laughed, an ugly laugh. 'That's not important – now.'

'It's important to me. It's my neck we're talking about.'

Fernando stood. Paco, no tall man, towered over him. And knew he was dominating him. Whatever those paintings were, Fernando had to see them since the Council of State was looking at them right now.

The major-domo escorted them through the armoury and the little room called the tramway to the velvet-walled audience chamber. It was a large, bright corner room, its arched ceiling covered by a Maella mural. The majo-domo announced His Most Catholic Majesty, and the dozen or so men in the room knelt perfunctorily and then turned to stare again at the two mighty canvases propped against the far wall.

On the left was *The Second of May 1808*. Against a murky greenish sky loomed the buildings of the Puerta del Sol. Turbaned, wild-eyed Mamelukes on white horses fought off the assault of Madrileños wielding knives and sticks. The dead lay in their own blood. A French infantryman, on his back, dying, tried to reach for a bayonet. A man, knife poised, dragged a pantalooned Mameluke from his horse, blood streaming from wounds in the Mameluke's chest. Horses looked crazed, Mamelukes looked crazed, the mob looked crazed. All of it just under life-size, horses big and muscular, the fury and the killing everywhere, the bloodlust. Madrid rising against its oppressors in one chaotic, unplanned assault. The painting was chaotic too, with no focus, no design. An instant in time, anarchic as war itself, an impression, an incredibly vivid impression of carnage.

On the right was *The Third of May 1808*. The consequences,

early the next morning. A hill, like the scarred surface of the moon. Beyond it dimly a convent. A French firing squad in their hussar hats, bayonets fixed, lined up in a row in their greatcoats against the chill of the night. A pile of corpses on the ground, fallen any which way. Others waiting to fall before the withering blast of point-blank fire – one with his fists in his mouth; one tonsured, cassocked, on his knees, hands clasped in prayer. One, the central figure, catching the lantern light with his white shirt and outflung arms, his face a study in terror and pride. In a moment he will be dead. In a moment they all will be dead, their executioners faceless, in a line like a wall, the rifle barrels gleaming. In a moment, yes. But it is not yet that moment. Again an impression, the figures jammed together, the paint applied with palette knife and split reed and bare hand, brush strokes hardly in evidence. An instant in time, caught forever, out of perspective, haphazard, unplanned. Death has no perspective, no plan. Death strikes in the cold harsh glare of a lantern, from the waiting rifles, in the middle of the night. The central figure, with his arms outspread, with his terror and his pride, could have been Christ.

The glory of resistance, and the madness.

Fernando saw only the glory. They were Spaniards, killing heroically and then dying heroically. So that he could return.

The futility of war. The madness of it. He missed that.

They crowded around Goya – dukes, generals, the new Grand Inquisitor of the Holy Office. They smiled at him. They thumped his broad shoulders. They shook his hand.

'Christ, Christ embodied in a common peasant,' said the Grand Inquisitor.

'The war of independence,' said a general. 'Immortalized in two paintings.'

'They'll hang in Madrid as long as there is a Madrid,' said the young Duke of Osuna.

Fernando looked at all their faces and then gestured to Paco. They walked back silently through the tramway and the armory to the Hall of Tapestries. The room, with its four hangings, its Francisco Bayeu ceiling, its baroque furniture, seemed tawdry and vulgar. Fernando did not sit. He took snuff with trembling fingers.

'You planned that, didn't you?' he said, his face empty, his voice empty. 'I can't have you killed now. You know that.'

Paco did not reply.

'Deaf old fool,' said Fernando. He could not stop trembling. 'You were no fool today.'

33 513

Paco waited, wondering where Antonio Francisco was, wondering if the one called the Shoemaker knew, wondering if the Shoemaker would tell.

'You'll remain first painter to the king,' Fernando said with a murderous look in his eyes.

Paco made the barest suggestion of a bow.

'In name only, señor. Keep out of our sight.'

And then, because the two paintings had touched him as deeply as they had touched the others, Fernando said: 'If we did not admire you so much, we'd have you garotted.'

He was dismissed. He left the palace and walked quickly through the cold autumn afternoon to Café Apiñani. Juanito did not know where Antonio Francisco was. It began to rain.

The arm hung heavily like a slab of beef on a hook at the slaughterhouse. His shoulder was the hook and below where the musket ball had smashed the bone there he could feel nothing. Meat. Dead meat. Like what passed for his brain. The raid, the rescue attempt, had been a disaster. Everything had gone wrong.

Whether the guard had taken their money and then betrayed them or had taken it and been unable not to betray them was of no importance. The guard lay dead in the dungeon room in the Cárcel de Corte where Juan Martín, the Shoemaker, had died of a hemorrhage after they had done something ineptly and overzealously to his genitals. There was not much Juan Martín could have told the corregidor's police, Antonio Francisco thought, the pain at last beginning to lurch now in his smashed shoulder with every step he took. Maybe they just enjoyed poking a man's eyes out and doing that to his rectum and his genitals Juan Martín could have revealed nothing about the movement for the good and probably fortunate reason that there was no movement. Nobody would depose Fernando. Nobody could depose Fernando. But, God and Holy Mother of God Who Does Not Exist, there has been enough of killing. Even if we could. But we can't. We are nothing now. In the hills we were something. Oh, we were something. We were butchers like those who had done that to the Shoemaker. It is no longer worth it, even if we could rally our old people. Let Fernando reign. Let him take Spain to hell with him. Perhaps it is what Spain deserves.

The other wound, the one he did not want to think about because he knew it was very bad, felt like a knife slipping in through his ribs every time he breathed, every time he took a

514

step in the dark, cold, hard-raining night, the Shepherd on one side of him supporting him, the Grandfather on the other side, a fleshwound in the meaty part of his lower leg and the Grandfather making a steady keening sound like the wind that lashed the rain at their faces. The others were dead. The one called the Priest was dead. He had been a priest, too, when Napoleon had emptied the monasteries. He had worn his cassock in the Picos de Europa and led a band of a thousand men who had now gone their separate ways, back to farms and shops and forges, because the Desired had returned. The Priest had died against a wall in the dungeon, his hands clasped piously or protectively before his face, the musket ball smashing through his piety and entering his mouth and lifting the back of his skull off. The one called El Médico was dead. El Médico had never been a doctor as the Priest had been a priest, but he had had some skill in the treatment of musket wounds and knifings. It had not helped him in the dungeon where they had gone to rescue the Shoemaker before the Shoemaker, already dead, could reveal all their identities. A guard had plunged his bayonet into El Médico's belly, low, and with a single lifting motion had brought it up to slash through tendons and El Médico's breast bone all the way to the throat. The one called Trousers was dead. Antonio Francisco did not remember how he had died in the abortive attempt to rescue the Shoemaker who was already dead when they had got there and who had either talked or not talked before that overzealous atrocity committed on his genitals.

Three left, and the Grandfather suddenly a very old man who, when he wasn't making that keening sound like the wind that lashed the rain at their faces, was saying over and over in a dead voice, 'I'm too old for this, I have nowhere to go, there's no one to hide me.'

The second wound, the one that made the bloody froth escape his lips each time he breathed, was bad. The lung, he thought, not liking to think about it. A small matter of a musket ball in the lung. That and the arm that hung like meat from a hook at the *matadero*. He would be good for nothing for a long time. It did not matter. Nothing mattered. No one was going to rally the people for the simple reason that the people did not want to be rallied. Maybe they were right and he was wrong. The Shoemaker had certainly and permanently proved himself to be wrong. When free speech and public meetings are prohibited, you do not stand on the corner near the post office in the Puerta del Sol and exhort the people to

515

do this and that in the milk of the king's mother. You do not laugh in the face of the corregidor's police when they come to haul you away. You realize it is hopeless and you run. The people hadn't even been very interested. The Shoemaker had not run. He had been led away struggling. Bit one of the corregidor's police in the arm and they said by the time he reached the cárcel, his feet dragging, his face bloody from the beating they had administered, he had been foaming at the mouth like a mad dog. He had been the bravest and wildest of the guerrilla chieftains. Half that and half a brigand; he really hadn't been able to tell the difference after the first few years of the war. He had been doing a good thing and a bad thing and calling himself a hero. He was no hero now. Not even a martyr.

'I can't go on much longer,' the Grandfather said.

'Shut up, old one,' the Shepherd said. 'It isn't much further.'

'It hurts too much,' said the Grandfather, limping slightly in the rain.

'Look at him, you coward,' said the Shepherd with only faint contempt. 'He's not complaining.'

'He's young. I'm an old man.' But the Grandfather limped alongside Antonio Francisco, the side where his arm hung, while the Shepherd half-supported Antonio Francisco's weight on the other side.

Antonio Francisco was surprised that he could walk. Or rather, lunge and stumble and right himself and keep going. The Grandfather was useless. The Grandfather was a little old man with a big fear. What he had had in the mountains, in the Somosierra when Napoleon had passed that way, he had lost. The Grandfather was nothing.

They were all nothing, and they might be less than nothing before the night was over. The one called One-Arm had been left behind, dying, his splintered ribs showing bone-white and jagged through his coat, the stump of his left arm thumping the hard stone floor of the dungeon like a fish's flipper flopping on the ground out of water. One-Arm might live long enough to talk. One-Arm had always talked too much, a harmless enough propensity if you are talking to your lieutenants behind in the dungeon where they had done that to the Shoemaker.

'Not Apiñani's,' Antonio Francisco had told the Shepherd after they had fought their way up from the dungeon and out of the Cárcel de Corte and into the rain-lashed little Square near the Plaza Mayor. 'We'll implicate Juanito.' He liked Juanito, but it would not have mattered if he had not liked

Juanito.

'Then where?'

'I don't know where.'

The Shepherd had grabbed his good arm and they had lost themselves, the three of them, in the maze of crooked streets behind the Plaza Mayor. For a time they could hear the pounding of boots behind them and the shouting of the police, and then they could hear nothing except the rain and, when the wind dropped, the faint wheezing sound of the breathing through the hole in his chest the musket ball had made.

They reached a shack in an alley in the flea market. Water stood ankle deep in the alley. The door of the shack was locked. The Shepherd fumbled for his keys and dropped them and cursed and removed his weather-slung musket, one musket to fight the Desired and his police, the Desired and his army, the Desired and the people, and with the butt of the musket he smashed the flimsy door. They went inside into absolute darkness. The darkness did not matter. They knew the stairs and they knew the tunnel beyond the stairs, God Who Did Not Exist alone knew why it was there. The tunnel twisted but it was narrow and they could feel the rough wall on either side with their shoulders, the Shepherd and the reluctant Grandfather could, with Antonio Francisco between them. They were going to Café Apiñani after all and now, finally, Antonio Francisco hurt too much to argue. A few hours of rest. All he wanted now was a few hours of rest. In the tunnel the breathing sound the hole in his chest made was very loud.

Juanito had sent for Paco and for Dr Rodríguez-Perira. It would be, he thought, a night like this. Of course. It had to be a night like this when the skies open suddenly and the rain pours down and the patrons in the upstairs room linger, not wanting to face the rain, and when more come in off the wet, cold, rainswept street.

'Two beers.' He drew the beers.

'Tinto, hombre.' Five cups on the bar, and he filled them with red wine.

A priest came in. 'What a night,' he said.

'What a night,' Juanito said.

The priest sat with his broad backside to the olive wood fire and his cassock streaming. Black and white. A Dominican. A Dominican's all we need, Juanito thought. The Dominican ordered a jar of wine.

Paco, wearing a drenched woolen cape and carrying a stout

walking stick, appeared in the doorway. Juanito came out from behind the bar and went over to him.

'Antonio Francisco's downstairs,' he said in a voice softer than a whisper, his lips forming the words carefully. 'Wounded. I sent for Rodríguez-Pereira.'

Paco stared at his face and hurried downstairs.

A few minutes later the splashing clop of a mule's hooves could be heard outside. Rodríguez-Pereira entered. The men at the bar turned and looked at Doña Isabel.

'Who is it?' Rodríguez-Pereira asked.

'Musket wounds,' Juanito said in that voice softer than a whisper, this time with his lips hardly moving.

'A street fight?'

'Would you treat him if I said it was the police?'

Rodríguez-Pereira gave him a scathing glance. 'Where is he?'

Juanito jerked a thumb toward the stairs. 'Listen, hombre,' he said, in that less than whisper. 'It's the one they used to call Captain France. Goya's with him.'

The doctor waited.

'He's Goya's son,' said Juanito, and nothing showed on Rodríguez-Pereira's face. 'I don't know if Paco knows. I don't know if he ought to know. He's no young man. You understand?'

'Then why tell me?'

'He's dying, I think. He may say things. Paco's been through enough. Too much. ¿Comprendes, hombre? They're friends. Only friends. Goya marched with his guerrilleros in the mountains. That's all.'

All the times I could have talked. God Who Isn't, I wanted to talk. The way the painter cared for my mother, helped her, the special way he looked at the boy, her son, me. The resemblance. Nobody could mistake it. When I was a child it confused me. It did not confuse me later. I knew. I know. All the times I could have talked, but something always held me back. A perverse Spanish pride. Let him make the first move, the first gesture. I won't speak the words unless he speaks the words. My father. And now when I want to I can't. No, I can't. Words. I can't form words. I try. I keep trying. Tell him something. A word. One word. The breathing of the hole in my chest, and then plugged with a handkerchief by the Shepherd; at least that's over, I don't have to hear my body dying. Can feel it though. The froth, bubbly pink, when I breathe. Talk, damn you. One word. Let him know you know. A hard table under my back and it feels strangely soft so that if I don't hold on and grip with all my strength I will sink into it and keep on sinking and then I can never tell him that I know. Couldn't have picked a better father. So proud of him I could burst with it. Mucho hombre. War, the kind of war we fought, the kind of war we had to fight, is an abomination. Had to? Maybe we did not have to. But he had to see it. He had to draw it. He had to show it. To everyone. Forever is close now. I can feel it. Talk. Talk, God Who Isn't damn you. Show him you know. Look at those eyes. Young, but with all the world's sadness in them. Just watching me. The pride. In both of us always. The God damn Who Isn't pride. Well. Look. Here comes the doctor, who couldn't save me now if he was Jesus Christ himself. Who Isn't. Famous. I rate a good one. The one with the deaf-mute nurse. Doesn't look his age either. I bet I look my age now. I bet I look my age and then some. Give or take a few years. Mostly give. Yes, doctor, it is rather grave, isn't it? *Muy grave. Gravísimo Prognóstico nada.* That's all right, no, don't worry, you can't hurt me any more than it already hurts. Did you ever feel a knife sliding between your ribs every time you took a breath, doctor? But the woman's hand is soothing. Never had time for women. Never had time for anything. Hated the French because they corrupted their own ideas. Mother taught me. Good ideas. Enlightened, and then the corruption. We could use a little of that enlightenment down here. I thought it would be simple. Nothing is simple. The people don't want it, father. The people aren't ready. Perhaps they never will be ready. Show it, father. No one can show it the way you can, the way you had to. I understand that. Never told you. Never told you anything I wanted to tell you. The killing and the brutality were necessary. Tell yourself that often enough and you'll believe it. But you'd better hurry because you don't have much time left. Or much anything. It is too late to make him understand. See the funny old woman in the madhouse, the one over there all in black with white hair, all in black if the keeper keeps an eye on her; otherwise she is all in nothing and screaming she won't, she will, no she won't pose in the nude. The one time and the pointing fingers and the simpering laughter. Enlightened. I knew then that I had to kill. I had to kill and kill and kill and now I wish I believed in something because I would beg forgiveness. Of him? No. But if I could tell him. If I could say the words. They're talking, the doctor and my father. He's deaf. Reads lips. I'm deaf now too, funny, isn't it? Ears stuffed like that breathing hole. Do you find the breathing hole interesting, doctor? Sorry if I seem to be foaming at the mouth like the Shoemaker. I really am quite sane. But if only I could say it. Enough so that he will know that I know.

'I could remove the musket ball,' Rodríguez-Pereira said.
  'And then?'
  'He'd die in terrible pain. I could leave the ball where it is.'
  'If you did?'
  'He'd die. Less pain.'
  'How long?'
  'An hour. Two. No more.'
  'Don't operate,' Paco said. He looked down at the younger man's eyes, like looking into his own eyes. The eyes were trying to say something. They were trying desperately. There was a sadness in them, and an eagerness. The lips were moving but forming no words. Every time they moved the pink froth came out.

Paco leaned over him. 'Antonio Francisco,' he said. The desperate eyes, young, trapped, looked at him without comprehension. 'Antonio Francisco,' he said again. The trapped eyes examined his face. 'Antonio Francisco, listen to me. Those things you did. The war. You had to do them. Everybody knows that.'

The trapped eyes looked at him and looked at him.

'I want you to know. I want you to know, Antonio Francisco – '

But the eyes, the trapped eyes, were finally too much. He felt his heart beating in his throat, beating in the ears that could not hear, and he turned and fled upstairs and when he went to Juanito the tears were streaming down his face.

'I can't,' he said. 'I can't. He's dying.'

He thought he had whispered the words. He had shouted them. The men in the bar looked at him. The Dominican looked at him. Juanito gave him a large cup of cognac. 'Chico,' he said. 'Chico,' his hand on Paco's shoulder.

Paco drank the cognac in a single eye-stinging, chest-warming gulp. He heard, he actually thought he could hear, the rain pounding on the cobbles outside. It was the pounding of his heart, the pounding in his ears, and then the terrible creaking in his ears, the creaking screaming howl of the witches of his nightmares, and for a long moment everything went away and then everything came back and he saw the Dominican fingering the big crucifix around his neck and walking downstairs.

Paco ran after him. The Dominican had neared the table where Antonio Francisco lay dying. The Dominican raised the crucifix and began to mumble words that Paco could not hear and that Antonio Francisco did not want to hear.

Paco grasped his shoulders, beefy under the thick cassock, and spun him around. 'You! You! Get out! Leave him alone, you!'

The priest's eyes looked grave and then they looked mean, but he shrugged and went back to the stairs and climbed them.

Paco stood near the table. He reached out and took Antonio Francisco's hand in his two big square hands. The hand was cold. Antonio Francisco's face had a pinched look. The pink froth bubbled from his mouth. The eyes looked up. The blue lips moved and formed no words.

The hacked and mutilated corpses, Paco thought. If only I didn't see the hacked and mutilated corpses like toys while they hacked and mutilated them, and Antonio Francisco watching and not stopping the hacking and the mutilation. But I want to say it. I have to say it. I cannot let him die without saying it.

'If you were my son,' he began. 'Can you hear me, Antonio Francisco?'

The eyes moved up and down.

'If you were my son,' he said, and his throat swelled and he choked on the words. The trapped eyes waited. They had taught him death. But afterwards, the two or three times Paco had seen him here at Café Apiñani, he had been so different. Gentle. Sad. Remembering.

Trying to forget.

'You did what you had to do,' Paco said, and knew it wasn't enough. He had said it before. But if he told him? His son would die hating him. Your mother. Your mother might have had a good life, except for me. She might have kept her sanity, except for me.

How did your mother die? She died in Paris.

The younger man's lips moved. Almost the pale ghost of a smile. And they began to form words. No sound, but words on the lips. The cold hand gripped his. He was barely aware that the ones called the Shepherd and the Grandfather had gone. The hand gripped tighter. 'Once I told you we would meet again, Don Paco.'

His throat swelled again. He could not speak, and then he could. 'If you were my son,' he said gruffly. 'You are my son, Antonio Francisco.'

And the lips moved one final time. 'I always knew, father. It made me proud.'

CHAPTER THIRTY-EIGHT

The House of the Deaf Man

THE OLD GARDENER was no witch. That much he knew. He ought to have remembered the old gardener's name, though. Some days he almost had it. He would sit in the sun on the hill looking down across the river at the royal palace or watching the old gardener working. The gardener was the oldest friend of his life, except for that one in Zaragoza. Tending the vines now, in the garden of the house above the river, or weeding the tomato plants. He really ought to have remembered the man's name. Sometimes the man would talk to him, patiently, but he would watch the lips and see no words and after a time he would resume his seat on the stone bench that looked across the river to where the king ruled Spain with an iron fist. From there the palace looked very small. A toy palace, like the toy figures hacked and mutilated so that Napoleon would have to send a battalion to escort a dispatch rider. The gardener was a marvel. He diverted a stream through the property and the stream fed a marble fountain in the garden and he would sit for hours watching the water rise and sparkle in the sunlight.

The witches came out of his ears and out of his dreams and were everywhere in the large, two-story, brick and adobe house. They had little figures of heads, arms, legs, other parts of the body. They had jars of cemetery earth. They had various burned objects to cause hatred, and they had human skulls and the dried hearts of pigs and frogs and the bones of birds.

They had a jar of earth from the deepest dungeon in the Cárcel de Corte. They had wax candles and grains of wheat and barley, and bread soaked in the blood of a living man. They had magical cords tied with three magical knots and they had a large sack filled with the feathers and beaks of hoopoe birds from the sanctuary of Doñana, where once he had loved the woman for whom, so long ago, he had bought this house. They had powders and drugs without number and they prayed nightly to the devil and no longer flew from town to town without God and without Santa Maria but stayed here in the house above the river, cackling in the ears that could not hear and trying to tell him he must do something to the house, the big, empty, cheerless house, so gloomy inside with its bare white-washed walls, but they did not make it clear what he should do. Whatever it was, they would continue to haunt the house until he did it.

Sometimes he remembered things. Long ago things. He remembered deeding the house on the Street of Disillusion to his son Javier, Javier a prematurely middle-aged man with a simpering wife. He remembered deeding most of his paintings to Javier. He kept the painting of the woman he had loved in the sanctuary, with the words 'Only Goya' written in the sand at her feet. He kept enough money for his needs. Occasionally a man came from the Banco Nacional, driven in a spectacular coach with two fine white horses, and there were papers to sign. He dutifully signed them, and a pouch of silver reales or gold escudos would be left by the man who came in the spectacular coach. The man's name was Meléndez and he said he was a lawyer, and he said Don Paco's investments were sound, the advice he had been given long ago by Cabarrús the banker had been sound. He remembered no one named Cabarrús. Soon the lawyer Meléndez had been exiled to France, according to the new bearer of the pouches of reales and escudos, a bulging-eyed old man named Cean Bermúdez who looked vaguely familiar and who always tried to talk and left with tears in his eyes.

He remembered the burial of his son. The burial was not in hallowed ground. He did not think it would bother Antonio Francisco. He remembered the old gardener had lost his café after the death there of Antonio Francisco. He remembered a meeting with the corregidor and threats of the garotte or exile, and the intercession of a man named – he thought the name was Wellesley, he was the British ambassador, brother of a general he once had painted. That was when he had deeded everything, or almost everything, to Javier. The next day the witches came out of his ears and were everywhere.

He remembered the old gardener and the pop-eyed man and a doctor with a nurse who could not talk discussing him as if he wasn't there. He still had enough interest to read lips then. Javier was there too, and when Javier said something he did not see, the old gardener said: 'If you suggest that again, I don't care who you are, I'll kill you.'

Javier, a flaccid, paunchy man – Santa Maria, how can a man have two sons so different? he remembered thinking – had turned pale and not mentioned it again, whatever it was that he had mentioned.

The doctor with the nurse who could not talk had said: 'No, there's no point committing him at his age. He'll be trouble to no one.'

'He's not coming to live with us,' said Javier. 'He frightens Mariano.'

'He frightens Mariano's father,' said the old gardener.

'He needs a quiet place in the country,' said the doctor, and the nurse who could not talk looked at him with the smile of an angel and for a moment he didn't hear the flapping of bats wings or the cackle of witches.

All that was years ago. The old gardener, who was not a gardener then, came across the Segovia bridge with him. For a time there was an old woman with the gardener, but one day she died and was buried in hallowed ground in Madrid, and he had gone across the bridge then to the funeral. The witches followed him, quietly, so that the others couldn't hear. They remained outside the hallowed ground, though. They were afraid of the hallowed ground. They waited for him just outside the cemetery.

He did not mind them. In a way they were his companions. He thought of painting them. He thought of painting other things. The old gardener hired a cart and went into Madrid and purchased an easel and canvas and pigments and oil and brushes and brought them back to the house above the river. Every day the old gardener watched him looking at them. Once in a while he might pick up a brush and examine it, or stare moodily at an empty canvas. The old gardener would smile at him and say words that were not words, but he would put the brush down after a while and go outside and sit in the sun and stare at the toy palace across the river.

'Why don't you paint, chico?' the old gardener asked him once. 'It is a good thing to do what you know how to do. A man becomes a ghost if he doesn't.'

That day he had condescended to read lips. 'Why didn't you fight the bulls?' he asked, and immediately wondered why he had asked it. Had the old gardener been a bullfighter? He wished he could remember things. He wished he could remember times and places and names. He wished he could remember to change his linen and wash his clothing and make his bed. The old gardener did those things for him sometimes. He wanted to pay the old gardener a salary, but the man smiled when he suggested it, a gentle smile, a forgiving, loving smile.

Once when Javier came with his grandson Mariano, he lifted the boy high over the wall at the edge of the garden so that the boy could stare down across the river at the toy palace, and he said, 'A wicked king lives there,' and the boy, high in the still-powerful arms, began to cry, and Javier took the boy away from him and the visit was short.

'I meant no harm,' he told the old gardener, bewildered.

The gardener shrugged. 'You had a son, and you have this one.'

He recalled, sometimes he recalled, the madhouse in Badajoz. He knew he belonged there, on a big stone slab on the floor, painting with an invisible brush on a non-existent canvas while the witches cackled. But the knowing, he asked himself, wasn't the knowing a sign that he really wasn't mad? A madman thinks he is sane, thinks the others are crazy. It would go away. It had to go away because he had work to do.

'You've had a full life, rich in pleasure and in pain,' the witches told him. 'Aren't you content?'

'No,' he said.

One day at noon while he was sitting on the stone bench in the garden he saw a mule-drawn cab cross the bridge and mount the dirt track to the house. A woman climbed down, a dark-haired, attractive woman, and not old. It was a warm spring afternoon and she wore a black mantilla and a black dress. She was big and strapping, and her face was handsome rather than pretty. She reached up and helped a little girl climb out of the cab. They walked up the lane to the gate. The cabman followed behind with two large cases. The gardener looked up from his vines and then looked at Paco, who went to the garden gate and told the woman:

'No one lives here.'

The little girl, six or seven years old, he thought, was hiding timidly behind the woman's skirts.

525

'They told me I'd find you here,' the woman said, and something compelled him to read her lips. 'They told me things about you, things I refused to believe. And if I refuse to believe a thing, it isn't so.'

'Go away,' he said.

The woman snorted. 'Look you,' she said, 'I came all the way from Barcelona. Even in Barcelona they were saying those things. A lot of nonsense, I said, and I still say it. Goya living like a hermit? Goya finished?'

She must have raised her voice, because it brought the gardener on the run. He said something and the woman told him:

'Keep out of this. It's between Goya and me. Who the hell do you think you are?'

The cabman, holding the two heavy cases, shifted his feet. 'You staying?' he said.

The woman took out a purse and paid him, and he shrugged and put down the cases and walked along the path. Soon the cab was descending the hill toward the bridge.

Paco looked at the woman. He said suddenly: 'Leocadia. Leocadia Weiss.'

'Don't call me Weiss.'

'Juanito,' he said, not even aware that now he knew the gardener's name, 'it's Leocadia. She marched with Antonio Francisco against the French.' It was the first time he had spoken his dead son's name.

'And one of these days,' said Leocadia, 'the king's justice will catch up with me. I ought to be in France. The French forgive. But I don't have the money to live in France. So I'm here, Goya. Rosarito,' she said, and the little girl's pretty face peeked out from behind the black skirt timidly.

'This is your daughter Rosarito,' said Leocadia.

Paco looked at the child. He must have been scowling fiercely, because the little face darted behind the black skirt again.

He did not hear the creaking in his ears.

He did not hear the cackling.

The face peeked out again. 'Is he really Papá?'

'The old hermit dressed in rags and smelling like he hasn't bathed in week is your father,' said Leocadia scornfully.

'He's not so bad,' said Rosarito. 'He just makes faces.' And she smiled up at Paco, a timid smile.

He looked down at her. He felt something happen to the muscles of his face. He reached out and lifted the child high in his arms and cried, 'Rosarito! What a beautiful name!' She shrieked with delight as he swung her.

He was smiling, a huge wreath of a smile that accepted the torment and the magic and the living.

Leocadia led them into the house, into the big dining room. Dirty dishes were on the table, dirty clothing in heaps on the floor. Flies buzzed at the shuttered windows.

'It will take a week to get this place in order. A month,' stormed Leocadia. 'I always told you you needed a keeper.'

She rolled up her sleeves.

After Leocadia and the child had been there three months, Juanito packed his meager possessions in a small case and told Paco: 'I'm going south. I want to feel the sun of Andalucía again before I die.'

Paco was startled. 'What will I do without you?'

'You don't need me. That Leocadia, she talks too damn much to suit me, but that wouldn't bother a deaf man. A cantankerous old deaf man,' said Juanito with a grin. 'For some reason she likes you.'

'For some reason I like her.'

'My brothers are raising bulls with horns as wide as a barn. I want to see them. I want to cape them. We've had some times together, chico.'

'Yes.'

He watched Juanito walking down the path to the river and the bridge. He prowled the garden for an hour. Then he picked up his crayons and began a drawing of Juanito Apiñani in his youth vaulting over a bull. Under it he scrawled: 'The skill and daring of Juanito Apiñani in the bullring at Madrid.' He began to draw other bulls and other bullfighters. He did the death of Pepe Hillo three times before it satisfied him. Ideas filled his head, and he knew he was going to etch a series of bullfight plates. The magic of a single man pitted against the dark forces of nature. Or fighting the beast inside himself. Or, like a medieval alchemist transmuting the baser metals into gold, changing the meanness and suffering of life into exaltation. Almost, he thought, like the crucifixion of Christ.

Soon he became robust again. He hadn't felt so good in years. Leocadia kept a neat, tidy house, and talked too much, and sometimes at night lay quietly in his arms. He didn't need Andalucía. Rosarito's smile was Almería the Golden, and Silver Jaén, and Sevilla that could be a man's whole life.

He walked with her along the river in the early winter when the sky was clear, sketch pad under his arm. He rarely opened it. 'My father is the deaf mute,' Rosarito would explain to the friends she made among the gypsies who lived on the riverbank. 'I live in the house of the deaf man.'

Before long the gypsies called it that, the House of the Deaf Man. It pleased him. The gypsies had never heard of him. He wasn't a figura. He was just the deaf man, Rosarito's father.

Leocadia scolded him when he forgot to shave or change his clothing. He would look at her handsome face and nod and not bother to read her lips. After a while she gave up.

'First Weiss, then you. I must be mad.' Then she smiled. 'But on the other hand, I never loved Weiss. Will you paint again?'

'They want me to.'

'Who wants you to?'

'The witches.'

He could talk to her about them. The witches spoke to him rarely now, but they spoke. She did not mind the witches.

'Call them that if you want,' she said. 'It's only the gift, the gift inside you. You have to paint. Witches! What do they want you to paint?'

'The truth,' he said, and heard the creaking in his ears.

But his paints remained untouched. He did not know what the truth was.

Across the river the king pretended to relent, and for a time let the liberals have their way. It was his way of making them come out of their hiding places. Soon the Segovia bridge was crowded with political refugees fleeing the city and heading north to France. Paco watched them from his bench in the garden.

That was part of the truth.

The war he did not like to think about was part of the truth.

Napoleon and Antonio Francisco were part of the truth.

Destroying Mariana when all he had wanted to do was love her; that was part of the truth.

Josefa wistfully watching the days and years of her life pass was part of the truth.

The midwife named Zárate was part of the truth.

Ramón Bayeu and all the mean little men like him everywhere were part of the truth.

Queen Maria Luisa was part of the truth.

Godoy living and Cayetana dead was part of the truth.

528

No. There was more. There had to be more. He stood. He shook his fist at the toy palace across the river. Bundled in greatcoat and muffler, he was suddenly cold in the chill of the late winter day.

Never having enough time was part of the truth. He was old.

> What is it in the jota, mother?
> Mother, what's in the jota
> That makes the young folk laugh
> And the old ones cry?

A spurious warmth invaded his chest, but he felt colder than before. The warmth burst inside him and he fell forward on his face.

Rodríguez-Pereira looked down at him. Doña Isabel was beside the bed. Leocadia stood behind her. He thought he saw Rosarito's head in the doorway. He waved weakly and his jaw muscles moved in what he hoped was a smile. Rosarito ran to him and covered his face with kisses before Leocadia could pull her away.

He slept with the witches and the truth.

Later, much later, Rodríguez-Pereira told him: 'It's your heart, old friend. Three months of absolute rest. Then we'll see.'

Paco said nothing. The witches said: 'You've got to paint and paint and paint, if you want to find the truth.'

They never spoke to him again. He did not need them any more.

In a month he was out of bed. Rodríguez-Pereira threw up his hands. Leocadia went on at length and shrewishly, the torrent of words unseen on her lips.

Rosarito said: 'Papá is well again.'

Papá was not well again. But soon he could walk around the house, and before long in the early spring he was walking in the garden. The Segovia bridge was still crowded with refugees.

He looked at the pigments and oil that Juanito had brought across the river. He looked at the canvases. They were too small. His eyesight was too weak. His hands trembled. What was the use?

He climbed the stairs slowly and went to his bedroom and found the leather case of dueling pistols. He opened it, and from red velvet the two ornate pistols stared at him. He put on his spectacles to see the intricate designs on the grips of the pistols. He lifted one off the red velvet and held it in his hand.

He was aware, without knowing how he was aware, that Rosarito had entered the room. He put the pistol in the case and shut the case and took the girl in his arms. They walked out together and he saw the big workroom upstairs with its bare plaster walls. They went downstairs and he saw the big dining room with its bare plaster walls.

Big enough to contain the truth.

Not for a king or another king, and certainly not for the third king. Not for his patrons, two generations of patrons with Goya paintings decorating the walls of their palaces and town houses. For himself? For his art?

Not even that. Sixty years. Santa Maria, he thought, sixty years he had lived for his art.

'Papá, you look very happy. Are you feeling better?'

He was feeling wonderful or mad or both.

Now he would live *in* his art.

Javier Goya felt a duty, a family obligation, to visit the House of the Deaf Man. He did not look forward to those visits, and he had stopped bringing Mariano. His wife never came. Twice a year, he thought, or maybe, if he could stand it, three times. The visits were never satisfactory. His father's insanity had terrified him as much as his father's subsequent calm pleasure in living quietly with that Leocadia woman and the child had annoyed him. Well, at least they had got him through the madness. Nevertheless, he did not like Leocadia. She talked too much. Her attitude toward Javier's father was too posses- sive: Her attitude toward Javier was scornful.

Well, he thought, driving his landau across the Segovia bridge on a warm summer afternoon in 1823, we will keep the visit brief. Father. Good to see you. You're looking well. He would do his best to ignore the little one, that Rosarito who his father pretended was Javier's half-sister. At his age!

And yet, reluctantly, Javier admitted to himself that his father was, or had been, a great man. That was the trouble. It was very difficult being the son, the only son, of a great man. Even if you accomplished much he would expect more, as if comparing you with another son you have never met because the other son does not exist. Thirty-nine, thought Javier. I'm thirty-nine years old, I have a wife, I have a child, I have an income, and unlike other rich men who die before giving an inheritance to their only son my father had the sense to give it to me while he was alive and could enjoy my enjoyment of if. If he does enjoy it. He never says so, but he's disappointed in me. I can tell. Thirty-nine, and I'm balding and the best tailor in Madrid can't hide this paunch. A life of genteel dilettantism. What's wrong with that? It could have been a life of debauchery, not that I was ever tempted. Unseemly. And then too the great man, the figura, the father, how could I have competed? He did everything, went everywhere, slept with all the beauties in Madrid and God knows where else. Never had religion. No belief in anything but himself and what he calls that magic of his. I believe. I go to Mass every day, went every day of my grown life. Kept my nose out of politics too, thank God. He had me worried, what was it, nine years ago? That trouble with the king. A collaborator, by God. I thought we might lose it all. Wouldn't do to be poor. There's a lot of living you can do in Madrid, when you have money. Nothing extravagant, of course, but still.

Pretty extravagant, that letter of Leocadia's. Your father's been decorating the house. Decorating? Did she mean painting? Her letter was short but full of hyperbole. With fire and thunder and genius was the way she had put it. I wonder if she realized how silly that sounded. I like the neoclassic mode myself. Better not tell Father that. He likes neo-Goya. Javier smiled, a thin-lipped Bayeu smile, as the open landau clattered off the bridge and began to climb the narrow unpaved road to the House of the Deaf Man. Neo-Goya. That's good. He's always learning, he says, with every stroke he paints.

Neo-Goya, and now he's close to eighty years old. Make it a brief visit. Promised Mariano I'd be home before dark. Look at the paintings, if they are paintings, say a word or two of praise, and then be on my way.

Family obligations are such a bore.

It was, Javier told himself an hour later, a lucky thing that no visitors came these days to the House of the Deaf Man. He wouldn't want it known in Madrid that his father was still totally and hopelessly mad. He had his own position to think of. Why, only last night he had entertained a friend of the young Duke of Osuna in his own home and the occasion had been enough of a success that he might hope to be included in the small, select, cultivated group invited to the Alameda for the last costume ball of the summer.

It was a lucky thing too that the old man had retired for his siesta before Leocadia had led Javier into the big dining room and then upstairs to the workroom to show the paintings. Javier would have been hard pressed to say that word or two of praise. What covered the walls of those two rooms was monstrous.

He felt sorry for Doña Leocadia. Just a touch of pity. It wouldn't do to let his emotions get out of hand. And there was the child to think of, that Rosarito who the old man pretended was his daughter. Ten years old at the most, an impressionable age, and she had to live with the madness.

Not that his father acted mad. He seemed calmer, on that hot summer day, than Javier had remembered in years. Younger too. Still doesn't look his age, not even after the heart attack, Javier thought. Hadn't talked about that magic of his either. Torment, he said, the word sounding perfectly rational, the tone of voice normal. Wanted to paint the torment outside himself and stand back and have a good long look at it. Like a priest exorcising a demon. Maybe, Javier had thought at first, his father had finally found religion. Then the old man had excused himself to have his siesta, and Javier had seen the paintings.

They covered the walls of both large rooms in the House of the Deaf Man, upstairs and down, painted directly on the plaster – if painted was the word. No brushstrokes were in evidence. His father had employed that split-reed technique of his sparingly, and his palette knife. Mostly he had worked and molded the colors with his hands, the blacks and muddy browns and dark blues and old golds. You could see the way his strong fingers had kneaded the thick pigments, like clay.

The dining room bothered Javier more than the big workroom upstairs. The little girl took her meals there, after all, and she had to look at those paintings every day, three times a day. She had followed Javier and Leocadia around the house, looking at the huge, dark, obscene, wall-covering monstrosities.

Even before they left the dining room to go upstairs, Javier had broken out in a sweat. He did not know what to say.

'No brushes,' was all he could say at first.

'God needed no paintbrushes,' Leocadia said.

Maybe, Javier thought, they're both mad.

But he had to tell someone what he really thought, and he would never dream of mentioning those paintings outside this house. 'Do you think he's quite sane, Doña Leocadia?' he asked.

'Because he has the courage to paint the truth? He's the sanest man in Madrid, you fool.' Leocadia, with that acid tongue of hers.

'Those paintings are the work of a madman,' Javier insisted in a shocked voice. He couldn't help himself. One of their mutual friends might give the old man a commission, and what if he painted something like what Javier had seen her today?

'You,' said Leocadia, 'should be so mad.'

She went outside with Javier to his waiting landau on the hot summer afternoon. 'You never have understood your father, have you?'

'Who could understand him now?'

Leocadia laughed. 'Go home to your little life, little man. Go home to your soirées and theaters and gaming tables. But just remember who made it all possible for you.'

She slapped the mule's flank, and with a lurch the landau careened down the hill toward the river.

Now he lay there in the little downstairs bedroom pretending to sleep. He watched Leocadia come in. She looked furious, until she realized he was awake, and then she shrugged.

'Well?' he asked.

'He thinks you're mad.' Leocadia related the conversation, and he remembered Juanito Apiñani's words. *You had a son. And you have this one.*

Leocadia and Rosarito went into the garden, and he got up and bathed his face with cool water because the afternoon was still hot. He walked slowly around the house. He lingered in the dining room and upstairs in the big workroom.

Walls thirty feet long and walls eighteen feet long, and he had filled them.

Santa Maria, of course Javier would think it madness. The dark soul of Spain, the beast in us all, no one is immune. Javier never understood that. Santa Maria. Strange, how he always used her name. In vain, Josefa would have said reproachfully. The Mother of God, if there is a God. Religion is an irrational thing, and he always hated the irrational, but it had tempted him too. The witches. No, there are no witches. A deaf man hears voices, that's all. He invents, to make the deafness bearable. He paints, to make life bearable. The witches, spanning one long wall of the dining room. The devil in the form of a goat, silhouetted in black, witches and warlocks all around him, subhuman, with bestial faces and mad, empty eyes. If there is a God, is there not a devil? Both live in human nature. Both contend for the souls of men, if men have souls. All in a thick swirl of black and gloomy brown, the gloom highlighted by old gold. And in a corner sits a young girl holding a muff. No part of the black Sabbath, she is still trapped by it. The individual, confronted by the madness of the mob. An eternal confrontation, and a hopeless one, until there are no more Pyrenees.

Across the dining room, another huge painting. *The Vision of the Pilgrims of San Isidro.* Madrid's patron saint, and the mob again. Always the mob. It is no gay holiday outing. Where is the singing and the dancing and the joy of the festival? He painted it that way, once, when he was young. But now the dark revelers are clumped together, black again with dark red and that mocking touch of old gold, going from light into darkness, a madness glazing their eyes, their faces contorted and joyless. If they sing and dance, and it is doubtful that they will, the singing and dancing will be a forgetfulness, not a rejoicing. The dark side of religion. He's seen that. The mob wants that. Fat black priests dozing in a dimlit church. But don't look, Javier. Don't try to understand. It's so much simpler not to.

High on one wall an old man leans on a stick while a demon shouts in his ear. He is deaf. He cannot hear the words. Perhaps it is just as well. Nada y nada y nada. Over the dining room door a witch stirs her brew while a man with a death's head hovers beside her. Upstairs, two horribly grimacing old women stare from their place on the wall at two toothless old men shoveling gruel into their faces. He can almost hear the insane laughter and the cackling. This, this will be us all, one day. There is never enough time, and never enough people who realize there is not.

Saturn, the monster-god of the Romans, over the dining room table. The classical ideal, steadfast, steadfast in the face of adversity. He smiled. That one must have given Javier some trouble. Saturn, eating his children so that he could reign in darkness forever as king of the universe. It was done before. Rubens did it, but being Rubens he managed to turn Saturn into one of his plump pink nudes, even though the plump pink nude was busily munching on one of his children. His own Saturn is all naked leathery limbs, wild hair, maniacal eyes, mouth bloody as he clutches a headless one-armed son and devours a limb. The figure is cut off by the border of the painting so that it seems to surge into the room from infinity. Implacable nature, creating for an instant, an eternal instant, and then destroying.

Is there no hope anywhere?

On the dining room wall, leaning against an iron railing, her handsome face serene, stands Doña Leocadia. A filmy black mantilla veils her face, the mysterious unpredictable face of Woman but there is patience in her stance, patience in her dark eyes. With her at his side, a man can do what he must.

He climbed the stairs again and saw, on a rock, bathed in golden light, a city. Perhaps it is the city of men's dreams, the Utopia all men seek but never find, the heaven on earth, the final citadel. The rock is unclimbable, but two figures float through the golden light toward it. Will they reach it? Is it forever unattainable? Below them, on a battlefield, soldiers wearing hussar hats take aim with their rifles.

An abstraction in brown and gold, deformed shapes, a few boulders strewn about by the hands of a careless unseen giant under the immensity of the sky. That one must have given Javier even more trouble. That one will give the critics trouble, if they ever see it. It looks incomplete. He is old. He wearied of the project. He filled the walls not with madness but with the memory of madness. Then he stopped, right in the middle of that final painting. But did he? Look again, Señor Critic. Barely visible against the thick, raw, hand-applied pigments, barely visible against the deformed shapes of earth, fighting them like a tired swimmer fighting the tide, seeking that immensity of sky, is a tiny mongrel dog. In a way a self-portrait, not that anyone will ever understand that, a final self-portrait of the old artist, trying to achieve more than he can ever hope to achieve, trying to see more, trying to understand more, trying to create more truly than anyone before him.

Don't get carried away, he thought, standing before the abstraction in brown and gold. Maybe he will fight free of the tides of earth and reach that immensity of sky.

This was the world. Well, it was part of the world. He had been born into it. That had not been his idea. But once there he had invaded it and suffered the torment and given it the magic. There had been much of the magic, and perhaps there was still a little left.

He had managed to survive, anyway. He had been lucky.

In the House of the Deaf Man, the house he bought for Cayetana, so long ago.

535

CHAPTER THIRTY-NINE

Paris, 1824

THROUGH THE PREDAWN MIST on the hill he can see the Arc de Triomphe rising against the brightening sky. Still under construction, it stands huge and ghostlike, Napoleon's dream of glory, where the Grand' Armée would march for all time into the Elysian Fields. It was begun in 1808. The year of *Dos de Mayo*. The year of the siege of Zaragoza. The year he met Antonio Francisco.

He is riding in a cab with the Prince of the Peace slowly past the Arc, the cab swaying gently, the dappled horse swaying, the cabman nodding sleepily at the reins. A lamplighter with his long pole dims the lights along the avenue. They go out one by one, summoning the day. Ahead looms a forest, the Bois du Boulogne, still night-dark.

The Prince of the Peace, sitting at his side, says nothing. He stares straight ahead, his tall hat squarely set on the once-handsome head, his hands folded on his lap. He wears yellow kid gloves. They are the height of fashion in Paris, in 1824.

Gloves that Javier would wear, if Javier were in Paris, Don Paco thinks.

Javier, who could not hide his dismay over the paintings in the House of the Deaf Man. Javier, who could not hide his dismay when the old man told him he was leaving Madrid.

'Leaving Madrid?'

'Leaving Spain. With the king's permission. To take the waters at Plombières.'

'France? What will you do in France?'

'I'll live in France.'

Letters have gone back and forth between the House of the Deaf Man and Leandro Moratín, in exile in Bordeaux. There is a colony of Spanish exiles in Bordeaux. They can live with

Moratín until they find a house. It is a pleasant city, Moratín writes. Almost has a Spanish feel to it.

There's a feeling of Spain in your work, of good red Spanish earth, I'd like to see it cultivated.

Leocadia and Rosarito leave with the third wave of refugees. A friend, once curator of the palace galleries, now the curator of the new Prado museum, where Goyas hang in profusion, informs them that Leocadia will be brought before the tribunal as an enemy of the state, as a friend of the one called Captain France, who wanted to fight the king and died at Café Apiñani.

Don Paco remains behind to settle his affairs. He deeds the House of the Deaf Man not to Javier but to his grandson Mariano, who is seventeen. He says no goodbyes. He takes the coach to San Sebastían and Bayonne and Bordeaux. He stays three days with Leocadia and Rosarito. He wants to see the exhibition at the Salon des Beaux Arts, he tells them. He wants to see Paris. The city of Diderot. The city of Napoleon. The city where Mariana died, but he does not say that. The city where the Prince of the Peace will die. He does not say that either.

Now he watches the first light of dawn bringing the autumn colors out of the darkness of the Bois de Boulogne.

The Prince of the Peace shifts his weight on the leather cushions and asks, 'It's Cayetana, isn't it? How did you find out?'

'Peral.'

'Peral?'

'Dying. Dying and confessing.'

The sky is suffused with pink. The old man turns and sees the rim of the sun appear in the central arch of Napoleon's monument to the Grand' Armée.

'I couldn't help it, you know,' says the Prince of the Peace. He does not sound frightened. 'Maria Luisa wanted Peral. She would have had him whether I sent for him or not.'

'You sent for him.'

'And where were you, Don Paco, when Cayetana was dying?'

He was delivering the plates and prints of the *Caprices* to the king. The king was explaining all about bullfighting to Juanito Apiñani. Cean Bermúdez was giving the king instruction in art. Very effective instruction. Don Paco was busy saving his own neck.

'We're not so very different, you and I,' says the Prince of the Peace. 'It's no long way from Badajoz to Aragon. It's a long way from either to Madrid. The Madrid we made for ourselves.'

Three days in Bordeaux, to see that Leocadia and the child are settled. Leandro Moratín was right. A pleasant city. A man could spend the rest of his life there.

Godoy living and Cayetana dead was part of the truth. For three nights he hardly sleeps. Thinking that. Only that. *Only Goya.* There is an incompleteness. An injustice. She was my life.

The post coach to Paris, and the cold rage growing.

'You disappoint me,' says the Prince of the Peace. 'It's no duel you want. Where are our seconds? Where's the doctor?'

'Does it matter?'

'No.' A shrug. A resigned shrug. 'I should have died in Madrid, when the mob killed Pepa Tudo. I had luck. The wrong kind of luck. They spared me.'

Sad old man in a garret room, writing his memoirs, trying to justify himself. A single suit of fine clothing and no money to live on. He's lived too long. He's glad I've come. It will be no duel. He's said as much. He wants me to kill him.

Santa Maria, that a man should want to die instead of live!

It is unthinkable. There is so much to do. There is never enough time.

Suddenly the city is behind them. The cab enters the forest and glides smoothly over the soft bed of autumn leaves. It is dim, almost night-dark again, under the canopy of trees. The avenue into the Bois is wide, but soon the cabman finds a narrow lane. He does not have to be told. Odd, Don Paco tells himself. Almost as if he can read our minds.

And if he could get inside my mind, what would he find?

Don Paco is no longer quite sure himself.

Why has he gone, first, to the Salon des Beaux Arts? To see Géricault, Constable, Delacroix? To see the fake classical junk they expected him to paint sixty years ago? Or the romantic foolishness that is the rage in Paris these days? First prize to the *Massacre of Chios*. Olé! for the *Massacre of Chios*. A rousing olé! to this French dauber who never saw the second of May or the third of May in Madrid, who never marched with Antonio Francisco in the hills above Zaragoza, in the Gredos Mountains, in the Guadarrama, on the Portuguese frontier.

The cab stops. It stands at the end of a lane canopied by great old trees, and beyond, a little way along a footpath, is a waiting glade.

Unexpectedly, the cabman turns and speaks. He is old, and his eyes are wise. 'Messieurs, this is not my affair. But may one ask? Is there no other way to settle your differences?'

'No,' the Prince of the Peace tells him.

'This is the nineteenth century, messieurs.'

'The nineteenth century,' says the Prince of the Peace, 'will do as well as any other.'

They climb down from the cab and walk side by side along the narrow footpath. Light filters through the dying autumn leaves overhead. The Prince of the Peace walks quickly, Don Paco at his side with the case of dueling pistols tucked under his arm.

They reach the glade. It is lighter there. Wet from last night's rain and the morning dew, the carpet of fallen leaves is slippery underfoot. It smells of decay and death.

'Here?' asks the Prince of the Peace. Still not frightened. Interested. With the look of a man who knows he has lived too long. With that special Spanish fondness for death. In a harsh land death is always close.

Paco opens the case, and they each take a pistol.

'Loaded?' asks the Prince of the Peace.

Paco nods.

'Then may I suggest that we change? Since you brought them?'

With a mocking little bow Paco offers his own pistol in exchange for the one held by the Prince of the Peace.

They stare at each other. The Prince of the Peace's eyes are already dead. He has only a moment or two longer to wait.

'Ten paces? Twenty?' asks Don Paco.

'Five.' The dead eyes look at him without hatred.

They turn their backs. They wait. Neither man can take the first step.

'Now,' says the Prince of the Peace.

And Don Paco takes a step.

Taunting death all his life with the icy blues of his palette, challenging it with the slashing blacks. Because it is the final enemy no man can escape.

Was it for this he ran into the Plaza of San Felipe in Zaragoza to show Martín the pouch of fifty reales, an artist's pay? Was it for this the Apiñani brothers saved him? For this the tolling of the wanderers' bell that sent him back to Zaragoza? For this his love of Mariana, born in a single beat of his heart? For this her dark red hair on his pillow and the sirens wet on his canvas? For this the death of Pascual Apiñani, for this

539

Tiepolo running along the crowded Alcalá after him, for this Padre Pignatelli, for this Josefa giving him back himself so that he could face anything, for this his flight to Italy and roaring his laughter from the dome of St Peter's in the middle of the night, for this the spilling of silver coins and gold on the bed in the kitchen of his parents' house, for this Santa Barbara and the Royal Tapestry Works, for this the love of his brother Juanito Apiñani, who had the magic, for this the foolish two-wheeled birlocho (to break his neck in) and Cayetana dancing the bolero with that arrogant elegance, for this Antonio Francisco thirteen years old and knowing his future (How did your mother die? She died in Paris), for this Sebastián Martínez's heathen artists with their magic, for this the wild ride in Andalucía and the deafness, for this the strange journey with Juanito and the *Popular Diversions,* for this the death of Francisco Bayeu and the death of the languid duke and the season of love with Cayetana in the sanctuary (the call of a wild sea bird – I'm free I'm free I'm free), for this the Virgin of Rocío and Tadea in his arms among the pines, for this the Lovers of Ugliness and the *Caprices,* for this the saints in San Antonio de la Florida with dirt under their fingernails, for this the death of Pepe Hillo, for this the patient love of Josefa, for this the *Dos de Mayo* and the *Disasters of War* (Once I told you we would meet again, Don Paco), for this Rosarito making him smile again, for this painting the torment out of himself like a priest exorcising a demon, for this the magic?

Five steps, with a pistol in his hand, with death in his hand, five slow steps, five seconds, almost eighty years of living.

For this?

He turns. The Prince of the Peace turns. They stare at each other.

And Don Paco slowly raises his pistol toward the canopy of autumn leaves, and fires. A branch falls at his feet. Some of its leaves are still green with life.

The Prince of the Peace looks at his own pistol. He looks at Don Paco. He smiles a faint, sad resigned smile. He discharges his pistol into the dead earth.

They walk together back to the cab. The old cabman is startled to see them both.

Already Godoy is gone from his life, as Paris will soon be gone, as the torment is gone.

Bordeaux, where Leocadia and their child await him. Bordeaux is new, a mystery. Bordeaux is life. He wants to capture

540

it and hold it and own it.

That new technique of lithography, he thinks. Why, I could put the slab of limestone on my easel and work as if I'm painting. I could do the bulls that way. I have some ideas about the bulls.

Or Rosarito. I've never painted her. Innocence. In a pearly light, the colors glowing, not a rendering of her beauty, but an impression.

He is eager to leave Paris. A vast impatience consumes him. There is never enough time. He has a few more paintings to paint.

With luck, he has a few more paintings to paint.

Afterword

FRANCISCO GOYA was born in Fuendetodos, near Zaragoza, in 1746, and died in Bordeaux in 1828. He had the luck he asked for in the final scene of this novel – four more years of life and work. He painted portraits of his fellow-exiles, lithographed a series of bullfight scenes now called *The Bulls of Bordeaux* and painted a stunningly impressionistic portrait of Rosarito as the *Milkmaid of Bordeaux*. He took up miniature-painting and taught it to Rosarito, who gained something of a reputation for herself in her early twenties. She did not have her father's luck. She died before she was thirty.

Little is known about the youth of Francisco Goya, and I have created a character or two out of whole cloth for his first stay in Madrid. For the rest, all major characters in this novel lived, and figured in Goya's life. Carlos III was likely the best king Spain ever had; his son was a fatuous dolt; Queen Maria Luisa was as debauched as she appears in these pages; Fernando VII was a monster. Dr Rodríguez-Pereira is a composite of several physicians who figured importantly in Goya's life.

In re-creating the turbulent history of the times, it was occasionally necessary for dramatic reasons to take small liberties with chronology. The Apiñani brothers probably made their appearance in Madrid fifteen or so years before Goya did.

Books have been written to prove that the Duchess of Alba was murdered. Books have been written to prove that she died a natural death. The manner of her death remains a mystery. Her on-again-off-again love affair with Goya, though denied by a few Spanish sources, is almost a certainty.

The 'black paintings' were removed from the walls of the House of the Deaf Man and carefully transferred to canvas in 1874. They now fill a room in the Prado. A visit to that room remains one of the moving experiences in the world of art.

If Goya had the luck he asked for, so did I. The writing of this book entailed living on and off for ten years in Spain, a country I love. It also entailed going everywhere Goya went, to make the background authentic.

I had the further good fortune to receive help from many people during the year and a half I spent writing *Colossus*. My wife Ann was always at my side, assisting with research and serving as first editor and critic. Many Spaniards, proud of their greatest artist, and the first really modern painter, were eager to do what they could for me. It would be impossible to list them all, but I especially wish I had been able to thank the late Don José Maldonado, Count of Aldana, who was always there with a valuable suggestion when it was most needed.

Guadalmar, Spain